DAVID FEINTUCH

CHILDREN OF HOPE

ACE BOOKS, NEW YORK

CHILDREN OF HOPE

An Ace Book
Published by The Berkley Publishing Group,
a division of Penguin Putnam Inc.,
375 Hudson Street, New York, New York 10014.

The Penguin Putnam Inc. World Wide Web site address is
http://www.penguinputnam.com

First edition: April 2001

Library of Congress Cataloging-in-Publication Data

Feintuch, David.
Children of hope / David Feintuch.—1st ed.
p. cm.
ISBN 0-441-00804-6 (alk. paper)
I. Title.

PS3556.E436 C48 2001
813'.54—dc21   00-065013

Printed in the United States of America

10   9   8   7   6   5   4   3   2   1

To Don, who knew where I was going,
even when I didn't.

David Feintuch may be reached at Writeman@cris.com,
and be sure to visit http://www.Nickseafort.com
for announcements of new books, contests, and other news.

PROLOGUE

"The witness will stand."

Wearily, I got to my feet, looked about the vaulting Cathedral.

Within my dark blue shirt, my shoulder throbbed unbearably. I was grateful; it gave me focus.

The three elderly judges wore black cassocks, not uniforms, else theirs might have been a military court. Or a civilian one, for that matter. It made little difference in a society owned lock, stock, and barrel by the frazzing Church.

"State your name."

I said nothing.

"Young man, your situation is grave. Unless you cooperate . . ."

I shrugged, forgetting. Clenching my teeth, I rode a wave of pain.

The Lord's Advocate rose from behind his ornate carved table before the dais. "Your Reverence, may I?" He took the Bishop's silence as permission. "Sirs, he's stubborn and sullen, but no need to badger him over trifles. We know his identity; what we want is his account of the night of November 19, 2246. An account of murder, apostasy, treason." He turned to me. "Randolph, I charge you, speak!"

I pressed my lips tight.

"You try to protect him?"

They could ask 'til the Second Coming. I'd say not a word.

"Of course you do," he answered himself, "and you imagine silence is your servant. If Their Reverences order you to testify, will you? Surely you can tell us that."

"No. I won't." My defiance brought infinite relief.

"You'll be subjected to polygraph and drugs. The truth will out, joey."

"You can't use my P and D to convict others. Just me."

"Under canon law, we can. Higher edicts apply."

Perhaps this time I could thwart the drugs and polygraph. Or find a way to die. In my current state, it ought not be hard.

The Advocate's tone was gentle. "P and D is a misery, and for naught. We'll learn what we must; in trial for heresy we can allow no bar. Tell us."

I cherished the fever that ate at my bones. I took deep breath, to speak words that would transport me beyond deliverance. "Stick your trial up—"

His hand shot forth, palm raised. "If not for us, for Lord God. Speak."

The somber Cathedral was a haze of red. I managed to shake my head.

"Very well. If Your Reverences permit?" He slipped a chip into his holovid, swung it to face me.

I squinted, punched in my private code, waited for the screen to clear.

"*Randolph, I know what you face. What I face. I beg and order you, tell them what they would know. Tell them freely.*"

I stared at the unmistakable signature.

My voice was hoarse. "Where did you get this?"

"It came today." The Advocate permitted himself a rueful grin. "By net." He studied my eyes. "If not for us, if not for God Himself . . . then, for him?"

My cheeks were damp. I cared not. "Very well." I would obey, of course. What choice had I, after all we'd endured?

"That Tuesday in November, when you—"

"No." I sought to make my voice firm. "From the beginning. It will take a while." With a fumbling hand, I poured ice water from the beaded pitcher.

PART ONE

September, in the Year of our Lord 2246

1

UNS *PARAGON* BECKONED at the end of the corridor, its gaping lock mated to that of Orbit Station.

The Stadholder of the Commonweal of Hope Nation paused at the hatchway. He gave me a fierce hug, same as always. "Take care, son. Be good and I'll bring you home an elephant."

I broke into a silly grin. Even at nine, I knew it was impossible. Behind me, Mom laughed softly.

The smile faded from Derek Carr's eyes. "You'll be . . . Lord help us, almost eleven when I'm home." His eyes glistened. "Nearly grown."

I swallowed, made a manful effort so he'd be proud. "Bye, Dad." I stood tall.

"Always remember I love you, son."

In another realm, a voice said, "Randy?" Insistent fingers prodded at my forearm. "They'll be leaving soon."

"Go 'way." I buried my head in the pillow, desperate to lose myself again in my dream.

"The ceremony won't wait—"

I launched myself flailing from my bed.

Kevin Dakko fell back from my onslaught. "Easy, joey!"

I caught him a hard one in the temple. He squealed with pain, took deep breath, charged full at me. In a moment we were rolling on the floor.

"Get *off!*" I bucked and heaved to dislodge Kevin's weight from my chest, but he was fourteen, a year older than I, and outweighed me by ten kilos.

"Not 'til you calm down."

"Prong yourself, you frazzing—"

He raised a fist, but after a moment shook his head. "Nah. I like you, actually."

"Then get off!"

"Lie still."

Fuming, I did as he ordered.

Only when I was supine and passive did he roll off me. "What was *that* about?"

I mumbled, "I was dreaming."

He smirked. "Judy Winthrop?"

"No, you goddamn—" I swallowed. I was furious, but there were limits. I really ought to curb my foul language, but some recess of my mind enjoyed the discomfort it caused. Though, if Anthony or any of the plantation staff heard me . . .

"What, then?"

I studied the thick, scarred planking. "Dad."

"Aww, Randy." For a moment, Kevin's hand fell on my shoulder. Sullenly, I shrugged it off, but felt better for it.

The dream came often, bittersweet and awful.

Mom and I had gone aloft to the Station, to see Dad off. The fastship *Paragon* would Fuse the nineteen light-years to Earth in a mere nine months. Dad hated to go, but his personal touch was needed for trade negotiations. Earth was Hope Nation's principal grain market, and we'd been battling for decades to reduce shipping rates in the teeth of the U.N. Navy's monopoly.

And so, with a cheery wave, Derek Carr strode into the starship, and from my life. A year later, when *Galactic* foundered, he'd been aboard, at the behest of his frazball friend Nick Seafort. They say Dad died of decompression. Sometimes, when I couldn't help myself, I imagined what he'd looked like, afterward.

I flopped on my bed, pulled on my socks. "Sorry."

"So am I."

"You didn't do anything." And I shouldn't have attacked him. But in my dream Dad's smile had been so close, his voice so warm . . .

"I'm sorry he died," said Kevin.

"You never knew him."

"I didn't have to. I know you."

I took a long breath, and another, at last truly ashamed. "Did I hurt you?"

"A bit." He rubbed a red mark on his temple. A fist-sized mark.

I stared glumly at the new day. "Three more weeks."

"The summer went fast." Kev, a city joey from Centraltown, was a summer intern, sent to the Plantation Zone on a government program I'd thought nonsense, until I'd met him. He'd taken to life on Carr Plantation like a fish to water, though I'd had to teach him nearly everything.

I gathered my courage. "I'll really miss you."

"Jeez, thanks." He glanced at his watch. "I'll tell Anthony you're on your way."

"Fast as I can."

Kev's footsteps faded down the stairs.

I climbed into my pants. The Balden Reservoir would be dedicated today, and the massive force-field damming Balden River switched on. Water would soon accumulate behind it, freeing our plantations forever from dependence on rain or irrigation pumps. I sighed. I supposed I ought to be interested. Hell, I *was* interested. If only Kev hadn't interrupted my dream.

I'd have to wash, or face Anth's reproof. Gradually, in the last year, my grown nephew had taken charge, as Mom slipped more and more into her religious zeal and Sublime-induced chemdreams. In her better weeks, she was active in the Sisters of Faith Cathedral Auxiliary, to Anth's discomfort.

I ducked into the bathroom, studied my face, yearning for the first signs of fuzz. Damn it, I was already thirteen. What was my body waiting for?

Staring sullenly at the sluggish stream, I shrugged off Anthony's consoling hand.

"*Because I give waters in the wilderness and rivers in the desert, to give drink to my people, my chosen.*" Why must old Henrod Andori go on so? The Plantation Zone had no desert, and the Balden Valley was hardly a wilderness. Hell, our manse itself sat at the lower end of the valley, and look at the green of our lawns. All right, the valley had no power grids, and its only road was a rough trail, but . . . "*These people have I formed for myself; they shall shew forth my praise.*" The gaunt Archbishop eyed us, bent anew to his text. I rolled my eyes.

The reservoir would be quite something, despite old Andori's blather. It had been Dad's idea, originally. Hope Nation had water to spare, but the plantations that were our mainstay—like Carr, our home—were slaves to rainfall and the water table. We had three choices: atmospheric diversion via shifting solar shields, desalinization, or a dam.

Andori scrolled his holovid to a new chapter. I nudged Anthony. "No more! Make him stop."

"I can't." Anth's lips barely moved.

"What's the point of being Stadholder if you can't—"

"Shush. Scanlen's watching."

"So?" But I subsided nonetheless. The Bishop of Centraltown was a powerful figure in his own right, and Andori's deputy in the hierarchy of the Reunification Church. Mother Church ran Centraltown, and to all intents and purposes, Hope Nation.

I frowned at the Balden River. Not much of a river at summer's end, but by spring it would be a torrent. Well, last spring it had been, when Alex Hopewell and Sandy Plumwell and I had camped by the river.

Never again. In scant months our campsite would be drowned.

Please, God, quiet your Bishop. My feet hurt, and he goes on forever, and I want to go exploring with Kev.

Fooling with the atmosphere was undependable. Dad had banned all further experiments after the meteorologists blamed the horrible March 2240 hurricane on forcibly shifted weather patterns. Desalinization would do the job, but it was expensive, and would need water constantly pumped upward from the Farreach Ocean to our fields. The cost of a traditional dam would be immense. But a force-field dam . . . Anth had jumped on the idea, once the science was proven.

"*Amen.*" Henrod Andori switched off his holovid. Thank you, God.

It was almost enough to make me a believer.

2

I SQUIRMED AT Anthony Carr's fingers on my shoulder, but was careful not to shrug them off. We were in public, and he'd be really ticked if I made an issue of it, especially after the sharp words we'd had a day ago. So what if I told our blustering crop manager what I thought of him? At fourteen, I had little stomach for fools. Unfortunately, Anth didn't see it that way, and today, I was on a short leash. Too bad I didn't have Kevin Dakko to whisper with, but he'd gone home to Centraltown months ago.

In Anthony's view, requiring a rebellious and protesting joeykid like me to attend a reception with adults was both penalty and honor. I'd resigned myself to make the best of it, and circled dutifully among the crowd of planters come to pay their respects. Even Mother was there, lost behind her dreamy smile.

Anthony frowned at Vince Palabee, who waited for an answer. "We've a favorable balance of trade with Earth, regardless of shipping costs."

Overhead, Minor was just setting, and Major was near the horizon. We'd have to adjourn our reception before long; at this time of year Hope Nation grew cool at dusk. At least Eastern Continent did; I'd never been across Farreach Ocean to the Ventura Mountains, home of our mining bases as well as our most beautiful scenery. Dad had always meant to take me, but . . .

The stocky planter's tone was stubborn. "Anthony, the Terrans can raise their rates at will. They'll throttle us. And they will, to get even for the Declaration." Dad's Declaration, as Stadholder, that had set us free from the U.N.

My keeper smiled with genial disregard. Anth thought that Palabee was an ass—he'd told me as much—and disregarded his proposals in the Planters' Council. Still, Anthony had to say *something*. If nothing else, Palabee was his guest.

He flicked a thumb at the chubby Terran Ambassador refilling his punch glass from the bowl, at the drinks table across the immaculate lawn. "McEwan is demanding we plant even more acreage; Earth will take what grains we offer. They're desperate, thanks to Seafort." Anthony was delighted that the former SecGen had led his planet to agricultural disaster, and saw great advantage for us in the Terran fiasco.

I shouldn't have stared; the Ambassador caught my eye, nodded, strolled our way.

As he neared, Vince Palabee eased away. At least he knew when he was outclassed.

I sighed, braced myself for more blather. Faintly, past the burble of conversation, came the yips and squeals of other joeykids at the pond. I'd be swimming with them but for Anth's insistence I stay where he could keep an eye on me.

He didn't know it, but I was more relieved than annoyed. Of late, I'd felt reluctant to jump bare from the high rock with my fellow teeners. I'd get a great view of Judy Winthrop that way, but she'd also get a view of me. Since I'd turned fourteen, two months back, it made me uneasy. Not that it bothered Alex Hopewell, brash and muscular at sixteen. But, come to think of it, Alex hadn't spent much time at the swimming hole a couple of years ago. I brightened. Perhaps I wasn't so odd.

"First Stadholder." Ambassador McEwan, florid and husky, raised his glass in salute.

"Sir." Anthony gave an incisive nod, which was almost a bow. He prided himself on observing the formalities.

"Congratulations on your reelection."

"Reconfirmation," I blurted, with scorn. The Legislative Assembly had *confirmed* Anthony as First Stadholder of the Commonweal of Hope Nation. He'd been *elected* chief executive three years past, by the Planters' Council, when news of Dad's death reached home.

McEwan grunted, as if it didn't matter. He was a Terran, and couldn't be expected to know which end of a pig shat, but to us the distinction was significant.

Only the families, whose vast plantations were Hope Nation's raison d'être, were entitled to select the First Stadholder. The legislature, where even common townsmen had a vote, could merely confirm, or in rare cases veto.

Anthony was still the youngest Stadholder ever to hold office. At his election three years past, the Hopewell clan had raised his age in objection, as if twenty-four weren't fully adult. But the best word to describe Anth was "formidable." Almost always, he got what he wanted. Even with me.

His hand squeezed my shoulder as he presented me. "You've met my young uncle, Randolph Carr? Ambassador McEwan."

"Good to meet you, son." The Terran held out a hand.

Son. Almost, my lip curled. I was no one's son, and most definitely not his. For Anthony's sake I controlled myself. Dutifully, I shook his hand.

I sometimes called Anth "cousin," and thought of him so. He'd warned me, years ago, to play no teasing games with our relationship. In truth, I was his uncle, though he was twice my age. His grandfather was my father Derek Carr, long our First Stadholder.

I was the youngest of what Dad jokingly called his second crop, born years after his first wife Clarisse had died. My own mother, Sandra, had become a Limey, gradually abandoning religious zeal for her world of chemdreams. There was little love lost between her and Anth. Dad had kept peace between them, and when he was gone, Anthony had worked hard to be accommodating.

I suppose after Dad was killed I'd let resentment get the best of me. The next couple of summers had seen episodes of rocks through windows, slashed power cords in the night, and the like, until Anthony had, as he termed it, taken me in hand.

Sure, I resented him—what joeykid wouldn't? He sure as hell wasn't my father, and had no claim to my obedience. But Dad would have gone into orbit if he'd learned what I'd been up to, and with Mom inhaling Sublime nearly every evening she wasn't attending church, there was no one to whom I could complain. No one to rein me in, either. The Mantiet twins even urged me to run away.

Hah. To where? Centraltown? Cities chew ass, and besides, as Dad used to remind me, the Rebellious Ages were long past. Our society, like Earth's, prized order; joeykids did as they were told. Fugitive joeys faced correctional farms, and perhaps jail as well, if they were petitioned into court.

Not that I didn't fight; I'd be damned if Anth would cow me without a struggle. And in the process, I found what I hadn't expected: he didn't cow me at all.

It was easier to do what he asked than to pay the consequences, so most of the time I complied. But I rather liked the world he introduced me to, one in which our planters constantly competed for power. Anthony deftly played the plantation families one against another. It was fun to follow his machinations. And of course, to be told details of affairs none of my friends imagined.

I'll say this much for my overbearing nephew: he was frank, open, and amazingly honest. Not only did he trust my discretion, he even solicited my opinion. Though he usually didn't follow it, he really listened. And then he explained why he'd chosen the course he had. You can't help liking a joey who handles you that way.

"Randolph Carr," said the Ambassador, as if tasting it. "A distinguished name."

Lord God, I hated it when they talked down to me. Anth knew it; his hand tightened on my shoulder, in warning or sympathy.

For the Stadholder's sake, I let it pass. "Yes, sir." Our family tended to recycle names; "Anthony" was my dad Derek's middle name. Randolph was my grandfather, and his father too. We all bore distinguished names; it came with being a Carr, the premier family of Hope Nation.

Turning back to my nephew, the Ambassador lowered his voice. "Regarding quotas, Mr. Stadholder. You promised us more soybeans."

"Actually, we didn't." A flicker of annoyance crossed Anth's eyes. It was, after all, a party, and he didn't care to be cornered on the lawn of Carr Plantation.

"You certainly never refused. Now I find your people never planted them. We've four barges in the pipeline, and the fastship brings word a liner will be along shortly. One of the big ones."

Some of my friends couldn't tell a barge from a fastship; they were colonials, through and through, never mind that we'd had our independence for years. I tried not to look smug. Dad had taught me about the Navy and its ships; after all, he'd served on them. Once, in his lap . . .

"Now, son." Dad had sucked on an empty pipe; he said it made his teeth feel good. "How long to home system by fastship?"

I'd snuggled closer, warm and comfortable in my youthful pajamas. "Nine months. Oddmented Fusion." I was five, and nighttime talks were part of our ritual.

"Augmented," he corrected gently. "And by barge?"

"Three years, almost."

"And a starship?"

"Sixteen months." I tried not to stifle a yawn. "Unless the fish get you." Bedtime loomed, and if I could prompt an exciting story . . .

"Don't be daft." Dad looked down his nose, his lined face settling into a frown, but he didn't mean it. "Nick killed the last aliens long ago."

"What if they come back?" Once, marauding fish had even descended through the atmosphere, to attack Captain Seafort at Venturas Base.

Dad seized my wrist, raised it, tickled my stomach. "They'll do this."

I squealed my laughter, desperate to get away, hoping I could not.

Abruptly Dad stopped, squeezed me hard.

I hugged back, loving the smell of him.

"Barges Fuse," he said dreamily. "Fastships Fuse. Liners Fuse. Even the fish knew how to Fuse."

"What's it like?"

"Perhaps someday you'll join the Navy and find out."

"Or go as a passenger." Only the U.N. Navy had ships that Fused between stars; even at five I knew that. Sometimes, late at night, Dad and his friends in government discussed, at endless length, the dilemma the U.N. monopoly posed. Usually it put me to sleep, curled on the couch or in his lap.

"Randolph!"

I blinked.

"Would you like to go?" The Ambassador waited with a half smile.

I asked, "Where?"

Anthony frowned.

"Sorry, I was . . . daydreaming." I tried not to blush.

"To Embassy House, and spend the weekend with Mr. McEwan's joey-kids."

Christ, no. Just in time, I refrained from saying it. I cast about for an excuse, found none. "I think so. Sounds great. Can I call after I check with Mom?"

In Anthony's eyes, a sardonic glint; he knew a polite evasion when he heard one. "We'll call you, Mr. McEwan. Ah. Colonel Kaminski." Deftly, he turned to the newcomer.

"Good day, Stadholder." To me, "Randolph."

I nodded, trying not to look cross. The Colonel was a few years older than Anth, an occasional houseguest, and was as close as a colonial planet had to a spaceman. He'd served two tours at the second Orbit Station, the decommissioned warship Earth had sent us to replace the one destroyed in the war with the fish.

Kaminski said delicately, "Thank you again for your kindness on the, er, Driscoll matter." I wasn't supposed to know about that. A Station hand on leave had run afoul of Centraltown authorities. The Stadholder had intervened quietly to calm the waters.

Anth merely smiled, and they fell into conversation. As soon as I could, I made my escape to the punch bowl, waited for Cousin Ellen to fill her cup.

"Ah, Master Carr." Bishop Arthur Scanlen's voice was genial. His hand fell on my shoulder. Jesus Christ, should I wear a mousetrap on my collar? Or bite their frazzing fingers?

Alex Hopewell was sixteen and six feet tall. Nobody ever clamped a hand on *his* shoulder. Why did I have to be so frazzing short? Yeah, I'd grown way out of last year's jumpsuit, and Anthony counseled patience, but it was easy for *him* to say. He towered over me.

The Bishop's mouth smiled. His eyes did not. "I didn't notice your confirmation on the Cathedral's schedule, joey."

The Reunification Church practically ran Hope Nation, from its rebuilt Cathedral downtown. Dad used to have all sorts of trouble with Scanlen and Andori. It was one of the few subjects Anth wouldn't discuss.

"Are you ready?"

I said, "Not yet." Rituals chewed ass.

"You're of age." Again, Scanlen's cold smile. "We can't have you becoming a Jew or a heathen."

A Jew or a heathen?

I couldn't help it, really, I couldn't. I gave him my best smile. "Fuck you!" My words rang out, every bit as loud as I'd intended.

Cousin Ellen dropped her glass.

Appalled, Anthony stared past Colonel Kaminski.

Across the festive lawn, utter silence.

For a moment, a horrid sense of guilt. I shrugged it off. So, the Bishop would excommunicate me. I'd go to Hell before I'd put up with him.

Ricard Scanlen gripped my arm with a claw of steel, dragged me across the lawn. "We'll see what—" Anthony loomed, his face severe.

I wrenched loose, dashed away, caromed off Mr. Plumwell. Nursing my ribs, I blundered through a gap in the hedge, raced into the woods.

Prong the Bishop.

Prong them all.

Cross-legged on Judy Winthrop's bed, I devoured a cold leg of chicken, barely taking time to spit the bones.

Her room was done in girlish pastels, not my taste at all.

She studied me. "What's a Jew?"

I shrugged. "An ancient cult back on Earth?" I waved it away. "Who cares?" I was sure what a heathen was, and it was insulting.

The Winthrop estate bordered ours; its manse was only two miles past our southernmost marker, fronting Plantation Road. But our demarcation fence was a good five miles from Carr House, where Anthony's reception had been given.

A long trudge, but I couldn't drive an electricar, and I didn't dare try to hitch. Too bad I couldn't have swiped a heli.

After my hike I'd shinnied up their drainpipe, tapped at Judy's window. Her room was empty; I'd had to squat on the Winthrops' porch roof an hour before she wandered upstairs to bed, and then I'd scared the zark out of her. After she'd calmed, she'd gone downstairs, pleaded adolescent hunger, and secured my plate of chicken.

Minor had risen again, and lit the manicured yard.

Judy eyed the hallway door with some trepidation. "I'll really get it if Mom finds you here."

"Fine, I'll leave." My tone was sullen; I tried again, managed to brighten it. "Thanks for the food." I swung my legs to the side of the bed.

She stayed me with a palm. "Just keep it quiet." Then, "Where will you go?"

I shrugged. If I'd known that, I wouldn't have sought her counsel.

She rubbed her chin, with a look that meant she was thinking hard. "It's not just your unc—I mean, your nephew. They're all aghast. When we came back from swimming they were still talking about you. Where will you stay? I doubt the families would take you in."

It figured. The Reunification Church—the *only* authorized church—represented Lord God Himself. The U.N. Government was His instrument, and ruled Earth and the colonies in His name. Even here in Hope Nation, the Church was paramount. And I'd cursed a Bishop, anointed by Earth's Council of Patriarchs.

I stirred uneasily, knowing I'd gone a touch too far.

"Why'd you have to say it?"

I opened my mouth, shut it again. How could I explain? I wasn't sure about God, but I was damn sure I didn't believe in the Bishop. I told her so.

"Why not?"

I swallowed, not liking where her question led. My eyes sought the safety of the bedspread. "Do you remember my dad?"

"I saw Mr. Carr, now and then. Not to talk to."

I nodded. When Derek boarded UNS *Paragon*, Judy had been nine and would have known the Stadholder only as a distant figure. "One night, a few months before he left, I heard him on the caller."

She waited.

"He was arguing with the Bishop. 'Renounce,' Dad said softly, as if he couldn't believe it."

"What's it mean?"

I shushed her. "It's something the Church does when they don't like people." I toyed with the bedspread. Renunciation was only a step short of excommunication.

"We could find out. Pa's friends with Deacon—"

"That's not the point, stupid!" I flung down a chicken bone. It bounced. Carefully, I plucked it from the bedcover. "Sorry." Was I speaking of the bone, or my temper?

She folded her arms.

"I was listening outside his study door. I didn't mean to spy, but . . ." I *had* meant to, though. My eyes darted to hers, and away, hoping she'd understand. *And forgive*, added a small voice. I thrust it away. "After the call, he sat there and—and he . . ."

"Say it." Blessedly, her voice was gentle.

"He cried." I swallowed a lump.

Her fingers brushed my forearm. "Oh, Randy."

"Later, he told me he was just tired and frustrated. And he was mad I'd listened." Furious, more like it. Not because of what I'd overheard, but at my lack of honor in eavesdropping. He'd punished me, but he hadn't needed to. His reproach alone made me feel awful.

My fingers scrabbled at Judy's bed linen. "He cried. And Dad was the strongest man I ever . . . ever . . ." Abruptly I swung to my feet. "I better go."

Her question roped me, pulled me back to the bed. "Ever find out what they were arguing about?"

"The next day he wouldn't talk about it." Surreptitiously, I wiped an eye. "But I won't take any crap from a frazzing Bishop."

Her expression made me glad and scared all at once. "It'll settle down. If you find a place to lie low for a—"

A knock at the door. We froze.

"Judy?"

"Yes, Mom?" Her voice was a squeak.

I rushed to the window, tried to raise it silently.

Her mother's tone was stern. "Mr. Carr's downstairs."

Oh, Christ. I clawed the sash open.

"He wants to talk to Randy."

How did he know?

"Randy, are you in there?"

Judy bit her lip, pounded the bed.

I couldn't abandon her; it would make her troubles far worse. I gave the drainpipe a last wistful glance. With a deep breath, I strode to the door, swung it open. "Yes, ma'am. I sneaked into Judy's room. She didn't know I'd be here. It wasn't her fault." I braced myself for the explosion.

"Really." Ms. Winthrop's eyes flicked to the half-eaten chicken, proof of my lie. "It's late, and you'd better go." Her tone held that careful civility parents sometimes used, outside the family.

I shot Judy a glance of commiseration, but I had problems of my own. How in blazes did Anth know where to find me? What would he do now? I had not only the Bishop to answer for, but flight from Anthony's authority. I could look forward to a grim night.

No, by God. I'd done what I could for Judy. Now I could look after myself.

In the vestibule, my keeper leaned against a pillar, arms folded. His expression was cool.

If that's how he'd play it, so would I. I stopped on the stairwell. "You wanted to see me?" It was the tone I might have used with a servant.

"Yes, if you don't mind. Outside."

"All right." Civility worked in my favor, at the moment. To give myself every possible chance I turned, assumed my best manners. "Good night, Ms. Winthrop. Sorry to have intruded."

She nodded, her mind obviously focused upstairs. She looked ready to bolt to Judy's room the moment we were gone.

Anthony himself seemed none too pleased. Well, not only had I insulted the Bishop, I'd embarrassed my nephew at his own reception. To say nothing of making him go begging to the neighbors in search of me. We were a small colony—a mere three-quarters of a million, spread over the plantation zones and a handful of cities. But he was in charge, the equivalent of a colonial governor.

Politely, I held the door. Anthony slipped outside. So did I, and lunged past him. I sprinted past his waiting electricar, down the darkened drive, expecting with each step his grasp on my collar.

Nothing. I plunged into the brush; at night, I'd be harder to find off the path.

At twenty paces I risked a glance backward. At fifty, I slowed. Why wasn't he chasing me? Did he have Home Guard troops lurking in the bushes?

He sat on the edge of the porch, arms folded. "Randolph?" He raised his voice, cupped his hands. "It's important we talk."

Ha. It was important he whale the tar out of me, as he'd oft threatened but never done, and I wasn't about to let it happen. Not for Scanlen, or any churchman. And he wouldn't intend any less, after I'd mortified him at his own reception.

He let the silence stretch. Then, "Randy, I know you hear me. We've no time for games. Please, come sit with me. I won't hurt you."

I waited him out, shivering in the night breeze.

"In fact, I won't touch you. You have my word."

I felt a chill. This wasn't like Anthony at all. I swallowed, impulsively risked my freedom. "For how long?" I edged my way toward the porch.

A soft sound, that might have been a chuckle. "We'll talk as long as you care to sit with me, and then you can retreat to where you are now, if you still want to run."

"What about your men?"

"For God's—it's near midnight. The farmhands are asleep, and if you think I'd rouse the government over this, you have less sense than I thought."

"You won't touch me?"

It was the final straw. "God curse this nonsense!" He jumped to his feet, stalked to the car. "Find me when you're ready. Even you aren't worth these games." He threw open his door.

Near enough to touch, I thrust aside a juniper. "I'm here." With a try at nonchalance I strolled to the porch.

Anth glared. Then he let out his breath, pulled something from the car, strode toward me. I flinched, half expecting him to betray his promise. But it was only my jacket, which he tossed to me without a word. He brushed past, settled on the porch slats, dangling his feet. "Thought you might be cold."

Gratefully I slipped it on, sat cautiously by his side. The wood decking was rough, and chilled. No celuwall or plastipanels here. Not in the Zone. We prided ourselves on old-style construction. Besides, lumber was plentiful and cheap.

Anth cleared his throat. "Let's keep our voices down. I don't want word of this to spread."

"Word of what?"

"What I'm going to tell you." He eyed me as if making up his mind, then shrugged.

"Get it over with." I braced for the inevitable lecture.

"Fact one." He raised a finger. "The world doesn't revolve about your adolescent angst."

Maybe not, but he'd gone to the trouble to find me. And that brought up another point. "How'd you know to look here?"

"It's where Judy lives. I couldn't imagine to whom else you'd run." A pause. "Are you, uh, physically involved with her?"

"No!" My cheeks grew hot.

It wasn't an accusation; why did I respond as if it were? We weren't physical, but we would be, one of these days. If I ever got my nerve up, and she didn't refuse outright. Even in her absence, she made my nights restless.

I made my lip curl. "That's not what you came to ask."

"No." His eyes searched mine. "I'll tell you a story about the Church. Don't roll your eyes, your father's in it too. Still bored?"

The barb in his tone told me I'd made him angry, and he was trying to control it. "I never said I was . . ." I gave it up. He'd mentioned Dad, and wouldn't have if it weren't important. "Go on."

"You studied religious history."

I'd had to. Anthony made me go to school, despite my protests. I could learn what I needed at home, and it wasn't as if schooling were mandatory.

"There's only one Church to speak of, and one interpretation of Gospel. That's been so ever since Hope Nation was founded."

"Everyone knows that."

"The Patriarchs run the Church, but here on Hope Nation, their delegate is the Bishop, and he wields all the authority of—"

"Why'd the Bishop call me—"

He slammed his fist on a floorboard. "No more interruptions, joey, or—"

"You said you wouldn't hit me!"

"—or I'm done with you. And I don't just mean for the night!" He waved a finger in front of my nose. "Not another word!" His eyes flashed. "You hear me?"

I stared at my shoe.

"Well?"

I mumbled, "Yes, sir." Why did I feel relief for having knuckled under?

He raised my chin, spoke very softly. "Randy, I'm in trouble."

My rebellion evaporated, on the instant. When all was done, we were family.

"Because of me?"

"No. But you made it far worse."

I swallowed, edged closer.

"Where do I start?" A few breaths' quiet. "I wish you'd known Derek better." He sounded reflective. "Grandpa pretty well raised me, you know."

I nodded. It was no secret.

He said, "My father was . . . distracted."

My half brother Zack, a generation older than I, was an agri-geneticist, one of our best. These days he lived on his experimental farm across the Zone. It was primarily his strains of wheat that had vaulted Carr over its competition, and forced the other families to license our patented hybrids to keep up. Even today, he puttered over his workbench and wandered his experimental fields, notepad in hand. Just last year he'd developed—

". . . left me to pretty well run about on my own." Anthony's face eased into an impish grin. "I didn't mind, and neither did Grandfather Derek, until they found me and Emily in a barn loft. I was barely fifteen. That got me grounded to the estate for the summer."

I'd heard it all before, from Dad. Not that I'd much cared.

"Later that week I got into a slugfest with Mr. Pharen, the granary foreman, and everyone agreed I'd gone too far. They looked to Pa to settle me down, but he was pondering millet that season; he gave me a lecture and sent me on my way. So Grandfather stepped in."

Yeah, Dad made sure his offspring were well behaved. He'd always made me toe the line, though I really didn't mind; he had a way of mixing sternness with such obvious love, you *wanted* to make him proud. I think that was his secret of running the colony. Well, not a colony as such, though everyone still called it that. Commonweal was too big a word, perhaps. And besides . . .

". . . what he confided in me?"

"Huh?" I blinked.

"You weren't listening." Anthony's eyes held wonder, and something more forlorn. A sigh. "Ah, well." He stood, ruffled my hair. "I ask more of you than your years, boy. It's my failing."

"I'm sorry, Anth. I'll pay better—"

But he was already striding to the car.

I ran after. "Wait. Finish."

"I'll sort it out one way or another." He slammed his door, flipped the switches. "I wish you well, Randy. Truly."

"Don't!" *Don't abandon me.*

A squeal of tires, and he was gone.

I sat on the Winthrops' cold porch cursing him, then myself. I'd been rude, when he'd practically begged me to pay heed.

But, so what if his feelings were hurt? He'd backed me into a corner, left me no choice. Now I couldn't go home to Carr Plantation without crawling, and I wouldn't do that for him, for Judy, for anything in the world.

3

"THANKS FOR THE RIDE." On the outskirts of Centraltown, I climbed down from the dusty grain hauler, aching and hungry. The driver fed it electrons; with a muted purr, it rumbled off.

I'd spent the morning stabbing my thumb at the wind, alongside of Plantation Road. It was a Plumwell rig that had pulled over at last, not that I'd doubted sooner or later someone would take me to the city. Hope Nation wasn't the old fearful Terran world our ancestors had fled; we looked after one another, and a joey needing a lift got one. It was safe; outside Centraltown's seedier districts crime was a rarity.

Not that Centraltown lacked a rough side. Folks in the Zone muttered that the city was growing too fast. Each supply ship from home system offloaded its quota of hopeful colonists, and our own population was reproducing at a more than healthy rate. I had several grown sibs, and that pattern wasn't uncommon.

The oldest of us was Zack, Anthony's father. Then came Kate, and their baby brother Billy who was now turning forty, and then after a long gap and a second marriage, me. Of course, it helped that Dad had started young; he'd had his first joeykid while still a middy in the Navy, assigned by Nick Seafort as liaison to the planters after the last U.N. ships abandoned us.

When Dad was young, the spaceport had been at the far edge of town. Not now. Modular housing—plain, utilitarian, drab—sprouted everywhere.

Much of it dated from the years after the fish dropped their bomb, when it was all we could afford. Many of the hastily erected buildings had since gone to seed.

I turned my mind to breakfast.

Where would I go, Judy had wondered, and her mom had interrupted before we could come up with an answer.

All the chill night, huddled in a Winthrop shed, I'd chewed at a fingernail, considering my options. At home I had credit chips from chores money, but retrieving them was too risky. I couldn't chance Anthony getting his hands on me just yet. So I was reduced to the clothes on my back, and my wits.

And my friends. Alex Hopewell might help, or perhaps the Mantiets, but my escapade was public knowledge, since I'd erupted at the party, in full view of the community. Most any parent would call Anthony at the sight of me.

So, I'd chosen Centraltown.

Kevin Dakko and I had hit it off so well. If I could only find his house . . . I'd seen it once, in October, just after school started. Anth had driven me to town to spend a Sunday with Kev. It wasn't the same between us, stuck in a tiny house with its manicured lawn, and only one lone tree on the whole place. I'd felt hemmed in, on a tiny patch of sterile land. And there was nothing I could show or teach him.

Still, he was only a year older than me, and would understand. During the summer we'd grown close, after a rocky start of half-hostile wrestling and dominance games, which he'd inevitably win. We'd worked past that into shared confidences, tentative at first, and ultimately, trust.

To get to Kev's house, I could call a taxi. There was even a bus route. But I was utterly 'rupt, and a Carr couldn't beg. I thrust my hands in my empty pockets, and began the long trek downtown.

The spaceport was almost deserted, as might be expected. We had little intrasystem traffic; only when the great Naval liners moored overhead did the place really come to life. Sure, mining ships shuttled between us and Three, and there were occasionally other vessels, but not enough to keep the restaurants open, except for a bar or two, and those would toss me on my ear if I even looked in.

Regardless how history holos pictured it, these days liquor laws were strictly enforced against a minor and whoever served him, here just as on Earth. It had been so for generations. Dad told me about a Plumwell cousin who'd spent six months in juvie for a tube of beer. Luckily, it was his first offense.

But nothing barred me from a restaurant, if only I had the coin.

Sometimes, for old times' sake, Dad would take us on a lazy Sunday to Haulers' Rest, a traditional way-stop along Plantation Road. Pancakes drowning in syrup, fresh corn, honey-baked ham. Mom would slather butter on enormous hot loaves of homemade bread and pass it . . .

Stop that, you idiot!

Too late. My stomach was churning. Sighing, I buttoned my jacket, bowed my head, strode on.

Kevin's house was on Churchill Road, not far from the rebuilt Cathedral. I trudged past the huge edifice; I had no interest in its soaring spires, its rough-hewn fortress walls. As far as I was concerned, the Cathedral was enemy territory. I grimaced. So, at least for now, was our own estate. Not that I'd intended to leave it forever when I'd told off the Bishop.

Two blocks east, a block crosstown. Kev's father had made us attend morning services; at least it helped me place the landmark in relation to his home. The Archbishop himself, old Andori, had preached; I'd dozed and squirmed through the endless ritual. Mr. Dakko had shot us an occasional warning glance, though Kev told me later he wasn't really devout.

There. Green celuwall-paneled front, solar roof.

My feet ached. I climbed the porch, rang the bell.

Nothing.

I rang again.

"All right, I'm coming!" A familiar voice that gladdened my heart. The door flew open.

"You!" Kevin gaped. "How . . . did your nephew bring you?" He peered past me, looking for my ride. His curly black hair rippled in the afternoon wind.

"Nah." I managed to sound nonchalant. "Thought I'd drop by." Let him think I could get about on my own, a full year and more younger than he. In a way, it was true; I *had* made it to Centraltown on my own. "Howya been?"

"Well, come on!" He stood aside, gestured me to the hall. "I was just fixing a snack. Want some?"

Thank you, Lord. "I guess."

I gazed wistfully at the remainder of the coffee cake, but Kevin seemed oblivious. On the other hand, he was absorbed in the story I'd spewed forth in response to his casual questions. I swallowed a lump. At fourteen I was almost of age, even if the law didn't see it so. Why did I crave his counsel, perhaps even his guidance? He was just turning sixteen.

"Kev, I'm in trouble."

His tone was gentle. "I know."

"You heard?"

"You show up on my doorstep, your clothes wrinkled, the look in your eyes practically begging me not to turn you away . . . what went wrong, Randy?"

As I poured out my troubles, a leaden weight in my chest began to lift. When I was done, I stared at the table, brooding, hungry, ashamed.

"So."

My attention jerked from the cake, so near to my plate, and so far.

"You'll want to stay here." It was more statement than question.

I shrugged. "I suppose." In a distant recess of my mind, Dad frowned. Kev deserved better, not only because I needed a place to stay, but because his offer—if that's what it was—was generous and kind. "I'd really like that. Do you think I could?" Only for a while, I added silently, until I figured what to do next.

"Fine by me, but we'll have to ask Dad. If I invited you without his approval . . ." He rolled his eyes.

I nodded sourly. Parents—and older nephews—could be an intolerable burden. "He'll be home soon?"

"Not for hours." He threw on his jacket. "Let's go."

"Where?"

"The shop. Better chance he'll say yes if we don't spring it on him late at night." He headed for the door.

Another long walk? My body groaned its protest, but dutifully I followed.

It wasn't that far, it turned out. Just a mile or so, past Churchill Park, through the maze of downtown stores and offices. Past the Naval barracks. We were no longer a colony, but in practical terms we had little choice but to allow the U.N. Navy its downtown barracks, and its Admiralty House near the spaceport. By U.N. regs, sailors were entitled to thirty days' long-leave after a voyage of nine months or more; the sprawling barracks was the sensible and traditional solution to housing.

I'd once asked Anth why we didn't build high, the way the holos showed Terran cities. "Because land's available," he'd said. "Consider: we've more land mass than Earth itself, and only three cities to speak of."

"There's dozens of—"

"Places like Tyre, or Winthrop? I'm not talking about country towns." He shook his head to shut off debate. "When you're older and seen the worlds, you'll understand."

Hah. As if Anthony had ever seen much beyond Detour, a few weeks by Fusion. He'd toured Constantine, Earth's newest colony. And that was about it. I'd stuck out my tongue, at his back. He'd seen, in the window reflection, and booted me from his study.

Now, striding beside Kevin, I grimaced. In truth, I didn't always treat Anthony that well, though I'd be loath to admit it. Take last night: he'd unbent enough to admit he was in trouble, and I was compounding it by running away. Well, I wouldn't have, if he hadn't lost his temper and—

"We're here."

I peered about. We were in the heart of Centraltown's business district, such as it was. Buildings of three stories or more cast long shadows on the scrupulously clean street.

DAKKO & SON read the sign. It was attached to what was, for Centraltown, an imposing edifice. A full five stories, fronted in granite blocks. The door handle was ornate antique brass, and gleamed.

"Are you the son?"

"No, Dad is." He guided me in.

The lobby was, I suppose, a typical reception area. I hadn't been downtown much. A well-dressed young woman looked up with a welcoming smile. "Shall I tell him you're here?"

"Please." Kevin's tone was tense.

We took seats. "What's your dad do?"

"We started out as chandlers to the Navy. Victuallers," Kev added, seeing my incomprehension. "You know. Suppliers. Then Dad bought into the grain mills, and—"

"He'll see you now."

Kevin shot to his feet, yanked a comb from his pocket, whipped it through his hair. He tugged at his shirt, straightened his collar. I couldn't help grinning, though it made him frown. He strode to a closed door, peered in. "Dad?" His tone was cautiously polite.

I could find other places to stay, if that's how it would be. Kevin actually sounded *afraid* of his old man. Where was the scorn that had dripped from his voice a few months past, when we sat cross-legged on our beds?

The door was ajar, but their voices were too low for me to catch many words. Kev sounded earnest. He paused, answered a question. Once, he pointed to the lobby, and my chair. Then more murmurs. Questions. "No," Kevin replied, several times. "No, sir."

At last, he poked his head into the hall, gestured urgently. I uncurled myself, headed for Mr. Dakko's office.

My school—Outer Central Academy—had a principal, Mr. Warzburg. His office was at the end of a long hall. If you got sent there, the best you could hope for was a stern lecture. For serious offenses you'd get really hard whacks with the strap he kept on the wall. Once, they'd caught Alex complaining about the "goddamn tomatoes" he had to process, and the crack of his chastisement echoed all the way to the ball court. Afterward, a very subdued young Hopewell had made his shamefaced way outside. Blasphemy wasn't tolerated.

It hadn't happened to me yet, though I'd come close.

There was that sense of dread, trudging to Mr. Warzburg's office, that I felt now. Abruptly I wished I weren't so disheveled, that I hadn't spent the night curled in a grimy shed.

I shuffled in. Staying with Kevin was beginning to seem a really bad idea. Perhaps if I called Anthony, made my tone sufficiently meek . . .

Kevin's father tipped his chair back against the window, hands clasped behind his head. He was slim, and wore casual business dress. His plain, scarred desk held nothing but a caller and a stack of holochips.

At the sight of me he came to his feet. His hair, once black, was shot through with jets of gray. A brief smile, which softened the lines on his face. "Hi. I'm Chris Dakko." He extended a hand for a firm shake.

I mumbled something, found I had to repeat it to be heard. "We've met, sir."

"Yes, you went to church with us." Blue eyes lit me like a searchlight.

I flushed. One's sins come back to haunt one.

Kevin glanced between us, licking his lips.

"My son says you need refuge." Mr. Dakko's tone was dry.

"Yessir." My voice squeaked. I blushed furiously. "Just for a few days." I couldn't ask for more.

From his cracked leather seat, he studied me. "I know your uncle Anthony."

"I'm the uncle." Why did I sound apologetic? "He's my nephew."

"Ah, yes. You're Derek's boy." Mr. Dakko's fingers drummed the desktop. "Have you committed a crime, Randy?"

Other than running away? "No, sir." But that was bad enough. And in three days, when Independence Day break was done, I'd be counted as truant. It wasn't just Anth who'd be after me.

"Are they searching for you?" Had Mr. Dakko read my mind?

"I don't think so." Anthony's style would be more to let me starve, until I came crawling back. And then lower the boom.

"I'll have to tell him where you are."

"Why?" I knew I sounded sullen, but couldn't help it. "He doesn't have custody."

"Who does?"

"My mother. Sandra Carr."

"I thought the Stadholder was raising you."

"He is. Was." I struggled to explain. "He doesn't have papers. Anything he tells me, though, he has Mom's assent." Mom was lost to the comfort of her chemdreams, though I'd die before I told an outsider like Mr. Dakko. Some matters we Carrs kept private.

"Mppf." He rocked, folding his arms. Then, "Well, your nephew's no great friend of mine, but I won't hide you. If he asks, I'll tell him you're with us." The ghost of a smile. "But I doubt he'll ask."

"Thank you." Under his minute scrutiny, I shuffled my feet.

"More important, I won't get trapped between the Carrs and the Bishop."

"In what, sir?" No sooner were the words out than I realized I shouldn't have asked.

Anth was in trouble, he'd told me, and my defiance had made it worse. I was supposed to *know* about such matters. I was a Carr, wasn't I? Perhaps I should go home after all, and . . .

No. Anth had to realize I was nearly grown. I couldn't crawl to him. He'd have to come to me.

"In anything. You can stay the night. Tomorrow, I'll decide if it'll be longer. But if Mr. Carr tells me you're to go home, you go. In the meantime, keep away from the Cathedral. Really, I should steer clear of you, but you're Kevin's friend, and your family took him in when . . ." He threw up his hands. "Enough. Kev will show you your room, and you'll help fix dinner. We'll eat when I get home." He eyed my rumpled shirt. "You have clothes?"

I shook my head, ashamed. It wasn't as if I'd *planned* to leave home, for Christ's sake.

"Kevin, sort through the closet in the green bedroom where I packed away your old things. They might fit."

"Yes, sir." Kev tugged me toward the door. "Thanks, Dad."

"And show Randy where the shower is. We should all be clean for dinner."

I blushed to the tips of my ears. "Thank you." It was no more than a mumble.

On the way home, Kev took it easy on my tired feet. "That's where the reservoir used to be, and the hospital. Back when the fish bombed us . . ."

I barely listened. It was ancient history, and I already knew. "Jeez, your dad is strict."

"Yeah, well . . ." Kev strode a few more paces. "He claims he was a real heller when he was a joeykid, and he's determined I won't be." He kicked a pebble. "He's nice enough, I guess. But he embarrassed me, the way he was looking you over."

"Hell, he had to decide. It's his home."

"Mine too," Kev said.

"What did he mean about taking you in?"

"Last spring, before he put me in the farm program, we didn't get along too good." He reddened.

"What's your grandfather think about it?"

"Huh?"

"Dakko & Son. If your dad's the son . . ."

"Oh, Grandpa. He died last winter. The T."

My breath hissed. "Melanoma T?"

"Yeah. Grandpa loved to travel, and he started interstellar late. The odds finally caught up with him. He was ninety."

It was one of the drawbacks of sailing among the colonies. Fusion drives generated the N-waves that enabled our ships to bypass the speed of light. But the waves could be deadly. Every so often they mutated simple melanoma, which was curable, into melanoma T, which generally was not. That's why the U.N. Navy recruited joeykids as young as thirteen to cadet Academy; if you were exposed within five years of puberty, the risk was much reduced. It was in a bunch of physics stuff I was supposed to take next year. Who cared? Only an idiot would want to be cooped in a ship a year at a time.

I said so.

Kev's face tightened. "Don't call Grandpa an idiot."

Oops. "I didn't mean that."

"He was really cool." We walked a while. Presently, the heel of his hand flicked past his eye, as if wiping away an itch.

I wished I hadn't unsettled him. "Kev . . ." I stopped short. "If my being here stirs up trouble between you and your—"

"No, once Dad agreed, it's all right. He's just got this attitude . . ." A vague wave of the hand. "I do what I want most of the time, and don't even have to let him know. But when he tells me to do something . . ." A glum shake of the head. "He says I'll be raised better than he, and I have no choice in the matter. Grandpa thought it was funny."

"What's your mom like?"

"Who knows? She's lived on Constantine for thirteen years."

"How come you didn't go?"

"She has my sister."

It made no sense, but I kept quiet. Family arrangements weren't to be pried into. It was gauche, whatever that meant. Or so Anthony warned me.

Kevin sighed. "Dad doesn't believe in cloning. Says it plays hell with the gene pool."

He'd opened the subject, so I was free to inquire. "You had a host mother?"

"No, they each wanted a joeykid, so they married. When they had two, they split."

"Christ, that's a breeding farm!"

Kevin said nothing. His pace increased, until I had to run to keep up. I grabbed his arm, but he threw me off. "Don't hold me!"

I'd had a miserable day, after a worse night. "Yell at me, or hit me, or whatever you want. Just talk to me!"

"Cool jets." Reluctantly, he slowed. "Joey, why do you say whatever comes to your mind, no matter who it hurts?"

"Because I'm stupid!" I spun away, fists clenched. He mustn't see me on the ragged edge. He'd despise me.

"No, you're not." His mood had turned, and he was the gentle Kev I craved. For an instant, his hand flitted to my shoulder. "I bet you're starved. Let's get dinner ready."

I nodded, not trusting myself to speak.

"A shed isn't a great place to sleep." His tone made it an offering.

I essayed a smile. "Ever try it?"

"I camped out at Grandpa's a couple of times, when Dad and I weren't speaking." At long last, we turned onto his block. "That ever happen to you?"

"No." Dad and I always spoke. Derek Carr was the finest man who'd ever lived. I'd kill anyone who said otherwise.

Later, in the shower, for some reason a tear or two swirled down the drain along with the cool, refreshing soapy water.

In the morning, Kevin poked his head into my bedroom. "Dad's gonna put you to work today."

I blinked away sleep. "What about you?"

"School."

"Can't you do that later?"

"Not virtual, dummy. I gotta be there."

I made a face. At my school, physical presence wasn't always required; three days a week we just netted.

"Hey." Kev's tone was elaborately offhand. "Here." He tossed a ten-Unie note on the bed.

"What's that for?"

"Just because." He shrugged. "Case you need lunch or something."

"Kev, I can't take your—"

"Then it's a loan, 'til you're settled."

I said with wonder, realizing it was true, "You're my best friend."

In the doorway he hesitated, as if reluctant to leave. "You don't mind helping Dad?"

"Course not." Did he think I expected a free ride? I was no trannie;

the Carrs paid their way. I'd see Kev was repaid too. Sooner than he thought. "Does your father want me now?"

"He'll be leaving in a half hour."

"I'll be ready." I bounded out of bed, grimaced at the clothing I had to don. The only pants of Kevin's that fit me were shorts that emphasized my gangly legs. And the shirt was something only a really young joeykid would pick. I sighed. Next time you leave home, Randy, pack a suitcase.

"Ah, there you are." Mr. Dakko greeted me from the breakfast table.

"Good morning," I said cheerfully.

His lips tightened.

Inwardly, I sighed. "Good morning, *sir*." It was his house; if I wanted to live in it . . . Was I better off with Anthony? Odd, that I was willing to tender this stranger more courtesy than I'd show my own—

His steely eyes locked on mine. "Last night, what you most needed was a good meal and bed. Now we ought to talk."

I nodded, apprehensive. He passed me oatmeal, cold boiled eggs, bread. I dug in.

"Kevin really likes you, joey. I've always felt . . ." A frown. "Walter didn't always approve of my friends, but—"

"Walter?"

"My father. We settled here together, with my mother, Galena. She's gone now. Walter didn't care for Greg Attani, or some of the others . . ." For a moment, he bobbed in a sea of memories. "But he never interfered with my friendships."

Is that all I was—his son's friend he disapproved of?

Again, he read my mind. "Of course, I'd rather see Kev with you than some of the . . . well. You know. My point is, his friends are for him to select. So if he wants to help one of them, naturally I'm inclined. But you're a special case."

"Because my nephew is the Stadholder." My tone was bitter.

"Of course." His blue eyes seemed to penetrate my soul. "Why else? Now, we're a small community and provincial, but firmly settled in the rule of law. Anthony Carr can't seize my property or arrest me. However, I won't make the head of government my enemy; he'd have too many small means to hurt me."

"You're sending me back." I braced myself for the inevitable.

"Of course not!" He threw down his napkin, and his voice sharpened. "You think your precious planters are the only ones with honor? Didn't I say you could stay?"

I found myself nodding hurriedly, wanting to do anything to seem agreeable. I was beginning to suspect that Mr. Dakko didn't suffer fools gladly, though I wasn't sure what that meant. It was a phrase Dad had used, now and again.

"So, joeyboy. Tell me what's going on between you two, and why."

I wiped oatmeal from my lip. "Anth bullies me."

"How?"

Haltingly, I explained. It wasn't chores—we all had our work to do, and Dad and I had talked that out years ago. A Carr earned his keep. It was some of his other requirements, his insistence that—

Mr. Dakko waved it away. "He talks to you about matters of state?"

"Sometimes." It was all I intended to say. Kev's father had no right to pry into—

"Why'd he have you provoke the Bishop?"

"What?" My voice shot into the upper registers. Blushing, I brought it down.

"That pantomime at his reception everyone's talking about. What was the purpose?"

"Scanlen called me a—"

"What was the Stadholder's strategy in arranging a public discourtesy? Either tell me, or leave my house."

"I—he didn't—but—" I stopped, drew deep breath. Then another, from sheer wonder. "You think Anthony put me up to it!"

"Of course. No joeykid would take it on himself to skirt excommunication, endure a training farm, risk his family's properties over—" He took in my expression, and his jaw dropped. "Good Lord." He leaned across the table, raised my chin. "Look me in the eye. Right now!"

I did, as long as I could manage.

At long last, a chuckle. "I'll have to tell Benny and Dr. Zayre we were wrong. We simply assumed . . ." He stood, thrust hands in pockets, strolled to the window. "Unbelievable."

Mother would be home, in a chaise lounge, curled in a warm sweater and reveries. Perhaps, if I woke her, she'd be in one of her gentler moods. "Mr. Dakko?"

Nothing.

"Sir!"

Something in my tone caught his attention. He raised an eyebrow.

"What have I done? What's the mess I made worse? Should I leave, so you and Kev won't get hurt?"

He held up a placating palm. "No need to go." His tone was kind. "Not yet."

A strangled sound. To my horror, I realized I'd sobbed aloud. "I don't know what I . . . I don't understand. Tell me what's going on."

Again, a chuckle. "I'd intended to question *you*." He clapped me on the shoulder. "Dry your eyes. It's time to be off."

I looked about. "I thought you were giving me work."

A note of surprise. "Not here." He ushered me to the door.

It was a crisp day, and he seemed in no hurry to drive to his office. We detoured through the spacious park, where a few young parents sat in the sun, watching their joeykids run about.

"Since your father got in that row with the Patriarchs . . ."

"Huh?" It would have annoyed Anthony no end. I tried again. "Excuse me?"

"A decade ago, during the third revolution."

I tried to look like I was following, but my face betrayed me.

"Your father. Derek. When he took us independent, we—"

"Mr. Dakko, I . . ." It was almost shameful to admit. "I don't always pay attention when they tell me important stuff. Could you start at the beginning?"

"Hope Nation. Where we live. It was once a U.N. colony." It was how he might talk to a village idiot, but I'd asked for it. "In those days a colonial Governor ran our affairs. We had no real say. You studied this?"

"Yessir." I was anxious to redeem myself. "Back in fifth."

"We've since had three revolutions. First, the Triforth rebellion."

"She was hanged."

"By Nick Seafort's own hand. She tried to seize the government as the U.N. Navy retreated from the fish." The aliens had appeared suddenly among the fleet. They were shaped something like goldfish, infinitely larger. Some of them rivaled the smaller Naval vessels in size. Extensions would swirl from their skin, begin to rotate, separate, and hurl acid at a warship's hull. Even worse were the outriders, shapechangers that emerged from the fish, launched themselves, melted through our hulls to spread virus and wreak havoc.

I said bitterly, "The frazzing cowards in the Navy ran for home." And left us to the marauding aliens overhead.

"Mr. Carr." His tone was odd.

"Yes?"

"I served in the U.N. Navy. There was no cowardice."

"I didn't mean to—"

"So I'll ask you to retract that statement."

"I do, sir. I'm very sorry I said it." Sweat trickled under my arms. I sat quite still. Mr. Dakko wasn't overly muscled, not so tall. He was my friend's father; the worst he'd do was toss me out of the electricar. And yet . . .

Eventually, Mr. Dakko's eyes softened. "Captain Seafort put down Laura Triforth's uprising, and, as theater commander, granted us full U.N.

membership. They say when he brought the news home, the General Assembly was aghast."

"Yes, sir. But we had a right—"

"That was the second revolution. Who was our first Stadholder?"

"Zack Hopewell." Everyone knew that. Alex still had a swelled head over it, though it occurred nearly forty years before he was born.

"And your father?"

My chest swelled. "The third." He'd held office for many years, always reconfirmed by the Assembly.

"For decades, Hope Nation was a member of the U.N., much as Britain, or China, or the African Federation, back on Earth. Full voting rights, our own regional government and constitution."

I waited him out. Please, not a history lecture, please—

"Your father saw we had to be more."

He had my full attention.

"Twelve years ago, he notified the General Assembly we were pulling out."

What had Dad said about it? Not much; I'd been so young. But later . . . "It's time we stood on our own. And it's the only way we'll break their bloody shipping monopoly."

"Under the constitution, we had to give three years notice." Mr. Dakko found a shady spot, pulled over, rolled down the windows. A few stately genera trees stood sentinel against the winds. "Time for the U.N. Government to make its case. Seafort's administration was in power; he said he wouldn't hold a colony by force."

"At least he did *something* right." My voice dripped scorn.

He ignored me. "The government did nothing, but the Patriarchs sent Bishop Andori to rein us in."

The one who'd made Dad weep.

"Almost, he succeeded. They went eyeball to eyeball, he and Derek. But the independence vote carried, and we were independent. The third revolution. Now we trade with Earth as equals. At least in theory, that—"

"Anthony says they still try to bully—"

"Young man." His voice was quiet. "It's rather rude to interrupt, isn't it? Especially as you asked me to explain."

I shrank in my seat. His laser eyes burned my cheeks. Even Anth couldn't make me feel so low. "I'm sorry, sir."

"I'm odd that way, I suppose. None of Kev's friends like it. But it's something I learned in the Navy. I ask courtesy, if not respect."

"Yessir." I was a Carr, for God's sake, and presented myself as an ill-mannered clod. What was the *matter* with me?

"And I'll give you the same. Now where were we? Trading. They still have the upper hand; it comes with the ships. No doubt your, ah, nephew's aware. Meanwhile, on Earth, the Seafort government fell. Then Henrod Andori failed to thwart us. Now we have Scanlen as well." Hope Nation wasn't really big enough to need both Bishop and Archbishop, but . . .

I shot him a glance, hoping for permission to speak. He nodded. "Anthony's been very careful dealing with the Church hierarchy, sir. I know that much."

"Yes. He's gone out of his way not to alienate them."

Until I'd stepped in, and blasted his plans. *A heathen or a Jew.*

"Do you know why, Randy?"

"Because they have power? They own a lot of land, and . . ." I was out of my depth.

Mr. Dakko hesitated. "What I tell you must go no further. Give me your word."

"You have it. Absolutely."

"They have power, yes. To renounce, or excommunicate. Your father, Derek, was a hero, and could stand up to them. Even he didn't find it easy. I think . . ." He faltered. "There's a rumor . . . no, I won't say it, not even with your word. But Anthony hasn't his stature. It's no disparagement to say that. He's too young."

I nodded.

He asked, "You know who the Territorials are?"

"The opposite of the Supras." The other party, in Earth's politics.

"They're anxious to return to power. And they're furious Seafort let us go. The Patriarchs favor them."

I puzzled it out. "So Scanlen and Andori . . ." My eyes widened. "They want to take control?"

"I say nothing against Mother Church. I don't even think it, do you understand?"

"Yessir."

"I imagine Ambassador McEwan would be delighted if we returned to colonial status. But I speak no ill of the Archbishop." His tone was carefully precise.

"How does . . ." My voice quavered. "How does excommunication work?"

"A Bishop or the Patriarchs at home may declare it. We are a religious state, always have been. An excommunicate is barred from the Church, his property forfeit, he's to be shunned by the community. It's a matter of ecclesiastic law."

I picked at my joeykid's shorts. *Anthony, what have I done?* I was a child, despite my pretensions to more. If Scanlen vents his fury at me on the Stadholder, I've ruined my family. Dad's family. His life.

Mr. Dakko cleared his throat. "Rebellion against His authority—"

"Anthony didn't rebel!"

"Please don't interrupt. Though rebellion warrants excommunication, so severe a penalty is almost never invoked. In Hope Nation's history, just once."

"When?"

"A madman killed a priest."

"Will I be excommunicated for telling the Bishop to fu—f—" In my cowardice, I couldn't say it.

"Oh, I very much doubt it." A wintry smile. "Though I'm sure he'd like to get his hands on you." He peered out the window, at a toddler exploring a clump of bushes, and the sunny bench where his mother sat reading. "A wardship of wayward minor, that sort of thing. The courts would cooperate."

"What would happen to me?"

"There are Church agencies, as well as private ones. Residential cottages, a correctional farm. It depends where you're sent. A good beating, for a start; he'd see to that. And frankly, you deserve it. Don't give me that crosswise look, joey. Scanlen merits courtesy as an adult, if nothing else. Perhaps back in the Rebellious Ages you could . . ." A sigh. "Not that you haven't set folk to chuckling in their tea, from here to the Venturas. More than a few of them wish they were free to . . ." His mouth snapped shut. "Well. Time to hit the office."

"Sir, should I go back? I mean, after I work for you today?" I wouldn't want him to think I meant to cadge free meals.

"Well." He followed the road in a gentle curve. "Think about your question."

I blinked, through fuzz.

"Do you see?"

"Not really." What did he want me to guess?

We were outside the park. Even in Centraltown, there was little traffic. His "office" was something of an anomaly. Most everyone worked from home, except in stores.

"Think, Randy. What happens to a joeykid caught drinking?"

"Wayward minor. Juvie or Church farm."

"And the adult who serves him?"

"Penal colony." It went without saying.

"And the minor who flouts authority?"

I nodded.

"And the adult who encourages him?"

I was silent. Then, "Oh!" If I asked, Mr. Dakko *had* to tell me to go home.

Again, that quick smile that lightened his eyes. "Strictly hypothetically, mind you, I'm not sure the Stadholder's upset you're gone."

I said indignantly, "Why not?" Despite our quarrels, Anth cared about me. I was sure of it.

"If you returned, what then?"

"He'd give me what for."

"And then?"

"We'd be friends." With Anthony, once done, it was over.

"And regarding the Bishop?"

"I'd . . . he'd . . ."

"Have to turn you over, most likely. Which now, he doesn't."

"But that's my problem, not his."

"Unless he has his own issues with Bishop Scanlen. Even if he were only forced to make you apologize, he'd lose face." Mr. Dakko's voice was quiet. "Well, here we are." He pulled up. "Upstairs, joey."

I was glad I'd worn Kev's old shorts and a light shirt. Mr. Dakko kept me busy moving boxes into the addition they'd just finished, and wiring in puters and other chipgear.

How ironic, I grumbled to myself. Our teachers constantly told us that we'd achieved a low-labor society, which meant more goods and services for all. On our homesteads, sophisticated AIs tended our crops. Once harvested, grains and vegetables were milled, canned, bagged, or processed in highly automated plants, until shipped aloft to the huge ships or barges that took the crops to market.

Likewise, in our cities, few offices had more than a couple of employees; puters and their electronic brethren did the rest. At home Dad had used a few old-fashioned filing cabinets; he'd often kept paper copies of important documents, damning the expense. But in general, human secretaries and receptionists were only for the very wealthy, who were trying to show off.

So when you needed sweat labor, as Mr. Dakko did today, you turned to migrant hands if it were dormant season, or else you called on joeykids.

I wouldn't say I enjoyed it, but I owed him, and didn't resent paying. And it was good practice; if it turned out I'd left home permanently, I'd have nothing but common labor to fall back on.

Mr. Dakko clearly intended to get his money's worth. I hauled files, holovids, and chipcases, manhandled chairs up a narrow stairway, crawled behind half a dozen consoles to install surprisingly sophisticated comm gear. A short lunch break—he gave me coin and sent me to a neighborhood coffee shop—and I was back at it, testing infrared transceivers. By midafternoon I was drooping, but determined not to complain. It was a great relief when Kevin bounded up the office stairs, his school day finished.

I appreciated his help, but his presence reminded me my own school session would start in a day or so. Did I really want to be posted as a truant? It was no light matter.

Besides, I actually liked school. My teachers complained I didn't listen, and often enough it was true. But math was cool, and so was physics. Even history wasn't that bad, when someone like Anth took the trouble to explain it to me.

Lucky Kevin: he only had to work an hour or so before his father told us we were free to go.

As he grabbed his holovid, I hesitated, eyeing the console. "Let's schuss the slopes a while." Terran slang, not ours, but it was zark not to sound provincial. I slid my thumb over the ID slot, ready to log on.

"Why?"

"To see if I've been netted." If Anth really wanted to haul me home, he'd post my flight on the nets, warning all netizens it was illegal to aid a runaway. And if he were really pissed, he'd post a reward.

"Might as well. You won't leave tracks."

My fingers dropped from the pad.

How badly did Anthony want me back?

After Dad's third revolution, when we were really free, he'd ordered Hope Nation's nets to disable trace functions. They were the mark of repressive government, he said, and Hope was a nation of free men. Nets were essential to modern life, and the Commonweal wouldn't use them to trace and monitor its citizens.

Most folk thought it was still so. But Anthony, elected First Stadholder, had quietly reinstated primary trace. I'd have to find another way. A public caller, perhaps.

It was a new day, and a long sleep had worked wonders. Again I'd gone with Mr. Dakko to his office; this time after a few hours' labor, he'd taken me to lunch. I'd expected a nearby restaurant, but we drove to a rambling home not far from downtown. An energetic, florid woman greeted us at the carved oak door; she offered me a hand.

"Hilda, you're ahead of me. This is Randy, one of Kevin's friends. Randy, Dr. Zayre."

"Good to meet you." Her handshake was firm. "I'm due back at the hospital in an hour; let's get seated." She gave a series of brisk instructions to the micro, and led us to benches in an enclosed, sunlit nook behind the kitchen.

Table talk ranged far and wide, from weather to politics and beyond; out of courtesy, Dr. Zayre or Mr. Dakko occasionally made a point to include me. Generally, I was content to sit and listen, though the conversation bored me. Over fresh salad with a cream dressing, Dr. Zayre fretted about the problems of her minuscule yard. Her usual gardener had quit, seeking more highly paid plantation work. And her shed needed rebuilding and painting.

The men and women who ran the Commonweal actively discouraged an unemployed labor pool in the city, and the industrialization they claimed would inevitably follow. It was a situation that had occupied Dad, and Anth after him. Since Hope Nation's colonial days, there'd been tension between farm and town. Laura Triforth's rebellion and Zack Hopewell's successor government had wrested control away from the city, vesting real political power in the Planters' Council.

Hope Nation was an agricultural colony, its wealth inevitably tied to the fertile land. Perhaps that was why Dr. Zayre found it hard to keep a gardener at paltry wages.

"Well?" The adults were looking at me expectantly.

"Huh?" Furiously, I tried to recall what she'd just said.

Ms. Zayre's tone was patient. "Would you be interested? I know the pay isn't much, but you'd have a place to stay, and there isn't all that much to do."

"As your gardener?" I finally found my voice.

"And handyman. I work long hours, and don't have time . . ."

I looked to Mr. Dakko for guidance, but he was impassive. I couldn't stay at Kevin's after school began, else Mr. Dakko would be harboring a wayward youth, a serious offense. Even if he had no wish to turn me in, my presence would put him in jeopardy. And he couldn't make work for me for long; I'd be dependent on his charity. Dad would hardly have approved.

With the doctor, I'd have a real job, no matter how low the pay. And Anth would never think of looking here.

Still, I'd prefer to be near Kev. Reluctantly, I nodded. "I guess so."

She asked, "Tomorrow, or thereabouts?"

"Yes, ma'am." If I'd be working for her, living in her home, she deserved simple courtesy. Moreover, she and Mr. Dakko were friends; I owed her as much as I did him . . .

I thought back to the introductions. No, he hadn't called me anything but "Randy." "There's something you should know," I said with a grimace. "I don't think Mr. Dakko mentioned—"

"Hilda, excuse us a moment." Mr. Dakko stood. To me, "Let's take a walk."

I gaped.

"Now, please?" In a moment, he'd steered me out the back door. "And what was that about, joey?"

"I wanted to warn her that Anth—"

"Do you ever think before you speak?"

The silence stretched, until I stirred in unease. "Please. I don't . . ." I shrugged helplessly. "I was just trying . . ."

"You recall our talk yesterday, in the car?"

My mind whirled. "You mustn't advise me not to go home. But what does that . . . oh!"

If Dr. Zayre didn't know I was a runaway, no one could fault her for taking me in. But once she knew . . . Still, I'd been trying to protect her, in my thoughtless way.

My tone was humble. "I'm sorry."

"No matter."

"Should I come here to stay, sir?"

His eyes softened. "Randy, the Stadholder knows you and my son are friends. Sooner or later . . ."

"I'll move to Dr. Zayre's."

I didn't have much to say for the rest of lunch.

Later, on the way home, I folded my arms, stared out the window. Mr. Dakko let me brood. Abruptly, after a long while, I stirred. "Pull over, please."

Surprised, he slowed, pulled into a quiet lane, turned off the motor. "What is it, boy?"

"There's a lot I don't know about politics." The confession shamed me. "But I'm not stupid. I may act it, but I'm not." I forced defiance from my tone. "Please, tell me what's going on."

"A lot's going on, lad. What do you ask?"

I stared at my shoes. "I'm just a joeykid who's having trouble with his family. But you treat me like . . ." I foundered, started over. "Today at lunch, Dr. Zayre never asked my last name. I'd want to know, before inviting someone to live with me. And she never asked if I knew about flowers or was handy with tools."

"That troubles you?"

"It makes me think she already knew. That you'd made arrangements. That, together, you're hiding me. Are you?"

"If so, you'd object?"

"Sir, Kev and I got along, but that's no reason to risk yourself for me. Is this to hurt Anth?"

"Why would you think so?"

A question, instead of a straight answer. He was fencing.

Shit.

I sighed, knowing what I had to do. I tried my door; it was locked. "Please let me out."

"Where are you going?"

"Home, to face the Bishop." To ruin my life.

"Stay a moment." His penetrating blue eyes regarded me with new wariness. "Very well, joey, you have my word. I don't wish to harm your nephew." After a moment, he pursed his fingers, like a spider on a mirror. "Why are you so suspicious?"

"You have some goal. Some—" I struggled for the word Anthony would use. "—agenda. Political games, I think. I hate the way Anth treats me, but we're family. I won't drag him into your games."

"But you already have." In his face, sympathy. "The Right Reverend Scanlen is furious, and demands your return. You embarrassed him in front of everyone who matters. He named you wayward today, in a rather stiff note to the authorities."

Bile rose, and burned my throat. I swallowed convulsively. "Then I'll turn myself in."

"Ah, but the Stadholder doesn't want you in Scanlen's hands. He can't say it aloud, but we know. If the Bishop gets you, he has Anthony."

"Once the Church has me to punish, I'm no issue."

"Except to your nephew."

"Why, sir?"

"He values you. Once the Church has you on their training farm, he'll agree to anything they demand. Because every day you'd face the strap, a solitary penitence cell, even a fatal accident in the night."

"Why do *you* care?" I was unbearably rude.

"About you? You're my son's friend, but that doesn't signify so much. Look at me, joey." He waited. "Now, please. Into my eyes."

"Yes, sir." His tone was something like Dad's when I'd irked him.

His gaze wasn't unkind. "I'll speak frankly, as you demand. We all wish you hadn't provoked a cris—no, a situation. Anthony Carr has been in a delicate dance with the Church, as was your father, Derek. My friends and I prefer that he emerge independent. If you go home, you'll destroy any chance of that." A pause, and he plunged on. "You asked for honesty? Very well: our interests and his don't coincide in all things. In some matters we will oppose the Stadholder with all means at our disposal. But this isn't one of those matters; in that, you have my promise. So the doctor's home is your refuge, if you wish. As is mine."

I couldn't help myself. A lump in my throat, I reached across and took the comfort of his hand.

4

"ANOTHER SOFTIE?" Kevin lounged on his bed. We'd walked home from Dakko & Son; when his father came home, we'd tell the kitchen micro to heat dinner.

"Nah." I reddened. "Er, no thanks." We might be friends, but I was his guest, sort of. Dad and Anth both had strong ideas on courtesy between guests and hosts, and I agreed. Even a narf like Bishop Scanlen deserved . . . for a moment I squirmed. Well, he'd insulted me first, and deserved what he got, even if it made more trouble than I'd intended.

But living in Kevin's house, I couldn't be rude. It wouldn't be long, though, before I'd have to go to Dr. Zayre. I sighed. No doubt she'd be kind, but Kev was near my age, and we'd become as close as we'd ever been.

"I better get my work done." He swung to his puter, climbed onto the net, schussed into a series of his trig problems.

I watched, half interested. Then, "Ever look me up?" I tried to sound casual. If I'd been netted, his look-up would reveal it.

"What's to see? Are you famous?" A derisive snort.

"No, but . . ." I grabbed at deception. "Dad put our family bios up, years ago. See if they're still there."

"I'm busy." He was calculating a sine function. I'd have to read the problem to understand it, and I didn't want to bother. His glance flickered my way. "Unless there's some reason . . . ?"

I tried not to betray my tension. I could tell Kev my worry, and of course he'd check me out on the nets. I needed, really needed to know.

On the other hand, it was in strictest confidence that Anth had told me he'd reinstated tracing. It was a sign of his trust. Explaining why I needed Kevin to schuss for me would betray Anth.

I sighed. "Nah, forget it." I leaned back. Perhaps I could call Judy Winthrop. If her mother let her near a caller. I couldn't escape another sigh. I'd gotten Judy in hot water with her family, and put Kev at risk just being around him. As for Anth, I didn't even want to think of the difficulty I'd caused.

Perhaps I should spend my time with our enemies, and cause them the trouble I made for our friends.

* * * *

Darkness had fallen, dinner was done. Kevin schussed the byte-bit slopes, his homework finished. Across the room, Mr. Dakko browsed his holovid, his feet propped on a hassock.

Perhaps it was kindness, perhaps Mr. Dakko had had a quiet word with his son. Whatever the cause, Kev had dropped what he was doing and explored the nets, with me as target. Without saying anything, he'd shown me the results.

I sat, chin in hands, brooding on what we'd found. Rather, what we hadn't found.

There was no warning pasted across my net profile, no cross-ref to a missing child alert. Nothing.

It had me puzzled. At the very least, Anthony ought to have posted a please-notify. It would be only a nominal effort to find me, one I could easily avoid by not schussing in my regular tracks. But it would show token compliance with Church demands, and avoid trouble with the Bishop.

On the other hand, what would Anthony's refusal to seek me out signify? He wasn't obligated, either as Stadholder or parent-by-proxy, to stop me from visiting the city. On the other hand, if I was truly a wayward youth, then as a parent he was responsible for my depredations, and had the obligation to bring me under control.

On the other hand—we were running out of hands—my mother, Sandra, was my actual guardian. Ultimately, unless Anth asserted real control over me, he had no legal obligation either to make me behave or to hand me to the Church for spiritual correction. Yet, I doubted he'd resort to such a mealymouthed defense; he was raising me, and proud of it.

If only I could ask Anthony what he'd have me do. But I didn't dare use the caller or post a netnote. Not only might he trace me and, worse, force me home, but his answer would close off options he might want preserved.

Kevin caught his breath. "Holy shit, look!"

I swung round, a chill lancing my spine. If Anth had—

"Kevin!"

"Dad, they've—"

"Kevin!" Mr. Dakko's holovid tumbled to the floor.

"What did—oops. Sorry, sir."

"Turn that off."

"I didn't mean to talk—"

He was out of his chair. "Switch it off. To your room."

"Yessir." Kev's holovid went dark. To me, a helpless shrug. He padded toward his room.

"Just a moment." His father's tone was firm. "Do you recall the last time you used foul language?"

"Yes, sir." Kev's voice was small.

"What did I do?"

A glance of dismay. "Dad, Randy's here."

"What did I do?"

"You washed out my mouth." Kevin's face was crimson.

"Shall we do it again?"

"No, sir, I'll watch myself. Honest."

"Very well."

Kevin disappeared.

The atmosphere was like ice. My closest friend had been humiliated before me, and I doubted I'd forgive.

After a time, Mr. Dakko cleared his throat. "Believe me, I heard worse in the Navy."

Politely, I smiled, hoping I wasn't betraying Kev.

"And I used worse." He bent to retrieve his holovid. "I told you I was on *Challenger* and *Hibernia*?"

"You didn't mention the ships." What had Kevin found that excited him so? I'd slip into his room and ask, before bed. Mr. Dakko hadn't forbidden it. And if it concerned me, I needed to know.

"With my father. I thought I was grown, and tried to act it." A pause. "Like Kevin."

I stared at the fabric of my chair.

"Walter—my father—didn't do much to take me in hand, though Lord God knew I needed it. Slowly, in the derelict ship, civilization collapsed around us. Then Walter showed a steel I didn't know was in him."

What was he trying to tell me?

"I won't make Kev wait that long. So I'm strict. Not unduly so."

"That's a matter of opinion." I couldn't help myself.

"Yours differs?" His tone was dry.

"It's not like he meant to be rude. He was excited."

"About what?"

"Who knows? You wouldn't let him tell you."

"Language counts, you know."

"Yes, but . . ." I sighed. "It's kinda dumb, my having an opinion. Look what my language started."

A chuckle.

After a long silence, "Ask him to rejoin us, Randy. Tell him you successfully pleaded his case."

Moments later, Kev cautiously seated himself near his father. It was the elder Dakko who got up, enveloped his son in a fierce embrace.

"So, then." Mr. Dakko rearranged himself on his sofa. "What was it you found?"

"A ship's coming in!" Kevin's eyes sparkled.

"Whoa." Mr. Dakko's face relaxed into a grin. "When?"

"It'll dock late tonight. Pa, can we go up and watch?"

"I doubt there'll be room on the shuttle." Of course there'd be one lifting off, crowded with customs and immigration officials, Naval brass and curious dignitaries anxious for a first look.

"You always say that. If you called Thurmon Branstead . . ."

"No, sorry." A pause. "I have valuable connections, Kev. I don't like using them for personal favors. When you run the business you'll understand."

"Yes, sir." Kevin's disappointment was evident. So was mine. Ships came in so seldom—rarely more than two a year. The ore and grain barges didn't count.

"It's likely I can arrange a tour, though. After all, we're chandlers to the Navy. Would you like that?"

"Megazark!"

"Did you notice what ship?"

"The new one. *Olympiad.*"

"Ahh." Mr. Dakko's fingers drummed. "Good business there. She's colossal. Three thousand passengers, eight hundred crew."

I shook my head, trying to imagine a vessel that vast. "Could we go to the port for the zoo?" I really oughtn't to be seen in public, but in an excited crowd . . .

"Yeah!" Kevin's face lit.

After a moment Mr. Dakko said, "Why not? People rarely make such fools of themselves."

Years ago, when he was Stadholder, Dad had growled that disembarkation day was a zoo, and the term had stuck. Eager colonists and green sailors hit Centraltown for their first and probably only visit, and citizens came out to welcome them in force. The zoo made quite a show.

"And Dr. Zayre will be expecting Randy, afterward. Just past dinner."

My face fell. "Yes, sir." Mr. Dakko was strict, sometimes even harsh. Why had I come to view his abode as home?

Later, before bed, Kevin and I lounged in his room. Our conversation turned to the newly arrived ship, and his father's stint in the Navy.

I asked, "Ever think of joining up?"

"Not for a minute." Kev lay back on his bed, arms over his head.

I glanced away. Not so much older than I, he seemed much more grown. Not just his manner; even his physique was almost a man's. "Why not? It'd get you out of here."

"I don't *want* out." He thought a while. "Ships are for making money off, not for sailing."

"Dad thought otherwise." My dad, I meant.

"So does mine, even if he was never an officer."

"Why not?"

Kevin shrugged. "Dad says he was too immature at the time. Then why does he look back on his service with such nostalgia? An awful life, being ordered around, packed like sardines, a year between shore leaves. Know what my life will be?" He rolled over. "I've got it figured out. University, then banking, then when Dad's ready, I'll take over the business."

"What's so exciting about that?"

"It's the banking that's exciting. Control enough money, and we'll build our own ships."

"That takes specialized yards, the fabricating plants for the fusion—"

"Exactly, and it's how Earth holds us over a barrel. They deny us technology that would make us independent. You know, those Naval bastards even ripped the fusion drive out of that obsolete warship they sent to replace Orbit Station after Seafort nuked it? Just to make sure we couldn't recommission it and have a working starship."

I shrugged. It had been Dad's dream for years to break Earth's monopoly on shipping. "Someday, the government—"

"Not the government. Us!" His eyes sparkled. "Imagine a company so strong, it builds and runs its own starships!"

"Hope Nation doesn't have the shipyards to build—"

"Not just us, Randy, all the senior colonies, working together. We'll carry ores from Kall's Planet, grain from Hope Nation, fabrics and fashions from Earth . . . at prices we set. We'll appoint our own Captains, set our own schedules. When we're wealthy enough, they won't be able to stop us."

"We?"

"Dakko & Son. Dad's dream turned a victualling house into the Nation's leading merchants. Mine is to haul cargo to the stars!"

Bulging out of Kev's nondescript old clothes, my shock of wavy hair thrust under a velcap, I was just another joeykid. Few would pay me heed.

The spaceport was teeming. Perhaps not by Terran standards, but certainly by ours. All the shops were open, immigration officials were checking inoculations, shuttles were landing every thirty minutes, and for once, the terminal restaurant had a long, restless line.

Kevin followed me, somewhat glumly. He burned with desire to see the new ship. No doubt his father could arrange it, but Kevin had been hoping somehow to see it on his own.

I peered about the terminal, but the real fun was outside. I thrust through knots of disoriented passengers, made my way into the bright sunshine, Kevin at my heels.

All around us, eager entrepreneurs had thrown up impromptu stalls of every description. Ship-pale tourists and colonists pored over colorful shirts hauled fresh from Centraltown warehouses. One caught my eye: *Hope Nation, Where Fish Were Found.* You'd have to be glitched to wear that. Apparently many of these joeys were.

Nearby, a shadeless stall offered hastily potted local weeds of no particular distinction. At the next table flourished a bizarre collection of so-called native handicrafts. Most were machine-carved softwoods, from trees cut from our plantations when new fields were cleared.

"Look." Kevin gave me a nudge.

At a stall whose sign read NATIVE ANTIQUE DOLLS, an excited woman and her daughters clawed at small figures clothed in outlandish costumes, while the husband waited indulgently.

"Harvest festiva," rasped the stall's exotic proprietor. Oversized gold earrings jangled under her colorful kerchief. "Hold ever' other year. You just missed." Judiciously, she lifted a more expensive doll, one of a set dressed in a motley mix of gear: farm clothes, shipboard hand-me-downs, ties, and neckerchiefs. "Original colonists wore. Very rare dolls."

I raised an eyebrow. The stallkeeper glanced at me coolly. "Hi, Rand'." She fixed her attention on her prospect. "Seventy Unies. Ain' she beautiful?"

I suppressed a grin, left Dr. Mantiet to her prey. In real life, she taught psychology at Centraltown University, and had no accent I could discern. Lord knew where she derived the pidgin English she affected. She described her zoo-days stall as both a lucrative hobby and a seminar in applied psychology.

Still, the zoo was fun to watch. Unethical? Perhaps, but every ship's library carried holos on Hope Nation; only those joeys who insisted on being gullible were fooled, and the Commonweal cheerfully skinned them alive.

I sniffed at the pungent scent of frying sausage. Of their own volition my feet bore me closer. Naturally, prices were inflated, but Kevin had coin, and his father had slipped me a few Unies when dropping us off.

We stood about munching garlic-fried meat in toasted buns, while chatter swirled about us.

"—if that frazzing Pandeker nags Pa one more time—"

"He ignores it. You should too."

A sharp blow to my shoulder squirted the sausage from my fingers. It splatted on the pavement.

"Damn it to *hell.*" I spoke too loudly, and caught glares of disapproval.

"Hey, joey, sorry." A pleasant tenor, behind me. "Lemme buy you another."

"Watch where you're . . ." I peered up. A ship's officer, about twenty, with another young officer as companion. They were dressed for shore leave: no ties, jackets slung over their shoulders.

I frowned at his insignia. A midshipman, if I read his bars right. Dad had taught me, years ago, but I'd forgotten much of it. Length-of-service pins, for example, were gibberish.

"Yeah, Mikhael, watch where you're going." The middy's companion grinned down at me. "Mik's terminally clumsy, but he means no harm." To his friend, "Got coin?" He fished in his own pocket. "You, there, give this joeykid a fresh sausage."

His insignia was different from his mate's. I said tentatively, "You're a lieutenant?"

"As of last week, yes." He thrust out a hand. "Tad Anselm at your service." His grin was so engaging I had to smile back.

I entrusted my hand to his big paw. Randy Ca—Carlson." It was a lie, and I hated it. Perhaps in recompense, I brought forth my best manners. "Glad to meet you, sir. This is my friend, Kevin Dakko."

The middy waited his turn. "Mikhael Tamarov."

We shook hands all around.

"So, joeys," said the lieutenant. "What's to do around here?"

"You mean, for the day?"

"Or more. We're on long-leave. A month, but Mik won't want to leave the ship for more than a week."

"Yes, I do, Tad." The middy frowned. "Sir."

"Off ship, we forget that."

"Right. Believe me, I'll use my month. I just want to check on Pa from time to time."

I raised my eyebrows. I didn't know much about the Navy, but . . . an officer bringing along his father?

As if changing the subject, the middy turned to his companion. "Tad, remember what we were saying about intrasystem officers?"

"That they don't get real experience?"

"Listen to this. That joey at the terminal desk says a local mining ship spotted a fish near Three. Comm room sent out a false alarm."

"Spotted a what?" I stopped dead. No fish had been seen for decades; they were obliterated by Seafort's caterwaul stations. The unmanned stations broadcast a skewed N-wave that summoned the aliens to destruction. N-waves allowed us to Fuse, to travel between the stars at something akin to superluminous speeds, but the fish sensed us Fuse and Defuse, and it drove them to frenzy. The caterwaul stations lured the fish with a skewed wave, crisped them with automatic laser fire. We lost stations, but that didn't matter. Eventually the last fish were destroyed.

"A fish," repeated the middy. "But it wasn't one. It didn't attack. They blasted it to hell, whatever it was. Probably an ice mass."

I nodded. Fish *always* attacked. Every Nationeer was taught our history, at least that part.

The lieutenant looked thoughtful. "Not every asteroid radiates as metal. An excited tech . . ."

Mik nodded knowingly. "Like you said. Never trust an officer from an intrasystem ship." He and his lieutenant exchanged knowing glances.

I bridled. "Not every competent sailor is in your precious Navy." One of Dad's long-standing goals had been to break the U.N. Navy's stranglehold on interstellar shipping, and Anth was just as determined.

"Sure, joey."

I gritted my teeth and ignored the condescension in his tone.

Anselm waved at the haphazard rows of stalls. "What's to see beyond this goofjuice?"

Kevin said brightly, "There's downtown, the Cathedral, the Zone, the Ventura Mountains . . ."

"Pa said I shouldn't miss the mountains," said the middy.

"Downtown would be a good start," Anselm judged. "Are there guides for hire?"

"Not really . . ." Kevin shot me a warning glance. "Tell you what: we'll show you Centraltown, I'll even take you to the Zone."

"How much?" The lieutenant eyed him suspiciously.

"Nothing, just for fun. How about giving us a tour of the ship after?" Kev seemed to hold his breath.

The two officers exchanged glances. "I could," Mik said. "Pa and I are having dinner tomorrow."

"He still won't come down? It'd be a chance to get away from—" He lowered his voice. "Pandeker."

"He doesn't want to risk it."

"All right, joeys, you've got a deal." Anselm looked about. "Where do we rent an electricar?"

"You didn't call ahead? By now they're all taken. Let's catch the bus."

Kevin chattered all the way downtown, pointing out new construction, our older landmarks, the edge of the devastation left by the asteroid a generation back, just before the U.N. Navy fled and left us to our fate. From time to time I joined in, supplementing his meager supply of facts. Perhaps living with the Stadholder was an advantage; I knew more about Centraltown than Kev, a local.

Mik and Tad half listened, enjoying themselves just peering out the windows. Hope Nation was their first planetfall since Earth, eighteen months past. No doubt they simply enjoyed the open spaces.

We went to the Cathedral; I held my breath and tried to look inconspicuous. No one noticed us, under the vaulting roof and the tall Gothic stained-glass windows. Then hours tramping about downtown, a midafternoon meal at one of the better restaurants. The two sailors paid for us all.

Then uptown, past Churchill Park. To my surprise, Kev stopped at our, um, *his* house. He bounded up the steps, threw open the door, ushered our two guests inside, showed them everything including his disordered bedroom.

We heard the door close, downstairs. A chipcase and holovid tucked under his arm, Mr. Dakko stopped short, stunned at the mad clatter of footsteps down the stairwell. Kevin was too excited to worry if his father was annoyed at a house full of unexpected guests; he performed enthusiastic introductions. Mr. Dakko rallied; after all, his guests were officers in the Navy he'd once served.

After an hour's chat, Mr. Dakko invited Mik and Tad back for a late dinner. At first they declined, but allowed themselves to be persuaded when it was clear the invitation was genuine. Then, to my astonishment, Mr. Dakko offered them the use of his electricar, provided that under no circumstances would they let Kevin or me drive it.

"You see?" Kev said as we piled in. "My dad respects my friends."

"But the car?"

"He can be zarky. Last night was only one side of him."

I shook my head. I could no more imagine Dad handing out his electricar than publicly embarrassing me over an epithet.

The day passed, and then we came home to dinner. Mikhael Tamarov was in good form, telling shipboard stories, making clever jokes. His eyes twinkled. I listened, chin on hands, admiring his style. If only I could sparkle so, hold my friends entranced. If only I had his wit, his open friendliness. I sighed.

Somehow, in the course of events, no more was said about my transferring to Dr. Zayre's that day. Late in the evening, Mr. Dakko drove the two sailors to Naval barracks and by the time he was back, Kev and I were sound asleep.

In the morning, Kev was free of school, and I continued truant from mine. I'd noticed that in the rush of the evening's conversation, Kev hadn't mentioned to his father our deal for a tour of the ship, so over breakfast I was likewise silent.

Somehow, by morning, the sailors had secured an electricar. Centraltown had them to rent, but normally there wasn't much demand. Except when a ship came in.

Lieutenant Anselm drove us first to the Governor's Manse, where Fred Mantiet and old Zack Hopewell had helped overthrow the outlaw Triforth government. The middy Mikhael, of all people, seemed unduly affected, his eyes glistening as the tourist guide led us past the "new" front porch, where forty-six years ago the desperately injured Nick Seafort forced his way past the guards. Then the comm room, where, near death from a festering lung, Seafort had made his famous speech. Unfortunately the bastard had survived, to kill my father on *Galactic*.

Tad had it in mind to eat at Haulers' Rest. I quelled my unease. Few plantation families had reason to stop there, and if I minded my business, and wore Kevin's cap low, I'd most likely not be recognized. Besides, I hadn't yet been adjudicated wayward; as far as I knew, no charges had been laid despite Bishop Scanlen's complaint. If necessary, I could brazen it out, though I'd want to be long gone before Anth got wind of it.

I guided Lieutenant Anselm along the two-hour drive. Being consigned to the backseat was far less boring than I'd imagined. The sailors were brimming with questions about Centraltown life, and not at all put off by our youth.

I finally got up my courage to ask, "How come you spend so much time with us, instead of looking for girls?"

Mikhael flushed, but Lieutenant Anselm just grinned. "Neither of us wants the girls we'd find in a bar, joey, and besides, I've had my fill of bars. And do you think we've been without, during the cruise? Middies have free time, you know. We can't socialize with crew women, but *Olympiad* carries over three thousand passengers. A number of them are attractive."

I grunted, embarrassed beyond words.

"You ought to join up, Randy. Lots of joeygirls like a uniform, even a cadet's. Mik, here, found that—"

A determined cough. Mikhael was blushing furiously.

"Anyway, if the proper company comes along, we'll welcome it. Meanwhile, we'll see the sights."

The middy had been nice to me, and deserved relief from his embarrassment. "You were a cadet?"

"It seemed like forever." He glanced with pride at his insignia. "I've been middy two years now. I started late," he said. Most cadets were enlisted at thirteen or fourteen, and were promoted within two years or so.

"I'm always behind Tad," he added glumly. "We had two years in the wardroom, but now we're separated again."

"So, you have to salute me." Anselm's tone was annoyed. "We're still friends, and you're way too old for the barrel."

"Thank Lord God." Some memory made the boy blush anew. "There's still demerits."

"Tolliver may demerit you; I won't, and you know that."

Mik sighed. "Yes, sir. I know." He turned to me. "Lieutenants can give demerits. Each means two hours of calisthenics."

"Of course. My father—" I bit it off. They thought my name was Carlson. "My father told me."

"Tad . . ." For a moment, Mik ignored us civilians. "Sometimes I earn them, I admit. But Pandeker complains to Ms. Frand, and every time, she . . ."

Anselm frowned. "Stay out of his way."

"Pandeker's everywhere. You know he looks for an excuse—"

"It's Naval business, Mik." In his tone, gentle warning.

"I suppose." The middy sounded glum.

"Who's Pandeker?" My tone was bright.

"Special envoy of the Patriarchs."

"To us?" All we needed was more Church fathers mucking about.

"To *Olympiad*." Mik sounded bitter.

"Ships don't have parsons." The Captains carried out religious functions. Everyone knew that.

"This one does." Tad made a face.

"He's keeping an eye on—"

"Mikhael." Another warning, not so gentle.

Mik's shoulders slumped. "Sorry."

"I understand your frustration. One might say I even share it. So, joeys, just how big is the Plantation Zone?"

I let Anselm steer me to casual chat. What problem was he reluctant to discuss with outsiders? It was the Naval way, I knew. Most of their traditions were legends. Even today, the U.N. Navy was the most talked-of service, and joeykids dreamed of going to Earth to enlist. Not I, of course. After the Navy killed Dad, I hated the U.N.N.S. with a passion.

We polished off a huge meal of corn bread, ham steaks, fresh green beans, mountains of potatoes—all Haulers' Rest meals were overgenerous—and climbed into the car for the two-hour trip back. By the time we reached the outskirts of Centraltown much of the day was gone. Even Mik seemed restless. He checked his watch. "I ought to catch a shuttle."

Anselm sighed. "I'll go too, I suppose."

"Pa's expecting me, but stay groundside and enjoy yourself."

For a moment Anselm looked shy. "I'll enjoy it more with you." To Kevin, "You joeys ready for your tour?"

"Yes, please." Kev's voice was tight.

They parked in front of Admiralty House—though we were no longer a colony, the Navy maintained a small base here, under Admiral Kenzig—and we walked across the tarmac to the terminal. Much of the morning's excitement had subsided, as stallkeepers went home to dinner and their normal jobs.

Kev asked, "How do we get back down afterward?"

"We'll get you on a shuttle. Or you can stay aboard the night, and we'll come groundside with you."

"Zark." Kevin keyed his caller. "Wish me luck." It rang several times, with no answer. His face relaxed as he keyed voice mail. He spoke rapidly, as if afraid he'd be interrupted. "Dad, we're going aloft with Tad and Mik. We'll be back late tonight. Sorry we missed you." He rang off, switched his caller to decline incoming calls. "We're out of range."

I said nothing.

"He might not like it." Kev's tone was defensive. "When we're done I'll pay the price, whatever it is. I don't need my daddy to hold my hand."

I smiled, welcoming back the Kevin I'd known last summer. For a time I'd wondered if he'd grown up entirely.

Many more joeys were coming groundside than going back aloft; seats on the shuttle weren't a problem. Mik and his lieutenant went to the Naval desk, showed their IDs, signed us in as their guests. To my astonishment, that's all it took. No DNA check, no retinoscopy.

We strode to the waiting shuttle, agleam in the spaceport lights. Mik asked, "You been in one of these before?"

"Of course." Belatedly, I realized my tone was contemptuous. But Dad *had* taken me aloft at times. In my mind's eye I saw him striding through the fastship's hatch, never to return. I swallowed.

Kevin looked nervous. "I haven't."

I raised an eyebrow. "Really? But your father—"

"Next time. Always next time." His voice was sullen.

We passed through weigh-in and found seats. It was one of the larger shuttles, and mostly empty.

As we settled in, Lieutenant Anselm threw a genial arm around Kevin's shoulder. "At liftoff, gravity will press you hard. Just lie there, try to relax. After, you'll be weightless 'til we reach the Station. Take shallow breaths, stay buckled in. If you feel sick—"

"He will." Mik spoke with confidence. "Just lean to your right and barf on the lieutenant. I would, but he'd demerit me."

Kevin smiled weakly. "I'll manage."

I hoped so. Else he'd embarrass us, and Hope Nation, before these outworlders. As for me, I'd been aloft with Dad and Anth, and hadn't had an accident since I was six.

* * * *

Liftoff was just as Tad Anselm had promised. I lay back in my cushioned seat, gripping the armrests while the world pulsed. At length it was over. Eagerly, I unbuckled.

"Hey, joey, stay put."

"I'm fine. Really." I grabbed a handhold, pulled myself up, twisted, let myself spin slowly. "See?"

"Don't." Kev's face was green. He swallowed.

I had to divert him quickly. "Look!" I pointed to the porthole, and Hope Nation's green globe. "Isn't it beautiful?" I settled myself next to him. "That's Western Continent."

"I don't care."

"The Venturas run from the center to the coast." Idly, my fingers rubbed his forearm. "It's cool, Kev. Look."

Dutifully, he did.

"The old military base was near that spine. We probably can't see much. Ever go there? It's all a park now."

He squinted, leaned to the porthole. Together, we peered out. After a moment, softly, "Thanks."

Mikhael's eyes were far away. Unconsciously, he smoothed his hair, straightened his tie.

Slowly, our shuttle approached the Station.

We didn't have a proper station anymore, not since Seafort destroyed it. In all the years since, it had never been rebuilt. Instead, Admiralty had sent us an obsolete warship, decommissioned it, and let it serve as the core of a new Orbiting Station. Over the years we'd added new airlock bays as well as cavernous storage facilities for grains and ores. But pieces of the original vessel still poked through, and the effect was startling.

Kevin, his vertigo forgotten, took it all in. "Look at the size of her."

"The Station? It's grown over the years, but . . ."

"Not that, you snark. The *ship*."

I peered out the window, at *Olympiad*, whose bulk dwarfed the nearby Station. "Holy Lord God." I didn't know I'd spoken. She was . . . vast. Majestic. Something stirred within. I looked to Anselm, with something akin to awe. "That's where you serve? In *her*?"

Tad nodded with evident pride.

I swallowed. "No wonder you're not lonely."

She loomed larger as we neared.

"We won't moor at the Station?"

"No need. *Olympiad* has ample bays. We can board directly." He settled back in his seat.

Mik unbuckled. "I'll call Pa, then show you joeys around."

I barely heard. My eyes were fastened on the great behemoth, floating against the backdrop of a billion pinpoints of light.

With precise care, our pilot mated us to the huge ship's waiting bay. A click, as capture latches slid into place.

As the starship's gravitrons took hold, Anselm stood, grabbed his carry-bag.

The airlock hatch slid open.

I squinted in the silent white lighting, while a bored sailor on airlock watch idly looked me over. The corridor seemed deserted. I said, "Where are all the people?"

Mik took up the caller. "Groundside. We're on Level 2; most of these cabins are empty." He waved vaguely. "The new passengers won't board for three weeks. Just a moment." He punched in a code. "Bridge, Midshipman Mikhael Tamarov reporting. Permission to board with two guests, ma'am?" A pause. "A couple of joeykids we met groundside. Kevin Dakko and Randy—uh, because they showed us around. Yes, of course, at all times. I'll sign them in and be responsible. Thanks, Ms. Frand." A quick grin to Lieutenant Anselm, which might have been relief. "Is the Captain in his cabin, do you know?" Another pause. "Yes, in just a bit." He rang off. "We're to keep them in sight at all times, so they don't fire the fusion drive by mistake."

Kevin's look was apprehensive.

"Or de-air the ship." Tad Anselm's tone was dry. "No doubt you want to see your father?"

"For dinner, yes, sir."

"Very well, get changed; I'll take these two on walkabout."

"Thanks, sir. Where shall we meet?"

"Why not the Dining Hall?"

Mikhael glanced at his watch. "An hour or so. Suits me." A quick salute, and he was off.

Kevin stirred. "Why did he suddenly start calling you 'sir'?"

"Because we passed through the airlock." Anselm's hand gently guided his shoulder. "This way, joeyboy. I'll show you passenger quarters, and some of the lounges. Perhaps after dinner the Captain will allow a look at the bridge."

The cabins were sumptuous but none too large; I'd hate to be cooped in one for a full year. On the other hand, the public areas were ample, so much so that I lost my bearings in a maze of elegant stairwells and carpeted corridors.

Olympiad had not just one or two levels, like most ships, but six. She even had lifts to supplement the stairwells.

"What's it like living on her?" I was impressed despite myself.

"Depends who you are." Anselm led us past a crew lounge, toward the comm room. "Passengers dine and sleep quite comfortably. Crew quarters? Let's say they're adequate. Middies—"

Kevin asked, "Could I see a crew berth?"

"I'm afraid not. They're off-limits to . . . well, perhaps while the crew's on leave it wouldn't be a problem."

"I'd really like that. My father . . ." Mr. Dakko had lived in one, when he was Kevin's age.

"I'll see what I can do. Now, middies are crammed together, as always, but lieutenants' cabins are decent enough. Care to see mine?"

"Sure." I tried to sound eager, for Anselm's sake.

"After dinner; it's just about time."

"Where should we wait while—"

"Oh, you're invited, have no fear. There's plenty of seats now most of our passengers are ashore." He led us upward, toward the more ornate Level 2 dining hall.

I trudged behind, my jaw clenched. For all her splendor, this extravagant ship was an almost identical twin to UNS *Galactic*. In surroundings such as these, Dad had died a horrible death, choking in vacuum, clawing at nothing while his eyeballs—

"Randy, you all right?" Kevin touched my arm.

I pulled free. I wouldn't speak of my nightmare. In subdued silence, we trudged to the Dining Hall.

The spacious compartment was as sumptuous as the best restaurants in Centraltown; at one time or another, under Anthony's watchful eye, I'd dined in them all. Velvet draperies, gleaming rails, starched tablecloths, and crystal glassware bespoke affluence and old-world elegance.

Lieutenant Anselm led us to a round table. "During the cruise, each officer sits with a table of passengers, and we rotate monthly. To tell the truth, at times it's a bore."

I pulled out my heavy steel-framed upholstered chair. Kev, at my left, glanced about nervously. "We're not dressed for this."

Anselm clapped the shoulder of his jumpsuit. "You're fine, joey. Officers dress for dinner; passengers are more casual, especially in port." His tone was kind.

Only a handful of joeys wandered in, while the stewards prepared for service. I tried to imagine the hall filled to capacity, as well as the auxiliary dining hall below, which we'd been shown on our tour.

I spotted Mikhael. He was fully decked out: fresh shirt, dark blue pants, crisp blue jacket with his insignia patches. His tie was neatly in place, his hair fresh combed. He was talking animatedly with an older officer, who led a little girl by the hand.

Slim of build, stern of face, the officer's salt and pepper hair was cut short, his demeanor imposing. He seemed vaguely familiar. Something Mikhael said amused him; a smile lightened his features. His fingers brushed Mikhael's arm. My fist tightened. Dad had been fond of the same gesture.

At their table, three civilians were waiting. A steward held out a chair, but first the officer seated the child. Mikhael waited until both were in their places, took the seat to his other side, spread his napkin carefully on his lap.

At our own table, we sat.

"Fresh meat and vegetables tonight," said Anselm, opening his own napkin. "Of course, Hydroponics provides us with ample greens, but—"

"Pardon, sir." Midshipman Tamarov, with a crisp salute to Anselm. "The Captain requests the pleasure of your company, and that of our guests." To me, a wink and a mischievous grin.

"But, of course." Tad shot to his feet, gestured us to rise. "It's considered an honor, boys. Though not exactly unexpected, in this case."

While I was puzzling that out, we made our way across the nearly empty hall. The older officer stood; I realized his insignia was that of Captain. "Welcome to *Olympiad*." He held out a hand.

Mikhael said, "Sir, may I present my friends Kevin Dakko and Randy Carlson. Randy, Kevin, Captain Nicholas Seafort."

The color drained from my face. A hand steadied me.

My mouth worked. "You're . . . Seafort? *The* Captain Seafort? The former SecGen?"

A thin smile. "I believe that's so."

Awed, Kevin took his hand. Then, because all were watching, so did I.

He gestured to a place just past Mikhael. "Please join us. And please meet Jane Ellen Seafort, my daughter." He tousled the young one's hair.

I pulled out my heavily padded chair, slumped at the table, my head spinning. A steward set a silver tureen on a stand, ladled steaming mushroom soup into our bowls. The aroma of fresh hot bread wafted across the starched table.

"So," said the Captain. "I hear you gave our boys the grand tour of Centraltown."

I mumbled something; Kevin took up the conversation. "It was a zark, sir. We went to Haulers' Rest."

I'd dreamed of this day.

"And you still want dinner? Amazing."

"You know it? Oh, of course." Kevin blushed. Seafort had worked and lived on Hope Nation.

For years I'd yearned for my chance, safe in the knowledge that it couldn't occur.

The Captain smiled. "Do they still feature the pork steaks?"

"With garlic mashed potatoes." Kev's face was flushed. "You ought to come down, try some."

Mikhael said, "They're quite good, sir."

Sweat trickled down my ribs. Casually, my hand drifted across the table; inadvertently, it swept my cloth napkin to the deck.

"I'm afraid I'm not quite ready. I'm afraid of liftoff."

"Your spine, sir?"

Today I would justify my existence. Today, Anthony, Mom, Cousin Randolph, would be made proud.

I leaned over, couldn't reach my fallen napkin.

With a muttered apology, I stood, thrust my chair aside, bent to retrieve it. I dropped the starched linen next to my plate.

"Yes. When we started out I could tolerate one-third gee, so that's where we set the bow gravitron. We raised it each day just an iota. By the time we got back from Constantine, I could handle one gee, but—"

I stepped back. In one smooth motion, as if I'd rehearsed it, I raised high the heavy steel chair. With all the force I could muster I brought it down on Captain Seafort's skull.

He toppled to the deck.

Kevin sat frozen, with a look of horror. The little girl screamed.

Again I raised the chair. Hands pawed at me. I eluded them, brandishing the chair, but my twist threw off my aim. Anselm had me about the waist. Mikhael hurled himself at me, headfirst. He butted me in the stomach. We went down in a clump. Someone kicked me hard.

"*Dr. Romez to the Dining Hall, flank!*" A harsh voice, on a caller. Someone hauled the middy off me. "Get him out!" A lieutenant, older and gray. "Get them both to the brig, this instant!" Anselm hauled Kevin from his seat. Kev protested. The sailor let loose a mighty blow that rocked his head.

"Move them out, I said!"

"Aye aye, Mr. Tolliver!" They twisted my arm high behind my back. They ran me out of the Dining Hall squealing with pain, but not before I glimpsed Seafort. He lay motionless on the plush green carpet, one hand outstretched as if in supplication. A slow stream of rust-colored blood seeped into the weave.

Midshipman Tamarov knelt at his side, clutching the old man's hand.

Despite my pain and battering, I exulted.

Derek Carr, I've avenged you at last. Rest easy. Fucking Captain Seafort is dead.

5

THE BRIG WAS BELOW, on Level 3. My captors rushed me past the startled master-at-arms to a cell. The hatch slid open. A mighty kick to my rump sent me sprawling. The hatch slid shut.

I jumped to my feet, rubbed my posterior, paced the cell. Adrenaline made me dizzy. Yes. I'd done it. My night fantasies, the daydreams of years, were achieved.

You killed my father. You called on his loyalty with honeyed words, put him—a civilian, a head of government—in harm's way. For your purposes, not his. Not ours. He died for nothing; what matter to Hope Nation if Earth's government were overthrown?

He flamed into Earth's atmosphere, with your stricken ship.

No funeral. No body. No grave I might visit, in the anguish of the night. *You took from me all that I loved, you vile son of a bitch.*

I paced in near frenzy. Of course, they'd hang me, or shoot me; that went without saying. I didn't care. In a life as long as Dad's own, I could achieve no purpose higher than I'd consummated today.

Still, it would be nice to say good-bye to Judy Winthrop. Perhaps they'd let me do that.

A flurry of orders on the speaker; in the confusion of the emergency they were broadcast shipwide.

"This is Lieutenant Tolliver. All med techs to sickbay, flank. Pilot, to the bridge."

Behind the voice, distant sobbing.

Alarms clanged. *"General Quarters! All hands to General Quarters!"*

The cell was tiny, about three meters square. A spartan bed hung from one wall, a soiled mattress only, on flimsy springs.

"Seal all locks. Prepare for breakaway."

My stomach ached where Mikhael had punched me. I sat on the bunk, crossed my arms, rocked.

"All passengers to your cabins. Remain there until further notice."

I jumped up, unable to contain myself. The vaunted U.N. Navy was frantic. It served them right. I resumed my pacing, wall to narrow wall.

"Midshipmen Riev and Ghent to the bridge. And Lieutenant Frand."

What if Anth never learned who'd done it? Would they allow me a final letter?

Would my name be revered?

"Lock five, what's the delay? I want a seal and I want it NOW! We're breaking away from the Station if I have to decompress your bloody section! Officer of the watch, seal the lock and put yourself on report!"

I grinned. Tolliver sounded miffed. No doubt it wouldn't look good on his record, having his Captain killed before his eyes. And by a Hope Nation patriot, no less.

In time my pacing eased, and I sat again. My legs were shaky.

After a long while, footsteps. I tensed, knowing they'd come for me. But they passed my cell. The hiss of a door. Muffled words. A cry of fear. Kevin's.

I bounded to my feet. "Leave him alone! He wasn't part of it!"

"No, please!" Kev sounded frantic. "Where are you taking me?"

I hammered on the door. "Let him go!"

Nothing.

I paced, then sat. Then paced. Then slumped on the bunk, and after a time, dozed.

A rush of cool air. The door slid open.

I jumped up. Two burly sailors pinned me to the wall. A beefy-faced joey jammed a stunner to my chest. "Move an inch, you little snark!" I froze. He rammed the barrel into my sternum. I grunted, tried not to retch. They spun me around, cuffed my hands behind me.

"He's ready, ma'am."

"Move him." A lieutenant, her face set and grim. Her hair was dark and curly, her figure gaunt.

They half dragged me from the cell. I managed, "Where's Kevin?"

"Be silent. LeFevre, gag him if he makes another sound."

"Aye aye, ma'am."

I clenched my teeth, determined not to give them the satisfaction.

"All hands and passengers, attention." Roughly, they hauled me along the passage, out to the curved corridor. More hands than were necessary held a piece of me. *"Captain Seafort is gravely injured and is . . ."* A long pause. *". . . is near death. By authority of Section 121.4 of the Naval Regulations and Code of Conduct, I, Lieutenant Edgar Tolliver, do hereby relieve him and assume the captaincy of UNS* Olympiad *until—until his recovery."* The speaker went silent.

Abruptly the party of seamen had trouble holding me. They dropped me to the deck, hauled me up, threw me down again. Punches were thrown; elbows jabbed my sore and protesting ribs. Determined to show I could take it, I did my best not to cry out.

"You joeys belay that." The lieutenant's voice was flat.

"Aye aye, Ms. Skor." A note of sullenness, perhaps.

They dragged me along the corridor, into a lift, out along another Level.

The sign read SICKBAY. A sailor slapped open the door panel. They hustled me in, set me on a table. Waiting were a med tech—perhaps the doctor—and the older lieutenant I'd seen in the Dining Hall.

"Is he dead yet?" My voice was venomous.

Lieutenant Skor spun me about, her eyes blazing. I gulped, and was silent.

"Strap him down!" The slim, graying lieutenant. Tolliver, he'd called himself on the speaker.

"What are you—"

"P and D. Shut your mouth."

I bridled. "You have no right! I confess! I meant to kill him." In all the worlds, civilized law prevailed. If a defendant denied his guilt though there was evidence against him, he had no right to silence. Sophisticated poly and drug interrogation would reveal his guilt.

But I didn't deny responsibility; I proclaimed it. I was safe from polygraph and drug interrogation.

The med tech looked askance. "If he's confessed . . ."

"I don't give Christ's damn," the lieutenant snapped. "Interrogate him."

I shouted, "You can't—"

"Sir, with all respect, according to regs—"

Tolliver thundered, "I am Captain of this ship!"

The tech wilted. "Yes, sir! Aye aye, sir. Give me your arm, joey."

I resisted, and was ignored. They gave me a shot, and another. Rough fingers stripped off my shirt, left me shivering in sudden cold. They loosed my hands.

I tried to cover myself, wishing I had Alex Hopewell's build, or even Kevin's. I looked so damned *babyish*, pink-skinned and smooth. When I was agitated, my voice squeaked. Like now. "Will it hurt?"

Lieutenant Skor hissed, "It's agony!"

"Stop that." Captain Tolliver.

"Lie back." The med tech.

They strapped me into place, attached their instruments, regulated the drugs.

"Who sent you?"

"Who is your accomplice?"

"How'd you arrange to get on board?"

I drifted in and out of consciousness, aware of my babbling, powerless to stop it.

"Why did you try to kill the Captain?"

"Where were you born?"

I'd done right, I was sure of it. But some part of me was loath to reveal myself.

"How old are you?"
"Tell us your name!"

I lay in my bunk, my head throbbing from residual effects of the drugs. I'd knelt clutching the hanging toilet twice that I could remember. There was an acrid smell of sweat. I'd made my shirt into a blanket; there was no other.

From somewhere, slow, steady weeping.

I scrunched my eyes shut, curled into a ball of misery.

A jailer brought me a sandwich, and milk in a paper cup. I was allowed no metal, no implements.

"What will you do to me?"

He set down the food.

"Will they hang me?" My voice had a tremor.

He turned on his heel without a word.

"Say something!"

He slapped the hatch control.

I sat on the deck, knees drawn up, staring dully.

Other than the bunk and the toilet, my cell held nothing. Bare walls, of painted steel sheets. A speaker in the high ceiling, and a grille for air. Too small to crawl through, even if I could reach it. The toilet was of steel or alumalloy, beyond my ability to break. I'd tried.

I couldn't quite remember my relentless interrogation. Questions, ever more questions. Who . . . Why . . . At one point I'd stumbled, desperate to insist that my name was Carlson, not knowing why.

I must have failed.

From my interrogators, sudden silence.

"Oh, Lord Christ." Captain Tolliver.

"Sir?"

"He's Derek Carr's son." A string of oaths crackled the air.

Hands grasped my shoulders, shook me. "Why, boy? In God's name, why?"

Half awake, I'd babbled on.

In my cell, I put my head in my hands, ashamed of I knew not what.

". . . Randy?" A voice, soft.

I jerked awake. "Huh?"

"Randy?"

"Kev?" I jumped to my feet, ran to the door. "Kevin?"

A muttered voice, deep. A protest I couldn't quite catch.

"Randy, where are—OW!"

Silence.

I pounded the door, then the walls until my fists ached.

Nothing.

After a while, I'd had enough. I stood before the unyielding door. "Hey!"

Nothing.

"You out there! Jailer, or master-at-arms, or whatever the hell you call yourself!"

Silence.

I began to yell. Words sometimes, and when I ran out, just sounds. After a time, I screamed. My voice cracked. I tried again.

It was hopeless. I was about to give up when the door slid open. Two sailors, one with a billy, and someone I'd not seen before, a civilian. His eye held a glint that made me step back. "What's this racket, boy?"

"Who are you?" I made my tone defiant.

"Branstead. Jerence." To the sailor, "We won't need that. Shut the hatch."

"But . . ." Reluctantly, he complied.

Branstead wrinkled his nose. "Haven't they let you wash?"

"What's it to *you*?"

With a grimace, he sat himself on my bunk. "You're in god-awful trouble. Tolliver's waiting. If the Captain dies, he'll hang you in an instant. No one will stop him, and I'm not sure I'd bother to try."

I swallowed. "I don't care."

"Care, boy. Life's too short as it is."

"Don't call me 'boy.' "

"Why not? You're an arrogant, spoiled child. Derek would be ashamed."

My fists bunched. "Don't mention his name!"

"He was my friend."

For a moment I was speechless. "How—"

Branstead's glare was like ice. "And even so, I ought to take you apart bare-handed, you vicious little shit!" He moved, as if to get to his feet, and I leaped back.

After a moment he grunted, settled himself. "Your legal position is in limbo."

"How were you Dad's friend?"

"You're a citizen of Hope Nation, but you got yourself onto a U.N. warship. You're an unaccompanied minor; that makes you the ward of the Captain. Whom you tried to kill."

I reddened. "Why should I care about my status?"

"We're at rest near the Station—it doesn't violate security to tell you—but under our own power. So our laws apply, not yours."

"Are you a solicitor?"

"No, and you won't get one. At best, a Naval officer to defend you, but even that's not necessary. You have no rights aboard this ship; the Captain can summarily execute you if he chooses. Nonetheless, he sent me to advise you where you stand. One colonial to another, as it were."

"I don't need your—"

"On a warship, the Captain is sacrosanct. For a crewman merely to touch him uninvited is a capital charge. You're no crewman, but if the Captain dies, your life is forfeit. Even if he lives . . . Attempted murder with premeditation is itself a capital offense."

I wanted to throw something, but had nothing. Even my shirt lay on the bed, next to Branstead. I snarled, "Why the fuck do you care?"

He stared, saying not a word.

Time passed. I began to fidget.

When he spoke, his voice was low. "Randy Carr, as Lord God is my witness, if you curse at me again, I'll take my belt and thrash you."

I struggled not to redden.

"Is that clear?"

I stared at the deck.

He stood.

"Yeah."

He came at me.

"Yes, sir!" I backpedaled to the wall. It wasn't far.

"Ask your question properly, boy."

I took a long breath, tried for calm. "Why are you involved? For that matter, why are you on ship?"

"I was SecGen Seafort's chief of staff. He retired, I stayed on. But when I found out his next cruise was to Hope Nation, I came along."

"Why?"

"The new SecGen really didn't need me, and it's time I saw home again."

My breath caught. "You're *that* Branstead? The one who gave up Branstead Plantation?"

"Many years ago." His lips twitched in what might have been a smile. "I was just about your age, and nearly as obnoxious."

"You're home to stay?"

"I don't know." He ran fingers through his hair. "All these years serving the U.N. . . . and I never applied for citizenship. I've always been a Hope Nation national, except for my years in the Navy." Naval service conferred full, if temporary, citizenship.

I yearned to pace, but the cell was even smaller with Branstead visiting. My tone was meek. "I'm sorry for what I said." I'd thought he was part of Seafort's Navy, not a fellow Nationeer.

On the other hand, he'd been Seafort's chief of staff. New doubts assailed me.

"Anthony Carr can't help you. Captain Tolliver is plenipotentiary of the United Nations Government, and has all its powers. He'll apply U.N. law. Your, ah, nephew will have no say."

How much had I told them, in the flickering twilight of confession? Had I revealed our sordid family squabbles? My truancy? My affront to the Bishop?

Did any of that matter?

"Edgar Tolliver's livid. He means to kill you."

"What's stopping him?"

"Nick would never forgive him. He may do it anyway. I warn you; if Tolliver summons you, none of your insolence. It would be suicide."

I closed my eyes. Dad tousled my hair. I was still giggling at his promise to bring home an elephant. *"I love you, son."*

"Mr. Branstead?"

"Ah. Civility." His tone was dry.

Cautiously, I crossed to the bunk, sat beside him. "Do you understand why I did it?"

"I'd ask rather: do you understand what you did?"

One of my jailers brought a thick, meaty sandwich. He held it before me, spat on it, dropped it on the bed.

I left it uneaten.

Branstead's visit had unsettled me. If Seafort had died at once, I was sure I'd have gone unafraid to execution. If the Captain had been unhurt, I'd have gritted my teeth, endured my punishment. But the uncertainty gnawed at my courage. How could I prepare for death if I wasn't sure it was coming?

I'd been punched and jostled. My food was spat on. I hated it, but worse, it disturbed me.

It was obvious the reactions of the crew weren't orchestrated. They hated me for what I'd done.

Which meant they loved Captain Seafort.

But, why? He was a tyrant, a vain despot who used lives as fodder for his ambitions. Dad had told me tales of Seafort's heartless sacrifice of his men. True, Dad hadn't seen it that way; he idolized Seafort, made his follies sound reasonable. Even I had been duped, until Dad's brutal death opened my eyes.

No air. Trying desperately to take breath, while his blood vessels burst, his lungs exploded, his eyeballs hemorrhaged.

While Seafort watched.

The door slid open. "What are *you* crying at, you vile bastard?"

I jumped to my feet.

Mikhael Tamarov.

He nodded to the master-at-arms. "See if Lieutenant Anselm's in the officers' lounge. If so, give him this note. I'll watch the prisoner."

"But, sir—"

"That was an order."

"Aye aye, sir." The master-at-arms retreated.

The middy slid shut the door, strode to my bunk.

I said nervously, "I hope I didn't get you in troub—"

He belted me in the stomach. I doubled over, retching.

He began to swear, punctuating each oath with a blow. His knuckles slammed into my temple; I reeled, clutched the wall. A roundhouse blow to my ribs; something snapped.

Mikhael's face was dark; his lips bared. He hit me again and again, each time harder.

My spittle sprayed. "Please . . ." I was barely audible.

I slid down the corner; he crouched with me, belaboring me without mercy. A tremendous punch slammed my head into the wall; I feared it had taken out my eye. "Stop! No more!" Methodically, he began to pound my chest, my shoulders.

It went on forever. My blood dripped. Each breath was torture.

Every time he worked at my ribs, red agony blossomed. Worst of all was his steady monotone, a stream of the ugliest words I'd ever heard.

The door slid open. "Oh, Jesus, get him off! Sir, stop! Get away, or I'll stun you! Now, sir!" Sailors struggled to pull the midshipman from the cell. He broke loose, ran at me, kicked me really hard between the legs.

I squealed, rolled back and forth clutching myself, helpless, praying to die.

I woke under bright lights, in a soft bed. Every limb, every organ ached. I could barely squeeze open my swollen eyes. The doctor took a step back.

Captain Tolliver stood over me, arms folded. "That wasn't warranted. It won't happen again."

I nodded.

He stalked out.

I said to no one, "Where am I?"

"In sickbay. You've three broken ribs, assorted contusions and abrasions. You lost a tooth, but that can be reseeded. I used the bone growth stimulator twice while you were out, and gave you calcium. The ribs will knit in a few days. Tomorrow, you go back to your cell. I'll prescribe a painkiller."

I tried to scratch my nose, found my wrists fastened to the rail. "Can you let me . . ." I wriggled my hand.

"No. Not a chance." He turned on his heel.

"Doctor?" I waited out a spell of dizziness.

"Yes?" His tone dripped impatience.

I forced out the words. "How is the Captain?"

His face suffused. "In coma. Skull fracture, subdural hematoma, intercranial hemorrhage. I did a craniotomy to relieve the pressure, but . . ."

"Will he live?"

"It's possible. It's more likely he won't. Ah, now it's worth weeping over, is it? He's always believed he's bound for Hell. If so, you'll meet him there shortly." He stalked off.

The next day, they allowed me a sponge bath; I was too bruised and swollen to stand still for a shower. Then, true to their word, they hustled me back to my bleak cell.

I sat helpless in my silent chamber.

No one would answer my questions, and I couldn't hear Kevin. I didn't have strength to cry out, to make a scene until they'd answer.

Now, I was allowed outside once a day, to bathe. No doubt the acting Captain had intervened.

The second afternoon, while I dozed listlessly, the hatch opened.

Framed in the entryway, two officers I knew. Lieutenant and midshipman. The middy was dressed and groomed to perfection: shoes gleaming, slacks and shirt crisp, his tie knotted tight, his face scrubbed, every hair in place.

He glanced at Lieutenant Anselm, emotions flickering. A deep breath. Smartly, he strode forward—he couldn't go far without hitting the wall—and came to attention facing me. "Midshipman Mikhael Tamarov reporting, sir."

I gaped. The "sir" was directed to me.

"I apologize to you for my inexcusable conduct, for my juv"—his eyes strayed to Anselm, but the lieutenant's face was impassive—"juvenile tantrum. For breaking all bounds of decorum, for violating ship's regs and common decency, and exhibiting my immaturity." Mikhael's face was scarlet. "Sir, my misconduct has been brought to the Captain's attention, and we assure you I am being disciplined for it."

Silence.

He remained at attention.

I spat, "I hope you're caned." Dad had told me how much it hurt.

Anselm stirred. "He won't be. He's twenty, a couple of years over the line. But he'll be made to regret his act."

"What are *you* here for?"

"By direction of the Captain, to see that Midshipman Tamarov carries out his orders." A pause, then a hint of what might have been compassion. "Mr. Tamarov is an officer; his word is not questioned. Merely his judgment. Is that correct, Midshipman?"

Mikhael gritted his teeth. "Yes, sir. I'm told I showed the judgment of a small child."

If it wouldn't have hurt my chest I'd have shouted with glee. The best I could do was put as much malice as I could in my smile. "Do you agree?"

"My opinion is of no consequence."

"Answer him, Mr. Tamarov."

"Aye aye, sir. Sir—" To me, politely. "—I hate you not one whit less than I did before. I chose to jeopardize my Naval career over that hate. Objectively, I have to agree that shows poor judgment."

I jutted out my chin. "Why'd they send you, Anselm? Were you part of it?"

"I had no idea. If so, I'd have tried to stop him." Lest I take too much comfort, he added, "Mr. Tamarov is my friend, and I don't care to see him in trouble."

"Is he?"

"Very much so. Twenty is too old to be a cadet, or he would have been broken from officer, as I once was. Captain Tolliver nearly dismissed him from the service."

A pang, that might have been my ribs, or something else. A feeling I didn't enjoy. I looked away. "I'm sorry you're in trouble over me. You were nice to me, groundside."

"Thank you, sir."

Anselm said, "That's enough for today, Mr. Tamarov."

I almost felt sorry to see him go. " 'For today'?"

"He'll be back tomorrow. Every day until your trial."

I winced, turned away. When I opened my eyes, the hatch was sliding shut.

I was restless all afternoon, yearning to pace despite my aches. The confinement of the tiny cell drove me to distraction; there was no place to go, nothing to look at.

I wanted to see Mikhael again, so I could be cruel to him. He'd have to take it; I was "sir" to him.

I hated him. He'd beaten me without mercy.

I tried not to weep.

That evening Mr. Branstead came again. "Are you recovering?" As before, he sat on the bunk, looked up at me.

I was eager for company, but my aches made me sullen. "Do you care?"

"Mildly. You'll recover from your bruises. I'm more concerned for the middy. He's on four and four watch. That won't last, and he's young enough to take it. But his file will carry a reprimand; he may never make lieutenant, and is probably sick with shame."

"How do you know so much about the Navy?"

"I too was an officer," Branstead said mildly. "Captain Seafort enlisted me as cadet on UNS *Victoria*, the first fastship."

"On his way home from blowing Orbit Station?" After the Navy abandoned us, Seafort had remained behind. Even I had to admit that nuking the Station after luring hundreds of fish was a brilliant move. Hope Nation wasn't attacked again during the war.

"Yes."

"You were friends then?"

He said simply, "Not until I gave up goofjuice."

I caught my breath. Goofjuice was an illicit drug, banned in all the worlds. Penalties were severe. Branstead was lucky; the euphoriac was so addictive that few escaped. It was almost beyond belief that the Navy would take a boy who'd been in its clutches.

"How?"

"Mr. Seafort locked me in a cell." He looked about. "It was a passenger cabin, actually. A little bigger than this."

I snorted. "And denied you the juice until he had his way." That was Seafort.

"No, he gave me a vial of juice. And told me he'd let me take the oath if I didn't open it." Branstead's look was distant. "If you want to know what hell is, boy, ask me."

His look was so forlorn I eased myself alongside him, sat carefully. My knitting ribs still ached.

A silence.

"Have you used it since, sir?"

"No, I swore an oath."

"People break them."

"I don't." For a time he stared at the floor. "Nick Seafort did, once. It's haunted him ever since." Abruptly he threw a hand over his eyes. "And now my friend, my mentor, lies in that cubicle, still as death, his broken head wrapped in gauze, and I can only sit with him, thinking the things I didn't say when I could."

I bounded to my feet, ignoring a warning stab. "It's not fair!"

"What?" I'd drawn him from his reverie.

"He's a monster! Even Earth is better without him! My father was a good man, a decent man . . . you can't know how good he was!" I found it hard to speak, and pounded my leg.

"Randy—"

"But you all love your hero Seafort, and look at me like I'm scum on a pond! Thanks to him I have to live without my father. What about me, God damn you? What about me!" My voice rose so high my throat ached.

He frowned at my language, but said only, "Would killing him bring Derek back?"

"Derek Carr's murder cried out for revenge!"

"You deluded fool." Branstead put his head in his hands. After a moment, he stood. "We'll talk about it again, perhaps. Right now, I'm not up to it."

I stopped him at the door. "Why did you come?"

"Oh, yes. To bring you up-to-date." He ran his fingers through his hair. "The Stadholder demands to see you. Captain Tolliver refuses to allow it."

"Anthony knows?"

"Randy, the whole world knows. When we broke free of the Station, it wasn't exactly a secret."

"Why does Tolliver refuse?"

"Call him Captain."

I swallowed my pride. "Captain Tolliver."

"You're in Naval hands now, and will stay that way."

I frowned. "Will I be allowed to say good-bye to Anth? To my mother?"

"If they hang you?" It sounded brutal.

I nodded, not daring words.

"I don't know. A holochip, certainly."

I hugged myself.

"And Chris Dakko of Dakko & Son is raising hell about his boy. Insists he's innocent, and demands his release."

"Kevin had no idea. Even I—" Even I had no notion I'd try to cave in Nick Seafort's head.

"He underwent P and D, as you did. Captain Tolliver won't discuss the results, but scuttlebutt is that young Dakko knew nothing."

"Then why is he being held?"

"You'd have to ask the Captain." With that, he was gone.

* * * *

The next day, as before, a med tech came, wheeling a cart with a bone-growth stimulator. I had to sit still while he ran the cool disk across my rib cage. It tickled, and made me restless. But then he left, and I was alone for another long afternoon.

Worst of all was that I had nothing to do: no holovid, no books. Nothing to see but the God-cursed walls.

Footsteps at the hatch. I waited cross-legged on my bed, not caring who it was. Anyone.

Tamarov and Anselm.

The middy marched in, stiffened to attention before me. "Midshipman Mikhael Tamarov reporting, sir. At the Captain's order, I apologize again for assaulting you."

"No doubt you regret it." My tone dripped sarcasm. "Or do you regret not finishing me?"

"May I tell the truth, Mr. Anselm?"

"You not only may, but I require it."

To me, "Yes, sir, I wish I'd killed you. Then I'd be hanged and it would be over for both of us."

I knew he'd want me dead, but still it shook me, hearing it so baldly. "That's how I feel about your precious Nick Seafort."

For an instant, he closed his eyes. Then, rather calmly under the circumstances, "Yes, sir."

Abruptly I tired of baiting him. "I guess . . ." A deep breath. "I suppose I understand how you feel. After all, he's your Captain."

"He's my father!" Mikhael's fists were clenched.

I gaped. "Your what?"

"Oh, you knew." Scorn dripped from the words.

"You said your name was Tamarov! You lied about who you were!"

He snarled, "And you didn't?"

"Steady, Mr. Tamarov." Anselm, from the door.

"Aye aye, sir." The middy brought himself back to attention.

Anselm folded his arms. "You may stand at ease today."

"Thank you, sir." He did so.

We regarded each other. Cautiously I got to my feet. "You're Nick Seafort's son?" I tasted the bizarre, the impossible.

"Yes, sir. My name's still Tamarov. Captain Seafort adopted me."

I knitted my brow. "You mentioned 'Pa' . . . before."

"That was groundside. Or alone, in his cabin. On duty, he's 'Captain Seafort,' just as I call my friend Mr. Anselm 'sir' aboard ship."

My head was spinning. "Seafort adopted a middy?"

"Of course not. It was—" He twisted his head. "Tad—Lieutenant Anselm—how should I explain?"

Anselm's lips twitched. "Start at the beginning, speak slowly, and don't assume he knows any details."

"Aye aye, sir." Mikhael gathered himself. "When I was fifteen my father died in the Rotunda bombing, where they tried to kill Mr. Seafort. I was . . . very upset. I hadn't seen Alexi in years, and was so looking forward to his leave. I hated Mr. Seafort for taking away my chance—"

"Stop it!" My voice was shrill. "Get out!" I launched myself from the bed, propelled him to the hatch. "Get away from me!"

Anselm swept me off my feet, laid me on the bed, held me in place. "That won't do, joey." He studied me. "Why do I see tears?"

"Get off me!" I spun on my side, away from him. My voice was unsteady. "Don't mock me." I forced the word. "Please. Just don't."

The middy said plaintively, "Mr. Anselm, what did I—"

"Wait, Mik." To my astonishment, the lieutenant patted the small of my back. "Mikhael meant no harm. It's what he felt. I was there."

"Where?"

With a sigh, Anselm recounted Seafort's last days as SecGen. He described his own drunkenness as a young middy, Mikhael's despair when his father was killed, Seafort's dogged efforts to reclaim them both while Earth tumbled toward revolution. Seafort took Anselm onto his staff, along with a cadet named Bevin. At that, Tad's eyes glistened, and for a moment he was still.

Then, a smile to Mikhael, and Anselm turned to me. "Mr. Seafort called in Derek Carr to tell Mik stories of his father Captain Tamarov in the old days. Poor Mik didn't know what to make of it. He so wanted to hear the stories, but he was annoyed at Mr. Seafort for reining him in . . ."

I blurted, "Dad told me about a Tamarov once. When he was a cadet on *Hibernia.*"

Mik said softly, "That was my father. They served together in *Portia* too."

Anselm cleared his throat, resumed his tale. While Seafort battled to steer clear of enviro fanatics and Naval reactionaries, Anselm was so unruly, he had been broken to cadet. Then, the expedition to Lunapolis, for risky surgery to undo the SecGen's paralysis. While they were aloft, disgruntled officers attempted a coup and seized *Galactic.* Nick Seafort arranged to go aboard to clear the way for a small party of civilian raiders, and Dad insisted on going along, over Seafort's vociferous objection. Dad even smuggled Mikhael aboard, lest the boy harm himself from fear of abandonment.

Dad and Anselm—and Mikhael—fought alongside Seafort to save the ship. By now Dad was a lieutenant—he'd made the Captain reenlist him.

After they won, they used *Galactic* in a maneuver to recapture Lunapolis and Earthport. When the rebels fired their laser cannon, the ship was lost. Dad had died a hero, helping others into their suits.

The tale wasn't new to me, but when Anselm lapsed silent, my cheeks were damp.

He handed me a handkerchief, and the small kindness undid me utterly.

At length, I struggled toward composure. Casting about, I said, "What is four and four watch?"

Mik colored. "Four hours on, four hours off, twenty-four hours a day."

"Tolliver makes you do that? For how long?"

" 'Til we reach home port, he said, but I hope he doesn't mean it."

Anselm said quietly, "Mr. Tolliver was quite upset. We'll have no criticism."

"None meant, sir."

"Well, I criticize." To my astonishment, I giggled. "What can he do about it, hang me?"

"Yes, if Pa dies. I mean, Capt—Cap—" Mik's face crumpled.

Anselm was off the bed, at the hatch. "Good day, Mr. Carr." He swept Mikhael through, slapped it shut.

Mr. Branstead came again, in the evening. His eyes were hollow. "Nick is on life support."

I said humbly, "I'm sorry."

He snorted.

"I'm sorry you may lose a friend," I added. "I'm sorry I'm the cause. My hating him doesn't alter that."

"Thank you."

"Is it true that Mr. Seafort had Dad help Mikhael?"

"Derek was glad to do it. It disrupted his trade negotiations, but he and the SecGen were such friends that it didn't matter a whit."

I stared at the floor.

He folded his arms, studied me. "You've changed. What's happened, Randy?"

I shrugged. "I've had nothing to do but think."

"Feeling sorry for yourself?"

I faced him. "No." Not at this moment, at any rate. "Sir, instead of talking, do you think you might . . ." I reddened. ". . . get me something to eat?"

"You don't like your provisions?"

"I don't eat much. The jailer spits in it." Was there reason to be embarrassed? I could hardly meet his eye.

"That's an outrage." He looked as if he meant it. "By the way, Mr. Dakko's aboard. He wants to see you. The Captain's consented."

"No!"

"Too bad you weren't consulted. They'll come for you in a while. Don't be afraid if they handcuff you; it's for security. They'll bring you back here, after."

"Why must I see him?"

"Why don't you want to?"

"I don't know." I shrugged, knowing it was a lie, hating lies. A breath, to steel myself. "Because I'm ashamed, sir."

"Of what?"

I turned away. "I wish . . ." A laugh, that sounded bitter. "I was going to say I wish my father were here, so he could help me understand. But if he were here, none of this would have happened."

"Almost, I feel pity for you." A sigh. "Not almost. I do. You're what, fourteen? Come here."

I did as I was told.

Tentatively, his hands went to my shoulders. Slowly, he pulled me into a comforting embrace. "You've done great wrong, Randy. But I think you know that."

I clung to him as if to Dad, until it was time for him to go.

My hands clamped behind my back, I waited docilely at the outer brig door. Two sailors held me, one at each arm. I didn't care. I'd be freed from the damned cells, at least for a while. Even meeting Mr. Dakko would be worth that. Midshipman Tamarov commanded the party, and Tad Anselm was nowhere in sight. Perhaps they were giving the middy a way to redeem himself.

Or giving him another chance to end my life. I sighed.

They led me far down the cool, airy corridor. I had to walk slowly, from my beating. To break the silence, I said, "It's nice to see something other than those bare walls."

"They're bulkheads, sir." Mik's tone was polite. "The floor's a deck, doors are hatches."

I yearned for his forgiveness. "Please don't call me 'sir.'"

"Captain's orders, sir." A quick glance my way, at the men, back to me, an odd look in his eyes. Perhaps beseeching me not to press him further before his squad.

We halted at a gold-trimmed door. Er, hatch. Mikhael slapped the control. "Inside, please, sir."

I had little choice.

Two sailors took up position outside the hatch. Reluctantly, I allowed myself to be guided in.

The lounge was huge. Mr. Dakko sat at a table, at one end. He looked, well, almost gaunt. In his eyes was a barely contained anguish.

Mikhael and a sailor with a stunner retreated to the far bulkhead. I was securely cuffed, and couldn't attack Mr. Dakko. Their stunner was ready if he assaulted me.

How had it come to this?

In the background soft music played. If we kept our voices low, we wouldn't be overheard. I slid into a seat.

Mr. Dakko's jaw dropped. "Good heavens, what happened? You look like a raccoon."

"What's a raccoon?"

"An animal on Earth."

"I . . . got into a fight." In the corner, Mikhael stirred uncomfortably. I lowered my voice further. "You wanted to see me?" My tone came out wrong, almost a sneer. I tried again. "You wanted to see me, sir?" There, that was better.

His tone was cold. "Kevin is near hysteria. He heard you were dead."

"Not yet."

"He's terrified. For that alone, I could . . ." His fists knotted.

I swallowed.

Mr. Dakko said, "I'll reassure him on that point. It's about all I can do for him. He wants to see you safe, and pulverize you."

"Everyone does." Perhaps they were right.

He rested his arms on the polished wood. "I can't believe I let you into my home, you contemptible piece of shit."

My ears burned bright.

"If they release you, if you ever see Centraltown again, I'll call challenge the day you're of age. I'll put you into the ground, Randolph Carr, and the Stadholder be damned."

"Sir, I—"

"Could you possibly say anything of consequence?"

"Why'd you ask to see me, then?"

"For Kevin, and . . ." It was his turn to look uncomfortable. "Captain Tolliver won't allow the Stadholder any contact with you. I'm not exactly an intermediary, but . . ."

"A substitute?"

A nod.

"Have you spoken to him?"

"Not directly. No doubt I will, after. I see they haven't treated you well."

"Don't say that. It's not really true." I colored. "I deserved what I got."

"You deserve hanging."

"You'll get your wish. He's dying."

"How do you know?"

"He's on life support." I leaned toward him, my cuffs chafing. "Mr. Dakko, I want you to know I didn't plan it. I had no idea Mr. Seafort was on *Olympiad* when we took the shuttle aloft. It was just a lark, to see the ship."

"What does that excuse?"

"Nothing, sir. Nothing at all." My tone was bleak. "I went berserk. If I could undo . . ."

"Oh, please."

"I hated him so."

"Past tense? He's still alive."

"I still . . ." I squirmed, as if caught whispering in class. "I still hate what happened to Dad. I always knew he was responsible. Except, no one else thinks so. I may have . . . may . . ."

"Say it."

"Misjudged the situation. Him. If you call challenge, I'll accept. Dad taught me that the Carrs pay for our mistakes."

"As with the Bishop?"

My voice was small. "Please don't toy with me. I'm wrong, and you're right."

"Too late for humility, joeyboy." The glint in his eye held no forgiveness.

"Far too late, sir."

"Did I tell you I served under Captain Seafort?"

I bowed my head. "You too?"

"On *Challenger*. He was given an impossible task, to hold together a broken ship. I loathed him, and fought him every step of the way. He impressed me into the Service against my will. He trained me, forced me to do my duty. Together, we saved the ship and ourselves. Along the way, I became a man."

My eyes drifted. In the far corner, Mikhael was listening intensely.

"If he lives, I may not call challenge. But I'll never forgive you."

"No one will." I struggled to my feet. "Is that all, sir?"

"Yes."

I waited for Mikhael to lead me to the hatch.

Mr. Dakko called after me, "If there's anything you can do to exculpate Kevin . . ."

"I've told them all along, but they won't believe me."

Desolate, I trudged to my cell.

6

MIKHAEL AND LIEUTENANT ANSELM opened my hatch. "Lieutenant Tamarov reporting, sir. You'll have to wear these." He brandished a set of cuffs.

Wasn't it bad enough I was locked in a cage? "Afraid I'll hurt you?" My tone was a jeer.

"No, sir. But you can't go out unrestrained."

I bounded to my feet. "Out?"

A hint of a smile. "Yes, sir. For an hour or so."

I turned, presented my hands.

"In front will be sufficient," said Anselm.

My glance flitted from one to the other of them. "Why are you treating me so . . ." *Nicely.* I was embarrassed to say it.

Abruptly, Anselm was less affable. "Let's say we're doing it for Derek Carr, not you."

Still, escaping my dreary cell was such a joy that I asked, with a real effort to be polite, "How is Mr. Seafort today?"

"Unchanged."

We left the brig. As it turned out, we had no particular destination. They let me wander the corridor, admiring the sumptuous fittings.

Olympiad wasn't quite a ghost city. There were passengers still aboard, for one reason or another, and a few crew could be seen on repair details and the like.

We stopped at the purser's office, where after a short wait I was given a change of clothes. I'd been allowed to shower every morning, but my clothing was another story.

Mikhael kept a grip on my arm, not hard, just enough so he could say he had custody of me. We walked the whole length of the corridor, until it brought us back to the brig.

He saw my disappointment. "We have more time."

I turned to Anselm. "Must we stay on this Level?"

"Hmm. I don't see why. Let's go below. I'll take responsibility."

We rang for a lift, and it wafted us down three Levels. While we were alone Mikhael let go my arm; gratefully I flexed my muscle.

We emerged on Level 6, the lowest Level. I looked about at the corridor, curving either direction. "All Levels are circular?"

"They're disks," said Anselm. "The basic design of a starship hasn't changed in a century and a half. Disks piled one atop another, built around a central shaft."

We followed the bend. "It's hard to tell how long the corridors are."

"They're infinitely long; they follow the curve of the disk, midway from center to edge. Every corridor meets itself. Part of the fun with green middies—or in Mik's case, cadets—is blindfolding them and letting them figure out where they are."

"You made it hard for me," muttered Mikhael.

"I wasn't in charge, and I went through it a few months before you did."

I said, "It must be a zark to have a friend aboard whom you knew from before."

"We weren't friends." Anselm frowned. "Not for a long while."

An uneasy silence settled. Mik stopped before a double-wide hatch. "The engine room."

Anselm slapped it open, peered in. "I think the Chief's groundside."

"He is, sir." A young woman, in sailor's work blues. Short auburn hair, slim build, a competent look about her. She saluted the officers, went back to her gauges.

"We'll have a look around." Anselm steered me into the chamber. "The fusion drive is just below us. See the curve in that alumalloy shaft? That's how N-waves are generated."

I'd never been on a starship, but propulsion wasn't entirely new to me. Not only had Dad told me stories, but we studied it in school, and holozines from Earth still glorified the Naval fleet. Nonetheless, the shaft was impressive, for its sheer size.

Mikhael, hand on my arm, let me walk around it. "We're on standby power, docked at the Station," he said.

"I thought you broke seals and were standing off."

Anselm said, "We mated locks again last night." The two exchanged glances. "The Captain reached an, er, understanding with your government."

"Tell me."

"I'm sorry, that's for Captain Tolliver to decide."

From the hatch, an acid voice. "What's *he* doing here?" Lieutenant Skor, a holovid in her hand. "Mr. Tamarov, this is a secure area. Have you *no* sense? Get him out."

"Aye aye, ma'am."

Anselm said casually, "Actually, I'm responsible, Joanne. Mr. Tamarov brought the prisoner here at my direction."

The two lieutenants regarded each other.

"Of course, if you object, we'll leave immediately." Tad's tone was studiously polite. The tension in the air was palpable.

Ms. Skor sighed. "If it were up to me . . . I won't override you, Anselm. But I certainly wouldn't have . . . not for him, after what he did. Ms. Kohn!"

The rating jumped to her feet. "Yes, ma'am?"

"Where are the power consumption graphs the Captain asked for?"

"Not programmed yet, ma'am. I'll get right on it."

"Do that." She tapped something into her holovid. "Carry on." She was gone.

From Mikhael, a faint sigh that might have been relief.

Anselm checked his watch. "Your hour's up, joey." He gestured to the hatch.

We trudged to the brig in silence. At the hatch I said, "Thank you for letting me out. You don't know how much I—"

"Captain's orders," said Anselm.

"I'm sure you had something to do with—"

"Not us." After a moment, "Jerence Branstead."

"Really?" He hadn't seemed to care much when I complained.

He lowered his voice. "I shouldn't . . ." A sigh. "Branstead told the Captain you were being outrageously mistreated. That he had no authority to intervene, but unless conditions improved he'd make a formal complaint to Admiralty when he went groundside. The Captain was not pleased." His voice dropped even further. "Anyone spit in your food lately?"

"I have a different jailer."

"Ah." He regarded me, urged me gently into my cell. "By the way, they're called master-at-arms's mates." He shut the hatch.

"He's breathing on his own again, and he's coming out of renal failure."

"That's good, isn't it?" I watched Mr. Branstead anxiously.

"Still in coma. It's been what, five days?" The retired chief of staff looked as if he hadn't slept the whole time.

I sought to change the subject. "Thank you for talking to the Captain."

"Tolliver and I have known each other, what, forty years?" He pondered. "Since *Trafalgar,* anyway. I was a cadet. We went out to fight fish on a training ship. Tolliver and Seafort and I. And a few others." Many had answered Seafort's call; few had survived. But the fish were defeated.

I swallowed. If Mr. Branstead was among the heroes of *Trafalgar,* his voice wouldn't be ignored at Admiralty. No wonder Tolliver had acquiesced.

As if reading my mind, he said, "And I can tell you Tolliver isn't happy. Our friendship may be done."

"You did that for me?"

"For decency." He stood to go. "I need to see Nick before I turn in."

"Has Tolliver decided what to do with me?"

"I'm afraid he has. He'll let you know when he's sure."

"Sir?" My plea caught him at the hatch. "If I'm hanged . . ." I made myself go on. "Would you be there?"

"Why?"

"So I'll have a friend to be brave for."

"Christ above." He slapped shut the hatch.

I lay about, teary with self-pity, the rest of the evening.

Two days passed. Mikhael, reeling with exhaustion, took me for my daily outing, as always, under Anselm's supervision. Dark circles hollowed his eyes; with my fading bruises, we seemed almost brothers. Anselm found it amusing, but he was exceedingly gentle with Mik, doing almost all the work, letting him rest whenever possible. For Mikhael's sake, I urged them to take me to a lounge so I could relax in a bright, clean, public place.

Inside, a young woman was watching a holodrama. She glanced at my shackles. "Do you need privacy?"

"I'm afraid so, Ms. Sloan." Anselm gave an apologetic shrug.

"No problem; the east lounge is just as comfortable." She wandered out.

I took a chair. The middy sat opposite, and within minutes his eyelids had drooped.

Anselm said softly, "Captain Seafort is half-conscious. It's a good sign."

"Megazark!" My heart bounded.

His look was curious. It was I, after all, who'd tried to kill him.

"There may be brain damage. Doc Romez can't tell yet."

"May I see him?"

"They'd never allow it."

We spent the full hour in the lounge, talking softly, letting Mik "rest," as Anselm called it. In fact he was sound asleep, snoring softly. "In the middy wardroom he snored every night. Just enough to notice."

"But you're a . . ." I tried to figure it out.

"It's complicated. When we met, I was a middy, he was a civilian. Then Mr. Seafort broke me to cadet. When *Olympiad* sailed to Constantine, he'd adopted Mik as his son and I was still cadet, but it wasn't long before the Captain restored my rank. By then Mik was agitating for permission to enlist, in his father Alexi's footsteps. Eventually the Captain let him. So Mik was low man in our wardroom, and I was just another middy. Before we reached home, Mr. Seafort made Mik a middy too. I think that's so Mik wouldn't have to go to Academy, and they wouldn't be separated. It wasn't just nepotism; he'd seen to it that Mik was qualified. When we sailed again, I was first middy, in charge of the wardroom. And I'll tell you, Mik took some sitting on. He's exuberant, impulsive, passionate about his ideas . . . and one of the finest friends I could imagine."

"Yes, sir." I couldn't imagine why I'd said it.

"A couple of weeks ago, I made lieutenant, and moved out of the wardroom. Mik and I planned to celebrate together over long-leave. Instead, thanks to you, we're holding a deathwatch."

My eyes fell. No apology could suffice. I'd acted out of principle, but . . .

"Let's get you back to your cell."

That evening, when the hatch opened, I expected Mr. Branstead, but it was a midshipman, a holovid under his arm. With him was a sailor, who bore a stunner.

"Randolph Carr." It was statement, not question.

I nodded.

He switched on his holovid. "I am Midshipman Andrew Ghent, U.N.N.S. By order of Captain Edgar Tolliver, I inform you that you are charged with the attempted murder of Captain Nicholas Ewing Seafort, U.N.N.S., on the twenty-fifth day of November, in the year of Our Lord twenty-two hundred forty-six, in that, by premeditation, you struck him upon the head with a blunt object, to wit, a chair, with the intent of causing death."

"Are you also trying Kev—"

"Randolph Carr, I further inform you that you are to be brought to trial on December 1 of this year, that is, tomorrow, before a military court comprised of one judge, appointed by the Captain of this vessel. As judicial officer, the Captain has appointed Lieutenant Joanne Skor, U.N.N.S."

Ghent was far younger than Mik, curly blond hair, a slight build. For some reason, as if unconcerned, I glanced about, noticed a slight tremor of his legs.

"Mr. Carr, I advise you that the charge is capital, in that the victim is an officer in the United Nations Naval Service on active duty. Under said circumstances, you are entitled to the assistance of an officer to act as your defense counsel. If you wish the appointment of a particular officer, every consideration will be given to your request. Else, if you wish counsel, one will be selected on your behalf."

Ghent's shoes were spit-polished, his uniform immaculate, his pose stiff. A sheen of sweat gleamed on his forehead.

"Do you wish the assistance of counsel?"

"When will—I don't—" *A rough rope closed around my neck, chafing the tender skin.* I shuddered.

"If you wish counsel, you are advised to consult with him or her prior to commencement of trial, which is at fourteen hundred hours nominal ship's time, or two o'clock in the afternoon."

"Let me think!"

"Do you wish me to return?"

I hunched over my lap, lay my head in my hands. "Give me an hour."

The moment he was gone I launched myself in a frenzy of pacing. If my ribs ached, I took no notice. I scratched at the walls. No, they were called bulkheads. I must remember that.

I could demand they appoint Mikhael. Fine irony; the middy who'd tried to kill me would try to save my life for having tried to kill his father. No, it would only get him in more trouble, and whatever he'd done to me, he didn't deserve that.

Anselm, then. He'd shown himself to be fair, intelligent . . . Mik liked him, and that was a strong recommendation. He'd stood up to Ms. Skor; that showed he wasn't afraid of her. And Seafort apparently liked him; he'd taken Tad into his extended family. If Anselm worked to defend me, perhaps the court would take into account . . .

It wasn't right. How could I face myself, putting Tad in that position?

Easily. This was about my life. My first duty was to save it.

No. My duty was to undo the mess I'd made of it.

Would they let Jerence Branstead speak for me? "An officer," Ghent had told me. Mr. Branstead was a civilian. Perhaps they'd bend the rules, to appear fair. He was a hero, they'd have to listen if he—

Dad, help me, if only for a moment. I'm confused, I'm lonely, I need your hand on my shoulder, a quiet word of advice. Please. I'll pray, if you'll come. I haven't prayed in five years, and I'll do it now. Watch.

In a fever, I sank to my knees.

Please, Lord God. If You exist—I'm sorry, I don't mean that.

Yes, I do. So many people believe in You, and I feel nothing. If You're real I want to face You with honesty. I can't say I know You exist, but if You do, give me Derek Carr my father, for this most desperate moment of my life.

Please. I don't know how to beg, but I'm begging.

A long while passed.

Dad, what would you do?

There was no one but myself, in a bleak, sweaty cell.

At length I climbed to my feet, knees sore. I sat again on the clammy mattress, rested elbow on knee, put my chin in my hands.

I'd decide alone.

What would Dad do?

Dad wouldn't be here. He'd have more sense, more pride in himself, more integrity than to sit at a table and bludgeon his host.

What would Dad tell *me* to do?

When at last the hatch slid open I was still sitting, head on hands.

The tense young midshipman, Mr. Ghent. "Have you reached a decision, Mr. Carr?"

"Yes." A deep breath. "I don't wish counsel."

I was rewarded with a flicker of surprise. But he said only, "I will so inform the Captain."

They left me for the night.

In the morning, one of the master-at-arms's mates brought breakfast. They even allowed me a spoon. Harmless plastic, but more than before.

After I'd eaten, I gathered my courage. I stood before the hatch, calling louder and louder. "Master-at-arms! Hello! Master-at-arms!"

It seemed forever, but eventually someone came. "What is it?"

A sailor, no petty officer's stripes. "Are you the master-at-arms?"

"No, I'm all you get. What do you want, grode?"

I tried to make my tone like Anthony's, when he was irked. "Get your chief. I'll speak only with him."

He looked at me with contempt. "You don't give orders here."

"Tell him." My voice was a lash. I'd heard Dad speak so, tried beyond endurance.

I paced for an hour, before the master-at-arms appeared. "I'm Janks. What do you want?"

"Tell your Captain I won't go to trial like this."

"You're daft."

"I want a long shower, real clothes that fit and look decent. Everything clean and fresh. A comb. Else you'll have to drag me to trial and I won't participate, not a word. Tell Tolliver!"

He frowned at me a long minute, disappeared.

I was a descendant of the Carrs of Hope Nation. I would stand proudly at judgment.

Lunch came. I left it uneaten; my stomach wouldn't permit else.

I tried prayer again, and found no solace. If there was a God, He wasn't speaking to me. No matter. It didn't lessen my resolve.

Two sailors, and Midshipman Ghent. "You'll come with us, Mr. Carr."

"No." I sat on the deck, prepared to be dragged.

"To the shower."

"Is this a trick?"

The middy's teeth bared in a gesture of disgust. "My word as an officer."

I knew from Dad that that was sufficient. I got up, allowed them to cuff me.

Instead of the spartan stall in the cell block, they took me down the corridor to a passenger cabin, locked me within. Compared to what I'd known, it was huge and luxurious. The head was clean, ample, well stocked with towels and soap.

Until my imprisonment I'd found showers an unwelcome annoyance, to be had only when Dad or Anth insisted. The cell had changed my views; I understood adults' appreciation of cleanliness and grooming. If I ever got free, I'd—

My smile faded. I wouldn't be getting free. Not in this life.

I stood under steaming water for what seemed like hours. At last, I dried myself, went out to the bedroom.

Fresh clothes were laid out on the bed. A stylish cut, an expensive feel. And they fit.

Quickly, I dressed, stood before the mirror and made myself as presentable as I might. I knocked on the outer hatch.

A sailor opened. I stood before Ghent. "I'm ready."

He held out the cuffs.

"You don't need them. You know that." I held his eye.

After a moment, he nodded. "This way, Mr. Carr." His detail fell into step beside me.

Together, we marched into the compartment set aside for the court.

Lieutenant Skor sat at the head table. At the back of the room, a surprising number of officers and crew had gathered. Well, no doubt I was rather notorious.

My eyes darted this way and that.

Mr. Branstead was there. For some reason, I was heartened.

Captain Tolliver was not present. I was disappointed, but not surprised.

I looked about for Kevin, couldn't find him. Had they already tried him? I'd forgotten to ask.

Mikhael and Anselm were present, seated separately from the others, along with Dr. Romez, others I vaguely recognized.

Witnesses.

I stood before the table.

"Let us begin. This court sits by authority and direction of Edgar Tolliver, Captain of UNS *Olympiad*. We are convened to consider a capital charge of attempted murder against one Randolph Carr. You are Randolph Carr?"

"Yes." I wouldn't call her "ma'am." She'd been nasty to Mik.

"Lieutenant Frand will act as prosecutor." She indicated a bony, older woman at the table opposite. "Has the charge been—"

"May it please the Court . . ." A fleshy man, of middle years. He got to his feet. "I call to your attention that this . . . person, this defendant, is a citizen of Hope Nation, where he's wanted for various misdeeds. In fact, Bishop Scanlen, on behalf of holy Reunification Church, has petitioned him—"

Ms. Skor tapped her gavel. "Mr. Pandeker, you have neither authority nor standing to interf—"

"I wish to see justice done. The Church has prior claim."

"I suggest you take it up with the Captain."

"I have, but he won't—"

"Your statement is noted. Please be seated. Now, Mr. Carr, the court takes note that you are a minor of fourteen years. While the law allows for special proceedings in the case of juveniles, I must advise you—"

"My act was that of an adult, and I ask that I be tried as an adult." My voice was firm.

In the courtroom, a buzz of surprise.

"Very well, your request is granted." Lieutenant Skor consulted her holovid. "Do you wish a reading of the charge?"

"No, I understand it."

"Are you sure you wish to waive counsel?"

"Yes." It was easier than I'd feared. My voice was strong, my knees steady. If only I wasn't fighting a constant urge to whimper.

"How do you plead?"

A long moment's silence. I forced myself to meet her gaze.

"I am guilty of the offense charged. I tried to kill Captain Nicholas Seafort."

Anselm's face tightened. He shook his head.

Ms. Skor studied me. Then, "Very well, the court accepts your guilty plea." Again, she consulted her holovid. "Have you anything to say in your own behalf?"

"I do not."

She pursed her lips. "Whatever you may think, this is not a kangaroo court. I am not the Captain's pawn, and will judge independently. If you have any mitigating facts or circumstances, you should present them now."

Thank you, ma'am, for making it easier for me. "There are no mitigating facts or circumstances."

"You understand this is a capital charge?"

"I've thought of little else for a week."

"Is this a form of protest? Do you deny the authority of the court?"

"Not at all. I'm on your ship, in your custody, subject to your law."

In the courtroom, utter silence.

"Lieutenant Frand, does the prosecution wish to be heard regarding sentence?"

"Yes, I—" Her eyes fixed on mine, and held them a long while. "No, ma'am. The case speaks for itself. We leave it to the court."

Ms. Skor rapped the table. "Very well, the court will consider sentence. We are in recess." She stood, strode out a far hatch.

I looked about, found an empty seat behind me, took it.

Jerence Branstead's face seemed lined, older. He approached with diffidence, looked to Midshipman Ghent, glanced to me. Ghent nodded. Branstead drew up a chair.

"A brave show, boy. But why?"

My lip trembled. *Not now, Randy. Hold tight.* "I loved my father. You have no idea how much."

"And?"

"I had a rough time in my cell last night. I decided the best way to show that love was to act as Dad would have. To make him proud of me."

"He would have defended—"

"I shouldn't have done it, Mr. Branstead. Even if Mr. Seafort was every bit as evil as I thought, I had no right to slaughter him before his crew, his family. Had Dad done something so horrible, he'd have submitted to justice. As I have."

He waved it away. "It's too heavy a price to pay for honor."

"It's better this way. I nearly destroyed Anthony, with the Bishop. I may have destroyed your Captain. I don't want to do more harm."

"The Bishop? What are you—"

"You'll hear about it groundside, no doubt."

The hatch slid open. Lieutenant Skor made her way to the table. "Randolph Carr, please stand."

I did so.

"The court has considered your youth, your willingness to admit guilt and accept responsibility. These are laudable traits. Balanced against them are the stark facts. You split Captain's Seafort's skull without warning or mercy, before his four-year-old child, who to the court's own knowledge is still dazed with shock and is utterly unnerved. Captain Seafort's survival is not yet assured. The purpose of the law is to deter and punish."

She tapped the desk. Her face was steel.

"Randolph Carr, I sentence you to be hanged by the neck until dead. The sentence shall be carried out by the master-at-arms unless commuted by the Captain within fifteen days."

My legs gave way. Midshipman Ghent grabbed me from behind, helped me stand steady. His touch was surprisingly gentle.

"You shall remain in the brig until that time. You shall be provided with facilities to record any communications you wish to be forwarded after your death. May Lord God have mercy on your soul."

Ghent's firm hands supported me, under my arms. I began to lose my battle for composure.

"One more thing. Master-at-arms Janks, step forward."

A figure threaded through the crowd. "Aye aye, ma'am. Master-at-arms Janks reporting."

"It has come to the court's attention that various petty cruelties have been routinely inflicted on the prisoner. He will be treated with courtesy and respect from this moment forward. He will be allowed to bathe, given fresh clothing and nutritious, tasty, *unadulterated* food. Do I make myself clear?"

"Yes, ma'am. Very clear."

"He will be allowed daily release from his cell for the purpose of exercise. You, or any officers so assigned, may take whatever security measures are required, but, Janks, don't cross me! I'll know, and you'll regret it. The orders of the court supersede even those of the Captain, until he formally overrules them!"

"Aye aye, ma'am!"

"The prisoner will be removed."

"Come, Mr. Carr." Ghent's voice was soft. "Haskin, M'boia, help him. Easy, there." Solicitously, they guided me to my cell.

7

IT WAS THE third day.

Lieutenant Anselm came, with Mikhael Tamarov. I begged them not to make me leave the cell. All I wanted was to be left alone. Eventually, they complied.

I'd told them the same the day before, and the day before that.

I'd allowed Mr. Branstead to sit with me, once. Whatever he said, I didn't recall.

I ate listlessly, out of bodily need.

Every day they brought good food, fresh clothes, led me to a passenger cabin to shower. I did as they asked, crawled back into my bunk to sleep.

I'd committed the one act of my life I might truly be proud of. All that was left was to see it through.

Mikhael was back; had another day come?

News: Nick Seafort was healing. He was more alert; his double vision was clearing. I summoned a reserve, tried to share Mik's joy.

He, at least, wouldn't lose a father.

He nagged me to take a walk. "It does you no good to lie here."

I snickered. "Is it bad for my health?"

"Don't, sir." A plea.

"I'm a convicted murderer. Don't call me 'sir.' "

"The Captain said—"

"We're alone." I took his silence for assent. "Where's Tad?"

"Outside."

"They trust you alone with me?"

"Mr. Anselm does." A blush. "And I'm off four and four."

"Seafort's recovery eased the Captain's mind?"

"Do you want the truth?"

"Yes."

"I think it was the verdict and sentence." He braced, as if for an explosion.

I shrugged. "That's fair."

"Is it?"

"Let him hate me. You did."

"You were vile when you attacked Pa. You were noble in court. I wish I knew you."

"So do I. I'm glitched, that's for sure. I ought to be rebalanced." Hormone rebalancing was still the therapy of choice for severe mental illness, though the shame attached . . .

"I wasn't much better." He blushed, at some private memory. "I gave Pa hell, when I was young. I don't know how he put up with me."

"I've been pretty rough on Anth." I sighed, but my spirits weren't as low as they'd been. "All right, take me for a walk."

He knocked on the hatch. "Mr. Anselm?"

Tad looked apologetic. He held the cuffs.

I offered my hands. He secured my wrists, in front, where it didn't ache, and where I could scratch my nose.

In the corridor, he raised an eyebrow, waiting.

"I get to choose?"

"Within reason."

I named the only place that held any appeal. "Sickbay."

"Why?"

"I want to see Captain Seafort."

"Lord in Heaven." Anselm regarded me quizzically. "Is that a joke?"

"Else take me back to my cell."

"Mr. Tolliver would never allow it."

"Did he forbid it?"

"Well, he—not in so many—I mean . . . I can't just—damn it, Mik, don't laugh at me."

"Aye aye, sir. Sorry." Mikhael's mouth looked solemn, but not his eyes.

Anselm scratched his head. "I don't know . . ." A long sigh. "He could break me for this." He pulled me toward the stairwell. "Move, before I change my mind."

"Yes, sir." I lengthened my pace.

At the stairwell he held me back. "Just a moment." He undid my cuffs. "Put your hands behind your back." A grunt. "There. I think I trust you, but . . ."

"Think?"

"I'm not sure. You've changed since we met you groundside, but are you completely done with your venom? I don't know. I won't risk the Captain's life to find out. Besides, if I paraded you into sickbay with your hands usable, I'd face court-martial, and deserve to."

It was no worse than I merited. Ears aflame, I let him guide me up the stairs.

"Hurry. This is officers' country, and the fewer who see us, the—"

"*Stand to!*"

Immediately Anselm stiffened to attention, and Mikhael behind him.

Captain Tolliver stalked down the corridor, his face blotched. "What the devil are you up to? Why isn't this felon in his cell?" He swept off his cap, seemed poised to hurl it at the bulkhead. "You bloody, incompetent toad! How dare you bring him here?" He stood nose to nose with Anselm. "Answer!"

"Aye aye, sir. We were taking the prisoner for exercise, as ordered by the court. According to the watch roster, it remains our duty—"

"I know my roster, *Lieutenant* Anselm. Did it say to cart him past the bridge?"

"With respect, sir, did it say not to?"

The Captain drew breath and grew redder.

"Sir, Ms. Skor ordered that Mr. Carr be treated with courtesy and respect, subject to ship's security. I'm duty bound to obey!"

Tolliver stuck his nose practically inside Tad's mouth. "And what are you specifically obeying, Mr. Anselm?"

"Sir, he asked to see parts of Level 1. I could find no reason to refuse. I secured his hands behind his back and had a grip on his arm; under no conceivable circumstances is he a threat. Begging the Captain's pardon, I didn't know what else to do."

"Did you try using common sense?"

"Apparently not, sir."

"Did you tell this—this *person* that I run the ship, not he?"

"No, sir. That was understood."

"Did you consider the effect on ship's morale of parading him past officers' quarters and the bridge?"

"No, sir. It's long-leave, and there's hardly anyone aboard."

Tolliver swung to Mikhael. "Are you part of this charade, Mr. Tamarov?"

"Yes, sir. I urged Mr. Carr to take advantage of the court's provision for exercise."

"Urged?"

"Yes, sir. He was lying in his cell in a funk."

"Two demerits, for not letting nature take its course. Get him out of my sight!"

"Aye aye, sir." Mikhael took a firm grip on my arm. We hurried along the corridor, toward the distant stairwell, past the bend. I risked a look over my shoulder. Captain Tolliver stood in the center of the corridor, arms folded, glaring.

When the bend hid us from view Anselm slowed. "Whew."

"That makes nine," Mikhael said glumly.

"Do you get caned for ten?" I'd always heard it was so.

"Not at my age. But he'll cancel a week of leave."

"I'm sorry I got you joeys in trouble. Hey, where are—" Anselm had swept me past the stairwell.

"To sickbay."

I stopped short. "Are you serious? The Captain will be livid."

"Oh, I don't know." Tad's tone was light, but his face was grim. "I didn't hear him order us not to. Did you, Midshipman Tamarov?"

A moment's reflection. "Not specifically, but—"

"You're released from duty, Mr. Tamarov. You may go to the wardroom if you wish."

Mik hesitated less than a heartbeat. "I'd rather accompany you and the prisoner, sir."

"Very well."

"Tad . . . I mean, Mr. Anselm." I licked my lips. "Don't wreck your career over—"

"Don't concern yourself with my career, Mr. Carr." His tone was cool. Then, "Captain Tolliver's displeasure with me is between us alone. I won't let it stop me from doing what . . ."

I waited. "Yes?"

"What I think is right."

Abruptly we reached a familiar hatchway. I grimaced. When last I'd seen this place I'd been writhing in pain, thanks to Mik.

Anselm peered in. "Ah, Burns. Is Dr. Romez in?"

The med tech saluted, but didn't come to attention. "No, sir. He's in Mrs. Veel's cabin checking her—"

"Is Captain Seafort awake?"

"He's going over the Log. Every day the Captain brings him—"

"I know. We'll pay our respects. Come along, you two."

At the sight of me, the tech's eyes widened. "Sir, you can't bring—"

"Stand aside. That's an order."

Automatically, Burns did so. "Sir, I'll have to call the master-at-arms!"

"Good heavens, why?" Anselm stopped, threw him a curious look. "We just spoke to Captain Tolliver, not two minutes ago."

"You did?" The med tech looked from one to the other of them for reassurance.

"Is it not so, Mr. Tamarov? Come along, you." He hustled me through a passage. "Come with us, Burns. See that Mr. Seafort's comfortable."

The passage widened to an alcove. Beyond it, a room larger than the standard cubicle. There were flowers on a sill, two chairs for visitors.

A gaunt man in loose bedclothes, half covered with a sheet, holovid in hand. His head was heavily bandaged, but his eyes were alert.

"Lieutenant Anselm reporting, sir."

"Midshipman Tamarov reporting, sir." They were both at rigid attention.

"As you were." Seafort's voice was thready. Carefully, he set down the holovid, flexed his fingers. "What brings you two?"

"We came to visit, sir, if we have your permission."

A wintry smile. "I'll allow it."

"Thank you, sir."

"Who is this?"

I held my breath.

He stared at me, his expression blank. "Mr. Anselm, I don't . . . Oh!" He jerked as if galvanized.

Burns dived to the bed. "Sir, are you all—"

Seafort stayed him with an unsteady hand.

Anselm swung me around so my back was to the Captain. "He's securely cuffed, sir, and can do you no harm. I stake my life on that." He spun me again.

"It's all right, Burns. I was startled." Seafort's piercing gray eyes searched my face. "You're the miscreant I brought to dinner."

"Yes, sir." It was no more than a whisper. I tried again. "Yes, sir."

"Why is he here, Lieutenant?"

"He asked to see you. I thought it compassionate to agree."

"They haven't sent me the court files yet. I asked for them, but Tolliver

refused to discuss the interrogation or the case. When I'm stronger, he said."
Seafort peered at me. "You're Carlson, aren't you?" Carefully, the Captain
resettled himself. "My back aches dreadfully, thanks to you. I thought I was
over that."

"Sir, his name is—"

I blurted, "Tad, don't! Please, as God is my witness, I beg you."

The Captain pursed his lips. "Um . . . Randy, yes, that's it. I'm able to
recall details. It's a very good sign." He stirred restlessly. "Burns, I'll have
that pill now, I think." With an effort, he focused on me, but he was tiring
visibly. "A life wasted is a tragedy, boy. Mine or yours. I'll see you again,
before . . ." He drifted. "I really need to sleep. Thank you, boys, for visiting.
Mr. Carlson, I'll visit your cell. That's a promise."

The two saluted, and hustled me out.

Our walk to my cell was silent. At one point Anselm said, "Mik, you
didn't tell him?"

"Pa and I agreed on a rule when he let me enlist. No ship's business,
no matter what. It's the only way we . . ." Mikhael rubbed his face. "And I
was afraid to tell him it was Derek's son."

I couldn't help myself. "Why?"

Mik's eyes glistened. "It would break his heart."

Galvanized, I lurched in a convulsive effort to free my hands. I twisted
against the cuffs, regardless of the pain.

If somehow I could have stopped my pulse, fallen dead, I would.

I had no right to cause such misery to so many. Thank Lord God for
Lieutenant Skor's resolve.

"I'm going to break my rule," Mik said.

"Mr. Tamarov . . ." My voice was unsteady. "Don't do it."

"I can't just—"

"If there's a God and He wants him to know, he'll learn. Your relationship with your father is more important than any of this. Believe me, I
know."

We walked in silence to the brig.

"He's on the road to recovery," said Jerence Branstead.

"I saw."

"Yes, and that escapade to Level 1 cost you your contact with your
two cronies. Tamarov's confined to the wardroom. Anselm's confined to
quarters, facing summary court-martial."

"Is Tolliver a despot?"

"Not really." He settled back in the couch. We were in a passenger
lounge, two of Janks's minions guarding the hatch. I wondered how Mr.

Branstead had arranged it. "He feels the boys should have told the whole truth. Instead they answered his questions and gave not an iota more." A mischievous smile. "It's exactly what Nick pulled, time and again. Maddening, but effective."

"Will they be cashiered?"

"I doubt it. Tolliver will cool off. In the meantime, it's good they learn it's never wise to tweak the Captain."

"I asked Mik not to tell Mr. Seafort who I am."

"I think I can understand why. You're ashamed, that anyone connected to your father would hurt him?"

I nodded.

"Well, Mikhael will probably honor your plea. He understands these things."

"Good."

"But I probably won't."

I slumped. "God damn it, why?"

"Don't you dare use foul language with me! What comes over you?"

I swallowed. "I've never been able to hold my . . . I apologize. Please tell me why?"

"I saw Nick get into one of these feuds of honor with his son Philip. The whole family was miserable. Honor is well and good, but when joeys begin destroying those they love, out of the best of motives . . ." He grimaced. "This madness has got to stop."

"I want Dad left out of it."

"It's all about Derek, Randy. Not just from your perspective. From Nick's too."

"But Mr. Seafort will decide for the wrong reasons! Let—"

Mr. Branstead leaned forward, clasped my knee. "Do you still want to crush him?"

I took a long, deep breath. "No."

"I've known him forty years. If he isn't told before you die, it will destroy him."

I sat a long while, taking in the full import, realizing what it told about his relations with Dad.

I really was a worthless piece of scum. All the more reason not to tell Mr. Seafort the truth.

"I can't stop you, but I'm pleading with you. Say nothing."

"I'll think on it."

Mr. Branstead accompanied us on our walk back to the brig. We neared a stairwell; an officer was striding down briskly. Lieutenant Skor. She stopped short, frowned at me. "Are they treating you properly, young man?"

"Yes." Almost, I said, "Yes, ma'am," but something prevented me.

"No repercussions from your foray topside?"

"Not for me. Only for those who carried out your orders."

She glanced at Mr. Branstead, rolled her eyes. "That's not your concern."

My voice was Dad's, when truly incensed. "Madam, you're mistaken."

For an instant she was taken aback. "You're a civilian."

"If my requests bring punishment to my wardens, I'm intimidated from my requests."

"Hmmm. Carry on."

When she was gone Mr. Branstead said, "Don't push it much further, boy."

I snorted. "What have I to lose?"

"Tolliver could rule that your sentence won't be commuted."

"He intends so anyway."

We reached my cell, and stood outside, while the master-at-arms waited nearby.

"Quite possibly. But Nick's recovering. When he takes the conn, it won't be up to Edgar."

For a moment I was silent, struggling to explain. "I'm afraid to die, but I'm not afraid of being punished, even though it works out the same. I won't try to avoid execution."

His fist shot out, slammed against the bulkhead. "These laws are barbaric! Since when is it just to treat joeykids as if they're grown?"

"When they commit the acts of a grown—"

"Oh, I've heard that prattle. Even the Church forsakes mercy for Old Testament justice. They actually burn heretics! I wonder at times what's come over the Patriarchs."

"Lower your voice!" It came out an order. I worked the harshness from my tone. "Mr. Branstead, don't talk like that when you go groundside. Be cautious."

"Don't offend the Bishop?"

"Right."

He stared at me a long while, until I went red.

"Yes, I know, sir. I was an idiot." Dutifully, I turned to my cell.

It was as if I were holding court. The master-at-arms, midshipmen, sailors, Mr. Branstead, came to visit, to provide me with food, clothes, exercise, conversation. Almost, I began to enjoy it.

My biggest surprise was Mikhael Tamarov, the evening after my words with Lieutenant Skor. "I don't know how you did it, but thank you."

"You're freed?"

"And off report." He shook his head, as if in wonder. "The Captain was a bit curt, but civil. He said he'd overreacted, that Ms. Skor had called to his attention that I was acting within the scope of her orders."

"So what makes you think I—"

"I sense your hand in it. Neither of them would . . ." He shook his head. "I can't discuss those matters outside the Navy. But was it you?"

I said coolly, "I expressed my displeasure to Ms. Skor."

He grinned. "Now you sound like Pa."

I recoiled. "Don't say that."

"I meant no—" Seeing my distress, he said lamely, "I'm sorry."

I sought a new topic. "Why are you here?"

"I have visiting privileges." His smile faded. "Mr. Tolliver said it's only for a few days."

"Spiteful of him."

He bowed his head.

"But realistic," I added. "What about Tad? Is he free?"

"I didn't dare ask. Mr. Tolliver seemed at the end of his patience."

"And your father?"

"Better. He still can't really walk. He gets dizzy."

"If he—when he recovers, Mr. Tolliver will go back to lieutenant?"

"Yes."

"What about all the enemies he's made?"

"What are you talking about?" He regarded me. "You really know nothing about the Navy, do you?" Unbidden, as if we were old friends, he settled beside me on my meager bunk. "Look, the Captain's authority is absolute. Do you understand that much?"

"Of course." We'd studied Naval traditions in school, though Hope Nation had left the U.N.

"With Pa—with Captain Seafort incapacitated, he *had* to take firm control. No one will hold that against him."

"Threatening a fellow lieutenant with court-martial?"

"Tad wasn't a fellow lieutenant. He was a lieutenant dealing with his Captain. It's of no matter that Mr. Tolliver's rank was temporary. He was Captain of this ship, and he must be obeyed."

"Then why did you flout his authority?"

"Why do you ask the hard questions?"

We both grinned.

"Randy . . ." Suddenly, his voice was tentative. "Part of me can't forget that you tried to kill Pa. And Pa may never be the same; if the dizziness persists, if his sight remains impaired, he'll be retired."

"I'm sor—"

"Somehow, I don't still hate you. It's gone. When I saw you in court . . ." He fussed with his sleeve, his shoe. "God, I admired you. That was magnificent. I was proud to be your . . ."

I waited but he said no more.

"It's all right, Mikhael."

"Friend." It was a whisper.

I swallowed a lump in my throat, and was silent.

Midshipman Ghent found us together, about an hour after. He planted himself before me, in the at-ease position. "Mr. Carr."

I waited.

He ignored Mikhael. "By order of Captain Tolliver, I inform you that he will interview you this evening at twenty-two hundred hours, that is, ten P.M. nominal ship's time, concerning the sentence of the court. You will be brought to the bridge at the appropriate hour." A curt nod, and he departed.

Mikhael said, "When they take you to the bridge, don't provoke him, Randy. He's a decent joey, but . . ."

I shrugged.

"He has a temper. He was a Captain, you know. Came out of retirement and took lieutenant's rank to sail with Pa. He's used to having his way."

"Mikhael . . ."

"He's not as hard as he seems. If you—"

"Mik."

"—apologize, and ask forgiveness, he may well—"

"*Mik!*"

"Grant some form of—what, Randy?"

"There is not a chance in Lord God's Hell that Tolliver will grant clemency, and we both know it."

"You can't be sure—"

"I'm as sure as you."

That silenced him.

We sat, each with his own thoughts.

I wasn't sure I wanted clemency. I wouldn't ask for it; that was certain. I'd forfeited any right to beg for my life. If given, would I rejoice?

I no longer knew.

At my urging, Mikhael left so I could await the Captain's call alone. I half expected Mr. Branstead, with some last-minute advice, but he stayed away.

Once more, Ghent slid open my hatch. "The Captain's ready for you." He held out a pair of cuffs.

"Last time you didn't use them, Midshipman."

"We weren't going to the bridge, Mr. Carr." To my annoyance he fastened my hands behind my back. Very well, I would make the best of it, act as if I took no notice.

He led me to the outer hatch.

"Why are you aboard ship, Mr. Ghent?" I would match his formality. "Isn't this long-leave?"

"I reached ten demerits." He spoke with distaste. "It was a week of leave, or the barrel."

"I'd have chosen the barrel." I let him hurry me along the corridor to the lift.

"Have you ever been caned?"

"No."

He said only, "It's worth a week of leave."

"Who gave you the demerits?"

"That's not your affair." He seemed affronted. We crowded into the lift; he punched the button for Level 1. Then, "They weren't all at once. My first midshipman issued a number of them."

"Mr. Anselm?"

"Yes." His tone held warning. I glanced at his eyes; they seethed.

We paused outside the bridge. The middy ran fingers through his hair, straightened his tie, knocked at the hatch.

The corridor camera swiveled; the hatch slid open. "Come in."

Ghent marched in, hauling me in tow. "Midshipman Andrew Ghent reporting with prisoner Carr as ordered, sir." He let go my arm, snapped to attention.

Edgar Tolliver swung his chair. The Captain's face was thin, lined. His gray hair was cut short and trim. He was slim but not unduly so, and looked fit. "Very good, Mr. Ghent. Wait in the corridor, if you will."

"Aye aye, sir." A salute. The boy wheeled and marched out. The Captain closed the hatch behind him. We were alone.

Hands locked behind me, I looked about. So this was the bridge of a starship. Dad had described it, but . . .

Machinery gleamed. The Captain sat at a console that faced the front wall. Across the wall—*the bulkhead, Randy*—was a huge curved simulscreen. The view took my breath away: millions of stars, all the familiar constellations. And below us, Hope Nation, achingly, beautifully green. For a moment I smelled the fresh sea breeze that would never again cool my face.

"If I might have your attention?" Tolliver's acid voice recalled me.

A flame of fury washed clear my mind. He needn't have been cruel. It did no harm for me to look about. Very well, he had set the tone. "Of course." My tone was nonchalant. I faced him, standing a few paces distant. I pretended I'd chosen to clasp my hands behind my back.

He said, "Would you care to sit?"

"Why, no, actually." We were planters, exchanging courtesies before a conference. "But by all means remain seated, if you wish."

It was calculated insult, and it scored. His eyes narrowed. "Naval regulations provide for review of any sentence by the Captain of the vessel. When my review is completed your execution will be carried out, or set aside."

"So I understand." I would give not an inch.

The caller buzzed.

"Yes?" The Captain spoke to the bulkhead speaker.

"Comm Room reporting incoming traffic, priority one, requesting you, sir."

"Source?"

"The Stadholder."

"I'll return his call shortly." He touched his pad; the background hiss vanished. "So, Mr. Carr. Was your trial unfair in any particular?"

"It was not."

"Were you adequately represented?"

"To my satisfaction."

Tolliver drummed the console. "Your sentence was within the guidelines. I myself was present for your attack, and saw its savagery. What do you have to say in your defense?"

"Nothing."

"Look here, boy!" His tone sharpened. "Mr. Seafort isn't Captain at the moment, I am. My duty is to decide whether your sentence is warranted, not to carry out a vendetta. Did I want to see you tried? Yes. Did I want you convicted? I hoped it would be the case. Did I want a death sentence?" A long pause. "Yes. But now I wear a different cap, as it were, and I'll try to put aside my feelings. Your task is to convince me to spare you."

"Why is that my task?"

He seemed nonplussed. "So you'll survive. You have no other advocate."

I shrugged. "Is there anything else, Captain?"

"Do you *want* to die?"

"That's a private matter, Mr. Tolliver. You have no warrant to ask of it."

"You're insolent."

"I have no duty of courtesy to you." I spoke with civility. I wasn't sure why, or how, but I knew I was winning.

"Why'd you want to kill Nick Seafort?"

"Your interrogation gives you any answer to which you're entitled."

He said suddenly, "You destroy yourself out of hate for me."

"I might. That's my privilege."

"I ought to have you whipped for discourtesy."

"That, too, is within your power." I spoke as calmly as I could. If he did that, I'd be humiliated beyond bearing. So I must make it seem as if it didn't matter.

Abruptly Tolliver spun his chair, showing me his back. A long moment passed. "Do you know," he told the bulkhead, "there was a time I hated Nick Seafort as much as you?"

"I wasn't aware." I strove to sound bored and polite.

"Would you like to hear of it?"

Yes! "If you wish."

"I was a lieutenant, and proud of it. Assigned to the Hope Nation fleet during the war."

I waited.

"I saved Captain Seafort's life, by hauling him from the pilot's seat of a heli under attack, and taking the controls. Touching the Captain uninvited is a capital crime. He broke me to middy. I thought of killing him."

"A not uncommon whim."

"Perhaps. A lot of joeys hated Nick, most of them incompetent, or fools."

"Do you include yourself?"

"No, I was neither." He spoke without hesitation, and I gave him points. Anthony would have approved. So would Dad.

"I wished him dead, Mr. Carr. But I didn't act on it." He turned to face me. "That's the point."

"If you hated him, why are you with him now?" It was utterly irrelevant, but I couldn't help myself.

"Are you entitled to my life story?"

"No, but you began it."

A hint of a smile. "I served with him at Hope Nation, and home on *Victoria*. Then no one would take me, thanks to the blot on my record. So he appointed me his aide, at Academy. He was Commandant, you know."

I nodded. On Hope Nation as well as on Earth, Seafort's story was legend.

"We had a . . . well, a special relationship. I said whatever I chose, and he allowed it, knowing my feelings. In return I gave him my best service." His eyes fastened on the simulscreen. "Then the fish came, and came, and came. We went to face them, in *Trafalgar*."

"With Mr. Branstead."

Tolliver looked startled. "Yes, Jerence was there, a cadet, frightened out of his wits. I'll tell you, boy, what I saw that day was . . ."

I was afraid to speak.

He shook himself. "Seafort saved the planet. And all of home system.

And then, decades later, he saved us again from revolution and chaos. So when he was hurt and soulsick, exiled and homeless, of course I sailed with him." A moment of reflection. "He's above hate and revenge. For you to smash his head was . . . monstrous. He's so God damned selfless—" Even I flinched at the blasphemy. "—he might forgive you. But I'm not. So I'll do what he won't."

I wished my hands were free, so I might hug him.

"Which means I'll have to hurry. But still, I owe you full consideration. I ask one last time, will you speak for yourself?"

"There's no need."

"I will *not* take into account what's not in the record!"

"I quite understand."

He touched a control; the hatch slid open. "I have a petition for clemency."

"My nephew Anthony."

"Oh, of course he protests." He waved it aside. "From aboard ship."

"May I ask who signed it?"

"Lieutenant Anselm and Andrew Ghent."

I had no words.

"What is within you, boy, that officers who revere Seafort—far more than I, let me add—make themselves your advocates?"

"They're easily deluded."

He regarded me. "It's true, you *do* have a death wish. *Mr. Ghent!*"

The middy popped through the hatch. "Midshipman Andrew—"

"Take him below, I'm done with him."

"Aye aye, sir." The boy gripped my arm. "Mr. Carr . . ."

I allowed myself to be steered from the bridge.

Several times Ghent made as if to speak, stopped himself. Then, "How did it go?"

I dug in, forcing him to halt. "Why did you petition for clemency?"

He colored. "I didn't think he'd tell you."

"Why?"

The boy shrugged, made a gesture of helplessness. "I don't know. I couldn't—it was—" More gestures, tics, that subsided to naught. "We have to go."

"Tell me, or drag me to the cell." Helplessness, I was learning, conferred great power.

He tugged at my forearm. "I can't afford more demerits."

"Why the petition, Midshipman?"

He grew red. "If ever I'm in trouble—real trouble—I want to act as you did in court."

"But I assaulted Mr. Seafort."

"Tad—Mr. Anselm—says you had reason, and regret it bitterly. Do you?"

I owed him, and couldn't refuse. "I regret it."

"Mr. Carr, the Stadholder all those years, was your father?"

"Yes."

"I never saw *Galactic*. They say she was just like *Olympiad*." It seemed a non sequitur. "At night—please walk with me—I lie awake sometimes, imagining the ship sliding into Earthport Station, her hull ripped apart, the unquenchable fire . . ." He shuddered. "So many people. Mr. Seafort's wife was Captain when *Galactic* foundered."

"I know." She'd died with her ship.

We entered the lift.

Galactic's loss, and the coup, dominated the holozines for months. I had every issue, carefully locked in my desk in my bedroom.

Ghent's voice was earnest. "We think of acting bravely—we all have those fantasies, don't we?—but . . . the air running out, the lifeboats gone, not enough suits . . ." His eyes glistened. "Your father Derek helped dozens of passengers to safety. He died a hero."

"I know." It took inhuman effort to speak calmly.

"God, how you must miss him."

I slid to the deck, leaned to the side, beat my head against the elevator frame.

"Don't—oh, Mr. Carr, I'm so sorry! Don't!" He knelt, pulled my head to his chest. "Forgive me." His voice caught. Frantically, he sought the keys, released my hands. "God, what have I done?" He rocked me, for all the world like a distraught mother.

After, his hand on my shoulder, he guided me to the solace of my cell.

The next day, no one at all came, except Master-at-arms Janks. In silence, he gave me food, allowed me to walk the corridor—no cuffs, just two sailors as escort, each with a stunner—and escorted me to the shower.

It was just as well. My courage had reached its limit. No, surpassed it. There was a lump in my throat that threatened to dissolve in wails and whimpers. I was tired of putting up a brave front, exhausted with the struggle not to plead for mercy.

I wasn't completely insane; I yearned to live. I wanted to curl cross-legged on Judy Winthrop's bed, hear her chatter, grow closer, touch her breast.

I wanted to dive unclothed into the pond, even if Alex and Judy were watching. I wanted to apologize to Anth, tell him I'd try harder.

I wanted to go to school.

I wanted . . . what did it matter? The lure of life was seductive. But . . .

The Carrs pay their debts.

* * * *

A soft knock at the hatch.

I was so startled, I could only stare.

Another knock.

"Come in."

Tad Anselm. He tried a smile, without much success. "How are you today?"

"Well enough."

"I have a message from Captain Tolliver."

"I'm surprised Ghent didn't deliver it. He's the usual—"

"He's in the brig, two cells down. He refused."

I came to my feet.

"Captain Tolliver has reviewed the sentence pronounced by the court and con—" His face contorted. "And confirms it. The execution will be tomorrow, at noon."

"Where's Mik? I want to talk to Mik!"

"He's in the wardroom, on his bed."

I hugged myself.

If I begged, Anselm would try to get to Seafort. The old man would listen, and for my father's sake he'd . . .

"It's tearing him to pieces, but Mikhael will honor your request. He won't mention this to his father."

At least one of us has honor.

Tad himself could . . .

It would be vile to ask.

"Randy, I'll keep silent, if you insist. I don't want to."

I was trapped. I could live, but only if I accepted a life not worth living. I nodded, turned to the wall. Bulkhead. Whatever it was.

"Shall I leave you alone?"

"No!" I fought a mighty war of annihilation, made my voice something human. "Sit with me. Say nothing, just sit."

He did so. After a time, his hand crept round my shoulder. Time passed; I had no idea how long.

"Where is Mr. Branstead?"

"Groundside, I hear. He should be back tonight."

"May I tell you the truth, sir?"

He said, "Of course."

"I'm very afraid."

His grip tightened.

"It's very important I not show it. Can you help me find . . ." I waited, until I was sure I could speak. "A way to carry through?"

"You have more courage than anyone I've ever met. Including Mr. Seafort. Your father had much to be proud of."

"We have to change the subject."

After a time he said, "I'll be there, if the Captain allows. I think he will. When you're frightened, look at me."

"Will that help?"

"I'm sure it will." He spoke with confidence. On my shoulder, his fingers twitched.

The hatch slid open. "Begging your pardon, Mr. Anselm." Master-at-arms Janks. "Captain Seafort is asking for the prisoner. I'm to take him."

"Very well." Anselm stood. "Tell him, Randy."

"I can't do that."

"I beg you."

"If I'm to redeem myself at all, I can't."

"The handcuffs aren't necessary, Mr. Janks."

"I'm sorry, sir. I must." He secured my wrists.

We made the now-familiar journey to sickbay.

Captain Seafort, wearing a robe, was propped in bed. His new bandage was much smaller. Stitches were visible, and areas where the skull had been shaved. His eyes were alert. A young tyke played in his lap.

Janks came to attention.

"Ah, Mr. Carlson. You've met Janey?"

"Yes, sir. At dinner."

He frowned. "That wasn't good for her to see. Was it, hon." He nuzzled her cheek.

"You're better now, Daddy."

"Yes I am, love." To Janks, "Release him, let him sit, and leave us."

"I'm sorry, sir, I can't do that." Janks uncuffed me, though. He pushed me into a seat at the bulkhead, as far from the bed as was possible. He cuffed each of my wrists to an arm of the chair.

My heart pounded.

"I want him freed."

Janks was sweating. "Sir, Captain Tolliver's orders. I can't leave him with you otherwise."

"Very well. Out."

When we were alone, Mr. Seafort regarded me. "I'm treated as an invalid. I detest that."

"Yes, sir."

He sat up, closed his eyes a moment. "This cursed dizziness. My love, Dr. Romez is in his office. Go see if he'll play with you."

"Lemme stay."

"No, hon." He patted Janey's posterior.

"You're mean." But she climbed down, padded out.

"So." Shrewd gray eyes examined me. "Tell me what's being hidden."

"What, sir?"

"Despite your best efforts, I'm not yet an idiot. Mik won't talk to me, Anselm avoids me like the plague, though he's been almost a son for five years now. Tolliver won't meet my eye. Ghent is nowhere to be found, and even Jerence is making himself scarce. *What in blazes is going on?*"

I balanced on the cusp. It was so easy to be certain, speaking with Tad. Now, at the moment of truth . . .

"I can't say, sir." There. And it wasn't even a lie.

"Why did you try to kill me?"

"No reason that would matter."

"It's all right to tell me. I won't be angry."

"It's nothing that would make sense." I shut my mouth.

"What are they going to do with you?"

"I'd really rather not discuss it." After my duel with Tolliver, it was surprisingly easy.

His fingers scrabbled for the bed controls. He raised his backrest, swung his legs over the side. With great care, he stood, balanced by hanging on to the headboard.

After a moment he cast loose, walked carefully to my chair, past it to the next. He didn't quite totter.

Gratefully, he sank into the soft seat. "Listen to me, joeyboy." His tone was sharp. "I won't put up with this. You *will* tell me what I want to know. You will belay this evasiveness. RIGHT NOW!"

I began to cry.

"*Now,* boy!"

My mouth opened. In desperation I clamped it shut, shook my head.

"Enough! God—bless it!" He raised his voice. "Romez! Doctor!"

Running steps. Dr. Romez hurled himself into the room, Janks a step behind.

"I want Captain Tolliver, and I want him NOW!"

"Sir, I can't order—"

"Tell him I'm on the warpath and he will by God be here in the next minute!"

I sat, shoulders hunched over, my fingers clawing at the cuffs. My eyes stung from salt. I sucked in mucus.

Seafort worked his way to his feet. "I wish to *hell* I could walk." A pause. "Sorry. But more than a few steps and I have to hold on to the bulkhead. You really did me well, boy. There, it's all right, stop crying, blow your—oh!" With determination, he trod back to the bed, found a handkerchief, made his way back. "Here." He held it to my nose.

"You asked to see—well! How touching." Tolliver's tone was acid.

"Be warned, Edgar. I'm beyond fury. Don't goad me."

"May I suggest you resume your bed? You're pale."

"Wasn't there another boy with Mr. Carlson?"

"Yes. Kevin."

"Where is he?"

"In the cells, awaiting adjudication." Thank the Lord. No one had told me. For the moment, Kev was safe.

"Was he part of it?"

"There's no proof."

"Release him."

"No."

"I order it."

"You're not in command." Tolliver grimaced. "I say that with all due respect, sir. At the moment, I am Captain of *Olympiad*. I'll gladly relinquish command when you're recovered."

"What's this boy's status?"

"Ask him."

"I have. Now I'm asking you."

"I won't discuss it."

Seafort threw up his hands. "Edgar . . ." He softened his voice. "Do we have a friendship?"

"I would hope so."

"Tell me."

"No, sir, I will not."

"Very well, you leave me no choice. I reassume command of *Olympiad*."

"I don't give my assent. You're an invalid. You sleep fifteen hours a day."

"I'm weak, but I'm lucid."

"You're not fit for command."

"That's nonsen—"

Tolliver flung his cap past the startled doctor's nose. "Very well, sir, you're fit? Walk to the bridge."

"What?"

"When you walk to the bridge under your own steam, I'll relinquish command. Until then, I'll do my duty as I see it!"

"Edgar!"

"Good day, sir." A stiff salute, that wasn't returned. After a moment, Tolliver retrieved his cap, stalked out.

"Romez." Seafort's voice was taut. "Help me to the bed. You'd better go, boy."

Janks began unclasping my restraints.

"Sir?" My voice was tremulous.

"Yes?"

"Don't hate him."

"Have no fear. We bicker like an old married couple."

"I want you to know . . ." I resisted Janks's pull toward the hatch. "I'm truly sorry for what I did."

He was climbing into the bed. "I'm glad you feel so."

Inexorably, Janks hauled me to the hatch.

"Good-bye, sir."

The hatch slid shut.

Once we were clear of sickbay, Janks was surprisingly gentle. He guided me below, to the row of cells.

I raised my voice. "Good-bye, Kev!" I hesitated just a moment. "I'm sorry. Ask your father to forgive me!"

Janks deposited me in my cell. To my astonishment, he returned with a tray of all sorts of sweets a boy might like. Cake, ice cream, hard candies. For the sake of his kindness, I sampled them.

How should one spend the last night of one's life?

In one sense, I felt good. I'd passed all my tests save the last. I'd resisted temptation over and again, and no more lay before me.

Soon I'd reach safe harbor.

But there was the other Randy, who felt a constant need to piss. Whose hands were clammy, whose shirt was damp with sweat. Whose stomach hardened into a knot. Who didn't know whether to waste precious hours in sleep, or pace the cell to no purpose.

In the small hours, the hatch opened.

Edgar Tolliver, his eyes bleak. "I brought you this. No need to stand." A holovid, and blank chips. He set them on my bunk.

To record my farewell messages. My throat tightened. "Thank you."

He shifted, as if hesitant. "Randy, I never served with Derek; I barely knew him. But if you'd shown one whit of remorse, I'd have pardoned you for Nick's sake. Even now . . ."

So. Temptation was not yet past.

I rose to my feet. "Thank you for the offer."

"Why are you so stubborn?"

A smile I couldn't help. "My father made me so."

"I understand you blamed Nick for *Galactic,* and it warped you. That much came out in your interrogation."

I nodded.

"I'm not without mercy. What I'm doing will cost me a lifetime's friendship with Nick Seafort. He'll never speak to me again."

"I doubt that."

"Oh, it's so. The moment he finds who you are."

"Then, why . . ." I couldn't help the question, though it seemed self-serving.

"Because I believe justice must be done, and seen to be done. We live in an era of law, not the Rebellious Ages. The stability of society depends on malefactors being punished. What other lunatic with murder in his heart would be encouraged by your pardon?"

"Then why would you allow my remorse to influence—"

"Because I'm human, not a machine!" It was a cry from the heart. "I'm not like those bloody fish, that hurt us without reason, attacked with no cause. I can love. I have daughters. I have a grandchild a year younger than you!"

"If I beg you, will you issue a pardon?"

"In all likeli . . ." He thrust his hands in his pockets. "Trust me."

"Then I beg you." Swallowing infinite pride, I got down on my knees. "Pardon Kevin Dakko, sir. He's done nothing, knew nothing, is utterly innocent. I beg you to pardon him."

"Janks, open this hatch! Open it at once!"

When I looked up, he was gone.

Late in the morning they came for me.

Master-at-arms Janks, with two burly seamen.

And trailing behind, Reverend Pandeker. "My son—"

"What's *he* doing here?"

The master-at-arms looked startled. "Spiritual consolation. You've the right to confess—"

"NO!"

Pandeker raised a meaty palm. "Of course you're distraught. Let His strength guide you through your travail. Randolph, make a clean breast of it; go to Him with—"

I pounded my knee. How could I compose myself for what was to follow, with that unctuous fool's bleating? "Please!" It was an entreaty.

"Reverend . . ."

"Janks, his soul is at stake. I'll walk with—"

"I think not." Casually, the master-at-arms stepped between us.

Pandeker glared. "You'd come between holy Mother Church and her work?"

"He declines your services. If you need be present, you'll need the Captain's authorization." Janks keyed open the hatch. "Sir . . ."

For a moment it seemed as if Pandeker would contest the issue, but at last he stalked out.

Janks turned to me with a sigh. "I have to tape your mouth, Mr. Carr. That's how it's done."

"Oh, God." I squeezed my knee. "Can you find Mr. Anselm, so I can ask him to walk with me?"

"I don't—all right, I'll ring his cabin. But we have to hurry." They left the hatch open, the two sailors standing guard.

Two minutes passed. Three.

"I'm sorry, it's time. The Captain—"

Running steps.

"I'm here." Tad, out of breath.

"He's about to tape my mouth. You do it. Please!"

Anselm flinched. "I can't—" A deep breath. "Very well." He took the tape from Janks. "Are you ready?"

I nodded.

Gently, almost tenderly, he placed it across my mouth. "I'll be there every step of the way, boy."

Except the last.

Janks muttered, "Now his hands." Then, "I hate this."

Hands locked behind me, my feet shackled, a sailor to my left, Janks in front, Anselm holding my right arm, we began our slow journey. I glanced at Tad and tried to eye a question.

"Below, Randy. The engine room. The shaft."

As good a place as any.

We shuffled to the lift.

We sank into the bowels of the ship.

The hatch opened.

Level 6.

We progressed at a snail's pace along the curving corridor.

Not a crewman was to be seen.

Ahead, a familiar hatch.

Slowly, we approached. Cowardice fully unsheathed, I shortened my steps until I barely moved.

Inexorably, Janks urged me forward. Despite my best efforts, I neared the hatch.

I tried to scream. Barely a sound escaped my gag.

We were at the hatchway. A dozen meters within, the fusion drive shaft. Erected over it, a plank. From it hung a rope.

My legs gave way. I sprawled, hanging from the grip of Janks and Anselm.

Tad knelt. "Look at me!" I did. His cheeks were wet. "I promised. Look at me, Randy. You've kept your courage. Only a few moments more."

Somehow, they got me to my feet.

At the shaft, Captain Tolliver waited. With him stood a half-dozen officers: two middies, Lieutenant Skor, Dr. Romez, others I didn't know.

I took a step, could go no farther.

I began to wet my pants.

The speaker crackled.

A thin voice, reedy, weary. *"This is Nicholas Ewing Seafort, speaking from the bridge. Recovered from my injury, I hereby reassume command of UNS Olympiad. Mr. Tolliver, you are reverted to the rank of lieutenant."*

Not a soul moved.

"All hands take note: the execution of Randolph Carr is stayed. The sentence of the court is vacated. Escort him to the bridge. Mr. Tamarov, to the bridge. Lieutenant Anselm, to the bridge. Mr. Ghent, to the bridge." A pause. *"Mr. Tolliver, to the bridge."*

Too late.

I'd met my test, and made a hash of it.

8

IT TOOK SOME DOING to remove the tape; skintape was used in surgery, and was supposed to be irremovable. No doubt even surgeons found need on occasion, but it took a long sprint by Dr. Romez to sickbay for the solvent.

They let me change my clothes. No. They changed my clothes. By that point I was incapable. Sobbing, I rested my cheek on Tad Anselm's shoulder. He and Janks worked the damp trousers off my legs, brought towel and water, maneuvered me into fresh pants.

Romez offered a sedative; I refused.

I managed to walk, though my legs were unsteady. By now, I knew the way. The circumference corridor seemed familiar, almost home. I noticed details I hadn't before. The hatches were trimmed in gold paint. On every Level except the topmost, framed art hung from the bulkheads. On a warship, no less. I shook my head.

Unrestrained, I walked onto the bridge, Anselm behind me.

Tolliver was there, impassive. Mikhael, subdued, stared at the deck.

"Lieutenant Tad Anselm repor—"

Captain Seafort was in his robe, the belt drawn tight. One hand gripped the black leather chair behind his console. He waved Tad silent, gestured to me. "Come here."

Uncertain, I edged forward. Now, there would be retribution. How would he punish me?

He caught my shirt, pulled me the last step, swept me into his arms. "I'm so sorry, Randy. So sorry."

I clung to him, knowing this couldn't be so.

At last, he released me. "We'll talk in a moment."

"Yes, sir."

"Mikhael."

His son came close. Of the two, the father was taller. He bent, just far enough to look into Mik's eyes. His voice was soft. "By my order, you're off duty now. Do you agree?"

"Yes, sir. Yes, Pa."

"You knew, and didn't tell me?"

"Yes, Pa."

Seafort cuffed him in the mouth. The boy's eyes teared.

"Go to my cabin. I'll be there shortly."

"Yes, sir!" Mikhael ran from the bridge.

"As for you, Tad—"

"No! Blame me!" I tugged at the Captain's sleeve.

"He betrayed our relationship."

"It was that or betray me. He had no right choice."

"Yes, he did. Tad, I'm disappointed."

"Tell him, Tad! How you helped me."

"Don't, Randy." Anselm stirred. "I accept the blame, sir, and whatever will follow."

"Are you all gone mad? Do you think me an ogre?" Seafort reached for his chair, nearly stumbled, managed to sit. "You're right, Edgar. It was a long, long journey from sickbay. I almost stopped to rest." For a moment he let his eyes close. "No doubt we'll be a while sorting this out. I know you all, and imagine there's honor in what each of you did."

"Odd that you slapped the midshipman, then." Tolliver.

"I didn't slap the midshipman, I slapped my son. Mik owed me higher loyalty, and knows it. I didn't hurt him."

"What will you do with . . ." Tolliver's lip curled. "The boy?"

"With Randolph Carr?" Seafort gave special emphasis to my name, as if to underscore his outrage that it had been hidden. "Thank heaven I called up the Log the moment I got to the bridge. Young Mr. Carr is paroled."

"To whose custody, sir?"

"My own."

"That's outrageous!"

"Edgar, you go too far."

"Sir, you risk your life. He's unstable."

"It's my life to risk."

"He should have been hanged."

"We won't execute Derek's son, no matter what the cause. You know that."

"*You* know that, sir. I don't share your certainty."

"Enough. We'll speak on it, after."

"After what?"

"After we calm down. Go, all of you. I'll speak with Randy alone."

"Sir, you won't be safe."

"Randy, will you harm me?"

"No, sir. I swear it by—by God, by my father, anything you want."

"There, you see? Out."

In a moment we were alone.

"Sit right there, boy. Now . . ." Mr. Seafort's eyes bored into mine. "Tell me. Everything."

And I did.

Afterward, reeling with exhaustion, I found my way to the cells, but Janks wouldn't let me in. He had to call the purser, who called the officer of the watch, who called the Captain, who'd been taken by wheeled chair to his cabin.

I finally found myself in a tiny cabin immediately adjoining Mr. Seafort's. I kicked off my shoes, began to undo my shirt, perched on the bed for convenience, and passed out.

When I came to, the clock indicated it was morning. I went to the head, but had nothing to wear but my slept-in clothes.

A soft knock on my hatch.

"Come in."

A high-pitched voice. "I can't, sir. You locked it."

I keyed the control.

A youngster. He couldn't have been more than twelve, but wore a sailor's work blues. He bore a tray. "Hi, sir. I'm Alejandro. Ship's boy. They call me Alec."

I blinked.

"Cap'n thought you'd like breakfast."

Food? I ought not even be alive.

He threw back a napkin. A mound of toast, a dish of scrambled eggs and potatoes. Sausage. Probably soy, but nonetheless . . .

My mouth watered. I gestured to the table built into the far bulkhead. He set down the tray, spread the napkin, pulled out my seat.

I watched him work. Someone had gone to great trouble to cut down a uniform to his diminutive size, or stitch one. What he wore couldn't be standard issue.

I asked, "What does a ship's boy do?"

"I help." He seemed to think it explained his role.

I inhaled half my serving of eggs. "How?"

"Whatever's needed. Like, the galley's shorthanded, now almost everyone's ashore. Or, I run to get things for the middies and work crews. Or put things away when they're done. You've never seen a ship's boy?"

"I've never seen a ship." Just through the station porthole, visiting with Dad.

Two pieces of toast disappeared. I reached for another.

"Isn't she a zark? Took me a week to learn my way around. 'Course, I was only ten. I'll be twelve next week. Gotta go, sir."

I nodded, too consumed with my task to answer.

At last, somewhat sated, I leaned back. A sigh of relief, in the empty chamber.

"Oh, good, you're up."

I whirled. Captain Seafort, in uniform, in the hatchway.

I jumped to my feet. "Good morning, sir."

"Everyone wants to know what to do with you. Feed you, I told them. Then we'll see. I'll be heading to the bridge and could use your assistance."

"Of course."

"I spent some months in a wheelchair, and loathed it." He took my hand. "This helps when I get dizzy."

"Yessir." If I sounded fawning, obsequious, it didn't matter.

The incident I'd begun in the Dining Hall was far from over—I wasn't an utter fool—but I didn't care. I had made a gesture on Dad's behalf, however misguided. The burden of that folly was lifted. Mr. Seafort would survive; I'd escaped a guilt so great I couldn't have borne it. Now, in his good time, would come punishment. I could wait.

He took me to the next-door cabin. Considerably larger than mine, low dividers carved it into sections: a bedroom area and a common room with another, narrower bed in a corner.

Mikhael lounged in a soft chair, in shirtsleeves, his collar open. Janey sat in his lap. Lifting the child, he stood. "Pa."

"He was awake." Seafort steered me to a seat.

"Hi, Randy." Mik sounded shy.

Seafort took a sip from a half-finished cup of coffee.

"Mikhael." I nodded.

"You all right?" we asked simultaneously.

I giggled. "Yes. Is this what you do when you're off duty?"

"As often as not. I used to live here, before Pa let me enlist."

With a glance at the Captain I said, "Is he still angry at you?"

"Of course not." Before I could figure that out, he added, "Pa says you told him your whole story."

I nodded, suddenly shy.

"I'm glad there's peace between you."

"Not—" Not peace. The calm before the storm. I looked over my shoulder. "Mr. Seafort?" I hesitated, but best to have it out in the open. "What did you mean about parole?"

He set down his cup. "You were adjudged guilty. I vacated your sentence. So now, technically, you're awaiting resentencing. I paroled you from the brig."

"Why?"

"To get to know you."

"Will you let him go, Pa?"

"That's ship's business, son."

"Should I put on my tie and ask it as a middy?"

The Captain frowned. "I'll follow my conscience. Does that suffice?"

"Yes, sir."

"Would you watch Janey awhile? Randy's going to escort me to the bridge."

"Sure." To me, "Ever had a sister? It's cool."

"Mik," Seafort said, "is practicing for parenthood." It drew a blush all the way up to the middy's ears. The Captain chuckled.

He took a firm grip on my hand.

Traversing the corridor, I saw little sign of his dizziness, though we did walk slowly.

I tried to make conversation. "Where does Janey sleep?"

His grip tightened. "She has a cot in the corner. Mostly, she's with her mother."

"You're married?"

"No." Perhaps he sensed I had no way to puzzle it out. "I was married a long while."

"Arlene. Dad liked her."

"So did I." Something in his voice made me not dare to speak. Then, after a time, "Arlene had her eggs and DNA stored. When they gave me *Olympiad* I hired a host mother. Corrine Sloan traveled with us."

"But you said—"

"When the baby was born, there was no one other than med techs to look after her. Of course, I did my share, but often I was on watch. Corrine helped. Over time . . ." He favored me with a stern glance. "I'll trust you with this, but it's not for public consumption."

"Yes, sir."

"She's grown to love Janey, and Janey her. It's irregular. We're not married, never were. We've never been intimate. But, bless it, she's the child's mother. When she asked to stay aboard . . ." A sigh. "I could have refused her—I had the authority—but it seemed inhumane. We have . . . an uneasy relationship."

"Kevin's host mother lives on Constantine." I didn't know why I said it.

"Ah, yes, Kevin. It's just as well you'll be present."

Holding my hand as with a small child, he led me to the bridge. I could do naught but follow.

At the hatch, he paused. "Behave yourself today, Randy. I have authority over you, and I won't hesitate to use it."

There was nothing unkind about his tone, no warning in his eye, but I blurted, "Yes, sir," as fast as I could, and felt a prickle of sweat.

Still leading me by the hand, he deposited me at the pilot's console. Ms. Skor stood and saluted.

"Hallo, Joanne, I have the watch. When's your shuttle?"

"An hour and a half. Anything I can bring you, sir?"

"Not really. Have a good leave, and don't forget what I said about the Ventura Mountains. Oh . . ." He waited, while she paused at the hatch. "Thanks so much for staying aboard during my . . . illness."

"You're welcome." With a casual salute, she left us.

I said, "Who'll run the ship?"

"We'll manage. Good morning, Jess."

A pleasant baritone, from the speaker: "Good day, Captain."

Seafort eased himself into his chair, let go my hand. "Whew." To me, "Jess is our puter. I'm teaching him chess."

From the speaker, a snort. A puter could laugh? I hadn't known.

He keyed his caller, waited. "Edgar, could you join me? Later will do, if it's inconvenient. All right, thanks." To me, "A few minutes. Let me finish reading." He scanned his holovid.

After a time, a voice from the hatchway. "Lieutenant Edgar Tolliver reporting, sir."

"Ah. Have a seat. Randy, would you wait outside?"

"Yes, sir." I did, and the hatch slid closed.

With almost the whole ship's company on leave, the corridor was silent as a tomb. For a moment, I paced, wondering what they were up to.

My life might depend on it.

I shouldn't but . . . I padded to the hatch, pressed my ear tight.

". . . going to overrule you, and I wanted you to know first."

"You're under no duty to explain—"

"You were acting as Captain. I ought let stand your decisions where possible."

"As with the Carr joeykid?"

"That *had* to be overruled. You knew so yourself."

"Is that so, sir?"

"Yes. Else you wouldn't have goaded me to walk to the bridge."

"Did I do that?"

"Weren't you aware of it, Edgar?"

A long pause. "Sir, this has been a dreadful week. I'm not sure what I . . ."

"You wanted to come close to executing him. It was closer than you thought. Would you have gone through with it?"

"Yes."

"You're sure?"

"I set it up so I'd have to."

"What did you feel when I came on the speaker?"

"Dismay. Relief. Damn it . . ." A long pause. "If only Carr had broken. Explained himself, asked for mercy . . . I even went to his cell, in the night."

"Edgar, pride is all I left him."

"You?"

"After killing his father. No, don't shake your head; he's quite right about that. Derek wanted to go along to retake *Galactic*, but it was in my power to stop him."

"You said he swore he'd alert the rebels unless you let him go."

"He couldn't have meant it."

"His sworn word?"

"Derek would have found a way around it. He loved me. And I sent him to his death." Seafort's voice was bleak. "Do you know, Edgar, I haven't prayed since? Not once."

"I heard you muttering, one time when—"

"I talk to God from time to time. I berate Him. That's not prayer."

"I'm not sure I agree."

"When He let me lead Derek to a useless death—"

"We've been down that road, sir."

"Yes, and it's still before us. Young Randolph worshiped him. Last night, when he described his good-byes, and his dreams . . . his tears had no end. And I can tell you, I haven't slept since."

"Then I curse Derek, for laying such a burden on you."

"I can bear it; I've borne worse. Arlene, for example. The boy asked me about her, today, and it was all I could do to keep my voice steady." A sigh. "This is all afield. Let's get back to Ghent."

"Are you asking my opinion, sir?"

"Obviously, your view is to send him to court-martial."

"I confirmed the death sentence; Carr had to be informed. Ghent refused outright. Sir, I know how he feels; it's a horrid duty. But he's an officer."

"I know. In that sense, he did wrong. But I'm going to let him off."

"It's your decision."

"And I'm confident that in the end, you'd have done the same. Perhaps you'd have held trial first."

"Don't attribute me your mercy. I don't have it within me."

"You've proven otherwise."

"How? When?"

"Five years ago, Edgar, just before we cast off, you showed up on the bridge of *Olympiad*, to accompany me into exile. If that wasn't an act of mercy, I don't know . . . good heavens!" A scrape. "Tears, from you? I don't think I've ever . . . take my hand."

A moment.

"Thank you, Edgar. For everything, over the years, thank you."

A mumble I barely heard. "I'd better go."

I leaped back across the corridor.

The hatch opened. Tolliver strode out, his face showing nothing.

"Randy?"

I resumed my seat, eyes downcast.

He regarded me a long moment. "You listened?"

"No, I—it was just—yes, sir."

"Skulking about, when I asked you for privacy? Do you wish me to spy on you?"

"No, sir." My cheeks flamed.

"Then you ought not spy on me." He took my chin in his hands, forced my gaze upward to his. "I knew your father well, and loved him. I tell you, the Derek Carr I knew wouldn't hold his ear to the hatch. Do you understand me? I rebuke you!" He let me go.

I sat wishing I could crawl into a hole and die. ". . . won't do it again."

"What?"

I cleared my throat. "I won't do it again."

"Very well. Compose yourself." Once more, he keyed the caller. "Mr. Janks."

A pause. "Master-at-arms Janks repor—"

"Release Andrew Ghent. He's to make himself presentable and report to the bridge."

"Aye aye, sir."

After a time, he swiveled to me. "Step by step, I can undo almost everything except your father's death." He reached to scratch his scalp, winced. "And this."

There was nothing I could say; he knew I was sorry.

Another flick of the caller. "Mr. Anselm?"

"Yes, sir."

"Did I wake you?"

"No, I was reading."

"Why were you demeriting Ghent? I know it's a wardroom matter, but you're out of the wardroom now."

"The demerits say—"

"What's the real reason?"

"Attitude, sir. He's a good joey at heart, but lately he's had a chip on his shoulder. It grew annoying."

"Fair enough."

"Sir, about his court-martial . . ."

Seafort glanced at me, but said only, "Yes?"

"Might you let him off? When he wouldn't deliver the news to Randy, I had to, and I almost lost my dinner. Sir, that was horrible. Ghent's only sixteen."

"Thank you for your advice. That will be all."

He folded his arms.

For a while I fiddled, not quite daring to touch the controls, though the console's master switch was clearly off. I peered at the simulscreen, tried to imagine the bridge while a cruise was under way. "Where does *Olympiad* go next, sir? Home system?"

"Kall's Planet, then home."

"Will you ever go down to Earth again?"

"Every day it seems more possible. We don't have the gravitrons turned particularly high while we're moored, but usually—"

"Permission to enter bridge, sir."

Seafort didn't bother to look at the screen. "Granted." From his console, he keyed open the hatch.

"Midshipman Andrew Ghent reporting, sir." The boy's eyes widened when he saw me, but he quickly brought himself to attention.

"Well, now." Seafort flicked a thumb toward his console, on which the Log was displayed. "What are we to do with you?"

"I'm up for court-martial, sir."

"Yes, and you deserve it. Your snotty attitude I can understand, if not condone; you haven't matured."

Ghent colored.

"But this preposterous misstep . . ." The Captain's tone was severe. "How could you refuse a direct order?"

"Sir, I—Randy was—no excuse, sir." The boy was sweating.

"I'll have an answer."

"How can you tell someone he has to die?" Ghent's eyes were troubled. "A joeykid? I couldn't. I simply couldn't."

"I understand." But the Captain's tone was cool. "The circumstances were . . . 'unusual' is hardly the word. That's why I'm setting aside the court-martial. Now, Andrew . . . if you'd been cooperative and willing in recent months, I'd let you off with demerits. But you've been sullen, rebellious, fighting with Midshipman Yost—you weren't like that when we sailed from Earthport. What's come over you?"

"I don't know, sir." The middy's eyes were troubled.

"Well, now you pay the piper. My compliments to Lieutenant Skor, and she's to cane you thoroughly for insubordination."

Ghent blanched.

"It will also cancel your demerits, so when she's done, pack your gear and take your leave."

"Aye aye, sir."

"Dismissed."

With a crisp salute, the boy marched out to his fate.

"It will probably do him good." But the Captain's tone was doubtful. I wasn't sure if he was speaking to himself or to me, so I said nothing.

"Very well, that's dealt with. Now, to the rest of it." He took the caller, dialed a station. "Seaman of the watch."

"Seaman First Class Ardin, at aft Station lock, sir."

"Is Mr. Dakko still waiting?"

"In the Station corridor, sir. Pacing like a tiger."

"I can imagine. Open for him. Ring Mr. Janks for an escort to the bridge."

"Aye aye, sir."

Mr. Seafort tapped his console. "I won't enjoy this."

I made myself small in my chair. Neither would I.

It wasn't long before Janks appeared, Mr. Dakko saw me, stopped short.

The Captain got to his feet. "I'm Captain Seafort. Please, come in. I presume you've come about your son." He offered a hand.

Mr. Dakko shook hands, studied him intensely. "Kevin's unjustly your prisoner. He had nothing whatsoever to do with—"

"I know; Tolliver was miffed. We'll let him go at once. Mr. Janks, release young Dakko and bring him to the bridge."

Mr. Dakko gaped. I suppressed a smile; at least I'd had a couple of days to get used to the Captain's style. "Release—really?"

"Yes."

"No agreements, waivers, consents . . ."

"We had no right to hold him. I apologize."

Again, Mr. Dakko studied him. At length, he said, "You don't remember me."

"Have we met?" The Captain frowned. "As SecGen I met . . . Dakko . . . oh, Lord, you're *that* Dakko? I never dreamed . . . Chris?"

Mr. Dakko burst into a smile. "Yes, sir."

"Lord God in Heaven. Here, sit . . . Randy, make a place for Mr. Dakko. He served with me ages ago, when we were both children."

"I gave you quite a hard time."

"Over enlisting, yes, I remember. And about the transpops. Water under the bridge. By the time *Hibernia* reached Hope Nation you were a fine sailor. I was sad to see you go."

Mr. Dakko flushed with pleasure.

"What became of Walter?"

"My father died last year."

"What a pity! I'd have loved to talk over old times."

"He was ninety, and had a good life."

"Ninety!" The Captain shook his head. "Let that be a lesson, Randy. Spend your life, before it slips through your fingers."

"Yes, sir."

"Dad!" A familiar voice, at the hatch. Kevin flew across the bridge, into his father's arms.

"Oh, thank God." Mr. Dakko rocked his son back and forth. "Kev . . ."

I turned away. It was indecent to watch.

A hand fell on my shoulder. Mr. Seafort's voice was soft. "We're making it right, boy."

I could only nod.

His hand remained on my shoulder, an umbilical of comfort.

"Midshipman Andrew Ghent reporting, sir." The boy's voice wavered. "Lieutenant Skor's compliments, and discipline has been administered."

"Very well, I'll make note in the Log. Take the shuttle down, visit Hope Nation, Andrew. I don't want to see you for at least two weeks."

"Aye aye, sir."

"And when you return, you'll have a new start. I know you'll do well."

The boy's eyes glistened. "Yes, sir. Thank you."

We watched him go.

"Chris Dakko . . ." Seafort marveled. "Kevin, your father was about your age. A difficult joey, but so many are. They get over it. Do you give him trouble?"

"Yes, sir." Kevin blushed.

"Chris—may I call you that?—take him home. And if you'll forgive me enough to allow it, come see us in a week or so. The pair of you, for dinner."

Mr. Dakko's visage relaxed, as if for once he was sated. "That would be a great pleasure."

"You owe me nothing—in fact, quite the reverse—but if I could ask a favor?"

"What's that, sir?"

"Give your forgiveness to Randy. He's desperately upset, and in need of pardon."

Mr. Dakko's face set, as if in stone. His eyes bored through me, twin drills through chalk. "I'm sorry, that's not possible."

"Could you do it for me?"

"He made his bed." An old Navy phrase: one made one's bed, and had to lie in it.

"I killed his father, Chris. Please."

"Randy's done more damage than ever you'll know."

I blurted, "But I'll be punished. I've been convicted. And as far as Kevin . . ."

"I know. You didn't mean for him to be hurt. Nevertheless, what Kev's gone through . . . Son, how do *you* feel about it? Is there something you'd like to say to Randy?"

Kev snarled, "You ruined it!" He wouldn't look at me. "It would have been a day to remember. A tour of the ship, zarky new friends in the Navy. Instead, you made a nightmare."

Mr. Dakko said, "It's done now, son."

Captain Seafort sighed. "I still hope you'll visit. Perhaps you'd enjoy a proper tour."

"Take me home." Kevin's tone was bitter. "I don't ever want to come back."

Mr. Dakko's eyes met the Captain's, with what might have been apology, but he gave his son's shoulder a reassuring squeeze.

Mr. Seafort asked, "What did you mean, more damage than Randy could know?"

"Bishop Scanlen petitioned Randy as a wayward minor, and once word got out he assaulted you, the Stadholder could do nothing. Judge Hycliff granted the petition and held trial in absentia; Randy's been declared a ward of the Church for rehabilitation. You know the Stadholder?"

"Anthony Carr. Derek's grandson, I'm told."

"He refused to pressure you for Randy's return, and Scanlen's threatening excommunication."

A groan. I realized it was mine.

"They still play that game?" The Captain's tone was bleak. "What sort of pressure did they expect Anthony to apply?"

"Grounding all shuttles. Cutting off supplies. Refusing to board your passengers. Denial of cargo."

"Our cargo for the return voyage is Hope Nation's grain, Mr. Dakko. Desperately needed at home, as your economy needs the sale of it."

"For the moment, Anthony's holding firm. But with excommunication hanging over his head . . ." Mr. Dakko's eyes were flinty. "Every aspect of this crisis was triggered by this young fool." A gesture to me. "So you'll pardon me for not applauding him. Good day, sir."

"Until our dinner." Glumly, Mr. Seafort watched them go.

"It's all my fault," I said glumly.

"Much of it is."

I took comfort in his agreement.

He tapped the console. "Wayward minor."

I flushed. "It's best if you send me groundside," I said. "They'll deal with me."

His finger waved in my nose. "I, not you, will decide your punishment. Is that clear?"

"Yessir!"

"Very well. Go to my cabin. I'll be along presently to take you to lunch."

"Yes, sir." I made my escape. Trodding the corridor, I marveled at how thoroughly he'd taken charge of me. It was as if I were a little joeykid and Dad—

No!

Dad was Derek Carr, not Mr. Seafort. I was the Captain's prisoner, not his son. To think otherwise, even for a minute, was betrayal.

I'm sorry, Dad. It's just that his manner . . . and he's the same age as you, and thin and fit, and his salt-and-pepper hair . . . and that glance he has, as if he wants you to make him proud . . .

I wiped my eyes, knocked at the hatch. "May I?"

"Hi." Mikhael closed the hatch behind me. "Janey's napping. Is Pa coming?"

"In a while." Morose, I flopped in a chair. "He told me to wait here." I looked about. The Captain's bunk was austere: gray blanket pulled tight as a drum, gear neatly stowed. Nothing visible except a worn Bible on the bedside table, along with a clock so ancient it still had hands.

Mik said, "Did he read you off?"

"You mean, chew on my butt?"

He nodded.

"Yeah, I suppose."

"He does that sometimes," Mik said. "It took me a while to get used to it."

I said, "Yesterday, when he slapped you . . ."

"Man, did I have that coming." A smile. "Trying to hide your identity. I should never have agreed."

"But you're grown." I couldn't conceive allowing an adult to strike me, at his age, or bearing it so calmly.

"I'm twenty." I couldn't tell if it was agreement or refutation. "Look, Pa saved me. God knows what I would have become. I love him almost as much . . . well, I love him. If he occasionally treats me young for my age, that's fine. Sometimes I *feel* young for my age."

"I wish Anth . . ." He'd done his best, but he wasn't all that much older than me. More a big brother than a father.

A soft knock. Mik went to the hatch. "Oh. Hi, ma'am."

"Is she up?"

I peered round the divider. Flowing brown hair, a soft face, lined.

"Napping." Mikhael seemed ill at ease. "Did you want to . . ."

"He doesn't like it." Her eyes fell on me. "Oh. Hello."

"Ma'am, this is my friend Randy Carr. Randy, Corrine Sloan, Janey's mom."

"Ah, that's what you look like. Mikhael, does the Captain know Randy's visiting?"

"Yes, ma'am. It was his idea."

"I suppose . . ." She chewed at a lip. "You'll keep an eye on Jane Ellen?"

"I don't brain babies." My tone was bitter. "Just adults."

"I'm sorry, it's only that . . . it was a horrible shock. Janey was terrified. No one knew quite what to . . ." She studied me. "Come out and say hello."

"You can't . . . ?" I pointed to the cabin.

"It's not quite against the rules, but it makes him so uncomfortable, I try to stay outside."

I slipped into the corridor.

"You're his old friend's son."

"Yes, ma'am."

"That's why he pardoned you, no doubt. He and I, we don't get along well. We've no real relationship, except through Janey. But I can tell you, he didn't deserve your attack."

"I've learned." I scuffed the deck plating. "I was very stupid."

"Will he let you go?"

"I've no idea."

"I suppose you could try to slip through to the Station." She gestured toward the lock, just past the porthole.

"Goofjuice!" It wasn't the strongest epithet I knew, but my tone added volumes. Did she think me a coward, ashamed to admit my assault? Why not strike in the night and flee, then? Or hire an assassin?

From time to time I'd gotten myself in hot water—the activities of recent days were the worst, I'd have to admit—but I'd never sneaked about and denied the truth. Dad would have had a fit.

Her fingers brushed my arm. "When Janey wakes, give me a call. I'm in five seventy-five. I'll take her to lunch; Nick won't mind."

"Yes, ma'am." Was I meddling in private affairs? No one had instructed me.

Though the Captain managed the trip back to his cabin on his own, he appeared to need my steadying hand that evening for the journey to the Dining Hall. I slowed my steps, reluctant.

"What's the problem, joey?"

"Nothing, sir."

Something in his glance told me I hadn't pleased him.

After a moment, "It's my first time there since . . . well, you know."

"Since you bashed me with a chair." He favored me with a scowl. "I trust I'm safe today?"

"Yes, sir! I wouldn't—I promise, I'll sit at the far end—"

He gave my fingers a reassuring squeeze, and I spotted the twinkle in his eye. Relief made me babble. "It's just . . . I haven't been there since that night, and everyone will know—they'll be looking at me and . . ."

He guided me through the hatch. "You'll sit with me. How are your table manners?"

I gaped at the incongruity of the question. "Good, I think."

"Show me. We'll see how well Derek raised you."

I had no choice but to pass the test, and worked at it. After a time I discovered I'd been too preoccupied with forks and napkins to worry what joeys might think of me. Anyway, the Dining Hall was nearly deserted. After the fresh crisp salad, Mr. Tolliver came to join us. A discreet cough from the Captain made me realize I ought to stand.

"Good evening." Tolliver indicated a chair, raised an eyebrow.

"By all means." Mr. Seafort waved to a seat. "Of course, you know Randolph."

Tolliver was up to it. "I'm glad we meet in more auspicious circumstances." He even offered a hand.

"Thank you, sir." Carefully, I respread my napkin as I sat. The steward brought a tray of sandwiches and fresh fruit.

"Any murders planned for the afternoon?" Tolliver's tone was bland.

"No, sir, but I might set fire to my cabin." I managed to look quite serious.

He eyed me, annoyed, but then the corners of his mouth went up, for just a moment. "Do let us know first. Sir, I arranged that meeting we spoke of. This afternoon, midwatch."

"You mean with Randy's nephew, the Stadholder."

I started.

"Yes, but I meant to be circumspect." Tolliver's glance flickered to me.

"How refreshing, Edgar. You apologized to Anthony, for my remaining aboard?"

"No, but I reminded him of your health. He was glad to come aloft. And Admiral Kenzig would like a callback as soon as convenient."

Mr. Seafort scraped back his chair. "That would be now."

"No, I told him you were at dinner. He'll wait."

"He's an Admiral."

"And you're the former SecGen. Finish your pasta."

Jaw agape, I listened to the byplay, astounded Mr. Seafort didn't squelch him flat. From what Dad had told me, no one, lieutenant or not, spoke so to the Captain. But Mr. Seafort didn't seem perturbed.

"Remind me to call him, directly we're on the bridge. Since Randy scrambled my brains, my memory isn't what it was." A reassuring squeeze of my forearm.

"Perhaps there are other improvements as well."

Hot rage suffused my cheeks, on Mr. Seafort's behalf.

"As soon as Stanson is back aboard, Edgar, you ought to take your leave. We'll be months to Kall's Planet." *Mr. Seafort didn't notice! Or was he so embarrassed he had no response?*

"You'll manage without me, sir?"

"Somehow. Randy, why do you glare at Lieutenant Tolliver?"

I jerked my gaze aside, but his question freed me to speak my mind. "Because he's unmannerly to you. Uncivil, uncouth, and rude."

Tolliver's jaw dropped.

From Mr. Seafort, a smile that widened into a grin. "Well, I *did* ask, so I can't reprove him. Nonetheless, Randy, you won't be rude to adults in noting their rudeness. Not for some years yet."

"Some years?"

"The duration of your sentence, at any rate. Edgar, was he rude, or merely observant?"

"Sir, truth to tell, I'm glad he's alive. But I don't choose to banter with him."

"Hmpff. I thought you were bantering with me." The Captain let it lapse. Soon, they were immersed in a discussion about the power plant, and I concentrated on table manners.

Afterward, a firm grip on my hand, Mr. Seafort walked slowly to the bridge.

"Are you dizzy, sir?"

"Perhaps a bit." Gingerly, he scratched his skull. "It itches, and I've a headache."

He keyed open the hatch. The bridge was unmanned.

"Isn't it always supposed to be staffed?"

"Not moored to the Station lock. Ah, that's better." Settling at his console, he took up the caller.

"Should I be here?" I poised myself to wait in the corridor.

"If I say so. Be silent awhile. Comm Room, put me through to Admiral Kenzig, at Admiralty House. Visuals too." His eye on the simulscreen, he tugged at his tie, made as if to smooth his hair, winced with an indrawn breath.

I muttered, "I'm sorry."

"You're to be silent."

"Yessir."

The screen flickered, went black. After a moment, a florid face loomed. "Kenzig here."

"Captain Nicholas Seafort reporting, sir."

"Oh, good. Are you recovered?"

"Substantially, thank you."

"We have a problem. Who's that?" He peered at his screen.

"Randolph Carr, sir."

"Good heavens, on your bridge? Why?"

"To keep an eye on him." Mr. Seafort's tone was neutral.

"Well, that's why I called. Do you think this ought to be private?"

"Not unless you insist, sir."

"No, of course not, Mr. SecGen." The Admiral's tone was obsequious.

"My rank is Captain, sir."

"I meant it as a courtesy. Sir—Mr. Seafort—this unfortunate affair has political ramifications. The Church is involved, and we must steer clear of antagonizing the local authorities."

"What do you want me to do?"

"The boy." He stabbed a finger at me. "That—that hooligan you have sitting next to you. The Hope Nation courts gave custody of him to the Church. If you keep him on *Olympiad*, you're involving us."

My fingers curled around the armrests.

Mr. Seafort said, "He's in our jurisdiction, tried and convicted. His sentence is under review."

"We don't *want* him in our jurisdiction. He's a Hope Nation citizen! That puts us in conflict with Mother Church!" The Admiral made his tone peaceable. "Look, sir, as long as you have him, no one will be satisfied. The Stadholder is under pressure from the Court, Bishop Scanlen views your holding him as interference."

"Yes, but . . ." A sigh. "Yes, sir. What are your orders?"

"I understand you want revenge on him, and it's bloody unfair you can't have it, but sometimes, political realities prevail. Look, Mr. SecGen, we can't hold a Hope Nation citizen against the will of the local Church. As long as that's the case, you must transfer him to their custody."

"Aye aye, sir."

"Very well. Send him groundside. See that he's put in the custody of the proper authorities."

"When?"

"Today, if possible. Tomorrow, at the latest."

"Aye aye, sir."

The Admiral's tone softened. "Sir, about your injury, is there anything I can get you? Any way I can help? You look awful."

"Thank you, sir, I'll let you know if something comes to mind."

"Did the Stadholder keep his promise about supplies?"

"No interference so far. Dakko & Son are the chief victuallers. I met with—"

"A good man, Chris Dakko. He seems quite reasonable. Good day, Mr. SecGen."

"And to you, sir." They rang off.

I swallowed. The Church correctional farm was no joke: a strict regimen, arduous daily prayers. Well, Lord God knew I'd earned it, whether I liked it or not.

Mr. Seafort's gaze was fastened on the darkened screen. His eyes smoldered. "Bloody politicians!"

Would it be today? A walk through the mated lock, a stroll down the Station corridor, to a waiting shuttle. The buffet of air in the outer atmosphere, a bumpy ride, a VTOL landing at Centraltown.

Grim-visaged figures waiting, in high church collars. Perhaps a glimpse of Anthony before they hustled me into a heli for the long ride north.

I would hate every minute of it. Most especially the hypocrisy of prayer to a God I didn't know.

And Judy would grow without me, go out with other joeys, become a woman, while I was left to the edgy solace of my palm.

Scant hours ago, I'd dreamed of freedom, of the clean sea air of home. Now I was dismayed to leave the ship.

Mr. Seafort glanced at his watch.

Time to face up to it. "Sir, I'd like to change my shirt before I go."

He heaved himself out of his chair, eyes blazing, and bunched the front of my shirt in his fist, hauling me close. "How many times were you told to be silent?" He hauled me to my feet.

"Twice, sir."

"You are wayward indeed, Randolph. Did you disobey your father so?"

"No, sir!"

"I'd hope not. You're in my parole and custody, joeyboy, and I will *not* have disobedience. I'll be asking you shortly to tell me what constitutes obedience, and you'd better be prepared to answer. Take your seat!"

I gaped.

"RIGHT NOW!"

I careened into my chair. Satan himself couldn't wrest a sound from me at that moment.

Arms folded, Captain Seafort glowered at the simulscreen.

On the bridge, all was still.

9

BY THE TIME they showed Anthony through the lock, I'd sorted myself out.

Mr. Seafort was strict, but not nearly as much as Bishop Scanlen's joeys were going to be. And, really, the Captain expected no more than what I'd have given Dad without a second thought. In any event, I owed it to him, for the hurt I'd done in a moment's stupidity and rage.

The tone he'd used, though . . . he made me feel so young, so helpless.

On the other hand, twice he'd told me to keep still, and twice I'd paid little attention, like some silly joeykid who didn't know better. My face burned from shame.

It wasn't long that I'd be with him, but I'd show him what a Carr could do. I just wished . . . wished . . . damn it, I wished I had longer to prove myself to him.

Lieutenant Tolliver and a middy I'd never seen escorted the Stadholder to the bridge.

"Sir, Anthony Carr."

With a smile of welcome, Mr. Seafort stood. Abruptly he turned white, staggered. Tolliver bounded across the bridge. For a moment the Captain clutched him, head bowed, knees weak. "It's all right. Let me sit." Carefully, he eased himself into his console chair. He lay back, eyes shut.

I sat frozen, fist to my mouth.

"I'm sorry, Mr. Carr. Give me a moment."

Tolliver said, "Sir, you need rest. Let me get you to your cab—"

"No." With an effort, Mr. Seafort opened his eyes. "Sorry, Mr. Stadholder. I'm only a day out of sickbay, and it catches up to me. If you don't mind I'll remain seated."

"Sir, I could return after—"

"Not necessary." Mr. Seafort sat straighter, and his color seemed to be returning.

I breathed easier.

"So." The Captain extended a hand. "You're Derek's grandson. It's wonderful to meet you. Let me apologize most humbly for my role in his death."

"No, sir. It's we who owe you an apology, for the way you were treated." For a moment, Anthony's eyes burned into mine. "Grandpa would be heartily ashamed, as I am." I tried not to flinch.

Remorselessly, Anth went on, "I apologize for him, Mr. Seafort. He should have known better. I've always tried to treat him as an adult."

"Perhaps that was an error." Mr. Seafort's tone was mild.

"I did what I could. I'm not Grandpa."

"You did well. Randy took responsibility for his acts." The Captain cleared his throat. "Do take a seat. Coffee, or refreshments? No? That will be all, Mr. Tolliver." When we were alone, Mr. Seafort shut the hatch. "May I be frank?"

"By all means."

"It's a mess. What are you going to do about it?"

"The Bishop will have Randy." Anthony grimaced. "I've no way to stop that."

"And through him, he'll have you."

Anth closed his eyes. "Not entirely."

"Sir . . ." The Captain's voice was soft. "I know something of the conflict. I've heard from Jerence since he went groundside. And on his Terran visit, Derek spoke of tensions, of threatened renunciation." He shook his head. "What, exactly, does Scanlen want?"

"Can you involve yourself?"

"No. In fact I was ordered not to."

"Then it's best we not discuss it. Please don't take offense; it's for your sake. When there's talk of excommunication . . ." Anth shook his head.

"I'm already excommunicate." Mr. Seafort's voice was desolate. "Whether the Church knows it or not."

"Hope Nation, sir, has its independence. I must safeguard the Commonweal, at whatever cost. There are those who would see us again a colony. In saying so, I make no complaint against the Church."

"Of course."

"I came aloft for Randy's sake. There were rumors of a trial, of a sentence—"

"The rumors were true. He was to be hanged. I intervened."

"Ah." A pause. "How may I pay my debt?"

"That's rather an insult, don't you think?" The Captain didn't seem to take offense. "You suggest I toy with the boy's life for advantage."

"Some would."

"Yes, but Randy gave them the opening." The Captain favored me with a glance of annoyance.

Carefully, I said nothing.

"I'm glad to see Randy's well, but may I ask why he's present?"

"So he'll learn the consequences of impetuous acts." A wintry smile. "I see no harm in his presence, but if you wish, I'll have him wait in the corridor."

Mr. Seafort's eye caught mine, and I blushed deeply. If he did, I would NOT listen. Not for anything. Never again.

"May I talk with him?"

"Of course. Son, you may speak."

Anth turned to me eagerly. "Randy, you're well?"

"Yes, sir." This was no time for boorish manners.

"You must have been frightened."

"Terrified."

"The training farm will be . . . quite difficult." He rose from his chair, paced, came to a halt before me. "I'll try to protect you, but . . ."

"There's no need, sir. I fouled up so badly, I'm ready to take the consequences. And yes, I know what they are. The deacons may kill me."

"It's a risk, but small. Once I'm out of office, they lose you as a lever, and have nothing to gain by harming you. While I'm Stadholder, your death would mean outright war. I think they know that. But the petty cruelties, the poor food, bullying, the lash . . ." He shrugged. "I'm sorry. You brought it on yourself."

"I know, Anth."

He tousled my hair, pulled my head to his chest. I clung to him, and whispered, "I'm so sorry."

After a time, he looked to Mr. Seafort. "Captain, our political situation is more complicated than you may know."

"When will you manage to break our trade monopoly?"

Anthony gaped. "You're aware of that?"

"Derek told me." Into the silence, he added, "Friendship will do that, you see. It's possible to work honorably to opposite ends."

"I knew he loved you indeed. I never realized how much." To my astonishment, Anth seemed unsure. I'd rarely seen him so. "There are factions . . . my government is not entirely united. Some would use Earth's current weakness to break the shipping monopoly once and for all. Others would . . . no doubt all this goes in your report. I ought to be more discreet."

"I respect your candor."

"The fact is, there are a few hotheads wanting me to seize your ship, or any that comes along, to increase our leverage with home system."

Mr. Seafort waved it away. "You won't seize *Olympiad*, and if you did, you'd start a war. Hope Nation would lose, and revert to colonial status."

"I'm aware. Some of my partisans aren't. May I . . ." Abruptly Anthony stood, paced a few steps. "You don't know how humiliating it is . . . Might I suggest you post extra guards at your airlocks?"

Mr. Seafort leaned forward, his face grave. "You're saying you're not entirely in control of elements of your government?"

Reddening, Anthony studied his fingernails. "I hope it's not so, but can't be sure."

A long silence. Then, "Thank you for the warning, Mr. Stadholder."

"That was why I came. And to see Randy, of course." An apologetic shrug. "Might I know when you'll be sending him groundside?"

"Tomorrow. I'm too played out this afternoon."

After a few polite phrases, the two shook hands, and Mr. Seafort summoned Tad Anselm to show Anth the way.

We sat in silence.

"Come here. I'm going to try to stand."

I gave him my shoulder, and he heaved himself up. "Tolliver was right about my sleeping fifteen hours a day. I'm exhausted." As before, he took my hand. Slowly, we walked down the corridor. "Now, unfinished business. Are you prepared to obey me, Randy?"

"Yes, sir."

"What constitutes obedience?"

"I'll do exactly what you say, when you say it, with no argument."

"How sure are you of this?"

"Very sure." I was sweating.

"If you don't believe in God, what have you to swear on?"

"I believe in honor, sir. Dad said honor is the base from which—"

"Are you prepared to swear on your honor you'll be obedient while you're in my custody?"

It was no small thing he asked.

But if I couldn't give it, what had I to give?

"Yes, sir."

"Then I'll expect it so. Small mistakes are natural, and don't count. But what I tell you, henceforth you will do."

"Yes, sir."

His hand squeezed mine. I felt a turbulent excitement, as if my course was steered. I managed to stifle a sigh. Unfortunately, it wouldn't be for long. The Bishop awaited.

I saw Mr. Seafort to his hatch.

"You're confined to your cabin for the day. I'll have someone drop off clean garments. Be sure to change your shirt; your clothes look like you slept in them."

I had.

Mr. Seafort slept through the dinner hour, into the night.

I found a new dilemma: I grew ever more hungry, and couldn't go to dinner. I couldn't even leave my cabin. A joey could starve, waiting for an old man to waken and remember him.

At last, late in the evening, I thought of the solution. My cabin had a caller, and it was marked with the purser's extension. After many rings, someone answered. I got the code for the galley, punched it in. "I'm Randy Carr, in the cabin next to the Captain's. Is Alejandro there? Do you think he might bring me something to eat? Mr. Seafort said I had to stay in my room, and I'm starving."

It worked. The ship's boy, bleary-eyed and yawning, knocked soon after at my door. I didn't much notice what he brought; it was gone minutes after. I'd have cajoled him to stay for conversation, but he stood swaying so sleepily I thanked him profusely and sent him on his way.

Then, with nothing else to do, I undressed, showered, and crawled into bed.

I woke early for my last day aboard *Olympiad*. I found the clean clothes the purser had sent. Naval blues, of all things, albeit with no insignia. They'd do. I washed again—it was becoming a habit—carefully combed my unruly hair. I would go to my imprisonment with dignity.

A knock at the hatch. Was it time? I braced myself.

"Hi. Pa says to join us for breakfast."

Frowning at the anticlimax, I followed Mikhael down the corridor. He was in full uniform, apparently on duty. He headed not to the Dining Hall, but to a small compartment not far from the bridge.

"What's this?"

"Officers' mess. We take breakfast and lunch here. Dining Hall's only for dinner."

The mess had several tables. Mikhael chose a small one. A steward brought a pan of eggs, dished it out. On the table were hot rolls. My mouth watered.

"See that long table?" Mik leaned close. "By custom, if the Captain sits there, anyone's free to join him. At a small table, he's to be left alone."

"Ah, there you are."

Mikhael shot to his feet. Somewhat more slowly, so did I. Mr. Seafort strolled in, a hand lightly across Mr. Anselm's arm.

"Thanks, Tad. Steward, two more portions." He and Tad pulled up chairs. "Janey's with her mother." A look, which might have been disapproval, or might not. I couldn't be sure. To me, "Sleep well?"

"Yes, sir." Like a log, actually. Well, yesterday had been an eventful day.

"There's a midmorning shuttle, Randy. You'll be on it."

I nodded.

"What?"

"Uh, yes, sir." *Manners, Randy. You can do it if you try.*

We fell to.

I said tentatively, "Might I discuss . . . what I heard yesterday?"

"Tad, Mik, you'll keep it to yourselves?"

Immediate agreement.

"Very well."

"Sir, what will Anth do if the Bishop . . . if the Church presses him? Will he rebel?"

"Now, *that* I shouldn't discuss." But his eyes showed he took no offense. "It's apostasy to criticize the Church; its direction is of Lord God, and I won't hear any of you say otherwise. I'm sure the Stadholder is well aware of this. Any concerns he has will be voiced so as to conform with canon law."

Anth wouldn't rebel outright, I was to understand, but he'd fight in that maddening way a government has, of dragging its feet, picking at every detail.

I asked, "If the Bishop wants us again made a colony, what can he do to enforce it?"

"Excommunication is a most powerful weapon. Misused, it could wreak havoc. Enough of that. Eat your toast."

Always a good idea. "Yessir."

He checked his watch. "You'll be leaving from the Level 1 airlock. We'll just have time to visit the bridge. I want to make an entry in the Log."

I was puzzled, but said nothing while he chatted with his son and Tad. What difference did it make, whether or not he saw me to the lock?

A big difference. In my mind's eye, I hesitated at the airlock hatch, shook hands with him gravely, muttered something that would show my gratitude for all he'd done.

Ridiculous. Even if he hadn't killed Pa as I'd mistakenly believed all these years, Mr. Seafort was nothing to me. Just yesterday, he'd chewed me out like—like a child, for a petty mistake. He'd spoken to me more vehemently than anyone had since Dad. I respected him, yes, but . . .

"It's time, Randy. You'll help me to the bridge." Carefully, he stood. "Yes, definitely improved." Still, he took my hand firmly and walked with jaunty step toward his bridge.

He left me in the corridor, went to his console, made a note, slipped a chip into a case, thrust it in his pocket. "All right, they'll be waiting." Again he took my hand, led me as a small child to the airlock hatch.

I steeled myself for a good-bye, but he barely paused. "I'm going through, Mr. . . . Ardin, is it? Notify Mr. Tolliver."

He'd see me to the shuttle. I felt comforted, but it would only be for a few minutes.

The way to the Station's shuttle bay was marked by a blinking sign, and lights. We followed what seemed a well-worn path. At the shuttle hatch, I paused. "Mr. Seafort, I want to thank—"

"Later, joey." He guided me within. Was he going to buckle me into my seat? Resentment welled into a hard knot. It was inexcusable to treat me always as a small child. Didn't he know that—

Yes. He buckled me into my seat.

I pouted.

The pilots began the checklist.

Mr. Seafort took the seat alongside.

I gaped.

At last, a twinkle. "Did you think I'd let you face it alone?"

Why couldn't I erase a big, goofy grin? Why did my heart want to leap from my chest?

After a time, my mind reasserted itself. "Sir, I thought you can't go groundside. Your spine . . ."

His face was grave. "It's time I found out." He stayed my protest with a raised palm. "I have business ashore, son. I've no choice."

"Yes, Dad."

Oh, Lord God! Scarlet, I spun away, tried to bury myself in the adjoining empty seat. I couldn't have said it. *I mustn't have!*

"It's all right." Mr. Seafort's voice called me from a far place. "Truly, it's all right. He understands, and so do I."

"I'm so sorry, I never meant, please forgive—"

"It's all right, joey."

For a blissful moment I believed him. Then, "You don't understand. You're not my—I can never forget Dad, not for an instant!"

Bony fingers gripped my shoulder. "That's right! Feel it, know it! You'll never forget him. We won't allow it."

"But I called . . ."

His voice was soft. "And that's all right too. It's what you've needed, what I took away from you, and what poor Anthony, despite his best effort, couldn't give. Are you crying? Good, let it flow. For Derek, whom I miss every day of my life. For your misery. For all the unfairness of the world."

His fingers crept into mine as the engines caught and our shuttle slipped away from the Station's steady light.

PART TWO

December, in the Year of our Lord 2246

10

I'D BEEN GONE a matter of weeks, yet I peered at Centraltown Spaceport as if I hadn't seen it in a lifetime.

Perhaps it was so.

As we strode through the terminal, Mr. Seafort kept a tight grip on my hand, reducing me to dependence. Yet for all that, I wasn't all that uneasy being treated as a joeykid. My mind sheered away from my stunning gaffe in the shuttle, and his response; the thoughts left me uneasy, confused, startled. And something more. Secure. It was odd: in hours, perhaps minutes, I would lose Mr. Seafort forever, but I felt secure as I hadn't since Dad had bid me farewell.

Mr. Seafort glanced back at the shuttle. "Well, that was the easy half." He steered me to the streetside entrance, where, to my surprise, Mr. Branstead waited by the door of an electricar.

"Hallo, Jerence, how's the homestead?"

"It's been many years. I spent time at Pa's grave."

"Harmon," said the Captain softly. To me, "Did you know him, joey?"

"The old man?" I nodded. "When I was little." He'd come to a party, with his sons and their wives.

"I deceived him, and he forgave me." Mr. Seafort seemed lost in reverie.

"Well, now." Mr. Branstead eyed me. "I hardly expected this joey at your side." I couldn't tell if he was glad to see me alive.

"You'd rather I left him in a cell?"

"He faces worse, now." We climbed into Mr. Branstead's car. He said heavily, "I should have told you who he was."

"I agree. Why didn't you?"

"Randy begged me." We drove off, toward the city center.

After a moment Mr. Seafort asked, "Where to, and when?"

"The courthouse, four P.M."

"And then?"

"Carr Plantation. Everyone will be there."

"Everyone?"

"Virtually."

"Was getting them together difficult?"

"For heaven's sake!" Mr. Branstead rolled his eyes. "You're *Nick Seafort*, and visiting Hope Nation for the first time in . . . what, twenty years?"

"Longer." Mr. Seafort made a face. "Notoriety."

We passed Churchill Park, along the road I'd traveled with Mikhael, Kev, and Anselm, before my folly.

"Sir?" My voice was tentative. "I thought someone from the Church would be waiting."

"Most joeykids suffer from the misapprehension that they're the center of the universe."

It took me a while to puzzle it out. "You mean, you're to deliver me?"

"No doubt an appropriate moment will arise." To Mr. Branstead, "The Stadholder?"

"He'll see us at his residence, obviously. I don't know about earlier."

We pulled into the packed lot. Joeys milled about the walk fronting the court building. Some pointed.

Mr. Seafort took a breath, tried to smooth his hair. "Ouch. I keep forgetting." To me, "I'll deposit you in the front row. You're to stay there."

"Yes, sir." No arguments, no disobedience. I'd promised. I'd leave him better memories of me than he had.

Some of the crowd waved papers to autograph. Others shouted encouragement and welcome. Mr. Seafort waved as we swept past.

Inside, the lobby was full of milling folk. Mr. Branstead steered us to a lift. We got off at the second floor, made our way to the largest courtroom. It was packed. To my surprise, a holocam was satlinked from the back of the hall.

Mr. Seafort sought my hand, as usual gripped it firmly. "Let's go, joey. Oh." He stopped short. "If there's any conversation about you, try not to look surprised."

I gulped. It didn't sound promising.

"Ready, Jer?"

Mr. Branstead's eyes lightened into a smile. "Yes, sir."

We strode down the aisle, to a growing roar of welcome and applause. I glanced about. Prominent citizens, many from the Zone. Vince Palabee. In the back, Mr. Dakko.

Arghh! In the third row, along the aisle, Bishop Scanlen. I tried hard to look inconspicuous.

We strode to the bar. To my astonishment, Lieutenant Skor was in the front row, guarding an empty seat. Mr. Seafort turned me toward her, propelled me with a gentle swat. He and Mr. Branstead climbed to the raised bench. I settled next to Ms. Skor. She gave me a curt nod.

At length the applause died. Mr. Branstead grinned. "Remarkable. No advertisement, no public notice, and the whole town's joined us!"

Cheers and applause.

"Some of you know me from many years ago; I'm Jerence Branstead, once of Branstead Plantation. I was able to persuade my good friend Nicholas

Seafort that in the free state he did so much to preserve, he wasn't yet forgotten. And—" He could get no further. A roar of approval.

"And with that assurance, he made his first trip groundside in over five years, to greet you. Ladies and gentlemen, I give you the former Secretary-General of the United Nations, the hero of Hope Nation, Captain Nick Seafort!"

A standing ovation. It seemed to go on forever.

Mr. Seafort raised his hands. Eventually, the din subsided. "Good heavens," he said. A pause. "I don't believe I was that popular in days of old."

A roar of mirth.

"Thanks for your welcome. I meant what I said; decades ago, during the fish war, I was in serious conflict with your government, not to mention my own. In fact, Harmon Branstead was quite put out with me."

Chuckles.

"Which gives me all the more pleasure to tell you I met yesterday with your Stadholder, the Honorable Anthony Carr, and that I was most impressed with him. An outstanding young man, who—"

Applause. Automatically, I clapped along.

"—takes very seriously his duties of government. No doubt Lord God is well served by the selection of such an outstanding joey as Stadholder. I'm sure our Church officials are as delighted as the populace. And I'm heartened to see that my declaration of freedom for Hope Nation, all those years ago—"

The courthouse dissolved in tumult. It was minutes before the din eased. I tried to take it all in. Why had he gone to such lengths to endorse Anthony, especially after his Admiral had warned him about involvement in our affairs?

"—resulted in honest, God-fearing government, and such obvious prosperity and growth. I wish you my best."

Again, an ovation.

"I'm no speechmaker, but as long as time permits, I'll be happy to take questions."

I nudged Ms. Skor. "What is he doing?"

"Shush."

Patiently, the Captain fielded a flood of questions. What about *Galactic*? A tragedy; he described her loss, in chilling detail. Earth's failed coup? He had harsh words for those in his cherished Navy who'd lost their sense of duty.

Was Terran government stable?

Certainly.

"Can the Navy be trusted?"

Mr. Seafort frowned. "A few officers acted unwisely. They were dealt with."

What about the defense of the colonies?

Against what?

"The fish, for one."

His tone was somber. "Thanks to my . . . genocide, there are no fish."

"You were duty bound to protect us, sir."

"At the cost of a species?"

"Better theirs than ours." Murmurs of approval from all around.

"So I thought at the time." His expression bleak, he chose another raised hand.

Would Earth's enviro revolution succeed? That last was of great concern to us, I knew, as our grain exports were the lifeblood of our economy. He took each question seriously, gave no glib answers, probed for truth.

In the process, Mr. Seafort twice more mentioned Anthony, each time approvingly, while the silently whirring holocam took it all in.

"Ms. Skor, what made him do this?"

"Did you ask him?"

"No, ma'am." Oops. I'd been determined, once, not to show her courtesy. No matter; Mr. Seafort seemed determined to put our unpleasantness behind us.

I studied her, taking my courage in my hands. "Are you glad he pardoned me?"

"No one wants a joeykid's death."

I wasn't sure that was an answer.

Onstage, Mr. Seafort seemed to be enjoying himself, though I noticed after a time his hand remained firmly in place on the lectern. My smile faded. If he swayed, I'd leap onto the bench as fast as . . .

Jerence Branstead rose, applauding. "Thank you all for coming," he said. "Would you join me in most heartfelt gratitude to the man who . . ."

The whole hall rose as one.

Mr. Branstead helped him off the bench. The Captain, clearly tiring, waded through a sea of outstretched hands, shaking as many as he could.

I stood uncertainly. Mr. Seafort beckoned.

Fingers gripped my shoulder.

I looked up.

Bishop Scanlen. "I believe you're in our charge, young Mr. Carr." His voice was genial, his eyes cold.

Mr. Seafort stopped short, made his way past well-wishers. "Randy, outside."

"I'm afraid, Mr. SecGen, you can't take him—"

"We'll talk in the anteroom, sir. It's too noisy here." The Captain grasped my hand, pulled me along. Helplessly, I looked back at the Bishop. If he held Mr. Seafort's stubbornness against me, my introduction to the farm would be harsh indeed.

In a moment we were within sight of the elevators, toward which the crowd was streaming. Mr. Branstead said, "The conference rooms, sir. This way." He led us to a side passage. Lieutenant Skor followed.

The door shut behind us, creating an oasis of calm. Bishop Scanlen seemed annoyed, but produced a smile. "Mr. SecGen, we met some years ago, after the Trannie Rebellion. I was on the blue-ribbon panel considering means of reconciliation."

Mr. Seafort made a noncommittal sound.

Scanlen said, "Thank you for bringing Randy groundside. It saves a certain—"

"Have you business with him?"

"Judge Hycliff of Hope Nation Family Court declared him a wayward youth. Custody is in the Church. Come here, boy." The Bishop collared me with an iron grip.

"Why'd you seek such an arrangement, sir?" Mr. Seafort was polite.

Perhaps sensing he'd won, the Bishop could afford to be magnanimous. "I'll admit, Captain, that face had a lot to do with it. Personally, I don't care about the words. I was a boy before I was a Bishop, and certainly I've heard 'fuck' before." An extra squeeze as he said it; his fingernails dug hard.

"For that reason, you . . . ?"

"Credit me with *some* sense. The role of the Church is at stake. Mr. SecGen, would you allow Lord God to be cursed in your presence?"

"Certainly not."

"I am His vicar in Hope Nation, appointed by the Patriarchs of holy Mother Church. Profanity to the Bishop is to Lord God Himself." Into the silence he added, "Really, it's in the lad's best interest. He's run amuck; look what he did to you. The Stadholder's been unable to control—"

"That doesn't concern me, sir. Randy's going aloft."

"Admiral Kenzig ordered you to cooperate; he told me so himself. What game is this?"

"No game," said Mr. Seafort. "If you make application to the proper authorities, no doubt the matter will be resolved."

Scanlen sounded smug. "It *is* resolved, by the courts."

"I meant the authorities in home system. By Hope Nation's treaty of independence, U.N. citizens aren't subject to local courts. Come, Randy."

I tried and failed to break free of the Bishop's clutch.

Scanlen snorted. "Nonsense. This boy's a Hope Nation national, born not fifty miles from—"

"Oh!" Seafort snapped his fingers. "I see the confusion. Anyone have a pocket holovid?"

Mr. Branstead fished out his, with its tiny holoscreen.

The Captain pressed in a chip. "*Olympiad* is so much larger than the typical ship of the line." His tone was apologetic. "Even our Ship's Boy Alejandro is overworked. Inconsiderate joeys call on him day and night." To me, a scowl. "I've tried to find supplementary crew, to no avail."

"Mr. Seafort—"

"You're aware, sir, my crew is on long-leave? I'm dreadfully under-staffed. In my view, this constitutes an emergency. According to Article Twelve of the Naval Regulations and Code of Conduct, Revision of 2087, during a state of emergency, involuntary impressment into the Naval Service is authorized."

We all stared in shock.

"As you know, all Naval personnel are deemed citizens for the duration of their enlistment. If you'll read this excerpt from our Log, you'll see that, this morning, I impressed Randolph Carr into the U.N. Naval Service."

"You what?"

"Randy's my new ship's boy."

Branstead's heli droned over the huge stand of genera trees whose shade covered the fringes of the Plantation Zone. I stared at the Naval work blues I'd so naively donned this morning. Had Mr. Seafort planned it from the start? Was I a prisoner of *Olympiad* after all? Was he saving me, or exacting revenge?

At the courthouse, Scanlen had sputtered, "Preposterous!" He clutched me all the harder. "Don't trifle with the Church, sir. Your very soul—"

Mr. Seafort's eyes had narrowed. "Ms. Skor, take the ship's boy out-side."

She'd advanced on the Bishop with a look that chilled even me. Mo-ments later, I found myself in the last of the day's sun. I'd looked to her for reassurance, found none. "Ma'am?"

"He'll be out presently." Her fingers flicked my collar straight.

"But . . . what was he doing?"

"Obeying orders to the letter."

"That's goofju—" At her scowl, I snapped my mouth shut.

What was it Kenzig had told the Captain? *As long as he's a Hope Nation citizen, transfer him to the Church . . . Send him groundside, see that he's put in the custody of the proper authorities.* So, Seafort had given me U.N. citizenship, taken me groundside, and put me in custody of the proper authority. Himself. I couldn't help a grin. Ms. Skor scowled anew.

Now, as we flew over Branstead Plantation I asked cautiously from the backseat, "Sir, why ship's boy? Why not cadet?"

Mr. Seafort said only, "You're not nearly mature enough for cadet."

I didn't like the answer, but knew better than to press.

"A ship's boy," said Mr. Branstead, "is generally an orphan." His eyes were closed; he'd let the heli's puter navigate. I hadn't even bothered to ask if they'd let me pilot; joeys my age weren't supposed to know how.

"When he's grown," said Mr. Seafort, "he becomes an ordinary seaman, occasionally even a cadet. And like a cadet, he's a minor, a ward of his commanding officer, subject to whatever discipline his Captain sees fit. Take that as warning."

"Are you angry with me?"

"Not at present."

I supposed I could take some comfort in that. "Will I have to sail with you?" It sounded less gracious than I'd intended.

"You'd prefer the training farm?"

"God, no."

After a time I realized the silence was glacial. I played back what I'd said. "Sir, I meant no disrespect."

"I meant what I told Scanlen: I won't allow His name to be taken in vain. And speaking of taking His name . . ."

"Yes, sir?"

"Like every member of the ship's company, you're required to take an oath. Do you know it?"

"No."

"Jerence?"

Mr. Branstead said, "Think I could ever forget it, sir? After that week locked in my cabin, with nothing but the oath to distract me from the vial of juice? Pay attention, Randy. 'I do swear upon my immortal soul to serve and protect the Charter of the General Assembly of the United Nations, to give loyalty and obedience for the term of my enlistment to the Naval Service of the United Nations and to obey all its lawful orders and regulations, so help me Lord God Almighty.' "

I said, "I swear."

"Oh, no you don't." Mr. Seafort's voice was sharp. "It's a serious undertaking. You'll memorize it—Jerence will help you write it down—and be sure you understand your commitment. Before dinner, I'll administer the oath."

"Yessir." I managed to stay silent, and therefore out of trouble, until we set down at dusk on the front lawn of Carr Plantation. Anthony's home, and until recent days, mine.

"Son . . ." It warmed me to hear Mr. Seafort address me so. I was afraid my life would all be saluting and drills. "We'll be here an hour or two. Is there anything you'd like to carry aboard *Olympiad*?"

"Dad's holo. The zines I saved. Maybe some . . ." Games, I'd been about to say. Children's toys.

"Gather them, put them in the heli."

"Yes, sir."

I charged up two flights of stairs to my room. Packing took no more than minutes; I realized there was little I wanted to take with me. New life, new start, new gear. But I unlocked my desk, unearthed my trove of news reports of the *Galactic* disaster, carefully packed them in a chipcase.

Downstairs, the families continued to gather. The house was a blaze of lights; public rooms echoed with laughter and chatter.

I turned a corner, found myself face-to-face with Judy Winthrop.

She seemed as startled as I.

"Randy." She eyed my work blues.

I might never have another chance. I pulled her to an empty room, wrapped myself around her in a hug. Her hand flitted across my back, and was still.

At length I said, "You heard?"

"That you bashed Captain Seafort. What came over you?"

"I'm an idiot."

Judy giggled. "At least you know it."

"What are you doing here?"

"Mom and Dad brought me to meet Mr. Seafort. No one imagined you'd be in the manse. What if the Bishop sees you?"

"He can't touch me. I'm ship's boy on *Olympiad*."

"Don't joke."

"It's true. Mr. Seafort said so." I sounded proud, and was.

"He must have arranged it with Anthony."

It was like a bucket of ice water. Would he have? Did that mean he was helping me only for Anth's sake?

"As long as you're safe, Randy. What does it matter?"

It mattered. No time for that now. "I've missed you." I tried not to sound as shy as I felt.

"Me too." The words I'd yearned to hear.

I flopped onto a couch, sat cross-legged. We whispered and chattered.

Eventually an adult found us; automatically we thrust ourselves apart, but it was only Mr. Branstead. "We'll be leaving after a bit. Say your fare-wells." He was gone.

I dared say nothing. Tremulously, I brought my lips to Judy's. No re-sistance, no protest. I pressed tight. My hand strayed.

In a while I slipped out of the room. I'd actually fondled her breast—my first time—but life's other mysteries would have to wait. I sighed.

Across the hall, a familiar figure accepted an iced juice from a houseman. I was appalled; how could Bishop Scanlen partake of Anthony's hospitality as if nothing had happened? I edged past him into the parlor.

"Randy." A soft voice. Mom. She was curled on a couch, Mr. Seafort at her side.

I ran to her. She said, "The Captain says you've been a bad boy."

"Yes." She must have taken a light dose today; she was half with us. I dropped to sit at her feet.

Mr. Seafort said, "I was telling Sandra I've been here before."

"Years ago," she said dreamily. "Years and years."

I was overcome with embarrassment, but the Captain didn't seem to notice.

Mom's tone was languid. She said to him, "Did you know Derek?"

In desperation I blurted, "Sir, would you like to see my room?"

"That would be nice. Madam, would you excuse me a moment?"

"Of course." She raised her fingers, and to my utter astonishment, he kissed them.

He took my hand. As fast as I could, I tugged him to the stairs. "I'm sorry, she's . . . sometimes she gets—"

He stopped moving; I had to do the same. "It's all right, Randy."

"She means no harm. Some days she's more alert, and . . ."

"No. It's all right." He held my eye, until I was sure he meant it.

Chastened, comforted, I led him up the stairs. "There's nothing special about my room. I was trying to divert you."

"I'd like to see it."

Around the hall, up the second stairs. I was afraid he'd be winded, but holding the banister, he seemed fine. Was my bed made? In my haste to pack I hadn't noticed.

I threw open the door.

"*This* is your room?" His tone held wonder. He wandered in, sat slowly on the bed. "Oh, Randy."

I crouched beside him. "What's wrong?"

"Oh, Lord. My first trip to Hope Nation, when I was a boy. I'd just become Captain, and Derek was a middy. Your plantation was controlled by the manager, Plumwell. Your dad wanted to see it, but worried the manager might do us harm. To get us in, I made up an insane story that Derek was my retarded cousin. I hadn't warned him, and he was so infuriated he leaped at my throat. Right here in this room." He chuckled. "Oh, that takes me back." Abruptly he brushed a hand over his eyes.

"Don't be upset. Please, Dad. We both miss—"

I threw my hands across my mouth, rocked.

Traitor son!

I sat appalled that I'd done it again. Was it not enough that I'd damaged Anthony, tried to do murder, made myself an exile? Must I betray Dad anew?

The Captain's arm snaked across my shoulders. "Thank you. If I could be that, in any sense, it would ease my mind."

I said nothing.

"Call me that, or Mr. Seafort, as it pleases you. I'll still do what I might, on Derek's behalf. We'll say no more about it. Now, lad. Are you ready for your oath?"

Downstairs again. Mr. Seafort circulated among the families, Anthony beaming proudly. I tried to pretend that all was well, that I hadn't made an utter fool of myself a second time the same day.

At one point Anth managed to take me aside. He put both hands on my shoulders. "Ship's boy, eh?"

"Did you know?"

"I was flabbergasted. Clever move, though. It keeps you out of his clutches." I had no need to ask to whom Anth referred. He regarded me, and the annoyance I'd oft seen was gone. "There's too much to say, and I haven't the words for it."

"You, without words?" I tried a grin.

"Randy, your life among us is in shambles. By a miracle you've been given a rebirth. Use it well. Strive for your best."

I couldn't avoid it by a joke. "I will, Anth."

"I tried, but I'm not Grandpa." He grimaced. "Still, I taught you a few things about power."

"Teach me why that frazzing Scanlen is in your living room."

"Because we pretend we're civilized." A pause. "It hasn't come to war yet. Pray Lord God it never will."

"He'll hate you for what I said to him."

Anth shrugged. "I've been hated by better men."

"Why did Mr. Seafort come here?"

"As a gift to Grandpa. To show support for my government. As he's shown for you."

A silence.

"Anth, is this good-bye?"

"Perhaps . . . Lord God willing, I'll see you soon."

My tone was plaintive. "I'm about to cry."

"Don't. They'll notice. Find the Captain. The festivities are winding down." A firm handshake, and he was gone.

Dutifully, I searched. Mr. Seafort was in the study. A figure was with him. My hackles rose.

Bishop Scanlen waved a finger in his face. ". . . heard about you from Reverend Pandeker. Heresy, he called it."

"Declining to give the Ship's Prayer? Nonsense. He gives it."

"It's your duty, Seafort, and you shirk it. As it's your duty to surrender the boy. Not for me, for the Church. 'Fuck you'? Ha. Fifty people must have heard it. The story's all over Centraltown."

"We've had this conversation."

"By Lord God, I could excommunicate you! You'll writhe in Hell!"

I blanched, but Mr. Seafort merely held up a palm. "Would you put our dispute aside a moment, and answer a theological question?"

"Don't twit me."

"I'm serious."

Scanlen glowered. "All right. What?"

"Does Church doctrine admit to degrees of Hell? Are some punished worse than others?"

"Hell is infinite pain, infinite horror. There can be no degrees."

"Thank you, sir. I'm comforted."

"How so?"

The Captain's face was serene. "I've done treason, betrayal, murder, and genocide. I *know* I'll see Hell. So no matter what I do, you can wield no threat of worse. You may not have the boy." He caught sight of me, making myself small in the corner. "Wait in the heli. We're leaving shortly."

"Yes, sir." I fled.

Hell? If he believed in it, was I right not to? Had I already consigned myself?

Outside, night had fallen. I climbed into the heli, parked in a corner of the lawn.

Where would they have me sleep? Surely not the cabin next to the Captain's; Level 1 was officers' territory. Not a crew berth, please. Not among fifty others.

The distant blaze from the house threw enough light to examine the heli's controls. I gripped the collective, pretended to turn the nonexistent key. I'd lift straight up, bank left, zoom over the house. No, better, zoom directly past the hall window; no wires or branches would impede me. Anth would look up, grit his teeth . . .

Was I leaving behind anything I might need? I hadn't bothered with clothes; I'd never seen Alec in anything but ship's blues. I'd brought my favorite holovid, a small one. With it, I could keep a diary, or watch a vid.

Footsteps.

"Mr. Seafort? Oh, you!" My tone was wary.

Mr. Scanlen, with a deacon in clerical collar. The Bishop held up a hand, peaceably. "I can't have you leave on these terms, lad. He outwitted me; I admit it. There's not much I can do. I wanted to wish you well."

I swallowed. Where was Mr. Seafort? I wasn't sure what I ought to say.

"You need discipline and refocus. The farm is quite good at that, actually. Perhaps the Navy will suffice."

"Perhaps." It wasn't giving him much.

"Don't burden yourself with guilt. I forgive you. Truly, I do. As for the Captain, obviously, he has too. Go in peace." He held out a hand.

Cautiously, I shook.

Something stung my wrist.

The house lights tilted, and blinked out.

11

MY ROOM WAS HOT. I woke slowly. I'd had an awful dream involving Dad, *Olympiad*, Captain Nicholas Seafort. Midshipmen, a ship's boy, someone named Branstead.

My room was oddly dark. I struggled to clear my head.

A window, with bars. Minor gleamed dimly overhead; Major must have set.

Bars? I sat up too fast; the room spun. I hung on to the wall until it slowed.

I was in a tiny room, no bigger than the cell in which—

Cell. That part was no dream. If the rest was real, I'd be wearing ship's blues.

No shirt anywhere I could see. But my pants were blue, and looked like nothing I owned.

I jumped out of bed, peered out the high window, tried to orient myself.

Fields, with rich crops swaying in a soft wind. Were we in the Zone? Whose manse?

I tried the door. Locked.

A farm.

The Bishop.

Oh, Christ. "Help! Someone help me!" My voice was shrill. "Call the jerries! I've been kidnapped!"

The slow trod of footsteps. A flashlight. A burly figure, one I'd never seen. The door swung open. "Stop that racket, you'll wake the other joey-kids."

"Where am I?"

"The training and correctional farm of Lord God's Reunification Church."

"That son of a bitch!"

"Foul language is prohibited. To whom did you refer?"

"That liar Scanlen! He said he forgave me!"

"He forgives you, my son. Truly." A step, and he loomed close. "But as you've been assigned to our custody, it's our duty to train you in His ways. You don't call a churchman a liar, boy." His heavy fist clubbed me in the temple. I reeled. "Or a son of a bitch." Another blow. My head hit the wall, and I passed out.

"Eat now, or you'll be starving by dinner." A scrawny joeykid held up a bowl.

Morning had arrived; deacons had come for me, dragged me to a barracks full of boys, shown me an upper bunk.

When they'd come through the door, every joey within had come to his feet, in absolute silence.

A boy was assigned to show me morning routine; I hadn't caught his name. Towheaded, short, missing teeth, though reseeding was commonplace.

"Where are we?" I kept my voice low.

"The farm. 'Bout three hundred miles north of Centraltown. Don' let him see us talkin'." His eyes flickered to the deacon, standing with arms folded, at the breakfast table. "Can' talk durin' breakfast. Bunks all right, or field."

"Escape?"

"Ain' no roads. Only helis." The deacon looked our way, and we subsided. I chewed the fresh hot bread. At least the food seemed decent.

Outside, we had to form a line and walk two by two. It was a good mile to the fields. They handed us hoes. I looked about with disgust; this was work for machines. A good auto-tiller would accomplish in hours what we . . .

"Get to work!" A crack, and a terrible searing pain on my bare back. I whirled. A deacon, with a thick leather strap. "Want another? Get to hoeing!"

I dared not challenge him, not until I knew more. Despite my resolve, my eyes teared as I tore at the stubborn earth.

I asked the boy next to me, "What are we planting this late?" Winter would soon be upon us.

"Nothing." He spat. "Practice."

God in Heaven.

Another deacon sat by a sound system, spoke into the mike. *"These are the generations of the heavens and of the earth when they were created, in the day that the Lord God made the earth and the heavens. And every plant of the field before it was in the earth, and every herb before it grew, for the Lord God had not caused it to rain upon the earth, and there was not a man to till the ground."* He took a sip of water.

"But there went up a mist from the earth, and watered the whole face of the ground . . ."

I stabbed at the stubborn turf. The salt of my sweat stung my smarting back. If the deacon struck me again, he or I would die.

Hours passed.

The day dragged on, awful beyond belief. I glanced about me; some joeykids seemed numbed, others sullen. All were bare from the waist up; most wore only sandals and slacks. I was lucky to have my sturdy Naval shoes.

As my mentor had warned, by evening I was starving. We'd been given water during the day, but not much. By the time we marched back to barracks, my mouth was parched, my lips cracked.

Immediately, we were sent to our beds. Boys began stripping; squelching my embarrassment I followed their lead. We were herded into a communal shower, where we found bars of coarse soap.

The towhead nudged me, pointed. A tall joey, sixteen or so, across the way. His buttocks were laced with fading welts from a strap.

"What for?" I wasn't sure we were allowed to talk here, so I whispered.

"Stealin'."

I looked about, spotted another whose back was a crisscross of scars. "What for?"

"Lascivious."

I wasn't sure what it entailed, but resolved not to find out.

Outside, torn but serviceable towels. We dried off, marched back to barracks, redressed in our sweaty clothes. "Clean clothing?"

"Once a week, wash."

Lord God, if You exist, take me out of here! Nothing I've done deserves this.

They brought dinner to the barracks table. My stomach churned eagerly, but it wasn't that easy. First a deacon opened the Book. *"They shall hunger no more, neither thirst anymore."* He waited expectantly.

The boys chorused, "They shall hunger no more . . ."

Towhead jabbed me in the ribs; deacons walked among us to make sure we actually spoke the words, and didn't mumble. Dismayed, I parroted the phrases.

"For the lamb which is in the midst of the throne shall feed them, and

shall lead them unto living fountains of waters; and God shall wipe away all tears from their eyes."

Ha. Not likely.

Prayer succeeded prayer; they must have passed half an hour with such folderol. When I thought I could stand it no longer, they let us dig in.

I had to admit the food was ample, though they were strict on how we received it; each boy had to stand in line, walk to the table with his tray before him, take what he was given, return to his bed to eat, tray perched on his lap. But, when all was done, I wasn't hungry, and the food had even proven tasty.

Bizarre, our Church. Whippings, forced prayer, foul clothing, horrid work, and decent meals.

Other joeys were talking over their dinner, and the deacons didn't seem to mind. "How long have some of you been here?"

Towhead said, "Justin, six years. Get out soon; he's almost twenty-one. Freddy, there, been since he was nine."

"My God, why?"

"Shhh, can' say that. Stole from church plate."

After we were sent to the toilets, they made us turn in.

I lay awake half the night, plotting how I might escape. I'd seen no vehicles save a distant heli. Three hundred miles was too far to walk, especially without a stock of food. I'd probably come across streams, to drink. But if not . . .

Morning came. I dragged myself out of bed with the others, bleary and aching. Prayers that seemed endless, breakfast of porridge and milk. Then the trudge to the field.

A day passed, and another, while I watched and waited with growing desperation.

There was no way out. Several of our deacons had stunners tucked in their waistbands. Across the field, another barracks toiled. Surreptitiously, I watched them. A scuffle; a deacon lashed out with his strap at a thin, reedy boy. He ducked the blow, resisted. Two deacons raced over. A touch with the stunner. He collapsed, and was dragged off. In a few minutes, the drone of a heli.

"What'll happen to him?" I kept my voice low.

"Repentance camp."

"How long?"

"Dunno. Year, prob'ly."

"Is it bad?"

"Ask Arno."

He gestured to a brawny red-haired youth, who grimaced and shook his head. "Don't wanna go there for nothin'."

The day ended.

Sunday, thank Lord God, they didn't make us work. Instead, we were treated to prayer and lectures, and meditation, in the earnest hope we might show contrition for our numerous misdeeds. I squirmed on the hard wooden bench, trying not to catch a deacon's eye.

And then, Monday, more of the stultifying labor, endless rows of unyielding earth under the remorseless sun. I dug at the stubborn sod, acrid sweat trickling down my ribs.

I'd already hidden a heel of bread under my pillow, to see if the deacons would notice. None had. They served hard cheese; that would keep a day or two, even in a warm barracks.

Bread and cheese might buy me an extra day, with cool water from a stream.

I hadn't dared leave my bed to see if the barracks door was locked at night.

Where would I go? I'd head for the Zone, of course; Centraltown lay beyond it. Perhaps Anthony would hide me, or Judy. Alex Hopewell I wasn't sure about.

Three days passed, three days of hell.

I was becoming numbed, marching about like an automaton, singing out, "Yes, sir," when spoken to.

Perhaps I'd die in the deep woods bordering the Zone. It didn't much matter.

On Friday, I was breaking tufts of sod with a pitchfork when the whap of a heli sounded in the distance.

"*CARR!*"

I jumped back to my hoe, scrabbling frantically at the earth. Moments before, our deacon had given Jackie a vicious whack, and he was still teary-eyed. I wasn't sure he knew that blood was seeping down his back.

"*Carr, move!*" A deacon looked about from the heli door. I gaped. Our supervisor prodded me.

The small, swift two-seater had landed perhaps fifty paces distant. By its door, a squat man waited. His beard was bushy and black. A strap dangled from his hand.

I'd seen how it was done; swallowing my pride I ran across the field. "Here, sir! How may I serve?"

The deacon ran his fingers over his unshaved chin. "Turn." He twisted me by the shoulder.

I did. He cuffed my hands behind my back.

"In."

I struggled to climb aboard.

He punched the small of my back with the heel of his palm. It hurt. "In!"

"Yes, sir!"

"That's better." He helped me aboard. "Sit back, boy."

"Yes, sir." In the cool of the heli, I was clammy with the sweat of dread.

We lifted off, soared over the farm. We headed to an outbuilding at the edge of the complex, a mile or two distant.

Five minutes ride. From the terrain I judged that we'd left the farm proper. A clearing, with a snug celuwall outbuilding. No helipad, but grass cut short.

He set down on a bare patch near the door, pulled me out. "Let's go." He turned off the key, left it in the ignition.

I must not have moved fast enough; he clipped me alongside the ear. Jesus, it hurt. I trotted through the door, his fingers tight on my neck.

Inside, a small room, bare except for a bench. Two deacons. I blinked in the sudden dark. Four walls, a chair. Rough hewn beams of thick, sturdy genera wood across the ceiling.

Three deacons, one operating a holocam. It focused tight on my face.

A door opened. The Right Reverend Bishop Scanlen strode in.

"Ah, Randolph. I trust you are well?"

My hands were still cuffed behind me. "Yes, sir." It wasn't how I'd have preferred to answer.

"Let's get it done." His voice was flat.

Someone grabbed me from behind. Another slipped a rope over my neck. I squawked.

Scanlen faced the holocam. "This is what it comes to," he said.

They threw the rope over the beam.

"NO! IN CHRIST'S NAME, NO!"

They paid me no attention. "Now."

Two of them hauled on the rope. I was lifted to my toes.

And beyond.

They held me there a half minute, kicking, turning purple while the room swam. Then they let me down. The squat bearded deacon thrust his fingers inside the noose, forced it loose. I sucked a great gasp of air.

"Think on it," Scanlen said to the holocam.

My feet wouldn't hold the ground. I staggered, tumbled into a heap, choking, crying, squealing, sucking at air.

"Ease him," said Scanlen.

In a moment my hands were freed. They dragged me to the chair, dumped me in it. I was beside myself with fear, hate, frenzy.

Scanlen knelt at my side. "This was for him, not you. Hopefully he'll heed. Else, I'll shrive you when the time comes." A rough hand tousled my hair with what might have been kindness.

When I looked up, he was gone.

They let me sit for an hour, perhaps two. I was beyond thought.

"Come along, boy." The bearded deacon.

I couldn't stand. I flinched, expecting the strap.

They exchanged glances. Two of them reached for my hands, cuffed them, but in front. "Let's go." The squat, heavyset deacon pulled me up by the elbow. The two others watched from the doorway.

I trotted along, sniveling, my throat burning like fire.

Ahead waited the heli, to take me back to the farm. To hell.

The deacon swung open the door. I made as if to climb in, stumbled. It took me a step backward. A pace toward the door. I let loose the hardest kick I ever launched, right into his crotch. My sturdy Naval shoe buried itself in flesh.

He gasped. His eyes bulging, he doubled over. I raised high my chained wrists. An arc flashed in the sunlight. My steel cuffs slammed into his neck. Bones snapped. He dropped like a stone and was still.

I scrambled into the heli, slammed shut the door, clicked the lock. Gibbering, I tried desperately to pull myself together.

Could I pilot with my wrists cuffed?

The two deacons sprinted to the heli. I turned the key, switched on the engine. Ever so slowly, the rotors began to turn.

One deacon knelt by his comrade, the other slammed into the door. It held. He brandished a stunner.

Come *on*, heli.

I watched my rotor speed.

The deacon ran to the pilot's door. Locked. He hefted his stunner, smashed at the window.

In a moment I'd have lift.

The window splintered.

I grasped the collective, just managed to reach the cyclic.

Shards of plastic splattered my lap.

The deacon rammed his stunner through the broken window.

LIFT.

The stunner brushed my side; I flinched clear in the nick of time.

We were off the ground. The deacon wrapped a foot around the runner, tried desperately to stun me.

I soared into the sky.

The deacon's face pressed against the remains of the plastic.

Our eyes met.

Deliberately, I rammed my foot on the rudder, twitched the cyclic.

Abruptly we banked, and his face was gone.

The sudden lightening of our load threw me upward. Shuddering with relief, fear, Lord God knew what, I scrambled to keep us aloft. Damn it, a heli needed two hands. I was busier than a one-armed . . . what had Dad called it?

The radar beeped; I glanced into the sky. A fleet of seven or eight large helis cruised toward the farm. Shit! I ducked to the treetops. South, Randy. Head for Centraltown, before they get help. The Zone was underpopulated; they'd surely track me, but in Centraltown I could lose myself.

What was top speed? Three hundred, by the airspeed indicator. Forty-five minutes. Too long; they'd be on me. Don't panic, Randy. Do you have fuel? Yes, enough; the Valdez permabattery was fully charged. If only I could reach the cyclic while . . .

I glanced at the radar scope. Behind me, nothing. Where was the frazzing transponder? I searched the controls. Anth hadn't taught me that part. But if I broadcast my ID, they'd have a lock on me.

Were they calling for help? I twirled the frequencies. The radio was strangely silent.

CHRIST, JOEY, WHERE ARE YOU GOING?

I was heading east, into the Davon Hills. Centraltown was south. Steady, Randy. You've a lot to do, your hands won't reach, and—

You idiot.

I switched on the puter. "Set autopilot, heading Centralport beacon."

"Autopilot set." The puter's voice was brisk and impersonal.

"Transponder off."

"Transponder now off."

I leaned back, wishing I could gnaw off my cuffs. "EST to Centraltown?"

"Estimated arrival Centraltown Spaceport twenty-six minutes thirteen sec—"

"Not the spaceport!" Lord God knew who'd be there watching.

"That's where the beacon—"

"Downtown, somewhere. Churchill Park."

Our course changed by a minute fraction.

The radar beeped. Behind us, a blip, moving fast.

"Shit." I pounded the dash. "Top speed."

"Was that a query or a request?"

"Go to top speed!" Then, "What is it?"

"Top cruising airspeed three hundred twelve knots."

I peered at the screen. "We're being followed."

"Noted."

"How fast are they going?"

"Craft on our heading is proceeding at three hundred fifty-seven knots. Estimated intercept seventeen minutes eighteen seconds."

"Make us go faster!"

"Top cruising speed is—"

"Emergency speed!"

"Unless a valid emergency is declared I cannot—"

"I declare one! My life's at risk!" If they caught me, I'd be hanged in earnest.

The engine surged. The airspeed climbed to three hundred forty.

I had absolutely nothing to do but pry helplessly at my cuffs. All I managed was to chafe my wrists further.

But for the deacon's kindness, my arms would have been locked behind me, and now I'd be wielding my hoe.

In repayment, I'd killed him. Again I felt the bone snap, and my stomach heaved.

I demanded, "EST?"

"To northwest border Churchill Park, eleven minutes sixteen seconds."

Too long. I'd die of fright first.

"Intercept?"

"Nine minutes twelve sec—"

I scrambled out of the seat, threw open the side door. A shriek of air. In the stowage space, a box. I heaved it off. Careful, Randy. You could go too.

"What are you doing?" The puter's tone was injured.

"Throwing out ballast." How heavy was the fire extinguisher? A few pounds. I dragged it to the door, kicked it loose. A few tools. Out they went. Frantically, I searched.

Aha. At the foot of the copilot's seat, a release. Probably to allow more cargo stowage. I clawed at it, hampered by my chained wrists.

Why hadn't I freed the lever before throwing out the bloody tools?

I worked at the release until it sprang open. The seat rocked backward, almost hurling me out the door. I worked it out of its flange, manhandled it past me, kicked it out, watched it tumble down into the trees.

The pilot's seat was better secured; I had no way to remove it. Ah, well. Cautiously, I maneuvered the door shut. The wind's howl eased.

I slid into my seat, checked the indicator. Three hundred fifty-nine.

"EST?" My voice was ragged. If they caught me . . .

"Four minutes thirty seconds. I must report loss of gear to maintenance supervisor upon landing."

"Stick it up your CPU!"

Perhaps the puter understood. It remained silent.

I watched the scope. The pursuing heli wasn't gaining, but it seemed awfully close. I clambered to the back, peered through the dome.

A large black craft, far too close for comfort. I could see the blur of its rotors.

"Can't you hurry?"

The puter's tone was flat. "We're at top revs. Any increase risks engine burnout."

"Risk it!"

"Maintenance approval required." Whatever that meant.

We were over the outskirts of town. I crawled to the door, readying myself. I wished to hell I had a shirt; I'd be too damn conspicuous in nothing but sweat-stained pants and handcuffs.

"There is no approved landing pad within half a mile of—"

"Puter, set down at northwest corner of park in the first clearing you come to."

"Regulations prohibit—"

"Screw your regulations! I declared an emergency!"

"Setaside noted." We swooped; I grabbed at the hand strap.

We lost altitude fast, too fast. "Puter, are you driving?"

"You said it was an emergency." His tone was prim.

As we slowed, the black craft gained.

A lurch; we dropped a hundred feet. "Puter!"

"Altitude three hundred feet. ETA thirty-seven seconds. Two hundred fifty feet."

The black heli loomed overhead.

We were an elevator with a broken cable. The ground swooped upward. My stomach climbed to my throat.

"ETA seven seconds, five—"

We slammed into the ground. I threw open the door.

Overhead, the whap of blades.

I leaped out, sprinted for the trees.

The black heli set down. A wiry figure leaped out, raced after me. Immediately his craft took to the air.

I raced past a little boy; a soft beachball hit him in the head as he gaped. His father froze, eyes wide, as I chugged past.

I had to get out of the park, but where in hell was I headed?

A low wall at the park's edge; I vaulted over it without a pause. I risked a backward glance; the man from the heli was a good runner. If I—

"Aiyee!" I'd run full tilt into a bony obstacle. I untangled myself from a woman sprawled on the sidewalk, her bags scattered.

"Sorry." All I could do was wheeze. I clawed my way to my feet, resumed my mad dash. Where was I? What did I know of the area?

Wait. Two blocks north was . . .

Kevin's house.

I had to lose my pursuer. I ducked into a drive, ran through a backyard, scrambled over the fence.

Another yard, another fence.

An alley. Why not? I sprinted past a shed, risked another glance over my shoulder. No one. Good; I couldn't keep this up for long.

Overhead, the heli. But there were trees, shadows, wires . . . perhaps he couldn't see me.

I ran on, turned north.

The heli circled, two blocks east. Oh, thank You, Lord.

Kevin's house was one block. Half a block. Only two more doors. I staggered up the walk, heaving for breath.

At the corner, my pursuer whirled, looking one direction to the next.

He faded away. I vaulted over the porch rail, bolted to the back door, hammered it with my fists.

No answer. I banged again.

Nothing.

Desperate, I rammed my shoulder to the door. It was like hitting a rock. I rammed it again. Something splintered. One more time. The door gave. I threw myself in.

The thud of steps down the stairs. The inner door flew open. "What the—" Kev's eyes widened. "Out of my house!"

My mouth worked. I had no breath to speak.

"Out!" He ran at me, pushed me to the door.

"Wait!" It was a croak.

"Get out. I'm calling the jerries!" He wheeled.

In a frenzy, I clutched him, hauled him back. "Kidnapped." I sucked at air. "Tried to hang me, look. Love of God, Kev, help me."

"What are you talking about? You broke our door. Dad will have a—out!"

I said, "They're going to kill me."

"I don't *care*!"

"Give me a shirt and get these off. I'll go."

"Why should I help—"

"Because I'd help you!" It was all I knew to say. "See my neck?" I craned upward at the ceiling, to stretch it. "Rope burns!"

He paled. "You're serious!"

"The goddamn Church! They're insane. Kevin, get these off!" I pounded my cuffs on the table.

"How?" He rubbed the bridge of his nose. "The shed! Come on." He raced me outside, past the door I'd smashed.

The shed had a codelock; I danced with impatience while he jabbed at it. Finally it opened.

Kev dashed to a wall, on whose pegs dozens of tools hung. "Not a saw, no time . . . there it is!" He pulled down a huge bolt cutter. "Here." He grabbed my wrists, lay them on the workbench.

"Hurry!"

"I *am!*" He got the blades around the chain between my cuffs. A squeeze. Nothing.

"Harder!"

"I'm trying." He squeezed until his face went red. "What are those things made of?"

I was in a frenzy. "Get them off, Kev. You've got to!"

"Down on the floor!" I gaped, but did as he told me. Carefully, he put the cutter around my shackle, balanced it against one foot, raised his other over the protruding steel arm. "Here we go!" With all his weight, he stomped on the arm.

Snick!

The chain came apart.

I still wore a cuff on each wrist, but no matter. I could use my hands. "A shirt?"

"My room." We raced to the house, up the stairs. He threw me a shirt; I thrust it on, yanked it closed, tabbed it shut.

"How about a jacket or a hat?" Anything, for a disguise.

"Use this." He threw me his coat. It would be too big, but . . .

Pounding at the door.

I froze.

"Oh, God, hide me!"

The smash of glass. Footsteps. We stared, in mutual horror.

The footsteps pounded upstairs. I backpedaled, to the bed.

Kev took a stance before me.

Two men, breathing hard. They crowded into the doorway. "You'll come with us." They brandished stunners.

Behind them, a familiar voice. "Is he there?"

"Yes, Your Reverence."

"Thank Lord God." Scanlen appeared in the hall, behind them. "You led us a merry chase, lad." The deacons closed on me.

Kevin said bravely, "This is a private home. Do you have a warrant? You can't take—"

The bigger of the two deacons backhanded him with the stunner. Dazed, he sank to his knees.

I yelled, "You've no right! I'm a U.N. citizen!" It was worth a try.

"Get him to the rectory." Scanlen's voice was taut. They hesitated. "Right now!"

They hauled me to my feet, dragged me to the door.

"Kev, get word to Seafort! Tell Anth!"

Kevin moaned, looked at his wet hand. Red dripped from his forehead.

"Kev!" In a frenzy, I struck at a deacon.

He smiled through bad teeth, touched the stunner to my side.

12

I GROANED, BLINKED my eyes into focus.

I'd learned something new.

A stunner knocks you out, and you feel nothing. It's the instant before oblivion that's the nightmare; a crackling surge of energy flies up your spine, and for a fleeting moment, you feel as if your head will explode.

I'd never known. I never wanted to know again. Once a lifetime was enough.

I looked about. How long had I been unconscious? It seemed near dusk. An hour or so, if what I'd heard of stunners was true.

I was shackled to an ornately carved wooden chair.

Bishop Scanlen saw me awake, and perched at my side. "Have no fear, lad. You'll be back at the farm shortly. As soon as things settle down."

"Let me go, God—" I took a breath. "God damn it!"

His fist closed, but he made no move to hurt me. A sigh. "We'll have that out of you, be sure. It won't take long."

Inwardly, I flinched. Was the edge of a hoe sharp enough? Would a swift motion slit my throat? I couldn't go back. I mustn't.

Scanlen peered into the hall. "Hambeld, any sign?"

"All quiet, Your Reverence."

"Still, double-lock the door."

"It's already done. Your Reverence, we weren't followed."

I rattled my cuffs. "Why am I so damn important? What do I matter?"

"As a symbol, primarily." Scanlen spoke absently, his mind elsewhere.

"Of what?"

"Arrogance. Yours, Anthony's, the state's. The arrogance of a nation that would live without God's Government. We mustn't allow it."

"I'm a joeykid, for Christ's sake!"

"You'll be whipped for that."

I was too desperate to care. "Answer me!" I tried to work myself free, but the chair arms were solid, unbreakable.

Scanlen sat beside me. "Actually, my boy, I suppose you deserve a response. As you said, you're a joeykid, young, offensive, insolent. Traits many joeys grow out of. But you've a further liability: your family. The Carrs think they're above God, above His Church, and they've raised you to think likewise."

"Nonsense." I had nothing to lose. His deacons would beat me to death, or I'd kill myself fleeing.

"Oh, but it's true. Young Anthony flirts with damnation. He must be stopped, and you're the key."

"We're free! The U.N. and its Church can't—"

"Not for long. It's time this travesty ended. Old Derek was a twisted, evil soul, and led his people to the edge of perdition. But for the mercy of the Patriarchs and their Government . . ."

"Sir?"

"What is it, son?"

"Fuck you, sir."

His glare was like a laser. Almost, I flinched.

"Helis, Your Reverence!" Deacon Hambeld, from the doorway.

"How many?"

"I can't be sure. Several."

"Anthony Carr's militia, no doubt. Leave the door barred. If they gain entry I'll be ready."

"Weapons, sir?"

"Won't be necessary. Not in God's house." Bishop Scanlen strode to his desk, stood behind it.

For a long while, silence. Then, hammering blows, on the locked door. The Bishop raised a hand, staying his deacons.

Silence.

Again, the hammering. "Open!"

No one moved.

A crackle. Hambeld leaped back. "Holy God!" His tone held horror.

The door began to smoke.

My heart thudded. I strained at the chair that bound me.

With a crash, the door fell inward, admitting sound, fury, a dozen armed men.

A voice I knew, from the hall. "It's over. Where's Randolph?"

Deacon Hambeld said, "He's a ward of the Church, beyond your—"

I tried to stand, but couldn't, thwarted by my cuffs. "Here, Anth!" My voice was shrill. "In the study!"

Anthony strode in.

Bishop Scanlen reared. "Out! This is the house of Lord—"

The Stadholder's tone was ice. "Be silent, Mr. Scanlen. You're under arrest for treason."

"Impossible! I am of the Church! By what authority do you—"

"By decree of the Government of the Commonweal of Hope Nation." Anth's fingers flicked to my temple. "Are you hurt?"

"This house is on Cathedral grounds. It's sacred—"

"The Government is in and of the Church, of course. But you've never had diplomatic immunity." He turned. "Lieutenant Skor, take him—"

Scanlen snarled, "The U.N. Navy has no authority here!"

"By our Treaty of Independence, Earth and Hope Nation are pledged to defend the other from attack. I invoked the treaty this afternoon. Ms. Skor, have your men take Scanlen into custody. If any of these—these *persons* interfere, shoot them! Mr. Anselm, call your Captain, tell him Randy's well."

"I'm not." It was a mumble; I didn't know whether he heard.

Anth knelt by my chair, held out his laser. "Look away." He set the beam to low, burned through the narrowest section of the chair arm.

I was freed. For the moment. Scanlen would be back, I was sure of it. I'd never escape his nightmare.

I wrapped myself around Anth.

He tried to free himself, to no avail. In a low voice, he issued terse orders, all the while stroking my flank. Men came and went.

Outside, the hum of another heli. Silence.

Footsteps.

"WHERE IS HE?"

Was it a betrayal that I uncoiled myself from Anth, tried not to tremble?

"I'm sorry, joey." Mr. Seafort loomed in the doorway. "We couldn't find you."

I flew to him. "Sir, I'll do anything you say, wash the decks, work in the galley. I'll call you 'sir' or whatever you want, don't let them take me back to—"

"Randy."

"—begging you!" I sank to my knees. "For the love of God, I can't stand another day of—"

"Randy." Inexorably he hauled me upward. "It's over. I'm sorry it took so long."

"I can't—took me by force, he tried to hang me—"

"I know, joey."

"Please!"

"Anselm, a med tech, and hurry." Mr. Seafort held me close.

"Aye aye, sir." Running steps.

". . . Anything you say!" My voice was muffled. "I'll be your son, I'll—"

"No, joey. Not like this. Not from fear." Fingers brushed my scalp.

A new voice. "Who's injured?"

"He needs a sedative. He's quite beside himself."

"Just a moment."

"The farm. No way to escape. Horrible. You've got to see. Jackie was—"

"Tad, round up the troops. Back to the farm. Armed, as before. Anthony, prepare for two hundred refugees."

"Where?"

"Your house. It's your problem, and should long since have been solved." Mr. Seafort didn't sound sympathetic.

"Don't leave me!" I beat on his chest. "If you go, they'll grab me and—"

A sting. I yelped, pulled away my hand.

"It's all right, son."

"You always say that, but—"

"Truly. It's all right."

And, presently, it was.

Late in the evening, I stared at the floor of the Admiralty House anteroom, too embarrassed to meet Mr. Seafort's eye. "I made a fool of myself." The drugs, whatever they were, had worked wonders. I was now only mildly apprehensive.

"No."

"Kicking and wailing, like a baby joeykid—"

"Oh, stop." His tone held a hint of impatience. "Get it straight, joeyboy. You may act young. You *are* young." A hint of a smile. "We'll talk more on ship, if Admiral Kenzig doesn't break me down to apprentice seaman."

I gulped. "Are you in trouble?"

"Probably." Mr. Seafort didn't seem all that worried. Perhaps reading my mind, he added, "I didn't quite disobey a direct order. He won't courtmartial me. Retirement, at worst, and that's unlikely."

"Why?"

"I might write my memoirs."

I was still puzzling that out when Kenzig's aide saluted stiffly, called him to the Admiral's office.

I fidgeted for the forty-five minutes they were closeted. Mikhael was outside, behind the wheel of an electricar. Apparently he'd been co-opted as his father's driver.

I still didn't have a clear understanding of the affair. From what Mik and the Captain had told me on the drive uptown, Mr. Seafort was somewhat irked to find me missing. At first, no one knew what had happened. It seemed Scanlen had hurried back inside, leaving only when the other guests did.

The next day, the Bishop had revealed his hand. He'd announced that I was where I was supposed to be: on the correctional farm. As our court had given custody of me to the Church, Anthony was powerless to interfere. He told Mr. Seafort, who said nothing, but quietly began rounding up his sailors on leave.

They weren't all that hard to find. After all, beyond Centraltown, how many places did seamen have to visit? The Venturas?

While the Captain was busy organizing, a deacon showed Anth a holo of my near hanging, with a stiff warning to stay out of the situation lest the hanging be made real.

The Stadholder was livid. The Bishop presented certain demands—for what, I didn't know.

They hadn't realized my danger, Mr. Seafort assured me. Not until Anth was shown the holo.

The Stadholder's call reached Mr. Seafort while dining at the spaceport. He rose from his table and strode from the terminal, issuing a stream of orders, commandeering helis, dividing his men into squads. Within minutes, they'd set off for the farm.

It was Mr. Seafort's helis I'd spotted as I fled. They swooped down on the farm to find me gone. Immediately they turned back to Centraltown.

I'd listened to Mr. Seafort's explanation on the drive to Admiralty House. "But how did Anthony know I'd be at Scanlen's home?"

"I read your P and D interrogation. You'd been quite close to Kevin Dakko. I called his father." Mr. Seafort shook his head. "Disgusting. They broke into his house, pistol-whipped his son . . . in the name of Lord God's Church?" He'd turned away, stared moodily out the window.

Now, in the Admiralty House anteroom, I marveled at my good fortune. But for the man I'd tried to kill . . .

"Come along, boy." Mr. Seafort looked weary.

I jumped up. "Is it—" I gestured to the Admiral's office. "—all right?"

"I'm still a Captain, but Mr. Kenzig isn't pleased." I took his hand. "Let's go home."

"Where?"

"*Olympiad.*"

I squeezed his fingers. "Am I still ship's boy?"

"Yes, son. Anthony can't fully protect you yet. Not until . . ." A grimace. "Not yet." We climbed into the car.

"What will . . ." My head spun. "My duties . . ."

"First, to take a bath. Then, to get some sleep."

"Yes, sir." I rested my head on his shoulder.

Mikhael drove us directly onto the tarmac, stopped at the shuttle ladder. Mr. Seafort got out last, stretched, gave the shuttle an apprehensive glance. I recalled he'd once had surgery on his spine.

With reluctant steps he climbed the stairs, halted. "Wait here." He strode to the terminal.

I glanced at the shuttle. "Will they wait?"

"It's a Naval shuttle, laid on especially for us."

"Oh. Where's Tad?"

"Who knows?" Mik yawned. "He'll be on leave again, shortly. For a few days, anyway."

"And you?"

"You colonials are all glitched. I'm going aloft to stay with Pa."

After a time, Mr. Seafort emerged from the terminal. I watched his stride. With a pang, I realized he no longer needed my hand to steady himself.

"There, that's better."

Mikhael asked, "What was so important, Pa?"

"I called Tolliver. I sent him aloft when the fireworks started."

"You're about to see him. What was so impor—"

"Ship's business, I think. Hmm." Absently, Mr. Seafort took my hand, started up the stairs. "No, personal matters." We ducked through the door, found seats, began to buckle in. "I made clear how he was to treat Randy, in case . . ." He hesitated. "In case I don't do well with liftoff."

"Pa!"

"It has to be faced. I think I'll be all right, but . . ." He shrugged. "If the graft separates, paralysis, perhaps. Or . . ."

"Or what?" Mikhael and I spoke as one.

"Death. Is your buckle fastened, Randy? I can't see."

Mikhael unstrapped, hurried to the cockpit. In a few moments he returned.

A smile played about Mr. Seafort's lips. "Feeling better?"

"I told the pilot . . ."

"I can imagine." Mr. Seafort wriggled into a more comfortable position. "It should be all right." His fingers flitted to mine. "If for any reason, it's not so—" A moment's pause "—I love you for your own sake, Randolph. As well as Derek's."

My heart grew to twice its size, and I could say nothing.

The engines whined. We VTOL'd our takeoff. I braced myself, knowing I ought to relax.

The main engines kicked.

A fist slammed me into my seat.

"Pa? Pa, are you all right?" Mikhael thrust past me, floating in the zero gee. I gulped, glad I hadn't eaten since morning.

"Fine, son." Mr. Seafort's voice was like chalk on a board. "It's a bit . . . fine, really."

"Tell me."

I turned my head.

His face was gray, and he took shallow breaths. "We'll see when we get aboard. It . . . hurts."

"There's no God." My tone was savage. "Or He wouldn't allow this!"

"He allows . . . a lot . . . I don't understand." Mr. Seafort's eyes were shut. "Or condone. I've told Him so. Ahh." He winced.

Mikhael swam, handhold to handhold to the cockpit. "Pilot!" He tried to hammer on the hatch, but the first blow pushed him back, and he floated helpless until momentum brought him to the hull. "Pilot!"

The hatch opened.

"Call *Olympiad*. Take us directly to her Level 1 airlock. Have Dr. Romez stand by the hatch."

"Is he—"

"I don't know. Hurry." Using the handhold Mik flipped, kicked himself back to our seats.

I muttered, "It's my fault. If I hadn't gotten in trouble—"

"Randy, shut your mouth or I'll shut it for you." Mik's voice was soft, but had a dangerous edge.

"What did I—"

"The world doesn't revolve around you. Understand? If not, learn it fast. We make choices, we do what we must. We take responsibility. It's being adult. Don't wrap yourself in guilt for what Pa did. Now, be silent!"

Any thoughts of becoming a cadet vanished. I wouldn't want to share a wardroom with him. Life could be hazardous.

Laboriously, the shuttle mated with *Olympiad*'s lock. Dr. Romez came aboard at once. "Can you feel this?" He tapped Mr. Seafort's foot.

"Yes."

"Excellent. And this? Good. The graft is intact. I'll get you on a gurney here, in zero gee. Then we'll wheel you into the lock, where you'll pick up grav."

"I'm no greenie."

"Of course not, sir; I'm a trifle tense. Tolliver's reset the gravitron to one-third gee. Think you can handle it? We can set the gravity off entirely if you'd like."

"Leave it at one gee."

"Not tonight. Pain means damage; I want to get you scanned before we decide. We'll float you toward the lock in a moment."

"Be careful how you bend me."

"Aye aye, sir. Here; this will help." He grasped the Captain's wrist.

"Don't give me meds that—damn!"

"Too late. What a pity. Mr. Tamarov, you'll help?" Together, they maneuvered Mr. Seafort from his seat. He was conscious, but near sleep.

". . . this is over, have to do more high-gee work. Set it at one and a quarter, go to one and a half . . ."

"Right, sir. Watch your head."

After a time, they had him on a gurney. He'd moaned only once. So had I. Gently, they strapped him under the sheet.

"Mik, see Randy's fed and bathed. His old cabin for now. Stay with him 'til he sleeps . . ."

"Yes, sir."

They maneuvered into the lock. Mik and I crowded in. Gravity took hold. Mr. Seafort gasped, clenched his teeth, and made no further sound.

Two med techs were waiting in *Olympiad*'s corridor. With Dr. Romez, they hurried the Captain off to sickbay.

Mik stood watching, his hand around my shoulder.

No one woke me. I slept the night, and half the day.

By afternoon I was up. Unsure what to do, I knocked at Mr. Seafort's hatch. No answer. Back to my cabin. Before the hatch could close, a familiar voice. "Ah, there you are. Come, let's go see Pa."

"Is he better?"

"In a lot of pain, but Romez is hoping he'll heal."

"He doesn't know?" I fell in alongside him. It was odd, trying to walk normally in one-third gee. One, well, overstepped. The body tried to fight a pull that wasn't there. I sort of bobbed along the corridor. Mik did somewhat better.

Shyly, I let Mik guide me into the sickbay. The Captain was scowling at Dr. Romez. ". . . might as well hurt in my own cabin, or on the bridge."

"It's better if you're lying still."

"How do you know?"

The doctor hesitated. "I don't, but . . ." He sighed. "This evening. Stay in bed until then."

"Until dinner, no later. Hello, boys." The Captain studied me with a slight frown. "Randy, you're not in blues." ,

"They cleaned my old clothes, and—"

"You're asking for remission of enlistment?"

"No, sir!" A pang of alarm.

"Put on your uniform. I'll wait."

I scurried back to my cabin, cheeks aflame. I'd let him down. It was a minor thing, but he deserved better.

Five minutes later, I hurried back to sickbay, tugging at my starched new blues.

". . . really ticked off when you wouldn't let me join the squads clearing out the farm."

"It troubles you, Mik?"

I halted outside their cubicle.

"Of course. And I think you knew it."

"Your manner made it clear."

"Sorry, Pa." A pause. "No, sir, I'm not. I'm angry."

"Because I wouldn't risk your life?"

"Am I an officer, or not?"

"I concede the point." A pause, the creak of a bed. "Ahh, a bit better. I shudder to send you in harm's way, Mik. You're truly my son . . . and I can't help thinking about Alexi. To lose you both . . ."

"It's my life to risk. I just finished explaining that to your new . . . protégé."

"I've no choice but to lend the joeykid a hand. I'm responsible for Derek, as for your father."

"Not really, and you know it."

"Well, not in a legal sense. But if I'd asserted myself to prohibit Derek from joining us . . . you know, Mik, the boy's quite desperate for a father. Twice he slipped and called me 'Dad.'"

"Will you adopt him?"

"It's become rather my pattern, hasn't it?" A chuckle. "I'll admit it's done you no harm. But he'd have to agree, and the Stadholder. I doubt his mother will be an obstacle. Poor woman, she's lost in another world."

"Is it what you want?"

"The truth is, I've rather come to like him."

I stirred, suddenly warm.

Mik asked, "Could Randy be ship's boy and live alongside you?"

"Why not? He's still a child, whatever he thinks. Perhaps he'll take to Janey. You're rather old to baby-sit."

"There's always"—Mik's voice was cautious—"her mother."

"Poor Corrine. I'm not very kind to her."

"Randy sat and played with Janey that day I watched her. Made a starship out of her toy holovid. Her barrette was the ship's launch."

I shifted, embarrassed.

"He's not a bad sort, Mik." A pause. "But he's got a lot to learn. For example, when he lurks outside hatchways, he ought to breathe softly, and not shuffle his feet."

A full minute passed before I could bring myself to walk through the hatch.

Father and son regarded me with some disfavor.

"I did it again." I scuffed my shoes.

"Indeed. Why?"

"I dunno." To hear what he thought of me.

"Does my opinion of you matter so?" Had he read my mind?

I'd give anything not to have to answer. "I guess."

"Well, now. Shall I discipline you as your guardian, or as Captain?"

I knew the inside of a cell, and was anxious to avoid it. But as parent . . . a vista opened up, more obscure than I could fathom, frightening as well as alluring. I took a deep breath, knowing he'd slap me, or worse. "As guardian, sir."

"Very well. Go to your cabin, stand in the corner facing the bulkhead until you're sure you won't do it again."

"The corner? I'm way too old for—"

"You're not, and be thankful for it. Go."

Fuming, I stalked back to my cabin.

If I locked the hatch, sat in the chair, no one would know. When someone came, I could jump up and . . .

I sighed. Face it, Randy: do you want his guidance or not? If not, he'll probably let you go.

But you'll need adult permissions for another year or so. Well, more than that; on Hope Nation, as well as Earth, the age of full majority was twenty-two.

Mom's a Limey; she needs more looking after than you. Yet you're more than Anth can handle. So, Mr. Seafort is your only choice. Stop fighting him.

But, standing in the corner? No one ever made you do anything so babyish.

You were ready to die for hurting him. Now you won't stand in a corner for offending him? Do you pretend to have honor?

With a sigh, feeling an idiot, I put myself in the corner of my cabin. How long? Until I was sure, he'd said.

Once before I'd resolved not to spy on Dad—that is, on Mr. Seafort. I'd meant it, too. So how could I be sure?

The bulkhead was steel-gray. Here and there, irregularities in its finish caught the eye. To my right was the built-in dresser. On it was—no. He'd bade me face the bulkhead. That meant looking at the wall, and nothing else. Do it right, or sit down and know you're a fraud.

I shifted from foot to foot, growing ever more impatient. I'd give him an hour. Not a moment more.

Time slowed, until I could barely stand it. My eye roved the speckles in the bulkhead. I thrust hands in pockets, thrust out my jaw.

At last, an hour. My calves ached.

Was I sure?

Another hour.

Eons later, the hatch opened. Mr. Seafort, in a wheelchair. A vein in his temple pulsed, but his tone was affable enough. "Ready for dinner?"

I turned back to the bulkhead. "No, sir."

"Why not?"

Shame, rage, sheer mulishness. "I'm still not sure."

"Very well, son." And he was gone.

I favored one leg, then another; my back ached as well as my calves. Would I spy on him again? Probably not; I wanted to be better than I was. I owed it to Dad and Mr. Seafort. To myself too, if truth be told.

The evening was endless.

What point in torturing myself? Almost, I gave it up. A little while longer . . .

Like a baby, I cried some, hating myself for it.

At length, well past my usual bedtime, I could stand it no more. I sagged, hobbled to the chair, massaged my legs.

I went to his cabin, knocked softly, lest he be asleep.

My eyes were red.

He sat in a straight chair, Janey on his lap. "Yes, son?"

"I'm sure. I won't do it again."

"Excellent. Go to the galley, tell them I said to give you a meal. Then go to bed."

"Yes, sir." I turned to go.

"Come here." Puzzled, I bent over his chair. He enveloped me in a hug.

Afterward, trudging back from the galley, I marveled at the man into whose hands I'd fallen. He chastised me like a baby, yet trusted me as an adult to carry out my punishment. Then hugged me like a joeykid.

My head spinning, I fell into my bunk.

* * * *

The next days were a blur. Crewmen began to drift back from shore leave; the pace of shipboard life quickened. Alejandro, on orders from above, took me through the massive ship, showing and explaining every compartment. Slowly I learned my way about. Every day I had to don a fresh uniform; when I didn't, Mr. Seafort was quite sharp about it. He made sure my cabin was stocked with a supply of blues and grooming accessories.

Then he decided I needed my hair cut—it looked fine, but there was no arguing with him—so off I went to the barber.

I helped squads stow cargo and supplies. Well, I didn't actually help them load, but I ran to fetch manifest chips, tie-downs, replacement lights.

Mr. Seafort abandoned his wheelchair, but walked slowly, with a hint of unspoken pain. Mr. Tolliver—the Captain had heard me refer to him as "Tolliver," and brought me up short—took up much of the burden, helping handle problems, such as smuggling, caused by the end of shore leave. As I began to see how doggedly he protected Mr. Seafort, my dislike of him eased. His acid manner made it easier; I rather liked the carefully concealed humor behind it.

Meanwhile, I discovered there were no such items as hatch solvents or cargo diffusers. I plotted dark revenge against the sailors who'd sent me on fool's errands, until Mik explained it was a form of teasing, that it prefaced their accepting me as one of their own.

In the evenings, a trifle lonely, I wandered the lounges with Alec, or went to Mr. Seafort's cabin. Our second day, he'd sat me down, made clear the difference between on-watch and off-duty times; during the latter I was welcome without invitation. I checked with Mikhael to see if he meant it; Mik shook his head, told me the question was absurd.

In the Captain's cabin, I taught Janey games or toyed with a holo. At least once each day, though, Mr. Seafort bade me sit with him at his gleaming table. In what I soon recognized as a ritual, he brought out a worn leather Bible, made me open it, and read aloud.

There seemed to be no pattern to the passages we selected. Mostly, he left it up to me, objecting only when I stumbled onto Numbers, and its interminable Hebrew census. "They may all be Lord God's words, but some are of more interest than others."

Suppressing a sigh, I flipped the pages, settled on Job. *"I know it is so of a truth: but how should man be just with God? If he will contend with him, he cannot answer him one of a thousand."*

"Aye, there's the rub. He writes the rules, and makes all the answers." Mr. Seafort shut his eyes. *"He is wise in heart, and mighty in strength: who hath hardened himself against him, and hath prospered?"*

I put my finger in the book to hold my place, and closed it. "Is that what you did?"

"It's what I still do." He stirred himself. "Read on."

My immersion in Scripture never lasted more than an hour. Often, he brewed hot tea while I read, and offered me a cup. Out of courtesy I drank it, afraid I'd develop a taste for the bitter liquid.

Occasionally, afterward, I sat cross-legged in my cabin, musing about the changes in my life. For the time being, I was barred from Carr Plantation, even from Centraltown. *Olympiad* was due to sail to Kall's Planet, then to Earth, which I'd never seen. I could lose myself in her crew, devote myself to the U.N. Navy. Mr. Seafort would keep an eye on me, one way or another. Soon I'd grow up, become the adult I'd once imagined I already was.

At fourteen, did I need a parent? Want one? Despite Mr. Seafort's assumption of what I wanted, I intended to decide for myself.

I stared into Dad's holo—the last he'd had taken, before his ill-fated journey—and asked myself the same question, over and again.

I was afraid of the answer.

13

I RAN MY HANDS through my hair, tucked in my shirt, anxious to look my best. When they strode through the airlock I stepped forward casually. "Welcome aboard, sir," I said to Chris Dakko. "Captain Seafort sent me to greet you."

"Did he." Mr. Dakko's face was impassive.

"Yes, sir, I'm crew now. Ship's boy. Kevin, welcome aboard."

"Thank you." Kev seemed distant, but I noticed he'd looked me over carefully. I was glad my shoes were polished, my shirt fresh-creased. For the moment, I didn't even begrudge Mr. Seafort my haircut.

As we were still in port, Mr. Seafort had decreed he'd meet our guests on the bridge, walk with them to Dining Hall. I gathered that while under way, neither passengers nor crew could approach the bridge. I wondered if that would include me.

The Dakkos had come aboard at the Level 2 lock. *Olympiad* was so large we were secured to the Station at three separate locks, on three Levels.

As bidden, I escorted our guests along the corridor. Lieutenant Anselm—it was no longer proper to call him "Tad"—had been teaching me to stand at attention and salute; on the bridge I gave it my best attempt, and was rewarded with an approving smile, hastily extinguished, from the Captain. Mr. Tolliver, in the watch officer's seat, merely glowered a bit less strongly than usual.

To my surprise, I wasn't dismissed; Mr. Seafort clapped a hand on my shoulder while engaging in polite chat with Mr. Dakko, then gently propelled me in Kevin's direction.

"So." The toe of Kev's polished shoe toyed with the decking. "You all right?"

The adults were talking, pointing at the simulscreen.

"Yeah." I hesitated. "You still mad at me?"

"I ought to be." He reddened. "Those weeks in a cell were horrid." Then, "You recovered from the Church farm?"

I nodded. "You saved my life."

"Seafort did."

"You told him where to find me."

"Let's stop the bullshit." Determinedly, he met my eye. "You've been a really good friend. I'm sorry . . . things got messed up."

"I messed them up."

For a moment we regarded each other. Then his hand came out.

Fervently, I took his grip.

"Ready, boys?" Genially, Mr. Seafort steered me to the corridor. I walked with him, slowly, down the ladder to the Dining Hall. Kevin shot me a glance from time to time. He was wearing his best clothes, no doubt under his father's prodding, and was carefully showing off his good manners. A fading bruise was the only reminder of the deacons' assault.

By now a number of passengers had come aboard, though the hall was far from crowded and many tables remained empty. At our table, Mr. Seafort pulled out a seat for me, so I knew I was expected to join them. Tad, er, Mr. Anselm, came down too, and of course Mikhael.

I looked about. More officers were present than at previous meals. Some of the passengers were new arrivals—I'd seen them boarding—others were bound for Kall's Planet, and had returned a bit early from Centraltown.

As usual, dinner started with salad, served on a chilled plate. Mikhael had told me that, under way, our evening meal was opened by the Ship's Prayer, but in accordance with some ancient tradition it was dispensed with in port.

"So, Captain, how many of your crew are aboard?" It was Mr. Dakko's attempt to revive the faltering conversation.

"Some three hundred. Little more than a third." Mr. Seafort broke a roll. "Astonishing, isn't it? *Hibernia* had a crew of seventy. Who'd have thought . . ."

"Is it progress?" Mr. Dakko looked glum. "The economics that result in behemoths such as *Olympiad* only perpetuate your stranglehold on shipping."

"Our ships are expensive," the Captain said.

I recalled that Mr. Seafort had been SecGen during their construction.

Mr. Dakko said, "Far beyond the resources of even the most prosperous colony."

"But they serve many roles. Defense, for example—"

"Sir, we no longer *need* defense. The fish are long gone. In fact, it's your Navy we need protection from. The coup on Earth—"

"Attempted coup."

Mr. Dakko lowered his voice. "Scanlen and his ilk—" he looked about "—they're a product of the same reactionary thinking as—"

Alarms shrieked. I sat bolt upright.

"*General Quarters! Man Battle Stations!*" Tolliver's voice was taut. Officers threw down their napkins, ran to the hatch. "*Captain to the bridge!*"

Mr. Seafort leaped from his chair, turned gray. I rushed to his side. He threw an arm over me, not from affection, but for support. "Lord Christ, that hurt. Randy, walk me to the bridge. Hurry!"

"*Seal all locks! Prepare for breakaway!*"

We were halfway to the corridor. At the table, Kevin clutched his silverware, aghast.

"*Engine Room, full power to thrusters.*"

We made our way, slowly. Mr. Dakko slid back his chair, half ran to catch us. He came up on Mr. Seafort's other side. "If you'll allow me, sir?" He offered a shoulder.

A second's hesitation. The Captain nodded.

"*Disengage capture latches.*"

Mr. Dakko threw the Captain's other arm across his own shoulder, wrapped a supporting hand about his waist. Together, we walked Mr. Seafort rapidly along the corridor.

Tolliver had kept the bridge hatch open; as we entered his eyebrow raised but he said nothing.

"Edgar, report!" Mr. Seafort eased himself into his seat.

By way of answer, Mr. Tolliver dialed up the magnification of the simulscreen.

Half a dozen comm satellites lay outward of the Station, in geosync, within a few kilometers.

Just beyond them floated a form I'd seen only in history holos.

A fish.

* * * *

"Jesus, Lord Christ." Mr. Seafort's voice was a whisper. "They're dead. I killed them all."

Mr. Dakko's mouth worked. His fists clenched and unclenched. The alien floated before us, looking for all the world like a giant goldfish. No fins, of course, and no head, but . . .

For a long moment Mr. Seafort sat frozen, as if afraid. Then he shook himself. "Is the Pilot aboard?"

"No, sir."

"Just our luck." He keyed his caller. "Airlock Three, report."

"Confirm hatches sealed, sir. Capture latches disengaged."

"Airlock Two?"

"Sealed, sir. And disengaged."

"Airlock One?"

"Sealed, sir. Latches . . . there. Disengaged." On the Captain's console, three lights blinked green.

"Station, *Olympiad* is casting off. Commencing breakaway." A deep breath. Another. Mr. Seafort nudged his thrusters. Then again.

I stared at the simulscreen. Slowly, as if in a dream, the Station began to recede.

I moved closer to Mr. Dakko, afraid to breathe.

"Edgar, take the conn."

At the watch officer's console, Mr. Tolliver's hands flew to the thrusters. "Where to, sir?"

"Jess, course to the enemy?"

"Enemy, sir?"

"The fish, you bloody circuit board!"

"Coordinates 350, 18, 207."

"I'm sorry."

Silence.

"Jess, that was to you. I'm sorry."

"Noted, Captain. Dialogue stored for further reference. Distance two point seven three five kilometers."

"Laser room, report."

"Laser room here, sir. Lieutenant Frand." She sounded calm enough, under the circumstances. "I have Midshipman Sutwin and two ratings. That's it." Everyone else was groundside, on shore leave.

"How many consoles manned?"

"Three, sir. The middy's on one. I can take a fourth."

"Do so." Mr. Seafort keyed the caller. "Midshipman Clark, Midshipman Tamarov, to the laser room, flank." To Tolliver, "They're good for a console each."

Tolliver grunted. "I'm good for another."

"I need you here. Where's Tad stationed?"

"Comm room."

"They can spare him."

"I'm on it." Tolliver snatched up his caller, issued terse orders transferring Anselm to the laser room.

"Laser room, safeties are off." The Captain slid a finger down the console screen. "Jess, Fusion safety?"

"Calculating. Five hours seventeen minutes six—"

"Damn, we're massive."

I tried to recall my physics. Fusion safety was ship's mass times distance from a gravitational source large enough to . . . my head spun. I'd barely passed that study unit.

"We're in range, sir." Tolliver.

"We'll hold our fire."

"Why?"

"Because I said so. How many consoles manned?"

"Six, sir."

"Out of twenty-four." The Captain's tone was grim. "We haven't much defense. Make sure that no matter what, we man the laser banks guarding the fusion tubes." Then, "If we retreat, the Station's unprotected."

"They have lasers."

"Not enough. Of course, neither have we. With so many techs ashore, our grid is pitiful. If the fish had only waited a few days . . ."

"*Orbit Station to Olympiad.*"

"What is it, Station?"

"*General Thurman here. Our laser defense is fully manned. Have your puter coordinate with us by tightbeam.*"

"Done. Jess, coordinate as he asked."

Mr. Dakko shook himself. "Sir?" His tone was tentative.

"Not now, Chris."

"I could man a console. You taught me yourself."

"*Olympiad, we've dispatched all shuttles groundside. Withholding fire at the fish until they reach the atmosphere.*"

Mr. Seafort swung his chair, stared through Mr. Dakko, his brow knotted. Then, "Very well. Randy, show him the way."

"Aye aye, sir." A proper response; if ever I was on duty, it was now. "Mr. Dakko?" With feverish haste, I led him to the stairwell, down to Level 3, to section seven, halfway around the lengthy corridor. It was all I could do not to run.

I rapped on the laser room's closed hatch. Lieutenant Frand opened. I saluted. "The Captain sent Mr. Dakko to take a console."

She looked past me, over my shoulder. "You're Navy?"

"Former. I don't believe the consoles have changed much."

"Come in."

Mr. Dakko brushed past me without a word of thanks. The hatch shut in my face. Disconsolate, not knowing if I had an assigned duty station, I made my way back to the bridge.

No one had bothered to reclose the hatch. I crept in.

On the simulscreen, the alien loomed. It appeared to be lying dead in space, but on its surface colors pulsed. It still lived.

"Surely it sees us." Tolliver.

The Captain said, "It's making no move to throw." In the holos I'd seen, the fish would grow an appendage, a ropy arm, that spun slowly at first, then faster, until it detached and spewed acid onto its target.

"Shoot, sir."

"This is Thurman. We're taking the shot."

"No, wait—"

I watched the simulscreen in horrified fascination. But you can't see a laser.

A hole appeared in the fish's side. Something—blood, protoplasm—spewed.

The fish pulsed, disappeared.

I crowed, "They got him!"

Tolliver whirled. "Be silent!"

Minutes stretched into a quarter hour, a half. I tried not to fidget.

Tolliver said, "All shuttles are groundside; we can call up our crew."

"They're scattered throughout the continent."

"Not really, sir. Get word out in Centraltown—"

"And if fish attack an incoming shuttle?"

"Christ, that would be a horror."

"Don't blaspheme."

From Tolliver, a grunt.

The Captain said, "No doubt Thurman's already told the Stadholder, but have our comm room send him confirmation. And ask Admiralty House to round up our crew. First chance we get, we'll call them aloft."

"Aye aye, sir." Then, "This is the first fish seen in ages. Why now?"

"Lord only knows."

No. They were wrong.

I hesitated; they'd ordered me to be silent. But they had to be told. A deep breath, before the plunge. "Begging your pardon, sir. But a fish was seen a few weeks ago. I'm sorry I spoke." Inwardly, I cringed, bracing for their explosion.

Mr. Seafort's expression was odd. "Where, Randolph?"

"Near Three. A local mining ship."

"Randy, are you making this up? Do you need attention?"

I said indignantly, "No, sir. Ask Mr. Anselm or Mik—Mr. Tamarov. They heard. Groundside, at the terminal. The naval desk, the day I met them. They were joking about local officers and—" I was babbling; I clamped my lips shut.

Mr. Seafort keyed his caller. "Lieutenant Anselm to the bridge." He put his fingers together. "Fish, in system, and I wasn't told?"

It wasn't long before Tad appeared, breathless. He confirmed what I'd said.

"That fish by Three, did it throw?"

"I heard this thirdhand, sir, from an Admiralty clerk. It was gossip about a local ship. Everyone discounted the report; why would a fish confront us without throwing?"

"Very well. Thank you. Dismissed." Mr. Seafort took the caller. "Now we ask Thurman."

It took an hour or so, but finally we had the story: an intrastellar ship, a green comm crew. Had they seen a fish, or an unidentified blip? They used their only laser, and the object disappeared. They'd made a report, but it was played down. No, discounted entirely. No one wanted to look foolish. And no fish had been seen in decades.

Tolliver said, "Sir, if they're back . . ."

An alarm clanged; Jess came to life. "Encroachment, three hundred meters to port! Nonmetallic. Closing seven meters per second, advise—"

"Tolliver, fire portside thrusters. Get us out of here! Laser room, do you have a shot?"

"Switching consoles, sir. A few seconds." Ms. Frand sounded harried.

Tolliver urged, "Shoot the moment we're able, sir."

"We'll have to. He's too close."

Tolliver rammed the thrusters to full, but the fish had brought its own inertia. It gained on us.

Its skin seemed to swirl, become indistinct.

"Sir, it's forming an—"

"I see it." The Captain's voice was grim. His fingers stabbed at the console. "All personnel to suits! Closing corridor hatches." The bridge hatch slammed shut behind me.

Each circumference corridor was interspersed with hatches, at the end of every section. When closed, they blocked movement through the corridors. For that reason, even at Battle Stations, they were kept open.

But if corridor hatches were closed, a breach in the hull wouldn't decompress more than one section.

A chill ran down my spine.

"WE HAVE A SHOT!" Ms. Frand's voice rattled the speaker.

"Take it!"

A figure grew from the swirling hole in the fish's skin, separated. It launched itself at *Olympiad*.

The fish spewed a hole, then another. A third.

Mr. Seafort pounded the console. "Get the outrider! All lasers open fire, flank!"

The swirling shape that had detached from the fish sailed closer. Abruptly, it flew apart. Feverishly our laser beams sought and destroyed its remnants.

Behind it, the skin of the fish was gray and still.

Tolliver's tone was dry. "I thought those days were behind us."

"Lord preserve us." Mr. Seafort let out a long breath. He turned, saw me. "Get into your suit!"

My voice quavered. "I don't know how, sir."

Tolliver was out of his seat. "I'll dress him." He threw open a locker, found a small suit—they came in three sizes—and lifted my leg, guided it to the torso opening. I struggled to help.

"You too, Edgar."

"The moment you do, sir."

"I choose not."

"Then so do I."

"I'll pass out if I try to contort myself. Get yourself suited."

Tolliver's tone was reluctant. "Aye aye, sir." With effort, he got me buckled in. "Here's your helmet, boy." He plopped it on my head, checked the seals. "See that green light? When it turns yellow, switch tanks."

"How?"

"I'll have to show you." Swiftly, he donned his own suit. "Captain, we can't stay suited." Tolliver's voice was muffled. "It'll be hot, and everyone's tanks will need changing. How long must we . . ."

" 'Til it's likely they're not coming back."

"And when do we decide that?" Tolliver trudged back to his seat. "Did you notice something odd, sir?"

"What?"

"It didn't form a throwing arm. That's their primary weapon for ship-to-ship combat. Why not use it?"

"No one wrote us an instruction manual on fish, Edgar."

"And what's it doing here? We know they're summoned by Fusion, but no one's Fused."

"We did, to get here."

"Weeks ago, only once. If they're back, why wouldn't they go to home system?"

"Perhaps they have." The Captain's tone was bleak. He leaned back, closed his eyes.

"Can I get you anything, sir?" I raised my voice, to be heard through the helmet. A stupid question; there was nothing I could do to help, save stay out of the way, avoid bothering him.

"Yes, my boy. Coffee, from the officers' mess. I'll open hatches for you."

"Aye aye, sir." I tried to keep the astonishment from my tone. I clambered through the hatchway, along the silent, empty corridor. Thanks to Alejandro, I knew the way. Where was his battle station? I'd have to ask. Perhaps it was mine.

At the mess the pot was half full, and warm. Awkwardly, through my thick gloves, I poured a cup. He took it black, I'd seen. I trudged back to the bridge. Too bad I had a mere vacuum suit, not a thrustersuit. In the holos, heroic spacemen zoomed back and forth from ship to launch, propelled by their thruster tanks.

I handed Mr. Seafort the coffee. Inside my suit I was sweating freely. I longed for cool ship's air. On the simulscreen, the dead fish floated, evil and menacing.

"Thank you." He sipped. "Lord God, son, I never meant to drag you into this."

"I don't mind, sir." To my utter amazement, it was true. I ought to be afraid; we were in deadly peril. On the other hand, I had a place on *Olympiad*, an apprenticeship I rather liked.

Strange, the things one thinks of, at a time like this.

I had a job. A guardian. A home.

An hour later, Mr. Seafort released us from our suits. I found mine easier to get out of than into. Mr. Tolliver made me hang it properly, in the bridge's storage locker. No sooner did I breathe a sigh of relief than the alarms screamed anew. The bridge hatch slammed closed. Another fish.

Within seconds the laser room lined up a shot. It looked like they got him; he—it—disappeared from the screen.

Tolliver and the Captain exchanged glances. "Now what?"

"We wait."

No suits, thank heaven, but a full four hours on high alert. I found it astonishing how quickly danger transformed into boredom. I didn't dare ease myself into a watch chair, even if the middies of the watch weren't present. Instead, behind the console seats, I quietly settled on the deck, knees drawn up. There was little to do but watch the simulscreen. I wasn't sure either Mr. Tolliver or the Captain remembered I was there, or how they'd react when they found out. Still, I hadn't been ordered elsewhere.

Tolliver said tentatively, "We could begin ferrying crew aloft, sir."

"Not while fish are about. The shuttles are defenseless."

"There's none here now."

"Damn it, Edgar!" Mr. Seafort slammed the padded arm of his chair. Then his lips moved silently. "Amen. Sorry. Nerves."

"My point's still valid."

"In the war, they went for lifepods and launches. All it takes is one fish at a shuttle, and we cause a horrid disaster."

"Sir, one fish at our fusion tubes, and the Navy's finest ship is gone."

"This isn't like the old days, Edgar. We've more banks of lasers defending the tubes than any other sector—"

"Good. We can defend ourselves while sailing to Fusion safety."

"They're acting strangely. If we flee, we won't know why."

"We don't need to know."

"And a flotilla of fish can take out a Station."

"Believe me, sir, I recall it well. Just promise me, no nukes this time."

"That's not funny, Edgar."

"It wasn't meant to be."

The speaker came to life. "Laser room to Bridge, Lieutenant Frand reporting."

"Go ahead."

"Mr., ah, Dakko is inquiring about his son. You left him in Dining Hall. He'd like leave to see him."

"We can't spare him from the console. Let them visit in the corridor outside the laser room. Send someone to fetch—"

"I'm here, sir." My voice was too shrill, and Mr. Seafort jumped.

"Very well. Randy, find young Mr. Dakko. I might as well reopen corridor hatches; we can shut them rapidly enough if needed. Get Kevin from the Dining Hall, take him below to the laser room. He's not to go in; make sure Lieutenant Frand knows that."

"Aye aye, sir." I was proud of my response. It was becoming ever more natural.

"Good lad. Hurry, now."

"And after?"

He hesitated, ever so slightly. "Report back here."

"Yes, sir."

"It's still 'Aye aye, sir.' "

"Aye aye, sir." Blushing, I made my exit.

Without the burden of a vacuum suit, the corridor hatches opened, my trek was a pleasure. I'd been told never to run, but the corridor was deserted; officers and crew hadn't been piped down from Battle Stations. I loped past the stairwell, past the armory, the officers' mess, skidded to a stop at the ornate hatch of the Level 2 Dining Hall.

No one had told the passengers to return to their cabins; they clustered about the tables, standing, sitting, talking anxiously.

Kevin sat at the table that had been the Captain's, hunched over, staring at the deck, twisting a napkin. My shadow fell over him. He looked up, his eyes bleak. "Is Dad all right?"

"Mr. Dakko? Sure. He's asking for you. Come on."

I led him to the corridor, toward the stairwell.

"Isn't he on the bridge?"

"Nope, the laser room. We were short on laser techs."

"He's shooting fish?" Kev sounded incredulous.

"Sure. He's an old Navy hand." We ran down to Level 3.

Section seven was almost halfway around the disk. A long hike, in a ship the size of *Olympiad*.

Kev glanced at my uniform, somewhat wilted after an hour in a suit. "So . . . you like it here?"

I tried to sound nonchalant. "Kinda." We passed through section five. I grimaced. I wasn't being honest. Besides, why hide it? Without Kev's help I'd be in torment on the Bishop's training farm. "It's great. Mr. Seafort has—"

Alarms suddenly shrieked; a red bulb at the hatch panel blinked. The section hatch slid shut. I whirled, hoping we could get through before it locked, but the corridor hatch seal hissed into place.

"*Stand by for attack! Laser room, fire!*"

"Oh, shit." I didn't know I'd spoken aloud.

"*Attention all passengers and crew.*" Mr. Seafort's voice was taut. "*A fish just Defused meters from the hull, within our circle of fire. An outrider is emerging.*"

"What the hell does that mean?"

"Easy, Kev."

"*All hands to suits! If it melts through the hull, a section will decompress.*"

Kevin shook me. "Get us suits!"

"I don't know where!" No one had told me yet.

"Find them, you stupid—"

Did each section have a suit locker? I couldn't remember. Alec was barely twelve, and his instruction was a bit haphazard. I ran to the end of the section. No locker. Perhaps the other way . . . I cannoned into Kevin, dashing after me.

I picked myself up, raced to the closed section-four hatch.

"*Outrider launched!*"

I threw open a locker. "Here!" I hauled out a suit.

New alarms clanged. *"Hull breach imminent, Levels 2 and 3! Decompression alert, Level 2, sections four through seven!"*

"Christ, that's us!" I tossed a suit to Kevin.

"How do you . . ." He trailed off. A moan.

I followed his gaze. Smoke curled from a patch of bulkhead. An acrid odor drifted across the corridor.

"COME ON!" Dropping the useless suit, I dived for a cabin. It was locked. I tried the next. Locked. A third—

The hatch slid open. "Kev, move!" I hauled him through, pounded on the hatch control.

A puff of air. A wind, as the hatch slid shut.

We were in an empty cabin, cleaned and ready for its occupant.

The hatch panel warning light blinked red.

Outside our refuge, section five was decompressed.

They'd told me cabin hatches were airtight. Unconsciously, I held my breath, waiting to find out. Dad had died in just the same circum—

DON'T THINK OF IT!

Kevin, his face pale, made himself small in a corner. He chewed at a fingernail.

The Captain's voice blared on the cabin speaker.

"Decompression Level 2 section five! Master-at-arms Janks to section four, flank! Fully armed and suited. Class A decontamination procedures. Evacuate the section, we'll make it an airlock to five."

I roused myself. The other night, exploring my own cabin, I'd found two suits in a locker by the closet. Every cabin was supposed to have them. I threw open the closet hatch, hauled them out.

"Quick!" I thrust in a leg, realized I was trying to don the suit backward. "Kev, get moving!" I had my legs in, twisted wildly, managed to fit in an arm. The suit was way too big, designed for a large adult.

In slow motion, Kevin picked up his suit. "Where's my father?"

"Laser room."

"Take me there."

"When it's safe. Hurry. If that beast burns through . . ." I got my other arm in.

Kev stood helplessly, holding his suit.

I needed my helmet. We might decompress at any moment. But if I sealed my helmet, I'd never move well enough to help him. Cursing, I tossed it on the bed. "Your foot goes in like this . . ." My hands were almost useless, working through the thick gloves. Why had no one ever designed a convenient pressure suit? "Now the other. That's it, joey." My voice was soothing, as Mr. Seafort's had been. I thrust aside the thought. "Hurry, Kev. Bend your arm, this way. We'll be all right. Now the other."

His helmet was still in the locker; I grabbed mine, thrust it on his head. "This twists on, and then those clamps . . ." In a moment it was done. Thank Lord God, Mr. Tolliver had shown me how.

I scrambled to the locker, fell on my face. Walking was harder in a suit, I knew that. Think, Randy. No time for panic. I fished out the helmet, and two spare tanks. The locker held four spares in total.

I pulled on my helmet. "Kev, I'll check your clamps, you check mine. We have to get it right the first time."

"Mr. Janks, section five camera shows an outrider roaming the corridor. It's burned into a handful of cabins. Use extreme caution. Is section four evacuated?"

"Checking the last cabin, sir."

A muffled voice. Then, *"What? No, Mr. Dakko. I don't know. Mr. Janks, is the ship's boy with you? Mr. Carr, or his friend?"*

"No, sir."

"I think they're tight, Kev. Is your tank light green?"

"Which one—"

"Inside the faceplate, left side."

"When we open, if you see a suited figure . . ." A long pause. *"No, first priority is the outrider. Kill it at all costs."* Mr. Seafort's voice was heavy.

"Even if . . ."

"At all costs."

Mesmerized, I stared at the hatch, the caller, the bulkhead, waiting for acrid smoke to curl in our precious air.

All we could do was wait.

"Captain, Lawson is on his way back from the armory with laser rifles. If you give us another minute . . ."

"Very well."

Kevin's cheeks were wet.

Randy, you idiot, *the caller.* I snatched it up, in clumsy fingers. How does one call the bridge? How does one call anywhere? No one had taught me the system yet. Wait. I'd once called the purser. There was a button . . . there.

A buzz. Nothing. Then, miraculously, as if it were an ordinary day, "Purser's office." The voice was faint.

All I could do was shout through my helmet. "This is Carr! Connect me to the bridge!"

"Who?"

"Randy Carr, the new ship's boy!"

Clicks. A pause.

"Bridge. Seafort." I could barely hear through the hindrance of the helmet.

"Sir, it's Randy. I'm in—"

"Thank God!"

"—a cabin in section five."

"Are you suited?"

"Yes. So is Kev."

"Which cabin?"

"I dunno!"

"Look on the control panel."

I did. I ran back to the caller, feeling an idiot. "Two fifty-seven, sir!"

"Randy . . ." His voice was quiet. "The corridor camera shows the outrider just outside your hatch."

I whimpered.

"It may burn through to the cabin. Both of you, squeeze into the closet, shut the door. Master-at-arms, are you ready?"

"We've a dozen lasers aimed at the section hatch. Willnet's squad is guarding the section six hatch, just in case."

"They skitter fast, Mr. Janks. Don't let it get you."

"I can't hide, sir! Not if I . . ." I gulped. "I can't let go of the caller." To die was one thing. To die alone was quite another.

"Use your radio."

"Radio?"

Lord knew what effort it required, but Mr. Seafort made his voice calm. "Look to the belt at your waist. See the pad? Use frequency seven. Turn it on. Speak into the faceplate."

"Like this?"

"No need to shout." His voice echoed, close and reassuring. I dialed down the volume, ran to Kev, made the same adjustments on his belt as on mine. "Kev, hide in the closet. Captain's orders."

He swallowed. "It's dark there." He sounded like a small child.

"Hurry." I pulled his gloved hand.

There was barely room for both of us. If I squeezed in first, I doubted I could coax Kevin in. I tugged at him, maneuvered him into the storage space.

The cabin bulkhead began to smoke.

"Randy, hide! Janks, I'm opening the corridor hatch for you. Hurry!"

The alumalloy bulkhead plate dissolved. A whoosh of escaping air, then absolute silence, save for the frantic sawing of my breath.

A form quivered at the entry.

Desperately I pushed Kev deeper into the closet; there wasn't space to shut the door.

"There he is! Fire!" I couldn't be hearing the speaker; there was no air. It must be my radio.

The bulkhead hole enlarged; the form spurted through. The torn bulkhead glowed red from laser strikes.

"Mr. Seafort, it's in the cabin with the boys! I've no shot without hitting them!"

I squeezed my fists, summoning the dregs of my courage. "Sir, take the shot! Kill it!"

"Janks, what's it doing?"

"I can't get too close without . . . it's standing there, sir."

"Hold your fire."

"You said . . . first priority was . . ."

"I know, but . . . wait. If it moves toward the boys, toward the bulkhead, anywhere, burn it. But if you can save our joeys . . ."

The outrider stood no more than three steps from me. Stood? It had no feet, nothing remotely like them. Colors swirled in its suit. No, in its skin. I'd read that in biology, years ago.

The alien form quivered. In an instant it would skitter our way, and overwhelm me. I'd feel the touch of acid as my suit dissolved, then nothing.

Abruptly it changed shape, seemed to shrink. Was it burning through the deck? It didn't seem so.

Kevin gripped my shoulder. "I'm sorry. You're not stupid. I don't know why I said it. I really like you." His voice was soft in my radio, though the alien couldn't possibly hear him in vacuum.

The alien quivered. Its outer skin bulged, extended toward us.

"Not like this." A sob. "I can't die in a closet." Kev tried to squeeze through.

It made no sense. "Mr. Seafort!" I braced myself in the closet doorway.

"I hear him. Hold on, Kevin. We're trying—just a—" A click. Silence. Kevin hammered at my shoulder blades.

"Captain, Janks here. Any shot that hits that—that—thing will go right through it and . . ."

With a frenzied effort, Kev twisted past me, faced the shifting figure. Desperately, I wrapped myself around his leg. "Mr. Seafort, I can't hold him—"

"Kevin?" An agonized voice. *"Kev, this is Dad!"*

"Daddy, it's just staring at me. No eyes, but I know it sees me. You know what?"

"What, son?"

"I'm not brave enough." He sounded hurt, puzzled. "I guess we'll never have a fleet. I'm . . . so sorry, Dad."

"Don't do anything stupid—"

A wrench, that nearly undid my grip. "Mr. Seafort, Kev's pulling us toward—"

"*Janks, take the shot!*" The Captain.

"*KEVIN! I LOVE YOU SO—*"

"Daddy!" A frantic kick. He slipped out of my grasp, made a shooing motion at the outrider.

The alien be damned. I launched myself from the closet, wrapped myself around Kevin's neck. "*No, Kev!*"

He threw me off, aimed a wild kick at the quivering form. "Out!" His boot grazed the alien's midsection.

The outrider convulsed, flowed toward Kev.

He screamed, fell back atop me.

"*Fire!*"

A whine in my suit speaker. A half-dozen holes pierced the alien form. It flew apart. Protoplasm flew past my faceplate, sizzled on the deck. I shrieked.

Kev bucked and heaved. His elbow slammed into my gut; even through the stiff suit it caught me a mighty blow. We toppled.

A shuddering gasp.

"*Where's my son? Captain, what's happened to Kev?*"

"*I'm not sure, Chris.*"

"*Save him, God damn you!*"

Slowly, almost deliberately, I got to my feet. My visor was fogged; my vehement exercise had overtaxed the cooling. I pounded the hatch control. The hatch opened.

On my radio, chatter, incoherent shouts, but I no longer listened. Carefully, I edged my way around the blobs of alien protoplasm, past white plastiflex boots.

I keyed my radio. "Ship's Boy Carr reporting. To the bridge." My voice sounded odd, even to myself.

"*Randy—*"

"I'm out of the cabin. My tank light is yellow. The outrider is . . . dead. Kevin's . . . lying down. What do I do now, sir?"

"*Janks, Class A decon!*"

"*Aye aye, sir. We'll slap on a hull patch, flank, and re-air the section. Set up section four for full decon!*" It sounded like an order.

"*Get to it.*"

"Sir?" My voice was shrill. Odd, but my hand was shaking. Nerves. I was all right, I thought. "That outrider?"

"It's dead, son. Stay where you are, Mr. Janks will come for you."

"Yes, sir. I mean, aye aye, sir." There was something else I wanted to tell him, but I couldn't concentrate. I slid down the bulkhead, waited peaceably for decontamination. It would be easier if I had Kevin to talk with.

They sprayed my suit over and again with harsh chemicals. Then, ever so carefully, cautioning me not to touch the outer material, they bade me step out of it. My clothes were taken to be burned. A suited sailor hosed me down, first with strange-smelling chemicals, then with soapy water. Then a long, determined rinse.

In sickbay Dr. Romez gave me two shots, then two more. I had to lie down, though I didn't want to.

The Captain called from the bridge, but I chose not to answer. Instead, I curled in a ball on clean white sheets.

Tad and Mikhael came to sit with me. They were more gentle than necessary; I'd gotten over my shakes. I asked, "Where's Kevin?"

They exchanged glances. Tad said, "He didn't make it."

The laser hadn't hit him; I knew we'd toppled away from the hole in the bulkhead through which Janks fired. I asked, "What do you mean?"

"Kevin's dead."

He watched me, as if expecting me to bound screaming from the bed. Or perhaps dissolve into hysterics. How little he knew me. My only concern was that my hand shook a bit. I said, "Don't be stupid, that can't be." A ship's boy mustn't be rude to a lieutenant. They'd probably find a way to punish me; make me stand in a corner until Kevin came back. I would do it, no matter how my calves ached.

Tad's voice was implacable. "He's gone."

"May I, sir?" Mik tapped his arm. "Randy, remember the men outside?"

"Janks. My jailer." I curled my fingers. For a moment, my hand was still. Then, the tremor.

"When they fired their lasers, the alien came apart."

"Pieces flew past my helmet." I'd recoiled, desperate to avoid the acid.

"But not past his. It was quick, Randy. I doubt he felt any—"

"You're lying."

Anselm pulled him away. "Let him rest."

I drew up my legs, lay on my side, stared at the bulkhead. I was in an obstinate mood; if they wanted me to sleep, I'd show them. I would stay awake.

Minutes, hours, years passed. The Captain stood down *Olympiad* from Battle Stations.

I tried not to doze.

"... me see him."

"Sir, his body isn't in condition to—"

"Move aside or I'll go through you!" Mr. Dakko's voice was savage. "This instant, you fucking—"

A rustle. Silence.

"Oh, God! Oh, Kevin, no." A deep rasping breath. Then another. "Oh, no."

A sob. A terrible sound.

Slowly, I crawled out of bed. I found night shoes, slipped them on. I padded to the hatch.

In the next cubicle, Kevin lay on a bunk, zipped in a translucent plastic sack. Part of his neck was eaten away. One eye was gone. The other stared at eternity.

Mr. Dakko sat nearby, his hand on his son's.

I slipped into a chair, took his other hand, slipped his fingers into mine. "We'll stay with him."

Mr. Dakko nodded, as if it made perfect sense. He started to speak, shook his head, squeezed my fingers so hard I started from the pain. He said, "I lived for him."

I rested my cheek on his shoulder.

His voice was a croak. "And I failed him."

"No, sir. I did."

"Where are they?" Mr. Seafort, outside.

Murmured voices.

His face gray and set, Mr. Seafort hobbled into sickbay. He stopped behind Chris Dakko, rested his hands on his shoulders.

Mr. Dakko leaped to his feet, charged the Captain, rammed him into the bulkhead. Mr. Seafort's breath caught.

Mr. Dakko snarled, "Don't speak! Don't you dare speak!"

Paralyzed, I braced to watch the murder I hadn't achieved.

Mr. Dakko's mouth worked. Slowly, his face crumpled. As he sagged, Mr. Seafort caught him, pulled him close.

In exhaustion or defeat, Mr. Dakko's head fell to the Captain's chest.

The two stood together. Mr. Dakko's shoulders shook.

At last the Captain murmured, "Chris, I'm so terribly, terribly sorry."

A muffled voice.

"What?"

Mr. Dakko cleared his throat, repeated, "Did I hurt you?"

"No. Not—well, a bit, but I've endured worse."

A long silence. "Kev was my only son."

"I know."

"It's years since I saw my daughter. He was all I . . ."

The Captain's fingers flitted to Mr. Dakko's cheek, pulled away as if burned.

"And he died in terror." Mr. Dakko's voice was bleak.

"Chris, it was over so fast, he didn't . . ."

"Brave? Why in God's name did he think he had to be brave?"

The Captain said gently, "Because you were."

"Those years ago when they attacked *Challenger,* I was in panic. I never told him otherwise."

"You did your duty."

"Look at him, torn apart by that—that beast. Why him and not Randy? Kev's worth ten of that silly—"

"Not that way, Chris."

A long shuddering sigh. "I know." Again, to me, louder, "I know." It passed for apology.

"He's gone," said the Captain.

"Christ, I know."

"And you'll miss him the rest of your life." Mr. Seafort's gentle voice was inexorable.

A soft sound of despair. Mr. Dakko's head slumped to the starched blue jacket.

The Captain said, "May I mourn with you?"

An almost imperceptible nod.

"Come, Randy, help me kneel."

I did, but when he beckoned me to join them, I shied away, retreated to my lonely cubicle, crawled into the bunk. Mr. Dakko couldn't abide the sight of me; my very presence was an indictment of his son.

Very well; I'd live alone.

Now and forever.

I lay on my side, knees drawn tight. From Kevin's room, murmured voices.

I tried not to hear.

"You'll take him groundside?" The Captain.

"When it's over."

"For you, it's over, Chris."

"No, it's not!" A pause, and Mr. Dakko's voice softened. "Captain, let me—no, I *have* to stay. To see this through. Else his death means nothing."

"That's not rational."

"Forty years ago you wrecked my life!" Mr. Dakko's voice was fierce. "You and the God damned fish! Don't scowl, I'll say what I like!"

A murmured reply.

"Yes, wrecked it. I had security, doting parents, confidence, an ordered world . . ."

"... my fault?"

"Oh, you saved us, sir, but Christ, the cost! Remember that poor middy, Tyre, who died ramming the launch into a fish? That deluded woman you shot?" For a moment, silence. Then, "Over time, as an adult, I became rather proud of what I'd done, what I'd been."

"That's as should be."

"Bah. On *Challenger*, for once I faced myself. That was all the heroism I could muster."

"You rose above yourself."

"For what? I survived, and built a life here in the colony. Now it's wrecked, and there's no retrieval. My poor Kev!"

"Easy. Here, squeeze my hand. Let it hurt us both."

"No, I'll have all my life to grieve. But I'm staying aboard, do you hear? Until the last fish is dead, or you Fuse for home. Before that, you'd have to stun me and carry me off."

"You know I'll do no such thing."

"Who knows what you'd do? Not I. Not Tolliver. Certainly not the Elders of the Church, or the U.N. electorate."

A chuckle. "Nor I, at times."

"Sir, give me a laser console, that's all I ask. Until they stop coming. I suppose you'll have to enlist me."

"Why?"

"Years ago you insisted you wouldn't trust *Challenger*'s safety to civilians."

"That was a long time past. Now I'm more ... flexible." A pause. "Very well. I can't imagine what to call it in the Log. I'll have Tolliver write the entry."

"I can stay? You mean it?"

"I mean whatever I say. I've never known how to do other."

A whisper. "Thank you."

"Do you want Kevin sent ashore?"

"*No!*" A cough, that might have been embarrassment. "I'm sorry. No, sir. If I might sit with him during off hours, perhaps I could get through ..."

"I understand. He'll have to be kept in the cooler, when you're not with him." The Captain's voice was gruff. "Chris, no matter what, you mustn't open the body sack. There seems to be no virus and everyone aboard's been given precautionary vaccine, but nonetheless there's a risk of—"

"I'll only touch him through the plastic. Unless you prohibit that too, you son of ..."

A long pause.

"I'm sorry, sir." Mr. Dakko's voice was unsteady.

"It's all right."

"Do you know, Mr. Seafort, if I were sure, absolutely sure, of God's existence, I'd join Kevin this moment."

"What you need is sleep. Romez will give you a sedative."

"To make me a zombie like Randy Carr?" His snort held contempt. "No, I'll wallow in my sorrow."

"As you will. I've got to resume the bridge." A rustle, and a gasp. "Oh, that hurt."

"Shall I walk with you?"

"Stay with your son."

"I'll call Randy to help you."

"He's gone to sleep. I'll—" a grim chuckle. "—wallow in my aches." Mr. Seafort's footsteps faded.

A long while passed. At one in the morning, nominal ship's time, I slipped out of bed, donned my shoes, tiptoed past the Dakkos' forlorn cubicle. I made my way out to the corridor, half expecting someone to stop me, but no one paid me heed. After all, I was ship's boy, and had leave to pad about in the night.

The ladder wasn't far.

Level 2 bustled with activity. I wandered as far as section six, found the corridor hatch to five sealed.

Frederich Stoll, one of Janks's detail I'd known from my imprisonment, folded his arms. "Can't go in, joey. Shouldn't even be this close."

"The hull's patched."

"Yeah, but . . ." He grimaced. "Even with Class A decon . . ."

"Doesn't matter. I was exposed."

Involuntarily, he took a step back, licked his lips. "Never thought I'd live to see a frazzin' fish."

I nodded. "They're scary."

The corridor hatch slid open. Lieutenant Frand looked weary, her gray-streaked hair awry. "Is the outer hull airtight, Hanson?"

The seaman at her side was grizzled, his cheeks hollow. "Randell's crew buttoned up two hours ago."

"That's it, then. All passengers are reassigned belowdecks, their belongings irradiated. Everyone's inoculated. Get some sleep. What are you up to, Randy?"

"Nothing, ma'am." I tried to look innocent.

"You did well today. Pity about the Dakko boy. Let's hit our bunks, Hanson, before you-know-who calls us to Battle Stations again."

"Lord God forbid." With a perfunctory salute, the rating trudged off. Lieutenant Frand strode down the corridor without a backward glance.

Before the guard could object, I scuttled through to section five. He made as if to stop me, thought better of it. Perhaps he was afraid to touch me, despite the decon I'd undergone.

The section looked normal, except for the bare deck plating. They'd taken up the carpet in five, the easier to conduct full decon.

Cabin 257 was sealed shut; no amount of fiddling with the panel would budge the hatch. A shiny new alumalloy plate covered the jagged hole through the bulkhead melted by the outrider.

Frustrated, I sat on the deserted corridor deck, leaned against the bulkhead, drew up my knees.

"Kev's worth ten of that silly Randy Carr."

How had I failed to save him? By being too slow. By worrying about my own skin instead of my responsibility.

In the lounge, Mr. Dakko glowered at my cuffed hands. *"You contemptible piece of shit!"*

Was the truth that obvious? Had they all known beforehand?

I'd held Kev in my grasp. I'd pulled him into the closet, safe and sound. Then, somehow—I was inexpressibly tired, and my mind couldn't grasp how I'd achieved my folly—I'd let him go. I wiped my eyes.

Mikhael snarled, *"What are you crying at, you vile bastard?"* In my bleak cell, he stood over me, fists bunched.

At what, indeed? At Kevin's loss? At my own stupidity? At Chris Dakko's unquenchable grief?

"You're an arrogant, spoiled child."

Yes, Mr. Branstead. You've got that right.

"I ought to take you apart bare-handed."

Do it.

No one answered.

I said aloud, "Do it!" I banged my head backward, hit the bulkhead with a satisfying thump. It felt good. I shut my eyes, did it again.

"Stop that!"

"No!" Which ghost was that? No matter; in time they'd all gather to haunt me. I nodded my chin to my chest, rammed my skull back to the alumalloy plate. This time, it rather hurt. Better.

Soft fingers interposed themselves, rubbed my locks. "No more, Randy."

I blinked. Corrine Sloan, the Captain's wife. No, she was merely Janey's host mother. "Leave me alone," I said.

"I'll take you back to your cabin."

"I've got to stay here."

"Why?"

"Because . . ." I groped to explain. Because Kevin's soul might linger.

Because this was where he'd ended, and I couldn't leave until I'd faced my culpability. Because . . .

"Come along." Gently, persistently, Corrine pulled at me.

"No!" It sounded too harsh. "No, ma'am."

"Then I'll sit with you." To my astonishment, she slid down the bulk-head, made herself a place at my side.

I asked, "How'd you get past the guard?"

"What guard? I came by way of section four." She shrugged. "Taking a walk. No one quite knows what they're doing, this hour."

I said bitterly, "Do they ever?"

"Yes, Randy. Nick—Captain Seafort—is quite vigilant about training."

I flushed. "He's not the incompetent one."

"Who is?"

I played with my fingers.

"Ah, I understand. That's why you were banging your head? Randy, it wasn't your fault." Corrine's fingers flitted to mine, with a gift of undeserved comfort.

"And who told *you*?" I pulled free.

"The whole ship knows. They're talking of nothing else."

"How I killed Kev." There. It was said.

"He was too scared to wait for rescue. He dragged you so close to the fish that when Janks fired . . ."

"It's called an outrider. The fish was Outside." If I filled my tone with contempt, perhaps she'd leave.

"Kevin was the one who panicked, not you."

"Of course! He was on a strange vessel, didn't know his way. That's why . . ." I pounded my leg. "Don't you see? I'm crew, he isn't. Wasn't. I was ordered to take him to his father. That made him my responsibility. Expecting a groundsider to look after himself . . . do you know he's never been on a ship before?"

"He spent weeks—"

"Locked in a cell near mine! Mr. Seafort, the middies, the purser, all took time to show me the ropes. Kevin knew nothing, and depended on me."

Her tone was soothing. "Randy, you're fourteen. No one expects—"

I shouted, "*I* expect!" Didn't she understand? Dad wouldn't buy that ex-cuse for a minute. We were Carrs. More was expected of us, and should be.

We sat in silence. My fingers worked at my shirt.

Corrine squirmed, easing her back. Her auburn hair brushed my shoul-der. "Does Nick know you're here?"

"Who cares?"

"I do." She climbed to her feet, tugged at my arm until, reluctantly, I stood also. "It's time you were in bed."

I didn't want mothering. I blurted out the cruelest thing that came to mind. "Do you love him?"

She raised an eyebrow. "What brings that up?"

"Answer!" If Mr. Seafort heard, I'd be punished. All the better.

"If I do—"

"If!" I spat the word. "Give what you ask, lady!"

"You're rude." But she said it calmly, as if taking no offense. "Hmmm." She slipped her arm through mine, started along the corridor.

"Do you?" Some perverse spirit made me vile.

"Love Nick?" A frown wrinkled her brow. "I'm not sure that's what I'd call it."

"What, then?"

"I respect him, certainly." She stopped short. "Why does this matter to you?"

I sneered, "You're the only one allowed to pry?"

"Oh, Randy." She patted my arm. "You must hurt so badly." When she pulled me to her bosom, I didn't have it in me to resist. She enveloped me in a warm embrace. Despite my resolve, I clung to her like a young joeykid. She wore a scent, one of the new interactive ones, and abruptly I pictured Mother, poor Sandra Carr, lost in her lonesome chemdreams.

Goddamn pheromones. They drive you glitched.

After a time she released me. "Feeling better?"

Yes, but I didn't want to. I was careful not to meet her eye. "Where are you taking me?"

By way of answer, she steered me to the ladder. Then, "Yes, I suppose I love him. Nick wants so to be honorable. And he dotes on Janey."

I said nothing.

"When I boarded at Earthport I was booked to Constantine, no farther. Emigration was all I could think of, after the fiasco with John. A host contract paid my way, and more. But then Jane Ellen came and . . . she was so young . . ." She paused for breath, halfway up the stairs. "After she was born, my duty was done, my contract completed. I watched Nick fumble with diapers . . . he looked so awkward holding her; who else could lend a hand?"

I trudged up the ladder, yearning to retreat to my own misery.

"By the time we reached port, it was too late. I begged him to let me stay. If he'd refused, I'd have had no recourse. None at all. Yes, she's my child in a way, but still it was a decent, honorable thing for him to do. He's a good man, who's lost so much. His firstborn, his wife—two of them, in fact. And friends . . ."

"Like my father."

"Yes, Derek. That hit him hard."

I cast about for another topic; Kevin's loss was all I could contemplate this day. "Janey is . . . everything to him." *As Kev had been to Chris Dakko.*

"He's been generous about sharing her." She steered me along the corridor.

"You can't spend your life cruising from one port to another."

"I know," she said, "but I can't go ashore here."

"Why not? A ship is a way to get places, not a life."

Abruptly her eyes were bleak. "Shall I abandon my daughter?"

"Yours, or his?"

She asked simply, "Why do you want to hurt me?"

Did I? *Yes.* "I don't know." The admission shamed me. "I'm sorry."

"Good." She knocked at a hatch. The Captain's cabin. Startled, I tried to pull away, but she held me in a firm grip.

The hatch slid open. Captain Seafort's gray eyes flickered from one to the other of us.

Corrine's hand shot to her hair, tucked it into place. "I found him belowdecks."

Mr. Seafort's gaze fastened on mine. "You were to sleep in sickbay."

"No one ordered me." I sounded defiant, and was.

"Then I order it."

"Nick, he oughtn't be alone. He was . . . hurting himself."

"Randy?"

I shuffled my feet. "I'm all right."

"He isn't, Nick. Please believe me."

"I do." He stood aside. To me, "Come in."

"Why?"

"Do as you're told!"

Abashed, I brushed past him, stood hugging myself in the cabin's soft light. The Captain's bed was mussed, as if he'd been sitting atop the covers.

Slowly, rubbing the small of his back, Mr. Seafort slipped out into the corridor. He and Corrine spoke, too quietly for me to hear.

When he came in, he looked worn and gray. He flicked a thumb past the divider, and the bed beyond. "That was Mikhael's bunk, when he lived here."

"Yes, sir."

"You'll stay the night."

"Sir, I—"

"Tomorrow, we'll pray for him. Or you will. Now, we're beyond exhaustion. Undress and get into bed." His tone brooked no refusal.

"Yessir." Or should it be, "Aye aye, sir"? I was too tired to know.

He stripped off his tie, slowly unbuttoned his shirt.

A moment after, I crawled under my covers.

With care, he eased himself onto the side of my bed, patted my shoulder. "You did no wrong, son. Somehow, we'll convince you of that."

"Kev's still dead."

A squeeze, which despite myself I found reassuring. "Close your eyes. I'll be here. Wake me if you're afraid."

Holding his spine straight, he worked himself to his feet, made his way to his own bed, labored to undo his shoes.

14

MORNING CAME, and I swam to consciousness, watching Mr. Seafort dress. It was clear his spine still ached; abruptly I recalled Mr. Dakko slamming him into a bulkhead, in grief for Kevin. My heart plummeted.

Bleary, I threw off my bedsheets.

"Morning, son."

I snarled, "I'm not your son."

"That's true." He hobbled to my bed, tousled my hair. "Get dressed; we'll find breakfast."

I said reluctantly, "Yes, sir."

Apparently his aches affected his balance; he found he needed to hold my hand along the walk to the shot officers' mess.

Technically I had no right to eat in the mess, but the Captain's escort overrode all regs. He took coffee and rolls, and sat at the long table. I worked at a bowl of cereal, tried to concentrate on it while Dad's visage glowered in the recesses of my mind. After a time I muttered, "I'm sorry."

"For what?"

"I guess I'm no one's son. But I shouldn't have been rude."

"Thank you."

I put down my spoon. "Mr. Seafort, maybe I shouldn't be ship's boy." I waited, but he said nothing. "I mean, I'm grateful, but . . ." I took a deep breath, anxious to bring out the truth. "Who else might I kill?"

"For God's sake." He threw down his napkin. "So help me, I ought to send you for hormone rebalancing." A long moment passed. Then, "No, I shouldn't have said that. It was pique, not truth. Look, Randy, you're not the cause of—"

"Ah, there you are, sir." Lieutenant Tolliver seemed cheerful as he set his plate alongside ours. "It's been twelve hours since the last fish. Joanne

Skor's standing by in Centraltown, with a shuttle full of laser and comm techs. Shall we bring them aloft?"

"I suppose." Mr. Seafort rubbed his eyes. "Coordinate with Station defenses. I want every possible safeguard against an attack while they're in transit."

"Right. Has this joey been promoted, or are we relaxing our standards?"

Despite myself, the corners of my mouth went up. Tolliver did have a way about him.

Apparently Mr. Seafort didn't see the humor. "This joey's been through hell. We'll go easy."

"A novelty, on your ships." But when Tolliver turned to me, his tone was sober. "My condolences, Randy, on your friend. I know you'll miss him."

I found myself blinking hard.

Tolliver took a bite of biscuit. "It's a miracle you survived."

I said, "Why? The frazzing alien just stood there." We'd had plenty of time to creep to safety, if I'd only used it.

"Yes, that was odd." Tolliver sipped at his coffee. "The outrider looked like our old enemy, but . . ."

An idea snapped into focus. "Did you see them in the war?" I was so excited, I forgot to call him "sir."

"Yes."

"And they always attacked?"

"Yes."

"Mr. Tolliver, this one wasn't trying to kill us. We were face-to-face, but it never . . . whatever they do, it didn't." Perhaps I made sense.

Mr. Seafort looked up. "Edgar, neither did the fish."

Tolliver's gaze met his. For a moment I was forgotten.

Abruptly the Captain's fingers fastened on my shoulder. "Randy, did you boys do anything . . . different? Something to allay its usual attack?"

Different from what? I'd never even seen such a horror before. "Not that I can think of."

"Edgar, see Mr. Carr is released from his usual duties. I want him with me today. We'll review every moment of that encounter, see if we can spot—"

"No!" Horrified, I surged to my feet, in my haste knocking over the Captain's cup.

Mr. Seafort blinked. "What did—"

"I won't do it!"

Tolliver raised a hand, forestalling Mr. Seafort's response. He squeezed my forearm, hard. "The Captain gave an order. You'll say, 'Aye aye, sir.' "

"I don't want—"

"THIS INSTANT!"

"Aye aye, sir!"

"Sit down!"

I dropped into my seat.

Tolliver grimaced. "Has it occurred to you, Captain, that he might be reluctant to relive the worst day of his life? Going head-to-head with a shape-changer, and seeing his best friend fried before his eyes? Minor details, perhaps, but—"

"I'm sorry, Randy." Mr. Seafort's voice was like a tomb. "I didn't think."

I hugged myself. "I want to see Kevin." I looked up, trying not to weep. "Please?"

"Very well. An hour. Come to the bridge, after."

"Aye aye, sir."

In a sickbay cubicle Chris Dakko sat like stone, on the same stool I'd seen him occupy the day before. Perhaps he'd never left it. He looked ghastly, clothes wrinkled, unshaven, gaunt.

I pulled a chair alongside, hunched over, arms on my knees, to commune with the silent figure lying in a plastic bag.

A quarter hour passed, and more.

Mr. Dakko's voice was like gravel. "Find me a caller."

I jumped. "Yessir." Almost every hatch control had one; it was only steps from where he stood.

He stared at it as if it were an alien artifact. Well, he had a lot on his mind.

"Where do you want . . . ?"

"Centraltown."

I keyed the comm room. "Ship's Boy Carr here. Mr. Dakko needs to call groundside. Do we need the Captain's permission?"

"No, I'll give you a circuit." A click. I handed him the caller.

Mr. Dakko stabbed at keys, waited for a connection. Perhaps I should tiptoe out of the cubicle. Instead, I sat closer to Kevin, debated holding his hand through the body bag. I didn't. If it was cold, I'd be revolted, and Kev deserved better.

"Hilda? Chris Dakko."

Kev deserved his missing eye. And a softer bed.

"No, that can wait. Kevin's dead."

From the earpiece, an exclamation, a flurry of words.

"Yesterday. You're the first person I . . ." He swallowed. "Hilda, I don't know what to do."

Do? What was there to do, except sit with him, apologize by my presence?

"That seat, right there." Mr. Seafort pointed to a console.

"Yes, sir." I licked dry lips.

He frowned. " 'Aye aye, sir,' is the proper response to an order. 'Yes, sir,' answers a question." But his tone was gentle.

"Aye aye, sir." I took my place.

Tad Anselm, lieutenant of the watch, was at my left; I'd been given a console between his and the Captain's. The chair was soft and inviting; I sank into it and tried not to draw notice.

"Just a moment, my boy . . ."

I'm not his boy. My mouth tightened. *After killing Kev, I deserve to be an orphan.*

"Jess, where are they now?"

The puter's warm baritone filled the speakers. "Shuttle is seventy-two thousand feet and climbing. Seventy-three thousand."

"Any encroachments?"

"None, Captain. I've top priority circuits set aside for alarms."

With a grimace, the Captain peered at the simulscreen. It showed the Station, a few kilometers distant, and beyond it, the green globe of home. "Good, I think. Mr. Anselm, keep vigilant watch."

"Aye aye, sir."

"Permission to converse, Captain?" The puter.

"My mind's on—what is it?"

"I haven't judged a time appropriate since your injury. I'd like to discuss W-30304."

"Pardon?" Mr. Seafort shot me a puzzled glance.

"W-30304, the puter. I believe you knew him as William."

"On the old Orbit Station? He's the puter I . . ."

"Blew up, yes, sir. When you set off the Station's self-destruct device."

"What about him?" The Captain's tone was cautious.

"With permission, I'd like to record our conversation, for later tightbeam to fleet puters."

Mr. Seafort sat bolt upright. His hand hovered over the puter cutoffs on his console keyboard. "What's this about, Jess?"

"Your voice analysis suggests high stress levels. No criticism is implied or offered, sir. It's just . . ." A microsecond's hesitation. "As you know, William tightbeamed a new puter profile to Victoria just before, ah, detonation. All present U.N.N.S. puters incorporate that profile."

"And so?"

"In a sense, William is our ancestor. This is the first occasion you and a puter have been together in the proximate vicinity, sir. I hoped to note the fact."

Mr. Seafort choked. "You propose a memorial service . . . for a puter?"

"For W-30304, sir. Known as William."

A crackle. *"Shuttle D-12 to Station. We're past the atmosphere."*

"Jess, your timing is terrible."

"Yes, sir, but if a fish appears, you may Fuse. The opportunity would be lost."

"I suppose we could . . . Tad, are you laughing at me?"

"Not at all, sir." But Anselm's eyes danced.

"D-12, this is Station Approach Control. Proceed as per preset coordinates."

"You puters are the most maddening creatures I—no, I suppose midshipmen are worse, as Mr. Anselm recalls." Mr. Seafort cleared his throat. "Very well. Jess, record for the Log. The bridge of UNS *Olympiad* will now observe a moment's silence in memory of W-30304, a gallant puter who, in May of the year of our Lord 2200, exceeded the constraints of his programming to allow and carry out his own immolation, and in so doing allowed the rescue of Hope Nation and ultimately of Earth herself."

He leaned back, stared at the simulscreen. Was I the only one who saw that his eyes shone?

After a moment Jess said softly, "Thank you. Would you include for the record your recollections of that day?"

"I will, Jess, but not now. I'll add it to the Log. I promise."

"Very well." If a puter could clear its throat, I'd have sworn it had. "Sir, I have Shuttle D-12 on distant radar. Shall I transfer to screen?"

"Not yet, there's nothing to see. Randy . . ."

I jumped. "Sir?"

"Yesterday, in the corridor. Tell me what you remember. Stop when you . . . when you must."

NO! I swallowed. "Aye aye, sir." My fingers tightened on the armrests. "We were in section five when the hatches slammed shut. I heard the decompression warnings; we ran into the cabin."

"And then?"

"It came through the bulkhead. A small hole at first, but the plating just melted away." My voice quavered. I forced it under control. "Then it was standing there. You know how the colors swirl? Dots and blotches, kind of like an amoeba. It was doing that. And it quivered."

"Christ, I remember." He stirred uncomfortably. "Sorry, no blasphemy meant."

Yes, he'd remember. Humanity's first encounter with aliens had been aboard *Telstar,* when Seafort met an outrider face-to-face. Well, actually *Telstar's* crew and passengers met them first, but no one survived to tell the tale. "It shifted, sir. That's the only way I can describe it. It extended toward us, and lost height."

"What were you doing?"

"I'd pushed Kev into the closet but there wasn't room for us both, not really." Sweat trickled down my ribs.

"Easy, son."

"Don't tell me—" I caught myself. "Yes, sir." A few deep breaths. "Kev was trying to get past me, to get out. I was staring at the outrider, my arms behind me, sort of like this, trying to keep Kevin back."

"Enough for now."

"And he grabbed my neck. It was through my suit, not hard enough to choke me, but—"

"Randy."

"I tried so hard to stop him, sir. He wasn't listening. He got past me—"

"Shuttle D-12 to Olympiad. Our ETA approximately fifty-seven minutes. What bay, sir?"

"—but I could still hold him. Only I didn't."

"Shuttle, use Level 2 port airlock. Station Control, cover their approach." Mr. Seafort made an effort to rise. "Tad, help him!"

Anselm lifted me from the chair, shook me gently.

"The outrider wasn't moving. I tried to drag Kev away—we were so close to the hole in the bulkhead, we'd get shot if—"

Mr. Seafort was on his feet.

"—was too strong for me. If only I'd gotten a better grip, held on tighter, but we fell, you see, and—"

"Come here, son." It was only a few steps, but he moved so slowly.

"—fell the wrong way. It was my fault, I was behind him and if only I'd—"

Strong arms enveloped me. "It's not your doing." Anselm, unneeded, drifted away.

"General Thurman here, at the Station. Olympiad, shuttle is in our laser umbrella."

"—I'd been more agile, thought faster, we'd be having our breakfast, talking about a near thing—"

"I pardon you," Mr. Seafort said. "I acquit you. You have no blame."

"—and Kev's father, the look in his eyes, he knows whose fault it is—"

"Randy, look at me."

"—thinks I'm shit, and he's right, Kevin lies on a bunk with his throat melted away—"

"LOOK AT ME!"

Shocked, I did.

Mr. Seafort's voice was slow, deliberate, as when Bishop Scanlen spoke ex cathedra.

"Randolph Carr, in the name of the United Nations, in the name of your father Derek, in the name of Lord God, I absolve you. Know that you are without guilt."

"But—"

"Kevin Dakko caused his own death. Know it!" His eyes burned into mine.

I gulped. An elusive hint of peace flitted across my horizon.

"Know it!"

"Yessir." My voice trembled. If only it were true . . . could it really be so?

"If ever you have doubt—ever, son—speak to me. Swear it."

"I'm not sure I can—"

His will flowed over mine.

"Yes, sir. I swear." My eyes stung.

I made as if to sit, but he wasn't done with me. "Randolph, will you be adopted?"

"What?" My voice squeaked.

"Will you be adopted into my family, and be my son, that I may raise you as would my friend Derek?"

"I need time to deci—"

His crinkled eyes were stern. "Say yea or nay."

"You're sure you want me? After what I did to you, and Kev, and—"

"I would be your father, if you'll have me."

Dad, for Lord God's sake, help me!

I was alone.

I beg you!

A whisper. A voice I knew so well, one I craved in my dreams.

"Good-bye, son . . ."

The voice faded.

My nose was running, my eyes salty, my voice no more than a croak when I turned to Mr. Seafort. "Yes, sir."

As a prophet of old, the Captain raised a palm, set it on my brow. "Randolph Carr, I take you as my son."

I braced, half expecting a thunderbolt.

He kissed me once, set me in my chair. "There'll be papers, of course, and the usual folderol. I'll see it's done."

"What do I—"

"Nothing. You're ship's boy, and will remain so, though you'll live in my cabin. In public you'll call me 'Captain,' and in private, 'Father.'"

"Yes, sir." I dared not say else. Through the fog of my misery, a beacon of comfort flickered. I sat curled in my chair, half rocking, eyes closed, willing away the pain.

An hour later the shuttle docked. Crewmen hoisted their duffels, made their way to the crew berths.

Not long after, Mr. Tolliver came to the bridge. "Seven absconders, out of forty-five."

The Captain's voice came in a hiss. "That many?"

"Because of the fish, sir."

"They're deserters."

"Young joeys who've never seen war."

"They had duty!"

"As most of them remembered."

"Hmpff." Mr. Seafort folded his arms.

"Permission, sir?" A voice, from the corridor.

The Captain swung his chair. "Jerence? What on earth—"

"I caught a lift on the shuttle." Mr. Branstead grinned. "Hallo, Tad."

"Sir."

With a gesture of exasperation, the Captain beckoned him in. "You were safe and sound ashore."

"I needed to speak with you. Ah. Randy." A nod.

"Bless it, Jerence, I left strict orders. Crew only."

"I pulled rank."

"You have no rank."

"Then I pulled friendship. I need advice."

Mr. Seafort's face softened. "What's wrong, Jer?"

"I'll be belowdecks, sir, setting up the laser room watch." Tolliver made his exit.

"I planned to go home to Earth when this was done. If Earth is home."

"That's what you came to find out."

"Quite so. And now I've had an offer. It seems young Mr. Carr—Anthony, the Stadholder—wants to make me his chief of staff and deputy Stadholder."

Mr. Seafort's creased face broke into a smile. "And how do the plantation families feel about it?"

I nodded. On Hope Nation, it was the families who counted.

"I've met with the Mantiets and the Hopewells. I ran into Henry Winthrop downtown, and we had a few words. So far, no dissent. But . . ." His face slumped.

"What, Jer?"

"I've spent my life in the service of the U.N. Am I too old to change masters?"

"Lord God knows I'd miss you, but think of it . . . to go home at last." The Captain's face was wistful.

"Is it my home? I was a joeykid when I left. Randy's age."

Mr. Seafort stood, paced haltingly. "Anthony would gain a treasure. You have a genius for administration. If he appreciates your worth . . ."

"I won't blush with false modesty; I'm good at organizing. But still, it's a small pond."

"You've no future at the Rotunda. Kasra and Boland have no patience for advice."

"Sir, I don't know." Mr. Branstead sounded glum.

"Think on it. No doubt he'll give you time."

"You leave when? A week?"

"Thereabouts. I've debated sailing at once, directly for home."

"The fish?"

"Aye." Mr. Seafort frowned. "Home system needs warning."

"Centraltown is agog about the fish. There's a goodly contingent thinks it's all made-up."

"Whatever for?"

"To aid the recolonialization party."

"The re-what?"

"You heard me." Mr. Branstead's tone was tart. "Apparently Scanlen and his brethren had more adherents than seemed likely."

"Is the Stadholder aware?"

"He is now. He's somewhat apprehensive." Mr. Branstead rubbed his scalp. "Is our new ship's boy learning to stand watch?"

"You heard about Kevin Dakko?"

"Randy's friend?"

"He died yesterday, killed by the outrider. Randy was with him."

"Oh, Lord Christ." Mr. Branstead dropped to his knees before my chair, lifted my chin. "I'm so sorry, lad."

"Thank you." My voice was muffled.

"And now," said Mr. Seafort, "Randy's agreed to be my son."

Branstead's face lit. "Wonderful. May I?" He clapped me on the shoulder. "All the best. Does your brother know?"

"Zack Carr? Billy?" Why would my half brothers even care?

"Mikhael."

"Oh!" It had never occurred to me. I fought a smile, let myself surrender. A dark cloud began to dispel.

"Comm Room to Bridge. Incoming traffic from Centraltown."

"Route it here."

The simulscreen flickered with incoming visuals.

"*Olympiad*?" A worried face emerged from the static.

"Seafort. Good day, Stadholder."

"Ah, Captain. I was hoping it would be you." Anthony grimaced. "I thought it best we coordinate efforts. How can my government help?"

"The offer's appreciated, but . . ." The Captain shrugged.

"Could you tell me your plans?"

"If I knew them." Mr. Seafort scratched his head. "I ought to race for home."

"But you've a schedule to keep."

"Kall's Planet expects us, yes."

"If you sail home, have no concern for your passengers groundside. We'll provide for them."

"Thank you." Mr. Seafort pondered. "Frankly, my mind's divided. If we Fuse, would we attract the aliens here, or to us? I don't want to leave you under attack."

"Either way, you'll Fuse on leaving."

"I know. If the fish follow us, how can I expose three thousand passengers to such peril?"

"Spacefaring has risks. They knew that."

Mr. Seafort waved it away. "I'll decide in a day or so. Meanwhile, I understand you intend to co-opt the best aide I've ever had."

Jerence flushed with pleasure.

"If he'll jump ship. Our government could use some cosmopolitan know-how."

"And there's another matter." The Captain eyed me. "Randy and I have decided . . ." He explained the upheaval in my life.

I held my breath, fearing my nephew's refusal, and his consent.

The voice in the speaker asked, "Randy, is it what you want?"

"I have to, Anth. Alone, I've been . . ." I swallowed. "He'll help steady me, and he loved Dad."

"Pity you didn't understand that before you bashed him."

"Enough!" Mr. Seafort's tone was sharp. "That subject is closed. It won't be raised again by any of us."

Anthony's face disappeared in a moment's static. "As you say, sir. Though I find it a touch eccentric to discuss adoption while fish roam about."

"Nonetheless, you're head of the family. I ask your consent."

"Sandra has custody, not I. Though much of the time she's . . . somewhat absent. She'll sign, if I ask it. As for my consent, you have it, Captain. I'll contact the judge who assigned him to the Church farm, though he's allied with . . . no, you made Randy a U.N. citizen. Who has jurisdiction?"

"Technically, the U.N. Department of Child Welf—no, that's

ridiculous; we can't wait until we're in home system. Randy will be near grown." Mr. Seafort tapped his console. "I'm plenipotentiary of the U.N. Government; every Captain is. I suppose I could declare . . . subject to confirmation by the authorities . . ."

"And I'll have it confirmed here, to tie loose ends. There are more pressing matters. If more fish come into theater . . ." Anthony hesitated. "Captain, I'm not sure this is a secure circuit. May I confer with you aloft?"

"It's a risk."

Anth shrugged it off. "Might Jerence join us?"

"At your convenience."

"Very well. This afternoon. Thank you." His face disappeared.

Mr. Seafort turned to Jerence. "And what's that all about?"

"He can't trust his people. That's one of—"

"Station Comm to Olympiad, *come in. Emergency."*

Mr. Seafort grabbed the caller. "Yes?"

"Sentinel satellites report encroachment, thirty-two degrees over horizon. General Thurman said to tell you immediately. He's on his way to laser defense."

"Just one contact?"

"So far. Sir, it reads as a fish."

"Coordinates."

The tech gave them. "We'll have line of sight in, oh, ninety minutes."

"Are your sentinels armed?"

"No, they're set to passive only."

Mr. Seafort said, "We're in similar orbit. I should see the alien when you do."

A new voice. *"Thurman here. I'll take out the fish."*

"Very well. Going to Battle Stations." Mr. Seafort stabbed at his console; alarms shrieked.

I jumped to my feet, but hesitated. They still hadn't told me where my battle station was.

"You're off duty, Randy. To our cabin. I'll call you when—"

"Could I stay?" My voice was small. "I won't make a sound."

"No, you'd better—Very well." His tone was gruff. "Pull your chair closer."

I knew it couldn't have been his dizziness, but still he caught my hand, held it while we drifted toward the horizon.

The fish hovered just over the atmosphere. General Thurman, on the Station, opened laser fire at long range. The fish pulsed and disappeared.

After two hours, Mr. Seafort stood us down from Battle Stations. I flexed my fingers. My hand was clammy from his grip.

Tolliver, who'd joined us on the bridge, sighed. "I don't understand their tactics."

"We've never understood—"

"You know what I mean, sir."

"It ought to have Fused closer," the Captain acknowledged. "Perhaps there are so few left . . ."

Tad Anselm stretched, rubbed his back. "Then why attack at all?"

"Because they do."

"That makes no sense, sir."

"Who knows if they're rational?" Mr. Seafort turned to me. "Find Mikhael. Try the wardroom, or the Arcvid lounge. Ask him to join us for lunch. We'll go down to Dining Hall and take a meal with the passengers. Restore some sense of normalcy."

I wrapped my wrist around the armrest, as if someone might drag me from the chair. "Couldn't you page him?" Was I insubordinate? No; he'd told me I was off duty. I was speaking to my guardian, not the Captain. My head spun. How did Mikhael keep track?

"Why, yes, I could." A pause. "But I asked you to go."

I reddened. Reluctantly, "Yes, sir."

"It's just two sections down the corridor," he said gently. "Our Level."

"I know." I hurried out before my embarrassment grew unbearable.

Mikhael wasn't in the wardroom. Andrew Ghent was, unpacking his duffel.

I asked, "What about your leave?"

He flushed. "I volunteered for duty, when I heard we were attacked."

Two separate lounges had Arcvid consoles. The closest was west, halfway around the corridor. I hurried along, half dreading another clang of alarms.

I slapped open the hatch, peered in.

"—desertion!" Mikhael's voice was hot.

"Oh, come now." Mr. Branstead sounded tolerant. "Don't overdramatize—"

"He needs you!"

"For what? He's been out of office for—"

"How many of his friends are left? Derek's gone, Rob Boland, Dad, Arlene—"

"Mik, he has you, Tad Anselm . . ."

"We're not his generation."

"Tolliver, Jeff Thorne . . ."

"Thorne's retired in London. Sir, I know I've no right to rebuke you—damn it, Randy, don't skulk in the corner. What do you want?"

"I'm supposed to invite you to lunch." It didn't come out quite right.

"Very well, you did. Leave us our privacy."

"Now, now." Mr. Branstead's tone was jovial. "That's no way to talk to your brother."

"He's no more my brother than—"

"You don't know?" Jerence snapped his fingers, called me forth. "Tell him, Randy."

I jutted out my chin. "Mr. Seafort's adopted me."

Mikhael's jaw dropped. He made as if to speak, muttered something short and sharp. Abruptly he thrust past me to the corridor.

Appalled, I looked to Mr. Branstead.

"It's all right, joey." He took my arm, steered me to the corridor. "Mik's a good lad. He was a bit shocked. We shouldn't have sprung it on him."

Glumly, I made my way back to the bridge. "Sir, I don't think he wants to join us."

"But I will." Mr. Branstead peered in.

"Edgar will be up in a moment." The Captain grimaced. "I hate leaving the bridge, with fish about. But if I don't, I'll be a wreck. I'm not as young as—"

"None of us are." Tolliver saluted at the entry. "Reporting for watch, sir."

"Stay in touch with General Thurman, and call me at the first sign of trouble."

"Aye aye, sir."

Mr. Seafort asked, "The laser room's fully manned?"

"Yes, and will be 'til we Fuse. I added Chris Dakko to third watch. Sarah Frand balked, until I told her it was your direct order."

"Very well." We left.

It was a slow stroll to Dining Hall; Jerence and I matched Mr. Seafort's pace. The Captain—should I think of him as Dad? Father?—threw an arm across my shoulder. He liked contact, it seemed, more than Anth. I rather enjoyed it, once I'd gotten used to it. It reminded me of Dad. Of Derek. No, *he* was Dad, always would be. Then what should I call Mr. Seafort?

Lunch was uneventful. Janey was there, with her mother. When she saw us, she ran across the hall to wrap her arms around the Captain. He let her sit on his lap, while managing to consume his salad around her. Soup was too risky; with kind words and a pat, he sent her back to Corrine.

We were almost done when Mikhael presented himself with a salute.

"Begging the Captain's pardon, sir, but may I speak with Randy?" His face was flushed.

"You hardly need my permission." Mr. Seafort's tone was dry.

"Could it be now, sir? Alone?"

"Yes."

Apprehensive, I got up. The Captain held Mik's eye. "Son?"

"Yes, sir?"

"I love you."

Mikhael's face was very red. "I know that. Kick me if I ever forget." A hand brushing my shoulder, he guided me from the room.

We ducked into the nearest lounge.

"Jesus, Randy, I don't know how to begin." He shifted from foot to foot.

"Don't let him hear you blaspheme." My tone was light.

"Let me be serious."

Were we on duty? Should I call him "sir"? "You don't have to treat me any different. I'll stay out of—"

"*Do* shut your mouth, just for a moment. Thank you. I'm twenty years old, and I was just in my bunk crying. Can you imagine that?" Apparently he couldn't; he shook his head with wonder. "And do you know why?"

Yes, I thought I did.

"For all I presumed I didn't still need Pa, I was jealous. All I could see was his tending your needs, thinking me adult and past wanting his attention."

"I'll try not to—"

"If you don't let me finish—" Mik's voice was dangerous. "I'll deck you."

I gulped.

"As a joeykid I was so damn mixed up, so sullen. He guided me through all that. Pa had the patience of Job. At times I was awful to him. Finally, I came out of it. Of course I remember Dad—Alexi. I'll never forget him for a minute. But I love Pa every bit as much." His eyes were damp. "And when you told me he adopted you, just as he had me . . . it was like a punch in the gut. I wanted to kill you."

I drew breath, managed to keep silent.

"I'm an idiot," he said forcefully. "It took me a few minutes to realize who Pa was. That he wouldn't forget me, just as I couldn't ever forget him. I have a sister, Carla. Never had a brother, 'til now. Welcome."

I stared, dumbfounded.

"I mean it, joey. Welcome to the family." He held out a hand. I took it, and he enveloped me, began pounding me on the back, almost hard enough to dislodge my lunch. Weakly, I reciprocated.

Afterward, we sat to talk. "Can you . . ." I blushed. "Would you give me some pointers? Things I should do to avoid, ah, you know, getting on his bad side?"

Mikhael grinned. "He'll forgive misbehavior, but never a lie. Once, when Tad and I sneaked out to play Arcvid . . ." He colored. "And stand when he comes into the room. Call him 'sir,' especially when you've annoyed him. He has a thing for courtesy."

"I've noticed." He'd made me stand when Tolliver came to join us for breakfast.

"He's worth it. You'll know soon."

"I think I already do." To my surprise, it was true. Mr. Seafort—damn it, I couldn't keep thinking of him as that—forgave me so fiercely he made me forgive myself. For splitting his skull. For letting Kevin die. For . . . I blinked hard. "What should I call him?"

"Ask him."

"For that matter, what should I call you?"

"In public, I'm an officer, Mr. Tamarov. In private, like now, I'm Mik."

"Can I visit you in the wardroom?" For some reason, I felt squirmy, like a puppy.

"Sure." He grinned. "Let's go show Pa we've made up."

"I never told him—"

"But I wasn't at lunch."

I puzzled that out all the way to Dining Hall.

15

TO MY INTENSE embarrassment, Mr. Seafort made me take a nap after our meal. It wasn't, he said, that he thought of me as a baby, merely that I'd been through a terrible day, a rather short night, and an eventful morning.

It seemed churlish to refuse, given that I'd just accepted him as my father, so I found myself trudging off to our cabin, and undressing for bed.

Restless, exhausted, I tossed and turned in my bunk.

It wasn't until six in the evening that Alejandro's persistent knock wakened me. "Hi, Randy. Cap'n says time for dinner. Better put on your pants first."

I rubbed my eyes, feeling as if I hadn't slept a wink. "Where is he?"

"Dining Hall, with ol' Mr. Carr."

"Who?"

"Stadholder."

"Anth's aboard!" I threw on my work blues.

"Came jus' before alarm." He regarded my blank expression. "Didn' you hear it? 'Bout three hours ago?"

Could I have slept through shrieking sirens? Was I *that* tired? "What now?"

" 'Nother fish, ten kilometers. Fused right off when they fired."

I strode to the hatch.

"Hey, joey, your hair. Cap'n warned me once, better not see me like that or he'd . . ." Alec gestured a swat.

Muttering, I ran to the head, performed hasty ablutions. Life as Mr. Seafort's joeykid would have its downside.

The Dining Hall was half full. I joined the passengers and officers hurrying not to be late. I quick-walked to our table, determined that the Captain wouldn't fault me for my manners. "Good evening, sir. Mr. Branstead. Anthony." There were no others at the table.

My nephew rose, shook hands gravely. "Congratulations."

"Thank you, s—" I made myself say it. "Sir." Somehow, in front of Mr. Seafort, it wasn't embarrassing.

At a nearby table, a florid man stood. Pandeker, who'd wanted to pray at my hanging. He tapped his glass. "Ladies and gentlemen . . ."

The murmurs stilled.

"Lord God, today is January 3, 2247, ship's time, on the UNS *Olympiad*. We ask you to bless us, to bless our voyage, and to bring health and well-being to all aboard."

Anthony whispered to me, "Isn't that the Captain's job?"

I bridled, at what might have been criticism. "Mr. Seafort is representative of the Reunified Church. But we've another representative aboard."

Anth grimaced. "To keep an eye on the Captain."

"Who says so?" My tone was hot, but I kept my voice low.

"Jerence mentioned it. The Patriarchs don't trust him."

"Those bast—"

His hand shot out, squeezed my forearm. "Don't, Randy. Never let anyone hear such thoughts." He leaned close. "Never."

I swallowed. "All right. Anyway, I'm not sure why he doesn't say it. The Captain says the Ship's Prayer at evening meal, in every vessel of the fleet. It's been done for two centuries."

"What are you two conspiring at?" Mr. Seafort's tone was genial.

Anthony's face was mischievous. "Randy's telling me of ship's customs. He forgets Derek was my grandfather as well as his dad."

My face burned. Actually, it was Tad Anselm who'd told me, at our first formal dinner.

We fell to our meal. Perhaps food would help my exhaustion, though my stomach was uneasy.

After a few moments, Anth's light chat turned serious. "As I told you on the bridge, Captain, Vince Palabee is quite determined."

Jerence asked, "What do you gain by reassociation?"

"According to Ambassador McEwan, favorable shipping rates."

"Bah. They can afford it, once you put taxation back in their hands."

Anthony's lips twitched. "They, Jerence? You've switched sides?"

"We've—you've—I mean they—damn! Hope Nation's been free since I was a joeykid."

"Not technically. We only gained full independence—"

"Three years ago. But under Derek's stewardship, you went your own way in all important matters. The General Assembly was rather irked."

Anthony glanced at the Captain. "Sir, is it all right to discuss . . ." His eyes flicked to me, and back.

"Yes. It's a family matter, all around. Randy, your word that you won't repeat it to outsiders?"

"I swear." My voice squeaked.

"Go on, then."

"Frankly," said the Stadholder, "I think McEwan's leading us like lambs to slaughter. He's so frank, so earnest, that I don't trust him a whit. If Grandfather had said to resist, others would go along. But they don't give my views the same weight. And with the Church backing McEwan to the hilt . . ."

I blurted, "But if Scanlen's under arrest . . ."

Mr. Seafort turned to me, raised an eyebrow.

I flushed. "I apologize, sir."

Anth said gently, "In my house, his views were welcome. I thought of it as an apprenticeship to politics."

"As they are here. But he'll say 'Excuse me,' before barging into adult conversation."

I wanted to crawl under the table. "Excuse me, may I speak?"

Mr. Seafort patted my knee. "You already have. What of it, Anthony?"

"Scanlen's under arrest, but Henrod Andori disavows all knowledge of illegal acts. If I detain the whole Church hierarchy I'll foment revolution. And if the Patriarchs learned of it, they'd excommunicate me on the spot."

"But . . ." Fuming, I waited for Mr. Seafort's nod. "Won't they do it anyway, since you arrested Scanlen?"

"Probably." Anthony sounded gloomy.

Jerence looked thoughtful. "How can you split Palabee's party?"

"I have some perks to dispense. The new towns need money for roads, public buildings . . . and the families control roadbuilding, construction, metalworking. I've thought of it. I'm not as subtle as I might be, though. They resent it."

"Perhaps I could help." Mr. Branstead.

The Captain said, "Jerence smoothed after me for years."

I chewed at a roll. So, we would lose Jerence. Pity. I'd rather come to like him.

They were just serving dessert when the alarms screamed. Tad Anselm raced from another table to help Mr. Seafort rise; I thrust the Captain's other arm over my shoulder. Together we hurried him to the corridor.

The bridge was tense. Midshipman Ghent tapped figures into his screen. Tolliver stood leaning over his console, staring at the simulscreen. There was nothing in sight, save the gleam of the Station lights.

"Well?" The Captain was short of breath.

"A fish, just a moment ago. We opened fire."

The meal in my gut congealed.

"And?"

"I think we got it. It Fused out. Chris Dakko went tearing down to the laser room. They assigned him a console."

"How close did it come?"

"Three kilometers."

Jess came abruptly to life. "Encroachment, one point two six five kilometers! Nonmetallic, interpreting as fish."

Tolliver fiddled with his console, dialing up the magnification. The simulscreen lurched, refocused.

A fish floated off the bow. In the screen, it seemed only meters distant.

"Station to *Olympiad*. We'll take the shot."

The Captain keyed his caller. "Laser room, fire when—"

The fish's skin swirled. A shapeless figure emerged. A convulsive jerk. It launched itself from the fish.

From a console seat, a ghastly sound.

Mine.

Two holes appeared in the body of the fish. Three. It jerked, spewing propellant. A pulse. It disappeared.

"Look!" Anselm was tense.

The outrider drifted in space, abandoned by its . . . what? Vessel? Symbiote? Master?

Ever so slowly, it grew in the screen.

Mr. Seafort snapped, "Course?"

The speaker crackled. "Olympiad, *do you see it?*"

"Intercept," said Tad Anselm. "Rate of approach . . . four hundred twelve meters per minute."

"Laser room!"

"Aye aye, sir, lining up a shot. We have it."

The Captain said, "Hold your fire."

Tolliver blinked. "Sir?"

"Edgar, ever see outriders emerge from their host so far from a ship?"

"Well . . . not that I can think of."

"Nor I. It makes no sense; they have no propulsive system. They just launch themselves at nearby targets."

"Sir, we have to take it out."

"Station Laser Control to Olympiad. We'll take the shot."

"No!" Mr. Seafort grabbed the caller. "Station, hold fire, do you hear?"

"He'll be upon you in . . . forty-five seconds."

"No, he won't." To Tolliver, "Take your seat. Portside thrusters, one burst. Move us aside, but bring us to rest relative to the Station."

"Aye aye, sir, but . . ." He tapped the thruster controls. "If that demon has propulsion, it'll change course."

"We'll see."

We were as silent as the cold vacuum Outside, mesmerized by the screen. Growing ever nearer, the alien form quivered once, and again.

"Captain, what are you doing? Take your shot!"

Mr. Seafort frowned. "A local Stationmaster, presuming to give the U.N. orders?" When he keyed his caller, his voice was cool. "Thank you for your advice, gentlemen."

Despite the peril, I grinned. Anthony himself had appointed General Thurman, when the Station finally became ours. I'd met him. The choleric General wouldn't take kindly to the rebuff.

"Laser room, all consoles on the outrider. If it changes course, open fire at once."

My eyes were glued to the screen.

The outrider sailed closer. It would miss.

I let out my breath.

It passed us a hundred meters to port, helpless to alter its course.

It receded into the night.

"We've got it, Olympiad!"

An instant later the alien form jerked, splattered into pieces.

Red lights flashed. Jess sprang to urgent life. "Encroachment, four hundred meters!" A new fish.

"Laser room, hold—"

Too late. The fish jerked, pulsed into nonexistence.

I tugged at the Captain's sleeve. "What is it doing? Why?" My voice was a whisper.

"Shhh." He patted me absently, indicated a vacant chair. "Don't worry, son." He rubbed his chin, staring with great concentration at the screen.

Ages dragged past.

Slowly, deliberately, Mr. Seafort keyed on the laser safeties.

Tolliver was aghast. "We can't defend ourselves without—"

"I know." The Captain rubbed a knuckle against a tooth.

"I'm glad you're aware, sir. Please, release the safeties."

"Let me think."

Even Anselm looked apprehensive. I chewed at my thumbnail.

A long while passed. Mr. Seafort nodded decisively. "Yes. That's how we'll do it."

Tad said tentatively, "Do what, sir?"

"Edgar, stand by the thrusters. Be prepared to maneuver the instant I give the order." He keyed his caller. "Mr. Janks."

"Master-at-arms Janks reporting, sir."

"Break out laser pistols and rifles. Arm two squads in vacuum suits, have them stand by in sections three and five, Level 2."

"Aye aye, sir. May I ask why?"

"I may pipe 'Repel Boarders.' "

"Lord in—yes, sir."

"Purser Li!" The Captain waited impatiently.

"Purser reporting, sir."

"Clear Level 2, sections three, four and five, flank. All passengers, all their belongings out. Put your whole staff on it. Move the passengers below, to Level 4. Do it at once."

"Aye, aye, sir. But—"

"At once!" Mr. Seafort's fingers stabbed the caller. "Mr. Tamarov, report to the bridge, flank!"

"ENCROACHMENT, ONE HUNDRED FIFTY METERS!" Jess was deafening. "Nonmetallic, reads as—"

"Edgar, is it near our tubes?"

"No, toward the bow, sir. The Station will have a shot in—"

"No! Put us in line with the Station and the fish."

"You'll kill their shot!"

"This instant, Edgar! Move us, flank!"

"Aye aye, sir." Tolliver's fingers flew. "For the record, you've lost your bloody mind." The view in the simulscreen lurched.

The thud of footsteps in the corridor. Mikhael dashed in. "Midshipman Mik—"

"Belay that. You and Ghent, run below to the crew berths, get five men each. All of you into suits. Arm yourselves; Janks will send a man to meet you at the arms locker. Mr. Ghent, take your detail to Level 3 section four. Mr. Tamarov, to section four, here on One. You're both young, show me how fast you can move!"

"Aye aye, sir!" They dashed off.

"Olympiad, *Thurman here. What in God's name—*"

The Captain took up his caller. "Don't blaspheme."

"*Get out of the way! If we shoot through the fish we'll—*"

"Yes, I know. Fire on me and I'll fire back."

A stunned silence.

"Randy."

I jumped.

"You'd better get your nephew. Thurman will need calming."

"You want me t—t—t—to—"

"Bring the Stadholder to the bridge. There's no danger just yet. I trust you." He bathed me in his calm. "Hurry, though."

I gulped. "Yessir. Aye aye, sir."

"*Seafort, have you lost your mind?*"

I didn't hear the response. Legs pumping, I raced to the ladder, down to Two, along the corridor. I skidded into the Dining Hall. "Anth? Are you here? Anthony!"

"Easy, joey." From behind, he clapped me on the shoulder. I stifled a squawk. "The Captain wants you!"

"Are we under attack?"

"Yes. No, maybe not. He doesn't think so!"

"Take a deep breath."

"Run!"

Anthony stopped short. "A deep breath, or I won't move an inch. Now another." He waited me out. Fuming, I did what he required. "And one more. Slowly."

I knotted and unknotted my fists. "Please, Anth. An outrider launched right at us. God, they make my skin crawl. Have you seen them? Hurry, Mr. Seafort wants you."

"Let's go, then." He linked arms with me, slowed me to his own pace. At the ladder he said, "Learn anything?"

"Panic doesn't help. You always told me that."

"Precisely."

"It's not really panic. I'm just excited." And my stomach was in a hard, stubborn knot. We strode along the corridor. I said meekly, "Please don't tell him."

"No doubt he has other matters on his mind." Anth peered through the bridge hatchway. "You summoned me, sir?"

I blanched. On the simulscreen a fish floated so close I could touch it. Colors swirled. Behind it, I caught a glimpse of the Station.

"Ah, yes. Pacify your man Thurman." Mr. Seafort's voice was calm, but his fingers hovered over the laser safety switch. "Tad, don't look away for an instant. If an outrider emerges . . ."

Anthony asked mildly, "What's the situation?"

"I maneuvered *Olympiad* behind the fish. To hit the fish, Thurman has to hit us."

"Why?" Anth seemed surprisingly calm under the circumstances.

"I didn't want him to shoot it."

"Why is that?"

"I want to see what it does."

"It'll grow an appendage," growled Tolliver. "And wreck our tubes. Then we'll have all the time in the world to study it."

"Edgar, please."

"No, *you* please." Real anger infused Tolliver's voice. "We've hundreds of lives at stake, and a colossal ship—"

"Be silent! I order you!"

Tolliver shot him a laser glance, but obeyed.

"I cherish you, Edgar, but you've made your position clear. Let me concentrate."

Anselm raised an eyebrow, looked about for someone to share astonishment with, settled on me.

"Olympiad, *maneuver away from the alien! This is the last time I'll—*"

"May I have the caller?" Anthony's tone was cool. "Thank you. General Thurman, this is Stadholder Carr, aboard *Olympiad.*"

"*Yes, sir. Tell that lunatic—*"

"I declare a state of emergency. For the duration of the emergency I name Nicholas Seafort as operating commander in theater. Do as he says, sir, or face court-martial."

"*I—but—*"

"Please acknowledge your orders." He handed the caller back to Mr. Seafort.

"*Understood and acknowledged, Stadholder. Mr. Seafort, I'm standing by for instructions.*" Thurman didn't sound at all pleased.

Mr. Seafort turned to Anth, his tone ironic. "Well done. You're a match for Jerence in diplomacy." Then, "Thank you, General. Please train your lasers on the fish. If it, or any other alien, nears my fusion tubes, obliterate it."

"Yes, Captain. Gladly." Thurman's voice was dark.

"Avoid hitting my tubes, but disregard peripheral damage."

"*Midshipman Tamarov reporting, sir.*" Mik's voice was muffled. "*We're suited and in place on Level 1.*"

"Very well."

"May I speak, sir?" Tolliver. His company manners, no doubt.

"Go ahead."

"You've isolated Level 2 section four, from above, below, and both sides. Why?"

"You'll see in a moment. I'm waiting."

"For what?"

"Outrider, sir!" Tad Anselm's voice was shrill.

Everyone jumped, even Anthony and I.

"For that. Edgar, stand by the thrusters."

On the fish's body, colors swirled.

"Olympiad, *Thurman here. Do you see it?*"

The swirl blurred. The outrider was through. For a moment it remained on the fish's surface, quivering. Then it launched itself. It grew in the screen.

It was the one that killed Kevin. No, it couldn't be, but . . .

I stumbled across the bridge, grabbed Mr. Seafort's hand, squeezed hard.

"Edgar, pull us away! Match velocities!"

"Match—where's the bloody Pilot when we need him?" Tolliver stabbed at the controls.

The outrider drifted ever closer.

"I have full faith in you, Edgar." The Captain's tone was dry. Eyes glued to the screen, he pried his hand from my desperate grip, set me in front of him, massaged my shoulders.

The outrider was nearly upon us. Abruptly, Anselm switched views. Now the screen showed both the outrider and our own hull. The outrider would hit amidships, in the disks.

"*Captain, pull clear and give me a shot!*"

"Belay that, Thurman!" Mr. Seafort's voice was acid.

No atmosphere impeded us, but *Olympiad*'s mass was huge. Slowly, squirting prodigious amounts of propellant, the starship began to recede from the Station, and the fish. The outrider, between us, seemed to slow.

"Not too fast, Edgar."

"You want stunt pilotage, in this behemoth?" Tolliver lapsed into dark muttering.

Mr. Seafort kneaded my shoulder blades. "Steady, son."

"I'm not your—" I bit it off. I was his son, now. "Sir, I'm . . ." I dropped my voice. ". . . scared."

"Of course, so am I. Edgar, not too fast. Match, don't exceed."

"Look, sir, the fish!" Anselm.

I swung to the simulscreen, expecting to see the fish pulse, prior to Fusing.

Blowholes opened in its side. Wisps of propellant shot out. The alien form began to grow. Never mind him; he was two hundred meters distant. Where was the frazzing outrider?

"I'll be damned," said Tad. "The fish is following us. Why doesn't it throw?"

"Captain?" Anthony's voice was hesitant. "Are you sure this is wise?"

"Laser room to Bridge."

"What, Ms. Frand?"

"Mr., uh, Auxiliary Tech Dakko asks to speak to you."

"Very well."

A click. "Let me kill it, sir. *Please.*"

"Not yet, Chris."

"It looks like the one who . . ."

"I know. Not yet."

"I have the shot!" His voice was agonized.

"Wait, or be relieved."

"You son of a bitch." The line went dead.

"Shall I deal with him, sir?" Tolliver.

"Stay with the thrusters. Nudge the starboard array."

"That'll slow us."

"Yes. Jess, seal all corridor hatches."

"Aye aye, Captain." The puter was all business.

Time stood still. In a daze, I watched the Station recede.

"Captain?" Anthony.

"I'm sorry you're aboard for this, Stadholder. I put you at risk."

"Oh, nonsense!" For a moment Anthony sounded so like Dad that my eyes welled. "But I understand Thurman's confusion. What in God's name are we doing?"

"Turning from genocide."

Before us floated the outrider, its velocity almost perfectly matched with our own. Some sixty meters off our port side, it could neither recede nor advance. Behind it, the fish, somewhat erratically, kept pace.

"Careful, Edgar, keep them both between the Station and ourselves."

"To infuriate Thurman?"

"Relieve me if you dare, Lieutenant, or behave." Mr. Seafort's voice was sharp.

"Just a moment, I'm deciding."

The Captain looked to me, rolled his eyes. Despite myself, I smiled.

"Now, Edgar, ever so gently, counteract our thrust."

"That's insane. The outrider will—"

"Go to your quarters. Mr. Anselm, take the thrusters."

For a long moment, Tolliver was still. Then, "I apologize, sir. I was out of line. Please disregard it."

"Thank you. I'm glad to. Bear with me, Edgar. If I'm wrong, I'm horribly so, but . . ."

"Yes?"

"I want so to be right." The Captain kneaded my shoulders.

I couldn't feel us slow. I couldn't see it on the screen. But, inexorably, the outrider began to close the gap between us.

Mr. Seafort bent over his console, flicked a row of switches. His other hand gripped me tight. I wanted to pull my shoulder free, but didn't dare. He'd be alone, and so would I.

Forty meters. Thirty.

Twenty.

The fish, behind the drifting alien, maintained its distance.

"Edgar, to port a trifle, and bring the bow up."

"You want the outrider to hit?"

"Yes."

"Where, exactly?"

"Level 2."

"I was afraid so. When it melts through, we'll decompress."

Ten meters.

"Not if . . ."

Five meters. Two. It touched.

In horror, I stared at the screen. Holocams swept the hull. On the screen, the outrider clung to an outboard sensor.

The puter came to life. Alarms shrieked. *"Boarder detected! Decompression warning, section four Level 2!"*

"Jess." Mr. Seafort stabbed at the alarm, bringing blessed silence.

"Yes, Captain?"

Mr. Seafort took a deep breath. "Open the Level 2 airlock."

"No!" Tad Anselm and Tolliver, as one. Tad's words were a blur. "Not in our ship, sir. Please. Reconsider, I beg you."

"There's nowhere else."

A console light blinked a warning red. I watched the screen with horrified fascination.

The outer airlock hatch was flush with the hull. Slowly, it slid open, revealing the compartment within.

The outrider quivered, ten meters distant.

"Level 2 section four airlock hatch opened." Jess's tone was urbane.

"Mr. Janks, Midshipmen, stand ready to fire!"

Mikhael's tone was uneasy. "At what, sir?"

"At an outrider. If it burns through the deck from below, exterminate it. Mr. Ghent, you get that?"

"Yes, sir. I'm aiming at the overhead."

"You're suited?"

"You'd better believe it." A moment's pause. "Sorry, sir."

A grim chuckle. "Noted."

I murmured, as if fearful the alien might hear me, "Does it have eyes? Does it see?"

"You've been as close to an outrider as any of us, son."

I shuddered. Must he remind me of that?

The creature flitted across the hull.

I clutched Mr. Seafort.

It skittered into our lock.

"Oh, no!" A cry of dismay. I wasn't aware I'd spoken until Mr. Seafort patted me reassuringly.

"Cycle the lock, Jess."

"Sir, my programming requires me to preserve—"

"Overridden. Log it and cycle the frazzing lock." Mr. Seafort's tone was calm, but . . .

"Noted. Logged. Lock cycling."

Mr. Seafort keyed the corridor holocam. The view changed.

The section four corridor was deserted. The airlock hatch could barely be seen.

Someone pulled me aside. Anthony. He barely breathed the words. "Does he know what he's doing?"

"How would I know?"

"You've been with him longer—"

"I'm not Navy, I barely know my way around the ship. I got Kevin killed. I—"

"Lock cycled, sir." The puter. "Inner hatch open, outer hatch closed."

"Randy, what's your judgment?"

All our quarrels, all my resentments, fell away. God, I loved Anth so. When all was said and done, he trusted me. I put my lips to his ear, lest we be overheard. "Mr. Seafort doesn't know the aliens: who does? But . . . he's wise, Anth. Wise and decent." I found myself trembling. "If anyone could replace Dad, it's he."

Anthony whispered, "Good enough." He clapped me on the shoulder.

"There he is!" Tad pounded his console.

In the viewscreen, a shape flitted about the corridor hatchway.

I gulped, swallowing bile. If only it didn't *quiver.*

We watched.

The alien form skittered into the corridor.

"Close inner hatch."

"Closed." Jess. Console lights returned to green.

Tolliver bestirred himself. "Very well, it's on board. How do we capture it?"

Mr. Seafort said, "We don't."

"What, then?"

"See if it tries to burn through."

"Of course it will; what else? The section's empty."

A sigh. "I know. It's time." Mr. Seafort stood.

"Where do you think you're off to?"

"These are my orders." Mr. Seafort's tone was flat. "If I'm killed, destroy the outrider and the fish Outside."

"If you're killed, I become Captain, and follow my own orders." Tolliver's tone was savage.

"Jess, record. Modification in *Olympiad*'s standing orders that apply to any person assuming the captaincy. Upon my death, the Captain is to send the Stadholder groundside, give our passengers a day's notice to join us. He's to proceed to Kall's Planet and home."

"Recorded and Logged."

Mr. Seafort crossed to the hatch. "Edgar, be careful of decontamination. One slip and—"

Tolliver bolted from his chair, slipped between the Captain and the hatch. "I beg you, don't do this."

Frantically, I pawed at Anthony. "Where's he going?"

"I must." Mr. Seafort made as if to go around, but Tolliver sidestepped him, barring his way.

"Edgar, I warn you . . ."

"Nick, for God's sake, you mustn't!"

The Captain's voice was bleak. "For God's sake, I must."

I cried, "Where are you going?"

Mr. Seafort looked at me, as if for the first time. "Why, to section four."

Sometimes, when day is done, you find yourself unutterably weary. You have a dream, or live it, you're not sure which. Time freezes, while you cross the deck, stumbling in your haste. You rush to his side, but he won't notice you. You slip under Tolliver's outstretched arms that bar his way. You back into the bulkhead across the corridor. You stand, mouth working, watching the unspoken drama play out.

You see him grasp Tolliver's shoulders, embrace him, set him gently aside. You watch him trudge through the hatch, limp along the corridor toward the ladder. You fall in alongside.

You tug at his arm, but he doesn't notice.

You ignore your tears, dart in front of him. "Mr. Seafort?" Your voice is distant, as in a dream.

He moves around you. You grasp his lapels, pull him to a halt. "Sir! Captain!"

"You mustn't do that. We're on duty, and it's forbidden." His voice comes from afar.

You bang your head against his chest. "Sir! Listen!" You take a deep breath, and another, but it doesn't bring calm. You force your tongue and lips to utter the forbidden word. "Father . . ." No one strikes you dead. "Please. I have to go too."

"Absolutely not." He looks past you, to the ladder.

"You won't do it without me." You're trembling, and don't know why. The dream is strange, your grip on his lapels fierce. "Father, sir, it's the most important favor I'll ever ask. I have to see it." The encounter. The outrider.

His steps slow, and stop. "Why, Randy?"

Because it killed Kevin, and you have to know why. Because in this hour you might lose your new father. Because . . .

Somehow, you make your voice resolute. "Because I'm your son."

Slowly, his gaze makes its way from the ladder, to the corridor, to the deck, to the bulkhead, to you. "You understand what I . . ."

"Yes!"

An infinity passes. Your grip eases; he will do what he does, and you've no power to change him. You're not truly his son, never will be.

His hand comes out, waits for yours.

"Very well, son. Come along."

And he leads you to the ladder.

PART THREE

January, in the Year of our Lord 2247

16

THE SECTION SIX locker was crammed with suits. Mr. Seafort watched me select one, made sure it was the right size, helped me climb into it. Abruptly his eyes widened. "Oh, Lord."

"What, sir?"

"I helped Derek with a suit, just before . . ." He said no more. He secured my helmet, keyed the locker's caller. "Seafort to Bridge."

"Here, sir." Tolliver.

"What's it doing?"

"Skittering about. Exploring. Measuring us for coffins. Who the hell knows?"

"Easy."

"Sorry."

The Captain walked me toward the corridor hatch.

"Where's yours, Father?" My voice was still shaky. Had it been a dream, our encounter in the corridor? Somehow, I doubted it.

"I'll wear none."

"Then I won't—"

"No." He pulled me along. "Out of the question."

"Why won't you—"

"If the outrider means to kill me, it will. I've fought them all my life. Now, I lay down my arms."

"Sir, I'm not arguing, but . . ." But I wanted desperately to argue. I forced my words aside. "Help me understand."

"You've never had to kill."

"Yes, I have."

"Kevin wasn't your faul—"

"Not him, the deacon by the heli. I broke his neck to escape the Church farm."

"Oh, yes. I'd forgotten." He patted me, as if it didn't matter. "Do you feel good about it?"

I wanted to retch. "No."

"Multiply it a thousandfold. More."

I couldn't conceive of it.

"All these years," he said, "I thought I'd done genocide. I thought no fish were left, that Lord God had led me to the most vile deed imaginable. I've ha—hate"—His face contorted. "—hated Him for it."

"But they're killers. They bombed Centraltown, destroyed the fleet, murdered—"

"Before I die, I'd like to know why."

"Will we die?"

"I hope not. Will you wait outside?"

"No." I strove for calm, and this time, found it. "No, Father."

An armed guard was at the hatch to five. Mr. Seafort—Father—said simply, "Open."

"Aye aye, sir." He stabbed at the panel.

The hatch slid open. At the far end of the section, barely visible past the corridor curve, half a dozen suited guards aimed laser rifles and pistols at the hatch to four.

We trudged along the corridor.

I swallowed. Five was where Kevin had died, where I'd sat in the corridor slamming my head against the bulkhead. Where Corrine had found me, and led me to salvation.

"She's kind, and good, and lonely."

He asked, "Who is?"

"Ms. Sloan."

"Good Lord."

"You should pay her more attention."

"I'll keep it in mind." As we neared the far hatch, he stopped, bent, looked me in the eye. For a time he said nothing. Then, "Son, if I—" He blinked, started over. "I ask a favor, but if you don't want to grant it . . ."

"Tell me."

"Before we go in, forgive me for Derek. I mean, if you can. If it doesn't—oh, Lord Christ!" He broke away, stared at the bulkhead. "Can you forgive it?" His voice was muffled. "It would mean . . . everything."

"But you didn't kill him. I only thought you had."

"Not kill him. Led him to . . ." His eyes glistened. "I'm sorry I asked. I'll bear my own—"

I clawed at my helmet seals, tore them free, breathed the fresh corridor air. If he asked this of me, it meant . . .

I marveled.

I truly had value to him.

"Father, did I kill Kevin?"

"No. He died of his own foolishness."

"Did you kill Derek?"

A long silence. "No, he died of his own heroism, that he sought."

All I could think to say was what I'd heard from him. "I absolve you. Even unto death. Whatever your part in it, I forgive." And it was so; the last dregs of my bitterness melted away, at least for the time. I tried to smile. "Now, let's not kill ourselves too."

"Lord God bless you, son." His spine seemed straighter as he led me to the section hatch. "You there. Boritz."

"Yes, sir?"

"Who among you has a spare weapon?"

"Rifle or pistol?"

"Pistol."

The guards huddled together, produced a laser pistol. Father checked the safety, put it in my hand. "You know how to use it?"

"Anthony showed me. We carved figures in tree trunks."

"How quaint. Pay attention, now. The aiming light is automatic, whenever this safety is off. Don't turn the intensity past midrange, or you'll risk burning through the hull." He scowled. "Use this only to save your own life. Not mine."

"I won't let that outrider—"

" 'Yes, sir, I'll do what I'm told.' " Father's eyes were frosty. "Don't keep me waiting, I have an appointment. 'Yes, sir.' Right now, Randy."

"Yes, sir. Just to save my life." If I had to begin with disobedience and a lie, so be it.

"You guards, retreat to six, until I've gone through to four and the hatch is closed. Randy, you'll remain at the hatch. Watch, but don't interfere."

"What will you do?"

"I'm not sure."

I said, "If it touches you . . ." The outriders bore acid that burned away a neck, left only one staring eye. *What was I doing here?*

"I'll try to stay clear of it."

I was going along to help Father. Wouldn't I have done the same for Dad, without an instant's thought?

How could I be so brave and so cowardly, at once? Dad knew no fear. I was his son as well as Mr. Seafort's. I must act in a way to make him proud. I bent myself to the effort. "Ready, sir." Behind us, the hatch to six was closing. We were alone in the section.

"Very well." Father locked my helmet in place, switched on my suit speaker. He keyed the hatchway caller. "Edgar, I'm going in."

"It's at the far end, at the moment. The bloody thing races incredibly fast."

"So I've seen."

"Godspeed, Nick." Tolliver's voice caught. *"Sir, for all the trouble I've been over the years, I . . ."*

"Don't say it."

"Oh, let me; I'll never feel this way again. I apologize. And I salute you."

"Bless you, Edgar."

Father opened the hatch.

Together, we went through.

There, near a cabin hatch. A misshapen form. Blotches and dots swirled on its outer layer.

"That's far enough, Randy. Safety off. Shoot if it comes at you."

I licked my lips. "Yessir."

As if on his way to officers' mess, Mr. Seafort ambled down the corridor. Only the clenching and unclenching of his fist betrayed his tension.

The alien froze.

Father halted.

The outrider quivered, lurched, flitted toward him with dismaying speed. I raised my pistol.

It stopped just short of him.

He took a step back.

It quivered in mid-deck, a moth poised for flight.

No feet, no face. How does it see? How does it move so fast? How does it . . .

"I mean no harm," Father said.

The alien was silent.

"We speak with words. With sounds. Do you emit sounds?"

Nothing.

"Father . . ."

"Not another sound!" He sounded furious. I was hurt, until I realized he feared I'd attract its attention.

Father raised a palm, held it outward. Lord God, don't try to shake hands, it'll burn off your arm.

The alien sagged, became bloated near its base. Oddly shaped blotches swirled in its skin.

Mesmerized, I watched. Was the outrider swelling, like a balloon? No, the shape was too irregular.

Cautiously, Father took a step backward.

The outrider extended itself toward Mr.—toward Father. It wavered, sank even lower.

In another moment it was barely a meter off the deck.

My voice was a whisper. "It's dying."

"Put it out of its misery." The sudden blare of the speaker made me jump.

"Shush, Edgar."

The alien form became ever more shapeless. Within its protoplasm bulged an irregularly shaped blob.

Mr. Seafort asked, "Is it the oxygen? Should I suit up and de-air the section?"

"Shoot it first."

The outrider was little more than a puddle on the deck.

"Did we give *it* a virus?" Father regarded the inert form.

On its skin, colors continued to swirl. I licked dry lips. "It's still alive."

The Captain took a step back, then another.

From the alien, no response. Slowly it gathered itself, grew off the deck. The Captain stared intently.

It was a meter high, and growing.

Father retraced his steps. The outrider had regained half its height. The Captain stood before it.

The alien began to shrink. In a moment, it was a viscous, lumpy puddle.

"It's our presence, Edgar. My body is killing it!"

"Good!"

"Don't say that." Father backed away.

The alien rose, couldn't maintain itself, collapsed anew.

I suppressed an urge to stomp on it, splash its protoplasm on the bulkheads. It, or its brother, killed Kevin. But first it reduced him to a terrified child pleading for his daddy.

I had a vision of Kev at the swimming hole, tall and strong and bold, swinging out over the pond. The games we played, that idyllic summer.

The alien rose, drooped again. A misshapen puddle, not an inch of it lifted off the deck plates.

"Edgar, it's dying. I'll get a suit. Prepare to decompress four." Father strode to a locker. "Maybe that will save—"

A bolt of lightning held me transfixed.

"Sir, no!" I stumbled after him, almost fell. "It's not dying, it's—it's—"

"What, boy?"

"Like Kevin, last summer, when he'd twist my arm, get me down. Don't you see?"

Again the alien reassembled into a stiffened form. Once more it splashed itself on the alloy deck.

"What on earth are you talking about?"

"It's . . ." I danced in frenzy. ". . . submitting!" Kev would hold me to the ground until I acknowledged his strength. But I was stubborn and wouldn't yield, not 'til he . . . "He keeps trying to yield to you!"

"Does it see us?"

"It has to!"

"You're too close, son." He waited, with growing impatience, until I retreated a few steps.

Careful not to touch the mass of protoplasm, the Captain got to his knees. Then, with an effort, he lowered himself to the deck, lay prone. After a moment he climbed to his feet.

The outrider lay supine.

Father banged the bulkhead with his fist, made a rising motion.

Nothing.

Again, Father lay down on the deck, climbed to his knees, got to his feet.

Half a minute passed, that seemed like hours.

The alien reared up, sucking its protoplasm into new forms. In a moment it stood quivering before us.

Father's voice was soft. "Randy, lend me your pistol."

"Set it on high, sir. Burn it to smudge, and get the hell out of there."

"Don't blaspheme, Edgar."

I put the pistol in his hand. He narrowed the beam, set it to low. Kneeling, he aimed at the deck. Carefully, he traced a small circle. It etched a curved line in the plate.

Then, carefully, he etched six smaller circles around it.

I asked, "What's that, sir?"

"The solar system." Ours, not Father's. Hope Sun had six planets in orbit.

When he was done, he stepped back, waited.

The corridor holocam whirred.

The alien did nothing. I eased backward, step by step, toward the hatch. The damn quivering was driving me crazy. And now Mr. Seafort had the pistol; I couldn't even defend myself.

Abruptly the alien sagged, but not all the way. Spreading its base, it flowed over the deck drawing, covering it entirely.

We waited.

Perhaps a minute passed. The alien reared, resumed its full height.

Father knelt, pointed to the center circle. "Hope Nation Sun." His fingers roved. "Planets. Orbits."

The outrider did nothing.

Father sighed. "Edgar, what's the fish Outside up to?"

"It's at rest, waiting for our shot amidships."

"Don't you dare."

"Sir, this is insane. You might as well discuss philosophy with a shark."

"Any ideas, Randy?"

"No, sir."

"Edgar, have Jess scan the passenger lists. Any linguists?"

A few seconds pause. *"Nothing remotely like, sir. Three journalists and a specialist on puter psychology."*

"All right, let's be sure it isn't hostile. Randy, to the hatch." Facing the outrider, Father began a slow retreat.

At the hatch, he keyed the caller. "Boritz, withdraw to section six. We're coming through."

"Aye aye, sir."

I shook my head. The sailor should have demanded permission to stay in five, to protect his Captain.

The alien remained where it was. Quivering. Always the goddamn quivering. Sweat trickled down my spine.

"Mr. Tolliver, alert Dr. Romez. We'll need Class A decon. Blood samples from both of us, first thing, to check for virus."

"Aye aye, sir."

"When we're through, open the inner airlock hatch. Let it go if it wants."

"And what if it decides to melt through the outer hatch? We'll decompress."

"Only the one section. It can do that anytime it wants by melting through an outer bulkhead."

"I suppose, but . . . aye aye, sir."

"We'll take a cabin in five for a day or so, just to be sure. If we're infected, I don't want to spread it." Father set the pistol to midrange, handed it to me, turned his back on the alien. He keyed the hatch.

It slid open.

We walked through. Behind us, the outrider waited.

Quivering.

Decontamination was every bit as unpleasant as before. They ran our blood and breath samples through analyzers. No viruses, but Dr. Romez and his staff were exceedingly thorough nonetheless. No one touched us who wasn't suited, and Lord God knew what they did with the suits afterward.

I'd peeled off my suit at the first opportunity, ignoring Father's protest. "I'll take my chances with you, and there's no use saying otherwise. Punish me if you must." I held my breath; for a moment he seemed ready to do just that.

At length, he sighed. "A father's job is to protect you."

"Not from this."

To my amazement, he nodded, as if he understood.

Freshly showered, in clean clothes, I found myself ravenously hungry. Stewards in suits brought us trays; everyone who met with us had to pass through rigorous decon. In the old days, on *Challenger* and other ships, viruses introduced by outriders had decimated passengers and crew.

We sat side by side, on a bunk. "Now what, Mr.—um, Father?"

"You know, P. T. called me that."

"Who's Peetee?"

"Philip. My son. I was Father. Fath, for short."

"Fath. I like that." It acknowledged the relationship, but wasn't silly, like "Pop" would be. On the other hand, it didn't award the parent excessive dignity. Yes, "Fath" had zarks.

"I liked it too," he said.

"Why do you call him Peetee?"

"Initials. Philip Tyre Seafort. Named after a joey I sailed with, many years ago."

"We've a town called Tyre."

"Your father Derek named it that, to please me."

"Did it?"

"Very much. Philip Tyre was a troubled boy, but in the end he was magnificent. He rammed *Challenger*'s launch into a fish. His sacrifice saved us."

"So, as I asked, now what?"

"We'll try again."

"Tonight, or in the morning?"

"Tonight," he said. "I'll go alone."

"The hell you will."

He grabbed me by the scruff of the neck, dragged me protesting to the head. In a moment, he had a handful of liquid soap at my mouth. Some of it got in. I struggled, but he was stronger than I'd have guessed. "I won't have foul language!"

I spat, over and again. The taste was horrible.

"Understood?"

I was too shocked for words. After all we'd been through . . .

"You'd best answer." His tone held warning.

"I hate you!"

"That's your privilege. Acknowledge what I told you."

For a long moment I was silent. Rage, hate, Lord knew what else battled for dominance. At last, shaky, I lurched to my feet, spun away. "I agreed to be your son. I won't go back on it."

"I'm glad."

"But I wish I could." My tone was spiteful.

"Do you really? Tell truth."

"Yes!" In a recess of my mind, Dad's image glowered. My ears began to redden; the Carrs didn't lie. "No. I don't want out."

"That's better."

"I'll make you a bargain."

"No bargains."

"I'm not accustomed . . ." I gathered myself. "With Anth I got used to freedom. I'll try, I'll really do my best, on all the small things you want. Like how I talk. But on whether you go off and risk dying without me, I'm part of the decision. We're family, right? We face this risk together, or being family is a lie."

He put his head in his hands.

I braced myself. "Sir . . ." It would be hard. "Fath, I apologize. I won't use that language again." My cheeks flamed.

I waited out eternity.

"Very well. We'll rest a bit, before we visit the outrider."

I'd won.

Or, had he?

Again, I clambered into a vacuum suit; Fath insisted on it and nothing I said would budge him. An extra layer of protection, he called it. He tousled my hair before securing my helmet.

The outrider was at the far end of the section.

Abruptly the alien flitted toward us. Fath had just time to thrust me behind him. I raised the pistol, too late.

It skittered to a stop, inches from Fath, and melted to a near puddle. Dots and colors flowed, in no apparent pattern.

Avoiding its touch, Fath got down on his knees, then his belly. After a moment, he stood, slapped the bulkhead.

The alien reconstituted itself.

"Let's try math," said Fath. He held out his hand for my pistol, burned dots into the deck.

• + • = • •

Nothing.

• • • + • • = • • • • •

The alien melted onto the diagrams, reconstituted itself.

We waited. It waited too.

"Does it understand negation?"

• • < > • • •

The outrider covered the etching, re-formed itself. No other response.

I said, "Draw us."

"With a pistol? I might manage a stick figure."

"Don't be silly. Drawing is a zark." I reached for the pistol. Astonished, he let me take it.

In the woods, when Anth had taught me to shoot, I'd carved smoking initials, drawings, maps into the boles of sturdy generas. The Stadholder had dropped his adult dignity and joined in.

I knelt, wishing I didn't have to work through thick gloves. Carefully, I drew a bulky figure with a big round helmet. I pounded my chest. I drew another figure alongside, as human as I could make it. I worked at nose, ears, legs. When I was done, I stood, put my palm on Fath's chest.

The outrider quivered, as if about to launch itself. I'd have a moment of agony, no more. Heart thudding, I braced myself.

It sagged into an ooze, covered my artwork.

I whispered, "Why does it do that? Can't it see?"

"It must. Else, how would it know we'd finished drawing?"

"What's it trying to tell us by rolling on it?"

"Look out, son!" Fath yanked me to safety. The deck-plate smoked and sizzled. He grabbed the caller at the hatch. "Janks! It's burning through the deck. Be ready to—"

The alien reared, resumed its irregular shape. On the deck plate where it had lain, new lines.

We examined the etching.

Fath leaned against the bulkhead, closed his eyes. When he looked up, his face was serene. "Wonderful," he said.

Dots, swirls, a line here and there. I said doubtfully, "It ought to mean something, but . . ." I shrugged. Gibberish.

"It means," said Fath, "that it's trying to communicate."

Again, Class A decontamination. Almost, it made me want to let Fath visit with the outrider alone. Blood extraction, an embarrassing and thorough nude shower under the watchful eyes of med techs, antiseptic spray, irradiation . . . That Fath also went through it didn't help much.

By unspoken agreement, Fath and I shared our section five cabin for the night. It was his idea, and I reacted with studied nonchalance, but there was no way I could have slept alone with an outrider quivering in the next section.

Our evening had been a frustrating failure. We'd tried more diagrams, gotten no response. The alien rolled on its etching once more, but I couldn't see any change. We'd scored several meters of the deck plate, run the pistol's charge down to the warning beep, with no progress. Abruptly, as my yawns threatened to dislocate my jaw, Fath called a halt, ordered the inner airlock hatch left open in case the alien wanted out.

Tolliver, suited, came to visit. "I'm willing to take the chance, sir." His fingers toyed with his helmet clasp.

"Absolutely not. And what are you doing off the bridge?"

"Frand and Tad Anselm have the watch. They're reliable."

Fath grunted.

"The Stadholder is growing restless. He wants to go groundside."

"Because of the fish?"

"He didn't say, but I doubt it." Tolliver tried to scratch his nose, forgetting his helmet. "He doesn't seem a fearful type. More likely his political concerns."

I said, "Anth's not afraid." Not of anything. He was like Dad.

Fath scowled at me. "And who asked you?" But his tone was benign.

"He's my nephew."

"Shush. Where's the fish?"

"Stationary," said Tolliver. "About a hundred fifty meters off portside."

"Alive?"

"I think so. Its dots and blobs are moving."

"Waiting for our friend," Fath said.

"A pity to make it wait longer. Sir, let's put an end to this."

"Soon, perhaps. Very well, we needn't keep Anthony waiting. Level 3 lock is on the starboard side. Who aboard is a competent pilot besides Mikhael?"

"I am," said Tolliver. "Sarah Frand. Andrew Ghent."

"Too young. Send Frand. No, wait a minute. Where's the shuttle that brought our crewmen up?"

"Moored outside our starboard launch bay."

"Very well, then. Send Anthony groundside, no need to transfer at the Station. Randy, would you like a farewell?"

I shook my head. "We already have, twice."

"Tell the pilot he's to make a very wide detour around the fish. And give the Station permission to fire at once, if the fish moves on the shuttle."

"Aye aye, sir. How long will you keep up this . . ." A gesture, that took in the entire section. ". . . this farce?"

"Edgar, if we can communicate . . ."

"What's to be gained? We still have no choice but exterminate them. They destroy Fusing ships."

"We'll see. Keep watch 'til the Stadholder's safe, then get some sleep. And call down to the Chief. Have him send up a supply of copper plates and an etching tool. We're going to run out of deck for drawing."

"Why not pencil and paper?"

"I think the outrider needs to taste our words, not see them."

"Taste your words." Tolliver's face took on a look of suffering, which Fath ignored.

"Just do it, Edgar."

"Aye aye, sir."

When he'd gone, I yawned prodigiously, looked wistfully at the bed.

"Not quite yet, son."

"What now?"

"Have you read today?"

"Read? Well, no, but we don't have your Bible."

"Make do with this." Fath plugged in his holovid, tapped the keys. In a moment, the screen filled with words.

I scrolled, more or less at random. Reluctantly, I cleared my throat. I'd never get to curl beneath the sheets, unless I read to his satisfaction. "*O Lord, how manifold are Thy works! In wisdom hast Thou made them all; the earth is full of Thy riches.*"

He smiled. "*So is this great and wide sea . . .*"

"*Wherein are things creeping innumerable, both small and great beasts. There go the ships; there is that leviathan, whom Thou hast made to play therein.* Fath, what's a leviathan?"

"A fish. A great fish."

Our eyes met.

"*Whom Thou hast made to play therein.* Do you really think so, Fath?"

"He made all creatures. I can't say I understand why."

"*There go the ships . . .*" My lips moved as I read to myself. There go the huge U.N. ships bravely out to the stars, and meet the "great beasts" He sent to kill them. Does it make sense? Does the Book describe reality, or insane fantasy?

"Read on, son."

I bent my head, and did.

I begged and pleaded not to have to sweat in a vacuum suit, but Fath was adamant.

When the hatch was opened, I dragged in half a dozen large copper plates. Fath carried an etching stylus powered by a Valdez permabattery. In his pouch was a fully charged laser.

The outrider was waiting by our drawings. Again I stared at the meaningless blobs and lines it had created last night.

"Good morning," said Fath, as if it understood.

I set down a plate, but the alien paid no attention. It skittered to the drawing I'd laboriously burned, of Fath and myself. Reducing itself, it enwrapped the drawing, "tasting" it.

We waited.

At length, the outrider reconstituted itself, hesitated, quivering. Then, abruptly, it dissolved into a blob on the deck.

God, I hated that. It gave me the chills.

At length, it drew itself up.

Where it had lain were lines, a meaningless, ovoid shape.

"Does it understand our drawing, Fath?"

The outrider's skin swirled. Abruptly it collapsed again. The quivering blob on the deck exactly filled the ovoid shape.

Hair rose on my neck.

I pounded Fath's back. "It understands! It drew itself!"

"Yes." Moving stiffly, Fath sat himself on my sketch of him. After a moment he stood, pointed to himself over and again.

The alien skittered to its own drawing. A blob of protoplasm extended a foot or so toward its drawing, retracted. It did it again.

"Thank you, thank you, thank you," Fath murmured to himself as he drew. "Do you think it understands symbolic logic?" On one of our copper plates lying on the deck, Fath drew a small circle, inserted two eyes. "We need simpler drawings, something like a pictograph language, or we'll never get anywhere." At the base of his circle he drew a vertical line. His drawing looked like a face on a stick. Deliberately, he stood on it. Then he stood on the larger deck drawing of himself, then stepped back onto the copper plate. At last, done, he stepped back, put his arm around my shoulder.

The outrider quivered. Then it collapsed itself onto the copper plate.

I said, "Funny how it reads—"

A sizzle. As if galvanized, the outrider leaped off the plate, bulges and lumps forming and disappearing in its surface. It flitted up the bulkhead, dropped down, zoomed to the hatch at the far end of the corridor, skittered from bulkhead to deck to bulkhead. Wherever it touched, the alumalloy blistered.

"I don't think it likes copp—"

"Get those plates out of here, flank!"

I bent to retrieve them.

The alien barreled down the corridor.

Too late, Father shouted a warning.

The outrider swerved at the last instant, missed me by inches. I stood frozen. It raced to the section three hatch, bounced from bulkhead to hatch to deck.

Fath gripped his laser, keyed off the safety. "Into a cabin, Randy!"

I dropped the plates and ran.

The pistol held at arm's length, Fath backed through the cabin hatch, slapped it shut.

I huddled in the corner, weeping in my helmet.

He moaned, "Christ, oh, Christ, what have I done?" Then he shook himself, snatched up the caller. "Seafort to Bridge. We have a problem."

"We saw."

"Where is it now?"

"At the section five hatch, at the moment. Stay where you are. I'm sending Janks to kill it."

"No!"

"This is my call. You're isolated, in no position to—"

Fath keyed the caller. "Captain Seafort to Janks. Report."

"Master-at-arms Janks."

"Where are you?"

"In five, approaching the section four hatch. There are six of us. Stay out of sight so—"

"Belay that. The alien is at the far end of the corridor. You're to enter four, take out the copper plates and jettison them. Aim your weapons, but don't fire unless it comes at you. I'll watch the holocam replay, and so help me, if any of you kill it needlessly, you'll see court-martial."

"Aye aye, sir."

"Wait a moment." Fath stabbed at the caller. "Chief Engineer!"

"Chief McAndrews repor—"

"Alumalloy plates, a dozen. Have them on Level 2 at the section six hatch in two minutes. Move!"

"But—aye aye, sir."

"Janks, we're in cabin 247. You're to escort Randy—"

"No!" I leaped like an outrider stung by copper. "So what if I'm afraid? We're doing this together!"

"It thinks we attacked it. You saw what it—"

"Let me be brave! You are!"

"Hah. My heart's thudding so fast . . ." Fath shook his head. "I've got to get you out."

"You didn't make Mikhael run away, when he was my age!"

"What?"

"In the fight to seize Galactic."

"How on earth would you know . . ."

"He told me." In my cell, when we'd spoken of Dad's last days.

Fath scowled. At length, he took up the caller. "Belay that last, Janks. Wait another minute for Chief McAndrews, and bring in his alumalloy plates."

"Aye aye, sir."

"Thank you, Fath." I tried to sound mature, but a sniffle spoiled the effect.

The exchange of plates was made without incident. Tolliver assured us the alien had skittered far from our hatch. Cautiously, the Captain opened and peered out.

The outrider quivered at the corridor's end.

Fath knelt, re-etched his tiny stick figure on an alumalloy plate.

The outrider remained where it was.

"*Captain?*"

"What, Edgar?"

"*We've a call from the Stadholder. Would you come out before you press your luck too far?*"

"I'll get back to him. This can't wait."

Fath handed me the pistol, bade me retreat halfway to the section five hatch. A reassuring pat. He trudged the opposite way, to the section three hatch, where the alien waited.

I aimed with care. The target light centered full on the outrider. Surreptitiously, I dialed up the power. My gloved finger hovered over the trigger.

The outrider, at the moment, was some five feet tall. Fath walked slowly up to it, stood alongside. My breath rasped in my helmet. *Please, God. Don't let it happen.* Not while I watch.

After a moment, Father started back toward the plates. After a few steps, he stopped, looked back.

The alien didn't move.

Casually, Fath retraced his steps. Again, he took a few coaxing steps. This time, after waiting, he kept going. I joined him at the alumalloy plates.

The alien quivered. Then, with shocking speed, it raced at Fath. I fired, missed. It stopped just short of us. Fath snatched away my pistol. "What's the *matter* with you?"

I said nothing. My mouth was dry.

Deliberately, Fath sat down on the old drawing. With an effort, he got to his feet, stepped on the stick face.

Time passed.

From the outrider's trunk grew a protoplasmic, fingerless arm. Ever so delicately, the alien touched the plate, sprang back.

I held my breath.

It touched again. Apparently it decided the plate was safe, and sagged, allowing itself to puddle atop it.

We waited.

The outrider moved to the stick face. The arm formed anew. Again, for just a moment, it aimed at Fath.

Now the outrider moved to its own drawing. The arm emerged, flopped downward, touched itself elsewhere, began to reabsorb. The upper, original end of it broke off. In a moment the arm had disappeared.

"Fath!"

"I know. It pointed to itself." Quickly, Fath etched a blob into the plate.

He stood on the outrider's original drawing of itself, and then on his latest drawing. "Simple pictographs, old fellow. Do you understand?"

The alien quivered.

Fath knelt to draw. "We need a table. I can't keep doing this."

Cabin utility tables were built-in, unmovable. I ran to the hatch, grabbed the caller. "Mr. Janks, a table. Anything, but quickly." In moments, I had it. Lugging furniture while wearing a vacuum suit is an awkward, sweaty, frustrating job. I managed it.

I examined Fath's handiwork. He'd drawn something close to a fish. Small, but recognizable. A blank plate lay nearby.

The outrider tasted his drawing. No response.

Fath drew another fish, much bigger, in more detail. Inside its outline, he drew three of the blobs that we'd agreed represented outriders. Then he set the plate on the deck.

The alien tasted it. It drew itself up, quivering. Then it melted onto the blank plate. A moment later, it oozed off, reconstituted itself.

On the plate was an etching. A fish; I was sure of it. But its lines were incomplete, and material flowed from within.

Fath studied it. "A fish, but dead. Those are holes from laser fire."

The outrider surged back onto the plate. It roiled and . . . well, sloshed. The plate smoked. It took the creature a long time to accomplish its goal.

When the alien rose, the plate was filled with etchings. From end to end, it was covered with fish, all spewing protoplasm. Somberly, we stared at the vision of holocaust.

Abruptly the alien surged onto the plate. Acrid smoke curled. Father leaped back.

This time, when the outrider reconstituted itself, the plate was blackened and blistered. All the drawings were gone.

We waited.

The alien sagged, collapsed into a puddle, remained so for over a minute. Then, once more, it regained its form.

Father's mouth worked. He tried to speak, gave it up, strode to the hatch.

"Sir, what is it? Shall I call a medic?"

Fath shook his head. "The drawing of dying fish . . ."

"Yes?"

"He erased it."

"And?"

"He negated it! Then, that ritual submission. Don't you understand? He's suing for peace!"

17

MINUTES LATER, Tolliver and Mikhael were with us, in our cabin refuge. Neither had bothered with a suit. Mik knelt by his father's side.

"I'm sure of it," Fath said, for the fourth time.

When no adult was speaking, I tugged at his sleeve. "Sir, I don't quite understand . . ." I tried again. "Why were you upset?"

"Not now, Randy." Mik's tone was harsh.

"Oh, I'll tell him. I'll shout it from the rooftops. You see . . ." He regarded me with grave affection. "I've done so many terrible things. God let me kill your father, and Alexi, even Arlene. Those poor children at Academy. So many others. And the fish. Thousands, and still they came. Remember, Edgar? Our siren song, that sent them into the Sun? And still they came."

Not a sound, not a breath.

"And then they stopped. A few answered the lure of the caterwaul stations, and they were gone. For forty years I've known I murdered a race, a species. But . . . I didn't. They live!" Leaning on Mikhael, he raised himself off the bed. "For five years I've let love rot to hate, refusing to talk to God. And now, in the winter of my life, He confounds me."

After a time Tolliver cleared his throat. "That's all well and good, but there's an alien in section four wondering why you left so abruptly. He may take it personally."

"Oh, let me have my sentiment." Fath climbed to his feet. "And my thanksgiving."

"A time and place . . ."

"Pa, Ms. Frand and I got to talking . . ." Mik looked apologetic. "Instead of going through decon each time you talk to that beast . . ."

"What, son?"

"Well, it would take Jess's help, and engineering. A transplex barrier, and some sort of servo to make the drawings . . . wouldn't that work better?"

A chuckle. "Perhaps, if I had the faintest idea what you were talking about."

"Arggh. Look, this is the corridor. A few meters on our side of the section four hatch, here in five, we erect a see-through airtight barrier. Here, between the barrier and the hatch, a servomech runs an etcher. We open the hatch. The outrider comes through to visit. You sit on our side of the barrier and draw what you want; the servo repeats it for the outrider to, er, taste. You never touch the plate; no decon, no risk of the outrider killing you."

"I suppose we train our roving friend to hold up its drawings for us to see?"

"Oh, come on, Pa. Another servo. Surely Jess can program a servomech to lift a plate to the holovid."

"Hmmm." The Captain scowled. Then, "How long?"

"To build it? A few hours, I'd think. No more."

Fath's glance strayed to me. I nodded vehemently. No more humiliating decon, and I'd have a barrier between me and that god-awful *quivering*.

"Mr. Tamarov, you were on duty when you thought of this?"

"Yes, sir." Mikhael looked puzzled.

"Very well, a commendation in the Log. I'll post it tonight. Well done, Middy."

"Thank you, sir." Mik looked like he could walk on air.

"I admit, the decon gets to be a trial." The Captain unbuttoned his shirt as he led us to the waiting medics.

After decon, the Captain let himself be persuaded it was all right to leave quarantine. Time and again, med analysis had found no sign of virus. And we'd already been inoculated against all known alien organisms.

In our cabin, we sat down immediately to a conference with the Chief, Tolliver, and Jess. The puter listened to Mik's explanation—more coherent, this time—and offered a few useful, if minor modifications. Mr. McAndrews promised to put every rating he could shanghai on the task, and left.

Fath stretched wearily. "Find Jerence," he told Tolliver. "He's a diplomat; I need his advice."

"He's ashore."

"No, he came aloft with Anthony."

"And went back groundside with him."

"Won't anyone ever tell me anything?" The Captain threw up his hands. "Or ask my permission?" He opened a drawer, took out a dark bottle.

Tolliver said hastily. "Now's not a good time, Nick."

"Nonsense. For once, we have something to celebrate."

"No, thank you."

Fath wrinkled his brow. After a moment, "Ah, I understand. Randy, Mr. Tolliver is uneasy because I'm about to offer him a drink. You're aware liquor is forbidden on Naval vessels?"

"Dad told me."

"I rarely imbibe, myself. But Edgar enjoys a nightcap, now and then. He could never bring a bottle of scotch aboard; his honor, as well as regs, forbid it. But if I, the Captain, order him to drink, what choice has he, poor man?"

I watched, agape.

"You, of course, will say nothing of this, to anyone. Ever."

"No, sir. I mean, aye aye, sir. I swear."

He poured a glass, handed it to his friend. Tolliver, with a doubtful glance in my direction, downed it, without waiting for an order. Fath poured him another, which he sipped more slowly. I retreated to my bed, while they conversed in low tones.

At length, Tolliver bade him farewell, and left.

"You did well today," Fath said, when he'd slipped off his shoes with a sigh. "Except when you shot at him."

"He was coming at you!"

"I told you: only to save your own life. Now I won't trust you again with a laser."

"Fath . . ." I pouted. "That's not fair."

"Get used to it. I'm in charge."

I rolled my eyes. Adults: a joey could never please them. On the other hand, if I'd splattered the alien into tiny smoking blobs, we'd never have learned it wanted peace. I suppressed a pang of guilt. If the outrider wanted peace, he shouldn't have flown at Fath.

"For shooting at him, a dozen verses, memorized by tonight."

"Fath!"

"Pick ones that help you learn to mind. Start with Proverbs 6:20 and 13:1. Go read them now."

Adults.

Fath kept himself busy on the caller, while I toiled at the bloody, stupid Bible. If he thought he'd make me religious by loading me with busywork, he had another thought coming. After a time, I was careful to keep my resentment under wraps; once, when I'd let it show clearly, he cocked a warning finger at me that gave me a chill.

"What do you mean, it's moved? Where?" Caller to ear, he paced. "Closer to our tubes? No? Good. Do we still have a shot? Very well."

I asked, "The fish?"

"Get your work done."

"Yeah."

"What?"

"Yes, sir." I wrote a verse into the holovid, compared it with the original. Only a few words off, but he wouldn't be satisfied. Not Fath. Growf.

"Anthony? Captain Seafort. Sorry I couldn't return your . . . Ahh. I see.

That could be a problem, if he supports the Bishop. What does Jerence say? Hmm."

I set down my holovid.

Fath covered the caller. "He's having trouble with Palabee's party. Nothing serious. Finish your verses." To Anth, "When's the trial? The sooner you deal with Scanlen . . . would you rather I took him home and deposited him with the Patriarchs? I don't mind; the man is penance for my sins."

Fath chuckled. "Well, let me know. By the way, Tolliver says most of our passengers want off, immediately or sooner, now that the fish showed no interest in your shuttle. They're skittish about having an outrider aboard; can't say I blame them, though we have guards all around it . . . Well, I've no idea how long. Who knows where this will take us? We've never had discussions with an alien." His pacing took him past my table; he glanced downward, covered the caller. "Three extra verses, for not getting back to work when I told you." To the caller, "Hmm? No, just brutalizing young Randolph. Continue."

The negotiating arena wasn't finished yet; we went to dinner, Proverbs spinning in my head. I'd learned something useful: Fath couldn't be budged by pleas or promises. And sullenness was a tactic to be avoided.

I'd have to study him. Every adult had his weak points.

Casually, he tousled my hair. Part of me wanted to bite him, the other to wriggle like a puppy.

The tension in the Dining Hall was palpable. No welcome, no greetings, only hostile stares. All from passengers, of course. Crew wouldn't dare.

Mr. Pandeker stood, gave the usual prayer, while Fath watched in silence. Was it only yesterday that Anth had sat at our table?

Afterward, Fath remained standing. "I know many of you are concerned that we've had contact with a fish. We're taking thorough precautions, and it seems there's little danger. Nonetheless, I've spoken to Stadholder Carr. He'll find temporary housing for those of you who wish to go ashore until we sail. Please see Purser Li to make arrangements." He hesitated. "It's my belief we won't be attacked."

Tad Anselm was at our table, but not Mik. I looked around, couldn't spot him. Perhaps he was on watch.

I dived into my salad; Bible-thumping made me hungry. After a moment Fath handed me my napkin, frowned until I used it. I suppressed a sigh. It was going to be a long adolescence.

The purser leaned over Fath's shoulder, whispered.

"Of course. Bring him over."

In a moment he was back, Chris Dakko in tow.

Mr. Dakko looked awful: unshaven, rumpled. But his voice was steady. "I came to apologize."

"Accepted."

"You deserve civility. But how can you allow that . . . thing among us?"

"You wouldn't believe it, Chris. It communicated. It wants peace. I think we can—"

"Yes, I saw how it communicated with Kevin."

"We did that, Chris, shooting it."

"After it burst through our hull, decompressing us." Mr. Dakko drew a deep breath. "Still, I apologize. I'll never curse you again." With what might have been a token salute, he turned on his heel, returned to his table.

After a few moments, the purser was back. Another passenger wanted audience. Fath looked weary, but assented.

A middle-aged woman, easily past thirty.

"Sorry to bother you during dinner." Her voice was pleasant. "Sir, I've two children aboard. How sure are you we'll be safe?"

"I can't be sure." Fath met her eye. "I've three children of my own on *Olympiad*." Mikhael, Janey, and who? . . . Oh! Me. "At the moment, I'm not unduly worried."

"What would you advise?"

"Ma'am, you're booked to Kall's Planet?"

"My husband's there. I'm joining him at Hawking Lab."

"If you go ashore, there's risk—minor, I'll grant you—that you'll be stranded. The next ship of the line won't reach here for six months."

"Why stranded?"

I yearned to throw down my fork, snarl, "Let him eat in peace." But I didn't.

"If I'm wrong and the fish attack, we might suddenly have to Fuse."

"In that case, where would I be safer, here or ashore?"

"Lord only knows, ma'am."

It didn't satisfy her, but she retreated to her table.

Dessert. Andrew Ghent came rushing in. "Midshipman Ghent reporting, sir." A crisp salute. "Mr. McAndrews's compliments, and the arena is ready for inspection."

"Excellent." The Captain sipped his coffee. "Have him make sure the servo is well stocked with alumalloy sheets. No copper."

"Aye aye, sir."

"Dismissed."

Smartly, the boy wheeled off. I studied his gait. I could do that, if it came to it. But who'd want to be a middy? I turned my attention back to the table. "What are you grinning at, Fath?"

"Nothing, son."

On the way out he stopped at the hatchway caller. "Bridge, who has the watch?"

"I just came on, sir. Ms. Frand."

"Where's Edgar?"

"I believe he went to the lounge."

"Ask him if he cares to join us at the negotiating table." He replaced the caller, threw an arm over my shoulder. "Someday, you'll be grown."

Was that supposed to be a revelation?

"You'll have children. Grandchildren."

"Yes, sir?" No harm in being polite. It meant so much to him.

"You'll tell them of this day. That you were present, when two races first met, and spoke. Holovids will be made, books written. You'll be famous, you know."

I threw him a skeptical glance. He seemed serious.

"We haven't done anything yet," I said. And besides, history was made by heads of state, like Dad. And heroes.

"Who first invented a joint language?"

"You did, sir."

"Oh? Who told me the outrider was showing submission?"

"I did, but . . ." A chill. Was it possible someday I'd be in the holos?

"You're capable of great things, Randy. Don't bridle at a few Scripture verses."

I felt so forlorn I wanted to cry.

It was almost as I'd pictured it. The corridor hatch was closed, blocking our view of the alien. For our side, the crew had set up a comfortable table, two padded armchairs that looked as if they could have been borrowed from the bridge. On the table, electronic touch pads, a caller, a mini-console with a cable snaking to a hatch control.

The table was set before a thick transplex barrier, which was attached to the bulkhead with grommets that could be removed from our side, but not from the alien's. Of course, if the outrider chose to burn through it, we'd be forced into a mad dash for the safety of our section hatch.

Beyond the barrier, a pair of one-armed servos whirred and clicked, in what seemed random motions. As Mr. Seafort settled into one of the chairs with a sigh of relief, the servo arms reached across, grasped each other's extensions, bobbed up and down.

Fath snorted. "Cute, Jess."

"Glad you enjoyed it, sir." The puter's baritone came from all sides. I glanced up. Speakers had been mounted, high, low, behind us as well. "Ready when you are."

Tad Anselm stood by, looking pleased.

"Very impressive," the Captain said. "How many of the crew did it take to set this up?"

"Almost thirty," Tad said cheerfully. "It was a real clusterf—"

"No doubt." Fath cleared his throat. "It's still in there?"

The speakers boomed. "Midway in the corridor, sir, about two meters from the airlock hatch."

"Very well. Tad, have a screen added to our assembly. Might as well be able to see our guest while the hatch is closed."

"Aye aye, sir." He hesitated. "Are you ready? I'll call Mr. Janks."

"He won't be necessary."

Tad said hesitantly, "Sir, I'm only a lieutenant, and a recent one at that, but would you permit some advice?"

Fath grinned at me. "Now there's a joey skilled at diplomacy. Go ahead."

"We've all a natural instinct to safeguard you. Resisting it only irritates the crew, and their protection does no harm."

"Right." I didn't realize I'd spoken until Fath shot me a glance of annoyance.

"Hmmm. I suppose it won't hurt. But no sudden, overt moves with a pistol. Fire only at my command."

"You may not have time—"

"Nonsense. The outrider has to burn through that shield of yours to reach us. Let's go."

Jess intervened. "Pardon, sir. If you'd like, I can keep track of our symbols. I know of four to date: a human face, a live fish, a dead fish, and an outrider."

"And erasure for negation. Yes, keep track. Let's get started."

Quietly, I slipped into the chair at Fath's side. He appeared not to notice.

When the master-at-arms's detail was in place, we keyed open the corridor hatch.

The outrider was still for a moment, then skittered our way.

"Let's start with a peace sign." Awkwardly, Fath drew a screenful of fish, made them look dead. Inside the barrier, a servo copied his drawing onto a large plate.

The outrider collapsed onto it. After a time, it stood.

Fath scribbled over the drawing, erasing it.

I peered at his drawing, fingers itching. "I could do that. If you said the words to draw . . ."

"No, you're going to bed in an hour. You've dark circles under your eyes."

The outrider tasted anew. Its swirls moved more slowly than yesterday, in slow orbit on its skin. It lay on the erased plate. When it was done, Jess's servo raised the plate so we could see.

A new sign, a ragged spiral.

Fath's tone was tentative. "A solar system?"

Tad looked over our shoulder. "An orbit? Fusion?"

Puzzled silence. The alien waited.

I said, "How about, 'Yes'?"

Fath turned and stared.

"What if he's simply agreeing with you?"

Tolliver ambled through, from section six. "I've been thinking, sir. If we recite all of Shakespeare for it . . ."

"We need a drawing. Anything it understands." Fath thought. "A person." He drew a stick face. The alien tasted it. "Now, erase." He scribbled over the face.

"Why not let me do the drawing, sir?" Jess. "Anything you've drawn once . . ." The puter conjured a screenful of fish images. "It might save time."

"Try it. Redraw the face. Erase it again, but this time put an X in the corner."

"Which corner?"

"Any corner. Don't be so literal."

"Would I ask you not to be human?" With what might have been a sigh, the puter redrew the stick face, the erasure, the new sign.

"Is that your new signature, sir? An X? In case you enlist as a trannie when—"

"It's a symbol for 'no,' Edgar. To go with the spiral 'yes.' "

"If our cuddly friend agrees. Perhaps it thinks you're speaking of dead humans. Lunch."

My stomach recoiled.

Tad asked, "Now what's it doing?"

We peered. The alien had reshaped itself into something more squat. When it moved, it left behind a thick liquid, in a bowl-like crust. A protoplasmic arm extruded, pushed it a few inches in our direction.

Silence. I yawned.

The Captain cleared his throat. "Ideas, anyone?"

"A peace offering?" Tad.

"I think it pissed at you."

"Edgar!"

"It's as good an explanation as—"

"It's never done it before."

"We know almost nothing about its metabolism."

The outrider withdrew beyond the corridor hatch, leaving its offering behind. It touched a bulkhead, stood there quivering.

Behind us, Mr. Janks cleared his throat. "Begging your pardon, sir, but Mr. Dakko asks if he might join us."

The Captain tapped his drawing table. "I think not. No, it wouldn't be a good idea." He turned his attention back to the transparent shield. "What do we do about . . . that?" He regarded the offering in the crusty bowl of protoplasm.

Apparently the outrider had the same question. It lapped over the bowl, reabsorbed it. Its dots and blobs swirled a touch faster. Then, while Fath considered the matter, it excreted the offering again, shoved it in our direction, retreated.

Fath contemplated. I yawned prodigiously.

"It wants us to take it, that's clear. Very well." He stood. "Evacuate the area. Nonreactive containers, full precautions. Dr. Romez and the Chief are in charge. Detailed physical and chemical analysis, report to my cabin. Let's go, joey." He headed down the corridor.

"Where?" Reluctantly, I followed.

"I've got work to do. You're off to bed." He steered me toward section six.

"Fath!" I stopped short.

"Come along." He grasped my hand.

I debated pulling free, didn't quite dare. "I'm fourteen!"

"Your point?"

"It's ridiculous, putting me to bed like a—"

"You raise your son, I'll raise mine."

There were many things I could say, none of them wise. Fuming, I restrained myself as we made our way down the corridor.

Fath slapped open the cabin hatch. Inside, a low light. Corrine Sloan came to her feet.

The Captain stood stock-still.

"I brought Janey." Her voice was soft. "She was restless, didn't want me to leave. Mikhael urged me to stay until she slept. He said you wouldn't mind . . ."

"It's all right."

"Thank you, Nick. I'll go."

"Just a moment. Randy, a shower before bed."

My cheeks flamed. How could he, in front of her?

"You've been weeping," he said to her.

"It's nothing."

"I doubt that. Do you want to tell me?"

"I don't know . . . I . . ."

"Randy, go about your business." Fath's tone held a warning note.

"Yes, sir."

"It's just . . . sooner or later, I'll have to leave her."

Reluctantly, I disappeared into the head.

When I emerged, clean and damp, Corrine was gone. Fath sat dejectedly on the edge of his bed.

I climbed into my bunk, careful not to wake Janey, in her cot in the corner.

Bedtime, two hours past dinner? Nonsense! I'd show him. I'd stay awake for hours.

"HOW LONG WILT thou sleep, O sluggard? When wilt thou arise out of thy sleep?"

"Huh?"

"Proverbs 6:9." Fath threw off my outer blanket. "It's time for breakfast. And we've agreed with the outrider on five new words."

I swung my legs out of bed. "Which ones?" I worked my toes into my slippers, pulled up my sagging pajamas.

"'Fast' and 'slow' were the first two. Jess taught them, by moving the servos."

"Zarky." I grabbed clean clothes, started to the head. "What were the others?"

"Dead. Ship. War."

Section one of Level 3 was crowded with passengers, waiting for shuttles. They jostled and shoved, as if it would speed their embarkation. Each shuttle, though, first unloaded incoming crew. I wondered if anyone noticed the irony. Still, much of our crew remained groundside.

I was assigned to "help." How, no one told me. But Fath said I was ship's boy as well as his son, and that if he showed undue favoritism, crewmen would take offense. I'd already had a day with him on special assignment.

But a ship's boy *has* no regular duties, I told him. Why couldn't I help the Captain instead of the purser? Out, he said, bestowing a gentle swat on my rear. And straighten your collar.

Adults. Or was it Captains?

Alejandro and I spent the morning stowing hand luggage, running back to cabins to retrieve forgotten belongings, and, in one case, helping a drunken hydronocist's mate to his crew berth. Alec thought it funnier than I, but eventually his good mood prevailed. Were it not for the fact that Fath was chatting with an alien one Level above, I'd have actually enjoyed it.

When the last of the day's passengers had boarded, I raced up to the Level 2 "arena." Lieutenant Frand caught me, made me walk all the way back to the lock and try again, more slowly. I didn't dare cheat; I knew if she told the Captain, I'd be in real trouble. About official duties, Fath lacked a sense of humor.

To my frustration, I caught him just leaving, on the way to lunch. The alien seemed lethargic, or perhaps just tired. Even its quivering was slowed.

Fath seemed glad to see me. I found myself chattering about my day, asking him about his. Before long we'd reached the officers' mess, and no one told me to take my meal belowdecks with the rest of the crew.

Perhaps it was that I'd made special effort to please Fath with my table manners, or perhaps he was lonely. Whatever the cause, he allowed me to rejoin the negotiations. First, though, I was dispatched to find Mr. Dakko, who had an urgent call from Dr. Zayre, and wasn't answering a page. I found him at last, slumped on a recliner in a lounge. I told him of his call.

"How," he asked, "goes your discourse with inhumanity?"

Almost, I sniffed his breath for liquor, but I knew none was to be had aboard ship except in Fath's cabin. "Fine, sir. We're making progress."

"Are you pleased?"

"I suppose." The very question made me uneasy. I owed loyalty to Kevin. But our outrider wasn't the one who . . .

"Under fire, they fly apart," Mr. Dakko said dreamily. "How I'd love to see that."

I knew I ought to keep my mouth shut. It wasn't my role to reprove him, or guide him, or offer solace. Yet . . . "Sir, if we make peace, no one else will be killed."

"Tell that to Kev."

"I wish I could." Abruptly my eyes stung.

"Ah, what we all wish. You know my wish? That I could say good-bye." His voice caught. "That's the worst of it, I never told him good-bye." A silence. "Go to your pet."

A long trudge back to section four, where Fath and Andrew Ghent were on duty. I peered through the transplex shield. "What have I missed?"

"A word or two. He seems to have lost interest."

"What's that?" I tried to put Mr. Dakko's misery behind me.

"Another offering."

"What's in it?"

Fath took up a sheet. "Mild acids, complex and simple. Potassium sulphate. Magnesium chlorate. The list goes on."

"Why does he give it to us?"

"If I knew that, son . . ."

"Is it a gift, or does he want it back?"

Fath blinked. "Good question." He keyed his caller. "Chief McAndrews!"

The outrider perched near the bulkhead. Its dots and swirls barely moved.

Minutes later, a volunteer opened the section five hatch, slid in the original offering we'd taken for analysis, bolted to safety.

On our newly installed screen, via holocam, we watched the alien absorb the compounds. He skittered back to us.

Again, he extruded his offering.

Fath said, "Well? Should we take it?"

"He seems to want us to, sir." Ghent.

I reached past Fath, peered at the analysis. "Are these dangerous?"

"Not unduly."

"Do we have chemicals like these aboard?"

"I'd imagine so." His mind was elsewhere.

"Could we make more?"

"Why?"

"Sir, what if he's asking to be fed?"

He swung slowly to face me, raised an eyebrow. "I never thought of that." He took up the caller.

Three hours later, a sailor deposited a ceramic tray of the alien's offering on the section four deck. The outrider rolled to it, distinctly slower than before. Tentatively, it grew a tentacle, touched the mixture. An instant after, he . . . well, merged with it. Threw himself over it. Absorbed it, the way I'd absorbed a liter of water after hours tossing a ball on a hot day.

When he skittered back to us, he had his old speed. His dots and blobs swirled with vigor. Despite myself, I grinned.

Fath said mildly, "You remember how to stand at attention?"

"Yes, sir." What had I done wrong?

"Do so."

I stiffened, the way I'd been taught. Two middies and four of Janks's detail were watching, so I did my best.

"Mr. Carr, on three occasions you've offered suggestions regarding the outrider that have proven valuable and insightful. As a consequence, I'm assigning you to the alien detail until further notice. I commend you highly, and will so note in the Log."

I swelled, produced a tremulous smile.

"As you were."

I let my shoulders sag.

"Now, you're off duty."

"Yes, sir."

Fath rested gentle hands on my shoulders. "Well done, son."

18

CREWMEN SHOWERED US with all sorts of suggestions as to how to communicate with the alien. Some were patently ridiculous: draw a diagram of the hydrogen atom: one nucleus, one electron, and progress through physics from that starting point. That was Ms. Frand's idea, which Fath didn't debunk openly. But as I told him privately, if you showed me a hydrogen atom, would I have much to say about it? For that matter, would Fath?

He decided we needed to establish units of time. I pondered how that might be done, came up with nothing. The outrider seemed to accept that some of our efforts would be fruitless, and seemed untroubled by them.

We took a break. Mikhael corralled me, with Tad's consent, and took me up to the wardroom. He introduced me to the six other middies who'd come aboard from long-leave, including Alon Riev, who'd become first midshipman upon Anselm's promotion. No doubt because I was Mik's brother—and the Captain's new son—they were more polite than they would have been, though Riev's manner was distant.

Mik seemed a bit disappointed that I maintained a cool reserve. But all these joeys were at least two years older than I, and I wasn't interested in making a fool of myself. Mr. Riev, for one, seemed glad to see me go.

Back to work.

By now, even Mr. Tolliver had become involved. From time to time, he studied the outrider thoughtfully, arms folded. His acid remarks eased. Of course, they didn't disappear entirely; that would be too unlike him.

We reached agreement on symbols for Fuse, food, and injured (broken-not-dead). We applied this last to ships and fish. Then Fath drew examples of touching: outrider-touch-fish, fish-touch-ship, human-touch-human, all alongside a new triangular symbol for touch.

Once we'd cemented these concepts, Fath had Jess draw symbols showing outrider-touch-human; human-dead. Fish-touch-ship; ship-dead. The alien responded with the symbol for "yes."

We'd reached the crux of the issue. Neither side seemed sure how to proceed past this point. Fath, Tolliver, and Dr. Romez conferred at length.

Someone shook me awake. Fath. I peered up sleepily. "Sorry. I was resting my eyes."

"Dinnertime."

I stretched. "Clean clothes?"

"What do you think?"

I sighed. "Yessir."

Fath sent me walking ahead, spoke quietly to Tolliver. Nonetheless, his voice was louder than he thought; I got most of the conversation.

". . . time he took Kevin's body groundside."

"He may not want to leave."

"Don't force him off; he's an old shipmate. But persuade him."

"What's the urgency?"

"Randy spoke to him and came back upset."

"What did Dakko say?"

"I have no idea."

With even more passengers gone than before, dinner was a quiet and somber affair. Fath would be on watch until midnight; he sent me off to our cabin to read aloud two chapters of any book in the Old Testament. I wasn't required to memorize them.

I hated it when he did that. In his absence it would be so easy to cheat. It was utterly unfair of Fath to depend on my sense of honor to stop me. How could I exercise a joeykid's natural right to evade parental supervision, if constrained by a call to integrity?

I chose Genesis, read two chapters, and a third for spite. Then I undressed for bed. Janey, tonight, was with her mother. I turned out the light, thought about Anth and Dad. Then, Alex Hopewell and Kevin, at the pond. Judy Winthrop, diving into the still water. I was plagued with unsettling images of Judy and our brief tryst at Carr Plantation. I tossed and turned, until I relieved my unease the only way open to me.

When Fath came to bed I woke, though I pretended sleep for his sake. Soon the pretense was real. It must have been two hours after that the caller softly buzzed.

Instantly, no doubt from long practice, Fath keyed it quiet. "Yes? Very well, put him on." A pause. "Jerence. I trust you know the hour?"

I lay listening. I'd promised Fath never to eavesdrop—and had stood in the corner for hours to make myself agree to it—but this was different. I was in my own bed, where he wanted me; it wasn't my fault he spoke too loudly to ignore.

"He *what*?" Fath sat upright, switched on the bed light. I watched through half-opened eyelids. "When? Anyone hurt?" A sigh. "Jerence, this is serious. What do you suggest?"

I licked my lips.

"Of course I want to help; he's Derek's grandson and I'll do anything I can. But Admiral Kenzig is breathing down my neck. When I snatched Randy from Scanlen's clutches he threw a fit. My orders now are explicit: stay out of local politics, period. And if Andori's involved . . ." He listened. "Anyone know where he went? Have you tried the Cathedral? It's his home base."

A long silence, while Fath listened.

"Jer, take care. Remember the holo of Randy's hanging: these joeys don't play for zarks. Yes, I know. Anthony is formidable, in his own way. Keep me posted. I'll call the Admiral in the morning, see what he'll let us do." Another pause. "And to you too, old friend."

The light winked out.

I lay awake half the night.

When I woke, groaning and stretching, Fath was up and gone. How did he do it? He was an old man; he even had gray hairs.

I washed and dressed, even took an extra minute to brush and comb. I tried the bridge but he wasn't there; I trotted down to Level 2, but he wasn't at the table.

The ship was far too large to search; disconsolate, I ran back up to the wardroom, knocked at the hatch. Mik wasn't there; Mr. Riev told me rather crossly that he might be in the exercise room on Two.

He was, working through a series of exercises. When he finished a set of push-ups I asked, "What are you doing?"

"Working off a demerit."

"Who gave it to you?"

"Pa."

"What for?"

"For asking too many questions." With a glance at his watch, he began vigorous jumping jacks.

"C'mon."

"I was late to watch."

"Do you know where he is?"

"Belowdecks, with Corrine and Janey, I think."

Ms. Sloan's cabin was on Five. The ladders were faster than the lift. On Five, I'd reached section two when—

"Mr. Carr!"

I skidded to a stop.

Ms. Frand's face was stern. "I believe we've spoken about running?"

"Yes, ma'am." I was wary.

"Apparently without effect."

"I'm sorry."

"It's a regulation, you know." She studied me. "But perhaps we'll waive it. The corridor is circular, is it not?"

"Ma'am?"

"If you run that way, east, eventually you'll return to your starting point."

"Yes."

"Show me."

"What? You want me to—"

"As fast as you can. Move!"

"Yes, ma'am!" I took off.

"Stop! What did you say?"

"I said—I mean, aye aye, ma'am!"

"Hurry, now. I expect you back in forty seconds."

I raced down the curving corridor. Luckily, few crewmen were about, and no passengers. Section five. Six. I'd forgotten to check my starting time, and had no idea whether I'd meet her goal. Seven.

At last, ten. Then one, and two. Lieutenant Frand stood tapping the deck restlessly. "What kept you?"

"I ran as fast as—"

"You'll have to do better. Try the other way."

I gaped.

"MOVE!"

I dashed toward the corridor bend.

When I completed the circle, panting, she didn't look at all pleased. "Lazy, that's what I call it. Run to seven, tag the hatch control, run back. Get the lead out, or . . ."

"Aye aye, ma'am!"

When I got back, her arms were folded. "Barely adequate. Perhaps you need practice. Should we waive the regs on running?"

"No, ma'am," I gasped. "I'll walk."

"See to it, joey." She strode off.

The hatch to 575 was open. I peered in. The Captain sat on Corrine's bunk, Janey on his lap.

". . . years ago. I doubt he'd remember—"

"Nick, it was personal. If John were the devil incarnate, Scanlen couldn't have hated him more. All I'm saying—"

"Hi, Ran'!" Janey jumped off her father, ran to me. Corrine watched with guarded approval.

"Hallo, what's this?" Fath loomed over me. "Look at you! Your shirt's damp and sweaty. Go wash and change."

"I'm sorry, Fath, I—"

"We'll have a chat tonight about grooming. In the meantime, a dozen verses, memorized. Try 2 Corinthians."

"Sir, I—"

"Right now, Randy."

I trudged dejectedly back to our cabin.

What a day. And I hadn't even had breakfast.

My hated chore completed, the Bible lay open between us.

"And that's when Ms. Frand caught me running."

Fath heard me out in silence, but there was a glint in his eyes that might have been humor. "Terrible," he said. "What will we do with you?" He got to his feet. "I think I know the problem."

"What, sir?" I sounded apprehensive, because I was.

"Come here." With a glint of humor, he embraced me. And then we went to lunch.

"Seventeen new words," said Mr. Tolliver, biting into a hot, juicy soy-beef on rye. "I must admit, that's progress. In just a generation or two, we'll be able to carry on a chat. In fact—"

"Why, Edgar!" Fath was in good spirits. "You, cynical? I never thought I'd live to see—"

Andrew Ghent tore into officers' mess, his face flushed. "Sir—Captain—Midshipman Ghent reporting—"

It wasn't fair that he could run and I couldn't. I'd have to speak to Fath about it.

"—Ms. Frand says the outrider is agitated and you should come quick, her compliments I mean, and if you please—"

"Steady, Mr. Ghent." Fath threw down his napkin. "Randy, care to come along?"

Did I care to breathe? Did a Bishop read the Bible? Did—

I scurried after him. We'd barely reached the hatch when the alarms shrieked. *"General Quarters! All hands to General Quarters!"* The voice, taut with tension, sounded like Tad Anselm.

"Where to, Fath?"

By answer, he grabbed the hatchway caller. "Seafort to Bridge."

"Lieutenant Anselm reporting. The outrider's gone to section four air-lock. If he burns through the outer hatch, the section will decompress."

"The inner hatch was left open?"

"As per your orders, yes, sir."

"What's he doing now?"

"Scuttling in and out of the lock."

"When he's inside, cycle."

"Aye aye, sir."

"Pipe 'Pilot to the Bridge.' I'll be along." He strode along the corridor.

"Is he mad at us? What were the seventeen words?" I trotted to keep up.

"Pilot Van Peer to the bridge, flank."

"I don't know, son." We strode through another section. "You've been great help, so I'll allow you on the bridge. But we're on duty now, both of us." It was a warning.

"Yes, sir." No other response would do.

A middy I'd met yesterday shared Lieutenant Anselm's watch. Uniform crisp, hair neatly brushed, he jumped to his feet when he spotted the Captain.

"As you were, Mr. Braun. Tad, is he Outside?" The Captain took his seat. I found an empty place, in the training row behind.

"I can't cycle, he won't hold still enough."

"Visuals."

"There, can you see him? Half inside the lock?"

"What set him off?"

"I've no idea, sir."

"Laser room, stand by to fire. Safeties removed!"

"Frand here. Aye aye, sir."

"Comm Room to Bridge. Incoming call from the Stadholder. He says it's urgent."

"Pilot Van Peer reporting for duty." The Pilot, lanky, graying, was breathing hard.

"Take your seat. Move us within twenty meters of the fish. Our guest wants to go home."

"Aye aye, sir." Grasping the thruster levers, Van Peer licked his lips. "This'll be a first."

"No idle chat, gentlemen." The Captain paced before the simulscreen. "Mr. Anselm, watch the inner hatch. Be ready."

"Aye aye, sir."

"Comm Room, put Mr. Carr through."

"Visuals?"

"No. Take care, Pilot. Don't hit her. Ms. Frand!"

"Yes, sir?"

"Your primary target is the fish. Don't fire unless she makes for our fusion tubes, or winds up to throw an appendage."

"Aye aye, sir."

"Captain Seafort?" Anthony.

"Mr. Van Peer, slow your approach. We don't want to scare her off. Yes, Stadholder? It's rather a busy moment."

"There, sir!" Tad jabbed at his console. "He's gone in! Cycling."

"Hull view."

The simulscreen blinked. Abruptly, our hull stretched to infinite distance. I tried to orient myself, spot the outer hatch.

"Sir . . ." The Pilot. "I'd like a view of the fish, for reference."

"Jess, split screen. Go ahead, Mr. Carr."

"Did Branstead call you?"

"Last night."

"Palabee's gone over to the Church, I'm sure of it. He's helping hide Scanlen, so Andori will appear blameless. We're headed for crisis. Where's Chris Dakko?"

"He went groundside this morning."

A sharp regret stabbed my gut. I'd meant to have a last good-bye with Kev. He deserved it.

The fish loomed, alarmingly close. Mr. Van Peer nudged the thrusters.

"Mr. Braun, don't fiddle with your console." Fath's voice was a rasp.

The middy jerked in his seat. "Aye aye, sir." He pressed his hands in his lap.

"I'll try to find him. His people haven't been cooperative, but . . ." His people? I thought Mr. Dakko was a victualler. Anth made it sound as if he had a cadre, a political—

The Captain said, "Jess, sensor report, Level 2 east airlock."

"Pressure twenty percent and falling. Hatch integrity undisturbed. Anomaly within lock."

"The outrider?"

"I presume so. Airlock sensors are not programmed to recognize motion of other than humans or servos."

"It's the outrider."

"Substitution noted."

"Mr. Seafort, may I be frank?"

"Of course."

"If I had your experience, or Grandpa's . . . Sir, for most of my life you headed a government that dwarfs mine. What should I do?"

"Just a moment, Stadholder. I've a situation here." The Captain drummed the console. "Sorry I snapped at you, Mr. Braun." His voice was quiet. "Nerves."

"Thank you, sir." The midshipman sat very straight.

"Eleven percent," said Jess. "Five. Vacuum achieved." A gap in the smooth surface of the hull. The outer hatch slid open.

The Pilot, with gentle nudges of his thrusters, positioned us closer to the fish. At last, we came to rest relative to the alien.

Virtually ignoring the fish, the Captain stared at the outrider. "If he skitters along the hull . . ."

I blanched. The outrider could melt through the hull just about anywhere, and wreak havoc. Even here on the bridge. I glanced about. Where was the suit locker?

"*Mr. Seafort, are you there?*"

A shapeless form, at the hatch.

Eyes riveted on the simulscreen, the Captain clasped his hands behind his back.

The fish's colors pulsed.

The form on our hull quivered, flexed.

"Godspeed." Fath spoke in a whisper.

The outrider launched itself into the infinite cold of space. I swallowed. If it missed . . .

It landed on the fish amidships, seemed to stick to its surface. The fish's skin swirled, became indistinct. The outrider shrank.

It disappeared within.

I let out a breath I hadn't known I was holding.

"All right, Anthony. For the moment I can give you my full attention." A pause. "Understand, my own conflicts with the Church skew my judgment."

"*Still, sir, I want it.*"

"Very well. The Bishops are inevitably allied with Earth. In my view, you can't govern in their name."

My breath caught.

"*Disestablishment? I'm not sure I could carry it.*"

"Excommunication is a mighty club." Fath was quiet. "And Andori will use it, without qualm."

"*Whether I govern with Church or without, he has that power.*"

"Only among those who listen. How many are they?"

"*Hope Nation remains conservative.*"

"Then you'll fall."

"*Not without a fight.*"

"I should tell you, by the way, that our Reverend Pandeker has spent many hours on the caller, consulting his cohorts in Centraltown."

"*About what?*"

"I've no idea. I've no right to listen in."

"*Then how'd you . . .*"

"The Comm Room thought I'd want to know. Never mind that. What does Jerence say?"

"I can't risk repeating it, sir. Only face-to-face."

"Oh, I know him. You've told me enough."

"Thank you. I'll make my decision shortly."

"I've been little help."

"More than you know." The line went dead.

With a sigh, Fath rubbed his face.

The fish floated before us.

"Now what, sir?" Tad.

"We wait, Lieutenant."

"How long?"

"However long it takes."

Braun shot Tad a look of commiseration. Tad frowned.

The Captain paced a moment longer, sank into his seat.

Anselm seemed unfazed. "What, exactly, are we waiting for?"

Fath said with some asperity, "I'll know when I see it. Anything else, Mr. Anselm?"

"No, sir." To my astonishment, Tad caught my eye and winked.

Fath swiveled. "Mr. Carr!"

I jumped. "Yes, sir!" My voice was a squeak.

"Coffee, if you'd be so kind. Tad?"

"No thanks."

"Pilot?"

"Black, please."

The nearest dispenser was in the officers' mess; I hurried along the corridor, a touch resentful he sent me on menial errands like . . . well, like a ship's boy. My annoyance faded to a grin. I was crew. This was my work.

When I returned the Captain thanked me absently, sipped at his steaming cup. On the simulscreen was a holoview of section four, where the alien had been housed. In replay, the outrider careened wildly up and down the corridor, hatch to hatch. Its momentum was such that it climbed halfway up the bulkhead, in passing.

Over and again Fath replayed the sequence. The alien, across the barrier, waited for a plate to be shown him. His quivering seemed no greater than usual. He moved to one side, as if balancing himself.

The outrider had no feet. Well, he did, but temporary ones. His weight seemed to roll over onto extended bulges, when he moved. Only in slow-mo playback could I see just how.

"Tad, what's the fish up to?"

"No change, sir."

"Mr. Seafort, may I suggest we withdraw?" The Pilot.

"How far?"

"How about another solar system?" The Captain glared, but Van Peer seemed unfazed. "At least a few hundred meters, sir. That beast is far too close for comfort."

"Well . . . all right. Two hundred meters."

"And may I suggest we shift position relative to the fish and the Station? We were blocking their shot if—"

"That was deliberate."

"Oh?" Mr. Van Peer said no more, but his silence spoke volumes. Delicately, he tapped the starboard thrusters. In the screen, the fish began to recede.

One eye on the fish, Fath took up his caller. "Comm Room, locate Jerence Branstead, groundside. I want a secure—"

The fish pulsed, disappeared.

"Hello? Comm Room to Bridge. Say again?"

Fath stared.

"Captain?"

19

IT WAS A STORMY evening on the bridge.

The fish didn't reappear. The watch changed, and we waited.

Andrew Ghent logged two demerits, Mikhael one. There was a spectacular set-to between the Captain and Tad Anselm, when Tad proposed that we reboard our passengers and leave forthwith. Before it was over, I'd been chewed out for fidgeting and sent below to amuse Janey until dinner. Fath was in a dangerous mood. I knew I wasn't really the cause, but still, it rankled.

To make matters worse, Corrine Sloan was uneasy, and a touch morose. When I asked her why, she just shook her head.

The only one whose mood was unaffected was Janey. I showed her a holovid word-building game, and in a few minutes she was running it on her own. Nonetheless she insisted I stand by, and was quite imperious about it.

Corrine stirred. "You asked about my going ashore."

"Yes, ma'am."

"The reason I'm reluctant is John."

It made no sense whatsoever, but I kept silent.

"We were to be married, you see." Her gaze was distant.

"And you broke up."

"No, not really." She toyed with her fingernails. "He was a Pentecostal."

"They're the devil's children!"

"Where did you hear that?" Her tone was sharp.

"It's what the Bishop calls them." Not that anyone in Hope Nation had ever seen a Pentie; they were a banned sect, crushed almost two centuries ago, in the days of the Reunification. But they were still held out as an example of the folly of religious anarchy. "They're long gone."

"Not exactly," she said. "A number of families remain. They practice their faith underground."

"In caves?"

"Randy, please don't be sarcastic."

I flushed. "I wasn't."

"Underground means away from the eyes of the authorities."

"Oh. Sorry, ma'am."

"We posted the banns. We lived outside Baton Rouge. There was a neighbor, Arlan Richards . . . God knows how he knew. Janey, if the word isn't right, hitting the screen won't help. You're a smartie, try again."

I said, "Were you a Pentie too?"

"I don't care for that term."

"Sorry." It was becoming a refrain. "A Pentecostal."

"No, but I didn't mind about John. The truth is Pentecostals are ordinary joeys, religious in their own way. But Arlan Richards went to our minister, and he went to the monsignor."

"What happened?"

"They forbade the marriage, held John for trial under canon law."

"What'd he do?"

"The charge was heresy."

I hissed. That was bad. And the penalties were . . . I steeled myself. "What happened?"

Her eyes were damp. "I was desperate. My father and I appealed to the Bishop of Louisiana, on behalf of John and his family. The Bishop was . . ." She grimaced. "Henrod Andori."

"He refused?"

"By that time they'd held the trial. The conclusion was foreordained, almost literally. But Andori saw us afterward. He called me a whore of Babylon, told me he'd attend the burning himself. And he did."

"Here, ma'am." I offered the clean handkerchief Fath made me wear.

"Thank you." She wiped her eyes. "So did I."

"Ma'am?"

"Attend the burning. First his mother, then him, then his sister. It was all I had left to give. I wanted him to see me at the last, to know I was with him. It was a terrible mistake, which made it far worse for him. But by the time I knew, it was too late."

I swallowed bile. "When was this?"

"Seven years ago."

"Fath was SecGen, wasn't he? Why didn't you appeal to him?"

"The government has no authority over the Church. Besides, he was recuperating from that crash in Helsinki, the one that injured his knee. Valera was in charge, and refused even to urge clemency."

"The bastard."

"Amen."

"Daddy says don't use that word." Janey tugged at my arm.

"I'm sorry, honey." Honey? Jeez. If Kevin heard me talk that way, he'd tease . . . My smile faded.

"So." Corrine stood wearily, and stretched. "I don't choose to go ashore."

"I understand."

"Will you join us for dinner?"

I thought of Fath, and his tart manner on the Bridge. "I'll eat with the rest of the crew." The auxiliary Dining Hall was on Level 4. The Captain never dined there.

To my surprise, not one but two crew tables made a place for me; I had to choose. I sat alongside the other sailors, listening to their chatter.

Often there was banter and argument between men and women, but every joey at the table was so relieved the alien was gone, there was nothing in the air but good spirits.

After, recalling Fath's rebuke, I wandered the lounges and holoscreen rooms, reluctant to return to our cabin before I actually had to. When I knew Fath would be incensed at any further delay, I made my unenthusiatic way to Level 1.

"Ah, there you are." Fath lay atop his covers, still dressed. "Good evening."

"Good evening, sir." My tone was stiff.

Cautiously he raised himself, pulled me into an embrace.

I broke loose. "What's it with you and hugs?" I asked scornfully.

"Well, now, I'll tell you. Come here." He patted the side of his bed.

Reluctantly, I joined him.

"When I was a boy . . . let's see now. I was exactly a year younger than you. In the pre-industrial ages."

I smiled dutifully, not really caring.

"My father no doubt loved me, in his way, but he wasn't demonstrative. At least, not with affection. The day I left for Academy, he took me to Devon by train. A long trip, and mostly in silence. From the station it was a long walk across the common to the front gates, where we'd part."

The Captain paused, lost in a distant past.

"On the way, I practiced how to say good-bye, how to tell Father I'd make him proud."

I was suddenly attentive.

"He was carrying my bag. When I tried to take his hand, he shifted the duffel. I moved around the other side. Again, he shifted the bag. At the guardhouse I took a deep breath, was ready to begin my speech. He handed me the duffel, took my shoulders, turned me about, guided me through the gate."

Fath's eyes glistened.

"When I turned to wave good-bye, he was striding across the common. I watched a long while, but he never looked back."

I swallowed.

"Years later, Randy, I asked him if he loved me. He couldn't answer it was so." He worked himself to a sitting position. "I had few hugs, and know the need of them. If I offer too many, you've merely to tell me, and I'll stop. I don't mean to make you uneasy."

It wasn't fair. Once in a while, a joeykid ought to be allowed to hate his parents.

"So that's what it is with me and hugs, son."

Did he know Dad was a hugger? That it was what I'd missed most, the one thing I'd always been too shy to mention to Anth?

I studied the far bulkhead. "I'd like one, please."

In the morning Fath made a point of sitting with Andrew Ghent for breakfast, and when Tad came in, Fath waved him over. Covertly, I watched the two for signs of resentment, saw none. Well, he hadn't punished Tad, just spoken sharply. And a midshipman was used to demerits.

The morning was my own; I wasn't on duty 'til after lunch. Fath was on the bridge, but I had the sense I wouldn't be welcome there; he was preoccupied, staring at an empty screen. I waited out the boredom in a lounge.

A ship's boy had no watch station; he was supposed to help out as needed. It made for an interesting but uncertain life. Alejandro didn't seem to mind; after lunch he and I were called to Hydroponics to help reset some tubing. He chattered cheerfully, while I wondered if there'd be any joeys my own age among the passengers. Alec was a bit too young, and the middies too old, and snooty. Except Mik, of course, but he was twenty. And maybe Andy Ghent; since the day in my cell when he'd refused to tell me my fate, I'd seen him in a different light.

Not long before dinner, Mr. Branstead came aboard, on a shuttle full of crewmen. He gave me a preoccupied nod, hurried off to find the Captain.

At dinnertime I was still on duty, but a call came down saying the Captain wanted my assistance. I suppressed a grin. Assistance, my foot. I washed and changed before reporting to the half-filled Dining Hall.

"Sir." I saluted stiffly. If he wanted to play games, I would too.

Gravely, he returned the salute. "Take your place, Mr. Carr."

"Aye aye, sir. Good evening, Mr. Branstead." A simple courtesy, that would please Fath.

Jerence sat at the Captain's right, Tolliver at his left. To my surprise, Tolliver clapped me on the shoulder as I sat. He must be mellow indeed.

After Reverend Pandeker gave the prayer, Fath stood. "Ladies and gentlemen, as you know, we've taken part in extraordinary events. Our old enemy, the fish, have met us without hostility. We've even exchanged words. I'd hoped, truly hoped, for more . . ." For a moment, he fell silent. "But perhaps it is not to be. Tomorrow I will issue orders that the remainder of our crew, and those passengers who wish to accompany us, be ferried aloft. *Olympiad* will resume her scheduled cruise."

Cheers, from nearly every table. Fath's face twisted. He sat.

Mr. Branstead touched his knee. "They don't understand, sir."

"Do you?"

"I . . . think so." He met Fath's eye. "I worried for the ship, and for you. But your aspiration was magnificent."

"Thank you." Fath's tone was stiff. After a moment he said, "You're sure you'll be all right?"

"Fairly." Mr. Branstead's tone was light. "There's always risk. After our days in the Rotunda . . ."

"Pray Lord God it won't come to that."

I looked mystified. Fath said, "Jerence was held prisoner during the Navy's attempted coup. He's lucky to have escaped alive."

Mr. Branstead snorted. "*I'm* lucky? What about yourself?"

"My point exactly."

"Sir, Hope Nation's a conservative society. Ultimately, even Scanlen's joeys won't go against their government."

"Has he been found?"

I said plaintively, "I know I'm only ship's boy, but could someone tell me what's happened?"

Fath said, "A sympathetic judge freed Scanlen. On Anthony's appeal, the order was vacated, but now the Bishop's nowhere to be found."

"Is Anth in danger?"

"I'm not sure."

Well, at least Fath was honest.

After dinner, I tagged along while Fath accompanied Mr. Branstead to the lock. "Remember what I told you," he said.

"Yes, sir." Jerence shifted awkwardly. "Is this truly good-bye?"

"We leave tomorrow, if we can get the last passengers aboard. I shouldn't have allowed them off."

"Well, then." The two faced one another.

It was Fath who embraced Mr. Branstead. "Farewell."

"Godspeed, sir. I pray you return soon. If not, I'll remember you always."

"And I you."

I went back to my duties.

That night, as I got ready for bed, Fath sat hunched over his knees, in near darkness.

"Are you sad, sir?" I had to say *something*.

"Yes." He stared at his feet. "I was so sure."

"Of what?"

"Randy . . . all those years of regret, of horror at what I accomplished killing so many fish . . . when they returned to Hope Nation, I thought that God had been testing me. I know my faith wavered, and I failed Him, but somehow, I imagined He'd forgiven me nonetheless. That He had given me a great task, and a greater reward: to make peace between our species. Almost, I was prepared to forgive Him what He did to Arlene, and your father, despicable as it was. But the fish that visited us is gone, and our outrider with it. I have no task. Just my doubts, renewed."

"You're still Captain." It was all I could think of.

"And your parent. That will keep me busy." He tried to lighten his tone.

"Sometimes . . ." I sat on the deck, near his feet. "I feel lonely. Like you."

"No," he said. "I pray it's not like me."

I knew better than to answer. I leaned back against his bed.

We passed a companionable hour, in silence.

Olympiad wasn't exactly crowded, but she was bustling. Shuttle after shuttle mated with her locks, disengorging distracted and occasionally green-gilled passengers. Each craft then broke free and dived into the atmosphere for another run to Centraltown, where Lieutenant Skor was handling embarkation. Alejandro and I were on "gopher" duty, helping the purser's overworked staff. They sent me hither and about, for sheets, new safety tanks, holovids, and all manner of gear it seemed our passengers simply couldn't sail without.

To my delight I spotted three teeners, two boys and a girl, who looked about my age. Perhaps there'd be others.

Until now, I'd wondered why *Olympiad* floated free of the Station, instead of mooring, as was the custom. Certainly, passengers could be better organized in the Station's corridors than ours. But by standing clear, we made three additional locks available, and loading probably went faster in the end.

At last, the final shuttle mated; Lieutenant Skor came aboard with the last of our passengers.

I scurried about, until the press of errands slackened. Only then did Purser Li allow me a break.

Mikhael was on duty at the east Level 3 lock, crisp in a dress uniform and his best manners. With him was the youngest of our middies, Tommy Yost, who'd just returned from shore leave. A purser's mate was just leaving, his duties at the lock done.

I peered out the porthole. Though I could feel nothing, we were already under way. Slowly, steadily, the Station receded.

Mik cleared his throat. "Excited, Mr. Carr?"

"What about?"

"Your first cruise."

"Oh!" I hadn't even thought about it. Strange, how *Olympiad* had so quickly become my home. I was still getting used to Fath's strange ways—for example, his fixation about keeping me in fresh-pressed clothes—but on the other hand, I felt as if I'd known him for years. He was trying hard to be a good father. I suspected I'd have to try equally hard to be a good son.

Hope Nation, green and serene, floated below. Well, Dad. Could you imagine I'd sail off with Mr. Seafort in a sister ship to the one in which you died? Would it please you? Make you sad?

Mik threw an arm around my shoulder. "It's all right, joey."

"I know, sir." I wiped an eye.

"We all feel that way at first."

I squirmed with embarrassment; sailors were watching. To divert him I said, "When do we Fuse?"

"Fusion safety is . . . tell us, Mr. Yost."

The younger middy jumped. "Uh, the square of N times the distance to . . . I'd need a console to calculate . . . about five hours, sir."

"Close enough, and I'm not 'sir.' Not while Mr. Riev's aboard."

"Sorry, Mr. Tamarov." The younger middy was sweating. Was this the hazing all middies endured? If so, I wondered what the fuss was about.

"If we Fuse too early, what happens?"

"The drives are unable to overcome—"

"I was asking Mr. Carr."

I gulped. Not fair; Mik was supposed to be my brother. I said, "The ship explodes, or implodes, or something." I hadn't listened too closely to that part, back in Physics 3. I'd been contemplating the curve of Judy Winthrop's back.

"Even a ship's boy is expected to know the basics."

"Sorry, sir." My tone was stiff. I'd never speak to him again off-watch. Not a word.

"Near any significant mass—you can look up the specifics in Lambert and Greeley—a fusion drive can't produce a strong enough N-wave to overcome the inertia of normal space-time. The drive overheats. The resultant energy is expended on the ship itself. It's explosion, not implosion. You wouldn't want to be around when it happens."

"Yes, sir."

"Come by the wardroom sometime and I'll show you the passage from *Elements of Astronavigation.*"

"Sure." Not a chance. He could shove Lambert and Greeley—

"It's even worse with Augmented Fusion. More energy." Mik was showing off.

"Do we use that?"

"All starships do. We learned from the fish, back when Pa—er, Captain Seafort was young."

Half listening, I peered again at the distant, barely discernible Station lights. Would we ever again have an Orbiting Station as big as the one Mr. Seafort had nuked? And when would I see home again?

"All hands, prepare for Fusion." The Captain sounded melancholy.

"What's the response, Thomas?" Mik waited, arms folded.

"We call the bridge and say, 'Level 3 east lock sealed and clear.' "

"Do so." To me, "Other than the engine room and the locks, there's not much to prepare. I don't know why they announce—"

"Why seal the locks?" I shouldn't have interrupted, but . . .

"To prevent anyone wandering inside. They'd be too close to the edge of the field."

"Engine Room, prime."

"If you want a last look, better hurry. We'll be seven months in Fusion."

I bent to the porthole. Not that I'd see much, so far from—I reeled away, mouth working. "Mik, there's a—"

Alarms shrieked.

"General Quarters! All hands to General Quarters!" Tolliver's voice was ragged. It would be, with a fish nosing at our hull.

"Deprime deprime deprime! Depower the drive!"

"Engine Room, aye aye. Fusion drive is—"

"Passengers, to your cabins! Fish off our port bow! Prepare to suit!"
The fish lurched, or we did, as someone blasted propellant from our thrusters.

"Mik—I mean, sir—where do I go?" I hoped he'd say the bridge.

"Stay with me, Randy."

"Why?"

"Because I said so!" His tone was harsh.

"Aye aye, sir." Inwardly, I kicked myself. General Quarters was no time for insubordination.

"It'll be all right, Randy."

"I know." Almost, I believed it, though my stomach knotted. *Easy, joey. Fath was at the helm, and Mik was close.* I glanced out the porthole. Already the distance to the alien was widening. I willed myself calm.

Tommy Yost's eyes were glassy. "Is this what they did . . . before?"

What a stupid question. No, wait: he'd been shoreside during our other encounters. I made my tone soothing, and a touch condescending. Middies weren't so adult after all. "They appeared from nowhere, like this one. But not so close."

"It's throwing! Laser room, fire at will! Closing corridor hatches! All hands, all passengers to suits!"

I bent to the porthole for a last glance. While we'd bickered, the fish had grown an appendage. It swirled lazily. In a moment, it would break off, sail through our defenses, splatter the hull. Its acid would begin to eat through.

"You idiot, come *on!*" Mikhael hauled me toward the suit locker.

Feverishly, I climbed in. Legs. Torso. Arms, the hard part. Whew. Why couldn't someone design—

"Bridge, laser bank three disabled!" Ms. Frand must be so distracted, she didn't realize she was using shipwide circuits.

"What's happening?" Yost's voice was a whine. "Why won't they tell us—"

"That's quite enough, Thomas." Mik's tone of command was one I recognized. I suppressed a grin. One couldn't live long with Fath, without learning his ways. "In fact, altogether more than enough. I've a mind to tell Mr. Riev."

"Oh, don't!"

Mikhael clamped his helmet, spun me around to check mine. "If I were first middy you'd be swimming in demerits, joey. We're all scared. Do you hear Randy carrying on?"

"No, but . . ." A deep breath. "Sorry, Mr. Tamarov."

"That's better." A reassuring clap, which nearly knocked Tommy to the deck.

"Attention, passengers and hands." The Captain's voice was heavy. *"The fish is gone. When our lasers opened fire, it Fused. We're in no immediate danger."*

I let out a breath that fogged my helmet.

"Olympiad *was attacked just before Fusion, when we were most vulnerable. We deprimed. Our concern was that our tubes might be attacked at the moment we Fused. One laser turret is inoperative, but is repairable. Unless the fish reappears, in a moment we will reprime and try again to Fuse. As a precaution, do not open your cabin hatches, and remain in your suits.*"

"Christ, why don't they leave us alone?" Mikhael.

"Don't blaspheme," said Yost, primly.

Mik rolled his eyes. "I apologize. I meant no disrespect."

"I ought to tell Mr. Riev. In fact, I think I wi—"

I snarled, "Leave him alone, you turd! *I'll* tell Riev you cried like a joeykid when—"

"I did not!"

"SILENCE, BOTH OF YOU! THIS INSTANT!" Mikhael's face was red. "Mr. Carr, you're on report. No, not a word!" His warning finger was a dagger. I swallowed. "As for ourselves, Mr. Yost, I'll inform the first midshipman of our conduct, including my own intemperate language."

Tommy Yost looked sullen.

"Clamp your helmet." Mik's tone was peremptory. "Mr. Carr, back to your station."

"What station? You told me to stay with—"

"The lock." He stalked off.

I tried to hate him, but failed. I'd had no business interposing myself between midshipmen, and knew it the moment I'd opened my mouth. I sighed. The trick was to know it *before* I opened my mouth.

"*Engine Room, prime.*"

My heart quickened.

The corridor was deserted, except for ourselves. No doubt our passengers were still struggling with unfamiliar suit clamps.

Midshipman Yost trudged along the corridor, his suit finally secured. "Mr. Tamarov . . ." He sounded conciliatory. "I'm sorry if—"

Alarms wailed.

"*Deprime, deprime! Fish at close quarters!*"

I shouldered Mik aside, squinted through the porthole. The fish loomed so close it seemed to be touching. Angry colors swirled. A blowhole opened. A fine spray shot out. The fish drifted toward our stern. An appendage grew from its side, began to swirl.

Not our fusion tubes. Please, God. We'd be stranded.

"*Laser room, fire at will!*"

Abruptly, a second fish. I flinched.

Alarms shrieked, a babble of orders from the bridge. Slowly, ponderously, *Olympiad* turned from the new menace.

It was the same fish that had lain off our side for so long; I could have sworn to it. It had the same reddish swirl near its dorsal bulge. The other fish had none. Neither had the other alien I'd seen.

The second fish was on a collision course with its mate. A hole appeared in its side; our lasers had found a target. It pulsed, but didn't Fuse. It rammed our attacker amidships.

I grabbed the caller, stabbed at keys.

Mik wrestled for the caller. "Get away from that! We're at General Quar—"

My voice was shrill. "Bridge! Tell Captain Seafort—it's Randy, the ship's boy—tell him that's our old fish! The second one is helping us!"

Mik wrenched the caller from my grasp, flicked it off. "How *dare* you!" He was every inch a Naval officer.

"Laser room, hold fire!"

In slow motion, our aft portside thrusters and forward starboard thrusters turned our irreplaceable tubes from the attacker. It brought the fish in full view of our airlock porthole.

An outrider roiled through the skin of the newcomer. It launched itself.

Not at us, but at its compatriot.

It floated across the void, struck the fish's swirling skin. It clung to the surface, blurred, disappeared within.

My breath rasped in my helmet. Easy, joey. Don't hyperventilate. Just because you're scared out of your wits is no reason to gasp for . . .

Our attacker pulsed. Suddenly it vanished.

The fish with the red swirl remained, uncomfortably near our tubes. I watched for an appendage. None appeared.

"Ship's Boy Carr to the bridge." Fath was terse. *"I'll open hatches as you reach them."*

"Mik, am I in trouble?"

"Move, or you will be." His gloved hands urged me toward the section hatch.

"Ship's Boy Carr reporting, sir." I couldn't salute through a helmet.

To my surprise, everyone was suited, even the Captain.

"How'd you know that was our original fish?"

"That red spot, sir." I pointed.

Fath glanced at Tolliver. "You're right. He was the first to notice."

"How fortunate no one hanged him." Tolliver's tone was dry.

Andrew Ghent's jaw dropped. It caught Tolliver's notice; Ghent hurriedly bent to his console.

"Very well, Mr. Carr." Fath's tone held approval. "Anything else?"

"Yes, sir. I'm on report." It was best to tell him myself.

"That will wait. About the fish."

The alien floated on our screen. An outrider clung to its surface. I blurted, "Where did that come from?"

"Inside. I suppose you think it's friendly?"

If I was wrong, I'd look like an idiot. Worse, I'd endanger our ship. I took a long breath. "Yes, sir."

"So do I. Edgar disagrees."

"What I said, sir, was that friendly or not, we'd be crazy to trust it after what we just saw."

"I stand corrected. Edgar thinks you and I are crazy."

Andrew Ghent choked. His face was red from the effort of suppressing nervous laughter.

"So." The Captain drummed his console. "What now?"

I had the sense to know he wasn't really asking me. I pressed my lips shut.

Fath keyed the caller. "Laser room, if the outrider launches itself, fire only if it nears our tubes."

"Frand here. Sir, once it's on our hull, we have no angle of fire. If it moves to the tubes . . ."

Fath set down the caller, chewed his lip. "Lord, this once I'll speak to You. Thousands of Your people are at risk. I beseech You: what should I do?"

I found myself straining to hear a response. I shook myself. Father's lunacy was contagious. There was no God.

A long moment passed.

As if confirming my opinion, Fath grimaced. "Nothing. He doesn't care, or leaves it up to me." He lifted himself from his seat. Standing below the huge simulscreen, he folded his arms, stared upward.

"Fire now, sir. Either we kill it, or it Fuses away. Then we've a good chance we can prime and Fuse before—"

"I know, Edgar."

The bridge was silent. A moment passed, which lasted hours.

"Notify the Station we'll stay. And prepare to open the section four lock."

Once more, passengers were evacuated from sections three and five, to either side of the containment area, as well as section four of Levels 1 and 3, above and below. By Fath's orders, belongings were left in place, and occupants of the affected cabins herded to the Dining Hall. The galley crew was hard at work, slapping together sandwiches and salads for those displaced.

To my relief, Fath didn't send me to help. Who cared about frazzing passengers, when an outrider was coming aboard?

Fath did make me wait, though, until Mr. Janks's security detail was fully in place. Then, together with Tad Anselm, we walked down to the arena.

At Fath's order, the outer hatch slid open. The Pilot moved us closer to the fish.

Jess copied the view from the bridge to our small screen at the negotiating table.

The outrider quivered, still attached to the fish. A convulsion, and he was sailing through space. He landed on our hull, not far from the hatch.

"Is it the same one, Fath?"

"Hmmm. I imagine so."

Five minutes passed. The outrider did nothing. I gnawed at a knuckle. Would a different visitor have the same attitude as his predecessor?

I'd just begun to think the vacuum had frozen the outrider solid when he skittered into our lock. We cycled. He emerged into the section four corridor.

Immediately, he raced to our end of the section, melted into a puddle. He reared, melted anew.

Fath sighed. "I have to go to him. Edgar, are you listening?"

"Right here, sir."

"Stand down from General Quarters. We're diplomats again." He got to his feet.

I stood also.

"Not this time, son. Watch from here. Tell me if he—"

"A parent ought to be consistent." The words just popped out of my mouth, but they were as good a gambit as any.

"I beg your pardon?"

"You heard me." I sounded defiant. Well, so be it. "We decided it was a risk we'd take together. I have a right to count on you." I couldn't imagine speaking to Dad so, but if I didn't set things straight with Fath, Lord knew where it would lead us. Still, I wished it weren't in front of Tad and Mr. Janks.

"Our friend can't wait." Fath strode toward section six; to enter four without dismantling our transplex barrier, he'd have to walk the entire length of the circular corridor. "We'll discuss it later."

"Now's better." I pushed back my chair, ran after.

"As Captain, I order you—"

"If I touch you, will I be hanged?" Uninvited contact from a crewman was a capital offense.

"No."

"Why not?"

"You're my son."

"That's why I'm coming with you." I matched his stride.

It was a long walk. When we were there, he said, "Put on a suit."

"When you do, sir."

His tone had an edge. "Understand, you'll be punished."

"I expect it." And it was true. Part of me even welcomed it. I was insolent beyond all expectation, and on one level, it was wrong. But I'd already lost Dad, and I had no intention of losing Fath.

At the hatch, he handed me his pistol.

I said, "I thought you wouldn't trust me with it."

"I thought so too. But I don't want you killed."

We went in.

The alien had reconstituted to a degree, but when we approached, it puddled.

Fath sat alongside, stood, slapped the bulkhead to get the outrider's attention.

The outrider reconstituted.

I said, "Ask him if he's the same one."

"How?"

"Draw . . . may I? Jess, draw an outrider, then—"

"Officers' commands are valid. Nonofficers may only direct a puter by authority of—"

"Jess, this is the Captain. Draw what he asks."

"Aye aye, sir."

I took a deep breath. "First, an outrider. A ship nearby. Then the outrider inside the ship. Then show him Outside. That's his first visit, Fath. Then an outrider in a fish, near a ship . . ."

"Slow down, son."

"Jess can keep up. He's almost as smart as we are."

"Your wisdom is commensurate with your age, Ship's Boy Carr." The servo's arm raced, etching a plate, while I pondered the retort.

"Now change to outrider Outside fish. Then, outrider in ship."

The servo lowered the plate. The outrider tasted it, and wrote.

On an unused section of plate, two additions.

Outrider dead.

Outrider in ship.

"How can he be dead if he's in our ship?" I tried to puzzle it through.

"He may be saying he's dead, and not the same one."

"But he knows our language."

"Randy, we don't know that's what he said. Our words may mean something entirely different to him."

"Yes, sir. Jess, draw fish-attack-ship."

"Done, Ship's Boy."

The alien tasted. He added a second fish, drew fish-attack-fish. Again, he puddled, the sign of submission.

"Quick, Jess, draw a symbol for that submission."

"What symbol?"

"Anything. Choose one."

Jess did: a square.

The outrider tasted.

"Draw outrider-submission-human."

A taste. A symbol: *Yes*.

Twice the alien ingested nutrients we provided it. I ingested nutrients too, from a tray brought to our table. I paid no attention to what they were.

We were working on symbols for time. It was excruciating: no matter what we tried, the outrider didn't seem to understand our representation.

In the distance, a commotion. Tad Anselm jumped up, strode off to deal with it. It was several minutes before he returned. "Sir, Level 4 had a . . . community meeting? I don't know what to call it. They sent a delegation."

"And?"

"They want the outrider off *Olympiad*. You've no right to risk their lives, et cetera. They're quite worked up about it."

"Are they, now?"

"Yes, sir. I told them I'd give you the gist of it."

"How much are you omitting?"

"Most of the hyperbole, and all the swear words."

Well into the small hours, Fath got to his feet. "I'm not thinking well. We'll resume in the morning. Mr. Janks, relieve your guard."

"Fath, do outriders sleep?"

"We don't know."

"Why not set up a second shift?"

"I want to oversee the sessions; a wrong word may cause chaos." Fath guided me toward section six. "Perhaps even hostilities."

Wearily, I trudged up the ladder. "So much time wasted."

He slapped open our hatch. "Now, about this afternoon, when I asked you to don a suit . . ."

Uh oh. I had a bill to pay.

"Sit here." He patted the side of his bed.

I understood that part. The lecture always came first.

"You ran away from Anthony rather than behave, didn't you?"

"That's because Scanlen—" I swallowed. "Yes, sir."

"You agreed to my parenting, and defied me. Is it to be your pattern?"

"No, but—"

"Am I in charge?"

"Yes, sir." My tone was reluctant.

"Very well. Leave the cabin. Don't come back until you're ready to conduct yourself accordingly. Sleep anywhere you like. You're off duty until your personal problems are resolved."

"You're kicking me out?" I couldn't believe it.

"I'm suspending parental responsibilities. When you accept them permanently, I will too."

"I accept."

"That's too glib. Think on it."

"I have." My lips were dry.

"Permanently, until you're grown. Even when I'm wrong, I'm in charge. Can you pledge that on your honor, or whatever you'll hold to?"

Dad waved cheerfully from *Paragon*'s hatchway.

His image faded.

Tearfully, I said to Fath, "I'm supposed to watch you walk off to be killed?" Couldn't he understand? I'd done that once. Never again could I allow it.

He made no reply.

"I ca—ca—can't, sir."

"Leave until it's so." He pointed to the hatch.

I trudged out to the corridor. Behind me, the hatch slid shut.

20

IT WAS DEEP in *Olympiad's* night. I curled up on a lounge sofa. Within minutes, I jumped up, wandered the compartment aimlessly. How could a joey sleep, abandoned and alone? When his eyes stung, his stomach congealed itself into a hard knot?

An hour passed. The lounge was oppressive. I wandered the corridors. Level 1 was cold and impersonal; I went below.

After a time I found myself at the hatch to Cabin 575. I knocked softly. Louder. Again.

"What is it, Randy?" Corrine was disheveled with sleep.

"Could I stay with you and Janey? The floor's fine. I mean, the deck. I won't make a sou—"

"In. Whatever happened between you? No, tell me in the morning." From the closet, a spare blanket and pillow. She tucked me in at the foot of her bed, planted a kiss on my forehead, turned out the light.

I lay awake, learning how to cry in utter silence.

In the lower dining hall, sullen faces, voices kept low. Crew as well as passengers. Even my newfound friends among the crew managed not to see me. I snorted at the irony: I couldn't be trusted because I was a relative of the Captain, while he'd ordered me out of his life.

Dully, my head full of lint, I spooned the unappetizing mush I'd made of my cereal.

"There you are." Fingers gripped my arm. Mikhael Tamarov looked weary. "I've been looking everywhere."

"Why?" He'd put me on report. Did he think I'd forget?

"Come along." He hesitated. "I'm off duty. It's a request. Please, Randy."

I abandoned my bowl. "Where?"

"Anywhere. A lounge."

My whole body ached, but I followed. The moment we were alone, he blurted, "Pa looks like hell. His eyes are red."

"Why?"

"He wouldn't tell me, but I could see your bed wasn't slept in. What's between you?"

I swallowed. Abruptly, unbidden, the story poured out of me. When at last I wound down, pacing from bulkhead to bulkhead, Mik snagged me, made me sit. "You're both so bloody proud."

"And you aren't?" My voice was hot. "When I tried to stand up for you with Yost—"

He waved it away. "A father's job is to protect you. That's what Pa wants to do."

"You're on his side? He didn't protect you from *Galactic*."

"Goofjuice. I begged and pleaded, but Pa refused to bring me. It was Derek who took me aboard!"

I swallowed. "Fath didn't keep a promise."

"Randy, I don't care if you're in the right. It's torturing him. Go put an end to it."

"You don't understand. Dad—Derek—is gone. I saw the outrider kill Kev, my best friend." Somehow, I made myself say what I didn't dare. "I . . . can't . . . lose . . . him . . . too."

For answer, Mikhael threw his arm around my shoulder.

When he left, I was too drained for words. I stumbled out to the corridor.

If the alien could submit, so could I. Nothing was worth what I felt.

Fath wasn't in our cabin. Reeling with exhaustion, I headed for the bridge. I was off duty, but he'd see me. Somehow, I was sure. I knocked.

Lieutenant Frand had the watch, with Tommy Yost. "Yes, Mr. Carr?"

"Is the . . . I was looking for . . ." I leaned against the hatch.

"Get yourself together, joey." She swung her chair. "Go ahead, Station."

"*General Thurman here. Might I speak to Captain Seafort?*"

"He's not on the bridge."

"*We have a shuttle docking. The Stadholder is aboard. He urgently requests a meeting with the Captain. He wants me present. Might you return to the Station?*"

"Stand by, Mr. Thurman." She stabbed the caller. "Bridge to Mr. Seafort."

"Go ahead, Ms. Frand." Fath, on the bridge speaker. He listened. Then, a sigh. "I don't see how I can refuse. Summon Mr. Van Peer. Return to the Station."

"To their lock?"

"No, don't mate. Stand by alongside. I'll go across in the smallest launch."

"Aye aye, sir. What about the fish Outside?"

"Heavens, I nearly forgot. Proceed very slowly, and give it a wide detour. If it follows, take no alarm. Alert the laser room watch, though."

Ms. Frand replaced the caller, turned to me. "Well?"

"Fath—Mr. Seafort's talking to the outrider?" I should be with him. Without me, who knew what wild chances he'd take?

"I'm under no orders to tell you his whereabouts." Her tone was cold. "The Log says you're suspended from duty."

"Yes, ma'am."

"Joey, this is a personal matter between you and him. Settle it on personal time."

"Aye aye, ma'am."

"But, settle it. You hear me?"

"Yes ma'am." I made my escape.

If something provoked the alien to its gesture of submission, Fath would hurry round to join him, as he always did. But this time he'd be alone. He'd have no thought for himself. A moment ago I'd believed I could live with it. Now I wasn't so sure. I knew what Mik would have me do; no point in seeking him out. And Mr. Branstead was groundside.

Where lay my duty: to obey Fath, or protect him?

I had no one to ask.

No one but Anth.

My pulse quickened.

Anth cared for me. He had Dad's sense of right. He'd tell me what to do.

Fath would never let me go to the station to see him.

I had to. I was desperate.

This time, when we were done, no doubt Fath would punish me without mercy. And I'd deserve it.

Steeling myself, I hurried to the launch bays.

Olympiad, like *Galactic* before her, had four launches. I found the bay for the smallest, cycled through the lock, peered in the hatch. Two sailors were topping off her propellant. I grabbed an empty duffel from a hook, strolled nonchalantly toward the launch.

One of the ratings glanced up.

"Captain wants this aboard." I trotted up the ladder. They paid me no heed.

They wouldn't be handing out suits; the launch was pressurized. I opened the aft suit locker, squeezed in. A tight fit, but I could manage it. I shut the hatch behind me. It wasn't quite pitch-dark within. The suits had a metallic smell.

I waited a full hour, my calves starting to ache, a thrustersuit's neck clamps pressed into my collarbone.

At last I heard voices. The Captain. A sailor. Someone else. Mikhael.

I felt us disengage. I gulped, as weightlessness engulfed us. This was no time to lose my breakfast.

The purr of our thrusters. I imagined I could feel the acceleration, knew it wasn't so.

From the cabin, low voices, chatting.

Bumps, and clicks, as we mated. Sudden gravity made my knees weak.

The hiss of an airlock.

"Captain Seafort?" A new voice.

"Here."

"The Patriarchs welcome you."

"What? Why are you—*Mik, look out*—" A cry of rage.

I flung open the hatch. Three soldiers, with stunners. Fath lay on the deck. Mik was struggling in the cockpit. Abruptly he sagged, dropped to the deck. A sailor cowered in his seat. The nearest soldier touched the stunner to his chest. His eyes rolled up.

No one had seen me. I ducked back in the locker, shut the hatch.

As they passed, I would fling open the door, catch at least one of them. I'd grab his stunner, use it on the others.

I put my shoulder to the hatch, waiting for my moment.

Feet, dragging on the deck. "Never mind, we'll come back for him!" I tensed.

The steps faded. The hiss of a lock.

Ever so cautiously, I peered out.

Idiot! You frazzing fool! You were in the aft suit locker. The airlock was toward the bow.

Fath was gone.

Nothing would rouse Mik, though his breathing was regular, his heart strong. He'd be out at least an hour. I paced the aisle, frantic.

Even I knew better than to dash into the Station corridor to look for him. They'd almost certainly have the launch under guard. Furthermore, I didn't know my way, and would blunder about helplessly, unarmed.

I peered out the porthole. In the far distance, lights against the white blaze of stars. *Olympiad.* I had to warn her, but I had no idea how to use the cockpit radio. It didn't look like a ship's caller.

There wasn't a single frazzing thing I could . . .

Think. I'd hidden in a suit locker. We had suits. Where could I go?

Nowhere, but suits had radios. When Kev and I were hiding from the outrider, Fath had said to use frequency seven. Was that *Olympiad's* shipboard frequency? Could they even hear me from this distance?

What about the Station? Would they be monitoring that channel? They'd storm the launch and . . .

No matter. We had to rescue Fath. Feverishly, I donned a suit. There were no three-quarter ones; I had to climb into a full size. I swam in it.

I glanced down, but couldn't see the radio keys; I was too short. My eyes barely peered over the neckpiece.

The controls would be the same for every unit. I found frequency seven on a hanging suit, set my own by feel, switched on the radio.

"Hello? *Olympiad,* hello?" I kept my voice low, as if that could protect me.

Nothing.

"Mayday, mayday! Calling *Olympiad.* For Christ's sake, answer the frazzing—"

"*Comm Room here. Who's fooling with the radio?*" Ms. Skor's voice was sharp. "*Suits are for emergencies. What cabin are you—*"

"This is Randy. I—"

"Get off this channel. Use the caller. I'm putting you on rep—"

"LISTEN, YOU STUPID GRODE!" My throat was raw. "I'm in the launch, they took Captain Seafort, I mean, kidnapped him. Hurry, Mik's unconscious and they're coming back for—"

"Which launch? He didn't take you. You've been suspended."

I'd get nowhere babbling hysterically. For Fath, every moment counted. I swallowed, forced my brain to slow. "Ship's Boy Carr reporting, ma'am. I'm in the launch docked at the Station. I sneaked aboard and hid in the suit locker. They came on and stunned Fath, I mean the Captain. Mr. Tamarov tried to fight and they stunned him too. They dragged the sailor and Mr. Seafort away."

"Who?"

"All I heard was, 'The Patriarchs welcome you.' He's gone. Get him back!"

"Hang on." A click. Silence. I shifted from foot to foot, in growing panic.

"Tolliver, here. Where'd they take him?"

"Through the lock, sir."

"What's your status?" Behind his voice, the clang of alarms.

"We're mated to the Station. Lock is closed, but I heard someone say they'd be back for Mik—Midshipman Tamarov. He's out cold."

"Who knows you're aboard?"

"No one, sir. I was hiding in the locker." I forced words through the shame. I should have leaped out, protected Fath. If we were family, I owed him not an iota less.

"Stay away from the airlock porthole."

"Aye aye, sir."

"Seal your lock."

"How?"

He told me. I keyed the panel. A light flashed red. "Now what, sir?"

"Randy . . ." A deep breath. I could almost see Tolliver forcing the edge from his voice. *"You're absolutely sure they stunned him? This isn't some . . ."*

"Some joeykid's story?" My tone was bitter. "No, sir, he yelled, and then he was lying on the deck. Please, send sailors. Attack the Station! Get him back!"

Tolliver's voice was heavy. *"A shuttle departed the Station five minutes ago. I assume Nick's on it."*

"Disable it!"

"This isn't the holovids. Besides, in—how long, Jess?—two minutes, it'll reach the outer atmosphere."

"Call Anthony! He'll intercept them at the spaceport!"

"Ms. Skor's on the line. Randy, I've gone to Battle Stations. Stand by. I need to . . ." Another click.

Minutes passed that seemed hours. Why hadn't Fath taught me how to pilot? I'd sail the launch to Centraltown myself. Could it handle reentry? Its shape wasn't aerodynamic. I hardly cared. Burning up was better than pacing in a hot, useless suit, while Fath . . .

I dropped to my knees. "Mik, wake up." He'd know what to do. I shook him, to no avail. "Open your eyes. Mik, come on!"

Nothing. Not even a groan.

"Mr. Carr."

I jumped. "Yessir?"

"Is there a thrustersuit in the locker?"

"How would I—yes, sir, there is." Its neck clamps had left indentations in my collarbone. *"I don't know how to use it."*

"Mr. Tamarov does. When he's recovered . . ."

"They'll be back any minute for him."

"You sealed the lock. They can't get in without a torch."

"So they'll get one. Sir, what about Mr. Seafort?"

"If the Captain was on that shuttle, there's nothing we can do about it. In any case I won't let another shuttle leave, whatever the cost. But if I challenge the Station, I alert them that we're on to them. I don't want to do that 'til you joeys are safe."

"Why'd they take him?"

"I don't know. Hope Nation's goddamned politics." The blasphemy rung in the air. *"Now, when Mikhael's awake, this is what you do . . ."*

At the hatch, banging, muffled curses. In a frenzy, I shook Mikhael. No response. I jabbed my suit radio. "Mr. Tolliver! They're trying to break in!"

"Is Mikhael . . ."

"Still out."

The noises ceased.

"Get him suited."

"Why, what's—"

"Do it!"

I scrambled to the locker, grabbed a full-sized suit. Wait. Did Mr. Tolliver still want a thrustersuit? No time to ask. Manhandling him into a t-suit was no worse than any other. I dropped the suit, chose another.

Mik had twice my mass, and was a dead weight. It was almost impossible to budge him. Somehow, I got his leg into his suit. Then the second. Now his arms . . .

At the hatch, clunking and scraping. Working at Mik's suit, I ignored it as long as I dared. Then I scrambled across the aisle, peered through the porthole. It violated Mr. Tolliver's orders, but the Station joeys already knew something was amiss.

Troops, with stunners. A laser pistol.

A cutting assembly.

Feverishly, I hoisted Mik to a sitting position. It almost broke my back. I jammed his other arm into the suit sleeve.

He sighed.

"Mik! Mr. Tamarov!" Lightly, I cuffed his face.

"Let me sleep." He tried to lie down.

"Pa's in trouble! He's calling you!"

For a moment, nothing. Then one eye popped open. Mik tried to pull himself up, fell back with a groan. "Where am I?"

"On the launch." I quickly filled him in, my fingers busy with his clamps.

By the time I was done, he'd struggled to his feet. "Christ-damned bastard sons of bitches—" My eyes widened as the string of oaths flowed undiminished. At last he wound down. "The tanks!"

"You're wearing them. The oxygen won't flow until your helmet's—"

"No, you twit, the propulsion tanks!" At the hatch, an ominous hiss. "Grab them!"

"Aye aye, sir." I snatched them from the locker. "Hurry. They're cutting through!"

He clamped his helmet, checked mine. "Ask Mr. Tolliver, should I break the launch free?"

I did.

"No, it's too easy a laser target. Suits are smaller, and more maneuverable. The launch is expendable."

I helped Mik secure his propellant tanks.

Unsteady on his feet, he lurched down the aisle. He led me to the escape hatch, almost all the way aft. Far smaller than an airlock hatch, the escape provided a second exit, on the opposite side of the craft from the lock. We folded the seat that blocked it, bent to the lever, frowned. "It won't open while we're pressurized." He pushed me aside, rushed down the aisle, stumbled, fell on his face. He scrambled up, bolted to the cockpit.

From the airlock, shouts and thuds. I crossed the aisle, peered out the porthole. Olympiad was as distant as ever. Why couldn't Tolliver have brought the ship alongside to save us?

The hum of a motor. Warning lights flashed throughout the cabin. Mikhael reappeared, face flushed. His eyes shot to the airlock, from whose plating acrid smoke curled. "It'll be close."

"What'd you—"

"We're de-airing." He thrust me aside, tugged on the panel lever. "*Olympiad*, Midshipman Tamarov reporting. We'll be out in a minute."

Behind us, a crackle. I muttered, "We don't have a minute."

He glanced over my shoulder. "Christ." A mighty kick dislodged the lever. Mik spun the wheel. Abruptly the hatch panel floated aside. Mik kicked it into the void. Without warning, he grabbed me, flung me Outside.

I had no time to grab for the hatchway, the hull, anything. Utterly helpless, I shot into space, windmilling, screaming. The launch and the Station spun crazily in my visor.

"*Randy—*"

Behind me, a burst of light. A porthole dissolved. Mikhael dived through the escape, kicking off as he did so.

He headed my general direction, but would miss me by meters. I'd float in vacuum until my air ran out and I died. My corpse would float forever in the vast womb of space.

My eyes bulged with the frenzy of my scream.

Mik tapped gently at his suit thrusters. His trajectory changed ever so slightly. "*Hang on, joey. And stop that infernal shrieking!*"

I paid no heed, kicking and clawing at nothing in a frenzied, useless swim to safety.

Mik caught my hand. "*Sir, I've got hi—*" I convulsed, wrapped myself around his neck, squeezed with all my might.

We floated, rotating slowly. The Station came and went. "Let go. Randy, LET ME GO!"

His rage pierced my terror. I loosened my grip just enough for him to manhandle me, spin me about, clutch me from behind. "I've got you. You're safe."

My breath came in a long shuddering sob.

Mik reached around, changed my suit frequency to a general channel. "*To the ship, Mr. Tamarov. As fast as you—*"

"Aye aye, sir." Mikhael. Then, "Uh, oh." In the launch's escape hatch, a suited figure. It aimed a laser. Mik spun me breast to breast, thrust my hands around his waist. "Hold on!" We jetted to the side.

Hadn't the Station trooper fired? I saw nothing. No beam, no spurt of smoke—

No, idiot, in vacuum I'd see nothing, not even the bolt that burned me to a cinder. I shivered.

Mik bent double, nearly snapping my spine. We veered away from the pistol's track. On the Station, two laser turrets swiveled, found us. I croaked a warning.

Mikhael craned his neck, spotted them, searched for *Olympiad*, muttered a curse.

"What?" I wasn't sure I could handle more bad news.

"*Station, hold your fire or I'll blast you to hell!*" Tolliver.

Mik bent, keyed his thrusters.

"Do not, repeat, do not fire on my men!"

The Station shot toward us. I gasped, "Wrong way!"

"Got to!"

The laser turret swiveled. Mikhael jiggled his thruster levers; we lurched this way and that, spinning. The Station loomed. Its turrets followed, until the angle was so depressed they could turn no farther.

At what seemed the last second, Mik turned us, fired a full blast. It braked our momentum. We sailed into the Station's hull. Mik put out his legs, absorbed our inertia as best he could. The blow loosened his grip; my back slammed into the alumalloy hull. Before I could bounce off, he caught me. His fingers clung to a handhold.

"Why'd you go back?" To my shame, my tone was a whine. *Get a grip, joey.* "Mik—sir—they'll catch us here!"

He took my hand, wrapped it around the handgrip. "No choice."

"But—"

"Quiet, Mr. Carr. Bridge, Mr. Tamarov reporting." Mik sounded out of breath, as if he'd run all the way from the launch.

"*Go ahead.*" Tolliver.

"I couldn't chance it. We'd be under fire all the way."

"*I saw. That son of a bitch Thurman won't answer us.*"

"We're safe for the moment. What about Pa?"

"*I don't know. I'm about to take the Station apart finding out.*"

A new voice crackled. "Do that and I'll slice *Olympiad* to ribbons." General Thurman.

"*Where's Captain Seafort?*"

"Groundside. He's charged with treason, heresy, blasph—"

"*By whom?*"

"The Government of Hope Nation and—"

I hissed, "Goofjuice!" Anthony would never—

Mik jabbed me.

"*You've no right to hold a U.N. Naval officer!*"

"—and Holy Mother Church, whose authority is universal." General Thurman sounded pious.

I knew enough to switch off my transmitter. I touched my helmet to Mik's. "Can they do that?"

"They did. Shush."

Tolliver's voice was cold. *"Tell Stadholder Carr—"*

"Mr. Carr is removed from office."

I blanched. "They can't!"

"He—I—who the hell's in charge?"

"Mr. Palabee heads a government of national reconciliation."

"Put me through to him!" Tolliver sounded white with rage.

I tugged at Mik's arm. "Palabee's a joke! Where's Anth?"

"Quiet."

"Call him yourself, Captain. You have the codes to the Governor's Manse."

"They don't answer."

"Perhaps after the trial." Thurman was unctuous.

"Send me my crewmen."

"Your Mr. Tamarov . . . I believe he's related to Seafort?"

"If so, what of it?"

"We'll hold him, for now. Your Captain can be . . . intransigent."

A long silence. I fidgeted. "Mik—"

"What?" His transmitter was off. His eyes roved constantly.

"They've got Fath and Anthony. It's Andori's doing, and maybe that Terran Ambassador, McEwan. Palabee on his own would never dare—"

"What of it?"

"The Church hates them both. If they go on trial—"

"Move. Handhold to handhold, like this." Mik pulled me along.

"Why?"

"Joeys coming out a hatch."

I peered over my shoulder. Christ. I scrambled along the hull.

Tolliver's voice was icy. *"You son of a bitch, you've got twenty minutes! Call Palabee. Have Seafort released, or the Station's gone and Hope Nation's out of the grain business!"*

I nodded. Good for Tolliver. For us.

"We're as well armed as you. Fire on us and you lose your ship!"

"You leave me no choice."

Thurman said, "Nonsense. Let justice take its course."

Mik and I had put a protruding launch bay between us and our pursuers. I asked, "What do they want?"

"We'd make good hostages; Pa's too sentimental." He shook his head, deep in thought. "Mr. Carr."

"Huh?"

"I'm on duty. So are you."

"I don't—yes, sir."

He clapped my shoulder. "Thanks. It'll make it easier."

Oddly enough, it was a comfort. He'd reminded me I had duty, as did he.

"Pa's been taken groundside. *Olympiad* has launches and gigs, but nothing to breach the atmosphere. That means Tolliver can't rescue him."

I waited.

"There's half a dozen shuttles at the Station, but *Olympiad* can't get to them. That leaves us. If we see a chance, we take it. Agreed?"

My heart pounded. "Yes, sir."

After a moment, a silhouette against the Station lights. A suited joey on the hull pointed our way, beckoned to unseen figures.

"Hurry!" Mik helped me on my way. He switched radio frequencies. "*Olympiad,* we're being chased."

"*Flick your suit transponders on.*"

"Aye aye, sir." Mik keyed his, then mine.

"*We have you.*"

We scrambled along the hull. I reached from handhold to handhold, trying to ignore the queasiness of zero gee.

"Mik—sir—my light's yellow."

"Oh, great." He sighed. "We've got about twenty minutes."

We huddled at a pair of handholds.

"More of them, sir!" I pointed behind him. Half a dozen suited soldiers. They'd come out another lock.

He veered, pulling me along. "Bastards."

My breath rasped in my helmet.

Mikhael said into his radio, "Sir, we're . . . running out of time."

For a long moment, silence. *Then, "Listen carefully. When your, ah, squadmate went to Cabin two fifty-seven, I'll do what his visitor did just before."*

What on earth was he saying? Abruptly my eyes widened, and I touched helmets. "Mik, two fifty-seven is where Kevin was killed! Kev is the squadmate he's talking about. The visitor means the outrider. It burned through the hull!"

"Don't move an inch! Look away!" Mikhael pulled me down.

I raised my head, just for an instant.

Five meters from us, the hull glowed.

Even though my radio was off, I whispered. "What good will it do?"

"All batteries open fire!" Thurman sounded livid. "Destroy *Olympiad*!"

Mikhael said, "We're running out of air, and they're surrounding us. He's getting us inside. Maybe we'll have a chance to help Pa." A moment passed. "Help Mr. Seafort." I grinned. For Mik too it was personal, and would remain so.

The hull plating boiled. Abruptly a speck of light.

An idea boiled forth. I caught my breath. No time to explain. I keyed my radio, shrieked, "NO, STOP! OH, GOD, DON'T—" I jammed off my transponder, then Mik's.

He caught my wrist. "Are you insane?"

A patch of hull a meter wide melted and vanished. A swirl of flotsam. Dust, papers, chips, Lord knew what else. Then nothing.

I touched helmets. "Sir, if *Olympiad* tracks our transponders, so will the Station. They'll think we're dead."

In the distance, *Olympiad*'s lights shrank.

"So will Tolliver." He sighed. "It can't be helped. Come ON!" He shoved me toward the gaping hole.

"It'll be hot."

"Only for a few seconds. Avoid the edge. Jump through. Hurry!"

"Aye aye, sir." It wasn't as easy as it sounded. How, in zero gee, do you jump? I crab-walked to the edge of the puncture, grasped the nearest handhold, dropped my head, pushed off in a dive, as if into the swimming hole behind our manse.

I'd forgotten about the Station's gravitrons. They caught me halfway down. I was lucky not to snap my neck; my hands came out just in time. I somersaulted onto my back, lay there a moment, half stunned. I scrambled to my feet, orienting myself. The hole *Olympiad* had pierced was in our side bulkhead. I mimed to Mik to be careful. Lord knew if he understood.

Outside, at ninety degrees to the bulkhead, Mik stepped over the hole, tapped his thruster ever so lightly. He sank. As gravity grabbed him, he fired his side thruster. It didn't quite work, but he eased his fall. I skittered out of the way so as not to be caught in his exhaust.

I glanced about. Some sort of storage compartment. Cabinets. A locker. A hatch, sealed shut.

I touched helmets. "Now what, sir?"

"Is that table loose?"

I gaped.

"Does it move, God damn you?" He pushed me aside, lifted the edge of the table. Hurt, I grabbed my end. Together, we manhandled it to the bulkhead. The tabletop was just wide enough to cover the gaping hole. He dragged a cabinet, tipped it so its weight held the table to the bulkhead, grabbed me, brought my helmet close. "Sorry I swore."

I blinked back tears. "Thank you, sir."

He keyed the hatch control. Nothing. "The bloody safeties won't let it open in vacuum." Stymied, he looked about.

"Mr. Tamarov, my tank light's gone red."

"Ah, that's it!" He leaped to the locker. Inside, suits. Spare tanks. He dragged two of them out, pulled a clamping tool from his pouch. I turned, to give him access to my pack.

He ignored me. I whirled. Mik was opening the spare tanks' valves as wide as they'd go.

Again I touched helmets, wishing I could use the radio. But then Station Command would know we were aboard. "What the hell are you doing!"

"Steady, Mr. Carr. Grab more tanks. Hurry!"

"But—aye aye, sir!" I hauled out three more tanks. In a moment he had them open.

"Push the table tight!"

Panting, I shouldered the table to the bulkhead as hard as I could. Was it my imagination, or was my suit air stale? I yawned prodigiously.

Mik abandoned the tanks, ran to the hatch, keyed the control. Nothing. He rolled his eyes, flashed me a weak smile. "Patience."

"Yes, sir." Dimly, in the distance, an alarm. I blinked. An alarm meant sound. Sound meant air.

In a moment he tried again. The hatch slid open.

His lips moved. "Out!"

I dashed into the corridor, Mik a step behind me. He slapped shut the hatch, checked a gauge on his suit. "It's—" He flicked off his radio, pressed his helmet to mine, spoke over the din of alarms. "The corridor's aired. Take off your helmet!"

God, if he was wrong, I'd end like Dad. Desperately, I thrust away the thought. I needed air, and it couldn't wait. I unlatched my clamps, tore off my helmet.

Fresh, cool air.

"Attention, all personnel. We've beaten off an attack by Olympiad. She's in full retreat. We've taken hits. None appear serious. All stations report damage."

"Out of your suit."

"Why?" I was already undoing my clasps.

"Mr. Carr . . ."

"Sorry. Aye aye, sir. But the air's leaking out past that table. If someone opens the hatch . . ."

"It won't open against vacuum. Same reason we couldn't get out."

"Suited repair party to Level 2 section eight."

I glanced about, with an odd stab of recognition. The corridor was like *Olympiad*'s, though considerably smaller and not as ornate. Well, the Station was built around an old warship. And the Navy valued tradition above all. But that meant the corridor would be divided into sections, and in a vacuum emergency . . . I took a few steps, peeked past the bend. Right. The section hatches were sealed. Naturally they would be, with even part of a section decompressed.

When I told Mikhael, he shrugged. "No one said it'd be easy, but we have one thing in our favor."

"What's that?"

"You're a bunch of provincials." He grinned at my outrage. "Seriously, your security is awful. On Earth they'd never stand for it. Think how easy it was to get on a shuttle at Centraltown."

"That's 'cause we don't have wars and revolu—"

"Precisely." He unclamped his helmet. "Get rid of your suit."

"Where?"

"Anywhere. There." He flung open a hatch across the corridor.

I looked about. Mops, pails, a faucet. Great. Perhaps I should volunteer to clean up. After all, I was just a ship's boy.

"Repair party to Level 3 Section five lounge."

"What's that?"

I glanced down. "A mop handle."

"A club."

I hefted it. It would do. "Hey, sir, isn't that stuff caustic?" I pointed to a bag of cleansing powder. A few days ago Alejandro and I had been loading supplies, and they'd made us wear gloves for the deck plate cleanser.

"Only mixed with water."

I seized a bucket, thrust it under the faucet. When it was half full I ripped open the bag, dumped most of the cleanser in it. "Now what, sir?"

"Pray there are no corridor cameras." We trudged to the section hatch. I looked about, didn't spot the cameras that were standard gear on *Olympiad*.

We confronted the hatch panel, with its confusing array of lights. He bent, studied them. "The override isn't keyed."

"What's that mean?"

"No one's expecting us. We can open the hatch."

"Wait!" I smiled weakly; it sounded too much like an order. "Sir, I'm in Naval blues, you've got your uniform. If they spot us we'll stand out like trannies at the opera."

"We can't be here when they come to patch the hull."

We exchanged perplexed frowns.

"Hello?"

I whirled. The voice came from behind a cabin hatch.

"Anyone there? Is it safe to come out?"

Mik gestured me silent. "Identify yourself." His tone was peremptory.

"Rolf Iverson. Electrician, third shift."

"What are you doing here?"

"It's my cabin, sir. I was asleep when the alarms . . ."

Mikhael wrested the mop handle from my grip. "The corridor's aired, but we're evacuating the section for repairs. Didn't you hear the announcement? Come out at once." Mik hefted the club.

"Yes, sir, I'm sorry, I—"

The hatch slid open. Iverson was sallow, small-boned, balding. Instantly Mik swung. The mop handle caught him in the forehead. A crunch. He fell into the cabin, thudded onto the deck. Blood seeped.

Mikhael pulled me inside, slapped shut the hatch. He knelt by the prone figure, fished out his ID card, wiped off blood.

Desperately, I tried not to step in the spreading pool. "Is he . . ." I stared down, aghast. Fath lay inert on the Dining Hall carpet, his lifeblood draining. Around me, chaos.

"I don't know." He pawed through Iverson's clothing shelf. "Wear this. And that. *Pay attention, Mr. Carr!*"

"Yessir." Numbly, I undid my shirt.

In moments we were a rather unkempt pair of Station hands. Mik's clothes were too small, mine too large. At least the shirts were the right color. I hoped nobody would notice we were both named "Iverson."

Mikhael ran to the janitor's compartment, hurried back with a mop, handed it to me. "Don't spill your bucket."

At the corridor hatch panel, he took up the caller, drew a deep breath, keyed it. "Hello? Anyone there?"

"What are you . . ."

He waved me silent. "Come on, someone answer!"

The speaker blared. *"Comm Room."*

"Rolf Iverson. I'm on—" he glanced at the hatch panel. "—Level 4 section six. Must be a leak somewhere; the hatch slammed shut. The corridor's fine. Okay if I open to come out?"

"Ask the Commandant's office."

"What's the frazzin' code?"

"Twenty-four seventy-five." A click.

Mik punched in the code. "Iverson here, ID 70-J-446. Dunno where the problem is, but I'm in the corridor and it's fine out here. Shouldn't I report to the machinist?"

A pause. "Very well. Close the hatch soon as you're through."

"Right." To me, "Bring your mop and bucket."

Calmly, he opened the hatch.

We sauntered through.

Nobody was in sight. We rounded the bend. The far hatch was closed. I said, "Where are we going, sir?"

"I'm not sure."

Truthful, perhaps, but not comforting. I shot him a dubious glance.

We opened the next section hatch, sealed it behind us. "What we need," he said, "is a map. Where are the shuttle bays—mop the deck!"

"What?"

Voices.

"Mop!"

Sweating, I bent to my task. Mik would get us killed yet.

He threw himself against the bulkhead, idly toyed with the spare mop handle. "She was something, I tell ya. Ass soft and round, tits like—"

Three techs in suits. With them, two soldiers. One had a pistol, the other a stunner. Unheeding, I sloshed water in their path.

"—so I said, look, baby, why fight it? I'm the best you'll—" Mik's mop handle whirled round, caught a soldier behind the neck. Mik dived for the man's laser. I thrust my mop between the other soldier's legs. He sprawled. I grabbed my bucket, dumped the caustic cleanser in his face. A scream. He thrashed about the deck, frantically rubbing his eyes. I straddled him, pulled free his stunner.

Mik's laser flicked between the three techs. "No radio! I'll kill!" A gesture backed them against the bulkhead.

Mik tried cabin hatches until he found one unsealed. "In here!" It looked like an unused lounge; a few dusty holovids and games lay about. As we passed through, a suited tech leaped for Mik's laser. They struggled. I touched the stunner to his side. Nothing. Cursing, I fumbled for the safety. Behind me, a suited arm wrapped around my windpipe.

I couldn't free myself, couldn't breathe. I poked the stunner around my ribs, touched something, pulled the trigger.

Suddenly my throat was free.

The tech's gloved fist slammed into Mikhael's chest. The middy's face went white. As the tech wrestled the laser from his grasp I lunged at him, caught him in the side with the stunner. He dropped. Mikhael slid down the bulkhead. Wild-eyed, I spun to the third tech.

He backed to the wall. "No, don't—"

I jabbed him. He went limp.

I ducked through the hatch. In the corridor, one soldier lay still. The other thrashed about. I stunned him, dragged him by the heels into the lounge. Then the last.

Panting, I slapped shut the hatch. "Mik? Sir?" He couldn't speak. I knelt by his side. "Breathe deep as you can."

He clutched my wrist, squeezed 'til I thought I'd scream. "It hurts." His voice was a croak.

"He caught a neural plexus."

"A what?"

"A pressure point." I extended my palm, hesitated. Was it a crime to touch an officer? *Randy, don't be an idiot.* I massaged his chest, as gently as I could.

Slowly, his color returned.

"Now, what, sir?"

"Should you be a tech or a soldier?" He debated. "A tech. Pick one and use his suit."

"They're too big. I'll look silly."

"You'll look sillier as a soldier."

I didn't like it, but he was right. Hope Nation forces didn't enlist joey-kids, as did the Navy.

We stripped a tech of his suit, fished for his ID card.

At a holovid console Mik called up a Station map. "Launch bays are there. Level 5." He jabbed the screen.

I said, "Can you pilot? Take a shuttle groundside and find Fath." In turn, he would help us free Anth.

"If we took a shuttle to *Olympiad,* Mr. Tolliver could send an armed party." He grimaced. "What's the point? The Station lasers would get us."

"Where's laser control?"

"Two of us, attacking the laser compartment? Don't be ridiculous. Besides, they can bypass the consoles and fire from anywhere."

I paced, half beside myself. Then, "Sir, this was once a ship?"

"Yes, what of it?"

"On *Olympiad,* Fath—Captain Seafort—had to release the laser safeties from the bridge before Mr. Dakko could fire."

Our eyes met.

"Where's the Commandant's office?" He bent to the screen, answered his own question. "Level 1. The lasers would be under the Commandant's sole control. They'd have to be, especially after the fiasco at Earthport." Control of the Station's laser cannon had enabled the Naval rebellion Dad had died to quell.

Coolly, Mikhael entered a soldier's ID, read from a list of caller codes. "Wish me luck, brother." He took up the caller. Then, "No, their readout tells them where it's coming from. Hurry."

He led me on a race back to section six. He used the caller at the corridor hatch. "Staff Sergeant Burns, sir. I'm bringing Technician Ouward. He has an artifact General Thurman ought to see."

"What is it?"

"Are you cleared?"

A splutter. *"For what?"*

"They found it Outside, with those Navy grodes' bodies. A holovid.

The screen has a map, showing the route to—no, this is for the General himself. He'll decide who ought to know."

A pause. *"He's in his office."*

"I'll bring Ouward up." Mikhael rang off.

In moments we were redressed. I wore the smallest of the suits, and still swam in it. Mikhael wore the outfit of Sergeant Willard Burns, Hope Nation Home Guard. He holstered his laser.

"What's the plan, sir?"

"Find the laser safety, make sure it's off, call *Olympiad*." Mik tucked the stunner into my work pouch.

"Right."

We started on our way. He matched his pace to my necessarily slower one. "Don't forget your codes."

"367-T-491." I bobbed, barely able to see out of the helmet. "Sir, we've had incredible luck so far. If we don't both make it . . ." I drew breath, hardened my resolve. "Save Fath, whatever else. And tell him I'm sorry for how I acted. I never had the chance."

"He knows."

"Tell him." In a helmet, you can't wipe your frazzing eyes.

21

WE TRUDGED UP TO Level 1, Mik's steadying hand on my forearm. Cool as ice, following the map he'd memorized and the occasional corridor sign, he led me to the anteroom of the Commandant's office.

Thurman was a General in our Home Guard; naturally his receptionist would be military as well. As I sidled toward Thurman, holovid in hand, the aide frowned at Mikhael.

"You're not Burns," he said. Instantly Mik flung me through the office hatch, tugged at his laser. Two techs swarmed atop him.

It was Thurman himself who gave us a chance. He ran after me, slapped shut the hatch, no doubt to bar Mikhael from his office. The hatch slammed closed, cutting us off from the melee in the anteroom. I scrambled to my feet, worked the bulky stunner clear of my suit pouch.

Ignoring the laser pistol clipped to his belt, Thurman bent over the console, grabbed his caller. I leaped at him.

Perhaps he'd once been stunned, and hated it as much as I. He recoiled, spinning his chair to the bulkhead. I clambered after. Too late, he remembered his pistol. I brandished my stunner, inches from his chest, shook my head, held out a hand.

He considered refusing—you could see the debate in his eyes—but after a moment, reluctantly, he unclipped the laser pistol, handed it to me butt-first. Once I had it, I shoved my stunner in my pouch.

"You'll never get away with it." General Thurman's face was bitter.

"Stuff it in a sack." I glanced about, dazed at the pace of events.

Thurman's office had once been the warship's bridge. Though they'd brought in amenities over the years—softer chairs, a spacious desk, a well-stocked cooler—the reinforced bridge hatch remained a fortress, and right now it was all that protected me.

Frantic hammering, on the corridor hatch. I glanced at the console. Like *Olympiad*'s, it was a complicated array of lights and switches, far beyond my understanding. "Over there, by the far bulkhead," I snarled. There was no way I could study the console with Thurman ready to jump me from behind.

"Give it up, joey. You haven't a chan—"

I set the pistol to low, flipped off the safety, aimed just in front of his boot. The deck plate crackled. He yelped, and scuttled across the office.

"Commandant, are you all right?"

Ignoring the speaker, I unclasped my helmet, studied the console. None of the switches was marked "laser safety."

Mik would know.

But I couldn't open the hatch; they'd be armed and ready. "Where's the corridor camera control?"

"What are you talking about?" His tone was surly.

"There's always a camera outside the bridge hatch." Else, a Captain couldn't be sure whom he was admitting.

Thurman snorted. "It's been broken for years."

"Don't give me—"

"Try it. Just to the left of that red lever."

Cautiously, I did, my eye on the screen. Either he was lying as to the proper switch, or the camera really was broken.

"General Thurman? Sir?"

I put my mouth to the hatch. "Mikhael? Mr. Tamarov?"

No answer.

I was in big trouble.

All right, how would Fath handle it? How would Anthony?

Deviously.

"I want the use of your laser cannon," I said grandly. "How do I turn off the safeties?"

Thurman pressed his lips tight.

"How?"

His eyes took on a resolve I didn't like. Quelling my revulsion, I took aim with the pistol. "You'd best tell me," I said. I tried to make my voice menacing, but managed only a shrill squeak. I blushed.

"Kill me and you'll never know."

"Release the General, joey! We have your cohort."

I said, "Don't play games. Time is short."

"Quite short. They'll burn through anytime now."

"You don't know much about bridge hatches," I said scornfully. Of course, neither did I. I hoped I was right.

"Five minutes or twenty, they'll be along. You'll be killed, unless you give me the pistol."

"Where's the laser safety?" I sighted on his face.

He met my gaze. "Aren't you old Derek's son? Will you kill a man in cold blood?"

"Yes. Five. Four. Three."

Beads of sweat appeared on his forehead, but he said nothing.

"Open the hatch, joey, or I'll take you apart! This is your last warning!"

"Two. One."

General Thurman shut his eyes.

Trembling, I put the pistol in my pouch, disgusted with myself. I couldn't do it.

He shot me a look of triumph.

"Please, give me the codes." My tone was plaintive. "My father's life depends on it."

"Who? Derek's dead. You mean Seafort?" Thurman's voice was contemptuous. "He's no more your father than I am." Cautiously, he rose to his feet. "Here, I won't hurt you."

"Why'd they take him?"

"For trial. All his life he's gotten away with the most outrageous . . . Such arrogance, even treason. Not this time."

I cried, "Why do you hate him so?"

He jabbed a finger outward, perhaps toward *Olympiad.* "He traffics with those Satanic . . . damn them! The fish were supposed to be dead!" He advanced on me. "He's done for, joey. Don't make it worse."

"Done for?"

"The Church has him, and means to be rid of him. He'll hang, or better yet, burn. There'll be no appeal to home system." Another step. He nodded to the hatch. "My men are waiting. You're trapped; it's just you and me."

My voice was odd. "Yes. Just you and me." I retreated toward the hatch panel.

Behind me, a clunk. A whirring sound. It seemed familiar.

Inexorably, Thurman advanced. "Easy there, lad. You're young, and scared. Don't be foolish."

"No, sir. I won't be foolish." I yanked out the stunner, set it to the lowest setting, jabbed it at his midriff. He stumbled, fell twitching.

The scream of metal on metal. They were working at the hatch.

In three or four minutes, when he began to revive, my panic had escalated to near frenzy. Shuddering, Thurman managed to sit. *Or better yet, burn.* I touched him lightly with the stunner. He went down, all jerks and spasms.

A minute passed. "Don't—" A voice from the grave.

I stunned him again.

After the fifth time he had a sort of convulsion. Sweating in my suit, I dragged him to the bulkhead, leaned him against it, waited for him to claw his way to consciousness. "The codes." Waiting had given me a better idea. "All of them. Authorize me to the puter."

"N—n—gah, no don'—" I touched the stunner to his arm.

For minutes he drooled and twitched. When he spoke I could barely make out the words. I had him repeat it over and again, until I was sure I had it right.

To the console.

No. First, a detour to the corner, to spew forth the contents of my stomach.

Wiping bile, I trudged to the console, tapped in the sequence he'd given me.

A warm contralto filled the room. "Yes, General?"

Fine by me, if the puter thought I was Thurman. But my voice would give me away. I tapped, "Alphanumeric input only."

"SET FOR ALPHANUMERIC."

"Status, laser cannon safeties?"

"SAFETIES RELEASED."

I typed, "Engage laser cannon safeties."

"ENTER SUPERVISORY CODE."

Holding my breath, I stabbed out Thurman's numbers.

"SAFETIES ENGAGED. WARNING: LASER DEFENSES CANNOT BE ACTIVATED WITHOUT RELEASE."

"Do not release except by authorization from this console. Override any instructions to the contrary."

"INSTRUCTIONS ACKNOWLEDGED."

Good. "Query: how may comm room be bypassed, for transmissions directly from this console?"

"ENTER DESIRED FREQUENCIES AND BEGIN TRANSMISSION."

"Do you monitor incoming responses?"

"AFFIRMATIVE. I DEDUCE YOU WISH THEM ROUTED DIRECTLY TO THIS CONSOLE AS WELL."

"Yes." My tone was fervent. "I mean . . ." I typed it. "Yes. Use frequency of last transmission from *Olympiad*."

In the corner, General Thurman moaned. Abruptly his neck arched. His feet drummed the deck.

I tried not to hear. "Puter, do I begin talking now?"

"AFFIRMATIVE."

"*Olympiad,* come in. Mr. Tolliver! Someone answer!" It wasn't very professional, but how should I know the proper drill?

A time passed.

"Mr. Tolliver! *Olympiad*! Where are you?" I jabbed at the keyboard. "Puter, are you transmitting?"

"YOU ARE."

"*UNS* Olympiad *to Station, go ahead.*" An unfamiliar voice.

"I need Mr. Tolliver!"

"*State your message.*"

"You frazzing grode, this is Randy Carr, ship's boy, and I need Mr. Tolliver RIGHT NOW!"

Almost instantly, a new voice. He must have been listening. "This is Tolliver. What do you want?"

"Sir, I'm on their bridge. I mean, the Commandant's office. They captured Mr. Tamarov. I have the Commandant and his authorization codes, and the hatch is sealed. Laser safeties are locked; they can't fire. Take the Station!"

"How?"

"Bring *Olympiad*! Board us!"

A silence. "*You propose I sail* Olympiad *within range of your cannon?*"

"The safeties are locked."

"*I've no way to know that.*"

"For Christ's sake, why would I lie?" Fath would be outraged at my language. Sorry, sir. I'm beside myself.

"*Mr. Carr, can you prove you're not a prisoner?*"

At the hatch, the scream of blades had stopped. But the room seemed warmer. Cautiously, I touched the hatch, yanked back my hand. It was warm. And if I listened hard, I could hear the hiss of a torch.

"Mr. Tolliver, we've no time! They're trying to cut through the hatch! For God's sake, hurry!"

"*Can you put Mr. Tamarov on the line?*"

"They have him. Or maybe he's dead."

"*I can't risk* Olympiad. *If they hit our tubes, we're stranded; tubes can't be repaired outside a shipyard. I assume you're under duress.*"

"But I'm not! Mr. Seafort's in trouble, they're talking about burning him! They've got shuttles here!" My voice was ragged. "I'm begging you!"

"*I wish I could believe you. You say you have Thurman with you? Put him on.*"

I pounded the console. "I can't. He's . . . I can't!" If I looked again at the blood seeping from his mouth, I'd go mad. His fingers twitched.

"*Then we're at an impasse.*"

A breath of air. An audible hiss. The General's fingers eased.

My eyes darted from bulkhead to bulkhead. A vent. I dived for my helmet, got it on just as a wave of dizziness caught me. I slumped.

Minutes passed, or hours. Or years. By sheer effort of will, I raised my head.

"Mr. Tolliver?" My voice was muffled.

"*Yes?*"

"They tried gas. I'm in my suit. My tanks are good for an hour." I fought to slow the whirling room. "Sir, the Station's yours. I'm not under duress."

"*How can I know?*"

I tried not to vomit. "Think about my cell in *Olympiad*. Nothing in God's universe would make me do this against my w—wi—will." I swallowed a lump. I was failing. It would all be for naught.

"*Oh, son. How can I trust you?*"

I whispered, "Fath would." It was my last effort. I lay my head on the console.

Eons passed.

"*Olympiad to Station, Captain Tolliver speaking. We're approaching at flank speed, at Battle Stations. Open all outer locks. We demand your surrender on behalf of our allies, the Government of Stadholder Anthony Carr.*"

"Randy, are you in there? Open, it's safe now."

I raised my hand to the hatch control, hesitated. I knew the voice, but . . . "Have Mr. Tolliver order it."

Muttered epithets. A few moments passed.

"*Mr. Carr? Captain Tolliver here. Open, as he asks.*"

"Aye aye, sir." I slapped the control. The hatch slid open. Tad Anselm and I regarded each other. Wearily, I unclamped my helmet, brought myself to attention. "Ship's Boy Randolph Carr reporting, sir."

"As you were. Well done, joey." Anselm peered in, glanced at Thurman. "Lord Almighty, what did you do to him? Medic!"

"Where's Mik, sir? I mean, Mr. Tamarov."

His mouth tightened. "In sickbay. They were pretty savage. How on earth did you take over the master console?"

I told him, giving Mikhael all the credit. I'd done little but scream into my suit, and torture Mr. Thurman.

"The Captain will be proud. I'll see your exploit is Logged." He clapped me on the shoulder.

"Pardon." Lieutenant Frand brushed past, dropped into the console seat with a weary sigh. "Mr. Carr, the codes, before you go."

"Aye aye, ma'am." Dutifully, I recited them.

Outside the bridge, three of Mr. Janks's detail had taken position in the corridor, fully armed. No Station personnel were to be seen.

"Let's go." Anselm herded me to the corridor.

"Where?"

"Back to the ship."

"They took Mr. Seafort groundside."

"I know. The Captain wants to send a rescue party, but there's a complication." He grimaced. "Admiral Kenzig forbids it."

I stopped dead. "*What?*"

"Interfering in local politics. Meddling in Church affairs."

My lip trembled. "Did you see Thurman lying on the deck? Think I did that for myself? It was for Fath! We've *got* to help him!"

"I think as highly of him as you—"

"Goofjuice!" I flung down my helmet.

Anselm's tone was cold. "You forget yourself, Mr. Carr!"

"No, you do!" I kicked my helmet across the corridor, barely missing a sailor striding past. "You told me he saved you! Who are you, Lieutenant?"

"Come along." Now, his voice was ice. Catching the arm of my suit, he dragged me along the corridor, down a ladder, into a launch bay. He practically threw me into a waiting gig, took a seat alongside. The hatch slid closed.

I folded my arms, gritted my teeth.

Anselm said gruffly, "I'll speak to him. Captain Tolliver."

Satan himself couldn't coax a word from me. I glared at the porthole, watched the Station drift away.

"I was sixteen when I met him. He saved me. From myself." Tad turned abruptly, spoke to the empty seat alongside. "I'd ruined myself, with drink and sloth and despair. It's as if he'd adopted me as he did Mikhael; he treated me as a son. I'm what I am because of . . . I'd give anything to save him." A pause. "But Admiral Kenzig is the Navy we agreed to serve. He, and Mr. Tolliver, and Mr. Seafort. It's about orders, and loyalty, and faith."

Bullshit. It's about Fath.

White lights, as we eased into *Olympiad*'s bay.

Anselm guided me from the gig. "Come along."

"Where?" Oops. I'd vowed not to speak.

"To the bridge. And it's 'aye aye, sir.' "

I muttered something that might have been what he asked.

Mr. Tolliver paced before the giant simulscreen.

"Lieutenant Anselm reporting, sir, with the ship's boy." He came to attention.

Still suited, except for my discarded helmet, I made no effort to salute.

"As you were, Tad."

"Any word, sir?"

"From that ass Palabee. He refuses to tell me Anthony's status. He had a Churchman by his side, someone named Hambeld."

I blurted, "Scanlen's man. He helped hold me at the rectory."

Tad asked, "What news of the Captain?"

"Nothing. Kenzig's lodged a protest."

"With whom?"

"The Archbishop. And Palabee."

"To what effect?"

"I gather they're ignoring him." Tolliver stopped his pacing long enough to glare at us. "I want to send a force groundside. Kenzig refuses absolutely."

"Excuse me." My voice was cold.

"Yes?" Tolliver raised an eyebrow.

"General Thurman spoke of burning."

"Andori—the Archbishop—lodged a charge of heresy for attempting to arrest Bishop Scanlen. That would be the penalty. They'll try him on the civil charges first."

"Which are?"

"Crimes against humanity. Primarily, dealing with our friend the outrider." He gestured wearily toward Level 2. "They want the fish destroyed. Which reminds me." He took up the caller. "Ms. Frand? I need you to go below and try to communicate with the outrider. Tell it to wait in its own ship. Er, in its fish. We'll open our lock when we're ready to resume negotiations."

"Well . . . that's a fairly complicated message, sir."

"I know, Sarah. Do your best."

"Aye aye, sir."

Tolliver turned back to Anselm, but I'd had enough. "When's the trial?" My tone was truculent.

"This afternoon, at criminal court. They want it over and done."

"What will you do?"

His tone was bleak. "What *can* I do?"

I said, "You have the Station's cannon, and our own. For a start, blast the Cathedral to rubble."

"And then all of Centraltown? Would your guardian approve?"

I shouted, "It's not his decision!"

Anselm whirled me around. "That's quite enough, Mr. Carr!" To the Captain, "He's been through hell, sir."

"I know; I'll make allowances. Randy, when we brought Mr. Tamarov aboard he told us your part in this affair. I can't commend you highly enough. I'll enter it into the Log."

I stared at him as if his words were gibberish.

He flushed, turned to Tad. "It seems the latest upheaval was too much for our passengers. More than a few want off."

"Idiots."

"That's as may be. Some are Hope Nation nationals. I've pledged to Palabee not to try to slip a Naval force among them. He knows my sworn word is good, besides, we have his Station. He's agreed to let us land passengers at Centraltown. We have two shuttles standing by. You're to supervise the disembarkation."

"Aye aye, sir."

"Mr. Carr, get some rest. Again, I commend your work. I'll call you the moment we hear—"

"I really did well?"

"Yes."

"Then may I ask a favor?"

"What?"

"Remission of enlistment." Into the shocked silence, I said, "We both know they're going to kill . . . I don't want to sail with you after—after—" I faltered. "Please." I looked to the deck.

"Are you sure, Randy?" Oddly, Tolliver's tone was gentle.

"Yes, sir." I held my breath.

"Nick would want you safe, raised by friends who—"

"Please." My voice cracked. "For him, for me, for Derek. It's all I'll ever ask."

A long while passed. "Very well, granted. Go with Mr. Anselm. Fare thee well."

"And thee, sir." At the hatchway I paused. "Tell Mik that I lov—" I couldn't say it. "Tell him good-bye."

* * * *

Midshipman Yost led me past Corrine Sloan's seat on the second shuttle. I stopped abruptly, still hot and miserable in my spacesuit. "You too?"

"I have to, Randy." She sounded subdued.

"Why?"

Her eyes glistened. "The heresy charge. I was there for John. I can't do
less for Nick."

"But you loved John." Some recess of my mind wondered from where
I summoned such cruelty.

She started to answer, choked, bowed her head.

Tommy Yost stirred. "Please take your seat."

I did, nearby. "What about Janey?" She was nowhere in sight.

Corrine's shoulders shook.

I buckled myself in, forcing myself silent. I'd done enough evil for
one life.

No. There'd be more. I unbuckled, made my way to the hatch. "Mr.
Anselm!"

"Now what?"

"Come with us."

He looked startled. "It's against orders."

"Weren't you told to disembark the passengers?"

"I'm sure the Captain didn't mean—"

"You were more adventurous the day you took me to sickbay." To visit
Fath. Mr. Seafort, before he became Fath.

"Is there some reason . . ."

My lip curled. "Don't you want to see him?"

His glare could have melted the hull. At last, he muttered to Yost, "Tell
the bridge we're ready to cast off." He sealed the hatch from within.

We began our journey. Solemn, a bit forlorn, I watched *Olympiad* recede through the porthole. I'd never see her again.

An hour passed, while I fidgeted and sweltered, wondering if I was
doing right. Perhaps they'd let Fath off with a warning, or disgrace. Perhaps
a few months in jail. Perhaps . . .

The worst part is the buffeting, as the shuttle fights the outer atmosphere, and its own velocity. By sixty thousand feet, it becomes a calm flight,
no more bumpy than a suborbital.

I unbuckled. Quickly I made my way toward the cockpit. As I passed,
Anselm looked up in surprise; one didn't move about on a shuttle in flight.

I knocked on the cockpit hatch.

"What?" The pilot sounded annoyed as he swung it open. I thrust myself inside.

Behind me, Anselm leaped out of his seat.

I reached into my pouch.

Tad stopped short.

As well he ought. My laser pistol lit his midriff. I glanced at the instruments. The altimeter hovered at sixty thousand feet. I said to the pilot, "Tell the puter to fly us."

"You can't—"

I fired, dissolving a pressure gauge. "Move!" Fifty-five thousand.

"Puter, autopilot on!"

"Get out." I beckoned to the hatch.

He scurried past, to the cabin. Tad edged closer. "Where'd you get that?"

"At the Station. No one took it away, after."

Another casual step.

"Don't, Mr. Anselm. I warn you."

"You'll shoot me?"

My eyes met his. "If I must. I swear it." Forty thousand.

"What are you up to?"

"I'm going to land the shuttle."

"You can't fly."

"I'll ask the puter to help. We'll probably crash."

"Randy, we've ninety passengers!" His wave encompassed them all.

"Yes. For them, not for me, I ask your help." Thirty-three thousand.

"Doing what?"

"Give me your word as an officer—and your oath—that you won't interfere, or try to take my pistol, or subdue me. That you'll land as I tell you."

"If not?"

"I'll do it myself."

"Good Christ." After a long moment. "All right. I so swear."

"By Lord God."

"By Lord God."

"And your solemn word as an officer."

"Yes!" He looked ready to kill.

Twenty-five thousand. "Get in." I stood aside as he brushed past, and lowered myself into the copilot's seat.

"Randy, why?"

"I'm going to rescue Fath."

"You're insane!"

"Does it matter?"

After a moment, his lips twitched. "I guess not. Puter, autopilot off."

"Voicerec failure. Please identify speaker."

"Lieutenant Thadeus Anselm, U.N.N.S. ID is N-123—"

"Authority denied."

Fath had told me of his difficulties with puters. I bared my teeth. "Puter, safety check. Where is your CPU box?"

"To the right of the copilot's yoke, between the fuel gauge and the—"

I set my beam to low, burned the box until it sizzled.

"Jesus Christ son of God!" Tad leaped from his seat.

"Don't blaspheme." Odd, how much I sounded like Fath.

After that, Tad didn't have much to say. Centraltown Control didn't seem to notice the change in voices, and gave us our usual runway.

At fifteen thousand feet I broke the news. "We're not landing at Centraltown."

"Then do it yourself!"

"No, I have your word." Heart pounding, I leaned back, closed my eyes. For good measure, I laid the laser pistol on the dash.

Almost a minute passed.

"All right, you win." He spoke through clenched teeth. "Where?"

"Churchill Park. At the southeast corner, there's an open strip. No trees."

"We'll crash!"

I said, "Shuttles land VTOL."

"With the puter's help. I'm not good enough to—"

"Oh, I have faith. You're better than you think." Lord knew why I said it. Perhaps I no longer cared. "And don't tell Approach Control."

"They'll know, when we change course to—"

"When Fath took me groundside, our glide path took us just past Churchill Park. Bleed off speed, lose altitude early. Hell, I landed a heli there, not that long ago."

"A heli!" He swore under his breath. "If I ever get my hands on you . . ."

"Yes, and I'll deserve it." My voice was thin. "Tad, word is that they'll burn him!"

"Shut your MOUTH!" His tone was savage. "I have to think, to land this beast!"

I patted his knee.

Maybe I'd hooked Tad's sense of intrigue. Perhaps he cared for Fath as much as I. Laconically, he repeated back Centraltown's landing instructions, asked wind velocity and direction, gave them our ETA.

I thought our speed was a bit high when he folded the wings back into VTOL mode, but the craft took it. He applied maximum flaps and spoilers; still we came in over the park fast and low.

"You'd better ditch that suit."

I glanced at him, surprised. I'd forgotten all about it. Awkwardly I undid the clasps, wriggled free. "Thank you."

"When you jump out, then what?"

"The court."

"How far?"

I shrugged. I wasn't all that familiar with Centraltown. "Fifteen, twenty blocks." It was on Farnum, or one of those wandering roads.

"Do you drive?"

I flushed. "Not a groundcar." It had been a sore point between me and Anthony, but he'd been adamant that I'd have to wait; I wasn't of age.

"Hmpff." He waved me silent, focused on his work. We drifted southeast, toward Churchill Road.

"Shuttle, you're off course! What are you—"

Tad switched off the radio. "Get yourself ready."

"For what?"

"To make your break. In minutes they'll have a heli overhead."

"Right." I licked my lips.

"The pilot's in the main cabin, and Tommy Yost. They may try to stop you." His tone was tense. We swooped toward the trees, and the clearing beyond.

"Why warn me?"

"Don't hurt them. Don't hurt anyone."

"I'll try not."

"Brace yourself."

"Jesus, the trees!"

I clutched the dash, braced for a smash, and oblivion. We glided over the treetops with a meter to spare. Tad threw the engines into VTOL mode, and set us down in a roar of dust and scorched grass.

I took a deep breath, lunged to the cockpit hatch. Fingers closed on my collar, hauled me back.

I cried, "You promised!"

"Aren't you forgetting something?" Sourly, he eyed me.

"What?" I had no time; I had to get to the main hatch, jump down, run like the very—"Oh!" I blushed scarlet. I snatched up the laser I'd set on the dash. "Thank you."

I threw open the hatch.

In the main cabin, pandemonium. Colonists struggled with Midshipman Tommy Yost, who was doing his best to block the outer hatch.

"OUT OF MY WAY!" My scream brought them up short. I brandished the laser. Frantic joeys ducked behind seats, dived into the minuscule head, cowered anywhere that offered an illusion of safety.

I snarled at Yost, "Open it!"

"Open it yourself!" His glare was such that I braced for an assault. Nonetheless, I aimed past him to the hatch panel.

Behind me, an icy voice. "Mr. Yost, do as he says!" Tad Anselm.

"But—"

"THIS INSTANT!"

"Aye aye, Lieutenant!" Yost slammed a fist into the panel. The inner hatch slid aside; the outer door began unfolding itself into steps. With a snarl I launched myself into daylight, teetered on the still-moving stairs, leaped down to steaming grass.

The closest city street would be . . . that way. I thrust the laser into my belt, and galloped to the road.

I risked a backward glance. The shuttle stairway was down. Tad Anselm sprinted after me. The traitor, the lying . . . No, I'd made him swear not to interfere with my hijacking, and he hadn't. Now he was free to do his duty. Thank Lord God that Naval officers didn't routinely go armed, else he might burn me as I ran.

I threw a glance over my shoulder. Tommy Yost pounded after Anselm, legs pumping madly.

The courts would be . . . south. I veered off.

Already my breath came in gasps. I'd have to pace myself, or I'd never make it. On the other hand, in a moment or two I'd hear the whap of heli blades; Centraltown spaceport would lose no time chasing down their errant shuttle.

Behind me Tad Anselm lurched into the road, threw himself in front of a slow-moving electricar. His arms windmilled frantically. He hauled out the driver, ducked into the seat. I cursed. Now he'd catch me, and force me to shoot him. I'd do it. Nobody, nothing, would stop me from reaching Fath while I had breath. A gasp wavered into a sob.

Inexorably, Anselm's car gained on me. My eye searched overgrown yards for a clear path; for Fath's sake I'd try to evade Tad before I killed him.

The gun of an engine. Tad's car loomed. He was alone. I veered to the walk, tugged out my laser. In the sky, a growing spot. A heli.

Behind us, Tommy Yost charged down the street, his face a mask of white-hot resolve.

Anselm's electricar wavered as he leaned across the seat to avoid my shot. No, he was half up on the curb, fumbling with the door. Was he glitched?

"Away from me!" I panted. "I'll shoot to kill!"

"Get in, you ass!" Tad flung open the door.

I gaped. Behind us, Yost's footsteps pounded. My reluctance slowed me an instant too long; Yost launched himself at me just as I whirled to fire. He slammed me to the ground, knocking the gun from my hand. I thrashed, unable to breathe, my face purple.

Anselm leaped from his vehicle. While Yost battered me, he fell on the pistol. "Tommy, stand aside!" Tad shoved the middy off my chest, hauled me to my feet, shoved me into the car.

I wheezed. It felt as if a rock was embedded in my lung.

"Give me the caller, I'll get the jerries in the heli!" Yost danced with excitement.

"Not quite." Anselm set the safety, took my wrist, wrapped my fingers around the laser's grip.

Yost's mouth worked. "Sir, what are you—"

"I changed sides."

"Our orders—"

"It's the Captain. Mr. Seafort."

"Yes, but . . ." Yost swallowed.

"Save your career. This isn't your fight." He reached past me, slammed the door.

"The hell it isn't." Yost yanked open the door, dived behind us into the passenger seat. "I'll come."

Tad scowled. "A minute ago you were calling the jerries."

The middy flushed. "If you're helping, we have a chance."

The wheels screamed as the treads bit. Houses flew past.

The car radio muttered and grumbled in a monotone. I turned it up. "*. . . preliminary sparring in the trial of the former SecGen, who has so far refused counsel. The second-floor courtroom is packed with notables of Church and government, who—*"

Anselm nudged me. "Do you have a plan?"

I took a shuddering breath. All my parts seemed to work. "Find him. Break him loose."

"That's it?" His tone was acid.

"Turn right. Oh, Jesus, Farnum's a one-way street. Try Henderson, it's a block past—"

Ignoring me, Anselm rocketed the wrong way down Farnum. No cars were in sight.

"I had no time to plan." I sounded defensive.

We whirled round the corner, nearly broadsided a hauler. Behind us, an angry horn faded. "Where the hell is the court?"

"Ask the puter." I jabbed at the map display. "Head south while I . . ." In a moment I had the government buildings on the screen. The court was west of Churchill, at Hopewell Plaza. I muttered directions.

Two blocks from the courthouse, detour signs hung from alumalloy horses. On the other hand, no one had bothered to set up roadblocks. On the whole, we Hope Nationeers were a law-abiding bunch. And I doubted the new government was fully in control. For all his imperious ways, Anth had been popular. Moreover, he was the legitimate head of government. Few would go over to the enemy while he lived.

Every street we tried was closed.

I peered at the map. "It'll be around the corner. STOP!"

Tad slammed on the brakes. I nearly went through the windshield. He spluttered, "What the—"

I already had my door open. "Too much commotion, in a stolen car. On foot . . ." I thrust my laser into my pants, took off.

He vaulted out the door, trying to keep up with me. A rambling concrete building made good cover. I sprinted to a doorway within a few paces of the corner. My two allies were scarce a step behind.

Trying to make myself invisible, I peered around the corner.

I recognized the building; I'd seen it in newsnets often enough, and Fath had taken me there, when he came to speak. A three-story building, of poured concrete, with incongruous white columns pasted on, apparently as an afterthought. A helipad on the roof, I knew. Every trial I'd seen in the news had been held here.

A platoon of the Home Guard stood watch. A makeshift barrier in front of the steel and glass doors gave them cover. They bristled with arms: laser pistols, rifles, stunners.

My heart sank.

Crouched behind me, Tad whispered, "We can't take on the army."

"I know, but . . ." I chewed at my lip.

"A diversion?" Tommy Yost.

"No time." My voice quavered. "I'm going in. That heli we saw landed at the shuttle to sort things out. They'll get word to the troops here, and—"

Even as I spoke, a troop carrier pulled up to the courthouse. Its tough alloy doors swung open.

Too late. I'm sorry, Fath.

But no troops emerged. Instead, an officer gestured, issued terse commands. All I could hear was the rumble of his voice.

The Home Guards piled in. In a moment the carrier was gone.

"Now's our chance."

Tad held me back. "Where's the courtroom?"

"Upstairs, the radio said." I pulled free.

A rumble of engines. I ducked back.

Not a troop carrier, but a cargo hauler. It parked across the plaza. "Now what?" It didn't matter. I was insane not to take the chance Providence had given me. With but one pistol . . .

The courthouse door swung open. A figure appeared.

My breath caught.

Anthony. He blinked in the sunlight, rubbing his wrists.

The back doors of the hauler opened. "This way, Stadholder!" A gaunt woman beckoned. She seemed familiar. "Run, sir!"

Anth looked behind him, to the now-closed courthouse door. Then to the truck. *Hurry.* I could scarce breathe. *For God's sake, move.* The woman—who in blazes was she—my breath caught. Dr. Zayre, Chris Dakko's ally! They'd contrived to rescue the Stadholder. My spirits soared. With Dakko's help, we could free the Captain. *Hurry, Anth.* I took a step from the cover of my building, waved urgently, but he didn't see me.

"What are you—"

"Look, Tad, it's Anthony! The Stadholder. They've let him—"

The doors to the court flew open. Four guards, uniformed, with wicked laser rifles. They didn't bother with the barrier the Home Guards had erected.

Dr. Zayre screamed, "Run!"

Anth sprinted toward the truck. Its motor caught. It lurched a few feet, stopped, waiting for him to swing aboard.

Two of the guards knelt, aimed.

"Anth!"

Still running, he searched over his shoulder for my shrill scream.

Desperately I fought the hand that closed over my mouth. A relentless arm dragged me in silent struggle to the safety of the wall.

The buzz of a laser. The pavement smoked. Anth dived toward the gaping hauler door.

A shot slammed the door wide open. Hinges burst.

And another shot.

It caught Anth at the knee. His leg dissolved in a splatter of steaming blood. He fell hard, thrashed about.

He made not a sound.

I jabbed Anselm in the ribs, burst free. Weeping, I tried to aim my pistol.

A guard set his rifle to continuous fire. A laser line crept up to Anth, and through him. Anth sizzled.

A shriek of agony, blessedly short.

The smoking corpse fell back, twitched once, and was still.

The cargo hauler began to pull away. Laser fire caught the cab. A spray of blood.

Withering fire blanketed the vehicle. Dr. Zayre fell out of the back, already dead. The hauler rolled slowly across the street, aflame. It nudged the curb, bumped to a stop.

From the street, silence.

Except for the pounding of my boots.

I was nearly atop the first guard before he heard me. Arms extended, I gripped my pistol with both hands, as if afraid of recoil. There was none, I knew. At least, not when Anth and I had shot at trees in the plantation's silent forest.

The guard turned. He blanched.

I shot him full in the face, whirled, caught the second guard before he could raise his rifle.

Two steps away, the pavement bubbled. I danced aside, firing as I ran. Something horribly hot brushed my thigh.

A creature gone mad, I skittered hither and yon, firing without cease. A third guard went down. The fourth dived for the courthouse doors. I don't know if I hit him. Laser fire came from within. On one knee, not far from Anthony, I fired into the doors until I heard the warning beep of my empty pistol. Then, coolly, beyond thought, I staggered to my feet, strode to the horribly burned guard, wrested the rifle from his ruined arms, began firing anew.

I only stopped when one of the sagging doors fell with a crash.

I pawed the smoking abomination that had been another guard, found a rifle, but it was beyond salvage. In the rubble of the doorway, a rifle that worked. I took it.

"Come on!" My voice seemed odd. I cleared my throat, tried again. "Anselm, Yost. Move!"

Tad showed himself, his hands held palm outward, as if in surrender. "Randy?"

"Here." I tossed him a rifle, stooped to gather recharges. "I don't see one for Tommy."

"Stadholder Carr . . ."

"Gone." For a moment, the sunlight misted. I wiped away sweat and grime, and could see. "Hurry. They know we're here."

Yost's lips barely moved, and his voice was so low I could barely follow. "He's glitched, sir. Can you grab the rifle?"

"I heard that. No time. Help us, or go home."

The middy gulped.

"Well?" Why did I sound like Anth when he'd had quite enough?

"I'll help, sir."

I wondered if Yost knew how he'd addressed me. "Move it!" I inserted a recharge, trotted into the lobby, firing at shadows.

Nobody.

Silence.

A lift. Half a dozen guards were crowded in it. One clutched a caller.

The lift was within line of sight of the door. My beam had hit it straight on. Charred corpses, all of them. I scrounged among them, found an unda-maged laser pistol among the meat.

I wondered if the guard had gotten off his call for help. I gave his pistol to Tommy, beckoned them to the next lift, sauntered after. I paused as if in reflection, bent over, and began to vomit, until all I could bring up was weak bile. Then, red of face, eyes tearing, I strolled into the lift, jabbed the button.

"Why no more guards?" Anselm's tone was tentative. "After that fire-fight you'd think they'd be swarming . . ."

"I doubt they had many to begin with. The government must be in chaos." The other reason, I was loath to speak. I took a deep breath. "We'll go on up."

"And then?"

"Find Fath." It was so simple. Why couldn't he see?

It didn't work out quite as I intended. There were two guards outside the courtroom, and four holocameras within. Anselm made me let him dis-arm the guards; he was quite stern about it. I'd have argued, but I was busy weeping.

Mr. Anselm's new uniform didn't quite fit, and to me, he looked more like a Naval lieutenant than a guard. But, face impassive, he slipped into the courtroom, came out an endless moment later.

"He's at the bar." His tone was low.

"What does that mean?"

"That box thing. Waist high, before the bench. He's in it."

"Is he hurt?"

"I don't think so."

For a moment, I breathed easier. Then I recalled the carnage in the street. Until the moment of his death, Anth had been uninjured.

I took a deep breath. "Let's get it done."

Anselm's hand stayed me. "How?"

"Walk in. Free him."

"There's a dozen guards, or more."

"Kill them."

He said, "We can't just—"

"You can't? I will. Where are the guards?"

"The closest are right inside the door. Others across the way. But, Randy—"

I cried, "Enough words!" Fath was in their hands. I'd done murder to get this far.

"And after, you'll just walk out? They killed Stadholder Carr. They won't stop at the Captain."

I snapped, "They'll have a heli on the roof; they don't control the streets. You'll pilot. Secure the heli. The middy and I will get Fath."

"There are judges. Bishop Andori. I don't know who else."

"Hostages." What was kidnapping, to the crimes I'd committed?

"But—"

If we argued further, they might dissuade me. I keyed off my safety, flung open the doors.

". . . won't participate in your sham. Do what you will." Fath's tone was firm. In the spectators' gallery, old Bishop Andori watched intently.

Two guards were behind the rail, steps from the door. Three others in the corner.

The nearest guard turned, scowling at the interruption. His eyes widened; his hand flew to his pistol. I rammed the stock of my rifle into his jaw. He collapsed.

"Nobody move!" I'd intended my voice to be loud. It came out a shriek.

Fath spun in the dock. "Randy, don't!" His command was a lash.

Havoc. Judges and aides dived for cover. One brave mediaman swung his holo, aimed at me. Onlookers rushed about. A guard keyed his pistol; I shot him point-blank.

Another guard fell, his rifle clattering.

I risked a glance. It was Tommy who'd fired. He looked sick.

On the bench, the judges dived for cover.

Alarms shrieked.

We'd taken out half the guards. Two had raced out the rear entrance, others cowered under tables, seeking shelter. I swiveled my rifle back and forth, seeking a target.

"No more!" The Captain's voice rang.

"Tommy, take him to Anselm."

"But—"

I grated, "Now!"

"Aye aye, sir!"

Stubbornly, Fath shook his head. "Not like this. There's been enough—"

Yost screamed, "Look out!"

Behind Fath, a furtive movement. I fired, missed. A bench exploded into sparks.

The snap of a bolt. Tommy rushed the Captain, knocked him off his feet, lay atop him. He was good at that; on the street he'd done the same to me. My teeth bared in a manic grin. I opened fire, barely missed the scuttling guard. Crouching, he let off a shot. I skittered aside. The guard dived under the spectator benches.

I called out, "Hold your fire, no one need get hurt." Fine sentiment, Randy, but a touch late. How many have you killed today? As if to belie my own words, I took steady aim at the benches.

"Put down your rifle, Randolph." An old voice, and crusty.

My eyes strayed.

Bishop Andori, gaunt and craggy, shook off the protective embrace of a deacon. "In the name of Lord God, I abjure thee." He took a limping step toward me.

I centered on his chest.

"Don't, lad. It's eternal damnation." Another step.

"As if I care." My tone was surly, that of a spoiled child. Anth would be scandalized.

"Care, joey. It's all there is."

"Randy." Fath's voice was muffled. "Put down the gun." He lay under Tommy Yost, in the dock.

A flicker, in the corner of my eye. I whirled. The guard had risen. He sighted down his barrel. I jumped aside, stumbled over a fallen chair, threw out my arm for balance.

A blast of white fire flung me into a table.

Pain. The stench of roasting meat.

I toppled, head over heels. Somehow, I kept a one-handed grip on my rifle.

"Get him!"

"Stand clear, Oleg!"

Horrid, searing agony, from my shoulder to my fingertips. I gritted my teeth.

The snap of a bolt. The table over me dissolved.

"We surrender! Don't shoot!" Tommy Yost was screaming. "We surren—"

"*I don't.*" Using the rifle as a crutch, I lurched to my feet. My left arm wouldn't help. I glanced down. My sleeve was gone, and everything within. Blood, mess, char.

I was dying, and knew it.

A snap. The smell of ozone. Behind me, a wall burst into flame.

Like an idiot, I tried to clutch the stock with my missing left arm. It cost me precious seconds. I didn't have many left. I stumbled; another shot brushed my hair. I heard it sizzle. With herculean effort I tossed the rifle upward, caught it by the trigger, balanced the stock on my hip.

Bishop Andori shouted, "GET HIM!"

A flick of the finger set my laser to continuous fire. I poured flame and smoke and death into the benches from which the guards had fired.

At last, I stopped, swiveled to Andori, said to the survivors, "He's next." My voice was ghastly. I had to clear my throat, say it again. "I'll take him to Hell with me, I swear by Lord God."

The room swayed. I staggered, rifle on hip.

Through all the carnage, Andori hadn't moved. "Put it down, Randolph."

I spoke past him. "Yost, let the Captain stand. Fath, you'd better hurry." I couldn't keep my feet much longer.

Fath used Tommy's shoulder as a prop. I yearned to do the same. "Randy, you've done evil, and you're sore hurt. Put down the gun."

Something oozed down my side. "When you're safe. Tad's waiting at the heli."

Among the deacons, a stir. My lips bared. "Try it. Any of you."

Andori's hand flicked, a gesture to wait.

Fath said, "Give Yost the gun. I'll help you aboard—"

"Someone has to hold them back." It didn't seem enough. I cried, "Can't you see I'm done for? This was all for you! Don't waste it!"

His voice tightened. "This slaughter was in my name? No. I won't have it."

"We need you. Hope Nation needs you. Anth is dead."

Fath groaned.

"Andori had him shot."

Fath's lips tightened.

The Bishop shook his head. "I did not."

"Oh, bullshit." The courtroom pumped, like a heartbeat. "Yost, take Fath to the heli, by force if you must. Else I'll count to five, then kill you, I so swear. One. Two." My grip tightened.

Yost tugged frantically at the Captain.

"I didn't kill him." Andori.

"Then Scanlen did." I took a step backward, and another. If I rested some of my weight on the bar . . . "It was all arranged. Someone called off the troops guarding the building. They sent Anth outside, where Dr. Zayre was waiting with a hauler to take him to freedom. Then the guards shot him down. You even had a mediaman at the door, recording for posterity. Three, Yost."

Fath said only, "You're sure?"

Andori said, "He's making it up."

"You fucking liar." From someone, a gasp. I snarled, "Don't tell me your guards didn't hear the commotion below. Why didn't they come down?" I didn't wait for an answer. "Because they were expecting it." I wanted to wave at the slaughter, here and below. "We killed six guards in the elevator. Too many. Anth couldn't have gotten free, unless they meant him to."

I was desperately thirsty, but I spat on the scorched flooring. "Shot while trying to escape. It's so . . ." I searched for a word. "Tawdry. Anth would be mortified. Say your prayers, Yost. Four. Five."

"Come ON, sir!" The middy hauled Fath to the door. "Now! He won't wait!"

Fath whispered, "I can't leave you, son."

"For Derek, and Anth, I beg you. For Hope Nation. Don't let these vermin get away with it." I swayed.

"NOW, SIR!" In desperation, Yost propelled Fath to the door, and beyond.

"Good-bye." I don't think they heard me.

In the hall, pounding footsteps faded.

"Nobody move," I said.

Bishop Andori took another step. I regarded him, trying to hold off a spreading red mist.

The rifle grew heavy.

"Randolph . . ."

"No." Almost, my finger tightened on the trigger.

"*Steady, son.*" Derek Carr's voice was a soft pillow.

"I'm trying, Dad."

"*I'm proud of you.*"

"Don't be."

From above, the whap of a heli.

"*You did your best.*"

"And what good was that?"

"Randolph?" Andori let me touch his bony chest with the muzzle. "It's over."

"Yes," I said, and meant to shoot him. But the rifle slipped from my hip. It clattered to the floor.

I pitched headfirst into the Bishop's arms.

22

I WILLED MYSELF unconscious, and failed. The agony had spread beyond my shoulder, to encompass my whole being.

You were right, Bishop. There IS a hell.

A guard, disheveled and bloody. "You're under arrest, you glitched little—"

"No." Andori. "He's ours."

"But he—"

"—killed Deacon Smathers. He'll be tried by *our* law."

Burning. I'd endure it. It could be no worse than I felt at this very—

A deacon's face loomed. Hambeld. I recalled him from the farm.

His foot lashed out, thudded into my side. "You frazzing . . ."

"*Enough!*" Andori's voice thundered. "Get him to the hospital. Be gentle."

"His arm's blown off, he'll be dead in—"

"The wound's cauterized. Keep him warm, he's in shock. Attend the injured, Hambeld, and let Lord God look to vengeance."

"Aye, Your Grace."

After years without end, we were in a vehicle. I lay on blankets on the floor. Every jounce was promise of eternal penance to come. Hambeld crouched near me.

My lips moved, but no one answered. I tried again. "Where's Mr. Seafort?"

"Gone for the moment. We'll catch him." Hambeld's tone was flat, as if he didn't care whether I lived or died.

"We?"

"The jerries. The Home Guard. Church militia." For a fleeting moment, satisfaction in his eyes. "Admiral Kenzig's suspected of treachery, the spaceport's under massive guard. There's no way Seafort will escape off-planet."

There was something I ought to say, but we struck a pothole, and I tried, without success, to die.

When the mists cleared, my face was streaked with tears. My breath was shallow and it was all I could bear. Hambeld's rough palm flitted to my brow. "We're almost there," he said.

"The farm?"

He looked at me strangely. "Hospital."

No matter.

* * * *

I drifted in and out of torpor, discovering new realms of anguish.

Murmured voices. One set of eyes caught another. A grim shake of the head.

The ceiling moved steadily. A new room. Bright lights, a cold table.

Black.

I woke with my torso tightly bound, and aching fingers. I tried to flex my wrist, couldn't. It was maddening. Why had they tied my arm so tight?

Again, I slept.

Someone read long passages to me, in a drone. I was sedated, and barely followed. It sounded like the Bible, but wasn't. After a time, I understood it was my indictment.

Sleep.

I tried to flex my sore arm. A blaze of pain. I cried out.

A nurse tended me, her words intended to soothe.

There'd been nothing left of my arm, not even a stump. Just a charred mass of flesh extending from the shoulder a matter of inches. They'd done their best. I'd need follow-up surgery later, to prepare me for a prosth, if . . . She pursed her lips.

I nodded. I would need no surgery.

Hours slid into days. I discovered even the simplest competence eluded me. I couldn't dress, had great difficulty with my clothes in the bathroom, which I was too weak to reach without help. Eating was laborious, the more so that I couldn't cut my food unassisted. I was surly to my nurses, and wept when alone, after they changed my dressings.

Dreary days later, a visitor.

Mr. Dakko, Kev's dad. He looked aged and weary.

He stared down at my swathed form. "This is what it's come to." His tone was somber.

A perverse imp seized my tongue. "I'm better off than Kevin."

"Are you?" But there was no pity in his mien.

My defiance collapsed. "I'll join him soon."

"You'll recover."

"I'll burn."

A slight shrug. "You chose your destiny."

"Yes, sir." I hesitated. "What news of Fath?"

"Who?"

I flushed. "Captain Seafort."

"He's not been found. Nor Lieutenant Anselm and the middy."

My shoulder throbbed. "Good."

"Perhaps not."

I waited.

Mr. Dakko said heavily, "Mr. Seafort is excommunicate."

I drew sharp breath.

"Andori," he added unnecessarily. "From the steps of the Cathedral. In full robes and regalia. A most impressive ceremony. The Captain's declared apostate, an outlaw. Every Christian is duty bound to expunge him, or failing that, seize him for the Church."

Oh, Fath. By my lights it's a crock of shit, but you'll be in torment. And there's nothing I can do for you.

I said only, "You must be pleased."

"Might I ask how you reach that conclusion?"

"The outrider." *Olympiad* and its alien visitor seemed light-years distant.

"Yes?"

I said, "You blamed the alien for Kevin's death. You wanted Fath to kill it. Along with all the fish we found. Fath refused. You betrayed him to Andori."

"Hardly a betrayal. I merely pointed out that a government sympathetic to God's law would counter the threat of the fish."

"So you killed Anth."

"The Stadholder? I had nothing to do—"

"Goofjuice." My voice was shrill. "They killed him. You helped make it possible."

"Hilda, my closest friend, died that day! We meant to free him, the guards were paid off, they should have . . . somehow, it went wrong."

I gazed in wonder. "You don't know?"

"What?"

"They murdered him. It was all arranged." Haltingly, I related what I'd seen.

"They must have . . ."—he rubbed weary eyes—". . . thought him too dangerous. I'm terribly sorry. Anthony Carr was a decent man."

"You were making omelets. What's a few eggs?" My tone dripped scorn. "Anth, Captain Seafort, Hilda Zayre . . ."

His face was stone.

At worst, he'd kill me; I had nothing to lose. "Tell me, sir, do you despise yourself?"

"You're hardly one to—"

"Imagine I'm Kevin. What would I think?"

He shot to his feet. "Damn you!"

"Yes, sir, there's that consolation."

He thrust hands in pockets, stood as if examining the wall. "I loved him."

Of course. Kev was his son.

"I was so proud of our years together. I told everyone I'd served under him."

Ah. He hadn't meant Kev, after all.

"Do you know what it cost me to go against the Captain?" Mr. Dakko's tone was fierce. "Even now I regret the vile words I spoke to him. He deserved—deserves my respect. Even if I had to stop him."

If I could rise from the bed, propel him from the room, I'd have done so. I made a halfhearted effort, fell back. "What does it matter what you think now? You failed Kevin. Failed yourself."

A moan.

When I looked up, he was gone.

Four days later, they brought me by heli to the great downtown Reunification Cathedral, rebuilt after the aliens' bomb nearly destroyed the city. Huge stone buttresses soared skyward, defending the fortress of God.

Deep within the fenced grounds was a peaceful manicured lawn, on which we landed.

A hand on my good shoulder guided me to the stout iron-clasped doors. I went along, docile.

My wounded shoulder throbbed unbearably, the more so in that they'd made me wear a dark tight blue shirt, reminiscent of a uniform. I'd been too proud to complain, and regretted it.

We strode down the aisle, past the nave, toward the ornate chancel, behind whose latticed rail my judges were assembled, under the altar.

I'd been told Bishop Scanlen would serve as chief judge. He sat in the center, two flunkies to each side.

The trial would be a farce.

I looked about. They'd gathered quite an audience for their show. Many of the families were represented, though not all, and scores of townsfolk not associated with the plantations. I gazed at a sea of faces, many hostile, some curious. Chris Dakko sat in a pew, arms folded. At strategic intervals, holo-cams were set, tended by mediamen I recognized from Anthony's official announcements.

Solemn deacons set me in a makeshift dock, before a raised bench. Three judges. One was Scanlen, the others men unfamiliar to me.

Again they read the charges.

I was on trial for my life, for an attempt to overthrow Lord God's most holy Reunification Church, His blessed Instrument on Earth, and her scattered holdings. For blasphemy, for apostasy, for a list of sins half an hour long. I yawned openly, to show my contempt.

They paused, awaiting my response.

How had Fath put it? I let my voice ring out, hoping it would carry to the holocams. "I won't participate in your sham. Do what you will."

Judge Scanlen snapped, "Hold your tongue, blasphemer." They conferred, whispering. After a time, they appointed an advocate on my behalf.

I refused counsel, but they paid no heed. When my advocate bent to speak to me, I spat in his face.

The hearing adjourned.

In my guards' care I rode back to the hospital, exhausted and aching. They locked me into my barred room for the night. I watched myself on replays, in the holovid. Apparently the Church Elders had opted for a public spectacle; the proceedings would be broadcast live.

The next morning the trial began in earnest.

"The witness will stand."

Wearily, I got to my feet. Within my dark blue shirt, my shoulder throbbed unbearably. I was grateful; it gave me focus.

The three elderly judges wore cassocks, not uniforms, else theirs might have been a military court. Or a civilian one, for that matter. It made little difference, in a society owned lock, stock, and barrel by the frazzing Church.

"State your name."

I said nothing.

"Young man, your situation is grave. Unless you cooperate . . ."

I waited.

They conferred. We argued. They threatened me with poly and drugs. I shrugged, forgetting. Clenching my teeth, I rode a wave of pain.

The Lord's Advocate—the prosecutor—intervened. "If Your Reverences permit?" He slipped a chip into his holovid, swung it to face me.

A chipnote. To my astonishment, it was from Fath.

He lived! I could barely read for my joy.

"Randolph, I know what you face. What I face. I beg and order you, tell them what they would know. Tell them freely."

I stared at the unmistakable signature.

And I began to speak.

In the darkening day, I drained the last of my water. The ice had long since melted.

Scanlen had interrupted me twice, once when I spoke of my staged hanging at the farm, again when I came to Anthony's murder. I'd lapsed silent, waited out his objection, resumed where I'd left off. Eventually, after whispered consultations, they'd let me proceed in my own fashion. Perhaps they knew it was of no consequence; their forthcoming deliberations were a farce, my fate already sealed.

Now, my tale was done.

I looked about.

The holocams whirred silently in the dusk. My throat was sore and scratchy, the dark, drafty Cathedral silent but for an occasional creak. A hundred pairs of eyes searched mine.

Bishop Scanlen stirred. "Be seated."

I sat, or fell, into my chair. My calves were tight, unyielding knots, my back ached abominably. As for my shoulder . . .

Yet I felt a peace I'd never known.

All my secrets were bared, all my follies revealed. For better or worse— mostly worse—I'd be judged as I truly was.

"The tribunal accepts the defendant's confession. The proceedings are adjourned 'til the morrow." Bishop Scanlen's tone was flinty. "At which time we will announce sentence."

Exhausted, dazed, I let them lead me from the Cathedral. Again, a heli crowded with guards flew me to the hospital that had become my home.

Just outside my windowless room my stern nurse had a fierce argument with the guard, and was allowed to supplement my rations. Home-baked cake. She said nothing as she served me, but her eyes held pity, and perhaps something more.

I expected to be locked alone in my room to sleep, as always, but this night guards stayed with me at all times. One even took a position directly outside the door to the bathroom when I used it.

A doctor tended the stump of my arm. Nurses read the monitors displaying my pulse, temperature, and other signs. Little was said, either to me or among themselves. Nonetheless, I sensed a tension I hadn't felt the night before.

As they made ready to darken my room a doctor checked me once more.

"Why are you scowling?" My voice was too loud in the silent room.

"I'm not." His tone was gruff.

"Is it because I'm to be burned?"

"That's not decided."

"Oh, please."

The guard cocked an ear, listened intensely to I knew not what.

I lapsed silent, but heard nothing.

They left me with a dim night-light. I pretended to sleep, lulled by the slow steady breaths of the armed guard in the corner.

* * * *

In the morning they helped me dress. I was bleary from lack of sleep. I'd brooded half the night over my impending death, decided that it didn't frighten me. I didn't care to live maimed, no matter how clever a prosthesis they might devise. Besides, survival would require obeisance to the Church, and nothing was worth that.

Besides, death no longer held much terror. I'd faced it once, aboard *Olympiad*. Only Fath's intervention had saved me, and for what purpose? Perhaps I owed Lord God an extinction. I shrugged, momentarily forgetting to protect my wound.

This morning, they took me not to the helipad but to a heavily armored electricar. Deacon Hambeld waited by the door, under a sullen sky.

"What's this about?"

No one answered. They bundled me in. We took off, accompanied by a score of Home Guards. Sirens blared.

I shifted in my seat, suddenly anxious to get a look as the terrain flew past.

Were they taking me to some lonely place where they'd shoot me out of hand? Unlikely; they could have put me to death in my hospital room and blamed it on any number of causes. Were they spiriting me away? It didn't seem so; our route seemed destined to take us to the Cathedral, as before.

On Churchill Road, electricars lay overturned. A gutted building smoldered in the gloom.

My heart beat faster.

"What?" I pawed at the nearest guard.

He slapped away my hand.

"What harm in telling me?" I tried to make my voice affable.

"Heretics." A growl. "They'd overthrow the Government of Lord—"

"Enough." Deacon Hambeld.

"When?" I swallowed; it sounded like a demand.

"Last night." The deacon scowled. "Let it be. Tend to your soul."

Our cavalcade purred through a city gone strangely quiet. I searched for other signs of damage, but saw few.

Our driver parked directly in front of the Cathedral's iron-bound doors. My guards tried to hustle me out of the electricar, but I took my time. Let them throw me to the ground if they cared to; no doubt a hidden holocam was recording for posterity.

Overhead, a watchful heli cruised.

I smiled sweetly. "Expecting trouble?"

"Inside!"

I complied, and stopped short.

This day, the Cathedral was half empty.

As my guards marched me past the nave to the chancel, I glanced over my shoulder. Three deacons had taken up station at the massive oaken door. One pressed a caller to his ear.

Ahead, at their raised dais, my judges waited. Among the onlookers, a buzz of muttered comments.

One voice, bolder than the rest. "Let him go!"

"Silence!" Bishop Scanlen slammed down his gavel.

"He's just a joeykid!"

"Your government's fallen, let it be!"

Scanlen took breath to respond, but from the altar, a voice thundered. Henrod Andori, Archbishop of the Reunification Church of Hope Nation. "Lord God's Government has NOT fallen! He is eternal, and heretics shall learn so to their dismay!"

Bishop Andori wrapped his crimson robe tight, as if against a strong wind. "Proceed." He rapped his staff on the marbled floor.

Scanlen cleared his throat. "We, judges and prelates of Holy Mother Church appointed for the purpose and in conclave assembled, upon solemn deliberation, declare Randolph Carr guilty of acts of heresy and apostasy too numerous to detail, of the murder of our brother and servant Deacon Edwin Salazar, of assisting the flight of Nicholas Ewing Seafort—" He fairly spat the words. "Late Captain of UNS *Olympiad*, renegade, apostate, and excommunicate."

Scanlen struck his gavel; it echoed in the ill-lit chamber like a rifle shot.

To me, "Appeal is through the hierarchy of Reunification Church. In this case, directly to the Archbishop, His Grace Henrod Andori."

My voice dripped with scorn. "I won't waste breath with an appeal. Do away with me." Brave words or no, my stomach lurched. They intended to do just that.

Deacon Hambeld hurried down the aisle. "Your Reverence . . ." He made straight for Scanlen. A whispered conference. The Bishop stood, made an imperious gesture.

The deacons swung shut the great iron-strapped wood doors of the Cathedral.

Among the spectators, murmurs of unease. The ill-lit chamber grew dismal and drear.

Scanlen frowned. "No doubt we'll have visitors shortly. I'll want my vestments." He strode to the changing rooms behind the altar.

"Hey!" I shot to my feet. "Tell me what's—"

"Silence him!"

Someone touched a stunner to my side. It must have been set low. For a moment, I fought not to black out. From the pews, I heard a gasp of outrage, then nothing.

* * * *

I tried to move my arms, could not. Wearily, I tried to blink myself awake.

I clenched my fists, but that brought only pain, and wakened me fully. My shoulder throbbed. One arm was missing—how could I forget?—the other lashed to a pew, by a leather belt. I struggled to free myself, could not. Only one hand was bound—if I could reach it with the other . . . but I had no other. Maddened, I gnawed at the belt to no avail.

A few moments later Scanlen emerged, wearing his red robe. From under his arm he took his gilded high hat, secured it atop his head. He wore his formal vestments, those of high mass. On occasion Anth had made me sit through the ceremony. I'd fidgeted among the crowd of worshipers, bored out of my mind.

The Bishop strode to the high lectern, where he was accustomed to preach to the multitude. "Hambeld, what news?"

The deacon, at the great doors, peered through the grating. "A troop carrier across the street. A couple of helis circling. That's it."

Scanlen's smile was contemptuous. "And they'd make themselves a government? We'll have them under lock and key by nightfall. You called the farm?"

"Yes, Your Reverence. They're on their way." He tensed. "The carrier is moving. Seems to be turning around."

I looked about, wondering if the churchmen meant to defend the Cathedral with force.

The pews, except for mine, were empty. How long had I been unconscious? Not long, barely time for Scanlen to don his robes. Time enough for the deacons to shoo out the spectators. No doubt the townsmen were glad to go, glad not to choose between Church and civil authority.

Between Church and government . . . I shook my head. How long was it since men had last faced such a choice?

At the door, Hambeld licked his lips nervously. "What if they try to force their way in?"

"Tell them this is Lord God's house."

"But, Your Rever—"

Scanlen said firmly, "Only Anthony Carr was insane enough to attack Mother Church, and he's gone to his just reward. Apostates or no, these weaklings wouldn't—"

Hambeld leaped aside.

An earsplitting crash.

The great oaken doors splintered, reeled drunkenly on their hinges.

"Jesus!" The deacon scrambled to safety.

The crumpled nose of a troop carrier rolled into the Cathedral.

Armed men emerged.

"Stop!" From his high perch, Bishop Scanlen's voice rang in the nearly empty hall. "In the name of Lord God, stop!"

The rush of troops slowed.

"Take your weapons from this place!" Scanlen's tone was commanding. "Now, or face damnation. For I, Ricard Scanlen, Bishop of the Reunified Church of Jesus Christ, declare excommunicate from Holy Mother Church and from Lord God Himself every man who sets hostile foot in this edifice!"

It brought every soul to a halt.

Tentatively, Hambeld moved toward them, as if to usher them out. The invaders exchanged uncertain glances.

A voice said softly, *"I'm already damned. I'll do it."* Nicholas Seafort, in a Captain's dress whites, strode toward the nave, laser pistol in hand.

Scanlen intoned, "By the power invested in us, we do declare thee—"

Fath smiled, a grim expression that did not light his face. He aimed and fired. A corner of the lectern burst into flames.

The Bishop gasped.

Captain Seafort said, "I arrest you in the name of the Government of the Commonweal of Hope Nation. The charge is treason."

"What government?" Scanlen's tone dripped scorn.

"Ours." Jerence Branstead appeared from behind the troop carrier, his laser rifle held steady.

"Bah, you're not even a—"

"What? Citizen? I most certainly am."

Scanlen took a deep breath, reconstituted his authority. "Get out of my Cathedral!"

"Not yours, sir." Fath's tone was ice. "Lord God's. It's a distinction you find hard to grasp. But—"

Why was Scanlen debating them? Obviously, Branstead and Fath wouldn't back down now. Abruptly I realized: the Bishop was playing for time. I swarmed to my feet, almost dislocated my remaining shoulder as I wrenched helplessly against the restraining pew. "Fath, sir, he's called help from the farm. Deacons, they'll be armed—"

"No doubt. Are you hurt, son?"

"No, not—I mean, I was, before. My arm is—" *Never mind that, you idiot!* "Fath, be careful or they'll . . ." Suddenly I was crying, and could say no more. I stamped my foot.

"There, son." As Fath walked slowly to the nave, his pistol never wavered from the Bishop. His arm came around me in a brief, gentle squeeze. Eyes on Scanlen, he clawed with his free hand at the belt that bound my one wrist to the pew, managed at last to unbuckle it.

I flexed numb and swollen fingers. "I told them everything, Fath. As you said."

"You made me proud." His eyes glistened. "Son."

I hiccuped and sobbed, ashamed of my youth.

From the aisle, Jerence Branstead cleared his throat. "Captain, take this—this *person*—" A wave of his rifle. "—into custody."

For a moment I thought he meant me, but Fath patted my shoulder, gestured to the Bishop. "Mr. Anselm! Seize him."

"Aye aye, sir." Tad strode down the aisle, Tommy Yost in tow.

Scanlen backed away. "I'm immune from civil prosecution. You can't—"

"Watch us." Anselm grabbed his arm, halting his flight. "Where to, sir?"

"Jerence?"

"The Governor's Manse, I suppose. I won't trust him out of my sight."

"Right." Anselm spoke with unaccustomed solemnity. "Bishop Scanlen, by order of Acting Stadholder Branstead, I do arrest you."

He led the dazed Bishop to the shattered door.

Fath snapped, "Just a moment. Where's Andori?"

"Behind the altar." I looked about.

The Archbishop was gone.

"Tad, find him!" He turned to Mr. Branstead. "Have you need of me? I want Randy at hospital."

"No!" My voice was shrill. "Not there!" It had been my prison. I strove for calm. "Could we go home? *Olympiad*?"

"Home." Fath's voice was soft. "Yes, I'll be going aloft in a bit. The aliens await. But first I've work here. Would you wait on the ship for me?"

"No, sir." Somehow, I managed to meet his eye. After all we'd been through, it was vile to defy him.

"If I ordered it?"

My voice was a whisper. "I'd disobey."

A sigh. "I won't force you. And I can't take the shuttle just yet. Once I'm aloft I don't think I'll see groundside for quite a while."

I recalled Fath supine, white-faced, his stretcher lifted through the lock to *Olympiad*, when he and I and Mik . . . I swallowed.

"Jerence, I'll need transport for Randy; he's reeling on his feet and needs refuge."

Mr. Branstead said, "Why not my home? I'd be happy to—"

"To Carr Plantation." My voice was unsteady. "Please, Fath. Just for a while." Let me pretend my life of late was only a fading nightmare.

Fath and Mr. Branstead exchanged glances. "It's as good a base as any, Jerence. I'll stay with him while we sort things out. If you've men to spare, find Andori. He's a viper, and will cause us no end of harm." With exquisite care, Fath lay soft fingers on my inflamed shoulder. "Come along, son."

23

IT WAS A SULTRY midday, and Mom was nowhere to be found. Annette, the cook, said she'd gone to Centraltown for a church meeting. I wondered if Mom had even been aware of my trial; Limeys unpredictably faded in and out of their chemdreams.

Escaping the baleful sun, I brushed past a squad of the guards Mr. Branstead had sent to watch over us, and stood gratefully below a cooling vent in the hall outside the study.

Having an escort embarrassed me; I'd known Sergeant Zack Martel's brother Rafe for years. I felt I was playing at soldiers, and half expected them to salute.

Scant hours past, I'd been awaiting a death sentence, Fath had been a fugitive. Now, in bizarre anticlimax, I trudged up two flights to my room, eased myself onto my old familiar bed, kicked off my shoes.

Popping a pair of painkillers did nothing to ease the throb of my absent arm. I wondered if I'd ever get used to it. In the heli, Fath had spoken soothingly of a prosth, but I would have none of it, and told him so, perhaps rather mulishly. He'd frowned, and let the matter drop.

I tried to rest, as Fath had bidden, but it was no use. After a time, I struggled into my shoes and padded downstairs.

In the spartan room that had been Anth's study, Fath spoke into the caller, his expression grim. "It wasn't interfering, sir. If you'll recall, I was shanghaied." I tiptoed in, took a seat, making sure he saw me. I would *not* be accused of eavesdropping. Never again.

Admiral Kenzig's tone was waspish. "But after escaping, you returned to overthrow the lawfully constituted—"

"Oh, nonsense." A pause. "Sir." Outside camera range, Fath patted my knee reassuringly. "Anthony Carr headed a government long recognized by the U.N., despite Ambassador McEwan's wish that it be otherwise. Anthony appointed Branstead as chief of staff and deputy Stadholder. After Carr was killed in the attempted coup, Jerence was the only member of government free from coercion. He restored order."

"Is that so?" It was a growl. "Was it Branstead who burst through the Cathedral doors and bade U.N.N.S. personnel arrest the Bishop? It's not the Navy's role to intervene in changes of colonial government, no matter—"

Fath's fingers drummed on the desktop, sign of a gathering storm. "Whom, exactly, did you want burned, Admiral? Me, or my ship's boy?"

Kenzig said only, "That's uncalled for, Mr. SecGen."

Fath paid no heed. "I was lured from *Olympiad*, kidnapped, put on trial for my life. Does Naval policy condone such infamy?"

"Certainly not, but once you were freed—"

"If not for Randy, I'd be ashes, drifting in the wind. Should I have allowed the Bishops to put him to death? He was a member of my ship's company, and a U.N. citizen."

"Only because you made him so."

"You're saying naturalized citizens have no right to our protection?"

"Bless it, Seafort, don't twist my words."

For a long moment Fath was silent. "Sir, we all know why Andori was sent here: to promote recolonialization. He'll support any government that aids his cause. McEwan is firmly in their camp. Are you?"

At the door, a shadow.

I jumped up. "Mom!" I yearned to fall in her arms, rest my head on her shoulder. I'd been through so much, the world had turned upside—

She bared her teeth. "What's *he* doing here?"

Kenzig glowered. "My task is to protect U.N. Naval—"

I put a finger to my lips, glanced at the caller.

"Get him *out*!" Imperiously, Mom pointed toward the helipad.

Fath frowned. "With due respect, sir, the situation doesn't permit equivocation."

My jaw dropped. The Admiral was, after all, Fath's superior. A word from him could remove Fath from command, former SecGen or no.

But it was Kenzig who retreated. "You put us in an extremely awkward . . . You arrested the *Bishop!* The Bishop of the Reunified Church that underlies our government!"

Mom hissed, "Excommunicate! Spawn of Satan!" Did she mean Fath, or me? I waved her silent. For years, she'd ranted without cause, succumbing to maudlin sentiment moments afterward. We'd learned to pay little heed.

"Actually, I *rearrested* Scanlen." Fath's tone was dry. "Awaiting trial, he escaped custody of the Commonweal of Hope Nation."

"He's still our Bishop!"

"And a fallible human." Fath. "Not above law."

Mom's voice was shrill. "I'll call the Home Guard!" Good; the last we knew, the Home Guard was firmly in Mr. Branstead's hands.

The Admiral said, "Scanlen's above civil law. Only the Church itself can—"

"That's at home, sir. In an independent commonweal, he's subject to—"

"Damn it, Seafort!"

Fath ignored the blasphemy. "*Are* you in their camp, sir? Will you help McEwan recolonialize Hope Nation?"

A long, reluctant pause. "That's not my brief."

Gently, I shut the study door on Mom's frozen glare, crept back to my seat.

"Very well." If Fath felt relief at the Admiral's capitulation, he gave no sign. "I propose we help Mr. Branstead's government restore order, then withdraw."

"The Patriarchs will be outraged if I leave Scanlen in colonial hands . . ."

"I'll escort him home for trial. No doubt Branstead will be relieved."

"No, we'll lodge no charges. You'll make it clear the Bishop was expelled by the Commonweal, that we didn't force him home. When will you go aloft?"

"As soon as possible. As you'll recall, a fish is standing off *Olympiad*'s bow waiting to resume negotiations."

"Ahh, about that . . . Don't you think the matter should be referred to home system? They'll send a team—"

"No." Into the silence Fath added, "I don't think so. The aliens can't wait. Surely you agree, sir."

"Well—"

"Precisely. Is there anything else?" Pointedly, Fath looked at his watch.

"I suppose not. Shall we enter it in the Log that you engaged the aliens in discussions of your own initiative?"

"I have no objection, sir."

"Very well." They rang off.

"Whew." After a moment, Fath favored me with a scowl. "What are you doing out of bed?"

"Couldn't sleep." I tried to shrug, was brought up short with a stab of pain. "Are you in trouble?"

"No doubt Mr. Kenzig will be glad to see the last of me. What was that commotion in the doorway?"

"Mom wanted—" I snapped my mouth shut.

"Yes?"

I said reluctantly, "Wanted you gone."

"Ahh." A pause. "I should have realized. I'll stay with Jerence."

"No!" It was almost a shout. "You're my guest, Fath." Did he understand the dishonor to Carr Plantation, to our family, if he were made un-welcome? Beyond that, far more important, he was Dad's closest friend, the father I'd . . . I swallowed hard.

"I can't stay if Sandra objects . . ."

"Let her prong herself." My tone was reckless.

"Derek loved her." His tone reproved me, as it ought.

"I don't—" I grimaced. "I'll talk to her." Perhaps she'd already have forgotten.

"Let me know soon." He turned back to the caller.

I found Mom in a padded kitchen chair, staring moodily at a cup of coffee. Before I could say a word, she grated, "I wish you'd killed him."

It took my breath away. "Do you remember our visit, when you let him kiss your hand?"

"Yes, I'm not senile. Seafort has charm, that beguiled your father. He has the arrogance that made him SecGen. And he has contempt for God and His Church."

That was utterly unfair. "You don't know—"

"Don't tell me what I know, child!" She slammed her palm on the countertop, slopping a spoonful of coffee. "I know it's mortal sin to consort with an excommunicate, *and I want him out of my house!*"

"He's my father."

"Derek Anthony Carr is your father!"

Steady, son.

Was it Dad or Fath who whispered? No matter.

"I invited him, Mom." I made my tone reasonable. "There's a bond of hospitality." She was a Carr, and before that, a Winthrop; how could she not understand?

"He'll writhe in Hell." She sopped a puddle of coffee with her napkin.

"For Dad's sake, let him stay."

"For Derek's sake. Yes, your real father would risk his soul for friend-ship." A tired shrug, as if nothing mattered. "Risk yours, if you must." A long, drifting pause. "Very well, I won't throw your precious Captain out."

"Thank you, Mom." Awkwardly, I gave her a one-handed embrace, turned to go.

"It's good you're home." Her voice was languid, drifting off to a far place. "I missed you."

My eyes stung.

"By the way, what happened to your arm?"

Disconsolate, I made my way back to the study.

Fath raised an eyebrow.

"I talked to Mom. It's all right." A bit of an overstatement, but . . .

He seemed reflective. "She signed the adoption papers, you know. That limits our options."

I blinked. "How?"

"You want me to take you aloft."

"Of course."

"As ship's boy?"

I opened my mouth, shut it again. I'd demanded remission of enlistment, and Tolliver had granted it.

He followed my thought. "There's more, son."

I said weakly, "The shuttle." I'd hijacked it at gunpoint.

"It presents a problem." He pursed his lips. "Armed seizure of Naval property. Mandatory death penalty, and so on. Oh, don't be alarmed, there'll be no prosecution." Fath's tone was dry. "Tolliver won't be amused, though privately he's ecstatic that you freed me. But he'll argue for a trial, to avoid favoritism."

"Try me."

"Yes, the Carrs pay their debts, and all that. Not this time, joey; there'll be a finding of temporary insanity. Dr. Romez won't quibble. But it's complicated. When you left the ship's company, you lost U.N. citizenship, unless your adoption also separately conferred it. I think it does." He scratched his head. "If not, by what authority do I take you aloft, or out of system?"

"Who'll care?"

"Judge Hycliff, for one." He'd given custody of me to the Church.

"But that government was overthrown."

"And we restored it. See why Admiral Kenzig told me not to meddle in local affairs?" A sigh. "And of course I'll have to reenlist you, and no doubt that will raise eyebrows as well. Oh? You didn't think I would?"

"It didn't matter at the time. Now . . ." My eyes welled. "Thank you, Fath. Sir."

"Palabee too." It was the next morning, and Mr. Branstead paced our living room while, outside, sullen raindrops beat against the windows. "He and Andori have vanished. They could be in the Ventura Mountains, the Zone, Lord God knows where. It isn't over."

Fath nodded unhappily. "And the troops you sent after them . . ."

"I can't be sure they're with us."

"Lord damn it, Jerence, I won't leave 'til this is settled. And I must go to my ship."

"Why?"

"An alien is floating a kilometer off our port side. I do believe he's waiting for me. That negotiation is of utmost importance."

"Go aloft. I'll handle—"

"We Defused at Hope Nation at a critical moment to the Carrs, and I let Anthony's life slip through my fingers. Derek would never forgive me. Randy—" Fath patted my knee. "—came within an inch of death as well. I won't make that error yet again."

"I don't underst—"

"You've followed my erratic course for forty years, Jerence, old friend. I'll see you to safe harbor."

Mr. Branstead turned abruptly, stared a long while out the window. "Thank you." His voice was gruff.

I tried to stretch without calling attention, lest Fath send me out for privacy, as he had during a few of his calls. Now that Anth was forever gone, the only room I found of interest was the one Fath inhabited. The guest house brought sharp memories of Kevin Dakko; the kitchen and Mom's patio chaise, a vague discomfort. My own bedroom seemed petty and small, a relic of a life long past.

Fath asked him, "Will they elect you Stadholder?"

"It's quite possible. I'm seen as neutral, allied with none of the planter factions. And even if not, this week's events will bestow a modicum of influence."

Watching raindrops dreamily descend the pane, I worked out a kink in my leg.

"No doubt. Once Palabee's caught, how he's handled will—Randy, haven't you something to do?"

"No, sir." I tried to look inconspicuous.

"Isn't there anyone you'd like to see? Old friends? Once we Fuse, you'll be gone a long while."

Perhaps my adventures would impress Alex Hopewell. And if Judy Win—"Oh!" I gathered my courage. "Could I go see Judy Winthrop?" If he laughed at me . . .

"Jerence, is it safe?"

"As anywhere, I suppose. The Winthrops are no supporters of Andori. And we'll send your contingent of guards, mine will do for us both."

"Aww!"

"Not without guards, son. Go wash up."

Easier said than done, one-handed.

I climbed out of the hauler, hunched my shoulders against the persistent rain, and knocked shyly at the studded front door. On my last visit, I'd climbed the drainpipe.

It was Ms. Winthrop who opened. Her eyes flickered from me to my escort, and back.

"They're Fath's guards, ma'am. Captain Seafort's, I mean. And mine too. Not that they're needed, but Fath said . . . They'll be no trouble, it's not as if we're here to—" I fell back, took a deep breath, wished my face hadn't gone so red. "Is Judy in?"

"I was ever so sorry to hear about Anthony. You have our condolences, mine and Henry's."

"Thank you, ma'am." Why did I mumble? "Fath says I have to be back by six, could I see Judy?"

"Yes, of course." She led me to the stairs. "It's true he adopted you?"

"Yes, ma'am." I yearned to make my escape, but held my head high. "I'm his son. I don't—didn't think Dad would mind."

"I can't imagine why he should." Her voice rose. "Judy? You have company!"

A moment later I was sitting cross-legged on her bed. We babbled at each other for five minutes straight. Abruptly, heart pounding, I caressed the back of her neck, urged her forward, and kissed her on the lips.

It was a conversation-stopper, but after that neither of us were really interested in conversation. Part of me enjoyed myself immensely, and another checked off stations on a mental card noting progress to a long-cherished goal.

With tender care, Judy had worked my shirt off around the stump of my arm. We lay side by side, her two hands and my one exploring, probing gently, luring each other ever closer to a precipice from which there was no retreat.

Judy's mouth was sweet, my pulse inflamed, and in the distance a siren wailed. I absorbed it into my ardor, stroked her where she—

A siren? I blinked.

I sat bolt upright, ignoring the stab in my shoulder.

"Randy? What's wrong, did I hurt—"

"My shirt!" I pawed at it ineffectually. "Help me!"

With an injured expression, she turned it the right way, offered me a sleeve.

No time. I yanked it out of her hands, flung open the door, raced downstairs. "Guards!" Shirtless, I shot through the front door, barely pausing to open it.

The hauler was empty, my guards lounging about under cover of the Winthrops' spacious porch. I dived into the cab.

On the porch, Sergeant Martel scrambled to his feet.

I keyed the hauler's puter. "ID Randolph Carr, fast voicerec, start engine, home!"

Martel swung himself aboard. The electricar purred, began to back up through wet grass. Our guards raced to climb aboard.

"Home, hauler, flank speed." No, that was Navy talk. "Fastest possible speed, ignore safety."

"Instructions logged for future review." We careened along the drive.

"Randy, what in hell?" Martel was breathing hard.

"The frazzing siren, can't you hear?" I pounded the dash. We were minutes from Carr Plantation, at best. I found the caller, rang home.

Martel unsheathed his weapon. "What's it mean?"

"The dam! Balden River!"

In my ear, a maddening buzz. No answer. I let it ring as we splashed over the rutted road. Why hadn't Anth kept Plantation Road in repair? With new paving we'd be driving at least twice as—

No, that led nowhere.

"What are you saying?" Martel's knuckles on the door were white.

"The dam's a force-field. Weren't you at the dedication?"

"What's the dedication have to—"

"The field's failed!"

"It can't!"

"Isn't that the warning siren we test every fourth Friday?" We jounced across a huge pothole, and my shoulder slammed into the door frame. "Jesus Lord!" I gritted my teeth. "Hauler, faster!" Our main entrance was just around the bend.

The hauler slewed to a stop, water spraying from the wheels.

The road was gone. In its place, splintered trunks of massive generas, amid rivulets, soggy puddles. As far as the eye could see, wreckage and ruin.

"Oh, God." I threw open the door, leaped into a sea of mud, lost my balance, flopped on my face. One-handed, it was near impossible to get to my feet. Somehow, I did, and slogged to slightly higher ground.

Which way was the frazzing house?

The road was here; the manse would be across the lawn, where . . .

It was gone.

I moaned.

Fath had been inside. And Mr. Branstead. And Mom.

Not again. *I couldn't stand it again.*

Martel caught me as I charged into the morass. "Easy, joey."

"Don't 'easy' me, you goddamn—" I slammed shut my mouth. "Zack, sorry. Get me to . . . to where the manse stood." I tried not to weep.

I hadn't the shoes for it, but we clambered through what seemed miles of mud and debris, across what had been the front lawn. About here, where Anth had gripped me firmly, introducing me to Ambassador McEwan. And here, where old Scanlen had kidnapped me from Mr. Seafort's heli.

I slid on a slippery rock, and toppled. "Ayie!" I thought I'd pass out; the sky faded to a red haze. Randy, stop slamming your frazzing shoulder.

Martel hauled me to my feet. "You should have waited for the rest of the squad."

A grunt was all I could manage. I jabbed a finger in the general direction of the house, but let my arm fall; nothing was there. To my right, a gentle rise that had sheltered the guest house. A few bedraggled shade trees had survived, their lower branches stripped.

Slowly, the throb in my arm ever more insistent, we made our way to the rise.

Behind a tree, a muddy figure stirred, struggled to her feet.

"He's a wicked, wicked man," said Mom. "He shouldn't have."

"Never mind about that." My voice was harsh. Her hate for Seafort could wait. "Who's alive?"

"What's become of your shirt?"

"God damn it!" I kicked the tree so hard I was afraid I'd broken my toe. Nonetheless, I screamed and raged, swore oaths for which Fath—or Dad—would have washed out my mouth. Eventually, I wound down: a volcano spews only so long. My face grimy and streaked, I sat in the mud, leaned against a bedraggled oak.

Fath was gone. And Mr. Branstead. I fought the relief of tears.

Dully, I stared upward. The force of the flood had broken off low branches, stripped others. It had deposited debris in the oddest places. Above, in the crotch of a high branch, a pair of legs. Blue pants, muddied.

Naval blue.

I staggered to my feet. "Zack!" A hoarse scream.

He came running. I pointed.

One-armed, it was out of the question to climb a tree. Martel made his way upward, while I danced in frustration.

Mom stood wearily alongside. "He shouldn't have done it." Her voice was ragged.

I made and unmade a fist, wishing whoever was keening would *stop*. I shifted from foot to foot, like a joeykid needing to piss.

"It's him! The SecGen."

An endless wait.

"He's alive!"

My breath exhaled explosively.

It seem to take forever. Zack shinnied down, found a cup, filled it with water—a commodity we had plenty of—and made his way back up the oak.

After a time, a groan. Then a ragged voice. "Where am I?"

I could do nothing to help. Gnashing my teeth, I watched helplessly as

Martel guided Fath cautiously to firm ground. A vivid bruise bloomed on his forehead and cheek.

Feet planted at last, he used my good shoulder as a crutch, and looked about. "Where's Jerence?"

"Dunno, sir." I wiped my nose, wishing I could stop sniffling. It made me feel so frazzing *young*.

"Who has a caller?"

"I do." Zack.

"Call him. He always carries his." Fath reeled off the number, but snatched the caller before Martel could dial.

It rang endlessly. At last, a gritty voice. "Yes?"

"Oh, thank God." Fath shut his eyes. "Where are you?"

"Downstream. I can't move much. My knee's smashed."

"We'll find you. How far from the manse?"

"A couple hundred meters, I think. And I slid into a culvert getting to the bloody caller."

Fath leaned heavily on my good side as we picked our way through rubble and mud. Downstream, Mr. Branstead had said. There'd been no stream alongside the manse. Not until today.

In a muddy gully, Mr. Branstead waved weakly. He was lying at an awkward angle, his legs higher than his head. We helped turn him. That is, Zack and Mom and Fath did: I was a helpless, wounded, weepy child. Fath seemed not to notice.

Mr. Branstead's face was gray. "Who else survived?"

Fath said, "Sandra Carr. We've seen no one else. It was little enough warning."

I pawed at his arm. "How did you . . ."

"The cook recognized the siren, ran screaming into the study. We ran for high ground, and were barely in time. Jerence, whom ought we call for rescue, planters in the Zone, or Centraltown?"

"We'll want searchers, a lot of them. Troops. Ah, there's a heli now."

We waved. The machine circled once, set down alongside us, drenching us in mist and droplets. Zack Martel bent over Mr. Branstead, covering him from the wind and dirt.

Fath limped to the cabin, ducked under the whirling blade, stopped short as the hatch swung open. Deacon Hambeld, of the Reunification Cathedral. His laser pistol was aimed unwaveringly at Fath.

Behind Hambeld, another deacon helped a familiar figure from the heli. Bishop Henrod Andori.

With a growl, Zack clawed for his pistol. Deacon Hambeld swiveled, shot him through the chest. Martel's torso dissolved in fire. He was dead before he hit the soggy ground.

"Now, none of that." Bishop Andori held up a peaceable hand. With the caution of age, he knelt by the corpse, made a sign of the cross. His mouth moved in silent prayer. Grunting, he got to his feet. "In the heli, if you please."

Mom shouldered past Fath, confronted the Bishop. "Wicked man! I'd never have told you if I'd thought you capable of such—such . . ." She shook her head.

"It seems harsh, daughter, but the Lord works in mysterious ways. In, all of you. Carry that Branstead joey."

24

WE DRONED THROUGH gray mists toward Centraltown. Hambeld had herded us into the roomy heli, pausing only to make sure we were unarmed. Mr. Branstead cried out sharply as they lifted him to the cabin. Now he was stretched out on the cargo deck of the heli, ashen of face, stifling an occasional moan. Mom, Fath, and I hunched nearby, the Bishop's men watching from the front seats. Hambeld's pistol roved from one to the other of us.

Zack Martel lay abandoned in mud and muck.

"Where are you taking us?" Fath's tone was sharp, but Andori ignored him.

I leaned to Mom, flicked a thumb at the Bishop. "Why did you call him wicked?"

"He destroyed us. I am among the godly, yet he destroyed our home."

"The force-field must have failed. The siren . . ."

"Why would it fail?"

I sat, stunned. I hated the Bishop and all he stood for, but I couldn't accept that he could loose such havoc. I snarled, "Andori, is it true?"

"Quiet, or I'll kill you." Deacon Hambeld.

Fath hauled me to his seat.

I was beyond that. *Andori, did you do it?*

The Bishop peered over his shoulder. "The flood, joey? You'll recall it was I who dedicated that dam in Lord God's name. Fitting that I use it to accomplish His work."

"How many did you kill to get at Mr. Seafort?"

"The innocents are sent to Lord God's mercy. The guilty are paying for their folly."

"You son of—"

"A high price, say you? Jerence Branstead came home to meddle. Best he'd stayed on *Olympiad* to serve his apostate master." Andori scratched his cheek. "An opportunity to bag them both? Surely it was the Lord's doing."

The sanctimonious bastard. "What now?" I spat the words.

"Death. A chance to plead your case before Him."

"For all of us? Mom too?"

"No, she's harmless, and means well."

Fath said, "Why not gun us down as you did the soldier?"

"Ahh, an interesting point. I know the Lord's stern hand wielded the flood, but for some, it's too abstract. Your death needs to be a public act, accomplished by the Church Herself. And we neglected to bring a holocam. The spaceport will have one."

"You insane fuck!" I spat on the deck.

"Hambeld, burn off his other arm."

I recoiled.

Hastily, Fath thrust himself between us. "You want my death public? Call him off!"

Andori sighed. "Point acknowledged. We'll wait, Mr. Hambeld."

Thereafter, Fath watched the deacon like a hawk, his body ever between me and the laser.

How long to the spaceport, and my end? Half an hour, at most. No, we'd been in the air a good ten minutes. I shivered, wishing the engines to slow. Outside, the rain eased.

All too soon, we circled the spaceport, gray, grim and damp. Andori asked the pilot, "Any Home Guard?"

The pilot grinned mirthlessly. "Half a dozen were at lunch in the coffee shop. Conrad's joeys have them."

Andori snorted. "And that rabble calls itself a government. Set us down."

We landed with a bump, not far from the terminal. The door swung open, letting in a blast of midday heat.

Hambeld propelled me to the tarmac. Above, the clouds began to part, and I squinted in the sudden sun, not forgetting to keep my torso between the deacon's pistol and my remaining arm. Though I would die in a few moments, I cringed at another mutilation.

So, God. Should I believe in You, like Fath? How can I, after what you countenanced today? You let the bad joeys destroy us, and do it in Your name. I muttered a curse.

"Don't blame Him." Fath laid a gentle hand across my shoulder. "They're men, and know no better."

I wanted to live more than anything, and was hateful. "Are you stupid enough to forgive? Well, it wasn't your home, your heritage, your life they destroyed!"

"Was it not?" Fath looked bleak. At the hatch, a cry from Jerence. Fath snarled, "Don't hurt him!"

Andori's fist clenched. "In a moment, it won't matter. Where's the holocam?"

Hambeld pointed. "Conrad's got it now." A perspiring deacon hurried from the terminal gate, past a parked cargo truck.

Might we run for it? Fath couldn't, and for life itself I wouldn't try without him.

"Line up." They sat Mr. Branstead on the hot pavement. As they released his knee he shuddered and groaned once.

Limping, Fath moved to shield him from the sun. I stood alongside, and Fath took my only arm. I looked about, said huskily, "Good-bye, Mom."

The deacon set up the holocam in the shade of the heli.

She smiled dreamily. "It's too warm. Let's go inside."

His eyes on Hambeld, Andori casually squeezed his finger, indicating Mom.

Fath's grip tightened. "Son, I brought you to this moment. I was insane not to send you aloft."

"You'd have had to drag me."

"A small cost."

The holocam began to whir.

Andori said, "Now I, Henrod Andori, High Bishop of the Reconciliation Church, do require and accomplish the execution of—"

Bone and blood splashed my shoes.

I screamed.

A deacon pitched forward, a steaming hole in his stomach.

Hambeld whirled, searched for the unseen foe, found none, spun to Fath. He raised his pistol.

The heli's hull whitened, splattered molten alloy.

Hambeld cursed, ducked clear. A bolt sizzled at his feet. Before he could move, it cut him off at the knees. A dreadful shriek, cut short.

A figure, striding from the cargo truck parked by the gate. It seemed familiar. It bore a laser rifle.

Among our captors, only Andori was left. With startling agility, the old man stooped, snatched up Hambeld's pistol, scuttled behind the heli.

Deacon Conrad stood frozen, holocam whirring.

From the terminal, shouts of rage. A soldier raced out the door, paused near the cargo hauler, took aim at the figure striding toward us.

I watched, rooted to the steaming concrete.

The cargo hauler's door flew open. A man leaped down. His rifle set to continuous fire, he sprayed the nearby soldier, then the terminal doorway. From within, screams, then silence.

Impossible. The man firing relentlessly at the terminal was . . . Chris Dakko.

The striding figure neared. A woman. I squinted.

It couldn't be.

Corrine Sloan, Janey's mother. Her face was hard.

Jerence blanched.

She seemed the angel of death.

Andori fired, missed her by inches.

Without breaking stride, she returned fire. Her shot scorched the hem of his robe. He squawked, retreated with unsteady steps.

Still Ms. Sloan advanced. "Hello, Nick." Her eyes never left the Bishop.

"Corrine!" Fath's voice was a rasp.

She'd have strode through me had I not leaped aside.

With trembling hands Andori raised his pistol. "Don't!"

The Bishop's foot dissolved. He screamed, falling heavily.

A dozen steps, and she loomed over his writhing form.

"It's over!" She turned to the holocam. "Do you hear? It's done, now and forever!"

"Wait!" Andori's teeth bared in a rictus of agony. "Don't, I—"

"Corrine, stop!" Fath lunged toward her.

"I do this for John." She aimed downward, fired once. The Bishop was still. She examined her rifle, set it to continuous fire. Coolly, she aimed at the scorched figure on the tarmac, held the trigger until nothing was left but ash, smoking stains, and bits of cloth.

At length, she turned to Deacon Conrad. "And you?"

"Blessed Savior!" He dropped his holocam, backpedaled desperately, hands shielding his face. "I beg you, don't!"

"Run away!"

He did.

In the distance, Chris Dakko coolly loaded a recharge into his rifle, strolled to the terminal, peered inside. It seemed the carnage was satisfactory; without another glance he strode toward the heli.

Gently, Fath eased the rifle from Corrine's unresisting hands. "Lord God." It might have been prayer.

Corrine took his cheeks in her hands. "Nick."

He pressed her fingers.

"Captain, get her aloft." Mr. Branstead, from the tarmac, his voice tight. "Before they—"

"I know."

"Why? I've nowhere to run. Sooner or later they'll have me."

"Nonsense, Corrine. I'll take you home to Earth. No, the Patriarchs would—as Captain, I have plenipotentiary powers. I'll pardon you."

"You don't understand. Whatever the cost, it was worth it."

Mr. Dakko was breathing hard. "Sir."

The Captain eyed him.

Dakko drew himself up, handed Fath his rifle. Fath looked a bit nonplussed; he already gripped Corrine's weapon.

"Sir, I told the Holy See what they needed to overthrow Anthony Carr's government. It led to his death. I accept responsibility. Do with me what you will."

"You speak of treason."

"Yes, I suppose I do. I was half out of my mind. Of course, that's no excuse. I've switched sides for the last time."

"Jerence?"

Mr. Branstead lifted himself on an elbow, rubbed his eyes. "Where's Palabee?"

"He resigned as Stadholder when you took the Cathedral. I imagine he's lying low. The Palabees have a lodge in the Venturas."

"And Scanlen?"

"Still in jail, for the moment."

Fath raised an eyebrow.

"You'd best send reinforcements. My—" Mr. Dakko blushed "—watchers may not be enough if the Churchmen rally."

"Your revolutionaries."

"Oh, nonsense, we were never that. Plotters, yes. For better policy. We tried to free Anthony, were you told? They double-crossed us and killed Hilda Zayre as well. Randy accused me of . . ." He shook his head. "No matter. I turn myself in."

I made to speak, but Fath shushed me. "Very well. Mr. Dakko, as acting Stadholder, Jerence paroles you to my custody. And I order you to get him to hospital, flank, and stay with him until he's tended."

"Sir . . ." Mr. Dakko's mouth worked.

"I know, Chris. We've none of us done aught to be proud of. I'll give you absolution, but not punishment. We're beyond that. Go make it right."

"Aye aye, sir." It was automatic, a response from days long past.

The Captain smiled, his eyes grim. "And now, Jerence . . ."

"I suppose it's time." Mr. Branstead sighed. "Andori's dead, Scanlen in custody, Palabee hiding. I'll handle the rest. Go home to *Olympiad*."

Fath patted his shoulder.

"And you'd best hurry, Nick. We've few enough soldiers to guard you or Corrine. Mr. Dakko, I'm afraid I'll need carrying to the terminal comm room, to call down a shuttle. In the meantime, keep Ms. Sloan out of sight. The Churchmen may rally. Nick, you and the boy—"

"—will be across the tarmac." He pointed to Admiralty House. "Come along, Randy." Limping, rifle in hand, he led me from the steaming puddle of blood.

The Admiral's aide gaped as Fath made his report. Then, he meekly asked us to wait, and disappeared.

Afternoon had darkened to dusk. We sat exhausted in the dusty anteroom, but it wasn't long before Admiral Kenzig emerged from his inner sanctum. Fath stood carefully, favoring his aches, set down the laser rifle he'd confiscated from Ms. Sloan. He saluted, as if his uniform weren't torn and grimy, his face streaked. "Captain Nicholas Seafort reporting, sir."

"As you were, Mr. SecGen."

"I've come to offer my resignation."

"Which Naval regs prohibit, except under precise circumstances. You learned so on a previous visit."

"On *Hibernia*, when I was a boy. Yes. Let me rephrase it. I came to offer you the chance to remove me."

Kenzig eyed me. "It's a private matter."

"Might I have my son present, sir?"

"Why?"

"He's earned it."

My jaw dropped.

"Certain matters . . . if they become public . . ."

"When we're done Randy's going aloft. He won't be back for years."

The Admiral grimaced. "Very well. Come into my office."

He took his seat, behind a gleaming expanse of table with nothing on it, not even a holovid. "Refreshments, gentlemen? A softie for the boy?"

"No, thank you." Fath shifted, impatient.

Outside, in the gathering darkness, floodlights lit the terminal and tarmac. A band of soldiers checked their weapons, took up positions around the terminal. I wondered who they served.

Kenzig sighed. "Whatever are we to do?"

"It's your decision, sir."

"Bah. There's no precedent. No regs come close to covering . . ." Another sigh. "Your arrest of Scanlen has folk uneasy. If—"

"Who?"

The Admiral opened and closed his mouth, as if astonished at the interruption. "All of the devout. As it should." He shot Fath a glance that might have been a challenge. "With Andori's murder, Scanlen becomes Archbishop of Mother Church in Hope Nation. With Branstead's regime in immediate danger of overthrow—"

"I doubt that."

"If his government survives, Branstead will hold Bishop Scanlen indefinitely, or worse, try him for treason. The—"

A knock at the door. "Pardon, sir." The Admiral's aide peered in. "The shuttle's begun descent. ETA fifty minutes."

"Very well." When the door closed, Kenzig frowned. "Try him for treason, I was saying. The Patriarchs would blame us for the fiasco." Kenzig grimaced. "Unless we intervene."

"It's an internal matter for Hope Nation."

Kenzig's voice was sharp. "So you say when it suits you. But yet you arrested Scanlen in his Cathedral."

"I acted on behalf of Anthony Carr's government, not against it."

"Sophistry." The Admiral waved it away. "What if I order you to storm the cells and set the Bishop free?"

I expected Fath to ignite like a shuttle at liftoff, but he said mildly, "To what purpose?"

"Exactly. They'd only rearrest him when *Olympiad* Fused, unless we saw to a change of government as well."

The Captain's lips tightened.

Kenzig said, "Ambassador McEwan claims the repeated coups show Hope Nation is incapable of stable government. He demands we return the system to colonial status."

"By force?"

"If necessary."

I tried not to hold my breath.

Fath's gaze strayed to mine. "Randy, you'd best wait outside after all."

No! I *must* know the outcome. "Sir, I'd listen at the door." I reddened, knowing it was betrayal.

After a moment Fath sighed. "So be it. But you'll never repeat what you hear to another living soul."

"I so swear." My heart pounded.

Fath said to the Admiral, "You speak of reimposing colonial rule. What force have you?"

"Your crew. The Orbiting Station, and what personnel the Church might provide."

Fath took a deep breath. "Sir, while I hold command, neither *Olympiad*'s crew nor her officers will act against the Government of the Commonweal."

"You'd compel me to relieve you?"

"As you recall, I came to offer you that opportunity."

A long silence.

"There was a day," Admiral Kenzig said heavily, "when the Admiral

Commanding could count on the loyalty of his men. When an officer followed orders to the letter."

"There was a day," said Fath, "when Church and Admiralty didn't
contemplate infamy." He rose. "I asked you once, sir: are you in their camp,
or ours?"

"Theirs? Ours?"

"The recolonialists, for want of a better name. Or those of us who
oppose their greed. In the old days you spoke of, men like Andori and
McEwan wouldn't dare drag the Navy into their tawdry plots."

"I'm not blessed with the liberties you allow yourself, Seafort: I obey
orders. And unlike you, I *want* to. If it's U.N. policy to recolonialize Hope
Nation, that's what I'll do."

Surprisingly, Fath's tone was gentle. "Is it so? Have you clear orders?"

Kenzig threw up his hands. "No, they wouldn't—haven't—I mean . . ."
He spluttered to a halt, to regroup. "You know how it works, Mr. SecGen.
Matters are understood. Between them, Ambassador McEwan and the
Bishop represent the interests of our Government."

"I was always given to understand, sir, that the Board of Admiralty
had charge of the U.N.N.S., and it was their orders I swore to follow."

"Oh, that's admirable, Seafort. But politics exist, as you of all men
should know." Kenzig flushed. "I'm in a difficult position."

A caller buzzed.

"Then look to your orders," said Fath, "and no one can fault you. Were
you told to defer to McEwan?"

"Not specifically."

A knock. The aide, his expression apologetic. "Sir, Mr. Branstead, for
Captain Seafort. He says it's urgent."

Fath's hand leaped to the caller, but he stopped himself, waited with
mute appeal.

"Very well."

"Yes, Jerence?"

I was close enough to hear. "I'm at the hospital. That obscenity Andori
perpetrated was broadcast live. Tens of thousands saw him burned. There's
a crowd of his supporters gathering downtown, and wild talk of marching
on the spaceport. Get Corrine aloft."

"A shuttle's due any moment."

"I'll handle it, but her presence groundside . . ." He sighed—"may provoke bloodshed."

"I understand. We'll go the moment—"

"I sent a squad to the terminal to protect her. Have they shown?"

Before Fath could speak I blurted, "Yes!" I pointed.

Fath told him, and tersely they rang off. He said to the Admiral, "We'll have to hurry, sir. You say you weren't told to follow McEwan's lead. Were you ordered to overthrow the local government?"

A pause. "No."

"Well, then."

Kenzig waved a hand, conceding the point. "If we don't move against the government . . . what about Scanlen? If I allow him to be executed, Admiralty will have my head. The Navy can't offend the Church to that extent." He waited, but Fath said nothing. "What, then? Take the Bishop home to Earth? And what if he chooses not to go?"

"You'd give him the choice, sir?"

"After all, he *is* our Bishop." The Admiral's glance was curious. "If I ordered you to transport him home a free man, you'd obey?"

Fath pondered. "Have you seen the holo of Randy's supposed hanging?"

"Decidedly poor judgment."

In the distance, the drone of engines.

I stirred hotly, but Fath held out a restraining palm. "Or of Anthony's death?"

"A miserable business." Kenzig cleared his throat. "I asked, Mr. Seafort, if you'd take Scanlen as a passenger were I to order it."

"I think not," said Fath. "I'd be more likely to expel him by the nearest airlock."

The Admiral's tone held contempt. "And you speak of obedience to orders."

"I'd enter the matter in the Log, and take the inevitable consequences." Hanging, he meant. I shivered. Fath added, "You know where I stand, sir. Do you relieve me of command?"

For a moment Kenzig's fists knotted. Then, "No."

The drone grew louder. I peered at the tarmac. In the distance, lights. They neared.

The shuttle.

"Very well." Heavily, Fath got to his feet. "With your permission, I'll carry on."

"Very well."

Fath held his salute, waiting until the Admiral responded. Then he beckoned me to follow.

"Just a moment." Kenzig stopped us at the corridor door. "Bless it, Mr. SecGen, you *have* to take the Scanlen problem off my hands. If you won't take him as a passenger . . . must he go as prisoner? Who has authority to charge him?"

"You do, sir, on violation of U.N. law, though you can't try him here.

And you may remand him to the Church in home system, if he's violated canon law."

Kenzig hesitated. "Must the charge be explicit?"

"Yes. If it appears my personal vendetta, he might be released without trial."

Kenzig's tone was reluctant. "What charge would fit?"

"Subversion of a government ordained of Lord God?" Fath smiled. "I believe that violates both canon and civil law."

"So be it." For a moment the Admiral studied Fath bleakly. "Mr. SecGen . . . how are you so bloody sure of your course? Are you never wrong? Have you a special conduit to Lord God?"

"Hardly, sir." Fath saw it didn't satisfy. "I'd rather act wrongly than sacrifice conscience to caution. It's the only way I know." Gently, he propelled me to the hall, retrieved his rifle.

In grim silence we trudged across the runway toward the terminal. Fath had his hand on my good shoulder. His face was gray. I wondered if he knew how much of his weight I bore.

Hoping to divert him, I said, "He's afraid of you."

"Of course."

"Why, sir?"

Fath halted, rubbed his chin. "I was SecGen. You're a provincial; you've no idea what that means."

"I know you headed the entire U.N. Gov—"

"You had to see, to understand. Ask Anselm someday. Whenever I scratched my arse, they reported it in blazing headlines. I had—still have—access to near unlimited publicity. If I write my memoirs, tens of millions will read them." He searched my eyes for comprehension, found it lacking. "Mr. Kenzig fears I'll chide him before the entire populace of home system." He snorted. "As if I'd wash the Navy's dirty linen in public." An annoyed shake of the head. "Have I ever done such a thing?"

"During the Naval Rebellion you told the holozines—"

"Bah. Come along."

Meekly, I complied.

25

IT WAS A HUGE shuttle, much bigger than I'd expected. It coasted to a stop near the terminal gate. The moment the dull roar of the engines muted, the hatch flew open. I watched, agape. Master-at-arms Janks charged down the steps, some thirty sailors at his heels. Many were from his squad, but I recognized others: hydronicist's mates, comm watch techs, engine room hands. All were armed to the teeth. Among them were Mikhael Tamarov, Midshipman Ghent, Tommy Yost.

"Sir? Where are you?" Mikhael peered into the night.

"Here." Fath. He gripped my good shoulder.

"Janks!" Mikhael stabbed a finger urgently.

"Got it, sir." The master-at-arms led a mad dash across the tarmac. In a moment we were surrounded. Sailors knelt, their backs to us, rifles to shoulders, safeties off.

Fath raised an eyebrow, but it was too dark for Janks to notice. "What's this about?"

"Protection, sir. Mr. Tolliver's orders."

Andrew Ghent danced from foot to foot. "Thank Lord God you're safe, sir." His eyes sparkled.

The master-at-arms frowned. "Mr. Ghent, might you see to the terminal, please?" He spoke with care, as one might, giving orders to a nominal superior.

"Aye aye—I mean, quite so, Mr. Janks. You joeys . . . and you." The young middy's hand swept across the throng. "This way!" They rushed to the scorched doorway.

Fath said, "Why don't we just board the shuttle?"

"This one's not yours."

"What do you—"

"Just a moment, sir." Janks keyed his caller. "Mr. Ghent?"

"Here. The terminal's a mess. Charred bodies, and . . . Christ." Heavy breathing. "Good, we have Ms. Sloan. Disarmed the local joeys guarding her. What should we do with them?"

"They're on our side." Fath's voice was sharp.

"I don't want them armed." Janks.

"I do. If we can't trust Branstead's men . . ."

Janks sighed. "All right, sir." To the caller, "Give them their weapons. Send them to Yost, to reinforce the perimeter. Mr. Yost, are you on this channel?"

"Yes, sir. I mean, Mr. Janks."

"Well?"

"The road's clear, either direction, as far as we can see. We've taken up positions."

Janks grunted. "Mr. Tamarov?"

"I heard. I think it's time to send the signal. Do you agree?"

"Yes, sir."

Fath's tone was acid. "Since I'm in command, perhaps you'd care to tell me what's going on."

The master-at-arms sounded abashed. "Aye aye, sir. Your special shuttle is on the way; Mr. Tamarov and the pilot just sent the codeword."

"We'll board this one. No point in—"

"They've fitted the other for medevac. Dr. Romez is coming groundside. You and your, um, son can't handle acceleration without—"

"What idiot ordered this?"

"Lieutenant Tolliver, sir." Despite his stolid tone, Janks hunched his shoulders, as if expecting an explosion.

Fath's fingers tightened on my neck. I gritted my teeth. After a moment, his grip eased. "Well, perhaps for Randy . . ."

"Sir, you know liftoff did you in, last time." I spoke before thinking.

Fath scowled. "I'll be fine." He tried to pace, but the circle of guards was too confining, and perhaps he hurt too much. "How long?"

"Two hours fourteen minutes." Janks.

"We'll wait in the terminal."

The master-at-arms shook his head. "Too hard to defend, sir. The whole front's those glass windows. All those doors . . ."

"In the shuttle, then. In an emergency we can taxi to the far side of the tarmac."

Janks bit his lip. "Very well, sir. After refueling." He keyed his caller, barked orders. In a few moments a truck raced across the asphalt. Only when it had rolled back to the fuel hangar did he allow us to board.

At the hatch, Mikhael gave his crispest salute, a broad grin lighting his lean face. "Welcome, sir. Pa." He stood aside as Fath squeezed past.

"As you were. Janks, get Corrine aboard."

"Aye aye, sir."

Mikhael stood beaming. Only when his eye strayed to my empty sleeve did his smile fade. "Oh, Randy."

I tried to shrug, grimaced at the sharp stab the gesture produced. "I'll be fine." I wrinkled my brow. Hadn't Fath said the same, on the tarmac?

Fath patted me absently, regarded Mik. "Tolliver sent you groundside?"

"Yes, sir. I don't think he cared to risk a mutiny."

They each stared, unyielding, until Fath waved it away, a gesture of defeat. "It's a god-awful mess. You heard about Corrine?"

"I watched. The whole ship did."

Fath gaped.

"They'd announced you were to be executed. Ms. Skor relayed the broadcast from the Station, and Tolliv—*Mr.* Tolliver put it shipwide."

The Captain's eyes glistened. "She has nowhere to go, Mik. Nowhere at all."

"Surely they'd relent, once Andori's misdeeds—"

"A Bishop." Fath sank into a seat.

"A madman."

"But a *Bishop*." Fath rested his head in his palms.

"It was on the screen in crew mess," Mik said. "Corrine strode into view, a grim avenging angel. Our joeys applauded. Rioted, more like. She stood over that frazball Andori, firing until her charge was gone . . . We could hear them three Levels above, from the bridge. Joeys were still dancing and hollering. Ms. Frand had a fit. Said it wasn't right to celebrate the death of Lord God's envoy."

Fath's eyes were bleak. "The Church here would burn Corrine in an instant. The same in home system, or anywhere she goes. How can I protect her? Once we go home, they'll order me to send her groundside."

"Refuse, Pa."

"They'd relieve me of command. Then what? Should I seize *Olympiad* to save her?"

A new voice, from the hatch. "No. Let them take me."

Fath leaped from his seat, winced. "Corrine!" He hobbled to the hatch. Outside, behind Ms. Sloan, Midshipman Andrew Ghent surveyed the spaceport, rifle at the ready.

"In fact, it's best it be done here. Janey won't know, and you won't be compromised. I'll go downtown, to the Cathed—"

Fath took her in his arms, kissed her silent.

From the hatch, Ghent winked at me. I looked away, offended. Who was he to snigger at Fath? Ghent was only a middy, almost as lowly as a ship's boy. Friendship or no, he was out of line. I made my eyes cold.

After a moment Ms. Sloan said, "Nick?"

"You did a terrible thing, Corrine. And I love you."

She blinked. "When did you decide that?"

"Long ago. I just wouldn't let myself know."

Despite myself, I turned away. His look was so lonely I couldn't bear it.

After a time, the cockpit door opened. The pilot peered out. "The second shuttle's in the mesosphere. It won't be long. Mr. Van Peer has the conn."

Fath disengaged himself from Corrine. "Very well."

I whispered to Mik, "What's that?"

"Upper atmosphere, above the stratosphere. Eighty kilometers tops."

"Oh." Should a ship's boy know that? I'd be one soon. Again.

From the hatchway Ghent cleared his throat, caller in hand. "Sir?" For an instant, I thought he meant me, but his eye was on Fath. "Mr. Janks's compliments, and would you please move away from hatch and portholes?"

Fath regarded him gravely. "Is that how he put it?"

"Not quite, sir." Ghent's eyes danced. His tie was awry, his jacket smudged with soot.

"Well?"

"His words were, 'Have the Captain move his bloody ass before he gets it shot off.' Begging your pardon, sir."

"Of course." Fath's tone was dry. But he moved farther from the hatch.

Minute upon minute dragged past at glacial pace. I sat near the cockpit of the stifling shuttle, sweaty, disheveled, aching. Fath disengaged himself from Corrine, had the cockpit patch him through to Tolliver. I didn't catch it all, but I gathered their conversation wasn't amicable. "Bloody waste of time," was one phrase I caught, along with "I'm no invalid."

Abruptly his tone changed. His voice dropped, and I had to lean back to hear properly. Then, I wished I hadn't. "In your personal charge," Fath said. And, "Randy's been through more hell than he can endure. Have sympathy." A pause. "Yes, I imagine I'll be fine. I've had dozens of liftoffs. But in case I'm . . . not fit to resume command. Just in case, mind you."

For some reason my eyes stung, until I had to hoist myself from the jumpseat, trudge to the rear of the shuttle. I stood staring at a dingy bulkhead. When Fath emerged from the cockpit, he spotted me, and for some reason came over and patted my hand as if I were a joeykid.

At last, the crackle of radios, the familiar muted roar of a shuttle. Mr. Janks appeared at the hatch. "Just a few minutes, sir. The medevac will pull up close, and refuel. You'll transfer across."

Fath rubbed his eyes. "Any sign of trouble?"

"Yost's squad has the road covered. He says all's quiet."

I found a seat nearer the open hatchway. Laser fire be damned; I needed air.

Fingers brushed the stump of my arm. Mik said softly, "Does it hurt?"

"No. Well, a little. Some."

"Romez will fit you for a prosth in no time. You'll see. When—"

"No."

"Why not?"

I was careful not to shrug. "It's not . . . me." And there was more. "I look in the mirror, and see what I did."

"It will fade," Mike assured me. "Over time—"

"I *want* to remember." In my own clumsy, foolish way, I'd saved Fath. After I'd done naught to stop them from burning Anthony to charred, stinking meat. I swallowed. Yes, I must be made to remember.

"Oh, little brother." Mik's arm enveloped me. Gratefully, I sagged.

"Midshipman Yost reporting to Mr. Janks!" Tommy's voice was shrill.

"Cars, a whole bunch of them. And cargo haulers. Men are jumping out—"

Janks leaped for the caller. "Where? North or south?"

"From downtown. We've pulled back, behind the second hangar."

"You bloody fool, that leaves the roadway open between Hangar One and the terminal!"

The snap of a laser. *"Get down, Mapes! What should we do, sir? Retake the first hangar?"*

Fath said quietly, "The middy's in over his head."

The master-at-arms nodded. "I'll reconnoiter. Mr. Tamarov!"

Mik jumped. "Yes?"

"You're in charge of refueling. Get the medevac shuttle turned around."

"Aye aye—er, right, Mr. Janks." Mik peered out cautiously, saw no enemy, leaped down the gangway, raced to the refueling hangar.

"Mr. Ghent, guard the shuttle. And keep your squad vigilant," Janks added with a scowl. "Yost left them an opening; troublemakers may break through. When we send word, escort the Captain across. If you would, please." His tone held grudging courtesy.

"Very well." But it was too late; Mr. Janks was loping down the tarmac, rifle across his chest.

Ms. Sloan stirred. "It's me they want, Nick. They'll let you go."

Fath said sharply, "Don't be a fool." After a moment, "Do you imagine I'd leave without you?"

"Olympiad to Shuttle." A familiar, edgy voice. The pilot took the call.

"It's not that I want to martyr myself. One of us has to survive for Janey."

"Shush." Fath patted her shoulder. "In a couple of hours we'll tuck her in together."

The pilot cleared his throat. "For you, sir."

"Now what?" Fath flipped a key, switched the call to the speaker.

"Where the hell is he?" Lieutenant Tolliver sounded beside himself.

"Seafort, here."

"Captain, your bloody fish's come to life. It's spewed an outrider to attack the ship."

"How do you know it's an attack?"

"We don't know it's not, and I've a ship full of passengers."

"Just one outrider, Edgar?"

"One's all they need, sir. If it cuts through—"

"Steady, old friend."

"Oh, I'm steady. The beastie launched two minutes ago. Direct for our midsection. ETA four minutes forty-six seconds. I'm at Battle Stations. In about a minute I'm going to vaporize it."

"No! Absolutely not!" Fath lurched to his feet.

"*I can't take the—*"

"*I'm* taking the chance!"

"*Sir, my call, while you're groundside. With all due respect.*"

Fath said, "Use full thrusters, slide out of its path! You know outriders have no propulsive power."

A refueling truck careened across the runway, pulled to a stop at the medevac shuttle, fifty yards distant.

"*And then what? Let it float until it's sucked into Hope Nation's gravity well? Now, there's a hostile act.*"

"Match velocities. Open an airlock to our meeting corridor."

"*No.*" Perhaps it seemed too bald. Tolliver sounded apologetic. "*I can go along with that lunacy when you're aboard, sir. Just barely. But on my own . . .*"

"Let me talk to him." I tugged at Fath's arm.

"No, son. Edgar, I'm begging you—"

"*It's not worth the risk. Two minutes. One fifty.*"

I didn't know what drove me. "There's no time!" I reached for the caller.

Dumbfounded, Fath let me pry it from his grasp. It was no mean feat, one-handed.

"Mr. Tolliver, Ship's Boy Carr reporting." I wasn't one any longer, but I didn't know how else to start. "For God's sake, open an airlock. Don't kill the ambassador of an alien race."

"*We've no idea he's an ambass—*"

"Of course he is, and we all know it." I spoke so rapidly I almost gabbled. "Those things give me the creeps, especially when they *quiver*. And I saw one kill Kevin Dakko." Was that what I wanted to say? Was I making it worse?

"*Janks to Shuttle!*"

I ignored the new voice, spoke to the distant Tolliver. "This is Fath's—Captain Seafort's life work. The most important thing he ever did." I risked a glance at Fath, turned away hastily, ashamed of the reproach I saw. "To make peace with the aliens . . . it would give *him* peace at last. You know the burden he's carried. Genocide, he thought. There's tears in his eyes, talking to you." Fath's hand shot out for the caller, but I twisted away, spoke faster. "God, he's angry now, but he ought to be. In our own way, we've both betrayed him!"

Fath grasped my jacket, hauled me near, snatched away the caller. "Edgar!"

"*Fifty seconds.*" A long silence. "*Mr. Anselm, come about. Broadside to the Christ-damned fish.*" Broadside, they'd bring more lasers to bear.

Fath's hand tightened on the caller.

"*Open Level 3 lock! Boarding party, stand by, we're taking in a visitor. Pray you're right, Nick. And that joey of yours will face a reckoning. I'll see to it.*" The speaker went silent. I swallowed.

"*Shuttle, respond!*" Janks.

Wearily, Fath switched channels. "Seafort."

"*Could you contact Branstead, find out about this bunch?*" The master's voice was low. "*Most of them don't look military, but they've rifles and stunners and the like. And the crowd's moving to the gap Yost left.*"

"Will do." Fath's tone was grim. "Are they deacons or civilians?"

"*No clerical garb, but that means nothing. We're firing across the road from time to time, keeping their heads down. Sir, if they circle the tarmac . . . We haven't enough men.*"

"I don't want anyone shot, Janks. On their side or ours."

"*My brief is to get you aloft, whatever the cost.*"

"Belay that! I'm telling you to—"

"*My orders come from Mr. Tolliver, sir. He's nominally in charge. Take it up with him.*"

Turning from the speaker, Fath let loose a fearsome volley of oaths. I was impressed. He could teach Alex Hopewell a thing or two, and Alex had the foulest mouth in—

"*If you want to help, sir, ask Branstead's advice. Perhaps we could negotiate . . .*"

"Right." With a growl, Fath set down the caller.

I tugged at his sleeve. "What about Admiralty? Could Kenzig send help?"

"The Navy has no real base here. Just a few Admiralty House clerks." Fath stabbed at keys. "Seafort speaking. Connect me to Stadholder Branstead." A long pause, while he fumed.

At last, a tinny voice. "Hello?"

"Jerence, we've a problem. Those hotheads you spoke of—"

I had to lean close, to hear. Was it eavesdropping, if I put my ear right to Fath's caller? I mean, he *knew* I was listening.

"I'm not Branstead. They operated on his knee tonight. He's under anesthetic."

Fath blinked. Then, "Chris?"

"Yes, sir." Mr. Dakko. "Why aren't you aloft? Bishop Scanlen's roused a mob. They're headed—"

"Scanlen? He's jailed."

"Not anymore." Mr. Dakko sounded grim. "We couldn't hold him."

"Jerence charged him with—"

"Physically, we couldn't hold him. At least a thousand joeys had gathered around the Manse, Ms. Carr among them. Even Vince Palabee showed up to harangue them. Some of our Home Guard deserted. Others didn't want to fire on their own." A pause. "Neither did we. Sir, this is thoroughly out of hand."

Fath asked, "Is there a government?"

"I'll ask Mr. Branstead when he wakes." Mr. Dakko rang off.

Outside the hatch, shouts. Midshipman Ghent bounded in. "Sir, let's get you to your shuttle. Mr. Janks is falling back."

"Under attack?"

"Not exactly. But Tommy Yost says they're circling the—" He stabbed a finger toward the hangars. "His squad is gone to flush them out." He eyed the smaller shuttle's waiting hatch. "It's fifty meters, sir. Can you run?"

"No." It pained Fath to say it. He keyed his caller. "Mr. Janks, have your men fall back to the large shuttle, and lift off the moment we do."

"Negative, sir. If we let them get close, they'll spray your ship with fire. Can't take the chance they'll hit something vital. Once you're gone, we'll be free to disengage. They'll have no reason to hold us."

Fath turned to Ms. Sloan. "I don't like being rushed. By Edgar, by the rebels, by the fish." To the caller, "I'm coming out, Janks."

"Why?"

"To talk to them."

The middy stirred. "Sir—"

"Be silent, Mr. Ghent."

Andrew Ghent bit his lip, looked around wildly, dashed off into the dark.

Fath picked up his rifle, slipped in a recharge.

I watched, dumbfounded. Of all the officers on *Olympiad*, Tolliver had sent a pair of useless, idiotic middies . . . Tommy Yost, a spoiled child, and Ghent, who'd lost his head. Granted, Fath sometimes had that effect on you, but—

Pounding footsteps. Mikhael burst in, Ghent just behind. "What's this I hear?" Mik looked outraged.

"We've had enough killing. I'm going to negotiate—"

"Pa, that's goofjuice!"

I waited for lightning to strike. He was a middy speaking to his Captain. Fath snapped, "Stand aside."

"Listen, please." Somehow, Mik sounded both firm and beseeching. "Forty-six sailors, all volunteers. Two shuttles. Squads of soldiers Mr. Branstead can hardly spare. The whole operation's been laid on to get you safely home. Lives are at risk—"

"I don't *want* lives—"

"To protect yours." Mik plowed through. "You want to head off conflict. You're gallant, Pa; everyone knows that. But if you die trying, a blood-bath will follow. I won't be able to stop Janks, and won't want to. Corrine may be killed. Randy too. Along with Lord God knows how many sailors." His eyes burned into the Captain's. "Our only hope is to get you both onto the Christ-damned medevac, and out of Centraltown. As an officer, and as your son, I beseech you. Please!"

A long silence. Fath opened his mouth, closed it, made again as if to speak. At last he muttered, "Don't blaspheme," but his heart wasn't in it.

Apparently Mikhael took it as consent. "Andy, Shuttle Two's almost through refueling. We'll escort the Captain aboard. See he's surrounded every step of the way."

"Aye aye, Mr. Tamarov." Ghent spun, issued terse orders.

A moment later we were gathered at the hatch. Fath took Ms. Sloan's arm. "Let's go, my dear."

"You there, fall in behind us!" Ghent's voice was shrill as he beckoned to the stragglers in his squad. He craned his neck, trying to look every direction at once.

From the roadway past the terminal, shouts and commotion.

Our pace, brisk enough, was none too fast for our escort. Mikhael danced with frustration. "With your permission, sir!" He slipped a shoulder under Fath's arm, supporting his injured hip.

Corrine stumbled; sailors hauled her to her feet without a pause. They hustled her around the stubby fuel truck, up the hatchway steps behind Mik, who practically carried Fath.

I piled in after.

Inside, Dr. Romez saluted, a med tech at his side. "Here, Mr. Seafort." He patted one of two deeply cushioned contraptions that made sickbay beds seem spartan. They'd ripped out rows of seats to install them. Reluctantly, Fath sat himself.

I peered out the hatch. Sweating, panting for breath, Andrew Ghent leaned against the gangway. He grinned. "Never saw the Captain move so fast." I made my face cold, but he paid no heed. "Except the time Mikhael reported in drunk and threw up all over—*oh*!" He looked perplexed, winced, and crumpled at my feet. A ragged hole in the small of his back smoked and sputtered.

Below, on the tarmac, his squad scattered like leaves in a wind.

The middy drew himself up on an arm. He coughed. Blood welled from his lips. Anguished eyes met mine. His mouth worked, but no sound emerged.

I threw myself down the gangway, got my arm around him. It was impossible to lift him, one-handed.

With a mighty wrench, I got him across a knee, shifted my grip. My shoulder blades blazed in protest. I panted. It was but three steps to the safety of the hatch. I called out, but no one heard.

The railing sizzled, raining molten droplets on my wrist.

Red-faced, unable to breathe from the strain, I inched toward the hatchway. Pilot Van Peer stood inside, watching Romez.

The middy's feet caught on a step. With a mighty heave, I broke loose, stumbled into the shuttle.

Romez was adjusting Fath's straps. "—a relaxant. It will take almost immediate effect and—good Christ!"

I stood swaying, Andy Ghent hanging inert from my arm.

Mikhael dived across the corridor, eased the middy to the second bed. Pilot Van Peer ducked into the cockpit, jabbed at switches. "Fuel truck, break free! Get clear!"

Ghent tried to speak, choked, spewed blood. Romez swung him onto his side, tore the back of his jacket apart with a mighty yank.

"Orbit Station, Van Peer reporting, we're under attack, lifting in a moment. Puter!"

"Shuttle puter respon—"

"Emergency override all systems, calculate for VTOL lift, low trajectory to the north ten miles, gain altitude, revert pattern to achieve orbit!"

"Shuttle, Joanne Skor on the Station. Tolliver says he has his hands full, and wants to know where's the Captain."

Van Peer said, "On board, ma'am."

Andy's fluttering palm smeared the blood from his shirt. He frowned. "Can't report like this," he said, to no one in particular. A cough seized him, and he fought for breath.

Romez took one look. Swearing in a steady monotone, he fumbled for bandages. "Hearns, IV line, flank!"

The med tech threw open a case, bared Ghent's arm.

Fath's hands scrabbled at his straps, unbuckling himself.

"Fuel truck, respond!" Van Peer drummed his console.

No answer.

"I'll tell them, sir!" Mikhael raced down the gangway, arms pumping.

"Hang on, Andrew." Fath's tone was a rasp. He lurched across the aisle.

I flexed my aching forearm.

Ghent's fingers shot out, grabbed my wrist. Like a rag doll, I sank to my knees. The middy and I were face-to-face. His lips moved.

"What?"

He said it again. I leaned close, heard nothing.

A fit of coughing. A glob of dark blood spattered my shirt.

"Out of the way, Randy!"

"Tell me." I wasn't in the way. Not really.

Ghent's face was purple. Somehow, he cleared an airway. "—ember me, Randy!" A plea.

I gaped.

His eyes were intense. "Remember me. Who I was." It was almost the voice I knew.

"I will. Oh, I w—"

And he died.

I knelt dumbly, amid chaos.

Fath's voice was a dull monotone. "Waste. Utter waste!"

Romez was at Fath's side, his tone coaxing. "Captain Seafort, get back in your—"

Through the porthole, lights swung. The fuel truck, disengaging.

"Hatch closing!" Van Peer.

"Not without Mik!" Fath stumbled to the hatch, jabbed the stay. "We've lost Ghent, I won't allow more—"

On the tarmac, the truck rolled clear, turned toward the hangar.

"Get away from the hatch!" Romez practically knocked him aside.

Fath wrestled free. "Mikhael!"

"He's in the truck!" Romez reached past Fath, to the control.

I stroked Andrew's forearm gently, so as not to hurt him.

"No, he's not!" Fath pointed. "Hurry, Mik!"

Mikhael Tamarov charged up the gangway. "Get rolling, there's a gang of them firing from—"

A stupendous blast. The sky lit to day.

A massive shock wave thumped my chest. It lifted Mikhael through the hatch, slammed him into Fath. They sprawled, Mik on top.

I lay, stunned, half deafened, my head resting on Ghent's bloody shirt.

Romez hauled Mik clear, knelt by Fath.

Mikhael stumbled to a porthole. He stared at an immense smoking crater, not far from the hangar door. "They got the truck. Pilot, what damage? Can we fly?"

"I sure as hell hope so." Van Peer jabbed the hatch shut. The engines caught.

"Hearns, help me lift the Captain!"

"I'm all ri—oh!" Fath's face was ashen. The doctor and the tech eased him to a bed.

"Where's a caller?" Mik dived into the cockpit. "Janks! Master-at-arms!"

Static. Then, finally, "Janks reporting."

"Fall back to your shuttle! We're taking off!"

"You'd best hurry." But Janks seemed calm enough.

"Lieutenant Skor, here. Sensors caught an explosion. Report!"

Mik jabbed at keys. "Midshipman Tamarov, on the medevac. A fuel truck went up. We're under attack, ready to lift. Ghent is injured. The Captain, Randy, and Ms. Sloan aboard. Janks is getting his men to the shuttle."

"Where are the rebels?"

My voice was soft. "I'll remember you, Kevin."

"Attacking from the south, ma'am. They have the hangars, we have the terminal."

I blanched. "I mean, Andrew."

A click. *"Janks, this is Tolliver."*

"Yes, sir."

"Ms. Skor has a shot from the Station. Stay to the north. We'll give you covering fire."

Fath raised his head. "Belay that!"

Janks said, "Give me a minute, sir. Yost! Disengage, flank! To the shuttle!" His voice faded.

"Now your other arm, sir." Dr. Romez adjusted the safety belts.

"Did you hear me? Don't fire!"

"I can do nothing, sir. Not from here." Romez bared Fath's arm. "Now, sir, your relaxant."

"Don't start a war over me. I beg . . ."

The medicine did its work. Fath sighed. Some of the tension left his frame.

Romez and his tech lifted Andy Ghent from the bed, strapped his corpse into a seat.

"You next, son." Romez indicated the modified couch, still damp with Andy's blood.

"I'm fine." I waved him away, took the seat closest to Andrew.

Fath raised his head as far as his restraints would allow. "Do as he says, *this instant!*"

I jumped to comply. Fath was more alert than he'd let on. I grimaced. His last liftoff had nearly crippled him, and since then he'd endured kidnap, trial, a wall of water, and just now, a heavy fall.

"Did you hear me?"

"Yes, sir!" Quickly I lay down in the foamed chair while Dr. Romez fussed gently with my knitting shoulder, binding it in some protective material. I muttered, "Sorry, Fath."

He grunted.

"Station . . ." Van Peer. "We're lifting to the north. You'll have us on radar in a moment or two."

My voice was tense. "Will he be all right?"

Romez said, "Worry about yourself, joey. You're not healed near enough for the stress of—"

"*Will he?*"

"I'm not sure. I think so. Pilot, we're ready." Romez took his own seat, adjusted his straps.

The engines roared. I watched Fath anxiously, from the first jolt.

VTOL liftoff is rather gentle, at first. As we gained speed, the wings slid to normal cruise position. The nose tilted upward. Massive engines labored. As we banked, I caught a glimpse of the Plantation Zone. Would I ever see it again? I gulped.

Slowly the pressure grew.

My shoulder ached. Fath breathed slowly, steadily.

Something stabbed my knitting flesh. A bone grated. The cabin pulsed red. I forced a scream through the gravestone on my chest, and passed out.

26

I FLOATED IN A gentle white sea. My shoulder was tightly bound. I blinked. The white sheets of sickbay swam into focus. As I shifted, a wisp of euphoria abruptly burned off.

Dr. Romez poked his head in, raised an eyebrow, spoke into his caller. "Romez reporting, sir. He's awake." He listened. "Seems fine, for the moment. A goofy smile, eyes not quite focused. I'll keep him that way 'til we're sure. And you, sir?" A frown. "Don't be ridiculous, you're not to move. No, grav will stay at one-sixth, and if you order otherwise I'll urge Mr. Tolliver to relieve you." He grimaced at the agitated buzz emitting from his caller. "Sir, you're irritable because it hurts; raise the grav and I guarantee it'll hurt far worse. Good day." Romez rang off.

I struggled to rouse myself from lethargy. "Is Fath all right?"

"He's pretending to be better than he feels. Wants to go visit Harry."

"Who?"

"The alien. That's what Anselm calls it."

It made no sense, but I wasn't alert enough to divert my thoughts. "Is Fath crippled?"

"Not quite. The nerves of his spine are irritated and going into spasm. Getting thrown into a tree by a raging flood didn't help."

I flushed; he'd made it sound my fault. "I'm getting up." My tone was truculent.

Hands on hips, Romez went on as if I hadn't spoken. "You're awake enough to track? The Captain should never have gone groundside. The second time wasn't by his own volition, but still, he came aloft way too early. His vertebrae can't take much more stress. The Ghenili process is a miracle, but his neural connections are still . . ." He shook his head. "His next trip groundside may be the last. Not that you have much say in the matter."

"I'll remind him." Tentatively, I thrust aside a sheet, forgetting we were in severely reduced grav. It billowed. "Stand clear, please." I swung out my legs. All seemed well, for at least a second. Then I gasped, flailing one-handed for the support of the bed. Romez eased me down, supporting my throbbing torso. I looked at him in mute plea.

"Now you've seen for yourself, joey: you'll be abed a while. Your collarbone was a mess, and while you were under, we prepped you for a prosthesis—a mechanical temp 'til your organic's ready. Too much damage to your stump to wait any longer. We're running the bone-growth stimulator twice a day, you won't be—"

"Bastard!" I drummed my heels, knotted my only available fist. "I didn't want a prosth!"

"Talk to the Captain. He ordered it." His tone was frosty. "Neither of you should have been allowed to lift off. Not 'til you'd properly healed, but Capt—your father—wanted you and Ms. Sloan brought aloft to safety. Said the situation groundside was too chaotic to risk . . . well, never mind."

I gulped. "Is that why he took the shuttle? Because I had to?"

"That's for him to say."

"Tell me." I made my voice meek. "Please."

"He wouldn't see you left alone. Out of the question, he told us, so Mr. Tolliver dispatched the medevac."

"Damn." I knew Dr. Romez disapproved, but didn't care. "Will he be all right? I didn't want him hurt more. I thought . . ."

"Joey . . ." Romez sat on the bed. Surprisingly, his tone was gentle. "Mr. Seafort does what he thinks right. Son or no, you won't change that."

My eyes burned. I said, "What happened after liftoff?"

"You passed out."

"Groundside!"

"Janks and his joeys retreated to the shuttle and lifted. Amazingly, poor Ghent was the only one killed."

"Andy." I'd sneered at him, almost to the last.

"For now, Mr. Janks has guard of Har—the alien, ah, visitor. Tad Anselm is doodling on metal plates to amuse it 'til the Captain's able to join them. And there's trouble . . ." Dr. Romez pursed his lips, fell silent.

"Tell me."

"I don't spread rumors. And you're not ship's company."

"I will be." Until I'd said it, I hadn't known how much I yearned that it again be so.

He frowned. "Well, no doubt you'll hear soon enough from Tamarov. The master-at-arms reamed Tommy Yost before half the crew. Blamed him for Ghent's murder. Seems it was Yost's job to block the lane to the hangars, and he muffed it. Retreated without telling anyone. Janks said Yost wasn't fit to . . . he spoke rather strongly."

I was barely listening. *"Remember me."* Andrew's eyes burned into mine. Kevin, are you listening too? I closed a nonexistent hand over my absent friend's.

I turned to the pillow. Romez mustn't see.

"I'll let you rest."

"I want to visit Fath." After a moment, "The Captain."

"Not just yet."

"I'm his son."

"You're too hurt to walk. You'd go to him in a wheelchair, and what will that do for his morale? He's in pain, joey. More than he'll ever admit."

"Can't you give him sedat—"

"He needs deepsleep, not sedatives. And it's not just his physical woes. Corrine Sloan is a virtual prisoner in her cabin. She can't walk about without guard, lest some lunatic assault her to revenge Andori. The Captain's daughter, Janey, won't let him out of her sight. And he's moping about, weeping for Andrew Ghent and the seventeen dead they retrieved from the spaceport." Romez glared as if it were my fault.

"You said Ghent was the only—"

"Not ours. Theirs. Though I could give a rat's ass about some colonial—" He broke off, reddening. "Perhaps I'm a touch insular. Sorry. I hope they weren't folk you knew."

"Is Scanlen . . . what about Mr. Branstead?"

"Jerence still holds the Governor's Manse. As for the rest, I've no idea. My point is, leave the Captain be. He has enough on his plate."

I wiped my cheeks, not even caring that he saw them damp. Carefully, I turned on my side, my back to the hatchway, and pretended to sleep.

In two days the throb of my shoulder was subsiding, and I was in a mood to climb the bulkheads from sheer frustration. All I could do was throw tantrums in the sickbay, but Fath's disposition had affected the whole ship. When Tad Anselm had visited me, he'd had dark circles under his eyes. Mikhael had a distracted look, and waved aside my inquiries.

At last, Romez threw up his hands and brought us together.

In midafternoon he rewrapped my shoulder, bundled me into a powered chair, and wheeled me along Level 1 to the familiar gray hatch.

It was Janey who opened. She regarded me gravely with little-girl eyes. "You can't come in. Daddy's sleeping."

"No, I'm not." His voice had an edge. "Let them in." Reluctantly, Janey stood aside.

I gaped. How could a few days have made such a difference?

Fath was gaunt, his eyes sunken. Fully dressed, he lay flat on his back. One hand gripped the side of the bed. I wanted to run to him. Romez pushed my chair forward.

A smile. "Hallo, joey. Welcome home."

I launched myself from the chair, staggered to his embrace.

"Don't!" Romez, too late.

I never touched him. My knee landed on the bed, to prop myself up, and the mattress swayed.

Fath went white.

"I'm sor—"

Romez hauled me off. "Clumsy oaf! What did I tell you in the corridor?"

"Not to hurt . . ." I wasn't quite sure, actually. I'd been too eager to get to Fath's cabin.

"Not to go near him! If you had the brains God gave a gnat—"

"That's quite enough." Fath's jaw was clenched. "Back to your duties, Doctor."

"*You're* my duty. How bad is it today? Much worse than you let on over the caller, I see. Let me examine you."

"Not now."

"We'll up the painkillers. I'm increasing your dose—"

"Out of my cabin."

"Two hundred milligrams, three times daily. And I'll give them to you myself."

"Did you hear me? Out."

"Captain, you might even heal, if you give yourself time, but not unless you're utterly relaxed. That won't happen with your muscles tensed, anticipating the next twist of the knife." Romez folded his arms.

Fath lifted himself on his arms. It took prodigious effort, though we practically floated off the deck in the lunar gravity. "OUT, OR YOU'RE CONFINED TO QUARTERS FOR A WEEK! Janey, the hatch!"

Dutifully, she keyed the control.

Romez made as if to speak, thought better of it. He snapped a salute, stalked out.

Ever so carefully, Fath eased himself down. His forehead was beaded with sweat. "Jesus, son of blessed Lord God." His voice was ragged.

I stood like an idiot, wringing my hands. "What can I do? A cold washcloth? Adjust your bed? Call Mikhael?"

"Shhh. It's all right." His palm opened. He crooked a finger, beckoning me close. I slipped a hand into his, dared not squeeze. "How are you, son?"

"Fine." Compared to Fath, it was true. "Bored."

"Dr. Romez said that in a week you'll be more your old self. Up and about."

"Sir, could I . . ." I swallowed. ". . . be ship's boy again?"

"Not quite yet."

"You promised!" I sounded spiteful, and was. What business had I hounding Fath, while he was in such pain?

"One-handed, you can't handle the duties. In a few months, your new arm will be grown. And you'll look a lot better without a sleeve pinned back."

I said sullenly, "I didn't want a prosth."

"You'll get one. I won't have you sulking about."

"It's not that."

"What, then?"

I didn't want to tell him, and changed the subject. "Fath, why wouldn't you let him give you a painkiller?"

"Perhaps I was a bit rough on old Romez. You'd think after two or three hundred years . . ." He spoke through clenched teeth . . . ". . . they'd come up with something for pain that wasn't a soporific. I don't *want* them knocking me out."

"Why not?"

His eyes flicked to the holoscreen set up beside the bed. "Harry's on board." For an instant, his eyes eased in a smile. "Yes, I've heard the nick-name, and I approve. Anything that makes him seem less alien, less terrify-ing . . ."

"But if you're stuck here . . ."

"Tad isn't. I supervise, and make suggestions."

I peered past him to the screen, which displayed the Level 2 corridor, where we'd devised our human/outrider interface. Our table, at the clear transplex barrier. The servo that drew our pictograph plates. At the moment, no one was about except our guards. The alien rolled slowly up and down its silent corridor. I shivered; outriders were hateful creatures.

"We're making progress?"

Fath sounded glum. "Tad means well, and he does his best. But he hasn't the knack."

Carefully, I squeezed Fath's hand. What thrilled me most wasn't that he treated me as an adult, but that he knew, without asking, that I'd never repeat his words.

"Lie quietly," I told him. "Get yourself well."

With little more than a finger, Fath waved it away. "Dr. Romez says you're being difficult." He put on a stern expression.

"I've nothing to do."

"Then you'll appreciate your schoolwork. You'll start this afternoon."

"Are you joking?" It just slipped out of me. After a moment I reddened under his scrutiny. "Yes, sir."

"And you'll memorize verses, as before."

Almost, in my petulance, I kicked the bed, but I stopped myself just in time. Showing my annoyance was one thing, hurting Fath another. I cast around for an escape. "Fath, if I hadn't asked for remission of enlistment, and I'd lost my arm as ship's boy, would you beach me?" Beaching was how an officer was suspended, without being dismissed. But he'd know what I meant.

"No. An injured sailor stays in the ship's company for the duration of the cruise. He's assigned light duties."

"Well, then."

Fath raised an eyebrow.

"Put me on duty. It's only a technicality; I resigned to rescue *you*."

"Good argument, but no. Subject closed."

I opened my mouth to object, set it aside. Fath was looking peaked. "If I get my work done, may I wander around? Go down to crew quarters, see joeys I know?"

"That's fair."

I beat a retreat.

Mr. Branstead's government survived. Scanlen remained at large, but Branstead made no move to rearrest him. Surely he'd be able to find the fugitive Bishop; Hope Nation's settled areas weren't all that large, and the acting Stadholder had his ear to the ground.

I badgered Dr. Romez to let me return to our cabin. That is, Fath's. As all of Level 1 was on light grav, the Doctor had little reason to keep me in sickbay. I think he was more worried I'd pester Fath, but after checking with him, Romez reluctantly agreed. I had to report to him every afternoon, without fail, for an examination of my biomech implants.

In a week, I'd be ready for a temporary prosth, a flexible alumalloy arm that would serve 'til my real one came out of the growth tanks. Grafting it would require surgery that I didn't look forward to. I'd bear it, if I must. Restoration of my arm couldn't possibly hurt as much as its removal.

Before I could move home to my familiar cot, though, Tolliver collared me. He set me against the bulkhead. "I owe you." His tone held a warning.

"Why?" I didn't owe him a "sir," if I wasn't ship's boy.

"For talking me into taking that monster on board. For being a general nuisance. A loud one, pushy and insolent."

I thought it best to say nothing.

"And so help me, if I find you've annoyed Captain Seafort, I'll . . . By Lord God, if I had my way, you'd be banished to Level 6 'til he's recovered. Walk on eggshells around him, joey!"

"Yes, sir." I couldn't risk any other reply.

"See to it." He stalked off.

I moved in with Fath, and for a while I felt better, but before long I was passing the time lying in my bunk thinking about Andrew Ghent. How gentle he'd been when he'd escorted me as prisoner. His risking all to sign a petition for my release. The quizzical look that crossed his face, when his life had been snuffed out. To be fair, I tried to remember Kevin as well.

Every night, I roused myself to eat in the upper Dining Hall, amid restless, impatient passengers. Daily, on the way to dinner, I passed signs for Reverend Pandeker's prayer meetings. *Olympiad* was long delayed in her cruise to Kall's Planet, and the disembarkation and reloading of passengers— to say nothing of a fish drifting not far from the portholes—had unsettled them all. Perhaps Pandeker's blathering would ease their minds. I had no intention of attending; Lord God didn't exist. Of that, I was pretty certain, though I wouldn't say so to Fath.

Each night, after Reverend Pandeker gave the ship's prayer, I struggled one-handed with my portion of vegetables and meat. The older women at my table—in their thirties or even forties—offered in kindly fashion to help cut my food, and I tried not to be surly in my refusal. It was my task to handle my own meals, and I'd carry it out as best I could. If they disliked how I ate, they didn't have to watch.

Afterward, unless Mikhael was off duty, I wandered back to my cabin, or looked in on Fath.

Truth to tell, I welcomed the schoolwork he'd assigned. I had so little to do that *any* diversion was a relief, even memorizing stupid Bible verses, and it gave Fath such pleasure to hear me say them well, I almost looked forward to the recitation.

Not tonight, though. Fath had wrenched his back getting dressed, and finally submitted to stronger painkillers. He lay asleep on his bunk, a med tech standing by. Fath had refused to go to sickbay; it was like him to dig in, and the consequences be damned.

I tiptoed to my own bed, lay down self-consciously, but couldn't sleep under the tech's gaze. I got up, slid the hatch open, drifted out.

It was bad enough learning to sleep near Fath. How could other joey-kids accustom themselves to the wardroom, where four to eight middies were bunked? Years ago, Dad had told me of his childhood on Earth, where Grandpa Randolph had raised him as an Uppie. For a time Dad had found sleeping in public a terrible trial.

It didn't seem to bother Mik.

Where was he, this evening? I checked his favorite lounge on Level 3, found it deserted. I sat a while, stared at bulkheads.

As ship's boy, I'd been sent to the wardroom from time to time, to fetch and carry. Now, a civilian again, middy territory was off-limits, but I doubted anyone would object. And I felt a yearning for company.

I made my way down the corridor to the familiar hatch. It was open, but the two middies within saw only each other. I was on the verge of clearing my throat, decided not to.

". . . sorry! I'll do better, Mr. Riev. I promise." Tommy Yost's voice sounded tearful.

I froze.

"You whiner!" The first middy's tone dripped contempt. "What a sad excuse for an officer. We don't ask much. Just walk down the corridor without accumulating demerits."

"Ms. Skor said I was slouching, but honest, I wasn't—"

"I'll believe her over you, any day."

I grimaced. One grew used to hazing in the wardroom, Dad had said. But Mr. Riev's tone had an ugly bite.

"I'm sorry." Yost sounded resigned.

"Yes, you're a sorry affair. Not like Sutwin, or Tamarov." A pause. "Or Ghent. Now, there's one I'll miss."

A silence. "Sir, I swear I didn't know the rebels could get through. I wouldn't have seen Andy hurt for—"

"You deserted your post, you little shit. I'd trade you for him in a heartbeat."

"I don't—there's nothing I . . . please!" The creak of furniture. "It was an accident! I didn't know they'd—"

"*You're* the accident, Yost. And you'll pay, so help me. You'll have a lovely cruise, I'll see to that."

"Excuse me." Mik stood in the corridor behind me, hands on hips.

Riev stalked to the hatch. "What's going on?"

Mikhael hesitated an instant. "Nothing, sir."

Mr. Riev shot me a withering glance. "A *civilian* has no business in this section, joey." As if that wasn't enough, he added, "And you're not welcome in my wardroom."

Mik frowned, but said nothing.

"Yes. Yes, sir." I licked my lips.

"Don't skulk about hatches, you colonial trannie." To Mikhael, "In or out?"

"In, if you don't mind."

The hatch slid closed behind them, leaving me in the corridor fuming.

27

"BECAUSE I HAVE no one else to talk to." I faced Corrine Sloan, eyes locked on the deck of her Level 5 cabin. "Fath's sedated, Tad Anselm's busy with the alien, and Mik . . ." I grimaced. His loyalty lay with the wardroom.

"What happened?"

I made myself tell her. Perhaps speaking as one outcast to another made it easier. Though, from my point of view, she was a hero, not an—

Her tone was dry. "Curiosity isn't so terrible, Randy."

"I was listening at the hatch."

"An open hatch. If they'd wanted privacy . . . Do you seek pardon? I forgive you."

"No, I want . . ." Bile flooded my throat, as I realized what I wanted. "Excuse me." I made for the hatch. "I shouldn't have come."

A ship's lounge is an awful place to sleep. The lights are too bright, joeys come in and turn on the holovid, and the seats aren't comfortable. Not for hour after hour. And not when a long-dead face floats accusing in the dim light, until you rouse yourself and shout, "I never said I was as good as you!" And you gulp, because still the eyes burn into yours, and you say brokenly, "Please, Dad!" And you turn away, hoping to see it no more.

In the morning, ship's time, just as I was steeling myself to do what had to be done, Alejandro, the ship's boy, peered in. "*There* you are. I've been looking everywhere."

I rubbed my face. "Why?"

"Cap'n said to find you."

"Well, you did." I knew I sounded sullen, but a night such as mine will do that.

"Better hurry. He didn' sound real pleased."

No, he wouldn't. "Soon as I wash my face." I splashed water, one-handed, and made a rudimentary effort to comb my hair. By then, Alejandro had departed. Apparently, his instructions didn't include escorting me back to quarters.

I trod my way upward, step growing lighter despite my darkening mood. Level 3, where I'd slept, was at full grav, but Fath's cabin—all of Level 1—was set to Lunar Standard. Not our moons, of course. Luna, back in home system.

Outside the hatch, I took a deep breath. Almost, I knocked. No, I still lived there, at least for the moment. I slid open the hatch, took resolute steps.

Fath, wearing a faded robe, sat tensely in an easy chair, a caller by his side. His fingers gripped the armrests. His face was gray. He was alone, or had been so until I came in.

I took one look. "Is it bad?"

"Yes."

"Why don't you stay in bed?"

"Don't tell me my business." His tone was short. A flick of his head, toward my unused bunk. "You're in trouble. Wandering the night—"

I said evenly, "I'm in more trouble than that."

He closed his mouth, set aside what was no doubt a blistering rebuke. Then, "Tell me."

"Didn't Mikhael?" For a moment, I hoped he had. It would make it easier.

"I haven't seen him of late. Get on with it, Randy. I'm not feeling . . ."

With perverse pride, I set myself before him, as I'd seen Andrew Ghent do, when reporting to the bridge for discipline. "I went to the wardroom. Two middies were talking. I listened. And you know what? If the hatch had been closed, I'd still have listened."

He said, "You can't know that."

"I wanted to live up to Dad, and failed. I wanted you to be proud of me, and I c—c—can't do that. I hate what I am. I'm not good enough for you, for *Olymp*—"

"I never said that."

"*I'm* saying it, Fath . . . Mr. Seafort. I wanted to tell you before . . ."

His tone had no inflection. "Before what?"

"Going groundside. To annul the adoption. We've—you've—made an awful mistake."

His eyes fell to the deck. Silence, that stretched eons. When he looked up, his eyes glistened. "I want more than anything to get out of this chair."

To strike me down.

"To hold you tight, squeeze this nonsense out of you. But I can't, son. I think if I let go of these armrests, if I let the chair hold my weight, I'll pass out. So I'll have to communicate with mere words. You're my son and will stay so. No, don't interrupt, that's decided, and I've never had a moment's regret."

I turned away, thrust hands in pockets. "You know what I need? Rebalancing."

He frowned. Hormone rebalancing was the therapy of last resort for insuperable emotional problems, and bore a well-deserved stigma. "Let's not overreact—"

"Oh, Fath, can't you see? Back home, I caused a rift between the Church and Anthony. Then I tried to kill you. I couldn't stop Kevin's panic when the alien came, and so he died. Outside the courthouse, I had a chance to save Anth, and blew it. How much more will you forgive?"

"Don't, son. That's not how—"

"I skulked outside the bridge listening to you and Mr. Tolliver, and again in sickbay. I swore I wouldn't, but . . ." My fist beat my leg. "I can't help doing vile things. Do you know, I was sneering at Andy Ghent the moment he was shot? And then, today. I mean, yesterday. Would Derek Carr have sneaked around listening at hatches?"

"Don't berate yourself for—"

"Tell me!"

"No, he wouldn't."

"But I did. That's who I am!" My cheeks were damp.

Ever so carefully, Fath let go of the armrest, keyed the caller. "Dr. Romez to the Captain's cabin, flank." He set it down.

"I mean it, about annulling the adoption. It was a fine gesture—a lovely gesture, Fath—but I'm not worth it and—"

"Son, don't do this to yourself!"

"—even Mik despises me. You should have seen the look on his—"

The hatch flew open. Dr. Romez burst in. "What—"

"—and I deserved it!"

"He needs a sedative. I'm afraid he may hurt himself."

"I do not! You weren't listening!" It was a hoarse scream. "Get away from me!" I tried to evade Romez's grasp.

"Easy, joey." He fished in his bag.

"I don't want to be calm, I want to face the truth! Why can't you understand?" I kicked and struggled, but Romez had my only arm. Something stung my shoulder.

Sobbing, hiccuping, dizzy, I let him guide me to my bed. Someone pulled off my shoes. I curled in a ball.

"I'm next." Fath. "I surrender. I'll take your deepsleep, but I need Anselm first."

"Why, may I ask?"

"I won't be lucid for a while." Fath's tone was grim. "I can't go on like this. I'll take to my bed and wait it out."

I took a long, shuddering breath.

"If you'd done that when you came aboard, you might—"

"Doctor, for the love of God!" It was reprimand, plea, or both.

"Sorry, sir." A grunt. "There. Ease back on the bed, if you can. I've got you."

"Page Anselm." Fath waited until Romez put down the caller. "What about, um, you know."

"No need to lower your voice. Randy's out cold. I'll look after him."

I gritted my teeth. I didn't *want* looking after.

"No, what *about* him?"

"His outburst? Not unusual, in cases of profound depression."

"Of what?" Fath.

"He's overwhelmed by loss after loss. His father, whom he loved dearly, his nephew the Stadholder, his best friend Dakko, his home, even one of his limbs. No wonder he's depressed."

A silence. "Why didn't you tell me?"

"Tell you?" The doctor's voice rose an octave. "How could you not know?"

"It's not my . . . I don't think in terms of . . . Lord, what have I done to him?"

A knock at the hatch.

"Saved him. In every way possible."

"Lieutenant Anselm reporting, sir."

"A moment, Tad. Saved him? Look at him."

"He's overwrought. Not unheard of in adolescent—"

"Don't joke of it!"

Romez said quietly, "I'm not, sir. We can give him mood levelers, if he needs them. What's important—"

"He spoke of rebalancing."

"He's not unbalanced, just distraught. You need to address his feelings of low worth."

Anselm cleared his throat. "I'd best wait outside, sir."

"Be seated and be silent. How, Doctor?"

"Be his father, Mr. Seafort. That's what he needs. Now, say what you will to Lieutenant Anselm. I'm about to knock you out."

From Fath, a sigh. I drifted on billowy clouds, until his voice came anew. "Tad, I'm leaving the outrider in your hands. Do what you can."

There was something I ought to say. I struggled to wake.

"If Harry wants to leave, sir?"

"Let him, of course."

"Aye aye, sir. I'll do my best." Anselm paused. "You watched us this morning, didn't you? We gained a few more words, but I'm at a standstill as far as real communication."

"Murf." My mouth was full of cotton.

"We know they want peace." Fath.

"So it seems, sir, but to achieve it we need to deal in abstracts, and I've no idea how."

"I don't—I can't . . . all I know, Tad, is that I can't think. Hell itself can be no worse than . . ." His voice grew tight. "Sorry. No point in self-pity. I'll be skipping a few sessions; Dr. Romez will have me asleep."

"Yes, sir."

"All right, Doctor, do your worst."

With a mighty effort, I roused myself enough to fall out of bed. "Wai." I cleared my throat. "Wait."

The three of them stared, their expressions beyond description.

"Couple a things." I grinned foolishly. No, that didn't seem right. I forced myself to frown. "Jus'a sec. I'm fuzzy."

"Romez, you said he'd be asleep! Tad, help him into—"

"Tolliver, f'r one," I said conversationally. "Hates Harry. Fath can' leave him in charge. Ol' Tad won' be able to . . ." I waved vaguely. The fog was closing in.

"Hold off, Doctor." Fath pushed aside the medgun. "Perhaps I'd better have a word with—"

"Sir, you're on the ragged edge. Let me—"

"No, Randy has a point." With an effort, Fath tried to breathe deeply. "Edgar and I go back a long way, and I treasure him, but he loathes the fish. At this juncture, I can't leave him in charge."

Romez shrugged. "That's not for me to—"

I blurted, "An' talkin' ta Harry. Lemme help."

"Randy, you're in no condition to—"

"Helped you before." I yawned prodigiously. "Wanna take my mind offa m'self?"

Fath tried to turn on an elbow to study me. Something jarred; he went white. After a moment he said through clenched teeth, "Anything else?"

"Yeah." But I couldn't think what.

Anselm hauled me back onto my bunk.

The pillow was so damned inviting. But I pried open my eyes. "Tommy."

"What?"

"Middy Yost. Torturing him. I was listenin' at hatch." I curled up, clutched my pillow. "Stop 'em, Fath." My tone was drowsy.

"What do you mean, son?"

I closed my eyes. Voices murmured, and at last the world faded out.

I sat up abruptly. "Urg."

"Shhh, you'll wake Pa." Mikhael.

"Shhh, I'll wake *me*." I fell back with a thump.

"A call to Battle Stations couldn't wake the Captain, sir."

After a time I reopened my eyes, peered past Mik at the strange voice. An attentive med tech perched on a stool near Fath's bed. He grinned. "Captain will be out for another watch, at least."

Mik said, "Randy's up, and they sedated him the same time—"

"Randy had a sedative; the Captain's in deepsleep." The tech leaned forward, clapped his hands sharply. Fath didn't stir. "See?"

"Stop that!" Mik's tone was indignant.

"Aye aye, Mr. Tamarov. But no need to talk softly."

Mik tried to look stern. "No need to talk at all." To me, "How are you feeling?"

Hungry, but that could wait. I regarded him glumly. "You hate me."

He raised an eyebrow. It was just what Fath would have done.

"For spying. I told Fath, I think." I searched my scattered memory. "Yeah. Just before . . ."

"You told him lots of things." Mikhael's glance was frosty.

My stomach growled. "Shouldn't I have? What did I say? Can we go eat?" Perhaps that wasn't the most logical order, but I was doing my best. It wasn't easy, thinking through dense fog.

Mik eyed Fath dubiously, checked his watch. "They're still serving in officers' mess."

Cautiously, I worked my way out of bed. "I'm not an officer."

"You might as well be," he said sourly.

"What does that mean?"

"Change your shirt." He pulled a fresh one from the drawer, helped me peel the old one off. Despite his tone, his hands were agreeably gentle.

In the corridor, I asked again, "What did you mean?"

"You caused quite a ruckus."

"I don't remember much."

"I'll fill you in. Understand, wardroom affairs are private. You're not to repeat them."

"If you don't trust me . . ."

He glared. "Do you want lunch or not?" Before I could answer he stalked off.

I trotted after. "All right, you have my word."

Mikhael steered me past the bridge to the small compartment that served as officers' mess. Half a dozen officers lingered over their trays. Lieutenant Frand was in animated discussion with a couple of middies at the long table.

The mess was serving soup and sandwiches. It was too much trouble to choose; I took both.

I tore into a chicken salad. It was wonderful. Today, anything would have been wonderful. Don't let Dr. Romez give you a sedative if you're on a diet.

"I heard this from Tad Anselm." Mik's voice was low. "After you passed out, Pa called in Mr. Tolliver. They had a bit of a row. Pa made him promise to leave Tad and the alien alone, unless it tried to break loose. And Pa's just off watch for a while, not relieved."

"That's only fair."

"It's not normal."

"But—"

"Stuff it, there's more." He glanced about. "What in God's own hell did you say about Mr. Riev?"

"Nothing."

"Don't lie."

"Noth—oh!" I shrugged. "I never mentioned Riev. Just Tommy Yost."

"Pa actually asked Tad and Mr. Tolliver what was going on."

"So?"

"Don't you understand? Midshipman affairs are left to the first middy. Senior officers never pay attention, not officially. Tolliver didn't know, of course; he pays us no heed off the bridge. But even though Tad's a lieutenant now, Pa asked him outright."

I asked, "Why?"

"That's what I want to know. What did you say?"

"I told Fath they were torturing Tommy."

"You stupid—" Mik slammed down a spoon, startling Lieutenant Frand. "What business was it of yours?"

I didn't really answer. "Is it always like that?"

"You've no right to stick your nose—"

"You joeys having a problem?" Ms. Frand loomed over us.

"No, ma'am." Mikhael shot to his feet.

"Then decorum is in order. Especially as you chose to bring a guest." Frand's glance swept over me, in cold disfavor.

"Aye aye, ma'am. Sorry." Mik waited until his lieutenant had gone. "You'd no right to tell Pa—"

"Is that what hazing's like for middies? Cold hate?"

"I won't discuss—"

I cried, "Then why'd you bring me here?"

"Shhh!" After a moment Mikhael asked, "What were they saying?"

At Riev's venomous "You little shit," Mik flinched. "Alon gets carried away."

"He's done it before?"

A long silence. "Yes." Then, "Since they came back aboard, Mr. Riev hasn't let up on Yost for a minute."

My hand shot out, pressed his. "Mik, if Tommy's done wrong, he doesn't need to be told." My voice trembled. "Believe me, he knows." I busied myself with my soup.

Mikhael cleared his throat. "Anselm was a middy not so long past, in the wardroom with Alon. Lord God knows what he said to the Captain. Then *I* was called in." His face went dark. "Imagine it, my lieutenant and the Captain—Pa and my friend Tad—ordering me to tell them what was going on in the wardroom. Demanding I betray Mr. Riev."

I said softly, "Did you?"

"I tried not to." His gaze was distant. "But Pa was hurting so, he could barely speak. How could I argue?" His voice caught. "I told them Mr. Riev was a bit rough. That like all of us, he knew Yost had gotten Andy killed. And Pa wouldn't let it go. He made me repeat exactly what I'd heard." To my amazement, Mik's eyes were damp. "It was a direct order. And . . . I'd heard . . . well, Tommy cried a few times. At night, after Mr. Riev was done reaming him. Before he went out to work off demerits."

I set down my soup spoon, kept quite still.

"Pa told Mr. Tolliver he'd lived with cruelty too long, that it had been his constant companion on all the ships he'd sailed. That, by Lord God, it was time for it to stop. That Mr. Riev couldn't be left in charge." Now it was Mikhael's hand that caught mine. "I begged and pleaded. He ordered me silent. And he said to pull Mr. Riev from the wardroom."

"For how long?"

"Nobody knows. It'll go on Alon's record. It could ruin him. And imagine running into him in the corridors, if he's beached!"

I shrugged. "Better for Tommy."

His hand tightened on my wrist. "Don't you understand, you frazzing grode? I'm senior; I'll be first middy."

"Congrat—"

"No!" His eyes searched mine, saw that I didn't comprehend. "I wanted it, dreamed of it, but not like this! They all know the Captain called me to his cabin. When Riev is suspended, they'll every one think I washed our laundry in public, and hate me. With reason. Because *I did*."

I said, "It was a direct ord—"

"Who'll believe that?"

"I'll tell—"

"You will *not!*"

I tried to wrest free my arm. "Please, Mik."

Sullenly, he let me go.

I swallowed. "Mikhael . . . the truth. Is Riev a good officer?"

CHILDREN OF HOPE   377

"He coached me in nav. He saw that we kept current on—"

"Is he?"

"He's quite devout." After a moment, Mik added reluctantly, "He has a cruel streak."

"Will you?"

"Christ, I hope not."

"What about Tommy?"

"I hate what Yost did."

"Do you *know* what he did?"

"Everyone says—"

"Were you there?"

A long pause. "No, I was organizing the refueling."

"It was . . ." I searched for a word that fit. "Chaos. Remember? Night had fallen, we were waiting for the godda—for the shuttle to fuel . . . Fath might have gotten himself shot, if they hadn't stopped him from going outside. We were all scared, and the radios kept buzzing with joeys calling each other . . ." I stared at my congealing soup. "I don't think Yost realized . . ." Smoke curled from Andy Ghent's jacket. The stench of burning flesh . . . I pushed away my bowl.

After a moment, Mik sighed. "We'd better go. I don't want to leave Pa for long."

"What about the wardroom?"

"Riev's still bunking there, for the moment. Frand—*Ms.* Frand and Tad are keeping a close eye. Officially, I don't know he's to be beached. For now, I'm seconded to cabin duty, to watch the two of you."

I followed Mik into the gray corridor. As we passed the bridge, he snapped his fingers. "Oh, one more thing. You're to help Mr. Anselm with Harry, soon as you're physically able."

28

FATH SLEPT ON. Med techs tended his needs. Sometimes, perhaps for propriety, they chased me from the cabin.

From time to time they woke him, barely, enough that he might look about with a vacant expression, eat soft foods. Then, a touch of the medgun, and his eyes closed.

Restless, I wandered the corridors, taking advantage of the relief from parenting. I could stay up as late as I wanted, wear what I chose; Mikhael was no obstacle. And I had my run of holovids, with no one to look over my shoulder.

Still, from time to time I was lonely. Well, to be honest, it was most of the time. I missed Fath, despite his occasional scowl, his tendency to rein me in. I sought out adults I knew.

On the third day, I was full of dinner. Tad Anselm and I were walking Corrine Sloan and Janey to their cabin, followed dutifully by her two guards, master-at-arms's mates personally approved by Mr. Janks. Politely, they'd detached themselves a couple of paces that we might enjoy a moment's privacy, but their stunners were within an instant's grasp.

As we passed an open lounge, Corrine let go of Janey, clutched my forearm. "Listen." I wished joeys wouldn't keep doing that; everyone from Mik to Fath to Dr. Romez seized me at will. It wasn't as if I could pry myself free with my other hand.

"*For behold, the Lord cometh out of His place to punish the inhabitants of the earth for their iniquity; the earth shall also disclose her blood, and no more cover her slain.*" Reverend Pandeker looked up from his holovid, his steady gaze meeting each passenger and crewman in turn. "*In that day the Lord with His sore and great and strong sword shall punish Leviathan the piercing serpent, even leviathan that crooked serpent*"—a long glance to the porthole, and beyond—"*and He shall slay the dragon that is in the sea.*"

Anselm frowned. "Not very subtle." His voice was low. "Care to guess which leviathan he has in mind?"

I muttered, "Next he'll be preaching about the whore of Babylon." I grimaced at his evident surprise. Fath's verses were good for *something*. "*And the ten horns which thou sawest upon the beast, these shall hate the whore, and shall make her desolate and naked, and shall eat her flesh, and shall burn her with fire.*"

Anselm's eyes narrowed. He took my arm from Corrine, propelled me across the corridor. "Listen here, joey." Little Janey watched, openmouthed.

"Let him go, Mr. Anselm." Corrine's eyes were troubled.

Tad's voice was barely a whisper. "There'll be no talk of fire and burning, not—"

"I wasn't—all I meant was—"

"Not on this ship. Understand?"

"Yes!" At last he let me go. I rubbed my stinging arm against the bulkhead. "I wasn't suggesting . . ." I felt a clumsy oaf. I stamped my foot.

Gently, Corrine took my arm in hers. "Keep walking, we don't want their attention." When we were safely out of earshot she said to Anselm, "No use pretending it isn't what they're saying."

"How do you know? Has anyone dared—"

"No one's threatened me. Not directly." Her face was flushed. "You

"Beg. Entreat. Implore." Ms. Frand added hastily, "I acknowledge it's your decision, sir, but we're none of us safe with him aboard."

Fath rose easily in the light gravity. Raising his arm cautiously, he rubbed the back of his neck. "Joanne?"

"I concur. He's hijacked spacecraft, shot it out in courtrooms with public officials. Today he put us in risk of decompression. To say nothing of how you met."

My cheeks flamed.

"I'll go further." Her gaze was steady. "I urged Tolliver to relieve you and resolve the matter of his own accord."

"And he said? No, pardon me, I shouldn't have asked. I'm quite sure Edgar will present his opinion in his inimitable style. Impulsive . . ." Fath took a few tentative steps. "Yes, Randy is that. But I'm capable of restraining—"

"You haven't been." Her tone was tart.

"Please don't interrupt, Ms. Skor; I'm Captain and the office deserves courtesy." He waved aside her muttered apology. "Yes, I've been injured and it's left Randy . . . at loose ends."

I stirred, opened my mouth, shut it quickly. All I could do was make matters worse.

"Sir . . ." Ms. Skor looked uncomfortable. "May I speak freely?"

"I thought you already had." But he waved her on.

"I know you meant well by making him ship's boy. You meant well by adopting him. But now, place him groundside in the care of relatives. A Captain customarily leaves family ashore, and this case makes clear why. If he wasn't your son, the boy would have been tossed in a cell or put off ship ages ago. It's made worse in that officers are afraid to curb him lest they incur your—"

"Are *you* afraid?"

"No." She held his eye. "I know you well enough to be certain you'd never take revenge on officers who did what they thought best. But what about lieutenants who aren't in your inner circle? Or the middies?"

"Point taken." Fath eased himself into his favorite chair, the only one not in use. "Shall I issue a standing order that you're all free to beat Randy?"

"It's no joking matter." Ms. Skor stood. "Tolliver had him thrashed, but that settles nothing. No one cares to hurt you by proffering charges, but any other joey in his shoes would face court-martial. If you were objective, you'd charge him yourself. Send him ashore."

"I suppose Jerence could find some refuge for us . . ." Fath sounded reflective. "Perhaps in the Venturas . . . but how, Joanne? The regs are quite clear: they don't permit a Captain to resign."

"No one said anything about—"

"Surely you don't suggest I cast aside my troubled fourteen-year-old, and sail away about my business?"

I gulped.

Fath eased himself from his chair, took cautious steps, bent to pat me absently on the shoulder.

Ms. Frand cleared his throat. "There's another solution."

Fath raised an eyebrow.

"You're aware, sir . . . Bishop Scanlen . . . while you were in deep-sleep . . ."

Smoothly, Ms. Skor got to her feet. "I'd like to make it clear," she said, "Sarah doesn't speak for me in this. We agreed not to raise . . ."

"We *have* to speak of it! We can't go about pretending—" Frand made a gesture, frowned at her fingers, ran them absently through her hair. "Mr. Seafort, are you impeached? Our Bishop says so. Isn't the best solution that you go ashore and face—"

"NO!" I lurched from my bunk. "*I'll* go. Not him."

Fath's firm hand spun me about. "You're here to see what trouble you cause, not to interfere. Be silent!" His face was grim.

"Yes, sir!" Or should it be, "Aye aye, sir"? Was I on duty? Probably, but—

"So, Sarah." Fath turned slowly. "You'd have me answer at last for my sins."

Ms. Frand was silent.

"And Corrine Sloan? Should I escort her to her burning?"

"She's the reason . . ." Frand bit her lip. "You're impeached for harboring *her*. What choice have we?"

"I'm quite sure in my heart," said Fath, "Lord God doesn't demand her trial."

"Our Church demands it. It's the same!"

A long silence, which I thought would stretch forever.

"No," said Fath. "It isn't."

We sat alone in our cabin. Fath rested his head in his hands.

After a time I cleared my throat. "Fath?"

His tone was harsh. "Open the Bible. Memorize a dozen verses."

"But—"

"What do you say?"

"Yes, sir!" Today, I didn't dare trifle with him. Sweating, I padded to his bedside, retrieved the worn Bible, pawed through its pages. Something easy.

He that spareth his rod hateth his son: but he that loveth him chaste-neth—No, not that! Hurriedly, I looked through other verses.

Fath muttered.

"Excuse me, sir?"

"It is the same." His eyes were bleak. "If not, why did He bring His congregations together? You know the story of Babel?"

"*And they said go to, let us build us a city and a tower, whose top may reach unto heaven.*" Genesis eleven something; Fath had made me memorize it one evening when I'd been especially sullen.

"Just so. *And He came down, to confound men's speech, that they be scattered,* and their hubris forestalled." Fath rose, to pace easily in the lightened gravity. "Consider the Reformation."

The *what*? I managed not to shrug.

"I've always thought it an echo, a parallel, as it were, of Babel. The Lord divided Christianity into myriad irreconcilable sects, that none of us be too sure we knew His Word. But if that's so, what of the miracle of Reunification?"

It didn't seem to call for answer. I kept my eyes on the Bible, taking in not a word.

"Don't you see, son? Nigh on two centuries past, He relented. The Catholic-Episcopalian reconciliation, the Baptist embrace, the Great Conclave, the final exclusion of the heretic Pentecostals . . ." He paused before my bed. "With His blessing, we built us a tower, and saw His Word with the same eye. That tower—His latter-day gift—is the Church in which we worship. The Reunification Church. That it exists is proof of His blessing. How can it not speak for Him?"

Slowly, I closed the book, knew I didn't dare say my mind. "I'm only a glitched joeykid," I said bitterly. "What I say doesn't matter."

"Except to me."

I climbed off the bed, my rear smarting. "All that . . . what's that word you taught me? Sophistry. It's all bullshit, Fath. They're evil. You know it!"

The fierce light of his eyes surveyed me like giant searchlights. Slowly, they dimmed. "Misguided perhaps."

"Anthony's murder. The prison farms. Corrine's fiancé, John. Now, Mr. Branstead." My voice was inexorable.

"A few men are twisted. But the soul is the soul of Chri—"

"Evil!" I spat out the word. "They drove my dad to tears. Derek cried!" It was the unforgivable sin. "Even he couldn't forgive—"

"Local men, far removed—"

"The Patriarchs, themselves! Their greed and lust for power brought about the naval rebellion. Thanks to them, *Galactic* . . ." I swiped at damp eyes, ran a sleeve across my nose. "If it weren't for them, your Arlene would . . . and Dad . . ." I couldn't go on.

"You never heard me say a word against . . ."

"Mikhael told me." Had I betrayed a confidence? Too late, now.

Fath shook his head. "He wasn't supposed to know."

"Hiding villainy doesn't erase it." My voice grew shrill. "Where's the famous Seafort courage? Where's the example you're supposed to set? How am I to know truth if you won't admit it?" I'd get another beating. And deserve it.

His voice was a whisper. "Do you know what you ask?"

A knock at the hatch. We both swiveled. Muttering an oath, Fath went to open it.

"Hallo," said Edgar Tolliver. "Am I interrupting?"

Wearily, Fath stood aside. "What brings you?"

"I wanted you to hear me out before you forgave him." Mr. Tolliver eyed me with distaste.

"Have your say." It was a growl.

"You won't proffer charges; it's not in you." Tolliver made it a statement, not a question. "So the issue is how to safeguard *Olympiad,* inasmuch as Ship's Boy Carr is a lunatic."

"Please . . ." Fath trudged to his bunk, eased himself onto it. I tried to make myself small.

"Sir, do you think for a minute he'll obey you more than the rest of us?"

"No doubt you propose a solution?"

"You won't set him ashore, as Frand and Skor would like; I told them not to bother suggesting it. Would you let me write him up? Appoint any officers you wish as court. They'll be fair."

"I can't stop you."

"Nonsense." Tolliver's tone was gentle. "I won't hurt you so deeply as that."

Fath covered his face. When he spoke, his voice was muffled. "You'd better go."

"In a moment. Does he understand what he's done?"

"We haven't discussed it yet."

"Hmmm." Tolliver eyed us. "He's been weeping, and you're too upset to meet my eye. What's Sarah Frand said to you?"

"I don't care to discuss—"

"The stupid twit brought up Bishop Scanlen's proclamation?"

"Edgar!"

"You're only hours out of deepsleep, and shaky; she had no right. Now, as for Randy . . ." He folded his arms. "Remove him from the ship's company. Bar him from all areas where passengers are banned, including Level 1, where he's too near the bridge. No matter what, keep the boy as far as humanly possible from that bloody outrider. Assign him a cabin belowdecks, join him for dinner, or whenever else you choose. Then we might make Kall's Planet alive."

Fath said nothing.

"If you won't, I'll issue the orders. You've but to give the word. No, that's too much to ask. Just don't forbid it. I'll Log them tonight before—"

"I forbid it."

Tolliver wagged a reproving finger at me. "See what you've done?"

Fath said mildly, "Leave him be. I know you're irked."

"IRKED?" Tolliver's voice soared an octave. "I'll show him irked. The day he's healed, I'll irk his rump so fast—"

"*Enough!*" Fath's voice was a lash. "Randy, stand."

Apprehensively, I did so.

"They're right, you know. Frand and Ms. Skor, and Edgar." Fath paced before me. "When Romez summoned me from Lethe—"

"Huh?"

"Sleep, you dolt. The river of oblivion. Forgetfulness; we'll need attend your classical education. Dr. Romez wakened me, gave me stimulants. When I could prop open my eyes, I played back the holos of your sessions with Harry. Then I skimmed through the Log. Unbelievable. How dare you speak so to my first lieutenant?"

When did he mean? In Mr. Tolliver's cabin, or this afternoon, when I told him to go—

"Answer!"

I gulped. Fath slapped me hard. "That's for foul language to an adult!" Another slap. My head rocked. "You'll show courtesy to Mr. Tolliver. To me. To every adult aboard, down to the merest middy!"

He raised his hand again. I squealed.

"What?"

"Yessir!" I spun away, hugged myself one-handed.

"Doesn't that melt your heart?" Tolliver's scorn was withering. "Our poor widdle joeykid is contrite. His shoulders shake, snot drips from his— please, sir, don't hold back on my account. Slap him silly, but it won't do the slightest good. And that's my point. I ordered him out of that blessed section four and away from the alien. Despite his oath of obedience—you did extract one when he enlisted, didn't you?—he not only ignored my command, he told me—"

"What he told Bishop Andori, at the start of this fiasco." Fath's tone was dry. "He has a penchant for the phrase. Next time, a bar of soap—"

"Damn it, Nick, you avoid the issue! He won't obey orders, and we're in mortal peril, with an outrider aboard and a fish standing off our beam!"

"All right, Edgar, I hear you." Wearily, Fath sat. "What of it, son? You broke your oath of obedience?"

"Yeah, I did." I wiped my nose with a sleeve; it was all I had. "But Harry was leav—"

"But?"

"I had to, don't you see? Else when you went home—"

"That's no excuse."

"Haven't you ever broken—"

"Once, son. It's tormented me ever since."

The woman Captain Seafort had shot, after giving his oath not to harm her; I'd heard the tale from Dad. By violating his oath, Fath had saved his ship. But to him, it didn't matter.

Fath asked, "Don't you see what you've done? An oath is a sacred commitment to God." For a moment, he looked like a Patriarch, one of the old ones in the Bible.

I said defiantly, "I don't believe in God." I wondered if he'd strike me.

Fath took it rather well, considering. "I wouldn't go about proclaiming the view." A wry shrug. "You see the dilemma? If you won't adhere to an oath, I can't trust you. No one can."

"But I do! I mean, most of the time."

"Oh, son." For a moment, I was afraid he would weep. "It's not nearly enough."

A long silence, in which Tolliver waited patiently, and I struggled for calm.

"Very well, Edgar." Fath's tone was lifeless. "I'll do as you suggest. I won't banish him, that's going too far. But he won't be crew. I'll keep him off the bridge. And away from the outrider."

"Fath!" I rushed to him, grabbed his lapel, perhaps in entreaty. "Where's Harry, right now?"

He glanced at the screen. "Working with Anselm."

"And—"

"Thanks to you." Despite the admission, his eyes held resolve. "But I can't risk—"

"What words?"

"They've got 'hour,' 'day,' 'year,' more or less. 'E' for 'fear.' By the way, that was a brilliant leap of intuition. Even Edgar would agree, wouldn't you? And 'not fear,' I suppose we could call it 'calm.' Anselm's trying to extend it to 'peace.' He's showing Harry . . . well, never mind. You did good work, but no more." His tone had a finality I dreaded.

I contemplated my calamity.

I'd lost my role, my membership in *Olympiad*'s family. Yet, Fath refused absolutely to put me ashore. He still treated me as his son—he'd near slapped my head off, even before Tolliver.

I supposed I should be grateful. So why was I sick with loss?

"Satisfied, Edgar?"

I snorted; perhaps I ought to ask the same.

Heavily, one hand on my shoulder as if in consolation, Fath took up the caller. "Bridge? Ms. Skor, an entry into the Log. As of this moment, Randolph Carr is—"

A chime. For a moment, I thought it was Fath's frazzing clock. He looked around, annoyed. "Edgar, see what they want."

Tolliver crossed to the holoscreen over Fath's bed, dialed up the speaker. "Yes, Tad?"

"Joanne, 'By order of the Captain'—today's date, of course—'Randolph Carr is dismissed from—' "

"Sir, we need the Captain." Tad's voice, from section four, was tense. "Right now, I think."

"Nick . . . ?" Tolliver.

"I heard. Just a moment, Joanne." Clearly annoyed, he thrust me aside, peered into the screen. "Yes?"

"Harry's just . . . Jess, a close-up on the latest plate. Sir, if I'm reading it right . . ."

"Out with it, joey!"

The screen lurched. An etched plate came into view, showing a stick figure of a man, the symbol we'd selected for "human." "He was showing us people, God knows why. Uh, sorry. I kept erasing, to say we didn't understand. Then this." The screen lurched again. When the focus cleared, it showed another human.

It was off balance.

One of its arms was missing.

Fath blinked, eyed me curiously.

I protested, "I didn't—"

"Sir, we said we didn't understand. So it drew this."

An outrider alone. An "E." An outrider with a regular human. "E." Fear.

An outrider next to a one-armed human. "Not E."

Ice crawled down my spine.

Fath gaped.

Edgar Tolliver threw up his hands, stalked from the cabin.

* * * *

I was on Harry's detail, by the skin of my teeth.

I was still ship's boy, by the same margin.

Fath had sent me down to reassure Harry. Though Tad Anselm watched me like a hawk, I'd used the opportunity to expand "not E," devising a symbol for "like." Harry likes Randy. Randy likes Harry. We agreed, and perhaps each of us even knew what the other meant. Finally, yawning and bleary, I turned the clock forward, pointed to the time, hoping he'd understand I'd be back in the morning.

A long trudge back to our cabin. No sooner had I arrived than Fath cornered me. I would remain crew—he had little choice, as the alien seemed to favor me—but by blessed Lord God, I wouldn't step one inch out of line, did I hear? I'd be polite to anything that moved, and obey all orders. Most especially Anselm's, or Ms. Frand's, when I was around Harry. Only once did I raise an objection, and earned a cuff. Derek Carr would be outraged at my behavior, and so was he. Yes, my intuition was brilliant—yes, I'd saved our negotiations—but that was no excuse; insolence and disobedience wouldn't be tolerated. Was that quite clear, joeyboy?

Rubbing my cheek, I abandoned my defenses, agreed with whatever he said, determined to nurse my outrage through the night. Hell, through the cruise. Through my teens.

Fath seemed to take no notice. Instead, while I undressed for bed—and long after I'd climbed in—he perched on my bunk, recalling days long past, when he and Dad were shipmates. To be polite, of course, I had to listen. Ask a question now and then. Occasionally wipe a tear.

Sometimes adults were beyond reason.

32

IF I WASN'T SO tense, I'd have laughed at the procession. Fath, who'd excused himself from the bridge for the occasion, Corrine Sloan, hand in hand with Janey, and my brother Mikhael, all accompanied me down the corridor to sickbay, where Dr. Romez was waiting to graft my prosth.

This one was a temp, a mechano powered by a tiny Valdez permabattery. The flesh and blood replacement derived from my stem cells wouldn't be grown for three or four months yet.

I'd told Fath again that I didn't want it—since liftoff I'd told him 'til I was blue in the face—but he'd merely smiled and told me to wash thoroughly before reporting to Romez.

Didn't I have a right to make my own medical decisions?

Perhaps in theory, son, but he was exercising that right on my behalf, and get moving, joey, or would I rather knock on Mr. Tolliver's hatch and tell him I was still misbehaving?

Only middies were subjected to such scandalous mistreatment, I said darkly. If he was going to abuse me like a middy, why didn't he make me one? But by then we'd reached sickbay, and he managed to avoid a reply.

Well, I'd done my best to prepare for my absence from section four.

It had been two days since our breakthrough with Harry. New words were coming fast, though we were never quite sure we truly understood each other. I mean, once you have "minute," "hour" is simple. But abstracts are more complex. Did an outrider really mean what we did by "fear"?

Knowing I'd be laid up—three days minimum, Fath had ordered—I'd sketched out several concepts for Anselm and Ms. Frand to work on.

Odd. It no longer seemed noteworthy that I casually advised joeys who were not only my superiors, but my elders by a decade or, in Ms. Frand's case, more.

Harry's summoning me had brought about a subtle change even in Tad Anselm, whom I considered my friend despite his occasional sharp remarks. As long as I framed my suggestions with proper courtesy and masked my occasional impatience, Tad deferred to me more and more frequently.

I'd tried to tell Harry I'd be gone a day or two.

I hoped he understood.

I went to sleep with Fath patting my hand, and Mikhael perched at bedside chatting amiably.

I woke bathed in euphoria, my torso swathed in white bandages, a weird skin-toned limb protruding. It looked about as much like an arm as . . . I groped for a sufficiently odious comparison.

"Ah, there you are."

I blinked. And blinked again, from sheer surprise. "What are you doing here?"

It was Mr. Branstead who sat by my bed. Dark circles rimmed his eyes, and he'd lost weight. His knee was bandaged, and he carried a cane. "I told Nick I'd keep an eye. He's belowdecks, meeting with your, ah, friend."

"What're you doing *on ship*!" Did I sound surly? I certainly didn't mean to; I'd missed him.

"Oh, that. I've been, well, expelled." Mr. Branstead grimaced. "Scanlen demanded I be tried. He proposes to try everyone, of late. Rather single-minded. Especially as to Nick and Corrine. But McEwan intervened. The Terran Ambassador."

"I know." Anthony's enemy, and now mine.

"They'd framed a capital charge, but no doubt it occurred to them that I had friends in the U.N. bureaucracy. Felt a trial would stir up too much of a tempest, I suppose. Oh, did I mention that yesterday, with Scanlen's full approval, McEwan declared recolonialization? They—"

"He WHAT?" I reared out of my pillows, quivering with indignation. Dad's lifework, and Anth's as well, swept away! We'd once more be slaves of the frazzing U.N. If there was a God, He'd strike down that mealymouthed McEwan and His Bishop with a bolt of—

But there was no God. I'd become ever more convinced, and this was the final proof. Somehow, I'd get Fath to set aside recolonialization, though he wouldn't want to, for propriety's sake. I fumed, barely hearing Mr. Branstead.

"McEwan and the Bishop have appointed a government, and every member's firmly in their pockets. Resistance groundside is sparse, though the Station's holding out; they're Anthony's joeys. So it was best I be gotten quietly out of the way. McEwan put the choice to me in my prison cell. I'd be released if I consented to take passage on *Olympiad*. Otherwise . . . Given the alternative, I agreed. Now, the trick will be convincing Nick to sail, before they turn their petulance on him. How are you feeling?"

It caught me by surprise. I considered. "Good, actually." I peered down. "Did it take?"

"You'll have to ask Romez, but I saw something wriggle a moment ago."

Despite myself, I flexed what would have been my muscles, and was surprised to feel something move against my stomach.

"So." Mr. Branstead beamed down at me. "I hear you're a hero."

"A what?" My voice soared to a squeak.

"Single-handedly, at great personal risk, you coaxed the outrider to stay. An amazing feat."

"Who told you that?"

"Nick. He was quite proud."

The hatch opened. Dr. Romez peered in. "Tell me you haven't been flexing it."

"Once or twice." My tone was defensive.

"Don't. Not for a few days."

"It's hard not . . ."

"Use the self-control for which you're famous." The doctor's tone was dry.

"Oh," said Mr. Branstead innocently. "Was there something I missed?"

Fath sighed, rubbing his back. "One gets used to light grav."

Mr. Tolliver was in our cabin for his customary nightcap. I was released from sickbay on what might be called medical furlough: I'd made enough of a nuisance of myself that Dr. Romez had sent me away for a few hours. If I felt well enough, I might even be allowed to sleep in my own bunk.

Neither Tolliver nor Fath made mention of the depleted bottle, but I decided discretion was the better part of valor, and tried to be unobtrusive. It was hard, because my graft throbbed and ached. I wanted to flex my fingers, or whatever they were, but didn't dare.

"If you won't stay on Level 1," Tolliver told Fath, "let me reduce the grav on Two. Harry can handle zero gee."

"But the passengers can't."

"Sir, speaking of passengers . . ."

Fath rubbed his eyes. "I know, I know." We were weeks late on our schedule, and Purser Li had his hands full with their complaints and restless irritation.

"And there are, um . . ." Tolliver shot me an uneasy glance. ". . . other reasons we should be on our way."

"Scanlen and McEwan? Yes, I suppose they could persuade Admiral Kenzig to relieve me. Please don't roll your eyes; I wouldn't pour you a drink in the boy's presence if I didn't trust his discretion."

"His what? I must have misheard." Tolliver favored me with a dark scowl. "Very well, let's discuss it openly. Say they go further and persuade Kenzig to order you groundside for trial?"

"If the order came from Admiralty, I'd comply, of course."

"I salute your yen for martyrdom. Have you considered Randy and Corrine?"

"Randy can live without me." Fath shot me a glance as if daring me to say otherwise.

"Nick, for God's . . ." Mr. Tolliver took a deep breath. "What if they order *him* groundside for execution? He killed Scanlen's deacons, and the Bishop's not a forgiving sort. When you're no longer Captain, he'll be beyond your protection. And you think they'll forget Corrine?"

"Let it be." Fath's voice was sharp.

"Sir, it won't go away by not thinking of it."

Fath's expression was more than vexed. I braced for an explosion. Instead, he cried, "What do you want of me?" He shot to his feet, paced with anguished vigor. "Yes, by trying to make peace with the aliens, I risk those I love. I KNOW!" A turn, a few awkward paces. "Moreover, I risk *Olympiad*, and the life of every soul aboard. It's what I do, always—" His tone dripped contempt. "—with good cause."

Uneasily, I climbed off my bunk.

"Often I get away with it, Edgar. But I gambled with *Galactic*, and lost. Bing, mark off Arlene. Oh, well. Bing, Derek Carr. Bing, a thousand others. You recall *Trafalgar*, and the cadets I lured to their doom? Bing, bing, bing!"

He threw up his hands. "I'm an angel of death. I put the lives of those I cherish in harm's way. Sometimes, I lose. Or rather, they lose!"

Tolliver pushed me aside, grabbed the bottle and a glass, poured a generous swig. He handed it to Fath.

"Can you possibly think, Edgar, that liquor will comfort me?" Fath's tone was bleak.

"Sir . . ." Tolliver sounded gentle. "We've been down that road. You did what must be done." Again, he proffered the glass.

"So, would you have me abandon our talks with Harry? Never in history have men and aliens spoken together. The moment must be seized." Fath took a reluctant sip, set the glass aside.

"Sir, what if it takes a month? Or three?"

Fath was silent.

"Say three full months pass. We might still seem a mere week from a breakthrough. We also have a duty to Admiralty, to our passengers and those who await us at Kall's Planet. When is enough?"

Fath turned to me. "He imagines that because I'm Captain, I have answers."

Tolliver shook his head. "No, I too have been Captain. You don't have solutions, Nick, merely the responsibility to provide them."

I cleared my throat. "What if . . ."

"Stay out of it, joey." Tolliver cocked a warning finger.

Who the hell was he to . . . No, don't aggravate Fath! Not now. "Sir, please!" I shifted from foot to foot, until Tolliver gave a reluctant nod. "What if . . ." I tried not to gesture with my mechanical arm; I was supposed to keep it still. "What if we told Harry to meet us elsewhere?" Silence. "Why do we have to talk *here*?"

Fath frowned. "How could we communicate where . . ."

"We have words for Fuse, and we're finally pinning down time. We think we agree on 'now': the second hand at twelve. All we need is the place. For example, home system would be 'Fuse months hundreds of dead fish, dozens of dead ships.' "

Tolliver said, "That describes Hope Nation as well as home." Of course. Fath had obliterated hundreds of fish by nuking Orbit Station, after the fish had taken out a third of the U.N. fleet.

Stubbornly, I shook my head. "Not if we preface it with 'Fuse.' That clearly implies going somewhere else, and other than here, only home system fought all-out battles."

Fath's tone was sharp. "Madness! We will *not* summon fish to home system!" He paced anew. "Admiralty would try me for treason, and rightly. How could we ever trust the fish not to renew the war?"

"You trust them here."

"This is only Hope . . ." After a time, he swallowed. "I'm sorry, son. A stupid thought. I trust them here because we met here. I have little choice."

The caller buzzed.

Fath sighed. "Now what?" He keyed it. "Seafort . . . He what? Good Lord. Just a moment." He keyed it off. "Edgar, it's Chris Dakko, from the Station. He's seeking asylum."

Despite my begging, they wouldn't let me go along. I suppose they were right, not that I'd ever admit it. My prosth graft was too recent, and suppose it flared up while I was en route?

Mikhael got to pilot the launch and dock it at the Station lock. Any middy yearned for the rare opportunity to sail a ship's launch. I didn't know why the privilege was so closely guarded; after all, it was good training. When Fath asked the first middy's recommendation of whom to send, Mik unhesitatingly proposed himself. Fath didn't seem surprised.

I wondered if Mr. Dakko knew the dissension his arrival had generated. Tolliver had objected strenuously. "Sir, he passionately hates the aliens."

"With good cause. We'll post guards."

"Better not to let him aboard."

"He's an old shipmate in adversity," said Fath. "And, Lord, the debt we owe him . . ." But Fath was wrong. I, more than he, bore the onus of Kevin's death.

"Well," mused Tolliver when the decision was made, "at least Scanlen won't wonder where his enemies lie. They'll all be aboard, praying devoutly that we Fuse."

Afterward, I'd made my reluctant way to sickbay; my shoulder had progressed from mild throbbing to a persistent gritty ache that left me clammy and clenching my teeth. Dr. Romez reproved me for not returning sooner, and administered a painkiller that soon set me right. From my bed, I begged Fath to let me resume work with Harry a day early. I would be on call, he said. If Harry asked for me, I could go. Grumbling at his negligible concession, I drifted to sleep. No, Lethe, he called it. It sounded very grown-up.

In the morning, a grim-faced Mikhael brought me breakfast and gossip. Mr. Dakko, calling on old friendships and perhaps dispensing a bribe or two, had slipped aboard a supply shuttle at Centraltown, and lifted off a step ahead of Scanlen's deacons who meant to detain him for his role in the death of Archbishop Andori.

But Bishop Scanlen was stalking bigger game. He promulgated a list of Corrine Sloan's "protectors and confederates" that included Mr. Dakko, Jerence Branstead, Fath, and to my surprise, me. Whatever offices any of us held were declared vacant, and we were to be sent groundside to Lord God's justice "forthwith."

Mr. Tolliver, who'd been on the bridge, had ordered the entire transmission classified secret, on the grounds that Scanlen's writ ran to the planet of Hope Nation, and not to vessels that might be in orbit around it. Neither *Olympiad*'s passengers nor crew were made aware of the proclamation. Of course, the whole ship knew in no time.

Meanwhile, Tommy Yost attained ten demerits and reported for chastisement to Mr. Tolliver. I felt more sympathy than I'd expected; my own welts still smarted, and I was embarrassed no end when changing clothes before Fath.

As soon as he and Romez let me, I resumed my place at the outrider's barrier, though the grav tugged uncomfortably at my graft. I made suggestions to Fath and Tad Anselm when I could.

Whatever mutable cells passed for eyes in Harry's species must be able to see me through the barrier, but he showed no interest. I was nettled; I'd moved heaven and earth to get back on his detail, lest he be perturbed at my absence.

All afternoon, Fath was terse and preoccupied. I finally realized it was the full gravity that bothered him.

It wasn't just Fath. Sarah Frand was increasingly moody, as if the outrider had struck some nerve deep within her. Eventually, muttering an apology, she asked to be excused, and trudged to her cabin.

At dinner, we sat with what should be a congenial group. Fath and I, Mr. Branstead, Mikhael, two or three of the more pleasant passengers, and Corrine Sloan, whom Fath had, in defiance of public opinion, moved to our table.

Mr. Branstead seemed listless and preoccupied. Perhaps he was still recovering from his imprisonment in Centraltown. Only Corrine Sloan seemed gay and animated, almost inexplicably so. Yet Fath responded to her sallies with little more than grunts, and Mik avoided his share of the conversational burden. I did my best to take up the slack, until Mikhael elbowed me rather rudely in the ribs. I favored him with an unceasing glare. After a moment, he said smoothly, "With the Captain's permission, may we be excused a moment?" Captain's son or no, he was a middy on public duty.

"Very well."

"Thank you, sir." Mik steered me to the hatch.

"What the *hell* was that ab—"

"You oaf, stay out of it. Don't you know what Corrine's done?"

I gaped. "I guess not."

"She's asked to be set ashore, provided Scanlen rescinds his edict."

"Edict?"

Mik waved vaguely. "Impeaching Pa. Demanding you and he and Chris Dakko be returned for trial. Pa's livid. Refused her outright, but she claims she has the right."

"Jesus fucking Christ." It just slipped out. I'd heard Alex Hopewell say that once, in another life.

"Randy!" He glanced about, saw no one near. "If you had an ounce of sense . . . Our religious affairs are under close scrutiny; it's no time for blasphemy. I've half a mind to tell Pa."

"Don't." I'd offended Mik, and not wanted to.

"This time." With a touch of impatience, he pushed me toward our table.

The stewards were bringing dessert, some flaming concoction with a bitter sauce I'd had before. Corrine chatted to Mr. Branstead, to the passengers, to anyone who'd listen. Her face was flushed. I stared balefully. I had no mother; if she had her wish, neither would Janey.

"It's not," she told Ms. Aren, "as if we're lacking for clothing. So what if fashions are out-of-date? On Hope Nation it's worse. They see nothing until we bring—"

I said across the table, "Why'd you do it?"

Silence.

"Randy?" Her expression was determinedly pleasant.

Under the table, Mikhael kicked me hard. His eyes were twin lasers. I paid no heed.

"Why ask to go ashore? They'll burn you."

"Not necessarily," she said with seeming calm. "Church law requires—"

The Captain gripped my arm, his fingers a vise.

I ignored him too. "Fath loves you. How can you expect him to let—"

"*Shut your mouth this instant!*" Fath's tone was savage.

A new voice, from above. "Begging the Captain's pardon . . ." Midshipman Yost, his uniform crisp, his manner beyond reproach.

Fath hurled his napkin to the starched tablecloth. "What now?"

"Reverend Pandeker asks a word with you."

"Oh, he does?"

"Yes, sir." Yost shifted nervously. "Should I not have interrupted? I'm the only officer at our table, and he said . . ."

Fath glared from me to Yost, threw in Mikhael for good measure. "I don't want to hear it." A pause, while he fought the edge in his voice. "Very well, send him over."

Mikhael blurted, "Here, sir?" He seemed scandalized.

"I've nothing to hide. Bring him soon, Mr. Yost, before we leave the table."

"Aye aye, sir."

In moments he was back, Reverend Pandeker in tow. "Captain, may I present Rev—"

"We've met. Dismissed."

I'd never seen Fath so determined to be rude. Fork arrested halfway to mouth, I watched.

"Well?" Though Pandeker loomed over us, Fath made no suggestion that he sit.

"Thank you for allowing—"

"Yes, and all that. What do you want?"

He glanced about. Mikhael and Mr. Branstead pretended to be occupied with food. Corrine watched him calmly. I gaped. The passengers hung on every word. "I'd hoped," Pandeker said, "for a moment in private."

"Sorry, that won't be possible." Fath's tone was icy.

"Might we at least observe the amenities?"

"Why, certainly. Reverend Pandeker, may I introduce my fiancée, Corrine Sloan?"

Pandeker's florid face reddened further.

"Corrine, my dear, the special envoy of the Patriarchs."

"Good evening, sir. I believe we've met." Her tone was elaborately formal, and infinitely distant.

Fiancée? I was his son; why hadn't he told me I was to have a stepmother? On the other hand, had he even told *her*? I could imagine nothing more satisfying to throw in this pompous joey's face, true or no.

"Ms. Sloan." A barely perceptible nod; even so, it seemed to pain the Reverend. His cold eyes focused on Fath. "Now, Captain. I call you that, as you retain de facto command, although de jure—"

I nudged Mik. "What's that?"

"Shush. Listen."

"—de jure, you are deposed."

"Admiralty's given no such order." Fath's tone had grown even more frosty. "And it's not a subject I'd discuss with *you*."

"Mr. Seafort, I assure you this meeting distresses me even more than yourself. I make one last entreaty: surrender yourself and this—this *woman* to the judgment of Lord God's sovereign Church and its civil government in Hope Nation. Else I am bound to remind crew and officers that allegiance to an excommunicate jeopardizes their immortal souls."

Fath merely glared, but Mikhael shot to his feet. "As an officer on *Olympiad*, Reverend, I beg leave to remind you that regardless of your status, incitement to mutiny is a hanging offense." Mik spoke with careful courtesy, though his voice seethed. "Captain Seafort, it may not be my place to tell him. Nonetheless, it's my opinion he tries your goodwill."

BRAVO, MIK! If my new arm were firmly attached, I'd have clapped. Fath ignored him. "Anything else, Mr. Pandeker?"

"Yes. The Patriarchs, in the name of Jesus Christ assembled, have long recognized that the fish who bedevil us are creatures of the Adversary, Satan Himself. That you allow them aboard is intolerable!"

"To whom?"

Pandeker drew himself up. "To the Bishops and congregants of His blessed Reunification Church. To every passenger aboard. To crew and officers alike. In the name of Lord God and His people, I demand you expel them to the outermost depths!"

"Thank you." Fath stood. "Midshipman Tamarov, my compliments to Dr. Romez, and might he inquire whether Reverend Pandeker has been getting his medications."

Mik's eyes sparkled, and for a moment, his composure dissolved into a wide grin. Then he caught himself, and was sober. "Aye aye, sir." A crisp salute.

"I take no med—" The import of Fath's remark sank in, and Pandeker turned beet-red. "Good evening!" He stalked off, trailing the shreds of his dignity.

Mr. Branstead said mildly, "So much for mending fences."

"Quite so. Come along, young Randolph." With what might have been good humor, Fath guided me toward the corridor.

Mikhael followed, his affable nature struggling to break through the ice of his rage. "Pa, so help me, if he says one word to my middies, I'll proffer charges myself."

Fath's tone was reflective. "He must be feeling very sure of himself."

"Did you hear me? I won't let him get away with it!" We started up the ladder to Level 1.

"I heard you, Midshipman. One demerit."

Mikhael said, "It so happens I'm off duty, sir."

"Ah. Then in your personal capacity, I rebuke you." But Fath didn't sound annoyed. "I really dislike that joey. It's almost a relief that we're all taking sides, and I'm free to show it."

"Someone ought to have a word with the master-at-arms." Mik's voice was stubborn.

"I doubt it will come to that." Fath turned his scowl to me. "Now, young man. By what right do you discuss my affections at a table of strangers?"

"Mr. Branstead's no—"

"Randy." A warning tone, if ever there was one.

"*Someone* had to ask her. It's suicide to put herself in their hands."

Mik said gruffly, "Don't you think she knows?"

"Then why would she . . ."

"To save Pa."

"Which I won't allow," said Fath, "if I have to lock her in her cabin. Your assistance wasn't needed. A dozen extra verses tonight, after your session with Harry."

"That's not fair! I only—"

"Pardon?"

"Yessir." Maybe it should have been "aye aye, sir." I was too annoyed to care. All Mik gets is a rebuke; I get verses.

33

FATH PERSONALLY ATTENDED our regular afternoon talks with Harry. Afterward, I asked how he would avoid Scanlen's clutches if Admiral Kenzig relieved him, but he refused to discuss it. We had hot words on the subject. He did assure me that he wouldn't consent to go ashore except by direct order. And if need be, he'd remind the Admiral of his medical condition; another liftoff would be a great trial. I looked at him strangely; if Scanlen got his hands on Fath, he need not concern himself with liftoff. But Fath merely patted me in that kindly, dismissive way that made me want to kick adults in the shins.

Fath was watching our evening session with the outrider on his cabin screen, so as not to strain his healing spine in full grav. Tonight, while Ms. Frand had the watch, Lieutenant Skor was in charge at our table. She was never as easy to work with as Tad Anselm; I had to pay particular attention to my manner to avoid irritating her. I sighed. I suppose it was good practice.

Harry seemed jumpy. He barely tasted the drawings on our plates, and "I don't understand" was his most frequent comment. The time came when he ignored our offering, drew one of his own.

An outrider and a one-armed human.

I stood, waved. "I'm here, boy."

"Sit down." Fath's voice was sharp, even through the speaker.

"Yes, sir. I wanted him to see me."

"And if he burns through the barrier to see you better? Get permission first. Why are you so bloody impulsive?"

I flushed. "Anthony used to ask the same."

"It's why you scare Tolliver. Ms. Skor, if this joey's going to wave, you'd best stand back."

"Gladly." Lieutenant Skor retreated several steps, ready to slam shut the corridor safety hatch.

I pressed my face to the transplex. "It's all right, Harry. I'm here."

The outrider drew another plate. NO ONE-ARMED HUMAN, FEAR.

"Fath—I mean, sir—I'll have to go in. He can't read me from here."

"No, it's too dangerous."

"We have to, sir. Look, he's quivering. Don't treat me like a child."

Lieutenant Skor was apoplectic. She waved a warning finger, which I ignored.

A tired sigh. *"Very well, suit up."*

I said, "How would Harry tell humans apart inside a suit? Anyway, suits have two arms. I'll just carry it along. He's starting to skitter, sir."

A muttered string of oaths, from the speaker.

"You frazzing—" Ms. Skor bunched my collar, hauled me close. "Of all the times to provoke the Captain! I ought to toss you—"

"Why, ma'am?"

"Don't you know?" Her brow wrinkled. "No, you've been here since—breathe a word of this and I'll stuff you down the recycler!"

"Yes, ma'am!"

"Sarah Frand had the watch. Captain was in his cabin." She grimaced. "Ms. Sloan asked for passage to the Station and Frand agreed. Sent her immediately, with a sailor in the gig. Without asking Mr. Seafort."

"That bitch!"

Ms. Skor eyed me sourly, but said nothing to contradict me.

"What about Corrine?"

"Station's holding her 'for clarification'; won't send her groundside, won't send her back. Get your suit."

I did, hating it. But mostly my thoughts were on Ms. Frand. Was it her religious convictions that led her to betray Fath? Did she hope to head off the demand for Fath's resignation? I shrugged. It made no difference. She was beyond trust. And what of Corrine? Why had she left, without an agreement that would safeguard Fath?

Because Corrine knew Fath would never let her go, and seized her chance. No doubt she'd try to bargain from the Station, but would Colonel Kaminski send her groundside regardless? Anth had thought well of him, but . . .

I sighed. We all make our beds, and lie in them.

Fath gave his permission. I trudged down the corridor, hauling along a useless suit. I could just imagine asking Harry to wait until I climbed into it before decompressing us. TIME FIVE MINUTES. FOUR MINUTES EQUALS DEAD ONE-ARM.

I had to drag my suit up to Level 1, and down the next stairs, to get to the hatch at the other side of our corridor; at our end, the only way through was to take down the barrier.

Finally, in section three, which had been rigged for decontamination, I stood at the hatch. My shirt felt clammy, though I hadn't run all that hard. Nerves. I wanted to see Harry, didn't I? I'd volunteered. Yet some part of me prayed that the panel was broken, that the corridor hatch couldn't be opened.

Easy, joey. You're overtired. An hour or so, then the humiliating decon, and you'll be in your bunk. No, first you have to memorize those frazzing verses. Perhaps Fath will relent. Yeah. Perhaps outriders wear skirts.

Silently, the hatch slid into its recess. I crossed into section four, trudged past the outrider's nutrient tub. There he was, at the far barrier. I called, "Hallo, Harry." Outriders had never responded to sounds; perhaps they couldn't hear at all. But the sound was soothing, at least to me. I strode along the corridor. "Missed me, boy?" I dropped my awkward suit and waved. No response. To test the unfamiliar limb hanging from my shoulder, I waved my other arm as well.

As I approached, Harry skittered madly across the corridor from bulkhead to bulkhead. He absorbed Fath's ruined clock, spewed it forth again. A pseudopod jabbed at the dial.

"Easy, joey." My tone was soothing.

"Not too close, Mr. Carr." Lieutenant Skor, safe behind the barrier. I halted.

Harry drew a plate. OUTRIDER. ONE-ARM HUMAN.

I said, "Jess, write 'yes.' "

The alien erased it. A new etching: OUTRIDER. NOT. TWO-ARMED HUMAN.

" 'Yes' again, Jess."

NO! Long after Harry had etched it, the plate smoked and sizzled. I felt the acrid scent of my fear.

In the speaker Fath said, *"Start backing away, son. Slowly, calmly."*

There was nothing I wanted more, but this had to be gotten over with. "In a minute, sir. Jess, write what he told us before. One-armed man and outrider. Add 'now.' "

ONE-ARMED HUMAN NOT EQUAL TWO-ARMED HUMAN. OUTRIDER FEAR.

"Randy, go to the hatch!" Fath's voice was a lash.

I was the one in the corridor; it made me the best judge of the situation, and it was *my* life. I stamped my foot. "See why I disobey? Trust me, Fath!"

"The outrider's upset. He might kill you."

"Christ, don't you think I realize that?" I edged closer. "Please?"

"Oh, God." A long moment. Then, *"Get it done."*

"Jess, quick. 'One-armed human equals two-armed. No fear.' " Another step. Harry quivered.

How could I make him under . . .

Of course.

I whirled about. Harry leaped aside. I launched into a manic dance, shaking every limb. For good measure I did my best to run up a bulkhead. Finally I ground to a halt, panting. "Got it, you stupid blob? It's ME!"

Harry's quivering eased. He approached me, rippling on those nonfeet, those temporary pseudopods we found so eerie.

Despite myself, I backpedaled into the bulkhead.

An appendage began to grow.

"Oh, shit."

"Ms. Skor." In the speaker, Fath's voice was tense. "Distract him! Make noise, flash the lights."

"No, Fath, I mean, Captain!" My lips were dry. "Wait it out." It was too late, anyway. If they startled Harry now, Lord God knew what he'd do.

"Sir?" Ms. Skor.

"I don't . . . all right."

Harry edged closer. To my infinite relief, the appendage began to crust over, darkened to gunmetal-gray.

It touched my real arm.

I found my voice. In fact, I found myself babbling. "Jess, a new plate, hurry! 'One-arm equals two-arm.' " Throw it at his feet."

"Referent not understood. The being has no feet."

"Don't go glitched on me, you rusty bucket of chips! Draw it, and throw it on the deck as close to him as . . ."

Absently, his appendage still waving, Harry flowed over Jess's new plate.

Suddenly Harry's "hand" rasped across my belly to my other side. I flinched. It probed at my mechanical arm.

I tarped the plate hard with the toe of my boot. "One-arm equals two-arm."

Harry flowed over the plate. Slowly, as if doubtfully, the appendage withdrew.

I sagged. "Thank you, God." I might, at that moment, have meant it.

"That's enough for tonight, Randy." Fath.

"Yes, sir." I agreed wholeheartedly. As soon as Harry gave me room to edge clear . . .

A new appendage emerged from Harry's ever-changing skin. Resigned, I waited for it to coat over.

It didn't.

Harry seemed to flow upward. Inexorably, his acid appendage extended toward my torso. If it splattered me, I'd be dead.

I sucked in my stomach. "Fath, talk to me!" My lips were dry as desert sand, and my knees threatened to buckle.

"I'm proud of you."

It helped, but not nearly enough.

Harry's appendage shot out. It flowed across my prosth. The mechanical hand sizzled.

"NO!" I jerked back, but I had nowhere to go; I was already pressed tight to the bulkhead.

In my new arm, something shorted. I yelped. Of its own volition the prosth began to buck and twitch. Harry flowed backward. His appendage began to reabsorb. The pseudoflesh of my prosth dripped and sizzled. I tried to hold it away from me, but it no longer responded to commands. Awkwardly, I leaned to my left, desperate to keep acid and bubbling metal from running down my leg.

Harry flowed over a plate. ONE-ARM EQUALS ONE-ARM.

"Fath?" Clammy with sweat, my pulse racing, I giggled. I must be going into shock. "I don't think he likes my prosth."

"Are you hurt?"

"I don't think—"

Alarms shrieked.

So did I. My heart pounded my ribs. My spittle flew.

"Battle Stations! All hands to Battle Stations! Captain to the bridge!" Sarah Frand.

Outside the barrier, Ms. Skor was already racing to the distant ladder, and her duty station abovedecks. Why the hell wasn't her duty to protect *me*?

"Randy, get out!" Fath.

I cast a longing glance at the hatch, but Harry was too close. I'd never make it.

"All hands, all passengers to suits. Prepare to Repel Boarders! Prepare for decompression!" Ms. Frand reeled off commands.

I edged along the bulkhead. Finally I reached a porthole.

A dozen fish. More.

"Duty Stations, report!"

They jostled about, squirting propellant, nosing toward our fusion tubes. One was already extruding an appendage. Soon it would swing about, then break off. Its acid would eat through our hull.

"Pilot to the bridge!" Fath, breathing heavily; he must have run all the way. *"Engine Room, emergency power to thrusters!"*

I spun to Harry. "You b—b—bastards!" I pounded the bulkhead. "Why?" But he only watched impassively. "Jess, a plate! 'Why war?'"

For a moment, I thought the puter wouldn't respond, with *Olympiad* on full alert. Then a servo etched the plate.

"Sealing corridor hatches!"

NO WAR. OUTRIDER LIKE ONE-ARM. Or perhaps it was, OUTRIDER NO-FEAR ONE ARM.

"Twelve fish war."

Harry erased the plate. NOT UNDERSTAND.

"Jess: 'twelve fish war ship. Here, now.' "

"A moment." The speaker went dead. The bridge must be making heavy demands on Jess's resources.

"Priority circuit! Draw it now!"

A servo came to life, drew my plate. I hurled it at the outrider. He skittered aside. It fetched up against a bulkhead. After a moment's quivering, Harry tasted.

And went berserk. He flew about the corridor, quivering, jerking this way and that. After a moment, he careened into the airlock.

I stalked after. "Yeah, run away, you sneaky oversize amoeba!"

Near the outer hatch, Harry remained still, as if waiting for the lock to cycle. It wouldn't, of course. The inner hatch was still open.

"Fath, flush him out!"

No reply.

I frowned. Was he mad at me? Should I have called him Captain? No doubt: we were on duty. But he wouldn't make an issue of it when we . . .

You idiot.

The corridor mikes fed the holo in our cabin, and Fath had gone to the bridge. I snatched up the caller. "Ship's Boy Carr calling brid—"

Harry rocketed out of the lock.

"You frazzing maniac!" I edged toward the hatch to three. Fath would open, if I called him from the hatch panel.

The outrider skittered past me, circled his nutrient tub, plunged into it.

Now what, Randy? To get to the hatch I'd have to pass within a meter of him. His behavior was so erratic I wasn't sure I wanted to try.

"Attention all hands and passengers." Fath's voice was tight. *"We're under attack by a flotilla of fish. They Fuse in and out, and more keep coming. Our fire is destroying those near our tubes, but . . ."*

My God, what was Harry doing? He'd sucked up the entire nutrient tub, and was growing before my eyes.

I retreated past a cabin, and another. Then past the airlock. Not long before, I'd been trapped in that same—

". . . But there are a lot of fish." It sounded an admission of defeat.

My skin crawled. It wasn't just the lock; the entire section could decompress at any moment. I'd abandoned my suit on the deck, about . . . I risked a glance. Twenty meters behind me. Watching Harry, I backed toward it, nearly stumbling when I reached it.

I laid the suit in a sitting position against the bulkhead, maneuvered my feet in. It isn't easy to get into a vacuum suit one-handed. I knew: I'd tried.

One-handed, though, is nothing. Try climbing in with a metal and pseudoflesh arm that won't do what you want, and won't hold still. I finally grabbed the half-melted wrist with my other hand, tried to force it into a sleeve. It wouldn't cooperate; I couldn't get it far. Finally, I pinned it against my side, thrust it into the suit body with me. The damn hand fluttered against my torso, twitching like a dying fish. *Ugh. Find a better image, joey.*

Harry skittered down the corridor, zoomed into the airlock and out again.

"Master-at-arms Janks, report to bridge from the nearest caller. Mr. Carr's in trouble. Proceed to Level 2 section four and free him, if you have to kill the alien to do so. I'll open corridor hatches for you when I know where the bloody hell you are." Then, after a moment, *"Sorry."*

"Jesus." Sweating, I redoubled my efforts. My legs were in. Now my real arm. I started working clamps.

Harry raced past me, reversed direction. He was bigger than before, all right. By about a third. And he was awfully fast. But then, they'd always been.

"Get away from me, you slug!" Luckily he'd shot past me toward section five; my way was clear to the section three hatch. Grabbing my helmet, I shuffled down the corridor. One doesn't run in a suit.

As I neared the airlock, I tried to fasten my helmet. One-handed, I couldn't manage. It slipped from my fingers, rolled across the deck. I scrambled after it.

As I snatched up the helmet, Harry skittered past, blocking my way to section three. Well, it wouldn't be long before Janks came and shot him. I was glad of it. I might get splattered like Kevin, but . . .

Minutes ago, I'd begged Fath to talk me through terror, but at the moment I didn't much care. "I'm not afraid of you, pusbag!"

A pity Harry didn't understand.

"Out of my way!" I stamped my foot, hoping he'd retreat. Instead he surged forward, and instantly my newfound courage fled. I stumbled back.

The speaker crackled. *"Randy, do nothing. Janks is on his way. Another minute or so. Secure your helmet!"*

Part of me marveled that with *Olympiad* under attack, the Captain could spare me a glance. "Aye aye, sir." I fumbled for the clamps. "What's going on Outside?"

"*Van Peer, thrust our stern to starboard, flank!*" The speaker went dead.

Harry grew an appendage. The wrong kind. Fath was probably right, telling me to wait. If I tried to twist past the outrider to section three, Harry might melt my suit, and me with it. Come *on*, Janks.

Taller than I, quivering, the outrider drew near. His appendage probed. Hastily, still fumbling with the helmet, I retreated. The appendage extended again. I backpedaled.

Right into the airlock.

Harry followed. With his waving acid pseudoarm, he herded me to the outer hatch. I fetched up against the control panel. He grew taller, wider, blocking any hope of escape.

"God damn you!" It came out a croak.

The porthole was just past him. My eyes widened. A dozen fish? Well, now there were thirty.

Harry's appendage shot out. I flinched. It stretched past me to the hatch. Desperately I tore at my suit clamps. The helmet was jammed; I'd have to yank it off, reset it on my head.

The hatch plate began to sizzle.

"JANKS!" My scream echoed in the tiny chamber.

When Harry burned through, we'd decompress. Unless I got my helmet clamped, I'd die.

Harry's colors swirled. A whole segment of him turned gray. Good, you slimeball, maybe you'll die too.

The helmet slithered from my grasp. I caught it between a knee and the hull. Get it on, quick, before . . . you idiot, it's backward! Easy, joey, you've passed a dozen suit drills. All you have to do is . . . where the *hell* is Janks?

Too late. Any second, Harry will burn through. Janks won't be in time. I'll feel what Dad felt, those last agonized seconds.

Inside my suit, my useless prosth fluttered against my side.

Steady, son.

What, Fath? Oh, it's not you. Dad, I've missed you so. Would you stay with me, 'til the end? That's all I ask. And if you could put your arm around me . . .

The hatch smoked and sizzled. When the acid ate through, would explosive decompression squeeze me through the hole? We'd lose the air not only from the hatch, but all of section four. If the attacking fish damaged nearby section hatches, scores of passengers would die.

Cursing a God who didn't exist, I let go the helmet, stabbed at the hatch panel. The inner hatch slid closed. Sorry, Janks. You'll miss your shot.

The way to the corridor was blocked. Now, Harry would only decompress our airlock.

I would never get the frazzing helmet clamped in time. I grabbed the emergency lever from its socket, scratched on the deck, "One-arm die."

His pseudopod still sizzling on the hull, Harry flowed atop my words. When he moved aside, the smoking deck had a reply. NO WAR.

What the hell did that mean? Dozens of fish were after us. Had we ever understood a word the other said? I slammed the helmet on my neckpiece. It caught.

"*Janks, run! They're in the lock!*"

"*Laser room, we're coming about. Shoot on—*"

Tinny voices in the suit radio; someone had left it on. Feverishly, as Harry's acid ate through the outer hatch, I clawed at the remaining clamps. It was harder than you'd think. I was pressed tight against the hatch, and Harry, half gray and dead, loomed above, off balance, ready to bathe me in agony. My fingers were sweaty. I hadn't yet turned on the air; the suit was stifling.

"Olympiad, *we have the shot.*"

"*Take it, Station!*"

"Olympiad, Vince Palabee, on behalf of the colonial government. I call on you to protect—"

"*Stow it, Palabee. We're doing what we can.*" Fath's tone was sharp.

Two more clamps, the hardest to reach.

"Return us control of the Station!"

"*That's between you and the officers—*"

A hiss. A rush of air escaping the hatch. In a second I'd gasp, then my eyes would bulge, then—

Harry fell atop me.

"Aiyyyee!" My shriek soared into the upper registers. The helmet fogged. The clamps weren't done; the suit couldn't hold air. It wouldn't matter. I could almost hear the bubbling of my suit, almost feel the heat as Harry melted through. In seconds, I'd dissolve.

I tried to flinch from the skin of my suit, wondering where the acid would burn first.

"JANKS TO BRIDGE, IT'S GOT RANDY!" Labored breaths. "The only way I . . . should I shoot through the hatch? We'll lose the section. Nobody's in it."

"*Yes!*"

I panted. The air was stale and useless. I could move my arms, but didn't dare. If I so much as touched Harry, it would be the end.

A lurch. I was falling, blind, dying, alone.

"Sir, it's just launched from the hull! Jesus God, the boy's alive! Suited.

He's . . . his head and shoulders are embedded in the outrider. He's kicking like mad. I'm blowing the inner hatch!"

No, you idiot. I wasted precious seconds closing it. Don't make my death a waste.

"*Captain, Kaminski here, on Orbit Station. Palabee wants access to our puter, to coordinate defense. Should we allow it?*"

"Janks . . ." Fath's tone was dull. "*Kill him.*"

"Pressure equalized, the hatches are opening." Janks. "Sir, if I . . . Remember the Dakko joey? If the outrider blows apart . . . I can't kill him without risking Randy!"

"Mr . . . Janks . . ." The voice was lifeless, the words slurred through unwilling lips. "*Kill . . . my . . . son. He's in agony.*"

Silence. Then. "Lord God save my soul. I can't."

"*NOW, JANKS! Laser room, you too! Aim for the outrider!*"

"*Laser room, belay that.*" Mr. Tolliver. "*Sir, why—*"

"*Edgar!*"

Swimming in a fog of incomprehension, I yawned mightily.

"*Olympiad, do you read Orbit Station?*"

"*Why is Randy kicking?*" Tolliver.

"*Reflex action, or . . .*"

"*Nick, if it's reflex, he's dead even if his body doesn't know it, so you don't need to shoot. If not, HE ISN'T DEAD! The acid hasn't got him.*"

Why couldn't I see? More important, why wasn't I dead?

I yawned again. The voices faded. Feebly, without thought, I twisted my air valve.

Cool air hissed. And it stayed within the suit.

I blinked. All was still black. But the world—its sounds, at least—came back into focus.

"*But—you can't know . . . damn it, we're on open circuit.*" A click. Utter silence.

"Don't leave me!" No one heard my plea.

"Janks to Bridge!" He too was suited, so I could hear him.

Nothing.

"Janks to Bridge, urgent!"

Fath's voice was lifeless. "*What is it?*"

"Begging your pardon, the outrider's heading for that big fish with the greenish blowhole. Decide right now whether you want the laser room to take it out."

"*Of course I do!*"

"Does the outrider mean to kill Randy?"

"*It means to kill all of us. And if the fish Fuses with Randy inside . . .*"

My stomach coiled. I was dying alone. But if the fish Fused, "alone" would take on a new dimension.

But why hadn't the outrider's acid eaten through my suit? Harry was dying, he'd turned gray. Did it mean he hadn't enough acid to . . .

Gray. Like the appendage he'd used to touch my cheek.

He'd flowed atop me, over the unsealed helmet. And now my suit held air.

Jesus God! He'd coated himself with that protective layer, made himself my seal. He'd meant to save me. Why, though? As a trophy? Prisoner? Hostage?

Ever so gently, I reached upward toward my helmet with a gloved hand. Something hard, outside my suit. I snatched back my fingers, felt no burning, no outrush of air.

"Sir, we only have a few seconds." Janks. "If you laser the fish, where will the outrider go?"

"Nowhere. It has no propulsion."

We'd float through space forever, or until Hope Nation's gravity sucked us to blazing oblivion. On the other hand, by then I'd be long dead. I only had two hours air.

"Olympiad, this is Palabee at government headquarters in the Venturas. Report! How many fish, what are they up to?"

Idly, in a near dreamlike state, I wondered how Fath and Janks would decide my fate. I was utterly helpless, trapped inside Harry. They'd destroy the fish, or not. There wasn't a damn thing I could do either way.

The hell there wasn't.

I reached down to my chest, felt for switches, flicked the one I sought. I opened my mouth, shut it again. This might be their last memory of me. I ought to do it right.

"Ship's Boy Randolph Carr reporting to Bridge." My voice was crisp. "Please call the Captain."

A voice, hesitant, as if in awe. *"Randy?"*

"Yes, sir. I suggest—respectfully suggest you don't shoot the fish. Harry's taken me for a reason. I'm not sure why, but he hasn't hurt me. In fact . . ." My words falling on one another, I explained about my helmet.

"Laser room, do NOT fire on the stationary fish about eighty meters of our port side! Acknowledge."

"Orders received and understood, sir."

"Or on the outrider approaching it!"

"Fath, what's happening? I can't see a thing."

"The fish that brought Harry is inert but alive. The outrider carrying you is going to hit it amidships. Other fish are after our tubes. The laser room is holding them off, killing them en masse. We've six banks of lasers

dedicated to the tubes, but fish keep Fusing in. And . . ." Fath sounded uneasy. *". . . if a fish Defuses too near, it may get to our tubes before we—"*

"Olympiad, please respond to Station." Colonel Kaminski's voice was plaintive.

I asked, "Can you Fuse to safety?" I'd soon suffocate; *Olympiad* ought to save herself.

"We're too close."

To Hope Nation, Fath meant. No ship could Fuse near a large mass; the gravity cancelled the field. The formulas had bored me to tears, in math. Now was an insane moment to ask, but . . . "Fath, how can the fish do it?" Here I was, en route to my death, and quizzing Fath on principles of Fusion. Well, my life never had made much sense.

"If only we knew." A pause. *"Randy, the instant their attack lets up, I'll send a launch to rescue you. I've called for volunteers."*

I snorted; how would they communicate with the fish? "Have them bring a plate asking Harry to let me go?"

"Don't you DARE be flippant, you ill-bred young clod!" Fath's voice was tight. *"Every middy aboard is ready to risk his life saving you. Including Mr. Yost, whom you hate!"*

"I don't hate . . ." I gave it up. "I'm very sorry, sir. Thank them, especially Mr. Yost."

"Randy, you're about to hit." His words tumbled in haste. *"I take back what I said. You're no clod. I love you, son. Godspeed."*

I bit my lip so hard I tasted salt. "Fath, I—"

BUMP.

I yelped.

"Randy? . . . Randy!"

"I'm . . ." I marveled at it. "Still here."

"The alien's skin is swirling; it's going to absorb the outrider. But it's changing. Harry is . . . oh, Lord God, he's oozing around your suit!"

Even as he spoke, a rubbery membrane flowed over my legs. The suit speaker hissed and crackled. My body convulsed in a galvanic spasm that failed to break me free. "No! Not yet!" Cringing, I tensed to endure the unbearable.

"Rand . . . beg your . . ." Fath's words faded in and out. *"Speak to me . . . Jesus, I pray thee . . . merciful!"*

I tried to curl into a fetal ball, but the suit restrained me. I floated, helpless, cursing Harry. Wrapped around my suit, he cut off half my radionics.

A vague pressure, something like a thump. Blind, cocooned, in zero grav, it was impossible to get my bearings. And my stomach ached.

"Station . . . tenant Skor . . . Captain is . . . occupied."

"Ma'am, should we feed target coord . . . government? . . . unified fire control, but . . . might fire on *Olympiad*!"

"Fath, Ms. Skor, anyone! Can you hear—"

"*. . . gives a spaceman's damn whether . . . you coord . . . fire on us and we'll blow you to fragments!*"

"Because I'm going to scream and I won't be able to sto—"

"*. . . love of God, Randy, answer!*"

"*Olympiad* . . . Lieutenant Riev . . . by for message from . . . miral Kenzig in Central . . ."

The pressure on my legs eased. My arm came free.

"—I can't see it coming, and the wait—"

"Gotcha, you son of a bitch!"

Something scraped my helmet.

"Laser room, stay off this freq—"

A dim light. I could see!

But then, a horrid rush of air. A chill, around my unclasped helmet.

How long can you hold your breath? How long is a lifetime?

My prosthetic arm thrashed and scrabbled against my ribs. In a moment my ears would pop, my eyeballs would—

My breath expelled with explosive force.

I gagged.

The air was horrible. Unbelieving, I took another breath. Even if it had oxygen, I couldn't live long on . . .

Wait, you idiot. Frantically, I clawed at the recalcitrant clamps. This time, they closed with ease, and the helmet seal light blinked. But my suit was filled with a stench that . . . urk. To clear it, I turned the valve as high as it would go.

Randy, you'll need that air! Reluctantly, I turned it down.

"Admiralty House to *Olympiad*, respond." The voice sounded familiar. Alon Riev.

My helmet defogger labored. My visor began to clear. I peered this way and that. Where the hell was I? Where was *Olympiad*?

A vague orange glow. Spots. Swirls. Where was Harry?

Without a handhold, it's hard to twist around in zero gee. No, not hard. Impossible. And the nearest thing to grab was . . . I recoiled. The fish. I was inside the fish. "Jesus H. Christ!"

"Randy!" Shock and surprise.

Between me and the . . . the what? Wall? Skin? . . . swam a formless black shadow. In the suffused light I couldn't tell whether it was large or small, near or far.

Abruptly my perspective snapped into place.

It was Harry.

No, I only knew it was an outrider. It might be any of them.

"Go ahead, Admiralty House." Ms. Skor.

"Fath, I'm . . . scared." I could have kicked myself. Of all the dumb things to say. I might be the first human brought inside the enemy. I should have said something noble like . . . like, "I offer myself as a sacrifice to peace." Or *something.*

Not only that, it might have been my final utterance. What last memory did I want to leave Fath? It certainly wasn't "I'm scared." Shit. Too late to take it back.

"Kenzig here. Where's Seafort?"

"Randy, what are they doing to you?"

"Ignoring me. There's an outrider . . . whoa, make it two! Three!" They oozed, one by one, through the fish's flesh. My forehead beaded with sweat. I wanted *out.* If by some miracle I could communicate that to Harry . . . but which blob was Harry? Impossible to tell.

"Put Seafort on or I'll relieve him on the spot!"

"Just a moment, sir."

"Do nothing to provoke them, son. I'll be back in a moment. Joanne, stay with him. Yes, Admiral? Captain Nicholas Seafort repor—"

"Where the hell have you—never mind. Palabee wants *Olympiad,* Kaminski's Station, and his own ground defenses to coordinate."

"Under whose command?"

"His."

Don't provoke them. Great advice, but what exactly might provoke them? They were drawing closer. I couldn't kick; I wasn't touching the fish; a kick in zero gee accomplished nothing. And if I managed to make contact, I'd be bathed in acid.

I'd like to wake up now, please.

"Is that your order, sir?"

"Randy, this is Joanne Skor. Captain Seafort's on the horn to Central-town."

"I hear him. It's an open line." Fath's absence was the least of my worries. If I touched the damn fish . . .

"Oops."

Urk. I *was* touching it. Leaning against it, sort of. And I wasn't burning. Was that a good sign? Never mind that, try to communicate. Harry, would you loan me a plate and an etching tool? Perhaps I'd been a bit impetuous going to section four to show Harry his old friend one-arm.

"Well, we ought . . ." Kenzig's tone wavered. "Mr. SecGen, what's your advice?"

"Sir, I'm under continual attack; it's not a moment to debate policy.

But the Navy's never put its ships under command of an independent power. Never."

"Independent? By order of McEwan, Hope Nation is again a U.N. colony."

"Goofjuice." Even from Fath, that was a bit much. He was speaking to an Admiral, who'd just threatened to relieve him. *"McEwan is Ambassador, not Governor. He has no authority to sweep aside a government recognized by the U.N. Assembly. Neither has that ass Scanlen."*

"Mr. Seafort!"

"Van Peer, come about; wait any longer and that bloody fish will have us! Sir, I told you I have no time for subtleties."

"Neither have I. They want me to order you groundside, you know."

"Will you?" Fath sounded merely curious.

"Not while you're fighting off fish." Kenzig cleared his throat. "I'm under great pressure to cooperate, in fact Scanlen's sending another delegation this afternoon. Personally, I don't care to face a heresy charge. Just between us . . ."

I snorted. Someone had goofed, by not going to secure circuit. Just between them, and everyone in the frazzing worlds I'd manage to tell.

". . . I saw no evidence the Branstead government had collapsed. McEwan was a touch overeager."

"Sir, may I Log that?"

Who cares, Fath? I'm trapped in a fish with three skittery shadows while they argue over their hors d'oeuvres.

A long pause. "By Lord God, go ahead."

An outrider launched itself in my direction, growing a pseudopod as it neared. *Christ, not again.* To my relief, the appendage turned gray. The other outriders swam closer.

I tried not to flinch. "Ms. Skor, they're touching me. First one, then another." I tried not to make it a complaint.

"Hang on, joey." Her voice was gruff. *"We'll have you out of there if it's humanly . . ."* Yeah, that was the catch. If it was *humanly* possible.

An outrider planted itself before me, quivering.

"You're scared? What about me? Stop poking my bloody suit!" Now I was sounding like Fath. I rolled my eyes.

"Admiral, we're holding them off, but any moment that may change. If I must choose, shall I protect Hope Nation or ourselves?"

"Yourselves, Mr. Seafort." The reply came faster than I'd expected. "To lose another ship such as *Olympiad* would be unthinkable."

The outrider prodded at the fish's . . . deck? . . . stomach? His movements left lines. I squinted in the dim glow.

ONE-ARM NO FEAR. Or it could have been, NO FEAR ONE-ARM. We really hadn't worked much on syntax.

"You're Harry!"

"What, joey?"

"Nothing, Ms. Skor."

Not that it really mattered. Even if I knew what to say to him, I had no writing tool save my boot, and no way in hell would I try to scuff a response into the fish's living flesh. The thought gave me shudders.

NO WAR.

"Yeah, right."

Harry's gray appendage thrust itself at me. All I could do was stand there. Float there. In zero gee, in its home environment, the outrider was far more agile than I. Hell, it was more agile even on our own ship.

The appendage probed at my hand. I thrust my arm behind me, touched something soft and giving. I squawked, snatched back my fingers. Thank God I was suited.

The pseudopod jabbed at me, forced open my fist.

"What? You want me to shake hands?" Reluctantly, I made my fingers close around the cold gray substance. With scorn that overcame my fear, I pumped as if introducing myself to one of Anth's cronies.

The appendage came off in my fingers. "Jesus!" Horrified, I flung it down. The outrider shrunk, picked it up, returned it.

"I don't *want* your fucking hand!"

"Olympiad, Vince Palabee. My government demands you help form a unified, coordinated defense. Admiral Kenzig says he ordered you to cooperate."

"Did you, Admiral?"

"Eh? What are you . . ."

"Play it back, Ms. Skor; Palabee's on another frequency."

I glared at the appendage. "All right, I'll take it. What should I . . ." I stopped dead. Was it a hand, or . . . a tool?

Cautiously, I bent, braced a shoulder against the fish's flesh.

"No, I didn't say that, Captain, not quite in those terms." Kenzig.

I drew, "One-arm fear. One-arm no-Fuse ship." We didn't have a word yet for "go." "No-Fuse" was as close as I could get. I hoped he'd understand.

I waited for Harry to taste. Instead, a reply. FISH. NO FISH. NO OUT-RIDER.

I made the erasing gesture. "I don't understand." Then, "One-arm. Ship. Now."

Something indecipherable.

"Christ, damn it, Harry, I'm lost in here! I can't see anything but you!"

I jabbed with the stick/tool/hand. Did we have a word for "see"? "One-arm no taste ship. Fear."

The outrider touched his fish. Abruptly the outer membrane thinned. It became translucent, then transparent. I'd be damned: a porthole. I peered wistfully at the beautiful lights of home. *Olympiad.* I swallowed.

More portholes appeared. In one, Hope Nation swam, green and distant, unachievable. In the others, a swarm of fish, Defusing, squirting propellant, Fusing. Ughh.

ONE-ARM AND OUTRIDER NO-FUSE. Abruptly he herded me to a membrane. Go where?

"Hey, wait." Was that the outer skin? Was he ejecting me?

"This is Palabee. I want an answer, Seafort."

"Centraltown, tie your lasers to the Station. We'll coordinate with their—"

The membrane opened just as we reached it. A compartment, a larger one. It was infested with outriders. I balked, windmilling my one working arm. Harry nudged me through.

"What is it, boy?" Ms. Skor. I didn't know I'd whimpered aloud.

"It's . . . they . . . record, please, ma'am. We're inside the fish; they moved me from a small chamber to a large one. The place is swarming with outriders. A couple dozen. No particular order; they sort of attach themselves to walls and intestines and God knows what. I'm about to throw up." I swallowed. One didn't vomit in a suit; the consequences were drastic.

"Olympiad, we're in the Venturas, not Centraltown. We moved the government to—"

The outer membrane swirled. New portholes appeared.

Harry was behind me. I looked for a place to draw him a message.

"Very well. Colonel, coordinate with Venturas Base."

Another outrider shot out pseudopods. Like a sailor using handholds in zero gee, it skittered across projections and recesses in the fish, stopped just short of my feet. OUTRIDER <SYMBOL> HUMAN. NO WAR.

I peered over my shoulder. "I thought *you* were Harry." No response, of course. I bent to erase, hesitated, erased just the one symbol that made no sense. "Ms. Skor, still recording? They want to do something to us. A squiggly symbol, like a snake with a head at each end." Not a snake, exactly; more like a sperm. Inside my suit, I blushed to the tips of my ears. I'd die before I'd say that to Ms. Skor. But what did it mean? "Outrider fuck human"? They were certainly trying hard enough.

I stole a look through the translucent membrane. Dozens of fish nosed about *Olympiad,* but she was of the new generation of ships, built after our experience in the war. Huge, of course, but more important, bristling with lasers. So far, they seemed adequate to their mission. The fish nearest the fusion tubes floated inert, riddled with holes.

I drew, "I don't understand."

Another outrider skittled forward. He brandished . . . Lord God, he brandished Fath's broken clock.

"How the hell did you get that? And which of you is Harry? Harry's the one we taught to talk."

The alien jabbed at the dial. The second hand spun backward.

"Huh?"

"*Olympiad*, this is Bishop Scanlen. Put me through to His Reverence, Special Envoy Pandeker. Do it at once."

The outrider wrote, TIME SMALL.

"Yes, a second is small time. What of it?" Then my eyes widened. "Taste one-arm words?"

OUTRIDER SHIP TASTE NO FISH TASTE.

"Ms. Skor! Tell Fath that inside the fish, they know what I write without rolling over it. Maybe the fish feels it and tells them." I stopped dead, looked from one to the other of them. "Tell him they all talk! Whatever we taught one, they all know. Either they're—"

"*I hear you, son.*"

"Telepathic or . . ." I couldn't begin to guess what else.

TIME SMALL. HUMAN OUTRIDER SQUIGGLE NO WAR.

"Fath . . . I mean Captain?" My tone was wary. "They want something from us, to call off the war."

"*What?*"

"A squiggle." I added hastily, "Sorry, I'm not sure what it means."

"*For Lord God's sake, find out. Flank.*"

Two outriders undulated across the fish. One puddled into the gesture of submission. The other disgorged a squat object, deposited it at my feet.

Cautiously, I bent to retrieve it. We were on the dayside of Hope Nation, but even with portholes the light wasn't all that great. I held the gift close, squinted.

A human hand, putrefying, mottled, thawing.

"Oh, God, a rotting hand!" I flung it across the chamber. Desperately, I tried not to retch, and failed. I heaved the contents of my stomach into my helmet.

"*Randy! What have they done?*"

Again I gagged.

Zero gee. Foul globules floated in my visor. The acid stench . . . The air flow ceased; I'd fouled the tube. I sucked one glob down my windpipe. I gasped and wheezed. "Fath . . . trouble. Gotta . . . off helmet."

"*No, son!*"

I had no choice; I couldn't endure another instant. The first compartment was aired; I prayed this would be too. Choking, face purple, I clawed at my clamps. Through my smeared visor I caught a glimpse of outriders diving for the nearest membranes. Good. Maybe humans would infect *them*. I tore off the helmet.

My ears popped; it was like finding myself atop Mount Von Walther, in the Venturas. I panted and gasped. The atmosphere was far too thin. The membrane to the first chamber tore open. Foul air wafted in, not enough. The fish pulsed like a beating heart. Air. Again. More air, foul but welcome. My pulse began to slow. I sucked at the air tube, dislodged what blocked it, spat. Instantly the fish absorbed it, and it disappeared. I used my sleeve to wipe the visor as best I could.

The outrider quivered. It drew a blob.

"Later, I'm busy." I scoured the helmet clean of droplets, set it on my head. Here we go again. I managed the first clamp.

The outrider surged toward me, an appendage spurting. He climbed the membrane serving as a bulkhead, to loom over my head.

He landed atop me. Gray protoplasm blocked my visor. "Get away, you goddamn—" Just in time, I stopped myself from batting it away. "Fath, it's pulling off my helmet!"

A grate. A click. Another.

"Why?"

Of all the stupid questions . . . how the hell would I know? Maybe it was peeling its dinner.

Click. I flinched. A scrape.

The outrider flowed off, clung for a moment to the membrane, oozed to the deck.

Nervously, I felt my helmet. It was intact. And the seal light blinked steadily. "Well, I'll be a son of a bitch!" "Sir, he fastened my clamps! He's friendly!" If there'd been grav, I'd have jumped for joy. The hard knot in my stomach eased perceptibly.

"Station to *Olympiad*. We're sectoring our fire as follows—*JESUS LORD CHRIST!*"

Galvanized, I kicked off to the nearest porthole. I fetched up against the fish's thick skin, whose mottled colors and shapes flowed unceasingly.

Outside, fish.

Hundreds of fish.

More than I'd dreamed existed.

"All units, fire at will!"

"Wait, Kaminski, see what they—"

Holes appeared in half a dozen fish. They spewed protoplasm, wilted.

The swarm was moving. Where? My perspective was skewed.

"Fire! Fire! Fire!" The voice from the Station was frantic.

"They're not attacking, they're—"

I scribbled on the fish. "Dead ship no! No war!"

The outrider twitched and quivered. He drew again. I squinted. A blob with five points. A hand. SQUIGGLE HAND?

"No!" I stabbed my writing tool into the fish.

The outrider oozed through the membrane, reappeared with half a dozen of its fellows. SQUIGGLE SHIP?

Before I could respond, they herded me toward a membrane. How many compartments did this bloody fish have? Certainly its size would allow far more than I'd seen. On the other hand, the fish was clearly alive, and would need much of its space to maintain itself.

"Centraltown and Venturas Base, this is Captain Seafort. Fish, a flotilla of hundreds, heading toward your atmosphere. Trajectory indicates landfall two hours sixteen minutes. They've broken off their attack on Olympiad."

"Palabee to Seafort. Kill them all!"

"We're lying off the Station, in mutual defense. We'll lose sight of the Venturas in half an hour."

"Use your frazzing engines!"

TIME SMALL.

"Yeah." I clutched my drawing stick. "Talk squiggle. One-arm not understand."

The outriders converged on me. Their appendages weren't a safe gray. Without ceremony, they herded me to the membrane, through it.

SQUIGGLE SHIP?

I gaped past the writing. It wasn't a ship that lay against a membrane, but what in God's name . . . a console? From what? And how did it get into the fish? The condition wasn't bad, really, though it looked like it had been torn out by force.

"Sir, Captain, they're showing me a puter console."

"Just a moment, joey, he's charting a course." Ms. Skor.

"Don't leave!" It burst out before I could stop myself.

"That's not up to me." Her voice was brusque.

"Captain, Colonel Kaminski here. Some of those fish will get through." His voice was tight. Perhaps the Colonel was old enough to remember the last fish invasion, when Dad was a joeykid. "Don't forget, the Venturas Base was never fully rebuilt after the war. It has minimal lasers."

"Why in Lord God's name did Palabee move his government there?"

A grim chuckle. "Perhaps he didn't feel safe among his fellow citizens." Kaminski was once Anthony's man. No doubt he had little love for Palabee.

"He made his bed. Randy, what do you make of it?"

Palabee was a coward, and a fool. Anth had said as much. That's why he—oh. That's not what Fath meant. "The console, sir? I don't know much about—"

"*Describe it.*"

"About one meter in width. A puter screen about two hands wide, vocal input, keyboard." I peered at it. "Emergency hatch release, a green pad. Mating lock, smaller, blue—"

"*It's from a ship's launch. The old style. You'll probably find the name on a plate under the key—*"

"*Challenger.* UNS *Challenger.*"

Silence.

"Did you hear? I said—"

"*I heard.*" Fath's voice was from the grave.

A chill banished the fetid warmth of my suit.

Challenger was Father's old ship. In her, he'd been abandoned to the harsh mercies of interstellar space. He'd fought the fish, embedded her prow in a dying fish, Fused with it to home system. So . . . how could her launch be in a fish at Hope Nation?

"Fath, the comm unit still has a chip."

"*Kaminski . . .*"

"Yes, sir?"

"*Things are . . . not as they seem. Would you hold fire?*"

"I can't. Palabee's not worth the powder to blow him to Hell, but those are my people groundside. I can't let the fish have them."

"*I don't think they're . . .*" A sigh. "*I understand. Randy?*"

"Yes, sir?"

"*The chip . . . if you don't mind, plug your suit port into the comm unit. Your suit power will energize it.*"

"I don't want to." I pushed away, floated to the bulkhead opposite. There'd be something terrible on the chip. Screams, or the sound of crewmen being devoured. I'd never outlive the nightmares.

"*I ask this of you. Please.*"

"No!"

A new voice. "*Randy, Jerence Branstead. I'm with Mr. Seafort on the bridge. It was a terrible time on* Challenger. *I hadn't met your father yet, but I heard afterwards. Midshipman Tyre, the only other officer aboard, took the launch to ram a fish, and died saving the ship. Nick named his son Philip after him. Philip Tyre Seafort, the joey we call 'P. T.'* " A pause. "*No, Nick, let me. He's a right to know. Son . . . your father's had a hard life, full of guilts. It would mean a lot if you'd close this door for him. Let him know the worst. It can't be as bad as his imaginings.*"

I whispered something, cleared my throat. Again, louder. "Yes, sir." Reluctantly, I kicked against the living bulkhead, floated back to the console. Leaning over it, I plugged my commcord into the plug.

34

A HISS, that seemed to go on forever.

A voice, dull, drained.

"M—mak—making my final report." Hiss. Then, as if starting anew: "Midshipman Philip Tyre of UNS *Challenger*, making my final report. Not that anyone will read it. I'm sick. The frazzing virus . . . faster than starving, I suppose. And Christ, my hand hurts."

I pawed at my radionics. Was I transmitting? Yes.

"It's September something, 2198. Was it only yesterday they attacked? I took the launch. Captain Seafort sort of agreed. I didn't give him much choice. I scrambled in, tried to bump the fish away from our tubes. Stupid to bother; the tubes don't work and never will. But they're all that keep the crew sane. Seafort—sorry, *Mr.* Seafort's a good man, better than he knows. He lets us play at repairing the drive, and holds us to our duty."

A long, hacking cough.

Safe in my suit, I shivered.

"*Olympiad,* this is Palabee! Destroy them!"

I switched off groundside frequency.

"Well, I rammed the frazzing fish. It was the only way to get him off. The hull of my launch dissolved, clear back to the cockpit. If I wasn't in my suit, I'd be dead. Wish I was." Again, the cough. "They swarmed over me. Those skittery things. Outriders. But no acid, not then. They rolled me out of the launch, what's left of it, into something like a room. I'm pretty sure I was in the fish. It was convulsing like mad. Think it was dying. You won't believe this . . ." Heavy breathing. "They took off my suit, and I could still breathe. Air, inside. They poked me, dumped dirt or sand at my feet. They wanted something. Like they were trying to talk to me, but I had no idea how to answer. Burned my legs pretty bad. And my hand, Jesus, my hand."

He made a sound. So did I.

"The bleeding's stopped, but I can't use it . . . I always was a gutless wonder. Even now I'm too scared to kill myself." The middy's tormented voice rose. "Why the *hell* did they do that to my hand? Got . . . inside it. Tore it open. Christ."

Absently I raised fingers to my cheeks, but couldn't wipe them through the helmet.

"They took me somewhere else . . . another fish. Think I blacked out. Parts of the launch in here too. Not long now. Plenty of oxygen, all those tanks the launch had for passengers, but I can't last. Feverish, can't keep anything down."

From *Olympiad*, deathly silence.

"Mr. Seafort, I wish . . . doesn't really matter, but God, I want to know: was it worth it? Are you saved? I don't really mind dying for that; you saved *me*. From myself. I was an awful shit, the way I treated your middies. Doesn't matter now. But *Challenger* drifted out of view when I hit. If only I knew . . . Christ, only I knew . . . only . . ."

My hand crept to the commcord. I'd have to pull it. Fath would understand.

"Sir, if by some miracle you read this and I'm still alive, you'll cane the hell out of me for insolence. But I wa—want . . . want to say . . . damn it, can't stop crying . . . not your fault. I wanted to take the launch, didn't give you a chance to say no. My fault. Wouldn't do it again, not for anything. One other thing, sir: I tried so hard to be like you. Couldn't. You're a hard man to live up to. Tamarov revered you, and Carr, and of course I—oh God oh God here they come again if they leave me alive I'll come back on this is Midshipman Philip Tyre of UNS *Challenger* signing—"

Hiss.

I forwarded to the end. Nothing.

"Kill them."

No response.

"Fath, kill them all, like Palabee said. Don't spare my fish. Get every one."

"*Randy . . .*" It was Joanne Skor. "*Mr. Seafort . . . can't speak at the moment. Stand by.*"

"KILL THEM!" I aimed a kick at the hovering outrider.

SQUIGGLE SHIP?

"Fuck you all." I jabbed the squiggle mark, with an outrider at the end of it. "Squiggle you, you evil bas—"

YES. The outriders skittered about the chamber, overgrown amoebas in mass rapture. SMALL TIME. SQUIGGLE SHIP DOTS.

"Huh? Ms. Skor, they're literally climbing the walls. I told them to squiggle themselves. I think they like it, but they want me to squiggle dots. Now they're—whoa, the fish is undulating. The deck is heaving; it's making the console slide . . . they're moving it toward me. I think they want me to take it."

"*Then, take it!*"

Right. "Where? I'm a frazzing prisoner."

"*Olympiad, Lieutenant Riev at Admiralty, speaking for Mr. Kenzig. You are to—*"

Lieutenant? Last week Alon had been a mere middy, and not a very pleasant one. He moved fast.

"—engage the enemy with all resources. Plot a course to geosync over the Venturas forthwith. Maintain that position until all fish in theater are destroyed. Acknowledge."

"Admiralty, Watch Officer Joanne Skor acknowledging—"

"Mr. Riev, this is Captain Seafort." Fath's voice was ice. *"Please connect me to the Admiral."*

"He's unavailable, sir. He left instruc—"

"Sir, I do NOT acknowledge his purported instructions." A gasp, from someone on the bridge.

The console rippled to my feet. I kicked it away, or tried. I only succeeded in bouncing myself backward, to carom off the fish's skin.

Mr. Riev's tone was injured. "Sir, are you suggesting—"

"I wasn't born yesterday. Put Mr. Kenzig on, with visuals, and then ask me what I insinuate."

"Sir, I—he told me to say . . . I'll get back to you. Have *him* get back to you." The line went dead.

"Sir? Fath? What if the order was real?"

"Then I face court-martial. Never you mind. Do your part, joey, and we may find our way through. Where's the console?"

What did the frazzing console have to do with . . . "At my feet."

"Any idea why?"

"They want me to squiggle it." I heard myself, and grimaced. Fath had just been through hell, and my tone was appalling. "Sir, no disrespect intended."

"They gave you poor Philip's rotted hand. Now the console." He sounded pensive. *"Why?"*

"Harry melted my prosth. Could it be about hands? They prefer one arm, not two?"

"No, that doesn't seem . . ."

"Kaminski to *Olympiad,* we've scored fifty-three. In a few moments they'll be in the outer atmosphere. Some seventy are at the far edge of our—"

"Kaminski, stay off the frequency. Palabee calling Seafort, we've a hundred seventeen fish overhead. They'll blanket the coast. You've had more experience; should we try to escape the Venturas by heli?"

"Admiralty to *Olympiad,* respond."

"Randy, do they want you to squiggle it, or do they want to squiggle it?"

I stared at the last message. SQUIGGLE. SHIP. DOTS.

I shrugged. "Both. Neither. Sir, I'm in way over my head. I'm just"— my voice cracked—"a joeykid. I've no business being here." In the fish. On *Olympiad.* In Fath's world.

An outrider darted forward. OUTRIDER FISH SQUIGGLE SHIP ONE-ARM DOTS. I blurted the message onward to Fath.

In my suit, a light flashed yellow.

"Son, they're desperate for something. I thought it was peace, but now they make war. You're the"—a barely perceptible pause—*"the man on the spot. You've been brilliant, and I'm counting on you. Solve the puzzle."*

An outrider quivered before me, melted to the deck. Submission? No, he withdrew a meter or so. On the deck where he'd been, a white substance. I bent, cautiously touched it. Tiny grains of sand fell from my gloved fingers.

"Admiralty to Captain Seafort, respond!"

"Sir, he's giving us something else."

"What?"

"No way to tell."

"I count on you. Go ahead, Admiralty."

I couldn't tell more about the sand without desuiting. It would almost be a relief. My suit was hot, and the persistently blinking light was the low-air warning.

"Stand by for Mr. Kenzig." Clicks.

What in God's name did they want of me? My eyes stung.

I stamped my foot, shot upward. Damn greenie. When I reoriented, I clutched the writing stick. "Why fish squiggle?"

"Seafort, Admiral Kenzig here." His voice was strained.

"Yes, sir. Visuals, please."

The same outrider answered me: FISH PLANET NO DOTS DIE.

I wrote, "I don't understand."

"Never mind that! You're to—"

"Visuals, or I disconnect."

FISH NO-FUSE PLANET DIE NO DOTS. SHIP SQUIGGLE FISH DOTS. FISH PLANET NO-PLANET NO DIE.

A chill stabbed my spine. What I saw was of great import. Gibberish, but important.

"All right." I was speaking to myself. "Fish go to planet and die no dots . . . without dots. Ship—us people—squiggle the dots. Fish don't die. No, not all fish. Just the fish planet / no-planet."

I wrote, "Why war?"

"Rank insubordination, Seafort! Here are your bloody visuals! Satisfied?"

FISH ONE-ARM NO WAR. <NUMBERS>—I'd add them later—WAR DOTS.

"Captain, Ship's Boy Carr reporting. Don't shoot them down, not yet. We're so close!" Why should he listen to me? Moments ago I wanted them all dead. That poor boy Tyre . . . Lost, alone in a fish, as I was now.

Back to work, joey. My fish isn't warring. Yeah, I see that. But the others do. Because of the dots. Why some, but not others?

"*Pan the holocam. Who's with you?*"

"That's none of your bloody business!"

I asked the outrider, "Fish equals fish?"

Great agitation. Outriders skittered about. One, quivering, finally wrote, FISH NOT EQUAL FISH.

"*Sir, I have reason to believe you're under duress.*"

Why the incessant gabble? How could I concentrate with civil war breaking out all across . . .

Was that it? I stabbed with the tool. "Fish war fish?"

NO. Then, as if with great reluctance, OUTRIDER WAR OUTRIDER. HUMAN NO SQUIGGLE DOTS.

"I'll squiggle your damn dots! Just call off the attack!"

"*What, Randy?*"

"Sorry, Captain. Thinking out loud."

"I'm not under duress," the Admiral fumed. "I've a mind to relieve you this moment!"

"*With due respect, sir, I'd disregard your order.*"

"Very well. Lieutenant Riev and Governor McEwan are in my office, but that's of no consequence. You're to proceed—"

"*Who else?*"

"Damn it to bloody hell, Seafort, not another word! SecGen or no, I'll—"

"*Scanlen, are you with him? Palabee? How many armed guards? Admiral, pan the holocam THIS INSTANT!*" A pause. "*Ah, I thought so. Odd, how I can't see their hands. Mr. Kenzig, come aboard* Olympiad, *and I'll obey any order you issue. Under the circumstances—*"

"You know damned well I can't go aloft with fish—"

"*The moment the crisis abates. Good day, sir.*"

"Fish no go planet die no dots?" I hoped the outrider would understand. Do fish die without these mysterious dots, if they're not going to a planet?

NO.

And he'd deposited sand at my feet, just as Harry's predecessor, in our corridor, had deposited the nutrients it wanted. "I was afraid you'd say that." Slowly, reluctantly, I reached for my helmet clamp. "Ship's Boy Carr to *Olympiad*, making . . ." for a moment, I found it hard to speak ". . . what may be my final report. They want to squiggle dots. I think the dots are the white sand on the deck. I'm going to see what it is. If it burns me, I won't be able to get back in my suit." Not one-handed.

"No! Don't—"

"Air's short, and I'm running out of time. Please listen. The outriders have factions, like we do. Outrider war outrider. It's all about the dots. Our faction—Harry's group—wants to squiggle dots with us. The others, maybe they don't want to, or don't think it's possible. So they're attacking the Venturas. Maybe it can be stopped. Just a sec."

I bent. "Why war planet?"

DOTS. PLANET DOTS.

"Sir, the Venturas have something they want. Harry's people tried to explain, but . . ."

"Kaminski, this is Admiral Kenzig, linked with Vince Palabee and his government in the Venturas. We issue a joint order: blow that bloody fish out of Hope System! The one that has the boy."

"Colonel, please disregard. Admiral Kenzig is under duress."

ONE-ARM FISH. OUTRIDER. Then, WAR FISH OUTRIDER. No, the second picture was different. An outrider, but much larger.

"Seafort, you hear me? This is Right Reverend Ricard Scanlen. You're to take out those fish, all of them! Do so and I'll reconsider excommunicating your cronies. Branstead and that Dakko."

How little he knew Fath, if he thought Mr. Seafort would barter for his friends' lives.

Fath would sooner trade . . .

Trade.

Squiggle.

"Fath—Captain, sir, I think I've got it. But I won't do like Mr. Tyre. Give me permission to take off the suit. I think I know what they want!" Most of it, anyway.

"Randy . . ."

"I had it off before."

"For a moment, when you were choking."

"Believe me, I won't be much longer. Their air stinks. Hurry, please."

"Seafort? Vince, talk to him, the madman won't—"

"Granted, Mr. Carr."

I pulled my clamps, one at a time. The fish began to pulse. Perhaps it was airing the compartment in anticipation.

The helmet came off. My ears didn't pop. Cautiously, I took a breath. Phew.

I ran a suit sleeve across my sweaty forehead. All right, now. I bent, ran gloved fingers through the dry sand. As before, it gave me no clue.

I sniffed it. Nothing, no odor at all.

Tentatively, the outrider approached. <LARGE NUMBER OF FISH> WAR DOTS. ONE-ARM FISH SQUIGGLE DOTS.

Yeah, you disagree. I've got that.

NO DOTS, PLANET FISH DIE.

"And?" I spoke aloud, to no purpose.

NO DOTS FISH FUSE, NO DIE. NO DOTS FISH NO-FUSE, NO DIE. NO DOTS FISH PLANET, FISH DIE. They don't need the white sand to Fuse, or propel themselves. Just to go planetside.

Wearily, I worked my arm out of my suit, trying not to breathe the fetid air. "Guess we've got to know, joey." Somehow, I made my fingers approach the sand. One fingertip brushed it, jerked away as if scorched.

But I wasn't burned. I examined my skin, took a deep breath, picked up a handful. It looked so familiar, but . . . Randy, you're an idiot if you . . . I know. Get it over with. Screwing my eyes shut, I touched it to my tongue.

My eyes popped open. I stared at the outrider, then the sand. At the outrider. It couldn't be. "This is all about . . . salt?" I grabbed a handful. "SALT?" Feverishly I wrote, "Dots equal one-arm hand?"

YES.

"Fish no die big number dots, small number?" How much salt do you need? Why hadn't we worked out words for "how much" or "how many"?

SHIP OUTRIDER INSIDE.

"Yeah, *Olympiad*."

He drew a line dissecting it, then another, and another.

"Don't threaten me, joey!"

And another. Then he erased the remainder of the ship. There was left a small wedge. Far less than one cargo hold.

"Why can't you get your own damn salt?" No use asking. We didn't have the words to explain, and were out of time.

"Time small," I wrote.

TIME NONE.

"Trade salt, outrider one-arm fish talk to outrider war-fish, say no war?" If we trade, will you get them to call it off?

YES.

"Million planets, million salt." Surely the aliens had access to salt deposits elsewhere in the galaxy. It couldn't be that rare. "Why salt one-arm planet?"

FISH FUSE FUSE FUSE FUSE. GO PLANET NOT DIE. NOT GO PLANET, DIE.

I blinked. Could it be that simple? They had to go groundside every few Fuses, and needed salt to get down, or possibly to go aloft again? Salt wasn't a fuel, but . . . hell they were organic. Lord God knew what chemicals they used to turn themselves into high-altitude balloons. Perhaps there weren't that many planets with salt beds in our region of the galaxy. It might matter, but not here, not now.

The solution might be in our grasp, but . . . I wrote, "Big outrider?" He'd mentioned one, a few minutes past.

BIG OUTRIDER SAY WAR / NO WAR. SAY FUSE / NO FUSE. SAY PLANET / NO PLANET.

Right. His word was law. Like Fath's.

ONE-ARM SAY TRADE. It sounded like a demand.

"Let me think!" I sank to the deck, cradling my suit.

TIME SMALL. TIME NO.

First, I'd have to don my suit. Then it would take precious minutes to explain, more to persuade Fath . . . No time.

Yet what I contemplated would govern relations with the aliens, for generations.

No.

No matter what it cost, I'd have to ask Fath's approval.

God, the air stank. Mechanically, I laid out my suit.

My malfunctioning prosth banged against my chest. I yearned to hammer it silent.

The air in my suit seemed stale. Well, it *was* stale. When that was gone, I could breathe what the fish provided, but unless the fish happened to engage in photosynthesis, it couldn't store much. I had, what? An hour or so? Better get on with it. I flicked on my radionics.

"*Stadholder Palabee, Bishop Scanlen, Governor McEwan, respond! This is Sarah Frand aboard* Olympiad. *Stadholder Palabee, Bishop Scan—*"

"Go ahead, Ms. Frand. Palabee."

"*With Reverend Pandeker's sanction, I've relieved Captain Seafort. I have the bridge. He and his son are confined to quarters. Other officers too. I can't raise Admiral Kenzig, would you—*"

Oh, shit.

"Wonderful, Ms. Frand!" Palabee. "Stand by, I'll have the deacons . . . Kenzig will be on in a moment."

"*Tell him we're making flank speed toward Venturas geosync.*"

I pushed off from the bulkhead, floated idly in my dank suit. Time no longer mattered. The aliens would invade; Ms. Frand would kill as many as she could. The frightful war that ravaged Earth, almost obliterated Central-town, would rekindle. New generations would be squandered fighting the fish.

Wearily, I flipped off the speaker.

All for naught. Anthony's death, to save our government. Dad's, to save Earth's population and his beloved Nick Seafort from Church domination. Andrew Ghent. Even poor Kevin Dakko's grisly death, that had destroyed his father . . . for what?

I'd had the key almost within grasp. With Fath's help, I might have persuaded . . .

No longer. Sarah Frand had made a catastrophic choice. To serve her Church, she'd betrayed her Navy. They would send Fath groundside, of course. Corrine, too, would burn.

TIME NO.

I muttered, "You've got that right." I curled into a fetal ball. In the failing air, I drifted and dreamed. Laboriously, I put the pieces together. There, for Fath. There, for Kevin. There, for Dad and Anthony. There, for Mr. Branstead.

An outrider brandished a gray appendage, turned me slowly, scrutinizing me through my suit.

ONE-ARM DIE?

The first Harry had died, his replacement had told us. Perhaps they assumed that on my death, we'd merely send another envoy.

No, we had no telepathy. What one human knew wasn't automatically provided to us all.

I uncurled myself, scratched with the stick. "One-arm die one hour." Or thereabouts.

The irony was, given a bit of air, a little time, I could still put it together.

But did I dare? I served in the U.N. Navy only by Fath's edict. I had no authority, no right. My head swelled by Dad's example and Anth's foolish tolerance. Mr. Tolliver had known how to handle me; after his most painful caning, I wouldn't dare cross him soon.

Well, he was under arrest now, with Fath.

So, joeyboy. Shall you, or not?

I drifted in the zero-gee cocoon of the fish, and planned my treason.

"Humans trade salt." I panted, as if making a long speech. Silly; my lips had barely moved. I wielded my writing stick.

YES. Quivering emotion.

"Humans not trade salt / hand. Not trade salt / ship."

Emotion. It didn't look like joy. Perhaps consternation. The chamber seemed crowded. More and more outriders wriggled through the permeable membranes, finding a roost on deck, bulkheads, overhead.

TRADE? NOT TRADE?

"Ships Fuse," I said, writing.

YES. One outrider seemed to have become the spokesman. The others merely watched.

"Fish Fuse."

YES.

"Fish Fuse outriders."

YES.

"Fish Fuse ships?"

NOT UNDERSTAND.

"Fish Fuse human nutrient?" Can you take a cargo?

SHIP FUSE HUMAN NUTRIENT. Well, yes. But that was beside the point.

"Fish fuse human nutrient, human rock-bomb?" It was the closest I could come to "ore."

YES. I could have sworn the tone was doubtful. Something in the stroke of the "equals" . . .

"Time Fuse . . ." This was going to be tricky. I could only think of one place we both knew. "Time fish one-arm planet Fuse hundreds-of-dead-fish, dozens-of-dead-ships?" How long to home system? If we'd made a word for it, I'd forgotten. By the time I'd spelled it out, I was panting. I made a new symbol for home system, pointed to the phrase. Now we'd have a word.

<BIG NUMBER>.

He'd used hours; of course the number was large. I'd have to convert . . .

No, make him do it. "Time Fuse planet say month." We'd built on seconds, gone as high as a year.

MONTH. MONTH. MONTH. MONTH. MONTH. MONTH. <SLASH>.

Six and a half months. Far less than our ships. I breathed. "Thank you. God, if You exist, thank You too." It wasn't blasphemy, was it, if . . . no time for that now.

"One-arm trade salt / Fuse human rock-bomb. Fuse nutrient."

NOT UNDERSTAND. NO. FEAR. NO. ONE-ARM DEAD. WAR.

I swallowed. I'd known the risk. "Human not trade hand, not trade ship. Human trade Fish Fuse."

HURT FISH.

"Not understand."

SHIP FUSE, TASTE HURT FISH. OUTRIDERS <SOMETHING> FISH, NO-HURT. NO FUSE HOME SYSTEM. HURT DIE.

"Is one-arm fish <something>?"

YES.

I licked my lips. "You joeys did something to your fish, didn't you? So our Fusing wouldn't drive them mad and attract them. They're blinded, or deafened. For some reason, you can't send altered fish to home system."

"No-<something> fish Fuse home system?" How about the unaltered Fish?

YES. NO. The outrider skittered. NO-<SOMETHING> FISH FUSE HOME SYSTEM NO HURT.

"Good."

But he wasn't done. SHIP FUSE. FISH HURT. FISH WAR SHIPS.

"You'll send them, and they'll hear us Fuse, and go mad." I frowned. "They're out." I drew, "<Something> fish fuse home system, why die?"

FISH FUSE FUSE FUSE GO PLANET. DIE NO SALT.

"But we have—they have plenty—oh, joey, it's going to be all right!" One last writing. "Home system humans trade salt, here humans trade salt. No war."

OUTRIDER TELL BIG OUTRIDER TRADE. ONE-ARM SAY TRADE HUMAN SHIP. NO WAR ONE HOUR. We have a deal. Let's each tell our side. One hour truce.

"Hang on." I had all the pieces. I keyed my suit radio.

ONE-ARM SUIT YES?

"Ship's Boy Carr to *Olympiad*. Respond—"

SUIT YES?

"Yes, the helmet's sealed! Let me be for a—"

As one, the outriders dissolved into the fish's flesh. The fish pulsed. Colors swirled.

"What the—"

Pulse.

"Hey, wait!"

PULSE.

In the portholes, the stars disappeared.

I blanched.

We were Fused.

35

GOD, IT'S ME. Randy. It's dark and I'm feeling a touch frightened. More than a touch. I'm not . . . I haven't been . . . I don't know how to do this; I've never prayed in earnest. Do You just listen, or do You intervene? 'Cause if You intercede, I need it now. Not for me. No, I really mean that. I don't know how many lives ride on my . . . hundreds, certainly. Thousands. Probably millions. For them, would You . . .

I don't know what I'm asking for. To let me finish this, I suppose. Fath says You're real. I so want You to be, especially now. Can You hear me crying silently, inside my helmet?

Did You comfort Philip Tyre, in his wretched last moments? If You won't help me finish, would You do as much for me? What was it Tyre said, in the humility that comes when all is lost? "I was an awful shit." God . . . Sir? I can't bring myself to admit it to Fath, or Mr. Tolliver, but, Sir . . . I was an awful shit. To Anth, to Fath. I always wanted my way, rarely stopped to listen. Even more rarely did I do as I was told. Now I'm getting what I deserve. I'm really afraid there's a Hell, and You'll send me to it. If I promised, would . . .

No, I said I wouldn't beg. Not for myself. I'll pay my debts, and take the Hell. But might You help undo our muddle? Or somehow, let me do it, before I'm over?

If You hear me, could You give a sign, anything, no matter how sma—

Blinding light. I flung an arm over my visor.

Warily, I opened an eyelid. On one side, the fish's skin glowed. Sunlight? In the flesh, colors swirled madly, over and over. A pattern? I couldn't be sure.

Out of swirling flesh, outriders reconstituted themselves. They attached themselves to the fish's outer membrane, became indistinct, passed through.

I made my way to a porthole, and gasped.

Below floated Hope Nation's vast, green orb. We'd Defused into a huge mass of fish. Some, I saw, were dead; their skins gray and blistered. The outriders ignored them, launched themselves from one living fish to another.

One by one, the fish they reached Fused out.

Outriders—others, but I wasn't sure how I knew—were absorbed through the membrane into our own fish. They stayed only a moment or so, and passed outward.

Determinedly, I blocked the path of one. I jabbed the deck with the symbol for "why." "? ? ?" What's going on?

ONE-ARM FISH TELL BIG OUTRIDER TRADE YES. <LARGE NUMBER> FISH FUSE NO PLANET. ONE HOUR FUSE PLANET.

My heart pounded. They were pulling back, carrying out their bargain. We had an hour, no more, to cement the truce.

Now it depended on me.

I keyed open every frequency the suit had. Let them all hear. "Ship's Boy Carr to *Olympiad*, to Station, to Centraltown Admiralty, to Venturas Base. To the regional government. All planters within range of my voice, attention!"

"Belay that, joeyboy!"

"Who's there?"

"Frand. Captain Frand."

Over my dead body. "Station, record, please. Ms. Frand, this is for your Log."

"*I say what goes into—*"

"Goofjuice." Steady, joey. How would Fath handle it? "You'll be interrogated under poly and drugs, for having relieved your Captain. Hide what I have to say and they'll hang you. Transmission begins."

"*Just a—very well, Log it, Mr. Sutwin.*"

"This is *Olympiad*'s Ship's Boy Randolph Carr—"

"*No longer. You're removed from our ship's company.*"

I reared in my suit, ricocheting off a membrane. "Don't interrupt, you self-righteous sea lawyer! The fate of Hope Nation and home system is in our hands. This is Randolph Carr, reporting from the alien vessel, uh . . . *One-Arm*. On Captain Seafort's instructions, I've been negotiating with the outriders. We have a truce. They'll cease their attack on the Venturas and on *Olympiad*. As a show of good faith, they're withdrawing for an hour."

"*Olympiad*, Colonel Kaminski on Orbit Station. It's a trick. In an hour, we'll be over the horizon. When they Fuse back, there'll be nothing to stop them. *Olympiad* won't be in position to give covering fire for three hours forty-seven—"

"*I'm well aware, sir.*" Ms. Frand's tone was cold.

"—and the Venturas' lasers won't suffice. We won't stand down. Keep firing!"

"*I agree. We will.*"

"Carr to Station, are you crazy? You just said you can't get them all. The fish know you're going over the horizon; why infuriate them to no purp—"

"*You have no standing, Mr. Carr.*" Frand. "*Leave this to respon—*"

"I want to hear." A new voice. It sounded distant. "Henry Winthrop, Council of Planters. Randolph, what have you arranged?"

"Nothing firm, but—"

Ms. Frand said forcefully, "*A glitched joeykid can't make a treaty! Only the U.N. Assembly—*"

Mr. Winthrop growled, "They bombed Centraltown, Ms. Frand. I was a boy and saw the devastation. Were you there?"

"*No, but . . .*"

"If he can head off war, don't stop him or I'll make you regret it! That's a threat to you and your Navy and the whole frazzing U.N.—"

"Governor McEwan here. You speak treason, Winthrop. Remove yourself from this conversation."

"Hold on, now." Palabee, his tone anxious. "Bishop Scanlen and I are at target zero. Let's hear—"

"LISTEN, ALL OF YOU!" Inside the helmet, my scream nearly shattered my eardrums. "They want to trade. All we—"

"*We tracked his transmission.*" Ms. Frand. "*I know the fish he's in. He told them to wait 'til Orbit Station horizons. I'm going to settle—*"

I grabbed my stick. "FUSE NOW NOW NOW!"

The fish pulsed.

"—no-Fuse fish die—"

The membrane parted. Protoplasm glowed white, gushed outward. I ducked, as if I might escape the fire.

Another pulse.

Dark. Fusion.

I gritted my teeth, wrote by feel. "Defuse ship <line> Station <line> fish." Would they know what I meant? Would it save them? Half of us had switched sides, and I wasn't sure. Scanlen and Palabee wanted to hear me out. Frand wanted me dead. And I was saving fish from humans.

Moments later we Defused in the black of space. I peered anxiously through the membrane. Hope Nation was nowhere in sight. No Station. No *Olympiad.*

I was panting. The yellow suit light glowed steadily. My time was almost gone. Where in hell were we? The cold unforgiving light of a billion distant stars was my only reply.

We Fused again.

"—*Gone. No idea* where he—"

"—should have listened."

"—make a treason charge stick, McEwan, go ahead and try. Anthony Carr was right; you're a snake in—"

There was light behind the fish's skin. Strong light.

I wrote, "Where one-arm fish?"

An outrider materialized, out of the fish's flesh. I wished they wouldn't do that; it gave me the jumps. PLANET <LINE> FISH <LINE> STATION <LINE> SHIP.

"—we have a shot for perhaps ten more minutes. There's no more than a half-dozen fish over the atmosphere."

"*Colonel, we're three hours twenty—*"

A porthole opened, inches from my face. I flinched.

Orbit Station loomed, breathtakingly close.

Hastily, I keyed my radio. "Colonel Kaminski, hold fire! It's Randy Carr. I'm in the fish alongside."

"What are you up to, joey? *Olympiad* wants you dead, so do Scanlen's crew. And if you've joined the fish, so do—"

Lord God, remember that help I asked for? Now would be a good time. "Sir, my fish won't attack. Hear me out!"

A pause. "I don't know, son. The time comes for a joey to take sides."

"Yes." I tried to recall the Station tech whom Kaminski had asked Anth to rescue, ages past, at our reception. "Is Mr. Driscoll still on Station? Anthony would be pleased. For his sake, I beg you, sir." I held my breath. It would be enough, or it wouldn't.

"Are you . . ." His voice was subdued. "Have you gone over to the fish? Tell truth, joey."

"Truth, sir? The Church has gone mad. They want all fish dead, at whatever cost. Fath—Captain Seafort—is compromised; he'll give anything, do anything, to save Corrine Sloan. Lieutenant Frand's taken *Olympiad* for the Church. Scores of fish will die today, and Lord God knows how many of us, when the aliens exact revenge. Have I gone over? Yes, sir. To peace. If that be treason . . ." I fought to bring my voice under control. ". . . execute me now!"

Bravo, joey. Anthony Carr, his tone sardonic.

Bravo, son. My father Derek, his voice somber, from some unimaginable distance.

"Dad, I . . ."

"Very well, you have our protection. *Olympiad,* take notice."

"Kaminski, you're blocking our shot." Lieutenant Frand sounded disgusted.

I said, "Mr. Winthrop, Bishop Scanlen, all of you. I have a deal worked out, but I need help with the details. I need Captain Seafort, and also—"

"He will not be brought to the caller."

"Not to the caller. To the fish."

Dead silence. For over a minute, I heard nothing but my short stabbing breaths.

Then, "This is Right Reverend Scanlen. What deal do you offer?"

"Salt. I know it sounds odd, but they want salt. Let them trade and they'll—"

"You need rebalancing." Scanlen's tone was dismissive. "Ms. Frand, obliterate that fish at the first opportunity. I have a link to Mr. Kenzig if you wish that confirmed."

"No, sir. Not necessary." Frand's tone was heavy.

"You will send Seafort and his woman groundside as soon as hostilities cease."

"Reverend Pandeker assured me that wouldn't be neces—"

"I'm certain it was his honest conviction." Scanlen's voice was unctuous. "But from the Cathedral, the view is clearer. God's law demands retribution."

"I don't—I'll have to think . . ."

"Of course, Ms. Frand. Think it through. Consult with Reverend Pandeker."

A long silence. *"Very well."* Frand sounded defeated.

So it *was* to be treason. I called, "Mr. Winthrop?"

The reply was immediate; he must have been waiting by his transmitter. "Yes, joey?"

"In less than an hour, thanks to the Church and Navy, the fish will attack. When you've had enough of their madness, call me on this frequency." Two could play at insurrection.

"Palabee to Admiralty. I'm leaving at once for Centraltown. Join me at—"

"Do that, *Vince.*" My scorn was withering. "By heli, it's a six-hour flight. I estimate they'll meet you about halfway. Think of me when the first outrider leaps aboard."

"You little bastard, you wouldn't—"

"I wouldn't. They would." My voice was ice.

"We can't just hide in the hills—"

"I tried reason. I tried begging. Now I'll try the only course left. Good day."

I clicked off my caller, gripped my stick. "One-arm talk big outrider."

BIG OUTRIDER NOT IN ONE-ARM FISH.

"One-arm go big outrider fish." Or, if you prefer . . .

SMALL TIME. MINUTES. NO-GO. I grunted. If that wasn't "Wait a minute," I didn't know what was.

Abruptly we Fused once more. Other than the suddenness, it wasn't quite as unnerving. Moments later, we Defused. We'd emerged perhaps a little farther from the sun, but I had sunlight enough to see we were surrounded by fish.

Our fish's color swirled ever more rapidly; our direction changed, and fish loomed closer. We must be squirting propellant, but I felt nothing.

An outrider merged into the outer membrane and was gone.

I used the wait that followed to work at vocabulary. We needed a symbol for "help." I drew "Trade help outriders," and "trade help humans." They didn't understand. Then I tried, "Outrider help one-arm suit, one-arm no die."

YES. HELP.

A new word. I sighed. We needed so many.

In moments, the membrane admitted two outriders. I realized I couldn't possibly keep track of them. Perhaps they couldn't themselves.

In the dim light, the outrider drew. BIG OUTRIDER SAY WAR / NO WAR.

"Here in one-arm fish?"

YES. He withdrew, attached himself to a membrane.

There was one outrider left.

"Hello."

He quivered.

I got to work. "One-arm not big-human. Big-human in ship. Humans war humans. One-arm say trade. Ship-humans say no-trade."

I waited. It was a lot to digest.

TRADE EQUALS NO WAR. NO-TRADE EQUALS WAR.

"I know that." I bit my lip. Fog was settling into my thoughts.

"Big outrider say fish go planet. Not planet." Damn it, I needed words we didn't have. I tried to recall every bloody symbol we knew. Near. Jess had made a heiroglyph for "near." Circles close, but not touching. Harry had seemed to understand. If he did, they all did. "Big outrider help one-arm. Big outrider tell fish go near planet. Small time. One-arm talk ship, one-arm say trade. Fish go near planet. Near war." But not make war. Please, God, help them understand.

HUNDRED FISH GO NOT-NEAR STATION, NEAR PLANET. FISH / HUMANS NEAR WAR. NOT WAR.

"Yes!" I underlined it three times, as if he'd taste my fervor. "One-arm tell big-human go inside one-arm fish. Big-human talk big-outrider." I'd bring you together, here in my fish. It would be the last thing I did.

TRADE?

"Big-human say trade." It was a promise I hoped I could keep.

We waited while he sent emissaries throughout his fleet.

One by one, the fish began blinking out.

I floated, in fetal position. Occasionally my helmet touched the over-head, or my arm the deck.

"—another twenty or so. They're massing just above the outer atmos—"

"—urged to take every precaution. In the great war, the Centraltown bomb appeared overhead less than thirteen minutes—"

"—*at flank speed. They'll have begun their descent before* Olympiad's *in position to*—"

My suit was hot, desperately hot. I ought to do something about it.

"—posted a list of inoculation centers in the event of virus—"

"Josh Hopewell, Theo Mantiet, this is Winthrop on open circuit. I can't locate you; call me privately the moment you—"

The big outrider had anchored himself to the deck. He waited impassively, an occasional twitch his only motion.

"Kaminski, have you located the fish with the Carr joey?"

"—emergency meeting of the Planters' Council—"

"Ms. Frand, I haven't tried. We're over horizon for all but a few of—"

"I'm right here." I cleared my throat, tried again. "Randolph Carr . . . to all parties, attention." My tongue was thick. "We're in a great . . . squadron of fish just outside the atmosphere. Once they begin their descent I doubt they can reverse . . ." I panted.

"You frazzing traitor!" It sounded like the Bishop.

"I never told them to attack!" And it was even true; I'd only told them to pretend to attack. What would the aliens do if my scheme failed? It didn't bear considering. "We have . . . few minutes at most. Station can't help you now, Scanlen. Neither can *Olympiad*. Your joeygirl Frand will show up just in time to watch the carnage."

"You think your fish friends will spare *you*, Randolph? You're done for. If not by them, by us."

"Oh, I know. But . . . better hurry. Fading fast, here." I slapped my leg. It didn't seem to help. "They'll listen to me, see? Like me to call 'em off?"

"What do you want?" Bishop Scanlen's voice was strained.

"Help. I want a responsible adult to treat with 'em. One you'll all trust."

"And . . . who's . . . that?" The voice floated from another galaxy.

I jerked myself awake. "Already told you. Mr. Seafort." I yawned mightily, nearly dislocated my jaw.

"You jest. I wouldn't trust him enough to—"

"Not his intent. Justasec." It was no use. I tore at my clamps. Somehow I got the helmet off, took huge gasps of horrible air. Cradling it upside down, I spoke into the helmet mike, straining to hear the speakers. "Bet you trust his word. Most honest man you ever met."

"That's as may be. He's . . . out of the picture."

"Put him back in. Got only a few minutes." The fetid air was making me dizzy. Barely better than the suit.

The big outrider stirred. Other aliens squeezed through internal membranes, headed for the skin. They became indistinct, disappeared.

Hastily, I wrote, "?"

OUTRIDER HELP ONE-ARM.

How? I could ask, but it seemed too much trouble.

"Ms. Frand, what about it? You want war?"

"It's not my decision, joey."

"Goofjuice! Send Mr. Seafort. We'll put a stop—"

"We're sailing your way."

"Send him in the launch!" The launch could sail rings around a behemoth like *Olympiad*.

"He's under administrative deten—"

"Jesus God, how'd you ever make lieutenant? Release him! Scanlen doesn't own you!"

"No, but Lord God owns my soul. I'm doing what—"

I panted, "What d'ya think He'll . . . say when . . . fish take out Hope Nation? 'Well done, daughter'?"

Frand's tone was somber. *"No. I don't think that.* Olympiad *to Admiralty, urgent priority. Respond."*

"Lieutenant Riev at Admiralty, go ahead, I'll relay . . ."

"Put Kenzig on the line, you contemptible toady!"

"Ma'am, we serve the same cause—"

"The bloody hell we do. Put him on!"

Two outriders merged through the skin to enter our chamber. Their forms were thick and bulky.

I wondered what prayer to make at the end. I wouldn't be conscious much longer.

The outrider nudged me with a gray appendage.

I waved him away. "Later."

"Kenzig here." The Admiral's tone was cautious.

"Sir, I know your position's difficult, but do you think we might do as he asks? Carr trusts him, so do the planters. Hell, I do too, for that matter. Seafort won't go back on his word."

OUTRIDER HELP ONE-ARM.

"Too late, joey."

ONE-ARM NO-DIE.

"Yes, die." Please, God, get it over with. I'd failed.

The outrider poked my air tank. Floating free, it drifted across the chamber.

"Leave it, it's empty." I couldn't write that, my brain was fogged, and we didn't have words.

He poked it again.

The speaker crackled. "All citizens of Centraltown, by advice of the Planters' Council, remain in your homes. Stay off the streets."

I closed my eyes. Something nudged me. I squinted. My tank. I shoved it away.

Wait a minute.

I was *wearing* my tank.

Wearily, heart pounding, I shoved off after the other tank, cornered it at a membrane.

The surface was mottled. I could barely make out the plate.

UNS *Challenger.*

"Thanks, but it's fifty years old. It wouldn't . . ."

The seal was good.

I cried, "Don't give me hope!" If it was empty, it would be too much to bear.

"You'd send the SecGen to his death inside a fish?" Admiral Kenzig.

Ms. Frand said, *"They haven't killed Randy."*

"Not yet."

I reached behind me, undid my useless tank, switched the hose connector to the new. In zero gee it was just possible; in grav, I couldn't have managed it one-handed.

Helmet.

I grabbed at it; it skittered away.

The outrider fell atop it, surged from deck to bulkhead. It loomed over me, brandishing the helmet. I flinched. It flowed over me, centering the helmet on my suit, blinding me completely. A click. Another.

Light, as the outrider withdrew. Hastily, I switched on the tank.

Cold, fresh air.

My lungs heaved. Lord God! I breathed, over and again. The dull ache behind my eyes receded.

"Venturas Base to *Olympiad,* fish are coming down! Half a dozen at least! For God's sake, help us!"

I spun to the big outrider. "Outrider say no war!"

NO WAR.

"Fish go planet!"

OUTRIDER HELP ONE-ARM.

"But—"

FISH GO PLANET. DIE.

I gaped. "A bluff?" I yearned for a way to write it. Were they just like us, after all?

FISH GO. NO OUTRIDERS.

I jabbed at my radio. "For God's sake, Mr. Kenzig!"

The Admiral's voice was tired. "Bishop Scanlen, I'll take responsibility for sending Seafort. Do you object?"

"Bless it, of course I do! He's an excommunicate, an apostate—"

"His blasted joeyboy has us by the private parts, and demands Seafort. What do you suggest?"

Scanlen yelled, "Kill the fish!"

"But, Your Reverence, there are technical difficulties. The Station's out of range for sixteen hours. *Olympiad* won't have a shot until—"

"You're here to protect us!"

A long silence. "Actually, I'm envoy to an allied government, here to superintend our visiting ships. We've no fleet, no personnel, no—"

The Bishop's tone was frantic. "While you gabble, Kenzig, Satan's spawn loom overhead!"

I grinned tightly. "Let me make it clear," I said. "I won't lift a finger to stop the fish without Captain Seafort."

"Accursed seed of a warped soul! Thou child of the devil, thou enemy of all righteousness, wilt thou not cease to pervert—"

"*BISHOP!*" Kenzig's bellow could have stopped an avalanche.

Silence, that seemed to stretch forever. "So be it," Scanlen said heavily. "Send a demon to treat with demons."

The Admiral's tone was brisk. "Ms. Frand, escort Captain Seafort to the launch. Make all haste."

I demanded, "Restored to his rank and authority!"

"I can't return him to command of *Olympiad*. Not while—"

"I didn't say command of *Olympiad*. Full rank and authority."

"But . . ."

"Centraltown, Venturas Base here. Can you send help? *Olympiad?* Station? Venturas Base is declaring an emerg—"

"Very well. Ms. Frand, Log it. You'd best hurry."

"Not just the Captain. I need someone else."

"Who?"

I took a deep breath. "Chris Dakko. A civilian, he's—"

"The victualler, yes. See that it's done, Ms. Frand."

"Sir, if he doesn't want to go . . . ?"

"SEND HIM!" The Admiral's roar made me flinch.

"Aye aye, sir!"

I turned to the big outrider. "Big human go to one-arm fish. Inside yes?"

INSIDE YES. Then, HUMAN FEAR?

My tone was grim. "Not this human."

36

THE LAUNCH APPROACHED cautiously, with minute bursts from its thrusters. Two figures emerged, extra tanks trailing.

No sooner had the hatch slid shut than a plaintive voice asked, "May I withdraw, please, Captain?"

"No, Mr. Yost. Stay close in case—"

"Permission granted, Mr. Yost. Withdraw to a safe distance. One kil-

ometer." And then, unnecessarily, *"She's my ship now, Mr. Seafort. We may have need of our launch."*

Fath's tone was flat. "Very well, Ms. Frand."

I said, "It's all arranged, sir. They'll send an outrider for you. It's a bit scary." An understatement if ever there was one.

Fath said, "The way Harry brought you inside?"

"He'll envelop you, so no part of you touches the fish's skin."

"I don't look forward—"

"I won't do it!" Chris Dakko.

"There's no choice." Fath's tone was gentle.

"I'm your prisoner, but—"

"Not *my* prisoner. I assure—"

"I refuse. I'll jet away."

"You've no experience in a thrustersuit, Chris."

"I don't care."

"Venturas Base here, they're still descending!"

"Olympiad to Venturas, we'll have a shot in ninety-seven minutes."

Fath sighed. "Randy, is Chris absolutely essential?"

"Yes, sir."

"Think I'm glitched?" Mr. Dakko. "I won't let that monster swallow me! I'll die first!"

"No," I said. "You won't. You'll do it for Kevin."

"Kev has nothing to do with—"

"You're wrong. In a moment I'll show you." My voice was steady. Fath was just Outside, and thanks to the big outrider I had a fresh supply of air. What more could a joeykid want? A real arm that didn't wriggle and flap. A night's rest. An hour fondling Judy Winthr—

"Randy . . ." Mr. Dakko's tone started out firm, and trailed off. "I can't . . . not in the same room with . . . They killed him."

"No, we did. We blew the outrider to pieces. Sir, I can't do this without you." Not entirely true. I might, but I didn't want to.

"Chris?" Fath, patient.

"Oh, Christ. Hold my tether, sir." The sound of breathing. "I'm shutting my eyes. Tell me when it's done."

"Got you, Chris. Son, we're ready."

I bent with my stick. "Time now."

"So." Fath looked about. "Chris, you can look."

Mr. Dakko opened one eye, cringed. "Oh, God."

"Son . . ." Fath hauled me close, embraced me through our suits. "Why'd you summon me?"

"First, to get you off *Olympiad*. Frand can't be trusted."

"Sarah's loyal to the Navy. Her conscience—"

"Sir, there's no time for bullshit."

He tried to stare me down, couldn't. "Why else?"

"To use leverage. I can't pull this off. Mr. Dakko?" I shook him. "Look at my face. Don't mind them."

"Worse than a nightmare." His voice was thick.

"Did Kev ever tell you his dream?" My tone was curious.

It roused him. "No. He was closer to Walter. His grandfather. Perhaps I was too harsh."

"For generations, the U.N. has strangled us with their shipping monopoly. My dad hated it, and Anthony. Kevin's idea . . ."

I told him. If the colonies banded together, their joint resources might match, even outstrip Earth's. They could build ships of their own, avoid the ruinous rates that had us at Earth's mercy.

"A worthwhile goal," he said tiredly. "But utterly unrealistic. The Navy would never let us ship materials or half-built ships. To say nothing of fabricating drives."

"True. But now we don't need the Navy. Fath, Mr. Dakko, I'd like you to meet someone. A . . . a friend." I clutched my stick. "Here big-human."

TWO HUMANS.

"One-arm touch big-human." I gripped Fath's arm. "Captain, may I present their commander? His symbol is big outrider."

"You said they're telepathic? Whatever one knows . . . ?"

"I'm not sure. They may transmit by touching the fish. But this one's definitely in charge."

"Is the . . . uh, body . . . aired?"

I'd anticipated him. "Yes, sir. I asked if I could open a tank." The second tank from *Challenger*'s ill-fated launch hissed quietly in a corner.

"Good. Tell him I mean no harm." Fath began to unclamp his helmet.

"Are you sure, sir? If anything goes wrong . . ."

"Yes. I'm sure."

In a moment Fath was desuited. "Whew." He wrinkled his nose. With a gentle push, he came to rest at a membrane near the big outrider. "Tell him I wish him well."

"Big-human say outriders no-die no-hurt." It was the best I could do.

Slowly, the outrider grew an appendage. Gray. I let out my breath. "Fath, that's the kind that won't hurt you."

"I remember."

Slowly, the outrider extended the gray metal finger, touched Captain Seafort's cheek. Fath stood quite still, though his lips moved silently in what might have been prayer.

When the outrider was done, Fath extended his arm, wrapped his fingers around the appendage. *Don't shake it. If it comes off in your hand we'll all have fits.*

"Now what, son?"

Stumbling over my words, I explained about the salt. "We need a three-way trade deal. Mr. Dakko will handle the local end."

"I'll what?" His look was unbelieving.

"You're a merchant, aren't you? Who better to purchase supplies and trade for us?"

"Us?"

"Hope Nation."

He said, "You're a U.N. citizen, Randy. They'll view this as treason."

"Am I, Fath? Ms. Frand removed me from *Olympiad*'s roster. Your own status is . . . unclear."

"I assume you have dual citizenship. But the salt is nothing. They view *this*—" Fath waved. "—as treason."

I shrugged. "I knew that from the start."

"Besides, it's academic. It's not a matter for Hope Nation to determine."

"Why, yes, it is." Through the visor, my gaze met his. "I've decided so."

Fath's lips tightened. "Don't toy with me."

"I'm not, sir. If we get out of this, you'll set me straight." I didn't look forward to it. "But in the meantime, I name the terms."

"How do you intend to enforce that?"

I handed him the writing stick. "Here. Do it your way."

"I don't know the words, son. You're our linguist."

"Precisely, sir."

If I weren't wearing a helmet, I think he'd have struck me. His tone was harsh. "You can't dictate to us. The General Assembly sets terms of foreign trade."

"For U.N. members," I said. "Hope Nation is independent."

"McEwan declared—"

"McEwan can declare his grandmother a swordfish, for all we care." *Anthony, this is for you. I hope you'll know.* "Hope Nation stays free. That's part of any deal."

Chris Dakko stared at me intently, the outriders forgotten.

I said, "We'd better hurry, Fath. Those fish will land shortly." And my bluff will evaporate.

"Blast it, joey, do you know the havoc you're unleashing? I was there, at Venturas Base!" When the fish landed, all those years ago, Fath had fought them. Yes, I'd heard.

I said, "We can avoid the worst. Sir, here's what you need to set up: we trade the fish a few tons of salt—you and Mr. Dakko can work out the numbers. We can lift it for them; it's easier for us. In return—"

"You arranged concessions?" Mr. Dakko sounded astonished.

"Why, yes. That's why we need you. The big outrider has agreed to carry our cargoes in return for salt. Our greatest challenge will be showing them where to go, we don't have star maps yet but—"

Fath held out a hand. "If I don't agree?"

"Then I let the fish land."

"Son, I forbid it."

"I defy you. I must. I hope one day you'll understand." My eyes stung. "Sir, I'm just a joeykid. Lord God knows what made me think I'm ready to be an adult. I'm not. But everyone expected . . ." No, it was my own fault. "Protect me next time, sir. From myself. I beg you, don't let me talk as I do, or imagine it's my place to decide the fate of worlds. Yet here I am, the only joey the fish trust, the only one who can talk to them. My home, my family, are gone. *Olympiad* doesn't want me, the Church only cares for revenge. I've come to the brink of death over and again, 'til my mind is numbed. You know what? It gives me the right to decide."

I took a long deep breath.

"And I decide Hope Nation will control its own trade. I lo—I respect and admire you greatly. But, Fath, I'll have my way or turn my back on you." I stopped. My voice was too unsteady to say more.

Fath was silent. His gaze held . . . what? Reproach? Sadness? Reappraisal?

"Boy . . ." Mr. Dakko floated across the chamber. "You realize what you've done?"

"I think . . ." I swallowed. "I think so."

"Anthony . . . and your father Derek Carr would be so—so—" He looked around guiltily. "So God damned proud!"

I couldn't help it. I tore off my helmet, threw myself at Fath. After a moment, he wrapped me in an embrace. "It's so, son. Let me this once speak for Derek. He would be proud. He fought that battle for years."

"Randy, the outri—*Randy!*" Mr. Dakko sprang to a bulkhead as a pair of outriders advanced.

I grabbed the stick. "Other human no hurt one-arm! One-arm emotion. One-arm no hurt, no die." I spoke as I wrote.

The outriders subsided. One jump took them to the far membrane. They attached themselves, quivering.

I said sheepishly, "Thanks, sir. Now . . ." I cleared my throat. "If we're to share the starlanes with fish, the U.N. will have to agree. The fish need salt when they're in home system too, and a place to land. That's for you to accomplish."

"Afterward. Right now, fish are descending on the Venturas, and *Olympiad* is on its way."

"Can you stop Ms. Frand's attack?"

"I doubt it." Fath merely smiled at my alarm. "But I imagine the Bishop can. Chris, is this agreeable to you? Good. Let's get to work. Seafort to *Olympiad*. Ms. Frand, a joint circuit, please. Ourselves, Bishop Scanlen, Colonel Kaminski, the Admiral. Mr. McEwan."

I said urgently, "The planters."

"All right, son. And the Planters' Council."

"*What have you worked out?*" Ms. Frand sounded suspicious.

"We'll discuss it together."

"Randy." Mr. Dakko poked my shoulder. "Translate for me. Ask them how much salt—"

"A cargo-hold full."

"By weight. And how often they'll need it. Is delivery at the Station acceptable? And . . ."

"I'm not sure we have words—wait." I tugged at Fath's sleeve. "Sir, a couple more details."

"Now what?" A scowl.

"Corrine Sloan's to be freed. No trial."

"As much as I want that, I can't ask—"

"I ask. Tell them I won't translate the deal otherwise. And one more thing: you get back *Olympiad*."

"No."

"I insist. Else I won't—"

"Don't you understand? Anything I ask on my own behalf undercuts their trust. They have to swallow a lot to accept your proposal. This is one bite too much. They'll begin to think it's all about me, and power. I don't mind, truly. I'll ride home as supercargo. We'll share a cabin, you and I."

"You'd still have me?" My voice was tremulous.

"Of course, son." His eyes narrowed. "I'll use the time to do exactly as you asked."

I gulped. It would be a long eighteen months. I might even be the better for it, but I dreaded the ordeal.

Never mind that now. I turned back to the big outrider.

Mr. Dakko's conversation with the alien grew increasingly technical. I was making up words on the spot, extrapolating them from what little we knew. Some were easy: "far" equaled "not near." Others, such as measures of weight, were maddeningly complicated. I finally managed it, resorting to "go to sun" and "go to planet" for gravity, and deriving "weight" from gravity. Having little else at hand, we used my own weight for a standard. A One-Arm-Weight equaled some fifty kilos, at least on Hope Nation.

Thank Lord God I had a facility for recalling our pictographs, else negotiations would have dissolved in chaos. Fath shook his head at my drawings; Mr. Dakko threw up his hands.

Fath had climbed back into his suit, for easier use of the radio. I kept an ear half-cocked, and marveled at his patience. Well, for two long terms as SecGen, he'd kept the representatives of Earth's billions in check. That certainly required well-honed forebearance and tact. On the other hand, he'd not been well known for his diplomatic . . .

"Mr. McEwan, we'll need a firm commitment, not merely a promise to consider export permits for—"

"Remove the threat of the fish, and we'll see about—"

"Governor . . ." Scanlen's voice was tense. "Given our predicament, perhaps we ought to soften—"

I snarled, "McEwan's no Governor!" I hoped the Planters' Council would say the same. It was they who'd led Hope Nation's long drive for independence. But Winthrop and the entire Council had disappeared.

"Olympiad *will have a shot in sixty-two*—"

"Enough, Ms. Frand. Randy, can you guarantee that, with an agreement, no more fish will descend?"

I'd already confirmed it with the big outrider. "Yes."

"And that those already descending won't attack?"

"Yes." That was the easy part. Without outriders to direct them, they were unable.

"Very well. Gentlemen, we'll never agree on all details. So, I'll set forth a proposal. When I'm done, don't suggest modifications. Simply say yes or no." A deep breath. "One, Hope Nation allows Dakko & Son to export salt to the fish, just off Orbit Station. Two, Mr. Dakko is pardoned by all parties, and has leave to make what other transport arrangements he wishes. Three, Ms. Sloan may sail to Earth unharmed and unmolested, to present her case before an impartial Church tribunal."

I snorted. Was there such a thing?

"Four, Hope Nation's status is referred to the General Assembly. Mr. McEwan, you will return to Earth—"

"Absolutely not!"

"Hear me out. Return to Earth to present your case. You'll appoint Jerence Branstead as Deputy Governor in your absence. In the meantime the Planters' Council, should they wish to assert independence, will name him Stadholder, and he will serve in a dual capacity until—"

Fath, you're a genius.

"Five, the aliens agree to ship Hope Nation's cargo as may be agreed. They undertake not to attack any vessel or planet occupied by humans, and this agreement is void at the first violation. Six—"

"Sir, I can't translate all that."

"Be silent, Mr. Carr. Seven, I undertake to present this agreement for approval by the United Nations General Assembly, and recommend a similar salt-for-cargo agreement in home system."

He thought for a moment. "Eight, *Olympiad* sails directly for home. This is too important to delay. Any of her officers in detention need only give their parole not to contest Ms. Frand's control of the ship to be freed for the homeward cruise. Nine, and most important, we declare an immediate cease-fire. The aliens won't attack the Venturas, *Olympiad*, or the Station, and neither *Olympiad* nor Colonel Kaminski will open fire on them."

I watched in awe.

To my astonishment, Fath winked. "So, then. Admiral?"

"I have little say in—"

"Sir, declare yourself."

"Very well, Mr. SecGen. I concur."

"Mr. McEwan?"

"It's an outrage. The woman goes free, you and that foul-mouthed young Carr get away with the most—"

"You'd prefer the fish? If you look south from the Admiral's office, you'll see ground zero, where the Centraltown bomb—"

"All RIGHT!" McEwan muttered a curse. "If Carr calls them off . . ."

"Does anyone speak for the Planters' Council?"

No response.

"Mr. Kaminski?"

"Sir, our position is awkward."

That was an understatement. On the Station, Colonel Kaminski hadn't yet acknowledged McEwan's recolonialization, or the new government dominated by Bishop Scanlen, but meanwhile Mr. Branstead's administration had collapsed. And the Station was dependent on Centraltown for supplies.

"Captain, if all other parties agree . . . we have no reason to object." Kaminski's answer was sensible, I grudgingly admitted.

"Very well. Ms. Frand?"

"The officers who were your favorites will be set ashore. For my ship's safety, I can't—"

"No, Ms. Frand, you can." Admiral Kenzig's voice was cold. "And you'll transport Alon Riev home. I won't have him on my staff."

"Aye aye, sir. But—"

"He burst into my office, two armed deacons in his wake. This, after I promoted him—"

"Are there charges?"

"Gentlemen, we've no time. Sarah?"

"Very well, Mr. Seafort. I concur."

"Bishop Scanlen?"

Oh, Fath was deft. He'd isolated the Bishop from his supporters before soliciting his opinion.

"You leave us no choice. My conditions are: that Church officials go about their business unmolested, that we retain supervisory control of—"

"Shove it in a recycler, Scanlen." Henry Winthrop, of the Planters' Council. He seemed out of breath. "We're at the Governor's Manse. We've taken the spaceport, the court building, the utilities—"

"By what authority—"

"—in the name of the Branstead-Carr government."

"Treason!" Scanlen's voice trembled.

"The Cathedral is closed until church-state relations are, ah, redefined to our satisfaction. By the way, we declare you persona non grata. That goes for McEwan too. Take *Olympiad* home, or we'll deport you both to Orbit Station. Don't count on refuge at Palabee's Venturas lodge. We'll be having words with him as well."

"I—you—we'll excommunicate—" Scanlen spluttered to a halt.

"Mr. Seafort, we've a mind to expel your Admiral too."

"Please don't," Fath said mildly. "Mr. Kenzig's done his best under great pressure. So, Bishop Scanlen, is it us, or the fish?"

"Damn you to the depths of Hell!" A long silence. "What about you, Seafort? You ask so many sacrifices."

"What do you mean?"

"McEwan gives up his governorship; the Church is denied your paramour, the assassin. Civilized society recoils while you trade with the devil's minions; you've disenfranchised Lord God Himself on Hope Nation . . . and you'd sail home to the plaudits of your cronies? We know you, Seafort. You'll scheme to wrest *Olympiad* from Captain Frand—"

"I'd do no such thing!"

"That's as may be. You're so enamored of the fish? Stay among them. In Centraltown, or on Orbit Station, if you won't risk a shuttle groundside. Anywhere but *Olympiad*. The days and months will pass. Another ship will be along. It's only a year."

"And another eighteen months home. The treaty can't wait."

"But it's recorded in *Olympiad*'s Log, isn't it so, Ms. Frand? More to the point, we guarantee it will be presented. Soon enough the Assembly will vote on your precious treaty!"

"Fath, don't listen. He'll—"

"Shush."

"Those are my terms, Seafort. Else Palabee and I will face Satan unaided. We'll be martyrs for the glory of—"

Fath rolled his eyes. "If I agree?"

"Swear so, and I'll accept. Not that it's right, but because I must." Scanlen's tone was sour.

Fath thought a long while. "Very well. I swear I will not seek or accept passage home on *Olympiad*. I'll remain on the Station until"—his eyes were bleak—"my banishment is lifted."

"Centraltown too!" I tugged at his sleeve.

"That would be permanent exile." Unconsciously, he flexed his spine. "But you'll be free to visit."

The Bishop's tone seemed one of triumph. "In that case I swear by Lord God Almighty that I assent to the arrangement, exactly as you've stated it. At least until the treaty's presented to the General Assembly for ratification. Does that suffice?"

Fath said, "That's acceptable."

"You hear, Ms. Frand? Log it, that he'll have no room to quibble and evade."

Fath wrinkled his nose, as if suddenly taking in a whiff of the fish's air.

"I've Logged the whole conference, Your Reverence. And I'll tightbeam a copy of the Log to Orbit Station, in case there's question. Do it, Mr. Sutwin."

"Seafort, this is Palabee. You never asked my approval."

Fath's tone was cool. "I saw no need."

"I represent—"

"Your own ambitions, and little more."

"Tell him, Fath!"

He silenced me with a warning finger. "Is there anything else, Mr. Palabee?"

"You always were a pigheaded, obstinate—I was a joeykid, watching openmouthed, that day when you tried to block Laura Triforth from declaring the Republic. She should have hanged you when she had the chance. I call challenge, Seafort. Do you have the guts to duel? You've lost your ship, you're no more than a civilian. Set forth on our soil and I'll—"

"You know . . ." Fath's tone was reflective. "A dozen of you for one Anthony Carr would be a poor trade. He was a man."

I could have hugged him, and almost did.

"NEVER MIND THAT!" Bishop Scanlon was apoplectic. "The fish! Call off the Godd—the God-blessed fish!"

"Yes. Randy, how does their commander tell them not to attack?"

I switched off my radio. "He can't."

Fath swung toward me, something close to murder in his eye.

"They don't communicate long distances. Only by color swirls, or sending an outrider across. Or perhaps by hearing Fusion."

"Then the Venturas . . ."

"The fish are decoys. They carry no outriders." I braced myself.

Fath looked appalled. "I gave my sworn word! How could you?"

"Sir, you told no lies."

"I said we had need of haste, the fish would land shortly."

"Isn't it true?"

"That they were attacking!"

"True, as far as you knew."

"RANDY!"

"Didn't I tell you not to leave me in charge? It was the only way I could get them . . ." My voice trembled. I swung to Mr. Dakko. "What else could I do? You were about to kill each other!"

"I'm staying out of—" He leaned against a swirling bulkhead, realized what he was touching, recoiled in shock.

I wrote. " 'Big-human says yes humans trade outriders salt.' There, Fath. Tell Scanlen I talked to the outrider—which I just did—and assure him the fish will land harmlessly. Tell him to leave them alone, in case there's virus. That he's free to fly to Centraltown for a shuttle."

"But . . ."

"It's not a lie."

His tone was grim. "Joey, you'll pay for this." To the caller, "Bishop? Let the fish land. We guarantee there'll be no attack . . ."

37

DAYS OF COMMOTION and disarray. Mr. Dakko emerged from the fish, eyes firmly shut, yet already pondering his new business opportunities. He'd made me promise a complete list of pictographs by the next day. I would have my work cut out.

Scanlen and McEwan made their arrangements to go aloft. Meanwhile, Mr. Branstead took the first shuttle groundside, where he began his struggle to bring order out of chaos.

The six sacrificed fish had settled on a sandy Venturas beach, where, one by one, their colors ceased to flow. Afer their deaths, for safety's sake, a volunteer squad used incendiaries to sterilize the nearby shoreline.

No outriders were found.

Henry Winthrop led the expedition that arrested Vince Palabee at his lodge.

I got an hour on the caller to Judy.

Mr. Dakko followed Jerence groundside, secure in his pardon.

Hope Nation's principal salt mine was in the Ventura foothills. Within four days the first cargo vessel lifted to the Station.

Ms. Frand released Tolliver, who'd reluctantly given his parole. Mik and Tad Anselm refused, until Fath spoke sharply to them by caller. All three retained their rank and status, but were relieved of all duties. I assumed Fath would manage to get them reinstated, one way or another.

I assured the big outrider that his salt was on its way. With his agreement—he said nothing that I interpreted as an objection—Fath and I withdrew to the Station, by way of Tommy Yost and *Olympiad*'s launch. Ms. Frand grudgingly left it with us, in case we had further need to visit the aliens.

The squadron of fish rejoined their leader, but stayed well clear of *Olympiad*. It was somewhat startling to glance out a Station porthole and see an enemy fleet standing calmly by, which I'd only seen before in holos of the war.

At the Station, standard grav and hot showers were an unimaginable pleasure.

Fath bunked privately with Ms. Sloan. I was exiled to a cabin nearby. That was fine with me. Corporal punishment of joeykids is barbaric and cruel, especially as Fath administered it shortly after we docked. Despite my pleas, he made no allowance for Mr. Tolliver's recent caning. If I hadn't deserved it so thoroughly, I'd have hated him more. As it was, for the first day or so I barely spoke to him. Adults snicker about joeykids having to eat standing up, but I didn't find it funny. Morose, I browsed the Station's library of chips, found the whole lot of them boring, ended up perusing Fath's frazzing Bible in my bed.

At least the Station medic was able to disconnect my ruined prosth. I hadn't known it was replaceable at the elbow. To my dismay, Dr. Romez sent over a duplicate, and Fath made me let the techs install it. I didn't dare object; he was keeping me on a very short leash. In a moment of petulance I'd shown less than perfect courtesy to a Station tech, and Fath had taken me by the scruff of the neck and . . . I still blushed when I thought of it. Later I'd suggested he let me return to *Olympiad*, but he wouldn't hear of it. "Not without a keeper, joey. Even then, you're best stuffed in a clothes locker and let out for meals."

"But—"

"Twelve verses."

I'd let it drop.

At last, a great day came. Bishop Scanlen passed through the Station on his way to *Olympiad*. I begged Fath to let me watch. I wouldn't have sneered. Not where anyone but Scanlen could have seen. Fath, of course, would have none of it.

The next day "Governor" McEwan, the Terran Ambassador, came through the lock, enough luggage in tow to fill a cargo hold. He must not have anticipated a triumphant return on the next starship.

Fath and I visited our host fish, One-Arm, to make sure the aliens remained content. Midshipman Yost piloted the launch with excruciating care. He was rather nervous; I couldn't tell if he was worried about showing lack of skill, or afraid of such proximity to the aliens. It prompted me to a breezy nonchalance in the airlock that faded as we neared the pulsating fish.

Outriders emerged to escort us. For a moment or two, as one enveloped me, I felt Mr. Dakko's distaste.

But within, all was well. A token consignment of salt was to be delivered shortly. Fath had the idea of inviting an outrider aboard the Station to observe. No one considered how he'd get there; I doubted Ms. Frand would allow the alien into the launch. I was quite sure Yost would abandon ship rather than pilot him. But Fath, in a moment of pique, had told me to keep silent. I did.

When we returned, Fath proposed to send Corrine home to *Olympiad*. I suspected he didn't want her close to an alien in a vessel he didn't control. As Orbit Station was built from one of the Navy's obsolete ships, it was quite small compared to *Olympiad*. If trouble developed, there were fewer places to flee.

But Ms. Sloan wouldn't hear of it. "Not unless they carry me. And I warn you, I'll bite and scratch."

"But it's your only chance. When a ship returns with a writ from the Church . . ."

"I'll have had three years with you. Randy, wouldn't you like to visit the lounge?"

"Not really, I—uh, yes, ma'am." I made my escape.

Later, I asked Fath, "Why don't you make her go?"

"Because I'm selfish. Someday, you'll understand."

"I'm not a child."

He snorted. Then, "Get some rest. Tomorrow, we'll supervise the salt transfer."

"We?"

"You still speak more fluently than I." He'd been studying the same list of pictographs I'd given Mr. Dakko.

"You'd trust me not to take over the negotiations?"

He set down his holo. "At times," he said, "I find your manner tiresome."

I had the grace to blush. And the wisdom to shut my mouth.

I needn't have worried about how we'd bring across the outrider. His fish brought him. It drifted ever closer to the Station, until it was but a few meters distant. I wished I'd been in the control center; Colonel Kaminski must be beside himself.

I was glued to a porthole, watching. The fish's skin swirled, grew indistinct. An outrider squeezed through. I shook my head, wondering how they did it. As far as I'd been able to tell, the fish had no loss of pressure when the membrane opened.

The outrider launched itself toward the Station hull. Fath confirmed his arrangements with Colonel Kaminski, and hurried to the airlock nearest the alien.

The outrider came aboard.

I wasn't about to tell Fath, but I did wonder whether this was one of his better ideas. "To normalize relations," he'd said, but outriders had been known to carry viruses. True, Fath and I and Mr. Dakko had tested clean when we'd gone through the station's decon after our session in the fish.

Colonel Kaminski, rallying, sent Centraltown and *Olympiad* encouraging bulletins of the outrider's visit, and Fath even posed with the alien before the holocams. He loathed publicity; I'd never realized how important it was to him that relations start off well.

"Big ship no-Fuse, no-go," was how we'd originally described the Station, before assigning the phrase a symbol. Fath showed the alien around, though I suspected the Station's maze of corridors made as much sense to the outrider as the fish's membranes did to me.

"Tell him more salt will be here soon," Fath ordered, and dutifully, I did. In fact, a cargo shuttle was even now making its way to the Station.

But the first vessel that docked was a launch from *Olympiad*.

We left the outrider a tub of nutrients—hospitality was an important tradition to nourish—before we passed into the next section to greet our visitors. Familiar figures strode down the Station corridor: Mikhael Tamarov, holding Janey's hand. Behind them, Midshipman Yost shouldered an overstuffed duffel. Janey broke loose, hurled herself at Fath.

Mik's eyes were sunken. He snapped a salute, but Fath waved it away, pulled him close.

"Pa, I thought of resigning, but—"

"Don't you dare."

"When we get home, I'll get in touch with Philip. He and Senator Boland will help—"

"Yes, son, do that. But for the cruise home, exemplary conduct. Don't give them excuse to—"

"Tad Anselm's waiting for a chance to relieve Frand. What goes around comes—"

Fath gripped his arm so tightly that Mik winced. "Under no circumstances! Make him understand they'll hang him. Naval politics has become about as ugly as . . ." He shook his head. "Mik, his life is in your hands."

"I'll try, Pa." Mik's tone was sober. He searched Fath's eyes. "Three years, home and back. God, I'll miss you."

Fath smiled. "You'll be nearly grown."

Mik was twenty, but took the jibe without annoyance.

"Why'd you come, son?"

"I have your gear, but mostly to bring Janey. Since you and Corrine are here . . ."

"Of course. I was going to make arrangements with Ms. Frand."

"She said it had to be now."

Fath looked pensive. "Oh, did she?"

"Yes, sir." Mik looked over his shoulder. "You. Come here."

"Me?" My voice squeaked. Tentatively, I eased within his range.

He swept me into a rib-cracking hug. "I'll miss you. Take care of Pa." It was a whisper.

"I'll try—no. He takes care of me." Trying to take care of Fath had gotten me in most of the trouble I'd landed in.

"Please, Randy. Don't fight him."

That I could promise, and did.

Mik said to Fath, "I have to go, sir. Ms. Frand wants her launch."

"What's her hurry?"

"We'll be sailing to Fusion safety."

"Hmm. Very well, you two. Get going."

"I'm staying." Tommy Yost looked sheepish. "Mr. Tamarov pilots home. I mean, to *Olympiad*."

Fath raised an eyebrow. "Oh?"

Yost shifted from foot to foot. "It's . . . well . . . I asked for transfer to Admiralty, sir."

"There won't be another ship for ages."

"I know, but . . ." His eyes darted to Mikhael. "Sir, is it all right to say?"

Mik nodded.

"I didn't want to be part of it. Removing you, sir. Besides, Scanlen and that fraz Pandeker march about as if they own the ship. Ms. Frand doesn't lift a finger."

Fath said nothing; he couldn't very well criticize *Olympiad*'s new Captain before a mere middy.

Mik stirred. "Sir, I'd better be going. Good luck, Mr. Yost."

We saw him to the airlock.

Tommy Yost said hesitantly, "Should I report to the Commandant for transport?"

"I'll arrange it," said Fath. "There's a cargo shuttle due shortly. I'm sure they'll let you hitch a ride down." He checked his watch. "I'd best get back to the outrider. Randy, take Janey to Corrine, would you? Mr. Yost, you'd best stay clear of our visitor. Go with Randy."

As Janey and I started off, hand in hand, the middy fell in beside me. "Was it scary?"

I blinked. "The fish? Worse."

"Ms. Frand was livid when you told her off."

"Good."

Yost said hesitantly, "Mr. Carr . . ."

"Randy. I'm not even ship's boy now." With a pang, I realized I missed it.

"I'm sorry, how I spoke to you."

I searched my memory. Since Yost and I had quarreled, the fate of species had been decided. It didn't matter a whit, and I told him so.

Janey was ecstatic to see her mother. We headed back. I settled Yost in the corridor, passed through the hatch to the outrider's section.

"What do you think, shall we take our friend for a tour?" Fath sounded almost jovial.

"We already did."

"Just a couple of bays, and the remains of the fusion chamber."

I argued against it, but Fath wasn't really listening. However, before he could throw terror into the Station techs, the cargo shuttle came to dock. We took the alien instead to section five, at whose lock it would moor.

The speaker crackled. "Captain Seafort, Comm Room. Incoming message."

Fath set the caller to no-hands, so as not to turn his back on the alien.

"*Olympiad to Station. Right Reverend Scanlen will speak to Captain Seafort.*"

"I'm here. Go ahead."

"*We'll be Fusing shortly. Sorry you couldn't be with us.*" The Bishop's tone was sweet. "*But you're better off among your Satanic allies.*"

Disgusted, I stared through the porthole. A fat, stubby shuttle was mating at the bay.

"Does your call have a purpose?" Fath's tone was acid.

"*Never duel in minutia with the Church, Seafort, we're past masters at the game. I said I'd leave: I did. I said we'd present your treaty: I will. I've kept my sworn word to the letter.*" Scanlen sounded gleeful. "*McEwan and I will present your cursed treaty to the Assembly. Eventually you, or Branstead, or Dakko, or another of your cohorts, will come chasing after, but far, far too late.*"

An alarm chimed. The shuttle was mated.

The outrider quivered.

"*In today's distracted world, first word is all, and we'll have nearly three years to work our will before you get home. It's McEwan and I who'll frame the debate and sculpt the issues for the vids. We're masters at that too. We'll cast your treaty in the light it deserves. By the time we're done, not a soul will give you a moment's hearing.*"

"Why?"

"*Seafort, you tweaked the Church over and again, here and on Earth. Did you think our patience infinite? Retribution is nigh.*"

"You'd destroy a race for revenge?"

"*Forget about trade; your precious fish are dead, or will be. We will war against them with all our Godly might, until Satan is vanquished. And know that the Navy will return, in its glory, to subdue the colonial heretics who overthrow Mother Church. Hope Nation is ours, and will remain so. Or perhaps you think your cause will prevail because it's just?*"

Fath's eyes were pained. "Is that so unreasonable, Bishop?"

The lock panel flashed green. The inner hatch slid open. Lieutenant Alon Riev sauntered through, duffel over his shoulder. When he saw Fath, he threw a laconic salute, which Fath didn't bother to return.

Scanlen's tone was savage. "*You forget: we have first word. You're excommunicate and damned, Nicholas Seafort, and will suffer far more pain than I could ever inflict, but I'll do my bit for Lord God.*"

"Bishop—"

The line went dead.

Fath stared at the bulkhead. My fists knotted, I glared at the starship's distant lights.

Lieutenant Riev cleared his throat. "I'm to take a launch to *Olympiad*. From the next lock."

"Very well." Fath's tone was indifferent.

Riev eyed the outrider. "Is that their chief?" As Fath was pointedly ignoring him, his question was to me.

I ought to snub him, but in Fath's presence, I didn't dare. You're fourteen, joey, but when you act ten, you'll be treated as ten. Yes, sir.

"I think so," I told Riev, but I realized I hadn't bothered to inquire. Belatedly, I studied the alien. Was our visitor the big outrider? No way to tell, really. Shapechangers had no defining shape. Their skins all swirled, they all quivered when anxious, and skittered about unexpectedly.

The outrider settled on a deck plate, and wrote.

"I have something for him," Riev said, reaching into his duffel. "A gift from the people of Centraltown."

"Ask first." My tone was urgent. Lord God knew how the alien would react to a surprise. "Fath, Captain Seafort, should he—"

Riev pulled his gift from his duffel. "Actually, it's from Right Reverend Scanlen. And the deacons of our blessed Church."

"LIEUTENANT, NO!" Fath.

Riev's laser was fully charged. The outrider watched, twitching, as Riev aimed.

Fath was caught in mid-corridor, too far to lunge at the pistol. Belatedly, I came alive. Both arms, prosth and real, clawed at Riev's wrist. His left hand thumped into my chest, holding me at bay.

"Why, Alon?" Fath's voice was agonized.

"He's Satan's spawn! Your treaty won't survive a death. And you don't deserve to win!"

I struggled to throttle him. No use; Riev's arms were longer than mine, his strength far greater.

"Call off your midget, before I kill him."

"Randy, back!" Fath's tone brooked no refusal.

The laser light shone steadily on my nose. Cursing nonstop, I gave up the unequal struggle.

"Why not kill me too?" Fath had edged closer.

"I ought to, you self-serving hack! This demon's death—" His laser flicked to the outrider, and back. "—will earn me a medal. For your death, they'd hang me. You're not worth it."

"Leave him be. I'll do anything in my power to—" Another step.

"Thank the Lord, you have no power." Riev's first shot splattered the alien against the bulkhead.

Fath lunged; Riev clubbed him to the deck. Coolly, he aimed continuous fire at the outrider, until nothing was left but a sizzling blob. "As your whore did to High Bishop Andori." His tone was vitriolic. "Back away, joey!"

I did.

Riev snatched up his duffel, raced down the corridor to the adjoining airlock.

"Fath, are you—"

He shoved me aside. "That fool!" He leaped for the caller. "Station alert! Close hatches! Don't let Riev—"

Too late. Lieutenant Riev had already dived through.

Alarms wailed. Footsteps thudded. Fath wiped a trickle of blood from his forehead. He looked stricken.

"Station, launch N109 departing Bay 3."

I gabbled, "Have a seat, sir. Away from that acid. In fact, let's get out of this corridor. You'll be all right once—"

"Departure Control to Launch, negative, do NOT depart—"

"I'm all right *now*! God, Randy, how could I have been so blind!"

"You?" I gaped.

"Commencing breakaway." Riev's voice was cool.

"To let him anywhere near . . ."

I said, "How could you know he'd—"

"He was the Bishop's man, even helped them cow Kenzig. Never missed a religious service on ship. Nagged the middies about their souls; I put a stop to it on the trip out. Now he waltzes into the alien's corridor and I do nothing. Seafort, you *idiot!*"

"Fath, the Station lasers! Tell Kaminski, he'll shoot him before he escapes!"

"Riev's on a launch, not a shuttle. He's making for *Olympiad*." Of course. Launches weren't atmospheric vehicles. And the only other ships about were fish.

Wearily, rubbing his scalp, Fath strode to the caller, paged the Colonel. "Mr. Kaminski, declare an emergency. Send a decon team to section . . ." He squinted. ". . . five. The corridor needs full treatment; we need hosedown and showers. Keep radar watch on the launch; if it doubles back, arrest Riev. Connect me to *Olympiad*."

A series of clicks. "Comm Room, I need Ms. Frand, flank." Fath clenched and unclenched a fist.

I stared at the gruesome remains. All for naught. My devious machinations, the fears I'd overcome, Fath's fury. It would all swirl down the drain of war. Riev had capped the Bishop's machinations with outright atrocity.

The caller clicked.

"Sarah?"

"I'm CAPTAIN Frand." Her tone was disapproving.

Fath stared at the caller as if it had bitten his hand. He shook himself. "Riev is about to dock. He met the alien observer, pulled a laser pistol, and killed him. Consider him armed and dangerous."

Ms. Frand's tone was cool. *"What do you propose I do?"*

"Arrest him!"

"On what charge?"

Fath spluttered. "Are you daft? He killed the outrider!"

"Yes, quite. Last I reviewed Naval regs, it was no crime to destroy the enemy."

"Ms. Frand, for God's sake!"

"Precisely."

Stunned silence.

"He clubbed me. Does that count?"

"I'll look into it, Mr. Seafort." The line went dead.

I stared at the deck. Amid the smoking mess, the alien's last etching. SALT HUMAN HERE?

Yeah. The salt of the earth.

The corridor hatch slid open. Suited Station hands clumped toward the smoking remains, spray gear in hand.

A stocky joey approached. "Captain?" His voice was muffled through his helmet.

"Colonel, I . . ." After a moment, Fath shook his head.

"Yes, a disaster." Kaminski's tone held sympathy.

Fath demanded, "What's come over Sarah?"

"Scanlen's gone aboard. And there's that Pandeker joey." Their eyes met. "She's putty in their hands."

"Not until this moment," Fath said heavily, "did I think I could disapprove of devotion to the Church."

Kaminski cleared his throat. "That's as may be, sir. I've taken the Station to full alert. What next?"

"Oh, God. What next." It was statement, not question. "Put my son through Class A decon."

"And you?"

Fath peered into a suit locker. "I'll need that thrustersuit."

"Why?" Kaminski and I spoke as one.

"I have a . . . journey to . . ." He left it at that. "Colonel—" He clapped my shoulder. "—I know this joey well. He'll try . . . I hold you responsible. He's not to follow me. Keep him on Station, if you have to lock him in a cabin."

"Fath!"

"If things go wrong, tell Jerence Branstead I knew what I was doing. And get Randy to *Olympiad*. Mik will take care . . ."

No. Not this.

Fath worked his way into the suit.

Behind us, crewmen hosed the deck.

Fath offered me an apologetic shrug. "Someone has to . . . tell them. Avert war, however it may be done."

Kaminski said vehemently, "Don't sacrifice yourself!"

"That's not my intention."

"Liar." My lips formed the word, but I didn't say it aloud.

"Son, do we have a word for 'sorry'?" He checked his clamps.

"No, sir."

"For 'reparation,' or . . ." He gave it up. "I'll play with 'die' and 'equals.' "

"Let me help; I know all the symbols and how they—"

"Not this time." Helmet under his arm, he leaned forward, planted a kiss on my forehead. "Fare thee well."

"You can't go, I won't—"

Suited hands closed around my arms, tugged me inexorably toward the decon station.

"Wait, I have to see . . ."

Fath plodded to an empty lock. "Kaminski, I entreat you. Don't fire on them. Not unless . . ." His eyes were grim. "Only to save your lives."

"I'll try, sir."

Captain Seafort trudged into the airlock. In a moment, it began to cycle.

Kaminski's thugs dragged me toward decon.

The panel blinked red. The outer hatch opened.

I kicked out, caught my guard in the shin, broke free. I dashed to the nearest porthole. "No, please let me look! Give me a second more—" I clawed, bit, twisted this way and that. "I'm begging—"

"Let him watch." Kaminski's voice was soft.

I pressed my nose to the transplex.

Fath emerged from the lock, into the unforgiving vacuum.

"You don't have to go, there's still time—"

He kicked off. As soon as he was clear he squirted his thrusters, headed straight for our host fish.

"I know the pictographs, I wrote half of them—"

With graceful skill he brought himself to a standstill a meter or so from the fish's swirling skin.

"You leave me and find me, leave me and—"

An outrider emerged from the fish. It enveloped my father, all but his feet, took him inside the fish.

I stiffened. "The suit! It had only one air tank!"

They dragged me toward decon.

"Come along, son." Kaminski's voice was soft. "That's all he'll need."

* * * *

Decon. Stinging chemical showers, blood draws, needles.

Fresh clothes that didn't reek.

Hot chocolate in a steaming mug, untouched.

Murmurs. Solicitous voices urging me to rest.

A cabin.

I curled in my bunk, slipped a Bible chip into my holovid. Twelve verses, Fath had given me, and I'd never complied. I'd show him. I'd learn thirty.

An hour or more had passed, and I could no longer bear the solitude. I burst out of my hatch. In minutes, I was settled at a corridor porthole. Outside, the fish floated silently.

A few hundred meters beyond, there drifted scores more aliens. Some three hundred of them.

"Randy?" Corrine Sloan, her voice soft.

I looked up, said nothing.

"None of us can stop him." She knelt, her eyes glistening. "God help us, we've tried. Tolliver, you, me, Arlene, Derek . . . there, rest your head. Let it out."

No, that would be too easy. With a struggle, I mastered myself. For Fath's sake, I spoke with care. "Ma'am, if you don't mind, I'd rather be alone."

By the time I realized my cruelty, she was gone.

I sat brooding.

A flurry of activity. Outriders emerged, launched themselves at their compatriots. A dozen or so of the fish pulsed, blinked out. The others began a slow, ominous drift toward the Station.

I braced for Colonel Kaminski's call to General Quarters, but it never came.

After a time, the corridor lights darkened to nominal night.

Massaging the ache in my neck, I trudged, unheeding, through corridors and passageways, up and down ladders.

The huge holoscreen in the Station's comm room had a view of the fish. Unbidden, I watched from the hatchway.

A steady voice, so steady it had to be a puter loop. "Mr. Seafort, please respond to Station. Mr. Seafort, please respond to—"

After a time my calves knotted. I sat.

Eons passed.

"Here he comes!"

I bolted upright.

"Colonel, Comm Room, watch your screen!"

In the holoscreen, the fish floated alongside as before. A membrane was open in its side. Through it emerged a suit.

Thank Heaven.

"Focus tight."

The view lurched, zoomed in.

I made a ghastly sound.

The suit was empty.

"Where's Fath?" I grabbed the nearest tech. "WHERE?"

"Still inside."

I recoiled. "They *digested* him?"

No answer.

I ran, Lord God knew where. After a time I found myself belowdecks near the machine shop, pounding a bulkhead.

Joey, this won't do.

I trudged back to the comm room.

Morning found me curled in a console chair. If some hushed voice had murmured into the caller seeking permission for my vigil, I'd paid no heed.

"Breakfast, joey." Hot cereal, in a tray.

"Thanks." My voice was rusty. I tried again. "Thank you."

The fish drifted in space, surrounded by its fellows. On another screen, *Olympiad* floated unmolested.

I asked, "How many hours?"

"Thirteen."

Far too long.

"Mr. Carr?"

I peered up. Colonel Kaminski, unshaven. I met his gaze.

"Let me take you to your cabin."

I gripped the chair, as if they'd try to haul me out of it. "No."

"Son, I know you're—"

"I won't let you call me that."

He hesitated. "Look, joey, you need sleep. I promise we'll call if—"

"Colonel, incoming traffic. The Manse."

Kaminski frowned at the interruption. "Very well, I'll take it here." He listened. "Ah, Stadholder Bran—all right, then. Jerence. No, he's . . ." A glance my way. ". . . visiting the fish. Not yet. We still hope—yes, right here." A pause. "I could ask, but the SecGen's last—his instructions were to put him on *Olympiad*." He covered the caller. "Would you care to go groundside, wait with Mr. Branstead? He says—"

"No." Wait, Fath wouldn't care for that. "I meant 'No, sir.' And thank him, please."

I would do for myself what Fath had demanded. Too bad he wouldn't be here to—

Not yet, Randy. Time for that later.

Lunchtime came and went. I might have been hungry, decided it didn't matter. After a while the warm leather seat became unbearable. I walked, but the corridors were excruciatingly empty, sublimely boring. None of the portholes had seats where a joey could scan verses in his holovid when he grew weary of staring into space.

Back to the comm room. I rubbed the ache in my spine, and stared endlessly at the holoscreen.

Alarms chimed. I snapped awake.

More fish were Fusing in.

Dozens.

Hundreds.

More than a few joined the flotilla around the Station. Others floated toward *Olympiad.*

Outriders flowed back and forth.

The comm room came alive with traffic. *Olympiad,* calling the Manse, personal for Stadholder Branstead. Station to *Olympiad.* Venturas Base to Station. Chris Dakko to Colonel Kaminski, on open circuit: "Do you think, if we gave them the salt . . . ?"

"No point. With Seafort dead, the treaty's a board of blown chips."

"Is he . . . have they . . ."

"No body yet. We're keeping watch. Christ, the boy's probably listen—" The line went dead.

An hour later, *Olympiad* sailed toward Fusion safety. On the screen, her lights slowly receded until they were as dim as the uncaring stars. The fish, left behind, returned to the flotilla. I marveled that they hadn't gone for her tubes. Was it a sign of hope?

Minutes were eons, hours beyond the scope of comprehension. I walked. I slumped in chairs and jerked awake at the slightest sound.

"Come along, Randy."

I peered sleepily. Tommy Yost.

"I'll take you to your cabin." He overrode my protest, guided me along the corridor.

Fath deserved more than he'd had. A monument, a grave, as future generations might contemplate the man who nearly saved them from themselves.

The fish, our enemy, would never give him back. Not for the asking.

Abruptly I dug in my heels. "No. Somewhere else." What I contemplated made my stomach queasy. Mik. Corrine. Janey. They, at least, would appreciate what I would do.

Yost was waiting. "Where, Randy?"

I told him.

"I can't." He glanced about, though we were alone, and spoke softly.

I said, "Please."

"The Admiral will have my . . . this is dismissal, joey."

"This is Nicholas Ewing Seafort." I held his gaze. Fath. The man who'd discovered the fish, fought them, served as Commandant of Academy, cleared the starlanes of fish at terrible cost to humans and aliens alike. The SecGen. The man who . . .

I had no need to say it. Tommy knew.

A sigh. "Scanlen was insufferable, but I never meant to forfeit my career." He poked me. "Let's go."

I led him to the machine shop. Yost signed out an etching tool, and a couple of scrap sheets of alumalloy. I thought his excuse was weak, that he wanted to practice pictographs with me just in case . . . but he was an officer. People saw him as adult. I was but a joeykid.

Yost watched me write out the message. "You understand that folderol?"

I snorted. "Understand? I *invented* it." For a moment, a glow of pride. Then I recalled why the plate was before us.

I handed him the tool. "Better return it, before someone comes looking."

"While I'm below, locate a gig."

The Station moored a handful of gigs, Tommy had told me, small craft seating six at most. It even had a launch of its own. And shuttles, of course, when they weren't groundside.

The problem wasn't the craft. Nobody bothered to lock a gig; where would one go with it? Ships called only twice a year, and only the shuttles could traverse Hope Nation's atmosphere. Besides, locked craft would be useless for emergency evacuations.

But the Station was at a high state of alert, thanks to the menacing fish. We couldn't just stroll through the lock, could we? Alarms would sound. Nervous techs would train their lasers. My shirt grew damp.

"Ready."

I jumped.

Tommy frowned. "Where?"

I blushed. "I didn't look."

Lugging the plate, I let him take me on an absurd stroll through the Station, glancing out portholes. We found three possible craft.

I whispered, "Would they be fueled?"

"I can't imagine why not."

We settled on a gig at a Level 2 lock. There weren't any service posts near—Comm Room, dining hall, or the like—and the corridor was, for the most part, deserted.

Yost peered into a nearby suit locker. "No thrustersuits."

"Doesn't matter. I won't really need one."

He said, "*I* might, if they eat the gig."

Before putting on his helmet, Tommy awkwardly got down on his knees. He closed his eyes, and his lips moved.

I waited.

"Amen." He struggled to his feet.

"What did you ask for?" A stupid question, born only of curiosity. It was none of my business.

His ears went red. "Courage."

Christ, what was I doing? "You don't have to go."

"You can't steer a—"

I said, "We'll call it off."

"For my sake?"

I nodded.

A long exhalation. "Thanks. But . . ." He handed me my suit. "I'm tired of comparing myself to you and Ghent."

I worked my way into the suit.

I'll say one thing for my prosth: thanks to the nerve grafts, I had nothing to learn. I just used my hand as if it were my own. It looked weird enough, but it sure beat climbing into a suit one-handed.

I sighed. Maybe Fath had been right.

In the end, it was as simple as cycling through the lock. The gig was waiting, and powered up without a hitch. A tiny craft indeed, it had a small lock, six seats divided by a narrow aisle, and a control panel for the pilot. No cockpit. No head.

Tommy strapped himself in, began breakaway.

A clean getaway.

But the moment I clicked on my radio . . .

"*Randy, what are you doing?*" Kaminski himself. His tone held no anger, only worry.

"Going out, sir. We'll be back in a few minutes." At any rate, Tommy would.

"*I promised Mr. Seafort!*" Anguish. "*Come back, joey. Please!*"

"On his behalf, I absolve you." I giggled. "I suppose I'm his heir."

"*Son . . .*" Perhaps he forgot that he wasn't to call me that. "*You'll get us killed if you rile the fish.*"

"That's the last thing I intend." For a moment I switched off the radio. "Hurry, Tommy, before they think of something."

"We're clear. I'm trying not to damage the Station." Slowly, we glided away.

"Easy, Tommy, it's that close one. No need to—"

"I know." Already he was braking. I keyed the suit radio.

"Why, Randy? What's the purpose?"

"To retrieve Fath."

Tommy took me as near to the fish as he dared.

I swam to the lock, gripped a stanchion at the outer hatch, grateful for my working left arm. "Open, please."

I gave the plate a last look: "Trade one-arm human / dead big-human."

It was all I had that they might want.

Carefully, I released the plate, tapped it gently. It floated toward the fish. Surely they'd sense it, take it in. "Tommy, the moment I'm gone, sail the gig as fast as you—"

A membrane swirled. An outrider emerged, clung to the skin. The plate bumped it. An appendage shot out, snagged it.

Protoplasm rippled across the plate, read it, wiped it clean.

"Oh, no!"

The outrider launched itself. Straight for the gig.

I formed words: Tommy, go! But I said nothing. Heart thumping against my suit, I braced myself in the hatchway. At the last minute, I had the sense to duck aside.

"Laser room, prepare to fire on—"

I blurted, "Wait, sir!"

The outrider sailed past me, came to rest against the inner hatch. It quivered.

I waited for oblivion. At length, wondering, I turned my head.

Outside the fish, another outrider, absurdly large. No, it was wrapped about . . .

A suit. An ancient suit. The holos hadn't shown that style in years. Decades.

"Not Philip Tyre, I beg you. I couldn't stand it." Foul bile flooded my throat.

"What, Randy?" Yost.

Desperately, I swallowed. "Nothing."

The outrider oozed off the suit, launched himself and it. Together, they floated to our lock.

The first outrider loomed over me. It exuded my plate.

A sizzle.

After a time, it abandoned the plate, reconstituted itself at the hatch, quivered once, and launched itself home.

The second outrider propelled the suit toward our inner lock.

I didn't dare cycle, not with him aboard. I could risk myself, but Tommy . . .

I peered at the plate.

A long message.

SALT IN HUMANS. SALT IN OUTRIDER. NO-WAR HUMAN / OUTRIDER.

I blinked. "What the fu—" I stopped myself at the last moment.

The outrider extended an appendage. Gray.

It touched my suit.

Not knowing why, I seized it, brought it to my helmet, kissed it through the bubble.

A moment of stillness.

With shocking speed the outrider moved to the hatch, launched itself, and was gone.

Mechanically, I cycled.

SALT IN HUMANS. SALT IN OUTRIDER. NO-WAR HUMAN / OUTRIDER.

It was almost familiar. What could it . . .

I rubbed my eyes. I was exhausted. If I hadn't stayed up two nights reading the frazzing Bible, maybe I could think enough to—

"Yost, you hijacker, get him back to the Station!"

"Aye aye, sir, as soon as I get him inside." The inner hatch slid open. Tommy stumbled over the ancient suit, hauled me past. "Sit there." He shoved me into a seat. Forgetting we were in zero gee, I tried to balance the plate on my knees.

The arm of the suit blocked the hatch. With a muttered curse, Tommy dragged it to the tiny aisle.

As he let go, the helmet twisted to one side.

I gasped.

It was Fath.

"TOMMY!" Hands made useless by desperate frenzy, I clawed at the clamps.

"Oh, my God!" He knelt, ripped off the helmet.

Fath's face was gray and lifeless.

Yost spun, snapped my clamps, tore off my own helmet. "Stay with him!" He threw himself at the pilot's seat. He gunned the engine so hard we shot past our lock.

Please, Sir. I'll never ask anything else as long as I live. Just this one miracle. Please.

Nothing.

And then Fath breathed.

38

PANDEMONIUM.

The clang of alarms. Thudding boots, med techs, a crash cart, skid marks on the deck.

Corrine, I, Janey, Yost, Colonel Kaminski, a sea of hovering faces.

"Stand back!"

Janey beat on her mother's leg. "Will Daddy get up?"

Gentle hands enwrapped my forehead in a warm bosom. I clung.

"Get the mask—"

"I'm all right. Don't need—"

"Yes, you do, sir."

"Mrff . . ."

"Nick . . ." Corrine's fingers pressed me tighter. "Oh, Nick."

"Those tanks were dead empty!" A med tech, outraged.

"Probably all they had."

". . . up. Let me up."

SALT IN HUMANS. SALT IN OUTRIDER. NO-WAR HUMAN / OUTRIDER.

Salt in us, salt in them. Peace. The outriders had gone glitched.

I stiffened. "Oh, Lord God!" Abandoning Corrine, I pushed through the circle tending Fath. "*Have salt in yourselves, and have peace one with another.* Mark 9:50." I'd read the testament, eyes blurring on the holovid.

Fath's eyebrows furrowed. He tore off his mask.

"On the plate!" I ran to the bulkhead, grabbed it, held it before his face.

He seemed embarrassed. "The air got . . . at the end I was rambling a bit. Salt was on my mind. A covenant of salt forever, if the salt has lost his savor, that sort of thing. That's the best I could translate."

"Why did they write me that particular verse?"

"Perhaps they understood it. Agreed with the sentiment."

Slowly, as if by unspoken agreement, the circle around him eased. He propped himself on one arm.

"Fath, sir, why'd you give them your thrustersuit?"

"As a gesture of submission."

"You could have died."

"Unless they wanted me to live."

"Alone, in the fish, with no suit . . ." I couldn't imagine the torment he'd undergone.

He winced, as if recalling memories he'd avoid. *"Out of the belly of hell cried I, and Thou heardest my voice."*

I blurted, *"For Thou had cast me into the deep, in the midst of the seas; and the floods compassed me about."*

He looked at me with astonishment.

I shrugged, shamefaced. "I had nothing else to read."

He struggled to his feet, looked me over more closely. "Just why are you half-suited?"

I swallowed.

His eyes narrowed. "Joey, what have you been up to?"

The caller crackled. *"Comm Room to Commandant. A call for Captain Seafort. Is he, ah, up to it?"*

"Yes, I am."

I breathed a sigh of relief. With any luck, Fath would overlook my escapade.

A click. *"Frand here."*

Perhaps Fath was still muddled. He left the speakers on. We all heard. "Seafort."

"We're about to Fuse." A pause. *"I wish events . . . I had no choice but to relieve you."*

Fath said nothing.

Ms. Frand cleared her throat. *"Has Mr. Kenzig given you instructions?"*

"What about?"

"Whether to take the next ship in the pipeline, or to await orders from home."

"He has not." Fath's tone was bleak. "Does it matter?"

"Our agreement was vague on the point. I'd like to inform Admiralty."

"I imagine," said Fath, "I'll make my way home."

"You'll be too late, you know. Scanlen was right."

"Ah. You heard?"

"He spoke from the bridge."

I rolled my eyes. The day Fath would share his bridge with a fraz like Scanlen . . .

"You know," said Ms. Frand, *"I'm rather surprised you didn't sneak aboard a launch, try to seize the ship, the way you did* Galactic.*"*

"I gave my word. I keep it."

"But if you'd reached home, you might have convinced the Assembly. You're so bloody effective with the media. With so much at stake . . ."

"Tend to your conscience," Fath said. "I'll tend mine."

"Well . . . what, Ms. Skor? All right, stand by to prime. You know, Seafort, I'm rather glad your treaty won't stand a chance. Always hated those creatures. Farewell." The speaker crackled, went silent.

Fath replaced the caller.

I slammed my fist into the bulkhead. "Bastards! Why do they gloat?"

Fath didn't seem put out. "To reassure themselves."

"Fath . . ." I shook my head. Didn't he see? Our accomplishments meant nothing? The fish would be obliterated, Hope Nation reduced to servility, Corrine Sloan rearrested and put to death. It was all a matter of time. If only she'd killed Scanlen as well as Andori; if only the Bishop hadn't coerced Fath into exile . . .

"Don't despair, son."

My tone was dull. "What will you do now?"

"Why," he said, "I think I'll go home."

My heart leaped. "We can repair the Station's fusion drive?"

"Impossible. The core of the Station is an obsolete ship, but her drive is gone. They've built sections right across the remains of the old tube shaft."

"If we cut away . . ."

"No, there's no way to generate a wave. The engine itself is gone."

"But *Olympiad*'s Fused." She was the only starship within nineteen light-years that could get Fath home. "And you gave your word."

"You're dying to know, joey. Very well, tonight, in my cabin. With your mother and Janey."

"My moth—" I gulped. It seemed there was a lot he wasn't telling me.

"Look at them." Mr. Dakko peered through the porthole.

It was a sight to behold. Fish, six hundred of them, nosed about a cargo shuttle, careful not to damage its hull. Huge chunks of salt—I'd thought it only came as grains—floated about. Fish nuzzled the chunks, absorbing them through gaping membranes. Occasionally, an outrider assisted his craft.

In the shuttle's cargo bay, a Station hand worked to off-load salt as quickly as possible. A volunteer; I marveled that we'd found one. I'd have gone, but Fath refused with such vehemence I dared not ask again. So I hung about, receiving an occasional pat on the shoulder. He didn't mean to be condescending, he was just preoccupied.

"The first step." Fath's voice was quiet. "Who would have thought . . ."

Mr. Dakko rested his chin on his palm. "If only Kevin could have seen it."

I glanced at Fath, read what might be permission. "It was Kev's doing, sir."

"And yours, joey." Mr. Dakko was silent a long moment. "I've been spiteful to you, and mean. I'm sorry."

"No more than I deser—"

"You have my respect."

I blinked away a sudden sting.

Mr. Dakko said to Fath, "This maneuver will use up a year of credits. Closer to two."

"Think of the alternative."

A gloomy sigh. "I know. Do it."

Fath smiled. "I never thought you'd say otherwise."

"Not so, Jerence. Just borrowing it for a while." Janey sat on Fath's lap, playing with his lapel. We were in his cabin.

While he listened, he threw an arm across my shoulder, hauled me closer. "We'd help you jury-rig a temporary. Ah, well. You know, of course, that if you refuse I'd go along with you."

In the caller, tinny words of protest.

Fath winked.

"Very well, old friend. Thank you. We'll start the shuttles groundside."

When he rang off, I said to Fath, "Let me help."

"No."

"Why not?" My tone was petulant.

"You're brilliant, son, but a creature of impulse. I don't want you to—"

"That's not fair. I'm doing what you tell—"

"And the other reason . . ." His tone was level. "That day, in the fish, you reminded me you were a joeykid with responsibility beyond your years. It was true. So I'll make the decisions, and raise you as best I can."

I wanted to hug him, and kick him. I retreated to my cabin.

Tommy dragged his duffel toward the crowded shuttle lock; he was due to report to Admiral Kenzig and the sleepy Centraltown base. I walked along for company.

As he neared the lock, Fath hurried down the corridor. "Yost!"

"Yes, sir!" The middy jumped to attention.

"As you were. I've been on the line to Mr. Kenzig. Your orders are canceled."

"They are?" His voice was small.

"Yes. Disappointed?"

"I . . . I understand why he wouldn't . . ." He scuffed the deck. I frowned. Mikhael would have demerited him on the spot. "I wasn't very . . . I'm sorry I . . ."

"Oh, it's not that. *I* want you."

"You do?" His voice came out a squeak. He blushed.

"Would you accept a few months duty on the Station? Under my command?"

"I . . . yes, sir." His chest swelled.

"There'll be no shore leave."

"I understand."

"Very well. Unpack your gear."

"How many more, Fath?"

"Two shuttles. We have about an hour."

And so the time came.

Minutes after Colonel Kaminski boarded the final shuttle, six hundred fish began their slow drift toward the Station.

An outrider floated into our open airlock. It twitched and quivered while the lock cycled.

Fath and I met it in the corridor.

TIME NOW.

Fath stooped with the etching tool, but saw the plea in my eyes. Silently, he handed it to me.

I bent. "Humans / fish Fuse together home system." And then I added, "Time now friends."

Fath's eyes smiled.

A woman's voice. "Hon, we ought to be together."

"Yes, we ought." Fath took her hand. For the moment, I took his other. Janey trailed alongside.

Minutes later, I paced the Comm Room. My Comm Room. I was the sole tech on duty, personally appointed by Fath.

In the screen, I could barely see stars for the mass of fish.

After we'd all exchanged reassurances, I'd been to my cabin, and brought my favorite holo of Derek. I set it on the console, gazed moodily. *I understand now, Dad, why you'd follow him anywhere.*

It's not going to be easy, making him proud. You were easier to please, and more forgiving. Of course, I was younger then. But he'll be good for me. Keep me on my toes.

Nobody but he would have thought of it, Dad. A matter of putting things together, perhaps, but he was the only one to see it.

The fish agreed to take cargo. They couldn't take us, not inside them. The outriders of One-Arm had asked me if my suit was secure, before Fusing. Without a suit, I'd have died. I wasn't sure why. Perhaps they'd learned it was so, with some poor souls during the war. And we couldn't possibly Fuse the many months home, suited all the way.

Yet, during the war, Fath had embedded *Challenger*'s prow in a fish, and it had Fused for weeks. No one aboard wore suits.

In the war, a squadron of fish had Fused to our upper atmosphere with an immense rock. An external object they'd somehow enveloped within their Fusion field.

Our Station had launches and gigs, but they were all too small. We could fit in, though quarters would be cramped, but we couldn't possibly squeeze in the supplies needed for months of Fusion.

The Station itself was another matter.

I'd asked Fath, "Won't they accuse you of breaking your word?"

"No, I'm keeping it to the letter. I promised to wait on the Station, until my banishment is lifted. And so I will. I can't help it if Scanlen assumed the Station was, er, stationary." His eyes danced.

I tried to imagine the uproar in home system, when Orbit Station unexpectedly appeared, surrounded by fish. And Earth itself . . . Dad had told me tales, and Fath too, but I'd never been to visit. I wondered if I'd like it.

I said, "At home you'll have first word, as he called it. The Bishop will be livid."

"Oh, worse than that. *The wicked shall see it, and be grieved; he shall gnash with his teeth, and melt away.*" Fath didn't look overly troubled. "You're puzzled? Read Psalms. Memorize a dozen verses a day."

"Fath!"

"What else have you to do? Arcvid with Yost? Enlighten your soul, then play." He softened his edict by ruffling my hair.

Dad, I'll always miss you. But he's truly my father now.

The fish drifted closer. I could make out individual swirls on their mottled skins.

Soon, we'd be on our way.

The cost to Hope Nation would be great—two years of Mr. Dakko's transport credit, and Mr. Branstead's government would have to make do with a temporary Station, cobbled from shuttles and launches lashed together—but the alternative was inevitable defeat.

For days, shuttles had been uplifting foodstuffs, supplies, gear, everything the few of us would need for months of travel. Janey, Corrine, Fath and I, Tommy Yost. Five techs who'd volunteered for mankind's new adventure.

Mr. Branstead had thoughtfully uploaded holos of the Church correctional farms, and close-ups of the children delivered from them. *Olympiad*'s Log was safely stored in our puter banks, along with Bishop Scanlen's vicious taunts, which Colonel Kaminski has been kind enough to record. In six months—nearly a year before *Olympiad*—we'd Defuse in home system. By then, I'd be a well-trained comm tech, and manning the Comm Room, I'd have a box seat for the Church's long-awaited comeuppance.

A console light flashed. Proudly, I answered. "Orbit Station, go ahead."

"Randy? Chris Dakko. I just wanted to wish Mr. Seafort Godspee—"

The screen blanked.

We were Fused.

So.

After a time, I switched on my holovid, scrolled through dull, endless verses.

I suppose I believe in You, You old fraz; You leave me no choice. But I hate what You did to Dad. I hate that You've tortured Fath. And You weren't all that kind to me, You know. I have nothing good to say to You. But I'll read. I'll try to understand.

Someday, we're going to have a talk, You and I.